THEY USED DARK FORCES

There, alone at the long narrow table, Bormann was sitting. Fixing his cold steely eyes on Gregory, he asked, '*Herr Major*, is it true that you predicted the crossing of the Rhine at Remagen by the Americans a week before it occurred?'

'*Jawohl, Herr Parteiführer*,' Gregory replied promptly.

Bormann stood up and said, 'The Führer requires an explanation of how you obtained this intelligence.' As he spoke he pushed open a door on his right and signed to Gregory to go through it. A moment later Gregory found himself face to face with Adolf Hitler.

DENNIS WHEATLEY

They Used Dark Forces

Mandarin

For BILL

Air Chief Marshal SIR WILLIAM ELLIOT,

G.C.V.O., K.C.B., K.B.E., D.F.C.

A small souvenir of a happy friendship which
began when he was Director of Plans (Air) in
1942

and for

ROSEMARY

A Mandarin Paperback
THEY USED DARK FORCES

First published in Great Britain 1964
by Hutchinson & Co. (Publishers) Ltd
This edition published 1991
by Mandarin Paperbacks
Michelin House, 81 Fulham Road, London SW3 6RB

Mandarin is an imprint of the Octopus Publishing Group

A CIP catalogue record for this title
is available from the British Library
ISBN 0 7493 0677 7

Printed and bound in Great Britain
by Cox & Wyman Ltd, Reading, Berks

I desire to state that I, personally, have never assisted at, or participated in, any ceremony connected with Magic – Black or White.

The literature of occultism is so immense that any conscientious writer can obtain from it abundant material for the background of a romance such as this.

In the present case I have spared no pains to secure accuracy of detail from existing accounts when describing magical rites or formulas for protection against evil, and these have been verified in conversation with certain persons, sought out for that purpose who are actual practitioners of the Art.

All the characters and situations in this book are entirely imaginary but, in the inquiry necessary to writing of it, I found ample evidence that Black Magic is still practiced in London, and other cities, at the present day.

Should any of my readers incline to a serious study of the subject, and thus come into contact with a man or a woman of Power, I feel that it is only right to urge them, most strongly, to refrain from being drawn into the practice of the Secret Art in any way. My own observations have led me to an absolute conviction that to do so would bring them into dangers of a very real and concrete nature.

Dennis Wheatley

Contents

Author's Note

In obtaining the factual background of the progress of the war,
the conspiracy to blow up Hitler and the detailed account of
the last weeks of his life, I consulted many books, but I wish
to express my indebtedness particularly to Sir Winston
Churchill's *The Second World War* (Vols. IV, V and VI),
Chester Wilmot's *The Struggle for Europe*, Milton Schulman's
Defeat in the West, General Westphal's *The German Army in
the West*, Gerald Reitlinger's *The S.S.*, *Alibi of a Nation*, *The
Von Hassell Diaries*, Fabian von Schlabrendorff's account of
the July bomb plot, Kazimierz Smolen's *Auschwitz* and H. R.
Trevor Roper's *The Last Days of Hitler*.

In my account of the attitudes and actions of Hitler's
personal staff I have taken only one liberty. At a certain point
in the story I have had Obergruppenführer Fegelein, Himmler's
liaison officer at Führer H.Q., relieved by Obergruppenführer
Grauber. But my description of Grauber's attempt to save
himself, and what followed, is exactly what happened to
Fegelein.

D.W.

A LETTER FROM GREGORY SALLUST

My dear Dennis,

I don't much like the idea of it becoming publicly known that for the best part of two years I was closely associated with a Satanist, but I appreciate that you cannot chronicle my adventures during the latter part of World War II without disclosing that.

It is very understandable, too, that as over eighteen million copies of your books have been sold, and nine of those books are about myself, many of your faithful readers should continue to demand that you should let them know whether my beloved Erika ever got free from her hateful husband, what happened to beautiful, wicked Sabine, and if my old enemy Gruppenführer Grauber met with his just deserts.

There are, of course, plenty of well-authenticated accounts of those terrible last days in Berlin; Goering's dismissal, Himmler's treachery and Hitler's savage attempt to involve the whole German people in his own ruin; but, although the faith he placed in astrologers is well known, no-one has yet described how his belief in supernatural guidance influenced his final decisions.

How much Malacou and I contributed to his committing suicide it is impossible to say; but Malacou was unquestionably a disciple of the Devil and, knowing your capabilities, I have no doubt at all that in recording those unforgettable weeks that I spent with Hitler in the bunker you will write a spy story to top all spy stories. So let me down lightly and go ahead.

Yours ever,

Gregory

P.S. Knowing your usual kindness in replenishing my cellar whenever you use my material, I may mention that I have developed a particular liking for the Moet et Chandon in the Dom Perignon bottles. No doubt you, too, have found it quite outstanding.

1

The Ace up Hitler's Sleeve

BY MIDNIGHT the aircraft was far out over the North Sea.
She was a Mosquito, fitted with extra fuel tanks for the long
flight to the Baltic coast of Germany. It was there, in about two
hours' time, that Gregory Sallust and his companion were to be
dropped. They were lying on their backs, side by side in the
narrow bomb bay. It was pitch dark down there, yet too cold
and uncomfortable for any hope of sleep. As the 'plane droned
on and the minutes crawled by, many thoughts drifted through
Gregory's mind.

He was thinking of the last time he had come in secret to the
Continent. It was now May and that had been in the previous
August. He had been sent on a mission to Budapest to assess
the possibilities of drawing Hungary into the war on the side
of the Allies. A number of Hungary's leading magnates had
shown willingness to commit their country, provided that an
Anglo-American force should land that autumn in France
and thus occupy such first-line German units as were not
engaged in Russia.

But Gregory had not got back to England until the end of
September. During his absence Churchill had persuaded the
Americans to accept instead his plan for occupying French
North Africa. By then every available division had been com-
mitted to Operation 'Torch', so the negotiations with the
Hungarians had had to be abandoned and in due course
Germany had forced Hungary to declare war on the Allies.

The delay in Gregory's return had been caused by his having
had the ill-luck to run into his old enemy Gruppenführer
Grauber. By the skin of his teeth and with the aid of the lovely
Sabine Tuzolto he had got away; but he had had to come home

via Turkey, and a journey down the Danube concealed in a barge is a far from speedy means of transport.

Yet, as he thought again now of those lost, sunny, autumn days chugging slowly down the great river, he smiled. For a few hectic weeks in 1936 Sabine had been his mistress. When they met again in wartime Budapest, no less a man than Ribbentrop had become her lover. That had led to complications. But, as a result of the Grauber episode, she too had been forced to escape from Hungary. Had they not shared a cabin on the barge, they would not have been human.

In a beauty contest the judges might well have hesitated between the dark-haired, magnolia-skinned loveliness of the Hungarian Baroness and the golden, blue-eyed, Nordic perfection of Erika von Osterberg. But for Gregory there had never been any question of choice. Between him and Sabine it had been no more than physical attraction and enormous fun; although fun that he had had to pay for dearly when he had got his entrancing Hungarian mistress back to London. Erika whom, for a score of qualities that Sabine lacked, he truly loved, had learned of his brief infidelity and he had come within an ace of losing her for good.

Sabine, too, had caused him one of the worst headaches he had ever had in his life. He had brought her to England in the innocent belief that he was saving her from the vengeance of the Gestapo. Where he had slipped up was in never having visualized the possibility that Sabine, convinced that Germany would win the war, had agreed to Ribbentrop's suggestion that, to rehabilitate herself with the Nazis, she should make use of Gregory to get into England as a spy for them.

Clever girl though she was, she had been caught. By most subtle intrigue, great daring and the reluctant help of his powerful friend and patron Sir Pellinore Gwaine-Cust, Gregory had enabled her to return to Germany, but had sent her back with false information about the objective of the 'Torch' convoys, which were then already on their way to North Africa.

When Gregory's age group was called up, Sir Pellinore had secured for him a post in the Map Room of the Offices of the War Cabinet and towards the end of November he had resumed his duties as a Wing Commander there. As he was not actually a member of the Joint Planning Staff, he was never officially aware of the forward plans under consideration. But owing to his constant contact in the famous fortress basement below Whitehall with those responsible for the High Direction of the war, there was little that he did not know about what was going on and differences of opinion between the Allies on the way in which their forces should be used.

It was one such difference that had deprived them, after the splendid initial success of 'Torch', of the magnificent achievement envisaged by Churchill. The original British plan had been for a third Allied landing at Philippeville in Tunisia, two hundred and fifty miles further east along the coast than Algiers. But the Americans had flatly refused to agree and insisted instead that the third landing should be made at Casablanca, a thousand miles away from the enemy on the Atlantic coast. Their excessive caution had cost the Allies dear. A force based on Philippeville could have seized Tunisia before the Germans had had time to reinforce it. Within a month Montgomery's Eighth Army, advancing from the east, could have joined up with 'Torch' and the whole North African coast from Morocco to Egypt would have been in Allied hands.

Instead, owing to transport difficulties the advance of the Allied Army from Algiers had been held up and, with their usual swift ability to take counter-measures at a time of crisis, the Germans had poured troops into Tunisia. Through the winter months, with growing depression, Gregory and his colleagues in the Map Room had seen the 'Torch' forces robbed of their great prize and become bogged down.

As Gregory's mind roved over the events earlier in the year on the other battle fronts, he felt there could now be no doubt that the tide had really turned in favour of the Allies.

During the second winter of the vast campaign in the East the Russians had taken their first revenge for the destruction of their cities and the brutal slaughter of their civilian population ordered by the Nazis. After their failure to take Stalingrad the German Sixth Army had been surrounded and virtually annihilated, only Field Marshal Paulus and ninety thousand men out of his twenty-one divisions surviving to become prisoners.

From the date that General Sir Harold Alexander had taken over as Commander-in-Chief Middle East, British fortunes had also prospered there. His offensive to pin Rommel's Army down while the 'Torch' landings were made had resulted in the great victory of El Alamein, and General Montgomery had lost no time in following up this success. In eighty days the Eighth Army had driven the enemy back over a thousand miles and on February 2nd General Alexander had sent his famous telegram to Mr. Churchill, the words of which Gregory remembered well:

Sir. The orders you gave me on August 15th 1942 have been fulfilled. His Majesty's enemies together with their impedimenta have been completely eliminated from Egypt, Cyrenaica, Libya and Tripolitania. I now await your further instructions.

Rommel, although boxed up in Tunisia, had by then the advantage of mountainous country defending both his flanks and a constant stream of reinforcements being poured in across the narrows from Sicily; and he still had plenty of kick left in him. But by March 28th Montgomery's Eighth Army had forced the Mareth Line, on April 7th his forward patrols met those of the U.S. Second Corps pressing south-east, on May 7th the Allies entered both Bizerta and Tunis, on the 13th Alexander could telegraph the Prime Minister: *The Tunisian campaign is over. All enemy resistance has ceased. We are masters of the North African shore.*

Had the Americans let Churchill have his way this triumph might have been achieved five months earlier, but when the final victory was gained its results were spectacular. A score of enemy Generals, a thousand guns, two hundred and fifty tanks and many thousands of motor vehicles fell into the Allies' hands; and nearly twice the number of the enemy captured by the Russians at Stalingrad were made prisoners.

To this splendid victory the Navy and the R.A.F. had both made great contributions. In fact, without their tireless seeking out and destruction of transports bringing succour to Rommel and key points in his defences its achievement would have proved impossible.

In other theatres, too, the Navy and R.A.F. had been getting on top of the enemy. The ability of Britain to continue to wage the war successfully depended entirely upon keeping open her sea communications and during 1942 the threat to them had increased to a truly alarming degree. By March 1943 Admiral Doenitz had no fewer than two hundred and twelve U-boats at his disposal and so great a number enabled them to hunt in packs, with disastrous results to our convoys. In that month sinkings rose to an all-time high and the Allies lost seven hundred thousand tons of shipping.

But in February Air Marshal Jack Slessor had been appointed to Coastal Command. By new tactics and devices he had forced the U-boats to come to the surface and fight it out shell for shell with his aircraft. The major encounters had taken place during that spring in the Bay of Biscay, so it had become known as the 'Battle of the Bay'. In April shipping losses had been reduced by nearly sixty per cent against those of the previous month and by mid-May Slessor had broken the back of the U-boat menace once and for all. The public little realized the immense significance of this victory, but in reducing Germany's prospects of winning the war it was second only in importance to the Battle of Britain.

Over Europe, too, fleets of British bombers by night and American bombers by day were now incessantly breaking through the enemy's defences to pound his cities into ruins. On the 17th of May, only a few days before Gregory had left the Cabinet Offices to go on leave prior to setting off on his present mission, he had seen the report of one of the most devastating raids ever inflicted on the enemy. Wing Commander Guy Gibson had led in sixteen Lancasters of No. 617 Squadron. They had been loaded with a new type of bomb and the Squadron had launched these powerful missiles on the waters of the two huge reservoirs controlled by the Möhne and Eder Dams that fed the heart of the industrial Ruhr. Early reconnaissance next morning had shown that the breaching of both dams had caused millions of tons of water to flood an area miles in extent, scores of armament plants had been rendered useless for months to come and thousands of munition workers' houses made untenable.

To this far brighter picture of the war in Europe it could be added that Japanese aggression had also now been brought under control. Between their treacherous massacre of the United States Pacific Fleet at Pearl Harbour in December 1941 and the summer of 1942 they had conquered Malaya, Hong Kong, Sumatra, Java, Burma, Borneo, the Philippines and scores of other islands, while their warships sailed unchallenged from Kamchatka down to the northern waters of Australia and from the Indian Ocean eastward two thousand miles out into the Pacific.

The Americans, by extraordinary feats of improvisation and daring, had first held the Japanese in the Pacific, then built up forces large enough to go over to the offensive.

The great clash had begun in August 1942 with battles in the Coral Sea, in the neighbourhood of the Solomon Islands and desperate fighting in the jungles of Guadalcanal. With magnificent courage and tenacity the famous United States Marine Corps had held on to these, against great odds, while the Australians in the jungles of New Guinea had rivalled their Allies' bravery. In the naval battles between August and January over forty warships had been sunk and hundreds of aircraft shot down, but by the spring of 1943 the Japanese had been driven out of New Guinea, Guadalcanal was firmly in American hands and now, in May, the enemy was everywhere on the defensive.

To outward seeming, therefore, it appeared to be only a question of time before both Germany and Japan were finally defeated. But those who were responsible for the High Direction of the war were far from being as sanguine as the public about the outcome. They had learned that a new development in warfare was maturing which might not only cancel out the superiority in men and material they now enjoyed, but reduce Britain's cities to ruins, render her ports unusable and make it impossible ever to invade and conquer Hitler's 'Fortress Europa'.

As early as the autumn of 1939 British Intelligence had reported rumours that German scientists were experimenting with some form of long-range weapon. From then on, at lengthy intervals, corroborative reports had come in; but it was believed that this new, secret weapon was still in its infancy and not likely to emerge from its experimental stage for several years, by which time it was anticipated that the war would have been won. Until December 1941 it had not even been known if the German scientists were working on a revolutionary type of cannon, a rocket or a pilotless aircraft; but chance had led to Gregory finding out at least that much.

In June 1941 Herr Gruppenführer Grauber, the Chief of the Gestapo Foreign Department UA-1, had become so infuriated by Gregory's series of successes as a secret agent that he had decided to lure him into a trap and put him out of the way for good. For this purpose he had used Erika's husband, who was a distinguished scientist. A letter from Count von Osterberg had reached Erika, informing her that, revolted by the inhuman method of warfare that would result from a project on which the Nazis had forced him to work, he had fled from Germany and was living in hiding in a villa on the Swiss shore of Lake Constance. The letter went on to say that since they meant nothing to one another Erika would probably welcome a divorce, and that if she came to live in Switzerland for three months they could secure one.

As Erika's dearest wish was to marry Gregory, she had asked Sir Pellinore to help her to get to Switzerland. He had agreed, at the same time urging on her the importance of endeavouring to find out about the project upon which her husband had been working. On reaching Switzerland she had been led to believe that it was a new and terrible form of poison gas, the formula for which von Osterberg had left in his castle on the other side of the lake. She had accompanied him back into Germany to get it, so had fallen into Grauber's trap; providing, as he had planned, the perfect bait to ensnare Gregory.[1]

Meanwhile, Gregory had been on a mission in Russia. On learning what had happened he had immediately gone to Switzerland, taking with him his friend Stefan Kuporovitch, the ex-Bolshevik General who had aided him on an earlier mission and then married a French wife and settled in London. At the lake-side villa they had killed the Gestapo thug who was acting as von Osterberg's jailer, and Kuporovitch had taken his

1. See *Come into my Parlour*.

place while Gregory went into Germany. There he had succeeded in blackmailing Grauber into giving up Erika. On their return, for a brief while, they believed that Grauber had shot the spineless Count, only to realize, when they recovered from their exhaustion, that the shot had come from a Swiss patrol boat. So Erika's husband was still alive.

While he had had the Count on his own Kuporovitch had forced him to talk. The secret weapon upon which he had been working was not a new poison gas, but a giant rocket weighing seventy tons. It was being constructed at Peenemünde, on the Baltic, and had a range of over two hundred miles; so from the French coast it could be used to bombard London.

That had been in December 1941. In the fifteen months that followed further somewhat vague and conflicting reports had come in about the Germans' activities at Peenemünde; but it was not until the previous April that serious notice had been taken of them. On the 15th of that month General Ismay had sent a Minute to the Prime Minister stating that, in the opinion of the Chiefs of Staff, German experiments with long-range rockets had now reached a stage when definite facts about them must be obtained, and recommending that a secret committee under the chairmanship of Mr. Duncan Sandys should be set up to carry out a full investigation.

Air reconnaissance over Peenemünde had disclosed that the buildings of the experimental station covered such a large area that several thousand people must now be employed there, and the aerial photographs had shown missiles of several different kinds assembled near the launching sites.

Suddenly, the need for full and reliable information became regarded as a matter of urgency. Sir Pellinore, who had a finger in every pie, was consulted. Although Gregory had never been an official member of the British Secret Service, most of the top people knew of the missions he had carried out for Sir Pellinore and the elderly Baronet had to admit that few men could be better qualified to find out the facts.

Between September 1939 and October 1942 Gregory had spent many months in enemy territory and had survived many desperate hazards; so Sir Pellinore, who loved him like a son, was most loath to ask him to risk his life again. But it now appeared that if Hitler's secret weapon were allowed to become operational millions of British civilians might be killed and the Allies lose the war; so the old man had decided that it was his duty to put the situation to Gregory.

Having thought the matter over, Gregory had decided that he would stand a better chance of success if he had a companion, and the stalwart Kuporovitch had agreed to accompany him. So on this night of the 30th May 1943 there they were, lying side by side in the bomb bay of the Mosquito.

As Gregory's mind roved over the past and speculated on the future, he thought it just possible that at Peenemünde he might come across von Osterberg and, if he were exceptionally unlucky, find himself once again up against Grauber; but it never even occurred to him that his mission might lead to his again meeting the lovely Sabine, much less that Erika would become involved, and that before the end all five of them would become enmeshed by the Fates, who had decreed that two of them must die.

It was a little after two o'clock in the morning when Gregory jumped from the aircraft and Stefan Kuporovitch followed him down into Nazi Germany—that land in which a growing fear of the consequences of defeat was making Hitler's fanatical followers ever more desperate and ruthless.

2

Back into the Battle

AS THE parachute opened, Gregory let his breath go in a sigh of relief. He had found by experience that at the critical moment of having to jump he could occupy his mind by calling a cheerful farewell to the crew of the aircraft, and statistics showed that although an unlucky landing might prove painful it rarely resulted in serious injury. But there was always that actually brief, yet seemingly interminable, wait before the time came to pull the ripcord. During it the heart contracted from the awful knowledge that should the cord fail to work nothing could stop one's body rushing to earth at the speed of an express train and being smashed to pulp upon it.

When the big inverted bowl of silk had taken his weight, and he began slowly to swing from side to side, he looked about him. The moon had risen and, several miles distant, its light silvering the sea enabled him to make out the coast line. Nearer and to either side of him the light glinted faintly on two divergent railway tracks. As the Pomeranian countryside was flat and almost treeless, except for occasional copses and orchards, he could follow the railways for some distance and what he could see of them satisfied him that he had been dropped as near to the place at which he hoped to go to earth as could reasonably be expected.

Before leaving England he had made an intensive study of large-scale maps showing this section of the Baltic coast and the country for fifty miles inland. That enabled him to get his bearings, for he knew that the two railway lines converged towards the north; so the dark patch into which, when almost meeting, they disappeared must be the town of Stralsund. Two other long gaps in the glinting rails to west and east of him must be where the lines passed through Grimmen and Greifswald. He strained his eyes towards the latter, for it was some seventeen miles further off in that direction that Wolgast was situated. From there a ferry plied to the island of Usedom, at the northern tip of which lay Peenemünde; but in the uncertain light he could not see even the narrow inlet that separated the island from the mainland.

As he descended, his range of vision rapidly decreased. The sea, the vaguely discerned towns and the nearest railway tracks disappeared one after another; then below him there was only a dim patchwork of fields separated by dykes.

In a night landing it is always difficult to judge height, and his feet struck the ground with unexpected sharpness. Instantly, as he had been taught, he coiled himself into a ball and took the next blow on his right shoulder. Although there was only a light breeze he was dragged some way, rolling over and over, but managed to haul himself to a stop a few yards before his parachute would have pulled him down the steep bank of a dyke.

Swiftly unstrapping his harness, he looked quickly round. Against the night sky he caught a glimpse of Kuporovitch's parachute some three hundred yards away, just before it partially crumpled as the Russian landed. Suddenly, a dog began to bark behind him.

Swinging round he saw, partially surrounded by trees, the roof lines of a farmhouse and some outbuildings. From the air he had taken the black patch for a coppice and had planned to hide the parachutes there; but now it held a menace. If the dog woke the inmates of the farm and they came out to investigate he and Kuporovitch might soon be in serious trouble.

Losing not a moment, he hauled in his parachute and thrust it down the bank of the dyke, then followed it until only his head remained above ground level. Pursing his lips he began to hoot, giving a fair imitation of an owl. There came an answering hoot and two minutes later the Russian scrambled down the bank beside him.

'You all right, Stefan?' he asked in a quick whisper.

'Yes, and you?' The reply came in French as, although Kuporovitch had picked up enough English while in London to make himself understood, he spoke French much more fluently; so they usually used that language when alone together.

'I'm O.K.; but it's a bad break our having landed so near that farm,' Gregory muttered anxiously. 'If our parachutes are found, the police for miles round will comb the district for us, and should the farmer come on the scene with a shotgun while we're looking round, we may have to bolt for it.'

The Russian shrugged his broad shoulders. 'We'll not be seen if we lie low here for a while. And I have already found a place to hide our parachutes. I came down near a haystack. We can bury them in it.'

'Good for you, Stefan. We'll be all right then. Unless some-one unleashes that damn' dog and he smells us out.'

Side by side they lay peering anxiously over the edge of the low bank. For four or five minutes the dog continued to bark, but no other sound disturbed the stillness of the countryside. Then the barking subsided into occasional growls. After giving the animal another five minutes to settle down they crawled out from their cover, collected their parachutes and, bundling them up, carried them to the haystack. Pulling the tufts of hay from one of its sides they dug a deep tunnel in it, thrust the parachutes in as far as they would go, then stuffed back the hay.

Having disposed of the evidence that two parachutists had landed, their next problem was to get in touch with the people at the base from which they hoped to operate. Before Gregory had set out he had been briefed for this mission by the little General who directed the activities of the Secret Operations Executive from his headquarters in Baker Street.

Anxious as was the General to help, he had been unable to suggest any means by which Gregory might get into Peene-münde and, while he had succeeded in establishing a wide-spread network of agents in contact with the Resistance move-ments in all the enemy-occupied countries, he had no such contacts at all in northern Germany. However, it was known that since Hitler's catastrophe on the Russian front, and his inability to protect the German cities any longer from devastating air-raids, several sections of the German people who had always been opposed to the Nazi regime had become much more active and, apparently, were now prepared to assist the Allies in defeating their country swiftly, rather than allow the war to continue until it was utterly ruined.

Between these groups there was no co-ordination, but some of their members were smuggling out useful information by way of Switzerland and Sweden. With a view to giving them encouragement and support the General had endeavoured to trace these messages back to their senders and in several cases had succeeded. One such was that of a Frau von Altern who lived at the manor house in the village of Sassen, some twenty-five miles south-west of Peenemünde; and it was from her that one of the reports had come that experiments with giant rockets were being made there.

Nothing was known about her except that she was the wife of an officer in the Pomeranian Grenadiers who between 1934 and 1937 had been Military Attaché at the German Embassy in Ankara. To have been appointed to a diplomatic post would have required Ribbentrop's approval; so von Altern must have been well looked on by the Nazis, and this was confirmed by Hitler's having decorated him at the Nuremberg Rally on his return from Turkey. In the circumstances it seemed strange that his wife should now be endeavouring secretly to damage the Nazi war effort; but that might be explained by the possibility that she had been born a Pole or had Polish connections, for it was a Polish officer whom she had helped get away, after he had escaped from a prisoner-of-war camp, who had brought her message out and delivered it to the British Embassy in Stockholm.

Unfortunately, the Pole could not be questioned further about her because he had been killed in a car smash shortly after arriving in Sweden, but it had seemed reasonable to assume that Frau von Altern's husband was absent on active service, and that if Gregory and Stefan could get in touch with her she would at least prove willing to receive them at the Manor temporarily, until they had a chance to decide on their next course of action.

Sassen, Gregory judged to be about five miles to the south, but he had no intention of walking in on Frau von Altern without warning. That would have been much too dangerous. For one thing, it seemed most unlikely that her husband was aware of her secret activities and he might be home on leave, or have been invalided out of the Army on account of a severe wound, so now again permanently living with her. For another, she might lose her nerve and, fearing to be compromised herself, give them away in a fit of panic. Gregory had therefore decided that their first move should be to the nearest town.

Alongside the haystack there was a cart track running roughly east and west. Pointing west along it he said, 'As far as I could judge we've come down nearer Grimmen than Greifswald, so it's Grimmen we'll head for.'

Both of them had light-weight suitcases strapped to their backs, but the contents of the cases were fairly heavy so, as they moved off, like two hikers with packs, they walked with their heads thrust forward. After a few hundred yards the track brought them to a road. Taking the moon as a guide, they turned north. Another mile and they reached a cross-road which enabled them to turn west again.

By this time it was getting on for three o'clock in the morning. The countryside was still deserted and so silent that instinctively the few remarks they exchanged were uttered in low voices. For about three miles they followed the road until from a twisting country lane it entered a broader highway. Soon afterwards scattered houses showed that they were approaching the town. It was now just on four o'clock and no-one was yet about, but Gregory halted and said:

'I'm sorry, Stefan, but the time has come when you must lug my case as well as your own.'

Gregory's caution was justified, as both of them were wearing captured German uniforms. His was that of a Major in the Artillery and it had been altered to fit him admirably, but that worn by Kupovovitch was an ordinary private's, selected as suitable to his massive figure, although in places a little baggy; and it might well have aroused suspicion if a German officer had been seen humping his own baggage while he had his soldier servant with him.

As they did not wish to give the impression that they had walked a considerable distance, Kuporovitch also unstrapped his case from his back; then they proceeded into the town. If challenged they had little fear of trouble, as Gregory was carrying forged papers showing him to be Major Helmuth

Bodenstein of the 104th Artillery Regiment, now on sick leave, and Kuporovitch had a forged Army pay book describing him as a Ruthenian *Hilfsfreiwillige*—as foreigners who had volunteered for service in the German Army were called—to account for his Slavonic features and the fact that he could speak only a smattering of German.

In this latitude, as far north as Westmorland, now that it was barely three weeks to the longest day in the year, dawn came early, and its grey light was now replacing that of the sinking moon. They were no longer walking side by side but with Gregory a pace ahead, and to a casual observer they would have appeared well suited to the roles they were playing.

Thin and wiry, Gregory was a shade taller than Kuporovitch and, although normally he inclined to stride along with his head aggressively thrust forward, which gave him a slight stoop, he had trained himself when wearing German uniform to square his shoulders and give an impression of habitual arrogance. Under his peaked cap his brown hair, with its widow's peak, was now cropped short, his lean features portrayed the habit of command and the old scar which drew his left eyebrow slightly up into his forehead might well have been received in a student duel.

Kuporovitch, by contrast, was thick-set and his heavy jowl gave the impression that he might be flabby. But that was an illusion, for he was almost solid muscle and immensely strong. His hair had become prematurely white but his thick eyebrows had remained dead black. Beneath them his blue eyes were again deceptive, as they had a mild, lazy look, whereas he was in fact extremely shrewd and completely ruthless.

They had first met when Gregory had been on a mission to Finland during the Russo-Finnish war in 1940.[1] He had temporarily become Kuporovitch's prisoner when that worthy was Military Governor of Kandalaksha up on the Arctic Sea. But the General had proved no ordinary Bolshevik. In that isolated post, eager for news of the outer world, he had treated Gregory as a guest and they had sat up all night drinking together.

During those hours of camaraderie Kuporovitch's story had emerged. As a young man he had been a Czarist cavalry officer.

1. See *Faked Passports*.

Like the majority of his kind he had lost all faith in the Imperial regime and, believing that sweeping reforms were long overdue, had welcomed the Democratic Revolution led by Kerensky. Six months later the Bolshevik Revolution had followed and the men began to shoot their officers; but he had been saved by one of his sergeants named Budenny, who had later become a great cavalry leader and a Marshal of the Soviet Union.

Having little choice, Kuporovitch had then sided with the Reds and later, as a professional soldier, given of his best; so in due course he had been promoted to General.

Later on in the night, when he had told Gregory about himself, it had transpired that although he had served the Communists he had never had any illusions about them. Under their rule, he declared, his beloved Russia had become a drab, dreary, poverty-stricken country that grew worse every year instead of better, and there was no longer anything in it that could appeal to any civilized human being. For several years past he had been secretly amassing foreign currency with the intention of one day escaping from Russia, his great ambition being to spend his old age in Paris, which he had visited several times when a young man and had come to love.

Gregory had had on him a large sum in German marks. Kuporovitch had agreed to exchange them, at a rate highly favourable to himself, for roubles. They had escaped from Russia and later worked together in Paris against the Nazis.[1] Since those days they had become firm friends, and trusted one another implicitly.

Now, with Gregory leading, they soon entered a street of mean houses, but all of them were still dark and silent. At its end they passed a small factory where lights showed that a night shift was at work. From the yard a lorry suddenly emerged, but the driver took no notice of them. As they advanced, the streets grew wider with shops and larger buildings. Nearly all of them dated from the last century; for Grimmen was not a progressive industrial town, but dependent mainly on agriculture.

They passed a cattle market and reached a corner from which they could see into the main square. Opposite them stood an

1. See *V for Vengeance.*

eighteenth-century building that was obviously the *Rathaus*. Leaning against the stone balustrade in front of it there was a solitary policeman. Before he noticed them they had drawn back and, taking a narrow side turning, come upon a broader street with tramlines running in the direction of the railway. As their first objective was the railway station, they followed the lines for some way. When a pony-drawn milk cart came rattling towards them they took cover in a still-shadowed doorway, and to pass a baker's, where new bread was being loaded into a van, they crossed to the other side of the street.

A few minutes later they reached the station. Somewhere outside it an engine was hissing, but there were no other signs of life. To the left of the station was a small park. Entering it they sat down on a bench, as they now had to wait until a train came in. Gregory got out his cigarette case and they smoked the last of his giant Sullivans.

While they were doing so the town began to stir. Lights went on in the buildings round the square and several people crossed it on their way to work, but no-one entered the park and a clump of bushes concealed them from passers-by outside. The sounds of shunting in the nearby railway yard raised false hopes in them now and then, but it was not until soon after six that they caught the unmistakable roar of an approaching train coming from the south. It pulled up in the station and remained puffing there for some minutes, then went on.

As it could now be assumed that they had arrived in Grimmen by it they left the park. For a long time past petrol had been so scarce in Germany that taxis could be got only with difficulty, and it would appear quite natural for them to have walked from the station to an hotel. Returning to the main square they decided that the *Königin Augusta*, which stood opposite the *Rathaus*, looked as good as any they were likely to find; so they went into it.

An elderly manservant who was sweeping out the hall fetched the manager. They produced their papers and Gregory filled in forms stating that they had come from Berlin. The manager then took them up to a large room on the first floor with faded wallpaper and old-fashioned furniture. Having shown it to Gregory he said that his servant would be

accommodated in a room on an upper floor and could eat
with the staff in the basement.

Leaving Kuporovitch to unpack their few belongings,
Gregory went downstairs to a stuffy lounge in which there were
two writing desks. Sitting down at one he proceeded to write
a letter, that he had already carefully thought out, on a sheet of
the shoddy yellowish paper which at this stage of the war was
all that hotels could provide. It was to Frau von Altern and ran:

*I have recently returned from a mission to Sweden and am
spending my leave in northern Germany because I have never
before visited this part of the country. I hope, too, to get some
fishing. Mutual friends of ours at the Turkish Embassy in
Stockholm suggested that I should pay my respects to you and
that you might be able to suggest a quiet village on the coast
where I could enjoy a fishing holiday. I am, of course, aware of
the security reasons which have necessitated restrictions being
placed on entry to the coastal zone in the neighbourhood of
Usedom, but hope there may be a suitable place somewhere near
Stralsund or perhaps on the west coast of the island of Rügen. If
you cared to lunch with me here tomorrow and give me the
benefit of your advice I should take that as a great kindness.*

Having addressed his letter he took it across the square to
the main post office and posted it himself. By the time he got
back the coffee room was open and, producing his forged
ration book, he made a far from satisfying breakfast of cereal,
a small piece of cheese and ersatz coffee.

Up in his room he found Kuporovitch who, in the meantime, had fared no worse but no better. Talking over their
situation they decided that, so far, everything had gone
extremely well. Their parachutes might have been seen coming
down by some night patrol, but they were now well away from
the place at which they had landed and no-one had seen them
enter the town on foot.

The cheerful Russian had met with no difficulty in establishing himself in the staff quarters, as in wartime Germany there
were countless thousands of foreigners—displaced persons,
imported labour and service men in the armies of Germany's

allies—so no-one had thought it strange that the Major should have a Ruthenian as his servant.

Gregory had got off his letter and received an assurance that it would be delivered first thing the following morning. To anyone into whose hands it might fall it was innocent enough; but his mentions of an Embassy in Stockholm and to security measures in the island on which Peenemünde stood would, he hoped, connect in Frau von Altern's mind, and prepare her for the possibility that his real purpose in coming to North Germany was his having been informed of the secret intelligence she had sent out to aid the Allies.

Having been up all night the two comrades intended to sleep through most of the day; so they separated and went to their respective beds. At about three o'clock Gregory awoke, but spent a further hour dozing, until he was roused by Kuporovitch coming into the room.

With a smile the Russian said, 'I just came to let you know that after I have drunk some of the muck that passes here for coffee I shall be going out.'

'I was thinking of doing that myself,' Gregory replied, 'but, unfortunately, we can't go together. It would never do for a German officer to be seen walking side by side with a private.'

Kuporovitch's smile broadened. 'When I went downstairs again after my sleep I got into conversation with a young chambermaid. Her name is Mitzi, and as it is her evening off she has agreed to have a meal with me later and show me the gay life of Grimmen.'

Gregory returned the smile. He had no need to warn his friend to be careful to say nothing which might lead the girl to suspect that he was not really a private soldier, but as Kuporovitch professed to adore his French wife, and had spent ten days' leave with her before leaving England, he did remark:

'Stefan, you are incorrigible. It is barely twenty-four hours since you left Madeleine; and I know you far too well to suppose that you do not mean to seduce this Fräulein Mitzi if you get half a chance.'

'*Nom d'un nom!* Naturally I shall seduce her,' Kuporovitch agreed amiably, 'and it should not be difficult. Have we not seen in the intelligence reports Hitler's announcement that it is

the duty of patriotic German women to give themselves to
soldiers on leave from the front? So, *Heil Hitler!*'

'That is no excuse for seizing the first chance to be unfaithful
to your charming wife.'

'Dear friend, you are talking nonsense. It is the Puritan
streak in you with which all Englishmen have been cursed.
Your morals are no better than those of the men of other
nations, but you have always to provide an excuse for yourselves before going off the rails. As for my little Madeleine,
since she is a French girl she has no illusions about men. And,
even if she would not admit it, the last thing she would wish is
that I should lose my virility through observing a monk-like
chastity while away from her.'

'Lose your virility, indeed!' Gregory laughed. 'You've had
little time to do that as yet.'

'Maybe, maybe. But one should never lose an opportunity
to keep one's hand in.'

'Good hunting, then. But don't give Mitzi a little Russian
if you can help it, or he'll become one more German for us to
have to kill off in the next war.'

When Kuporovitch had gone, Gregory dressed and went out
into the town. For the better part of an hour he strolled about
the streets, noting with interest that at least one in ten of the
people in them was a disabled soldier, evidently convalescing.
Their numbers far exceeded those that would have been seen
in an English market town, and were ample evidence of the
enormous casualties sustained by the Germans in the terrible
battles on the Russian front.

He noted, too, with satisfaction the scarcity of goods in all
the shops; but he had no difficulty in picking up a good rod and
other second-hand fishing tackle that was essential to his cover.
In the two suitcases they had been able to bring only necessities,
as the greater part of one case was taken up by a wireless powerful enough to transmit messages to London; so he bought
another case and, before returning to the hotel, half filled it by
using some of the forged coupons he had brought to make a number of additions to the wardrobes of Kuporovitch and himself.

When he got back he sat down outside the café that occupied the
ground floor to one side of the hotel entrance, had a drink there,

then dined not too badly off local-caught fish and stewed fruit. Afterwards he went early to bed with a copy of Thomas Mann's *Buddenbrooks*, which he had bought while doing his shopping.

Next morning Kuporovitch appeared at eight o'clock, in his role of batman, to collect his officer's field boots, belt and tunic. When Gregory asked him how he had enjoyed the night life of Grimmen he replied:

'*Pas de Diable!* It was even more depressing than I had expected. A shoddy little *Nachtlokal* where one could dance to an ancient pianola.'

'And Mitzi?'

The Russian shrugged his broad shoulders. 'When one cannot get caviare one eats sausage. You will recall that in Paris the French used to describe the German girls in uniform as their troops' "bolsters". By failing to join up, Mitzi missed her vocation. These German women are abysmally ignorant of the art of love and have no imagination. But she has pretty teeth, is as plump as a partridge and has the natural appetites that go with a healthy body.'

Three-quarters of an hour later, his buttons, boots and belt polished to a mirror-like brightness by the amorous ex-General, Gregory went downstairs to breakfast. After his meal he again went out to kill time in the town. The principal church had the bleak, uninspiring interior common to Lutheran places of worship; but there was a small museum in which he browsed for an hour over the weapons of long-dead soldiers, a collection of ancient coins and a number of indifferent paintings. At midday he returned to the hotel and, having told the porter that he was expecting a lady, settled himself at a table outside on the pavement in the row immediately in front of the café's plate-glass window, so that by sitting with his back to it he would not have to turn his head frequently to make certain that anything said there was not overheard.

Idly he watched the somewhat lethargic activities in the square while wondering if Frau von Altern would turn up, or if he would have to take more risky steps to get in touch with her. Owing to petrol rationing there were not many vehicles about; so, after he had been sitting there for some time, he noticed a rather battered farm truck when its driver parked it alongside a few others in the open space and, getting out, walked towards the hotel.

She was a tall, thin woman and, seen from a distance, appeared to be about forty. As she came nearer he saw that she had an oval face with high cheek-bones, very fine eyes, a mobile mouth and was considerably younger than he had at first thought. But her nose was fleshy, her complexion dark and, although he could not see the colour of her hair under the headscarf she was wearing, he felt certain that she was a Jewess. Knowing that ninety-nine per cent of the Jews in Germany had long since been rounded up by Hitler's thugs and pushed into gas chambers or were in concentration camps, he found the sight of one walking unmolested in a North German town most surprising, and wondered idly what price she was having to pay to retain her freedom.

The hotel porter was gossiping with a crony on the pavement, but the woman asked him a question and he pointed to Gregory. Instantly the alarm bell in Gregory's brain began to shrill. For no conceivable reason could any woman in the town other than Frau von Altern come to enquire for him at the hotel; yet this could not possibly be the real Frau von Altern.

Seized with acute apprehension, it flashed into his mind that the Gestapo must have got on to Frau von Altern and his letter to her had been turned over to them.

No doubt they had reasoned that for a true German woman to send important information to the enemy would have appeared to British Intelligence hardly credible; so their agent would expect Frau von Altern to be of foreign birth or, since the suffering of the Jews had aroused in them such bitter hatred of the Nazi regime, a German Jewess; so they had decided to use a woman of that persecuted race as their stool-pigeon.

The fact that she was free could be accounted for either by the possibility that she was the mistress of some Nazi official, or that she had been let out of a concentration camp and had agreed to impersonate Frau von Altern to save herself from the gas chamber. Probably she was hating the role she was being forced to play, but if her life depended on it that would not prevent her from doing her utmost to trap him. And he had seconds only to think of a way of saving himself.

3

Tense Moments

As THE tall, flat-chested woman came towards Gregory, he noticed subconsciously that the clothes she was wearing had once been good but were baggy from long use and that she had a generally uncared-for appearance. That fitted with the theory that she had been hurriedly released from a concentration camp. Suddenly, he realized that he was staring at her with apprehension. Swiftly he strove to compose his features and adjust his thoughts to this perilous situation.

Everything he had meant to say to her must remain unsaid. Instead, he must do his utmost to convince her that he really was an officer on leave, interested only in fishing. In making use of a Jewess the Germans, as was so frequently the case, had underestimated the intelligence of their enemy; but, even alerted as he was to his danger, how could he at such short notice explain his having said that he had come from Sweden, or give an account of his recent activities which could not immediately be checked up and found to be false? And, even if he could succeed in fooling her, for the Nazis to have sent her there meant that they must have seen his letter. That made it certain that Gestapo men in plain clothes were among the people at the nearby tables, covertly watching him, ready to pounce instantly should he attempt to bolt for it.

Knowing that his only hope lay in keeping his head, he succeeded in acting normally. Coming to his feet he clicked his heels and bowed sharply from the waist in the approved German manner, rapping out as he did so the one word 'Bodenstein'.

Searching his face with her large eyes, which were grey and unsmiling, she extended her hand. He took and kissed it, murmuring, 'Frau von Altern, it is a pleasure to meet you; and most gracious of you to enliven a lonely soldier's leave by coming to take lunch with him.'

'That we have mutual friends is quite sufficient,' she replied. 'It is in any case a duty to do anything one can to make our men's leave enjoyable. But you looked quite surprised at seeing me.'

Her voice was deep and she spoke German with a heavy accent, so Gregory was able to say, 'It was your appearance that took me by surprise. I—well, I had not expected you to be a foreigner.'

'How strange,' she remarked as she sat down in the chair he was holding for her, 'that our friends did not tell you that I am Turkish by birth. I married Ulrich von Altern when he was at the Embassy in Ankara. Perhaps, then, you also do not know that my beloved husband was killed six months ago on the Russian front.'

That von Altern was out of the way for good, so could not become a complication, was good news for Gregory, but he hardly gave that a thought so great was his relief at the earlier part of her statement. For a German while stationed in Turkey to have married a Turkish woman was in no way abnormal. Her Near-Eastern origin explained her features and their semi-Asiatic cast made her in Western Europe easily mistakable for a Jewess. Since she was not, there was no longer any reason to suppose that she had been planted on him by the Gestapo. Freed from his fears, he swiftly recovered himself, beckoned over the old, lame waiter and asked her what she would like to drink.

With quick, nervous gestures she fished a cigarette out of her bag, lit it and ordered *Branntwein*—an unusual drink before lunch—but Gregory made no comment and, as the waiter limped away, sought to make a new appraisal of her. At closer quarters he judged her to be in her middle thirties. She wore no make-up and her skin was sallow, merging into almost black shadows beneath her fine grey eyes. An untidy wisp of hair protruding from under her scarf now showed him that it was red. He decided that as a girl, when her nose would have been less fleshy, she must have been good-looking, but lines running from her nose and about her mouth now furrowed her features.

Although relieved of his sudden fear that he had fallen into a trap, he was still on delicate ground; for he had yet to make certain that it was she who had sent the information about Peenemünde to Sweden. So, having commiserated with her on her husband's death, he went on cautiously, 'It is not for us to question the Führer's wisdom, but one cannot help feeling that the sacrifices he demands have become almost unbearable.'

'You are right, *Herr Major*,' she agreed bitterly. 'Had my husband been killed while marching against France that would have been one thing; but for him to have died last winter in the snows of Russia is quite another. In *Mein Kampf* the Führer declared that never again should the German people be called on to fight a war on two fronts, and in that he betrayed them.'

To declare that Hitler had betrayed his people was a very dangerous thing to do, particularly when speaking to a person one had only just met; so Gregory assumed that she was giving him a cue and replied:

'Hitler having gone into Russia before he finished with Britain can end only in our defeat. Personally, I take the view that anyone who now does what he can to thwart the Nazis, so that war may be brought to an end before Germany is utterly ruined, would be acting in the best interests of our country.'

His words amounted to unequivocal treason, and S.O.E.'s briefing was not always reliable. If, after all, she was not the source from which they had received information, and her outburst had been caused only by resentment at the loss of her husband, she might quite well denounce him.

The forged papers he carried were adequate for all ordinary purposes, but the identity he had assumed could not stand up to investigation. German thoroughness in keeping records would soon disclose that there was no such person as Major Helmuth Bodenstein. If she turned him over to the police his mission would be at an end before it had properly begun. But he had known that sooner or later in their conversation, if he were to get anywhere with her he must offer her a lead and take the risk that he had been misinformed about her. Having made his gamble, with his heart beating a shade faster, he waited for her reaction.

For a moment her grey eyes remained inscrutable, then she said in a low voice, 'I was right then in assuming that you did not wish to meet me only to enquire about fishing?'

He nodded. 'Yes. There are other matters of interest up here in Pomerania about which I am hoping you may be able to tell me.'

At that moment the waiter brought her drink. She swallowed half of it at a gulp, then asked, 'Such as?'

'Such as that about which some weeks ago you sent a report by a Polish officer to Sweden.'

She gave a little gasp and looked round nervously. 'How . . . how do you know about that?'

'Through a certain Embassy.'

'In your letter you mentioned having friends in the Turkish Embassy, but it could not have been through them?'

'No. I put that in only to act as cover for both of us should my letter have fallen into wrong hands.'

Fumbling for another cigarette she lit it from the one she was smoking; then her voice came in a whisper, 'You are, then, a British agent?'

Gregory nodded. 'Yes, I have been sent here specially to contact you and ask your help in securing more exact particulars about these, er, long cigars.'

With a swift movement she gulped down the rest of her brandy, then she said, 'Can I have another? I must have time to think.'

Catching the waiter's eye, Gregory pointed at their empty glasses. Turning back to her, he said very quietly, 'In this our interests are mutual. You cannot wish the war to go on until millions more Germans are killed on the battlefields or blown to pieces in their homes by bombs; and I, naturally, am most anxious to prevent millions of British men, women and children from being obliterated by these ghastly secret weapons. If the two countries make it a fight to the finish there will be nothing worth having left to either side. Hitler has made his great gamble and lost it, but for this one thing. If you and I can prevent his using it peace will come while both nations will be little worse situated than they were in 1918 and a few years should bring full recovery to them both. It is a choice of that or destruction so terrible that those of us who are left will be living like pariah dogs in the ruins for decades to come.'

'I know it,' she murmured, 'but to secure this information you seek would be extremely difficult and entail great risks.'

'Naturally. But I have considerable experience in such matters; and, as far as risks are concerned, it will be for me to take the major ones. All I ask of you is to give me any lead you can and, if possible, provide a base from which I and the companion I have brought with me, who is posing as my soldier servant, can get to work.'

Her second brandy arrived at that moment. Taking it eagerly, she again drank half of it, then she said, 'I should like to help you, but I cannot give you an immediate answer. I must first consult my father.'

He gave her his friendliest smile. 'Thank you. How soon can you do that?'

'Petrol is precious. Having come in here I must not lose the opportunity to make a round of the shops for cigarettes. But if my father agrees, the sooner you leave Grimmen the better; so immediately I get back to Sassen I will speak to him then telephone to you.'

She finished her second drink and they went in to lunch. Over the meal, he learned that the von Altern estate covered several thousand acres. Before the war it had been farmed by her husband's cousin. When he had been called up she had taken over and still ran it with the assistance of one of the tenant farmers. It meant a lot of hard work, but had its compensations, as it enabled them to live very much better than people in the towns and cities.

Gregory tried to draw her out about herself, but she proved very reticent. All he could get out of her was that she had married von Altern during his first year in Turkey as Military Attaché, that to her great regret they had had no children and that her father, who was a doctor, had come to live with her at Sassen soon after the war broke out. For the remainder of the time they talked about the war situation, but exercised care not to express any opinions which, if overheard by anyone at the nearby tables, would draw unwelcome attention to them.

Shortly after two o'clock Gregory escorted his tall, somewhat untidy-looking guest to the entrance to the hotel and bowed her away.

At first he had been at a loss to decide what had attracted a Prussian aristocrat like von Altern, who also must have been a Nazi, to her; for she was both a non-Aryan and, he felt convinced, had had only a middle-class upbringing. But while sitting opposite her at lunch he felt still more certain that when a younger woman she must have been decidedly attractive.

During the meal she had eaten little but had chain-smoked all through it and, although he had offered her wine, she had stuck to brandy, even drowning her ersatz coffee in it; so he thought it probable that grief for her husband's death had caused her to take to drink. If so, that would account for the deterioration in her looks and her scruffy appearance. That she had proved intensely serious and had shown not a trace of humour gave him no concern, for he knew it to be safer to work with such a woman than one who was inclined to be light-minded and flirtatious; but he could have wished that she had a more pleasant personality.

Sending for Kuporovitch, he told him the situation and that he had better not leave the hotel that afternoon; then he settled himself in the lounge with his book to await Frau von Altern's telephone call.

She did not ring up till past five, but what she said was entirely satisfactory. 'My father is quite angry with me for not having asked you out here at once. He says it is unthinkable that we should leave an old friend of my husband's at an hotel and that you must spend as much of your leave with us as you would care to. Later we will make plans for you to get some fishing. Please be ready with your servant at half past six and I will come in to Grimmen to pick you up.'

Gregory politely protested that he did not wish to be a bother to them but accepted for a night or two anyway; then rang off. Kuporovitch was summoned and they went upstairs to pack. Now that they had a third suitcase Kuporovitch was able to put his few things in one while Gregory retained the other and that which contained the wireless transmitter. By twenty past six Gregory had paid their bill and they were standing on the steps of the hotel with the suitcases beside them.

They were not kept waiting long. As Frau von Altern brought the farm truck to a halt Gregory stepped forward, saluted, bowed and, indicating Kuporovitch with a negligent wave of his hand, said, 'This is my servant, Janos Sabinov. He is a Ruthenian, but speaks enough German to make himself understood.'

The Russian made an awkward bow, murmured, '*Küss die hand, gnädige Frau,*' put the suitcases into the back of the truck and scrambled in after them. Gregory climbed in beside the driver and they set off.

As soon as they were clear of the town and had entered a winding lane that ran between broad, flat fields, his companion said to him, 'I must now tell you something more about us. My husband's cousin, Willi von Altern, who ran the estate before the war, returned in the autumn of 1940. During the invasion of France he was blown up by a shell and seriously injured. He lost a leg and, although he was fitted with a false one, so can now get about quite well, he is no longer capable of running the place because his mind was also affected. We make use of him for simple tasks, but his memory is quite unreliable. He was never particularly well disposed towards me and my father and if his brain were still capable of taking in our sentiments I think he would betray us. But, fortunately, there is little danger of that.'

'All the same, I will say nothing of our business in front of him, just in case he might repeat it,' Gregory commented.

'Such caution is wise,' she replied. 'We, too, observe it. We are also careful in front of the farm hands and servants. They are peasants and I believe all of them to be loyal to the family. But, like most Germans, they still look on Hitler as a god; so to criticize him in front of them would be dangerous. I am thinking now more of your companion than yourself, as he will have to mix with them.'

'You may rest easy about him. Janos and I have done this sort of thing before, and both of us know that by failing to guard our tongues we would risk our necks.'

'It is a great comfort to me that you should be so experienced,' she sighed. Then, after a slight hesitation, she went on, 'Lastly, there is Herr Hermann Hauff. He does not live

with us but he comes frequently to the Manor. On his own
account he farms one of the largest properties on the estate, but
he also acts as our bailiff and handles matters for me that I
would find difficulty in dealing with myself. He is shrewd and
ambitious. He was among the first in this part of the country to
join the *Partei*; so has for long been the chairman of the local
Committee in Sassen and holds the rank of Sturmbahnführer in
the S.S. He is also a member of the area committee at
Greifswald. Most of these Nazi officials make their Party work
a full-time job, but to produce as much food as possible has
been so important since the war that he was encouraged also
to continue as a farmer. Having such an influential Nazi in
our employ is a great asset to us. To him we owe it that we get
top prices for our produce, a much bigger allotment of
fertilizers than we are entitled to for our acreage and in winter
of cake for our cattle; also he sees to it that no investigation is
ever made into the amount of meat, butter, eggs and so on that
we keep for our own use.'

'What a friend to have in these times,' Gregory remarked
drily. 'And does he do all this simply out of devotion to the
memory of your late husband?'

'No,' she replied quietly. 'He does it because he hopes to
marry me.'

'Then I congratulate you on your conquest.' There was no
trace of sarcasm in Gregory's voice, but she immediately took
him up:

'Were I as I was half a dozen years ago you might have
some reason for supposing that I had made a conquest, but you
surely cannot think that I now have any illusions about my
looks? Herman wants me for his wife only because that would
make him master of Sassen.'

'I'm sorry,' Gregory murmured. 'In that case, the situation
must be awkward for you.'

'Not at the moment. Fortunately, he has a wife already. But
it would become so should he succeed in getting rid of her.'

'Could he do so legally, or do you mean . . .?'

She nodded. 'His wife is an invalid, so more or less at his
mercy. Habit has made these local Party chiefs like Hauff
completely unscrupulous. They think nothing of having Jews

and people against whom they have a grudge beaten up so savagely that they die from their injuries. Anyone who holds life so cheap is capable of hastening the death of an unwanted wife.'

'That's true. But you told me your father is a doctor, and presumably in a small place like Sassen there is no other; so he attends Frau Hauff. Surely he would become aware of it if Hauff gave his wife an overdose, or something of that kind. And even Nazis cannot murder their wives with impunity.'

'My father is not a general practitioner. He is something of a recluse and goes out only twice a week to hold a clinic in the village. For that he is much respected because he is a very able physician and treats everyone who comes to the clinic free of charge. But he never visits patients unless called on in an emergency.'

They fell silent for a few minutes, then she said, 'You must do your best to gain Hauff's good will. Flatter him and imply that you have important friends in Berlin who might further his career if you put in a good word for him. In doing that lies your best hope of finding out what you want to know. Like most of these Nazi officials he is very vain and likes to make out that he is more important than he really is. That leads him to become boastful and, at times when he has had a good drop to drink, indiscreet. Everyone about here has known for years that there was an experimental station at Peenemünde, and more recently that there has been a great increase in the activity there. But the area is very closely guarded; so hardly anyone knows what the scientists are working on, and it was from Hauff that I learned about the rockets.'

'I'll certainly do as you suggest,' Gregory agreed, 'and, as I have met both Goering and Ribbentrop, I should have no difficulty in leading Herr Hauff to believe that they are good friends of mine.'

Ten minutes later they entered Sassen and, having driven through it, turned into a courtyard flanked by the backs of tall barns, at the far side of which stood the manor house. It was a large, two-storey building about a hundred and fifty years old and typical of the homes of the Prussian *Junker* families.

Leading the way into a low hall, on the wooden panels of

which hung a number of motheaten stags' heads and foxes' masks, Frau von Altern rang a brass hand bell. An old, bald-headed servant answered her summons and she said to him:

'Friedrich, here is our guest, Herr Major Bodenstein, about whom I spoke to you. His servant will take his bags up to his room. Show him the way and to the room he is to occupy himself, then take him down to the kitchen quarters.'

The old man shuffled away, followed by Kuporovitch, while she took Gregory into a long, low living room. The furniture was German Victorian and hideous. Evidently aware of that, his hostess remarked, 'As my husband was an Army officer he came here only for the shooting, so he would never spend any money on the place, but I hope you will not find your bed too uncomfortable.' As she spoke, she opened a pinewood chiffonier and added, 'We have just time for a drink before the evening meal.'

The choice was limited to *Branntwein*, schnapps and parsnip wine, so Gregory chose the brandy and water. His hostess had only just poured the drinks when a tall, flaxen-haired man of about thirty-five limped into the room. He was a strong-limbed fellow and had the 'barber's-block' good looks so often seen in the Teutonic male, but they were sadly marred by a terrible scar high up across his forehead.

Gregory guessed at once that he must be Willi von Altern and when they had been introduced the German said slowly, 'A friend of my cousin's? No, I do not remember you. But you are welcome.'

His pale blue eyes then wandered to his cousin's wife. Screwing up his face he stared at her for a minute with a puzzled expression then, evidently remembering why he had come into the room, he exclaimed in a sudden burst of anger:

'Khurrem, your drinking always makes you late for meals. To keep them waiting is not right. They have had a long day's work and are hungry. Come now!'

Frau von Altern merely shrugged her thin shoulders; but she tossed off her drink, waited for a moment until Gregory had hastily swallowed his, then led the way through a long corridor, in which the walls were stained with damp, to a barn-like hall with a timber roof at the back of the house. In it about a dozen

women, three elderly men and a few young boys were standing
on either side of a very long, solidly built table. Their mistress
took her place at its head, with Gregory and Willi on either side
of her, and said a brief grace; then, except for some of the
younger women who scurried into the adjacent kitchen to return with steaming dishes of food, they all sat down.

Gregory had been aware that at large farms in the more
sparsely populated parts of Europe some families who had
lived on them for generations still followed the ancient custom
of feeding with their farm servants, and he noticed with
interest that an empty space of several feet had been left
between himself and the nearest labourer; for it was there that
in mediaeval times would have reposed the dish of salt.
Kuporovitch, of course, was below it, but had placed himself
between two fresh-complexioned, if bovine, land girls.

The food was plain but good and plentiful; the dishes with
the best pieces being offered first at the top of the table. Willi
filled his plate high with masses of meat and vegetables and
gorged himself throughout the meal in silence. Khurrem von
Altern barely touched her food but carried on a desultory
conversation with Gregory about crops and the farm problems
with which she was called on to deal.

He later learned that her first name was Turkish for 'Joyous',
but few appellations could have been less suited to her. In the
present company she seemed particularly out of place, as she
never even smiled, whereas at the other end of the table the
clatter of knives and forks was constantly punctuated by
giggles at some farmyard jest and bursts of uninhibited
laughter. With the exception of Gregory, too, everyone else at
the table was a Nordic, so Khurrem's dark-complexioned face
contrasted strangely with the apple cheeks, blue eyes and corn-
coloured hair of the other women. Had she had black hair the
contrast would have been even more strongly marked. That it
was red Gregory put down to her having had a Circassian
mother, but that in no way disguised the fact that she was an
Asiatic.

When they had finished eating, Willi bade them an abrupt
'Good night' and went up to bed. Khurrem apologized to
Gregory that time had not allowed her to suggest that he might

like a wash before the meal, then took him upstairs and showed him first an eighteen-foot-square bathroom which had an ancient bath in one corner, in another an unlit wood stove and in a third a small basin; then, some way down a gloomy corridor, the room he was to sleep in. There she left him.

The furniture was in keeping with that downstairs, the principal item being a big, brass-headed double bed having only one blanket but two huge, square, down-filled cushions—such as were commonly seen in German houses in the last century—taking the place of an eiderdown. Dubiously he explored it to find, as he had expected, that instead of a spring mattress it had only a thin one of horsehair and below that a criss-cross of thin iron bands.

Kuporovitch had already unpacked for him, so, having made certain that the suitcase containing the wireless was still locked, he collected his sponge bag and walked along to the bathroom for a cold wash. Twenty minutes later he went downstairs and joined Khurrem in the long, low sitting room.

She had started a gramophone and was listening to a Beethoven symphony; so without remark he sat down opposite her. Once again she had a glass in her hand and by this time any normal woman must have shown signs of the amount of brandy she had drunk. That she did not he put down to the probability that she was an habitual 'soak'.

He thought it a little strange that, having consulted her father before agreeing to receive himself and Kuporovitch at Sassen, she had not yet presented them to him. But as she had said that the doctor was something of a recluse that would account for his taking his meals in solitude rather than in the communal dining hall; and it might be that he spent his evenings in study, so was averse to being disturbed.

For the moment Gregory was amply satisfied with the progress he had made. To have spent a night at the *Königin Augusta* in Grimmen without arousing the least suspicion that they had entered Germany clandestinely, to have successfully made the most promising contact in the area that S.O.E. could suggest and found her willing to co-operate, to be established already as a welcome guest in the home of a deceased Prussian aristocrat and have a lead to a Nazi official who must know quite a bit about what was going on at Peenemünde, was considerably more than he could have reasonably hoped for in so short a time; so, as the shadows fell, he settled down to listen to the records Khurrem put on until it should be time to go to bed.

But his experiences for that day were not yet over. Soon after darkness had fallen Khurrem suddenly got up, switched off the gramophone, stood as though listening for a moment, then said, 'My father now wishes to see you and your companion.'

Without waiting for him to reply she went out into the hall, rang the hand bell for the old houseman and sent him to fetch Kuporovitch. Immediately the Russian joined them she threw open the front door and beckoned them to follow her. As they crossed the courtyard she satisfied their curiosity at her having left the house by saying:

'We have not far to go; only a few hundred yards up the road to the old Castle in which the von Alterns lived before they built the Manor. The greater part of it is now a ruin. But my father likes solitude so we made a few rooms in it habitable for him and he is looked after there by his own servant.'

The moon had not yet risen, but, as they advanced, they saw a little way off the road, silhouetted against the night sky, the jagged outline of a crumbling tower and below it a huddle of uneven roofs. Leaving the road, they followed a winding path through some tall bushes until they came out into a small clearing adjacent to one side of the ruin. The light was just sufficient for them to make out a low, arched doorway mid-way between two arrow slits. Stepping up to it, Khurrem grasped an iron bell-pull and jerked it down. A bell jangled hollowly somewhere inside the ancient ruin. Almost at once the heavy door swung open and a swarthy hunchback of uncertain age silently ushered them in.

Without exchanging a word with him she led them down a dimly-lit stone-flagged passage and opened another heavy door on the right at its end. Momentarily they were dazzled, for the room into which they followed her was brightly lit by a big, solitary, incandescent mantle which, from its faint hissing, appeared to be powered by some form of gas.

The burner stood on a large desk in the middle of the room.

Behind it a man was sitting, but the bright light prevented his
visitors from making out his features until he stood up and
came forward. They then saw that he was tall and gaunt,
looked to be in his late fifties and had a marked resemblance
to Khurrem; but his hair was black flecked with grey, his nose
more hooked but thinner, his complexion darker and his full
mouth more sensual. His eyes were black and slightly hooded,
but his smile was pleasant as Khurrem said, '*Herren*, this is my
father, Dr. Ibrahim Malacou.'

'Major Bodenstein.' The doctor held out his hand to
Gregory. 'I congratulate you on your safe arrival here. In our
unhappy country it is a great joy to welcome men like yourself
and your friend Mr. Sabinov who have the courage to come to
our assistance in outwitting the evil men in whose hands
Germany's future now lies.'

When he had also shaken hands with Kuporovitch, and
Gregory had made a suitable reply, he motioned them to chairs,
then went on, 'My daughter has told me that our report about
the experimental work at Peenemünde reached those for whom
it was intended and that as a result you have been sent to secure
more detailed particulars. That will not be easy; but in your
endeavours I hope to aid you. Although I live mainly as a
recluse I have certain means which are not at the disposal of
others by which I can smooth your path. For one thing I have
a far larger-scale map of the areas in which you are interested
than any you can possibly have seen and a careful study of it
will certainly repay you.'

As Dr. Malacou finished speaking he stood up and, turning,
pointed to the wall behind him. Gregory had already noticed
that, whereas the two sides of the room were lined with shelves
of old books, the far one was blank except for two large maps.
While Khurrem remained seated, Gregory and Kuporovitch
joined her father in front of the maps as he went on:

'That on the left is of the von Altern property; the one on the
right delineates the northern half of the island of Usedom. On
it you will see marked the fords by which the creek separating
it from the mainland can be crossed at low water. One
moment, though. I will adjust the light so that you can see
better.'

While they remained standing within a foot of the wall he stepped back behind them. Next moment his voice rang out sharp and imperative.

'Do not move! I have you covered. Put your hands up above your heads. I have dealt with spies before, so I shall not hesitate to shoot if you disobey me. Khurrem, they are certain to be armed. Relieve them of the temptation to play us any tricks by depriving them of their weapons.'

4

A Strange Interrogation

GREGORY and Kuporovitch knew that the doctor could have stepped back no more than two paces behind them. They were two to one and by whirling round there was a fair chance that one of them could grab his pistol and force it downwards, so that as he squeezed the trigger the bullet would go into the floor. Then, between them, they could swiftly have overcome him.

Had they been amateurs, or the doctor a different type of man, they might have taken that chance. But both of them were old hands with firearms. Ample experience had taught them that in the hands of a resolute man only a split second is needed to blaze off with a weapon; and Malacou's command, given in harsh, heavily accented German, left no doubt in their minds that he would shoot without the slightest hesitation. Slowly they both raised their hands.

Swift glances to their rear had shown them that the doctor's brown, ascetic face, capped by its mass of dark, grey-flecked hair, was now menacing and the glint in his black eyes showed that he would stand no nonsense. Nevertheless, Gregory still hoped to get out of the trap into which they had fallen.

Khurrem could not remove the small automatic that he was carrying tucked into his left armpit without undoing his tunic. While her hands were occupied he meant to grab her and swing her round so that she made a shield for his body. He would then only have to drag her sideways so that both of them were between her father and Kuporovitch. His friend could be counted on not to lose a second in pulling out his pistol and, while the doctor would not dare to risk shooting Khurrem, shoot him.

Next moment his hopes were dashed. Malacou's harsh voice

came again. 'Attempt nothing while Khurrem searches you. If
one of you lays a hand on her I will instantly shoot the other.'

With silent fury Gregory realized that they were checkmated.
Before lunch that day he had had every reason to fear that he
had fallen into a trap; but Khurrem having turned out to be a
Turkish woman instead of a Jewess had swiftly exploded the
theory he had built up that Frau von Altern had been caught
out by the Nazis and another woman substituted for her.

That she was the real Frau von Altern he now had no doubt.
The natural way in which Willi von Altern and the servants had
behaved towards her was ample evidence of that. No. The trap
in which they had been caught was not one that had been
hastily arranged because his letter had been delivered to the
local Gestapo, leading them to suspect that a secret agent was
trying to get into touch with a woman they had already
arrested. It was a long-term, carefully thought-out plan.

In recent months the activities at Peenemünde had increased
so greatly that the Nazis must have realized that news of them
would have reached the Allies. They would then have reasoned
that an agent would be sent over to endeavour to obtain fuller
particulars. Instead of waiting for an agent to arrive unknown
to them, and perhaps succeed in his mission, they must have
decided to entice one over. Khurrem's husband had been a
Nazi and no doubt she had shared his political convictions; but
being of foreign origin she had made excellent bait for the
trap. They would only have had to tell her what to put in the
message she had sent to Sweden and await results.

As Gregory visualized the full extent of those results he was
almost tempted to swing round and make a fight for it. The
Gestapo would count on the agent arriving equipped with a
wireless. Having caught their man they would torture him
until he gave away the code with which he had been furnished.
When the messages were received in London it would be
thought that they were being sent by him and, as long as
they continued to come in, no other agent would be sent out.
But the messages would come from the Gestapo, giving false
information that the scientists at Peenemünde had met with
unforeseen difficulties; so the work there was making little
progress, while in reality it was being pressed forward with the

utmost vigour to bring wholesale death and destruction in Britain.

While these thoughts were rushing through Gregory's mind, Khurrem had taken his gun and had run her hands over his body to make certain that he had no other weapons concealed on him. As she stepped across to Kuporovitch, Gregory groaned inwardly, for a further deduction had occurred to him.

The man who had brought Khurrem's message to the British Embassy in Stockholm, whether he had been a Pole or only posing as one, must have been an agent of the Gestapo. His death in a car crash shortly afterwards had evidently been reported as a precaution against any attempt to trace and question him further; and, as all Gestapo operations outside Germany came under Foreign Department UA-1, this cunning plan to protect the secrets of Peenemünde must have been hatched by its Chief, Herr Gruppenführer Grauber.

Gregory was a brave man, but he blanched at the thought. The snare had not been laid for him personally, for Grauber could not possibly have known that he would be the agent sent; but now that agent had been caught he very soon would know, and his delight would be unbounded.

To have fallen into the clutches of the Gestapo was bad enough, but soon to be at the mercy of his most deadly enemy did not bear thinking about. Yet he could not prevent his thoughts racing on. Unless a merciful Providence enabled him to escape, within twenty-four hours or less he would once again be brought face to face with that pitiless sadist. Into his mind there flashed a picture of a gorilla-like figure, made doubly sinister by having the mincing gait and airs of an affected woman. He could even visualize the glint of triumph in Grauber's solitary eye. The other he had smashed in with the butt of a pistol.[1] Grauber had sworn that he should sooner or later pay for that by being kept alive in agony for months and allowed to die only by inches.

Khurrem had disarmed Kuporovitch and Gregory's nightmare imaginings were cut short by Malacou saying in a quieter voice, 'You may now turn round and lower your hands.'

As they did so, he motioned with the big automatic he was

1. See *The Scarlet Impostor*.

holding towards two chairs at opposite sides of the room, both
of which were well away from his desk, and added, 'Be seated,
Meine Herren. My interrogation of you may take some time.'

Swivelling round his own chair he sat down in it, looked
across at Gregory and went on, 'I will begin with you. What is
your real name?'

'I have nothing to say,' replied Gregory firmly.

Malacou shrugged. 'You are wasting my time. I have means
to make you talk; or, anyway, provide answers to my questions.
Tell me at least one thing. Have you ever been hypnotized?'

Gregory gave him an uneasy look, then shook his head.

'Then you would not prove an easy subject. I could, of
course, put you under if I summoned my man, had him and
Khurrem tie you up, then held your eyes open. And that is
what I shall do if you attempt to resist the measures I am about
to take. But I have no wish to spend half the night subduing
your will to mine. It will be much quicker and more pleasant
for us all if you quietly accept Khurrem as your mouthpiece.'

Extremely puzzled, Gregory stared at Khurrem as she came
towards him, then went behind his chair and placed both her
hands on his head. He knew that hypnotism was accepted by
the medical profession and now used by a number of practitioners for relieving pain and for other legitimate purposes. But
he did not suppose for one moment that by hypnotizing a
third party Malacou could get anything out of him and it was
evident that that was what the doctor now intended to attempt.
Swiftly Gregory decided that to let him try was obviously more
sensible than to allow himself to be tied up; since, as long as his
limbs were free, there was always the chance that his captor's
vigilance might relax and give him an opportunity to turn the
tables.

Malacou transferred his pistol to his left hand, rested it on
his thigh and, looking steadily over Gregory's head at
Khurrem, made a few slow passes with his right. After barely
a minute she said in a dreamy voice, 'You may proceed,
Master. I am with him.'

Transferring his gaze to Gregory, the doctor asked, 'What is
your name?'

Gregory kept his mouth tightly shut but, automatically, in

his mind he saw his usual signature on a cheque. Khurrem's low voice came again. 'It is a little difficult to read. Geoffrey, I think. No, Gregory. And his surname is—but how strange. It is that of the Roman historian, Sallust.'

Utterly amazed, Gregory jerked his head from beneath her hands; but Malacou raised his pistol and rapped out, 'Don't move! Remember that I can force these answers from you by having you tied up.'

With a sharp intake of breath, Gregory sat back. Once bound, even if he could resist the doctor's hypnotic powers, he would not be able to prevent Khurrem from again placing her hands on his head and, it seemed, extracting a certain amount of information from him. His only defence was to try to make his mind a blank.

As Khurrem's fingertips again pressed down on his forehead, Malacou waited for a moment, then asked, 'Where were you three nights ago at this hour?'

In spite of himself a picture formed in Gregory's mind. He jerked his thoughts from it and, visualizing a brick wall, strove to concentrate on that; but in vain. In flashes his mind persisted in reverting to the original scene, as Khurrem began to speak in a monotonous tone:

'He resists, but uselessly. It was a warm night and he was sitting in a garden. Seated beside him there is a fair woman. She is very beautiful with a strong resemblance to Marlene Dietrich. She must know that he is about to leave her for, although she smiles bravely, her eyes are red. With them there is another couple; the man Sabinov and a small, dark woman. She is younger than the other, also good-looking and wearing a nurse's uniform.'

'Mother of God, protect us!' Kuporovitch suddenly burst out in French. 'This is the Devil's work, otherwise it would be impossible.'

Malacou's thick lips broke into a smile and, using poor but fluent French, he commented, 'Instead of calling on the Holy Virgin in her remote serenity you would be well advised to speak with respect of the Lord of this World.' Then, turning back to Gregory, he reverted to German. 'Tell me, Herr Sallust, about this house at which you spent that night.'

Still hardly able to credit the existence of such psychic powers, Gregory stared in bewilderment at the doctor for Khurrem had given an accurate report of the picture that had floated through his mind. Before setting out on their mission he and Kuporovitch had gone up to spend their leave with Erika and Madeleine at Gwaine Meads, Sir Pellinore's ancient property on the Welsh Border. On their last night there, as it had been warm, the four of them had gone out after dinner and sat in the garden. Rendered more vulnerable by Khurrem's success he could not prevent his thoughts from flickering to and fro in response to her father's question.

Khurrem spoke again. 'It is a mansion. Far larger than Sassen and with many rooms. I see a spacious bedroom. In it there is a bed with a tall canopy. He shares it with the fair woman. I see her then in another room. It is downstairs and much smaller. There are many files in it and she is typing. In the more modern part of the mansion the big reception rooms now contain lines of beds. Young men lie in them and nurses move about among them; so it must be a hospital. I see another part of the garden. It is a big lawn and men in uniform are sitting about there, some with crutches. They are all officers of the British Air Force and there are no German guards to be seen, so this hospital must be in Britain.'

Malacou's dark eyebrows suddenly lifted. 'Khurrem, are you quite certain of that?'

Despite himself Gregory's mind slipped back to that scene as he had last seen it and after a moment Khurrem replied, 'It must be so. They cannot be prisoners of war. One of them is cleaning a shotgun.'

'*Donnerwetter!*' the doctor exclaimed, coming quickly to his feet and laying his pistol on the desk. Then, after making a few swift passes at Khurrem, to bring her out of her trance, he said to Gregory:

'Mr. Sallust, I owe you an apology. Your accent and performance as an officer are so impeccable that my daughter was completely convinced that you were a German. I, too, am fallible in such matters until I have had an opportunity to make use of my special arts and believed you to be one. It seemed so improbable that the Allies would trust a German with such an

important mission, we naturally jumped to the conclusion that
the Gestapo had become aware that we had sent information
about Peenemünde out of the country, and had planned to
plant you on us. May the Lord be thanked that neither you
nor Mr. Sabinov resisted when I held you up, for I certainly
should have shot you if you had. I fear, though, that by having
caused you to believe yourselves trapped I must have given
both of you a most unpleasant quarter of an hour. Please
accept my sincere regrets at having subjected you to such an
ordeal.'

An ordeal it had most certainly been, for Gregory had rarely
been inflicted with blacker thoughts about his probable future
than during those minutes while Khurrem had been taking
their weapons from himself and Kuporovitch. Even while the
doctor was making his apology his prisoners could scarcely
realize that their fears had been groundless, but now they both
felt an overwhelming sense of relief.

As the realization of the true situation came home to
Gregory, he felt that he must be losing his grip to have allowed
himself to be scared needlessly almost out of his wits twice
within a few hours. Yet on consideration he decided that in
both cases he had had ample grounds for his fears.

Coming to his feet, he said with a faint smile, 'Your mistake
was understandable, *Herr Doktor*. When I'm posing as a
German officer I always endeavour to live in that role and I've
had quite a lot of practice at it. Thank God, though, that your
methods of finding out the truth about people are so unorthodox and painless. I have often heard of thought transference, but never expected to witness such an extraordinary
demonstration of that gift.'

Malacou shook his head. 'It is not a gift. Anyone can
develop such powers, but, of course, training a medium like
Khurrem here to look into other people's minds is a long and
arduous business. Direct thought transference is a much
simpler matter. It was by telepathy that I told Khurrem when I
was ready to receive you here tonight, and by it I can transmit
orders to my servant. Be silent now for one moment.'

While they remained still he closed his eyes, but only for a
few seconds. Then he resumed, 'I am fortunate in having a

cellar here containing many fine wines. To cement our friendship we will drink a bottle of one of the great 1920 hocks. I
have just ordered my servant to bring it.'

After a moment Gregory asked, 'Am I right in supposing that
you could assist us in our mission by using your occult powers?'

Malacou nodded. 'Yes; and without such help I think it
almost certain that you would fail. The security precautions at
Peenemünde are quite exceptional. Since Khurrem learned
about these rockets from Herman Hauff she has cautiously
sounded out every one of her acquaintances in Grimmen,
Greifswald and Wolgast, hoping to secure further information,
but in every case she has drawn a blank. It is, too, her impression that they know nothing, other than the fact that the
number of men working at Peenemünde has greatly increased
in recent months.'

'There is no lead that you can give us, then; apart from Herr
Hauff?'

'None. And with him you must use great caution. He is both
shrewd and dangerous. I fear the only way in which you can
hope to succeed is for one of you to get into the experimental
station.'

'It was that I had in mind,' Gregory replied. 'But Sassen is
a long way from Peenemünde. It must be the better part of
thirty miles. I had been hoping that Frau von Altern would be
able to pass us on to someone who could provide us with a safe
base nearer to Usedom, from which during several nights it
would be possible to reconnoitre ways of getting across to the
island.'

At that moment the door opened and the hunchback came
in with a dust-covered hock bottle and glasses. Gregory could
now see that he had a bald head, large, limpid brown eyes and
a black moustache, the ends of which turned down. As he
placed the tray on a side-table his master spoke to him in a
foreign tongue that Gregory took to be Turkish. The man
replied in the same language, then left the room.

Malacou blew the dust off the label and showed it to
Gregory. It was a *Rauenthaler Steinhausen Kabinett Edelbeeren
Auslese 1920* but, in view of what had gone before, he felt no
surprise at this further manifestation of an unusual power.

While pouring the wine the doctor remarked blandly, 'I owe you both another apology. Tarik had orders to go over to the house, as soon as he had let you in here, and search your bags. He has just reported to me that they contain nothing that might give you away except for a wireless transmitter. He brought it back with him and I am sure you will have no objection to my looking after it for as long as you remain here.'

'Do you suspect, then,' Gregory asked, 'that someone at the Manor might also take an interest in our belongings?'

'No; no-one will spy on you there. But if you used your wireless—for example to report to London that you had reached Sassen safely and made contacts here who had promised to aid you—that could bring us all into considerable danger. Our enemies have listening stations. If they picked up a strange code they would swiftly get a fix, and in no time truckloads of them would be arriving to search the neighbourhood. The fact that you are a stranger here would draw their attention to you, and if there were the least thing suspicious about your papers that would lead to disaster for all concerned.'

Gregory felt that he could hardly blame his host for making quite certain that he made no use of his wireless while at Sassen; so as he took the glass of hock that Malacou handed him, he nodded his agreement. Then they all drank to the success of the mission.

After the first mouthful Kuporovitch smacked his lips and exclaimed, '*Herr Doktor*, this is magnificent! What a treat you are giving us.'

Holding his glass up to the light, Gregory admired the wine's deep golden colour and added, 'It's nectar for the gods. I've not tasted a hock so fine since I dined with Hermann Goering.'

Malacou raised his dark eyebrows. 'To have done that must have been a most interesting experience. You must tell me about it some time. And Goering's cellar is world-famous, so I thank you for the compliment. You are right, though, that it is something exceptional. Many of the 1921s were superb and it was a much bigger vintage, but the great wines of 1920 had more lasting power.'

After a moment, Gregory said, 'Since you cannot place us

with a fair degree of safety nearer to Peenemünde, in what way can you help us?'

'By seeking for you the protection of the stars,' Malacou replied promptly. 'Every one of us has his lucky and unlucky days. Many people who regard themselves as intelligent sneer at astrology and look on the daily forecasts that appear in the most widely read papers in all countries as no more than pandering to the superstition of the ignorant. Such forecasts can be no more than generalizations and so frequently liable to mislead a large number of their readers. But astrology is the most ancient of all sciences and an infallible guide to those who by prolonged study have learned how to make use of it. Naturally, to predict with accuracy the most favourable days on which to marry, or to commit a murder and get away with it, can be ascertained only by considering the case of the individual concerned. It is that which I propose to do for each of you.'

Gregory, like most people in this modern world, was extremely sceptical about the age-old belief that the stars influenced one's fortunes. That the doctor had hypnotized Khurrem with such surprising results still seemed to him to come within scientific acceptance; whereas he associated attempts to predict the future with charlatans who got money out of the credulous by gazing into crystals, telling the cards and suchlike dubious activities. None the less, it would obviously have been bad policy to offend his host, so he said:

'For this purpose I assume you propose to cast our horoscopes. If so, we should be most grateful to you.'

'Let us proceed, then.' The doctor took some sheets of foolscap from a drawer in his desk, picked up his pen and began to ask Gregory a long series of questions, including his birth date, his age and the exact spelling of his name. Having written down the answers in a small, neat hand, he put the same questions to Kuporovitch who, with some reluctance, but on Gregory's insistence, gave his real names. When Malacou had done he addressed both of them:

'You must not expect to receive overnight the results of the information you have given me. The influence of every planet that was above the horizon at your birth dates has to be taken into consideration, and the attributes of some at times conflict with those of others. Careful judgement and prolonged thought are, therefore, necessary before one can make a final assessment of the effect each planet may have upon your fortunes when it is in the ascendant. But it will repay you well to await my advice; so do not become impatient.'

'Is it likely to take more than a few days?' Gregory enquired.

'No. In the meantime you can be getting to know Herr Hauff, Willi von Altern and the more important people who live in the village, all of whom may later prove of use to you. I take it that the papers you carry are proof against any routine inspection?'

Gregory nodded. 'Yes, they show me to have returned from garrison duties in Norway and are good for an indefinite period.'

'How is that, when leave normally extends only for a fortnight?'

'Mine show me to be on sick leave, and that I am suffering from heart trouble.'

'While here as our guest, unless you commit some foolish act that draws attention to you, it is most unlikely that your account of yourself will be called in question. But should such a situation arise, and the authorities order you to go before a medical board, that might prove your undoing.'

'No, no!' Gregory laughed, 'I am too old a soldier to be caught out that way. In the First World War quite a number of men faked heart trouble by chewing cordite in order to escape from the horrors of the Western Front. It causes the heart to flutter. I have several strings of it on me and I should masticate one of them before I was examined.'

'Excellent. And, of course, as your soldier servant, Mr. Kuporovitch will be able to remain here as long as you do.'

Having refilled their glasses, Malacou went on, 'Now we have talked enough of our business for tonight. As you must know, the accounts of the progress of the war put out by Herr Goebbels' Ministry are very far from being accurate. By performing elaborate ceremonies my powers as an occultist enable me to learn the truth and, at times, secure glimpses of the future; so there are occasions when I know that battles reported by German propaganda as victories are, in fact, defeats. But to secure such information regularly through supernatural channels would require more time than I can give. So tell us please the latest news about the war.'

For the hour that followed Gregory did most of the talking, while Khurrem listened in silence and the doctor put in an occasional question or shrewd comment. Then he returned their pistols to them, they shook hands with him and he let them out himself. Khurrem led them back to the Manor and, shortly after midnight, they went up to their respective rooms.

It had been a long and anxious day for Gregory, but, with his usual resilience, he had by then recovered from the two periods of acute strain he had been through. Knowing nothing about the occult and never having even attended a spiritualistic séance for fun, he could still hardly believe that he had not been temporarily hypnotized himself and had imagined Malacou's extraordinary performance; but at least he was now fully satisfied that he had nothing to fear from Khurrem or her father and, within a few minutes of getting into bed, in spite of the hard mattress, he was fast asleep.

He had been asleep for about two hours when he awoke suddenly. The sixth sense that had often warned him of danger told him that there was someone in the room. Instantly he slipped his hand beneath the pillow and grasped his pistol; but a quick whisper came out of the darkness.

'*C'est moi*, Stefan.'

A shadowy figure advanced from the door and, as Gregory sat up, Kuporovitch seated himself on the end of the bed.

'What is it?' Gregory asked quickly. 'Are we in danger?'

'No; but I had to see you. Keep your voice low.'

In a slightly querulous tone Gregory murmured, 'Very well. But couldn't you have waited until the morning?'

'Dear friend, I am very worried. We must leave this house as soon as possible. There are still several hours to go before daylight, so we could get well away and find somewhere to lie up before dawn.'

'But you say we are in no danger. We've established ourselves here most satisfactorily, so why on earth should we get out?'

'I meant that we are in no immediate danger of betrayal or arrest. But if we remain here we shall imperil our immortal souls. The doctor is a wizard—a Black Magician in league with the Devil. I am certain of it.'

'Oh, come!' Gregory protested. 'The Devil was put out of business by modern science. Since the introduction of electricity and telephones nobody has believed any more those old wives' tales of a gentleman appearing to them in red tights, smelling of brimstone and with horns and a spiky tail.'

'You are talking nonsense, my friend. The Devil was a part of the original Creation. To suppose that he could be abolished by the invention of a few scientific gadgets is absurd. People have now become so materialistic that their minds are far less open to the influence of the powers of light and darkness than used to be the case, but that is all. Say if you like that the Devil has gone underground, but he still exists and has his servants working for him here.'

'There may be something in what you say,' Gregory admitted thoughtfully, 'and you certainly seem to be well up in the subject. Have you ever dabbled in the occult yourself?'

'Yes; in my youth many Russians did so. But I had an experience that convinced me that I was playing with fire, so I gave it up. By then, though, I had learned enough to be certain now that this man is a servant of the Evil One.'

'What makes you so sure of that? I admit that the way in which he extracted from me, through Frau von Altern, those mental pictures that I could not help forming of Gwaine Meads was positively astounding. But that's no evidence that he is a Black Magician.'

'I doubt if any ordinary hypnotist could have done so. But let that pass. Did you not hear him say to me that it was useless to call upon the Holy Virgin and that one should speak with respect of the Lord of this World? Surely you know that when God commanded Michael and his angels to drive the rebellious Lucifer out of Heaven he gave him the Earth as his Principality?'

'Yes, of course; still . . .'

Kuporovitch leaned forward and his low voice was intensely earnest. 'Believe me, we are in worse peril here than if we were being hunted by the Gestapo. Good cannot come out of evil. This man possesses powers that can be bought only by entering into a compact with Satan. Those powers would be withdrawn should he fail to honour his bond by doing his utmost to corrupt others. No good can possibly come to us by remaining in this house. To do so is to risk a fate that I would not wish upon my worst enemy.'

After a moment Gregory replied, 'Stefan, knowing your courage so well, I don't doubt that you feel that you have good grounds for your fears. But even if you are right about Malacou being a Satanist I cannot believe that he has the power to harm us. By that I mean harm us spiritually. At least, not as long as we retain our own faith and convictions in what is right; and I foresee no difficulty in doing that. For the rest, whether he be good or evil he is on our side against the Nazis and his help may prove invaluable. Situated as we are, we cannot afford to forgo help from any quarter, so——'

'There might be something in your argument if we could trust him,' Kuporovitch broke in. 'But we cannot. And you need no telling how dangerous it can be in our game to collaborate with a person who deceives you.'

'Why should you suppose that he is doing that?'

'Because he has already done so by leading us to believe him to be a Turk. When he learned the truth about us he should have told us the truth about himself, but he did not. While I was a young Czarist officer my regiment was stationed for two years down in Georgia, on the Turkish frontier. On two occasions I spent my leave in Constantinople, as we used to call it then. I never learned to speak Turkish but I picked up enough of it to know it still when I hear it spoken. He may have lived in Turkey, but he is not a Turk. When he spoke to that hunchback servant of his he used Yiddish.'

'You think he is a Jew, then?'

'I do not think; I am certain of it. The moment I saw his daughter my suspicions were aroused. Her red hair and the shape of her nose would lead any Russian to put her down as a Polish Jewess. I gave them the benefit of the doubt until he spoke to his servant. That clinched it. I'd bet my last *kopec* that he's simply adopted a Turkish ending to his name and that it is not Ibrahim Malacou, but Abraham Malacchi. For Jews to be still free in Germany is now unheard of. Of course, it's possible that the Nazis may believe these people to be Turks. But if the truth about them is known they can only have been left free as stool pigeons. Their having failed to come clean with us points to that; so it's my belief that we've fallen into a trap. Holding us up was just a clever act to win our confidence, and when they've got all they can out of us they'll turn us over to the Gestapo.'

5

Of Good and Evil in their Stars

FOR half a minute Gregory's brain worked overtime, assessing the degree of danger with which Kuporovitch's discovery might menace them; then he said:

'I don't doubt you're right about his being a Jew by birth, Stefan; and at my first sight of her I scared myself stiff by getting just the sort of idea you have in mind. But we do know that von Altern was Military Attaché in Turkey, so there are good grounds for believing that he met and married Khurrem while he was there. Jews have no country of their own and are a migratory people; so if Malacchi, as you say his real name probably is, was born a Polish Jew and emigrated to Turkey there would be nothing surprising about that; or that he should have changed his name to Malacou and taken Turkish national-ity. If he did he's got a Turkish passport and the Germans don't go out of their way to upset neutrals by throwing their subjects into the bin. As for Khurrem, she's in the clear because she would be on the record as a Turkish woman who married a quite high-up pro-Nazi. If I'm right I see no reason at all why the Gestapo should have put tabs on them.'

'But the Gestapo might get wise at any time to the fact that they are really Jews,' Kuporovitch argued. 'If that happened they wouldn't give a damn about Malacchi having a Turkish passport but come here and carry them off to a concentration camp. Then we too, as their guests, would indirectly become suspect. I maintain that he ought to have come clean and warned us of that risk.'

'I think you are making a mountain out of a molehill, Stefan. Remember, the Nazis' persecution of the Jews has been going on for ten years now, and it's six months since Frau von

Altern was deprived of any protection her husband could have
afforded her. If the Gestapo had found out about these people
they would have pulled them in months ago, so the risk that
they may do so now is negligible. I think, too, that it's quite
understandable that Malacou should have concealed from us
the fact that he is a Jew. After all, as far as he's concerned the
fewer people who know about that the better; and he must
have taken into account the possibility of our being caught. He
would be certain to reason that if we were, and had our
thumbs screwed off, we should betray him.'

The Russian sighed. 'Perhaps I have made too much of the
danger entailed by his having deceived us about being a Jew.
But there remains what is, to my mind, the far greater risk to
us in remaining here.'

'About that I have already told you my view,' Gregory
replied firmly. 'The very fact that these people are Jews makes
it much more certain that they honestly intend to give us their
help in getting the better of the Nazis. And we need their help
in whatever way they can give it.'

'Even if they are in league with the Devil?' Kuporovitch
asked dubiously.

'Yes. If Malacou communes, as you believe, with evil spirits,
that is his affair, not ours. We have secured what I believe to
be a safe base here, from which to proceed with our mission,
and if we left it we have no other we could make for. Besides,
you seem to have forgotten that he has our wireless. Without
it any information we may secure would be useless, as we
should be unable to transmit it to London.'

'*Mon Dieu*, yes! When he revealed that he had tricked us out
of that I was surprised that you made no protest.'

'I refrained because I was convinced that it would have been
useless. You can hardly blame him, either, for having taken
steps to make certain that we should not use it. As a matter
of fact I had intended to let Erika and Madeleine know, via
S.O.E. and Sir Pellinore, that we had landed without accident
and found safe harbourage. Malacou guessed I'd do something
of the kind and he was not to know that I'd have sent only a
single prearranged code signal, which it's certain would have
passed unnoticed in the general traffic.'

'Then you refuse to take my advice and leave this place that Malacchi has made a focus for evil.'

'Stefan, in the interests of our mission I must. But I'll not try to keep you here against your will. Since you feel so strongly about this I'll not reproach you if you decide to clear out. By morning I will have thought up some plausible reason to account for your disappearance.'

'No, dear friend, no,' said Kuporovitch heavily. 'As you are determined to stay, I will stay too. You know very well that not even fear of the Devil would induce me to desert you. But from now on I shall pray constantly to St. Nicholas to protect us from the dark powers that will seek to ensnare us.'

'Thanks, Stefan.' Gregory laid his hand on the Russian's shoulder and pressed it. 'I'd rather have you with me than any dozen other men, and between us we'll cheat the Devil, if need be, as well as the Nazis. Now let's try to put this business out of our minds and get some sleep, so that we'll be able to face up to any unexpected turn events may take tomorrow.'

The morrow brought no new fears or excitements. Gregory spent a good part of the day going round the home farm with Khurrem, while Kuporovitch loitered about, gossiping in his broken German with the house servants and the farm labourers. In the evening he paid a visit to the village inn and, in spite of the limitations of language, his genial personality secured him a good reception by the yokels. Although conversation was necessarily stilted he gathered the impression that, while everyone was aware that Frau von Altern had taken to the bottle since her husband's death, she still knew what she was up to as far as the estate was concerned; and that on account of the free clinic that her father held twice a week he was regarded with respect as a local benefactor.

On the second morning Gregory was standing with Khurrem von Altern in the big yard at the back of the Manor when an old but powerful car drove into it and a tall, florid-faced man of about forty got out. As he was wearing good-quality country clothes Gregory did not at once suspect his identity, for he would have expected any Nazi official always to wear uniform. But, striding towards them, the newcomer gave the Nazi salute with a shout of '*Heil Hitler!*' Gregory and

Khurrem promptly followed suit, then she introduced them and it transpired that he was Herr Sturmbahnführer Hermann Hauff.

Khurrem explained that her guest was an old friend of her late husband's and had come from garrison duty in Norway to spend part of his leave with them. Hauff showed his strong teeth in a friendly smile and said, 'I hope you will have a pleasant time here, *Herr Major*; but you must have found life in Norway pretty dull. I wonder that you should prefer to spend your leave in a remote country village like Sassen, rather than hit the high-spots in Berlin.'

Gregory returned the smile. 'Until quite recently I would certainly have done so; but unfortunately I have developed a weak heart and am on indefinite sick leave. All excitements and vigorous pursuits are now forbidden me; so I came here for a quiet time and hope to get some fishing.'

'That should not be difficult, although we are quite a distance from the sea here. Are you well acquainted with our Baltic coast?'

'No. I am a Rhinelander and have never before visited this part of Germany.'

Raising his fair eyebrows, Hauff remarked, 'There is good fishing to be had on the Rhine, and as you are condemned to a quiet life it must be a disappointment to your family that you have decided against spending your leave with them.'

'I would have, if I had one,' Gregory replied. 'But I lost both my parents when I was quite young and was brought up by a maiden aunt who has since died. I was, too, an only child and have never married.'

'Perhaps in that you were wise. Marriage is far from always proving a blessing. That is . . .' The Nazi's pale blue eyes flickered towards Khurrem. '. . . unless one can find the right sort of wife.'

Thinking it a chance to show his patriotism, Gregory said lightly, 'I may marry yet. In fact, since the Führer has said that it is the duty of every virile man to beget children to make good in the next generation the losses Germany has suffered in this, I have been seriously considering doing so.'

Hauff gave a sudden laugh. 'Your sentiments are laudable, *Herr Major*, but one does not have to marry to do that. There are plenty of eager Fräuleins and young war-widows about these days.'

Gregory laughed too, but shook his head. 'I fear my heart condition would not permit me to become a Casanova; but by being careful of myself I could father a family, and the idea has its attractions.'

A shade abruptly Khurrem cut in, 'Herr Sturmbahnführer Hauff has come to see me on estate business, *Herr Major*. So you will excuse us please while I take him to my office.'

'*Bitte sehr, gnädige Frau*.' Gregory stepped back, saluted her, shook hands with Hauff and added, 'I'll go for a quiet walk.'

As they turned away he decided that his first meeting with the Nazi had gone off well. Hauff had proved a more pleasant man than might have been expected. In spite of his rather close-set eyes he had an open face and genial manner, so it should not be difficult to get on good terms with him.

On the following morning at about ten o'clock, by his own mysterious means of thought transference, Malacou sent a message to Khurrem informing her that he wished to see their guests. Kuporovitch was summoned and the three of them went over to the ruin.

Tall, gaunt and slightly stooping, the occultist was standing beside the big desk in his lofty, book-lined room. On the desk lay two large parchments. On each had been drawn an inner and outer square, the border between them was divided into eight triangles and the whole was dotted with numerous figures and astrological symbols. When greetings had been exchanged and his visitors were seated Malacou pointed with a long, smooth-fingered hand to the two charts and said:

'There are your horoscopes. Since neither of you has any knowledge of astrology I shall not attempt to explain them in detail. But at least you will be aware that the Sun, the Moon and the Planets all have individual properties. It is these which govern our lives and make certain dates and periods either propitious or unpropitious for our undertakings. Anyone with knowledge of the subject is able to ascertain these, because from the most ancient times each of the heavenly bodies has been associated with a number.

'The Sun rules the number One, the Moon Two, Jupiter Three, Uranus Four, Mercury Five, Venus Six, Neptune Seven, Saturn Eight and Mars Nine. In an equal degree they are also

associated with all numbers which added together make their
own. For example, in addition to One the Sun also rules Ten,
Nineteen and Twenty-eight; the Moon Two, Eleven, Twenty
and Twenty-nine; and so on.

'The date of a person's birth, therefore, tells us the heavenly
body which usually exerts the greatest influence on his life and,
inevitably, his character is partially formed by its properties.
However, that is modified or, at times, intensified by the
number arrived at through the numerical significance of his
name, since that also attracts the vibrations of the astral body
with which it is associated.

'From the remotest antiquity, through the civilizations of
the Chaldeans, Egyptians, Hindus and Hebrews, there has been
handed down a code in which each letter of the alphabet is
represented by a number.' Beckoning them over, the doctor
added, 'I have a copy of it here.'

Standing on either side of him they looked at a paper he had
produced; on it was written:

A = 1	H = 5	O = 7	U = 6
B = 2	I = 1	P = 8	V = 6
C = 3	J = 1	Q = 1	W = 6
D = 4	K = 2	R = 2	X = 5
E = 5	L = 3	S = 3	Y = 1
F = 8	M = 4	T = 4	Z = 7
G = 3	N = 5		

While below the code both their real names and those under
which they were posing had been translated into their numerical
significance:

G = 3	H = 5	S = 3	J = 1
R = 2	E = 5	T = 4	A = 1
E = 5	L = 3	E = 5	N = 5
G = 3	M = 4	F = 8	O = 7
O = 7	U = 6	A = 1	S = 3
R = 2	T = 4	N = 5	
Y = 1	H = 5		
23=5	32=5	26=8	17=8

S = 3	B = 2	K = 2	S = 3
A = 1	O = 7	U = 6	A = 1
L = 3	D = 4	P = 8	B = 2
L = 3	E = 5	O = 7	I = 1
U = 6	N = 5	R = 2	N = 5
S = 3	S = 3	O = 7	O = 7
T = 4	T = 4	V = 6	V = 6
	E = 5	I = 1	
	I = 1	T = 4	
	N = 5	C = 3	
		H = 5	

23 = 5	41 = 5	51 = 6	25 = 7
5+5=10=1	5+5=10=1	8+6=14=5	8+7=15=6

When they had studied the figures for a few moments Malacou said, 'First we must consider your birth dates. These are of major importance because they cannot be altered; whereas by changing his name, or even insisting on being known by it with an initial between the Christian and surnames —as, for example, Gregory B. Sallust—a person can reduce a bad influence by attracting to himself that of a more favourable Planet.

'Yours, Mr. Sallust, is July 31st, therefore your birth number is 4, which comes under Uranus. However, the name Gregory Sallust gives the numerological value of 1, which is ruled by the Sun, and this is greatly strengthened by the fact that July 31st is near the middle of that period of the year which is known as the House of the Sun. You will note, too, that each of your names adds up to 5, the number of Mercury; so that Planet, too, must exert a considerable influence upon you.

'Uranus is not a fortunate Planet to be born under. Those subject to it have very positive views and opinions. They instinctively rebel against rules and regulations and often harm their careers by setting themselves in opposition to constitutional authority. But Uranus is regarded in astrological law as closely related to the Sun, and on that account frequently symbolized as 4 − 1. That being the case I am confident that your birth date is overruled by the combination of your name

number and the period of the year in which your birth took
place. From your appearance, too, any experienced occultist
would put you down as a Leo type; so we may take it as
certain that the Sun has played the major role in forming your
character and is the dominant influence in your life. The
affinity between the Sun and Uranus gives you an even stronger
individuality and makes you even more determined to go your
own way. But the Sun gives those subject to it resourcefulness
and determination, which nearly always bring success. Moreover, while everyone finds people with the same numbers as
himself the most sympathetic to him, No. 1 types are by
nature of a cheerful disposition, so get on well with nearly
everybody.'

Malacou paused for a moment, then went on: 'The
compound numbers formed by a name also have a considerable
significance; and about yours there is an unusual circumstance.
You will note that both your names give the same numerological value, 23. That number is known as "the Royal Star of the
Lion". Your having it places beyond all possible doubt that you
are subject to Leo; and it is a most fortunate number. That
both your names should add up to it is quite exceptional and
quadruples its potency. It is a promise of success, help from
superiors and protection from those in high places. Together
the two 23s give us 46. That again is a fortunate number and
has a special potency of its own. It indicates success in love,
reliable friends, sound partnerships and is a good augury for
your future.'

'Well, well!' Gregory murmured, sitting back with a smile,
'it certainly seems that I have been blessed beyond most people
in my stars.'

The doctor did not return his smile, but replied gravely,
'Remember, though, that "those beloved of the Gods die
young" and fortunate stars are no guarantee against an early
death.' He then turned to Kuporovitch and asked:

'Did you understand all that I said to Mr. Sallust?'

The Russian nodded his white head. 'Most of it, *Herr
Doktor*. I can understand German better than I speak it.'

'Very well, then. I will now interpret your numbers for you.'
Looking again at the papers before him, Malacou continued:

'Your birth date being February 11th, you are subject to the Moon; so your number is 2. Such people are imaginative and romantic. They are very sensitive and readily become subject to occult influences. This sensitivity leads to their becoming despondent and melancholy if they are not in happy surroundings. That, in turn, causes them to become restless and to crave both change of scene and feminine companions.

'Unlike Mr. Sallust, it cannot be said that several factors combine to place you under the domination of one heavenly body. The total value of your names adds up to 5, which represents the Planet Mercury. This makes you versatile and mercurial. You make friends easily and are quick in thought and decision. Gambling of all kinds attracts you and mentally you have great elasticity, so that you recover swiftly from setbacks and readily adjust yourself to new sets of circumstances.

'Your Christian name is the equivalent of 8, which is not a fortunate number; and in your case its influence is strengthened by the fact that your birth date also falls in the House of Saturn. Your surname is the equivalent of 6, the number of Venus. This gives you a magnetism that attracts others, particularly members of the opposite sex, a love of entertaining and a desire to see everybody about you happy. It also gives determination in the carrying out of your plans and a conviction that, if need be, you should die rather than fail in doing your duty.

'Now your compound numbers. 26 is again unfortunate. It foreshadows disasters either to yourself or to friends to whom you are devoted through your association with them. On the other hand 51 is, generally speaking, a propitious number. It is that of the warrior and is especially favourable to anyone engaged in a naval or military career. But I must warn you that it also carries the danger of assassination.'

Kuporovitch gave a solemn nod. 'I have no quarrel, *Herr Doktor*, with your assessment of my character and I cannot complain of the promotions I received while I was a soldier. To die by assassination presupposes a swift death; so if that is to be my fate I would not cavil at it.'

Gregory, having been greatly impressed by Malacou's accurate delineation of their personalities, said:

'And now, *Herr Doktor*, I would be most interested to hear how having changed our names may alter the influence the stars have upon us.'

'In your own case, hardly at all,' Malacou replied at once. 'Both of your assumed names, Helmuth and Bodenstein, have the value of 5; so added together again give us 10, which is the equivalent of 1. The uninitiated would consider that a coincidence, but there is no such thing. The influence of the Sun is so paramount in your life that when choosing a *nom de guerre* you were not permitted to escape from it. That is even more marked by the compound numbers of the German names you have taken. 32 and 41 have the same value. Both again reduce to 5 and have similar magical attributes as the fortunate 23.

'With regard to Mr. Kuporovitch, the name Janos produces for him another 8 and Sabinov a 7. The latter is the number of Neptune and affiliated to the Moon. It will increase his facility to make friends easily and his desire for change. His new composite numbers, 17 and 25, are both fortunate; the latter denoting success through strife and trials. But if these assumed names are used only temporarily they will have no marked effect on the activities of either of you.'

Malacou lit a long cheroot, then continued, 'Sun and Moon people are attracted to one another, as each is the natural counterpart of the other. This augurs well for your partnership. The fact that the total equivalent of Mr. Kuporovitch's real name is 5 and that all four of your names, Mr. Sallust, real and assumed, each add up to 5, greatly strengthens the bond between you, although it increases your liability to act rashly and take chances.

'There is another thing about which I must warn you. As your birth date, Mr. Sallust, is July 31st, you cannot altogether escape the influence of the number 4. Neither can you, Mr. Kuporovitch, altogether escape from the 8 you derive from Stefan and have now reinforced by adopting the name of Janos —another 8.

'The conjunction of the vibrations of Uranus and Saturn, which are represented by these numbers, inevitably brings disaster to those who are under their influence. Therefore, any 4th or 8th day of the month, or any date that can be reduced to either number, would be liable to result in misfortune if on it you were working together. This would prove especially so between December 21st and February 19th, which is the House of Saturn, and between July 21st and August 20th, which is the House of Uranus.

'However, it so happens that, as partners, you will receive compensation for that. Everyone has days in the week that are more favourable to him than others, because on each the influence of certain heavenly bodies is predominant; and it might well have been that the days favourable to one of you would have been unfavourable to the other. But the Sun and Moon, representing the male and female principle as they do, have a natural attraction and this results in the subjects of either enjoying the protection of both. Therefore, Sundays and Mondays will prove the most fortunate days for both of you. You will find, too, if these days coincide with dates ruled by your numbers, they will prove exceptionally fortunate. In consequence you should plan for your most dangerous activities to take place on the 1st and 2nd, the 10th and 11th, the 19th and 20th or the 28th and 29th of any month; and if those dates fall on a Sunday or Monday your ventures will almost certainly prove successful.'

Gregory nodded and said, 'Although up to now I've always thought of astrology as no more than a jumble of ancient superstitions, I've been most impressed by your exposition; and I feel it would be flying in the face of Providence not to accept your guidance. Can you tell us now what you think the chances are of our succeeding in our mission?'

Pointing to the two horoscopes on his desk, Malacou replied, 'To interpret these fully would take many days of hard work, but I can give you general indications. Your stars endow you with all the qualities needed to carry out your mission and your having the Royal Star of the Lion in both your names makes me confident that you will succeed in it. But not until August. Mr. Kuporovitch's horoscope shows that he will be of great assistance to you. Yet, through his association with the 8, the fact that August is the 8th month and that the greater part of it lies in the period of the number 4 Positive, he will bring you into grave danger. In fact, should you disregard my warning to take big risks only on your fortunate days, it is even possible that, owing to him, you may die in the hour of your triumph.'

At this, Kuporovitch, believing the doctor to have predicted that he would lead Gregory to his death, suddenly flared up and cried, 'How dare you attempt to undermine the confidence my friend has in me! I would be torn in pieces rather than betray him! You are a false prophet and have deceived us for your own evil ends. You are no Turk. I'll swear to that. Can you deny that you changed your name to Malacou from the Jewish one of Malacchi with which you were born?'

6

The Long Road to Peenemünde

GREGORY shot the Russian a startled glance. While he thought
it probable that his friend was right in believing the doctor
to be a Jew, he did not agree that they stood any risk of being
betrayed by him; and even if he owed his powers as an occultist to the Devil that was no affair of theirs.

What mattered was that he and his daughter were providing
them with a secure base from which to begin their operations.
This attempt to unmask him was, therefore, not only pointless
but dangerous. Rather than run any risk of their giving his
secret away, he might decide to rid himself of them. Into
Gregory's mind there flashed the memory that witches and
warlocks were said to employ poisons—and Malacou was a
doctor. . . . Swiftly coming to his feet, he intervened.

'Stefan, what on earth gave you such an idea? Before we left
London we were informed that Colonel von Altern had been
a Military Attaché in Turkey, and Frau von Altern has told
us herself that she is a Turkish lady. There is no basis whatever
for your imputation, and you have abused your position as a
guest by making it. Your faulty knowledge of German has
misled you, too. The *Herr Doktor* did not imply that you would
betray me; only that a certain combination of our stars might
bring me into danger. I insist that you apologize at once.'

As he spoke he held the Russian with his eyes, endeavouring
to convey to him that, although he had made a most regrettable
gaffe, Malacou might not take its implications seriously if he
were offered a complete withdrawal.

But before Kuporovitch could reply Malacou held up his
hand. His thick lips parted in a smile and he said, 'I might
have known that a Russian would smell out a Jew, since they

were for centuries the most pitiless enemies of my race. Of
course Khurrem and I are Jews by blood; but for obvious
reasons we take advantage, she of the fact that she is a German
by marriage and I that I am a naturalized Turk, to conceal it.
However, that makes no difference to the fact that we and you
have a common interest in destroying the Nazis.

'When I considered whether I should allow you to use
Sassen as a base for your mission I realized that if one or both
of you were caught my daughter and I would pay the penalty
for having given you a roof over your heads and that even if
we swore that we had no knowledge of your activities that
would not save us. So if now you gave it away under torture
that we are Jews our case would be no worse. That being so, I
see no reason why I should not admit that my name was
Malacchi and tell you why I changed it.'

'I assure you that I intended no slight upon your race,'
Kuporovitch put in hastily.

'Possibly.' Malacou's smile gave place to a frown. 'But you
are old enough to recall the treatment meted out by your race
to mine when Poland formed part of the dominions of the
Czars. That Hitler has since sought to destroy my people
utterly does not cause Jews of my generation to forget the
pogroms. I have only to close my eyes to see again the Polish
village in which I was born, a *sotnia* of Cossacks charging
down its narrow street using their knouts like flails on corn as
they drove the terrified people before them. Men, women and
children fell screaming beneath the hooves of the horses. Then
the houses were broken into, their poor furniture thrown out
into the street to make a bonfire, the men unmercifully flogged,
the women shorn of their hair and raped, the children forced
to defile themselves by being made to eat pigs' offal.'

It was a terrible picture that he drew, but Gregory remembered reading accounts of such purges in his youth; and
Kuporovitch knew it to be a true one. The latter said:

'I know it, *Herr Doktor*. But Russia has since endeavoured
to make amends for the old Imperial Government's persecution of the Jews. They now enjoy equal status with all other
Soviet citizens. In the past twenty years I have known a number
of Jews whom I respected and counted among my friends.'

Malacou shrugged. 'Oh, I do not hold you personally to blame. I recall those years only to explain why I left Poland in 1903.'

After pausing a moment, he added, 'If we are to work together we must trust one another. Sit down now, and I will tell you about myself.

'With the little money I could scrape together, I succeeded in joining an uncle of mine who had already established himself as a merchant in Turkey. During the First World War our business prospered and by 1919 I had amassed a small fortune. I had gone into commerce only as a matter of necessity; so I sold my business and as a man of independent means I was then able to give all my time to my real interests.

'Those were the study of the Microcosm and the Macrocosm, as occultists term the relation of the little world existing in each human being to the vast structure of the universe. I am not, in fact, a doctor of medicine, but my researches into the human body provided me with sufficient knowledge to practise as one; and I do so here in order to secure the goodwill of the local population. But that is a side issue.

'Seven, as you may perhaps know, is the mystic number and the key to the Eternal Logos. It is for that reason the candlesticks that stand in front of the tabernacle in our synagogues have seven branches. People who have the number 7 are by their nature more psychic than others; they have the gift of intuition and nearly always make good clairvoyants. As I was born on the 7th day of the 7th month I was exceptionally endowed with the power to make contact with supernatural forces. My name of Abraham gave me an additional 7, but Malacchi produces a 3. That is the main reason why I changed it. Ibrahim, of course, has the same numerical value as Abraham, but Malacou gave me yet another 7, and so increased the power of the vibrations which have proved such a great asset in my occult operations.'

'I see,' Gregory murmured. 'But in making the change were you not also influenced by your wish to pass in future as a Turk?'

'Certainly,' Malacou admitted promptly. 'In nearly every country Jews have the misfortune to be despised and misunderstood on account of their race. In 1907 I had married my

uncle's niece. Three years later I lost her, but she had blessed
me with a daughter. By the time I retired Khurrem was already
ten and I had great ambitions for her. When I changed my
name it was not difficult to select a Turkish ending to it
which would give me the additional 7 that I desired. Both
Khurrem and I by then spoke Turkish fluently; so when we cut
adrift from our Jewish acquaintances and moved surreptitiously
from Istanbul to Ankara we were accepted there as Turks.'

'Then von Altern had no suspicion of your origins,' Gregory
remarked.

'None whatever. Khurrem met him at a reception and at
once fell in love with him. As a race I have never liked the
Germans, but Hitler had then only recently come to power
and I failed to foresee that his animosity against the Jews would
lead to such terrible consequences for my people. Khurrem's
happiness was involved and I had always hoped that she would
marry a nobleman. Like many Prussian aristocrats, von Altern
had great pretensions but little money; so I used a part of my
fortune to buy him for her.'

'Father!' Khurrem suddenly broke in, 'did you need to tell
them that? Ulrich was a fine man and made me very happy.'

He shrugged. 'Daughter, our bona-fides having been called
in question, I wish to give the whole truth about ourselves to
these our friends. It is true that Ulrich, his political ideologies
apart, filled the role of a good husband towards you. Had I
not secured fore-knowledge that he would, I should never have
offered him the inducements which led to his taking you as his
wife.' Glancing at Gregory and Kuporovitch in turn, the
doctor added:

'When Khurrem left with her husband for Germany, Poland
had for eighteen years again enjoyed her independence as a
sovereign State. Turkey no longer had anything to offer me, so
to be nearer my daughter here in Prussia I decided to return
to Poland. Those of my relatives and old friends who had
survived naturally welcomed me. They were no longer being
persecuted and in various ways I was able to be of service to
them. But in September '39 there came this new war. Hitler
had by then made clear his unrelenting enmity towards all
Jews. To escape becoming compromised through my friends

there, who knew me to be a Jew, I used my Turkish passport to leave Poland and became a resident here at Sassen. As Khurrem was the wife of a pro-Nazi officer, no-one has ever questioned her Turkish father having come to live with her. There, *Herren*, you have my history and present situation.'

Gregory made a little bow. 'We are most grateful to you, *Herr Doktor*, for having been so frank; particularly as your private life is no concern of ours. Can you now advise us how best to proceed with our mission?'

Pointing with a long, smooth finger to the horoscopes, Malacou replied, 'These leave me in no doubt that in due course an opening will be given you. For the moment I can only suggest that you should pay a few visits to Greifswald and there scrape acquaintance with as many people as possible. One of them might provide you with a lead.'

'Why not Wolgast?' Gregory asked. 'That is much nearer to Peenemünde and the ferry to Usedom goes from it.'

Malacou shook his head. 'For you that is not possible. An area which is three miles deep from the coast has been sealed off, and a permit is required to enter it. Willi von Altern has one. Great quantities of foodstuffs are needed to feed the forced labour now at Peenemünde and he delivers our farm produce to Wolgast by lorry twice a week. But the two of you differ so greatly in appearance that you could not pass as him. However, he could take you to Greifswald and drop you off there.'

'Good. When does he make his next journey?'

'Tomorrow, Friday. But that is the 4th of June and in your case caution demands that the influence of both the 4 and 8 should be avoided. After that his next journey will be on Monday. That is one of the best days of the week for you; so propitious for starting to find out what you can.'

For a further hour Gregory and Kuporovitch remained with the doctor, studying his large-scale map of the Peenemünde neighbourhood and talking about the course of the war; then Khurrem took them back through the shrubbery and along to the manor house.

The weekend passed uneventfully. At Gregory's suggestion it was agreed that, while they stayed at Sassen, Kuporovitch should help on the farm. When Willi von Altern was told of this he became decidedly more friendly, as it seemed that his crippled mind was capable of concentrating only on various tasks that had to be done about the farm and in some of these a strong man's help would be very welcome.

Early on the Monday morning the lorry was loaded up and Gregory set off with him for Greifswald. After a drive of twelve miles through the flat country they reached the town and Willi dropped Gregory off in the main square. The place was much the same size as Grimmen and its buildings were similar in appearance. In the course of an hour he had explored all the principal streets and as by then it was still only a little after nine o'clock he was temporarily at a loss what to do.

By half past nine the usual queues were forming outside the food shops and quite a number of wounded soldiers were strolling aimlessly about. The sight of them decided Gregory to pay a visit to the hospital; so he spent the next half-hour buying from tobacconists as many cigarettes as they would let him have until he had collected several hundred. Then he went to the hospital and secured the willing permission of the matron to distribute them among some of her patients.

As he moved slowly down one of the long wards he spent a few minutes at each bedside talking to the occupant before leaving him a packet of ten or twenty. He was hoping that he might come upon a man who had received his injury as a result of an accident while on garrison duty on Usedom and, perhaps, get him talking about conditions there. But he had no luck. All of them had been wounded on the Russian front, so when he had exhausted his supply of cigarettes he made his way back to the main square.

Going into a small hotel there, which appeared to be the best in the town, he enquired of the landlord the price of a room, then said he was on leave and hoped to get some fishing in the great Greifswald Bay, which lay only a few miles to the north-east of the town. But the man shook his head and said:

'A few years ago, *Herr Major*, I could easily have fixed you up; but for a long time past the whole coast within fifty miles of here has been a military area. As you are an officer, you might perhaps get a permit from the area commandant, but I doubt it. They are terribly strict about letting anyone get even a sight of the big experimental station at Peenemünde.'

Gregory thanked him and said he would try his luck, although he had no intention of doing so except as a last resort. As far as he knew his forged papers were all in order, but the type of such documents was changed from time to time and there was always the chance that the ones with which S.O.E. had furnished him were not up-to-date.

In an adjacent café Gregory ordered a drink, then got into conversation with two convalescent officers who were sitting at a nearby table. After a while he again broached the subject of fishing. The elder of the two, a grey-haired Captain, shrugged.

'You'll get no fishing in these parts now, *Herr Major*. Only the local fishing smacks are allowed to go out, and then only on certain days, under escort. On others they would be endangered by the firing.'

'Surely that applies only when they are a few miles from the coast,' Gregory remarked. 'They couldn't come to any harm while far out in the Baltic.'

The younger officer laughed. 'If I were the captain of a trawler I wouldn't care to risk it. Big Bertha of the last great war was a pop-gun compared with this huge piece they are trying out at Peenemünde. It's said to be able to throw its shells two hundred miles.'

'Let's hope you're right and from the French coast it will destroy London,' remarked his senior. Then, with a warning glance, he added, 'But the Provost Marshal would have us on the mat if it got to his ears that we'd been talking about it.'

Gregory already knew that the secret weapon was not a gun, so obviously no information of value about it could be extracted from his companions. Tactfully, he changed the conversation and shortly afterwards left them to go and have lunch.

In the hotel coffee room there was a cold table of sorts. While standing at it and discussing with the waiter the possible merits of various kinds of sausage he succeeded in picking up a quite pretty young officer of the Women's Army. As she was on her own she agreed to share a table with him; then, after they had been talking for a while, he tried to pump her. But she had arrived there only that morning on leave from Brussels and was expecting to be collected that afternoon by her father, who owned a property some miles away. Talking to her made a pleasant break, but as it was over a year since she had been home she knew nothing of recent developments in the neighbourhood.

After lunch he returned to the café and scraped acquaintance with another convalescent officer, but again drew a blank. As he could think of no other avenues of covert enquiry, he remained there until three o'clock, when Willi returned from his thirty-four-mile trip to Wolgast and back, and picked him up.

For the next two days he kicked his heels at Sassen, puzzling his wits in vain for a way to establish himself nearer Peenemünde. Then on the Thursday Herman Hauff paid another visit to the Manor. On seeing Gregory, he expressed his surprise at finding him still there and asked why he had not yet made arrangements for his fishing.

Gregory shrugged. 'I had hoped to find suitable quarters at Wolgast, but am told that it lies in the prohibited area.'

'That is true. It applies to the whole of the coast north-east of here; also to the islands of Usedom and Rügen. But why Wolgast? If you went up to Stralsund, along the coast west of Rügen there are plenty of places where you could find what you want.'

'Perhaps.' Gregory looked despondent. 'But the coast there faces on the open sea, and even in summer sudden storms are liable to blow up in the Baltic. Alone, out in a motor boat, it would be no joke to be caught in one. Besides, before I came here an old friend of mine told me that the best fishing he had ever enjoyed was in those creeks between the mainland and the islands. So I had set my heart on it.'

Hauff fingered his knobbly chin thoughtfully for a moment, then he said: 'I could get you a permit to go into Wolgast. But whether you would be allowed to fish from there I don't know.'

'That's very good of you,' said Gregory gratefully. 'If you would get me a pass, at any rate I could go there and find out.'

On Saturday one of Hauff's land girls brought the pass over

to the Manor. That evening Gregory went over with Khurrem to the ruin and cheerfully told Malacou of the progress he had made. Then he asked to be allowed to borrow Khurrem's truck to drive himself into Wolgast next day. But the doctor would not hear of it. He pointed out that although it was a Sunday it was also the 13th, so like the 4th, 22nd and 31st a date under the influence of Uranus, which it was undesirable for Gregory to increase. Neither would he agree to Gregory's going into Wolgast with Willi von Altern on the Monday, but insisted that for this first venture into dangerous territory he must wait for a day upon which astral influences would give him maximum protection. That would not be until the following weekend of the 19th/20th, the latter as a Sunday being the better day for him; so, with considerable reluctance, Gregory agreed to wait until then.

Made irritable by the delay in getting to grips with his mission, he continued to lounge about the farm, spending most of his time reading or playing records. Then on the Thursday Hauff again put in an appearance. Greeting Gregory cheerfully, he asked, 'Well, what luck did you have in Wolgast?'

'I've not been there yet,' Gregory replied.

'Why not?' Hauff enquired abruptly.

'Well,' Gregory prevaricated, 'I thought I'd wait until the weekend. After all, my leave is indefinite and I'm having quite a pleasant time here. Besides, it has occurred to me that to explore all the possibilities will take more than a few hours and the pass you sent me is good only for the day. I really need to spend at least one night there. But perhaps you could fix that?'

Hauff frowned. 'I see. Yes, as you are an Army officer I don't doubt I could. And if you can get permission to fish there you'd need a permit as a temporary resident. Look, I have to attend a *Partei* Committee meeting there on Saturday. I'll run you in myself, then unless the authorities turn down your application we can get the whole thing settled.'

'That's fine,' Gregory smiled, 'and very good of you. I'll take my bags with me on the assumption that anyway I'll be able to stay the weekend, if not permanently. I suppose it will be all right for me to take my servant?'

'*Jawohl*. Being with me they will give him a pass at the barrier; and if you get your permit to stay on that will cover him, too.'

That night Gregory held another conference with the doctor and Khurrem, during which the latter raised a new aspect of the situation. She said:

'I think you will get your permit to stay, all right. Hauff will do his utmost to see that you do. He spoke to me about it after he talked to you. He was in a far from good temper and it wasn't difficult to guess the reason. He doesn't like your staying on here at Sassen.'

'Why should he be concerned about that?' Gregory asked.

'On account of me,' she replied, lowering her grey eyes. 'You may not remember it, but the first time you met him you mentioned the Führer having called on all German men to beget as many children as possible. You implied that your heart would not stand up to a series of young mistresses, but that you had been thinking of marrying if you met a quiet woman of a certain age.'

She gave a sudden bitter little laugh. 'Well, I suppose I could be described as that. And financially, as the owner of the Sassen property, I'm quite a catch. Then today he found that you hadn't gone to Wolgast to try to arrange about your fishing, and seemed in no hurry to do so. In consequence he has jumped to the conclusion that I'm the attraction that keeps you lingering here.'

Wild horses could not have dragged Gregory into making love to the scrawny, taciturn dipsomaniac that Khurrem had become, but he said tactfully, 'I see. Yes; that's very understandable.'

Malacou put in quickly, 'This is good. Khurrem is right. Hauff will now pull every string he can to secure you a permit to reside in Wolgast.'

Gregory remained silent for a moment, then he said, 'As he is so anxious to get me away from Sassen for good, I think we might make even better use of him. For me to be allowed to live in Wolgast is only half the battle. I've still got to get across the creek to Usedom. They'll never let me over the ferry, so I'll need a boat. For that it's certain that I'll require a special permit. If I play my cards properly perhaps Hauff can be manœuvred into getting one for me.'

By the Saturday morning Gregory had decided how best to play his cards. Hauff arrived in his old but powerful car, now dressed in the smart black uniform of a Sturmbahnführer of the Waffen S.S. Gregory got in beside him and Kuporovitch got into the back with their suitcases; then they set off.

Hauff drove at a near-dangerous speed for the narrow lanes, but he was a good driver, as he demonstrated in no uncertain manner on their entering Greifswald. With his klaxon blaring almost continuously he streaked through the town, forcing other vehicles to give way to him and making civilians jump for the pavement. A quarter of an hour later they reached the barrier, three miles beyond which lay the coast. To either side of it there stretched away across the flat country an eight-foot-high barbed-wire fence, behind which at intervals sentries were patrolling. Hauff spoke to a Feldwebel on the gate, then signed a paper making himself responsible for Kuporovitch and the Russian was given a pass to accompany Gregory.

Wolgast, as Gregory had known, was a smaller town than Greifswald. There were no wounded soldiers strolling about the streets but the place was a hive of activity, and the reason was not far to seek. Pre-war maps did not show any railway serving the little town, but one to it had been constructed and a railway bridge over the creek. On the Wolgast side there was now a big marshalling yard with at least a score of goods trains in it. As Gregory glimpsed them at the ends of several side turnings that the car shot past, the sight gave him new hope for his venture. If he were unable to get a permit to take out a boat they offered the chance that he might manage to conceal himself in one of the trucks and so get himself smuggled across to the island.

When they reached the creekside Hauff pulled up in front of a pleasant little hotel that had a broad verandah and said, 'You had better see if they can give you rooms here. I am going on to my meeting, but I'll return about one o'clock and we'll have lunch together.'

Owing to the crowded state of the town Gregory feared that all accommodation there might already be taken, but he

need not have worried. A stout woman behind the desk gave
a glance of surprise at his fishing tackle and said:

'We don't get many gentlemen here for the fishing these days,
and all the better-off ones who are here on warwork live in
their own hutments on the south side of the marshalling yard;
so half our rooms are always empty. We've no cause for
complaint, though, and I wish our dining room were three
times its size. We're always packed out with them for lunch
and dinner.'

Gregory booked rooms for two nights and a table for lunch;
then, while Kuporovitch carried up their bags, he set off for a
walk round the town. It must have been, he thought, a pleasant
little place in pre-war days, but there was nothing to interest
a sight-seer and in some mysterious way the neighbouring
marshalling yard seemed to have made it drab and depressing.
Deliberately he refrained from going near the railway tracks,
as he did not want to be suspected of snooping, and felt that
there would be plenty of time for that later.

Well before one o'clock he was back at the hotel and secured
a table on the verandah, which was now rapidly filling up.
Twenty minutes later Hauff joined him, a broad smile on his
chunky, rubicund face. Plumping himself down on a chair,
he said:

'Well, that's all fixed. I've got you a permit to stay here for
a month, with permission to fish in the creek. It can be renewed
for longer if you wish. To get that done you'll only have to
make an application at the Town Hall.'

Taking the papers he handed over, Gregory thanked him
profusely, then insisted on standing him as good a lunch as
the place could provide.

Hauff grinned at him. 'It will be pretty good, then, as I'm
with you. These innkeepers always have something up their
sleeve worth eating and they know when to fetch it out. I'm
a big shot in these parts and they'd soon hear about it if they
didn't treat me properly.'

His boast proved amply justified and soon afterwards they
were tucking into an excellent meal. On the previous occasions
when Gregory has seen the Nazi it had been only for a few
minutes, so this was the first time he had had the chance to

talk to him at any length. In due course he took the opportunity to mention Goering's name, then spoke of having dined with him at his palatial country home, Karinhall.

At this Hauff was greatly impressed and still more so when Gregory casually referred to having also supped with Ribbentrop at a night-club in Budapest. After lunch the Sturmbahnführer had to dash off to another meeting, but they parted the best of friends, Hauff wishing Gregory good sport with his fishing and adding that, although they might not meet again, should he run up against any difficulties he had only to let him know.

When he had driven off, Gregory walked round to the Town Hall, produced his permit to reside in Wolgast and fish in the creek and asked for the name of someone from whom he could hire a motor boat. As he had felt certain would prove the case, he was told that only by special permission were boats now allowed to put out from Wolgast.

That evening he and Kuporovitch both went to the local cinema, but occupied seats in different parts of the house. The newsreel reported a German victory on the Russian front, but nobody clapped; and when Goebbels was shown for several minutes giving a pep-talk the audience remained ominously silent.

Sunday the two friends spent in taking long walks along the bank of the creek, one to the south and the other to the north of the town. When they met in the evening and compared notes they found that in both directions the lie of the land was much the same. The country was low-lying, marshy and even at some distance from the landward side of the broad creek there were few clumps of trees. Across on the island bank, however, the prospect was very different. There, for a belt some two hundred yards deep, the land had been stripped of every bush and in a few places the foundations of cottages that had been pulled down could be made out. Beyond this field of fire stood a ten-foot barbed-wire fence, and along it at intervals tall posts carrying arc lights. It was evident that at night the whole area was brightly lit, and every few hundred yards sentries were patrolling. Behind the fence there was a deep screen of conifers. They were quite tall trees, so must have been planted several years ago when it had first been decided to establish an experimental station at Peenemünde. Owing to the flatness of the land they completely hid the interior of the island.

This reconnaissance depressed them both, as it now looked as though even if Gregory could get a permit for a boat he would stand little chance of landing on Usedom without being spotted. His thoughts reverted to the possibility of getting himself smuggled through in a railway truck but, as it seemed probable that the seaward side of the island would be considerably easier to penetrate, he decided for the time being to adhere to his original plan.

On Monday, after an early lunch, he paid his bill and, with Kuporovitch behind him humping the baggage, walked to the post office. There, as he had arranged without Hauff's knowledge, Willi von Altern, having delivered his load of produce, picked them up and carried them back to Sassen.

The next step in the plan was to adopt a masterly policy of inactivity until Hauff paid another visit to the Manor. His usual day for doing so was Thursday, so Gregory resigned himself to waiting with such patience as he could muster; but Hauff happened to be passing in his car on Tuesday, so looked in to speak to Khurrem about some matter connected with the farm.

Gregory recognized the powerful note of the car as it roared up, so strolled out into the yard. The second Hauff saw him his face darkened with a scowl; but now, believing that Gregory moved in high Nazi circles, he quickly controlled his features and said with forced joviality:

'Hello! I thought you were fishing at Wolgast. Why have you come back to Sassen?'

With a shrug, Gregory replied, 'I couldn't get any fishing after all. With that big marshalling yard and trains running over the bridge, for a mile or more either side of the town the water is filthy with oil and all sorts of muck. No fish could live in it, so I had to chuck my hand in and I got Willi von Altern to give mea lift back here yesterday.'

Hauff frowned. 'You had only to walk along the bank for a few miles either way and you would have got plenty of fish.'

'No doubt you're right,' Gregory agreed, 'but unfortunately my wretched heart doesn't permit me to walk far. I had expected to be able to hire a motor boat, but they told me at the Town Hall that even people with permits to fish are not allowed to take a boat out along the creek.'

'I see. Yes, of course, that is so. But why didn't you telephone me from Wolgast on Sunday? I told you I'd do my best to help you if you met with any difficulties.'

'I know; and I did think of that. But knowing how busy you must be with your official duties as well as your farm, and this place to look after into the bargain, I didn't like to bother you. The quiet life here suits me admirably and Frau von Altern makes a charming hostess. She very kindly said that I could stay as long as I liked, so I'm not really very disappointed about not getting my fishing.'

'But you would still like to go fishing if it could be arranged, wouldn't you?' Hauff could not keep the anxiety out of his voice.

'Yes,' Gregory replied, not very eagerly. 'Yes, of course, as that's what I came here for. But I'm afraid it's asking a lot of you to approach your Committee again.'

'*Nein, nein!* It's a pleasure to be of help, *Herr Major*. I can't guarantee anything. But the security officers and the top men who are working on . . . working over there, are allowed to take out boats; so I don't see why you shouldn't be. The best thing would be for you to go back to Wolgast, then after my weekly Committee meeting there on Saturday I'll let you know if everything's all right.'

Gregory shook his head. 'There's no point in my returning to Wolgast until I know if I may hire a boat, and I find it very pleasant here; so I'll stay on at Sassen until I hear from you.'

Against that Hauff found himself at a loss for any argument, so they shook hands and he went off to find Khurrem.

Until the end of the week Gregory had again to possess his soul in patience. By then he would have been exactly a month in Pomerania; he was still a very long way from getting into Peenemünde and he had not yet even been able to let his friends in London know that he and Kuporovitch had landed safely. But there was nothing he could do to hurry matters

and he knew that they had really been very lucky in finding
safe harbourage at Sassen and in being able to make use of
one of the most influential Nazis in the district.

All the same, he found time hung heavily on his hands.
Except for a few minutes now and then, when no-one was about,
he could not talk to Kuporovitch as a friend; while Malacou,
apart from going to his clinic twice a week, never emerged
from his ruin. After the evening meal Gregory had Khurrem
for company, but he could not succeed in drawing her out.
In vain he tried to get her to talk about Turkey, her life in
Berlin and Sassen before the war, books, pictures, politics;
it was no use. Even to remarks about music, which she appeared to like, she replied only in monosyllables or with little
display of interest, then put on another record or helped herself to another *Branntwein*.

Her heavy drinking did not noticeably affect her until about
ten o'clock in the evening, when her speech tended to slur
slightly and her fine grey eyes became dull. One night at about
that hour, when she stood up to get herself a fifth brandy,
Gregory said to her:

'Khurrem, it is not for me to question your habits. But I'd
like to speak to you as a friend about your drinking so much.
Only a few years ago you must have been a lovely woman, and
you're still quite young. This constant soaking must be ruining
your health and is destroying your looks. If only you'd stop it
you could soon get them back. I know the loss of your husband
was a great blow to you, but it's all wrong that you should go
on grieving for him for the rest of your life.'

She pulled heavily on her cigarette and looked at him with
lacklustre eyes. 'It is not only that. My life is a far from happy
one and I am constantly tormented by my thoughts. Drinking
enables me to forget them.'

After a moment's hesitation he said, 'Would you care to tell
me what is worrying you? I might be able to help.'

The ends of her untidy red hair waggled as she shook her
head. 'No. It is kind of you to take an interest in me, but my
troubles are something about which I cannot talk.' Then she
poured her drink and put on another record.

Sunday came at last and with it Sturmbahnführer Hauff.

With him he brought the permit for Gregory to take a boat out into the creek. Khurrem asked him in for a drink and to Hauff's obvious satisfaction it was agreed that Willi should take Gregory and Kuporovitch into Wolgast the following day.

In the evening Khurrem took both of them over to the ruin to say good-bye to her father. After they had reviewed the situation Malacou said to Gregory, 'Tomorrow is not only a Monday, so the best day in the week for Mr. Kuporovitch and favourable to you both, but also the 28th, a 1; so your best day and favourable to him. Therefore, in combination, no two people could make a real beginning to their mission under more propitious influences. You have now only to beware of taking risks on days in the middle of a week that are governed by the 4 or 8 and you will undoubtedly be successful.'

Again by thought transference the doctor ordered the bald-headed hunchback, Tarik, to bring another bottle of fine hock and in it they all drank to the frustration and damnation of the Nazis. Then, before they left, Malacou returned their wireless to them.

That night, at long last, Gregory was able to go to bed with a real hope that he might soon succeed in penetrating the secrets of Peenemünde.

7

He had been Warned

ON MONDAY, the 28th of June, Willi took the two friends in his lorry to Wolgast. By midday they were again settled in rooms at the pleasant little hotel. After lunch Gregory went to the Town Hall, showed his permit to fish from a boat and secured the address of a man who might hire one to him. The boat-master proved glad to see a customer. He said that for a long time past most of his boats had remained idle and were taken out only during weekends by senior officials from Peenemünde who had permission to hire them. Gregory selected a small launch with a cabin and paid a fortnight's hire for it in advance.

That evening he and Kuporovitch went out in it, heading south-west down the creek until they entered a big bay almost enclosed by the narrow waist of the irregular island. There they opened up the wireless set. In the lining of his leather belt Gregory carried a strip of stiff paper giving the code they were to use. He worked out the message; but the Russian, being much more knowledgeable about such an apparatus, tuned in to London. The message sent was brief and, starting with their code number, ran: *Both well first fence crossed but many obstructions to overcome will communicate when anything to report.*

They knew it to be highly probable that one or more German stations would pick up their coded message; but unless the listeners had been very quick they would not have been able to get a fix. Even if they had, as they could not plot it within less than a mile the transmitter might be at a place on either shore. In any case Gregory did not intend to send other messages from the same neighbourhood, and one of his reasons for being so anxious to get hold of a boat had been that in it they would be able to transport the set to different places several miles from Wolgast, without having to carry it, each time they wanted to send a message.

While Kuporovitch turned the launch round and headed her back towards the narrows Gregory quickly set about concealing the set under the bottom boards in the prow, as he thought it safer to leave it concealed there than to keep it with him in the hotel. When they had covered half the distance back to Wolgast, Kuporovitch cut the engine, Gregory threw out the anchor and spent an hour fishing. His catch proved disappointing, but it provided him with a few medium-sized fish to show on his return.

During the course of the week they set cannily about their prospecting. Some days Gregory went fishing only in the afternoons, on others the long, light summer evenings were ample justification for his going out again after dinner. Sometimes Kuporovitch accompanied him, at others he went for long walks to explore the surrounding countryside and memorize possible temporary hideouts in case some calamity forced them to seek safety in flight. But the problem of landing undetected on Usedom appeared to be insoluble.

The curiously shaped thirty-mile-long island consisted of two parts joined only by a neck of land scarcely a mile wide. The northern part, near the tip of which Peenemünde stood, was the smaller, but along the whole of its length on the landward side lay the lighted defence zone. The southern and much bigger part, on which was situated Swinemünde, the island's biggest town, had no defence zone, but Gregory soon discovered that it would be useless to land there because across the narrow neck joining the two parts there was a barrier at which anyone would obviously have to show a pass in order to be allowed through.

His hopes of making a landing on the seaward side of the island were also dashed, because, when he had attempted to pass out of the northern end of the creek he had been halted by a guard-boat, and told that his permit did not allow him to proceed out into the open sea. And even if in a single night he could have made the long voyage round the southern end of Usedom, as that was only divided from the mainland by an even narrower creek it was certain that another guard-boat there would turn him back.

The township of Peenemünde lay on the landward side of the island about two miles from the open sea and a good seven up the creek from Wolgast. When taking his first Sunday walk along the landward bank of the creek Gregory had not gone that far but had turned back after five miles, so it was not until he explored the whole length of the creek in his motor boat that he got a sight of the little town.

It had a small harbour, but little of the town itself could be seen, as the authorities had pulled down all the buildings on the water front and had built a twenty-foot-high concrete wall which screened all but a jagged outline of roofs and the church tower. At the entrance to what must have been the main street, leading down to the harbour, there was a big iron gate in the wall and a guard house with a picket of soldiers. As Gregory had expected to find the place heavily protected he paid little attention to it, particularly as he felt certain that the rocket-launching sites would be three or four miles away, on the seaward side of the island.

However, opposite Peenemünde, on the mainland about half a mile from the creek, stood the village of Kröslin; so he landed at the jetty that served it, walked to the village and had a drink at the only inn. As he dared not risk appearing inquisitive, the only information he picked up was that over a year before all the civilian inhabitants had been evacuated from Peenemünde, and the buildings in it were now used only as barracks for the troops who patrolled the open zone along the bank.

During the trips on which Kuporovitch had accompanied him they had surreptitiously made soundings at low water, in order to verify the places shown on Malacou's map at which the creek could be forded, although as long as they had the boat it did not seem likely that this information would prove of much use to them.

On the Tuesday they had seen several aircraft go up from the island and disappear to the northward over the open sea, and for some hours afterward they heard occasional explosions in the distance; so they knew that firing trials were being carried out. The same thing happened on the Thursday, but

for all the information it brought them the trials might as well
have been taking place on Salisbury Plain.

By Saturday evening Gregory had decided that there was no
way in which he could get on to Usedom by water, so he told
Kuporovitch that, as fewer people would be about on a Sunday,
he meant next day to reconnoitre the marshalling yard. But the
Russian shook his head.

'No, dear friend; not tomorrow. Remember what Malacou
told us. Although Sunday is your best day of the week,
tomorrow is the 4th of July, so a bad day for you to start
any new plan.'

Gregory gave him a quizzical look. 'Do you honestly
believe all that stuff? I can't really credit it.'

'*Mortdieu!* How can one not?' Kuporovitch took him up.
'Greatly as I dislike accepting guidance from a man in league
with the Devil, you proved right about his being on our side;
and I am sure that it is largely through following his advice
that we have so far avoided running into trouble. Remember,
too, that in the past I dabbled in the occult myself, so I have
had some experience of the potency of the stars. I beg you to
put off making any plan for smuggling yourself through to
Peenemünde until Monday.'

Somewhat reluctantly, Gregory agreed and on the following
day he was extremely glad that he had. As he came out on to the
verandah of the hotel for a drink before lunch he saw Hauff
and an officer of the Sicherheitsdienst seated at a table. Hauff
beckoned him over, introduced the S.D. man as Oberführer
Langbahn and said:

'*Herr Major*, I had hoped to see you here. Sit down and have
a drink. How goes the fishing?'

'*Danke Ihnen*,' Gregory replied with a smile. 'I'm doing
very nicely and as I give all I catch to the landlady she's looking
after me very well. Although I expect I owe that partly to
my first lunch here being with you.'

'Good. I should like to return today that lunch you stood
me, and we will have some of your fish. Feeling pretty sure I'd
find you here, I booked the table in the window recess so that
we can discuss our business without any risk of being overheard.'

Greatly intrigued, Gregory had a drink with them, then they

went in to lunch. When they had ordered, Hauff said, 'It's about that batman of yours. What is his native language?'

'He is a Ruthenian. They come of the same stock as Ukrainians and speak a form of Russian.'

'Enough to understand ordinary Russian?'

'Oh yes. Sabinov is a quite well-educated man and a die-hard anti-Communist, but he could easily pass as a Russian if he wanted to.'

'Do you consider him trustworthy?'

'Certainly. As the Ruthenians were a minority and oppressed by the Czechs, he hates their guts and joined up as a volunteer soon after we went into Czechoslovakia.'

'Could you do without him for a while?'

'I could if I had to,' Gregory hedged. 'Of course, he's had a pretty idle time lately, just polishing my boots and buttons and helping me with my boat. But I'm not at all anxious to part with him.'

'We'd fix it for someone in the hotel to do the polishing for you,' Hauff said quickly, 'and surely you could manage your boat on your own?'

'Yes, at times I go out without him. But I've had him with me for over a year. He's a good fellow and greatly attached to me. Still, what do you want to borrow him for?'

Hauff's senior, who ranked as a Brigadier, leant forward and said in a low voice, 'I will take on from here. My job, *Herr Major*, is Chief Security Officer at Peenemünde. It's no secret that the Todt Organization has many hundreds of Russian prisoners of war working there. Naturally, as they are kept on a very low diet they are lethargic and ordinarily my men don't have much trouble with them. But recently there have been certain indications that the prisoners in Camp C are plotting a mass break-out.'

The Oberführer took a drink of wine and went on, 'What these miserable creatures hope to gain by that, heaven knows. They couldn't possibly get away and we'd shoot them down like rabbits. But I don't want a number of my men to be taken by surprise and murdered, or to have to eliminate a valuable labour force; so I'm trying to find out who the ringleaders are; then I'd be able to have them shot and nip this business in the bud. I've got a few stool-pigeons working with the prisoners, but I'm anxious to put more of them on the job and it's devilish hard to find Germans who speak Russian well enough to pass as Russians. Hauff, here, happened to recall that you had a Ruthenian servant, and since you tell us he is a reliable man I want you to lend him to us for this work.'

Gregory had difficulty in concealing his elation at being presented with such a God-given opportunity to get Kuporovitch right inside the Experimental Station, but he did not wish to appear too eager to co-operate, so he said:

'To agree is obviously my duty, *Herr Oberführer*, and I do so willingly. But how Sabinov will take this proposal I can't say. Obviously he'll have to live and work among the prisoners and that's a pretty tough assignment. Of course, I could order him to do as you wish. But that wouldn't be much good if he is unwilling. Even for a short time such a life would amount to severe punishment; so from resentment he would probably keep his mouth shut about anything he did find out, just to spite you.'

'He would be well rewarded,' put in Hauff.

'*Ja, ja!*' added the Oberführer. 'I agree that such a task calls for sacrifice and fortitude; but he will be well paid for it, and if he is successful I'll see to it that he gets an Iron Cross, 4th Class.'

'Very well,' Gregory nodded, 'I'll put it to him.'

'When could you give me his answer?'

'I'll speak to him after lunch, but I think we ought to give him an hour or two to think it over.'

'That's reasonable. All right, then. I'll return here about six o'clock, and over a drink together you can tell me his reaction.'

For the rest of the meal they talked about the war and Gregory related some of his mythical experiences in Norway. Then, as soon as the two Nazis had left, he found Kuporovitch and took him into the garden at the back of the hotel. Having told him about Langbahn's proposal, he said:

'This is a marvellous break for us if you're willing to play, Stefan. But there's no getting away from the fact that it would mean hell on earth for you as long as you remain in that camp. The ordinary guards won't be told that you are a stool-pigeon, so you'll be treated just like the other prisoners. It's certain that you'll be starved and beaten, and if your fellow prisoners

rumble you they might quite possibly do you in. So I'll think
no worse of you if you regard it as asking too much, and somehow I'll get myself smuggled in on a train.'

'*Ventre du Pape!* You'll do nothing of the kind,' the Russian
replied stoutly. 'If you did you would like as not get caught
and anyway that wouldn't give you half as good a chance as
this will give me of finding out what's going on there. I'm
quite tough enough to take care of myself; and to bitch Hitler's
last chance of winning the war I'd willingly spend a year down
a coal mine on bread and water.'

'Good for you, Stefan,' Gregory smiled. 'I felt sure that would
be your answer, but I hate the thought of your having to go
through the mill like this while I'm just idling around fishing.'

'Don't give that a thought, dear friend. But this means we
shall be separated, and I will not be able to take the wireless in
with me. If I do get on to anything really worth while how the
devil am I to let you know about it?'

Kuporovitch's question presented a very difficult problem,
but after having discussed it for some ten minutes they agreed
on a line for Gregory to take when he saw the Oberführer
again that evening.

Langbahn arrived soon after six, and when they had ordered
drinks Gregory said, 'Sabinov is willing to play, if you'll
agree to certain conditions. He says that earlier in the war he
spent some time as a guard in a Russian prisoner-of-war cage
and that half of them died from starvation. I told him that the
labour gangs at Peenemünde wouldn't be as ill-fed as all that,
but he insists that he should be allowed out one day a week
to eat his head off. Rations being what they are, two or three
ordinary meals wouldn't be much good; but no doubt if you
had a word with the landlady here she'd fix things so that he
could stuff himself to the eyebrows. He realizes, too, that he'll
be letting himself in for a very tough time, so he wants to set
himself up each week by a day of real relaxation. There is
nothing he enjoys more than going out with me when I'm
fishing, so if you're prepared to let him come back to me on
Sundays, and arrange for him to have a real blow-out, he's
all yours for the rest of the week.'

For a moment Langbahn considered these terms, then he

said, 'I fully appreciate his point of view and I've nothing against his requests in principle. But it would look very fishy to the other prisoners if one of them were removed from their gang every Sunday, so make them suspicious of him and defeat our object.'

'That is a snag,' Gregory admitted. 'But surely there must be scores of gangs and quite a number of deaths that make it necessary to fill them up from time to time with new arrivals. Couldn't you place him with a different gang each week?'

'I'm afraid that's no good. In six days he wouldn't have been long enough with any set of men to win their confidence.'

Feeling that he now had to take a chance unless Kuporovitch's opportunities of securing information were to be rendered useless, Gregory said, 'The deal is off, then. He really dug his toes in about being given a break now and again.'

'Now and again,' Langbahn repeated. 'That's rather different. If he'd be willing to stick it for spells of a fortnight I'd agree to his terms.'

Gregory nodded. 'I might be able to persuade him to do that. Particularly if I were able to offer him some additional inducement. How about telling him that instead of a day a week he can have both Sunday and Monday off at the end of each fortnight?'

'That's fair enough.' The Oberführer finished his drink and stood up. 'I must be off now. Please put this new proposal to him this evening. If he agrees tell him to come to the Town Commandant's Office tomorrow morning at nine o'clock and report to me.'

Gregory too came to his feet and they exchanged a smart 'Heil Hitler'. But, having turned away, Langbahn suddenly swung round and said, 'One other thing. If he agrees I shall send him straight over to the island, so you won't see him again until Sunday week. When he has his days off I don't want him to come to and fro on the ferry, because there is just a chance that he might cross with a new batch of prisoners; and if one of them remembered his face afterwards they would tumble to it that he was a stool-pigeon. To avoid that I'll arrange for him to have a pass enabling him to go back and forth by the gate in the wall that we've built to screen Peenemünde. It's much nearer the camp, too. As you have a boat you can fetch him off at nine o'clock on alternate Sunday mornings and on the Monday evenings you must see to it that he's back through the gate before midnight. Will that be all right with you?'

'Yes. I'll miss him, of course, but I've nothing against such an arrangement,' Gregory replied truthfully. Then he added with a smile, 'I'll bring some cold food with me so that the poor fellow can make a hearty breakfast.'

That evening Gregory told Kuporovitch of this most satisfactory arrangement; and on the following morning, with very mixed feelings, he watched his friend march off to report at the Town Commandant's Office.

During the fortnight that followed, Gregory derived little pleasure from his fishing. He could not get his mind off what the loyal Russian must be going through and was in a constant state of anxiety about him. Only one event cheered him a little. As he was now able to receive the B.B.C. news bulletins on his wireless set without danger he listened in to them at various hours once a day; and on the evening of Saturday, July 10th, the successful landing of the Allied Armies in Sicily was announced.

From that he assumed that Churchill had finally lost his battle with the Americans and they had definitely vetoed his cherished plan for liberating Europe by a full-scale invasion of the 'soft under-belly of the Axis'. Had that not been the case the assault would obviously have been launched in the Adriatic, against the Balkans, or the first landings made in Sardinia as a stepping stone to the gulf of Leghorn and the classic road taken by Napoleon into Austria. The latter, Gregory knew, was the plan that had always been favoured by the Joint Planning Staff.

The Americans, on the other hand, had always wanted an invasion direct from Britain into France. It seemed evident now that they had got their way, and the operation against Sicily had only the limited objective of relieving Malta and freeing the Mediterranean so that Allied convoys could again be sent through it and thus be saved the long haul round Africa.

Throughout the next week Gregory listened eagerly to the bulletins and since the die was cast it comforted him to learn that in Sicily the Allies were sweeping all before them.

On Sunday the 18th he set out early up the creek in his

motor boat, praying that no ill had befallen Kuporovitch.
To his relief the Russian appeared on time, and he brought
interesting news.

As he devoured the *Brötchen* Gregory had brought he declared that during the past fortnight he must have lost at least
a couple of stone, and that the conditions under which the
prisoners had to live were indescribable. They were forced
to labour from dawn to dusk filling sandbags with earth
and making thick walls with them to screen the buildings in
which the scientists were working, they were brutally flogged by
their Nazi overseers if they showed the least sign of shirking and
fed only on coarse bread and soup made from potato peelings.
Daily, numbers of them died from exhaustion or malnutrition
and the huts in which they were quartered were pigsties, because they were too feeble at night to attempt to clean them out.

But he had seen the giant rockets, both from the distance
on the ground and during several trials when they had been
fired. They were, he estimated, as large as had been reported,
but more than half those fired had exploded prematurely.
It had not, however, been possible to judge the size of the
warheads they would carry when they became operational, for
these gave only a feeble bang before falling back to earth or
into the sea, which showed that the charges in them had been
only small ones.

His real news was about another form of secret weapon that
was being developed. This was a much smaller type of rocket
that had wings and looked like a pilotless aircraft. They also
sometimes miscarried and, having circled round, nose-dived
into the sea. But there were many more of them and, from their
performance, Kuporovitch judged the state of their development to be more advanced than that of the larger rockets.

So that no coded message sent out might be associated with
his release from the camp, they decided not to send one till
the following afternoon; and when they did send it they did so
from far out in the big bay to the south of Wolgast.

On Monday evening, at about half past eleven, Gregory
landed Kuporovitch at Peenemünde and watched him disappear through the gates there to face a further twelve days'
gruelling ordeal.

During those days Gregory was again a prey to all those anxious frustrations felt by a wife who has seen her husband go off to the war and can expect no news of him. But on Sunday the 25th news of great importance came to him from his wireless. Owing to the success of the Allies in Sicily, Mussolini had fallen. No details were immediately available, and for some days even the bare news was suppressed by the German stations; but towards the end of the month they had to release it, while the B.B.C. reported that the Duce had been forced by the Fascist Council to resign and arrested by the order of King Victor Emmanuel.

On the morning of August 1st Gregory again collected Kuporovitch and the Russian brought with him further valuable intelligence. While working with his group on erecting a wall of sandbags to protect a long, low building, two civilians had come out of it who, it seemed probable, were either engineers or scientists. They had halted within a few feet of Kuporovitch and stood for some minutes watching a firing trial that was in progress. When one of the small, winged rockets had been launched successfully one of the men had remarked to the other:

'At last we're beginning to get somewhere with these pilotless aircraft and I'm told that work on the launching sites in northern France is going well. Very shortly it will be only a matter of getting the new weapon produced in large numbers. With the priority that will receive they should be able to begin the bombardment of London by the winter, or perhaps even this autumn.'

The man had, of course, spoken in German and it obviously had not occurred to him that any of the miserable-looking Russians working nearby would understand that language. But Kuporovitch's knowledge of German had greatly improved during the past two months and he assured Gregory that he was prepared to swear that he had reported correctly every word that had been said.

This news that the first of the secret weapons might become operational within the next few months was highly alarming and Gregory felt that it ought to be passed on with a minimum of delay; so he went into the cabin and put a message into code while Kuporovitch took over the boat and steered her down the creek back to Wolgast. Shortly before they reached the town Gregory had the message ready and he sent it off at once.

Kuporovitch had gone through another very hard time, including a stand-up fight with a big bully in his hut who had attempted to rob him of his meagre ration. He had not yet identified any leader of the plot, but there were definite indications that one was afoot and, to keep in with his paymasters, he had reported these before leaving camp that morning to the junior S.D. officer under whom he had been placed.

For the greater part of the Sunday and Monday he either ate or slept, to recruit his strength for his next twelve days of hunger and hardship. Then, on the Monday, shortly before midnight, Gregory watched him disappear for the third time through the gates at Peenemünde.

He was due for his next release on Sunday, August 15th, and by nine o'clock that morning Gregory had the launch tied up in the little harbour, waiting to take him off. But he did not appear.

By half past, Gregory was extremely worried; then it suddenly entered his mind that Kuporovitch might have sent a message to the guard post to await him there; so he clambered up on to the quay. Outside the post, not far from the sentry, a Sergeant and several men were lounging in the sun. Quickly Gregory questioned them, but they could tell him nothing; so he asked the Sergeant to send one of the men to fetch his officer. Five minutes later an elderly Lieutenant of the Reserve came out of the gate. He said that he knew *Soldat* Sabinov by sight, as the man was on a list of people allowed to pass in and out of that gate; but no message concerning him had been received.

With growing fears that some misfortune had befallen his friend, Gregory remained there until eleven o'clock, making desultory conversation with the Sergeant and explaining his anxiety by telling him that Sabinov had previously been his servant, so he would be very upset if his failure to appear was caused by his having met with an accident.

Soon after eleven he decided that it was useless to wait

any longer and, returning to his boat, he made all speed back
to Wolgast. There, at the hotel, he was relieved of his worst
fears on finding a note that had shortly before been left for
him. It was from Brigadier Langbahn and read:

*I am sorry to tell you that your man was beaten up last night
and is in hospital. But his injuries are not serious and he will be
well enough for you to pick him up tomorrow. He has landed one
fish for us, but there is still trouble brewing, so I shall expect
him back at midnight on Tuesday.*

All that day it rained heavily and Gregory spent it indoors,
worrying about Kuporovitch; but when he collected him next
morning, apart from a black eye and a badly bruised chin, he
was in fairly good shape.

It transpired that in the last group to which he had been
allotted he had recognized—but fortunately without being
recognized himself—an ex-member of the O.G.P.U. Naturally,
he had had no intention of saving the Germans from riots by
denouncing any conspirator who confided in him; but he
knew that it would strengthen his own position if he turned
one of his fellow prisoners in, and several of his brother
officers who had been caught up in the Tukashevsky conspiracy had been tortured and executed owing to the activities
of this O.G.P.U. man. So Kuporovitch had avenged them by
reporting him as one of the leaders of the break-out plot and
had seen him hauled off to torture and death by the Gestapo.
Unfortunately other members of the group had suspected
that it was Kuporovitch who had 'squealed', so they had
attempted to do him in. As he had had the sense to shout for
help with all the strength of his powerful lungs, his bellowing
had been heard and the guards had arrived on the scene in
time to rescue him.

He had no fresh news about the secret weapons, but hoped
to pick up further information during his next spell inside;
and he had no special fears about returning to his highly
distasteful job, because he was to be put into a different camp,
to which it was believed that the trouble had spread and, of
course, he would enter it under a different name. Two days'

relaxation with plenty of good food and drink fully restored
him to his normal, cheerful self and, a little before midnight
on the Tuesday, Gregory landed him in front of the Peenemünde gate.

He pushed off at once and, not having heard the news that
evening, as soon as he had rounded the promontory just south
of Peenemünde he stopped his engine, then began to fiddle
with the knob of his wireless hoping to pick up a midnight
bulletin from a British station. He had been trying to get the
Continental wave-length only for a moment when he recognized his own call sign.

At once he pulled out his notebook and pencil, sent his
number and turned the set up. The message was short and having
taken it down it took him only a few minutes to decode,
because by then he had memorized quite a number of the
abbreviation symbols. As he worked by the light of his torch
he jotted down: *Tried to contact you three nights stop maximum
raid on P first suitable stop withdraw stop report results if possible.*

With swift concern he switched out his torch, returned the
wireless to its hiding place and turned the boat about. Somehow he must warn Kuporovitch, and they must devise some
way of getting him out. Perhaps they could say that, owing to
his injuries, he needed further time to recuperate. He had been
gone less than a quarter of an hour and he had a two-mile
walk back to his camp. There still might be time to catch him.

At full speed Gregory drove the boat back into the little
harbour and scrambled ashore. The arc lights were blazing
down, so the sentry recognized him at once and made no move
to fire. Running up to him, Gregory panted:

'*Soldat* Sabinov! I forgot to tell him something. It's important . . . very important. Get him back. Send someone
after him.'

The sentry shook his head. '*Herr Major*, I cannot leave my
post.'

'Then call your Sergeant! Call your officer!'

The man gave a shout and his Sergeant emerged from the
guard house.

Urgently, Gregory repeated his request that someone should
be sent after his man to get him back.

'I regret, *Herr Major*,' the Sergeant replied, 'but I have no authority to use one of my men for such a purpose.'

In a second Gregory became the typical German officer who is accustomed to be obeyed without question. Drawing himself to his full height, with all the authority of his rank, he snapped, 'Call your officer. Instantly; or it will be the worse for you.'

The Sergeant wilted. Calling another man out of the guard house, he turned, took a key from his pocket and unlocked the gate. Then he said to the man, 'Go and fetch the *Herr Leutnant*.'

A few minutes that seemed an age to Gregory went by. Suddenly the lights went out. In a flash he realized what that meant. It had never happened before during his seven weeks at Wolgast. It could be only because a warning had been received that an air-raid was imminent. The message had said 'first suitable night'. The moon was nearly full and now lit the scene faintly between drifting patches of cloud; so conditions could not have been better.

The gate was open. The Lieutenant might already be in bed. It might be ten or fifteen minutes before he had dressed and could be brought there. Meanwhile Kuporovitch was calmly walking back to the camp where within the next hour hundreds of men might lie dead. The thought spurred Gregory to immediate action.

Thrusting the Sergeant aside he dived through the gate. It gave on to a curving street. Expecting any minute to be shot in the back, he pelted along it, hugging the nearest side to take the best advantage of the deep shadows now cast by the moonlight. The sentry, bewildered by the sudden switching off of the lights and taken by surprise by Gregory's abrupt action, momentarily lost his wits and forgot that he should have used his rifle. The Sergeant shouted to Gregory to halt but, also taken aback, lost a few moments before drawing his pistol. By the time he blazed off with it, Gregory was round the first bend of the street and no longer a visible target.

In less than two minutes he was out of the deserted village and running hard along an open road. As he ran he caught the drone of an aircraft engine and knew that it must be a Pathfinder coming in to mark the targets. A siren wailed, then a score of anti-aircraft batteries opened up. Streams of tracer bullets streaked the night sky and shells began to burst overhead.

By then Gregory had covered a mile. The road dipped slightly and in a depression ahead a dark group of trees stood out. The fact that by now Kuporovitch would realize his danger and do his best to save himself did not enter Gregory's head. His one desperate thought was that before the friend who meant so much to him reached the camp he must manage to catch him up.

A dull droning was now audible from seaward. The mighty bomber fleet was coming in. In the distance, to either side of the group of trees towards which the road led, the darkness was stabbed by spurts of flame. The flashes lit up long lines of hutments and humps like giant golf-bunkers that must be the assembly shops protected by thick walls of sandbags. The Pathfinder had located his target and was dropping his markers.

Gasping for breath, but still running hard, Gregory reached the group of trees. His chest pained him terribly and he knew that his strength was flagging, yet he forced his aching legs to obey his will and thrust him on. When he was halfway through the trees the bombs began to fall.

From the sky there came a roar like continuous thunder. It was punctuated by terrific detonations. Searchlights streaked the sky in all directions. Anti-aircraft shells were now bursting up aloft at the rate of six a second. It seemed impossible that anything could live up there through such a barrage. Pieces of shell came whistling downward. An aircraft was caught like a tiny gnat in the beam of a searchlight. It was hit, burst into flames and came spiralling earthwards. In front of him, through the fringe of trees on either side of the road, Gregory could now see the camp clearly. Scores of brilliant flashes made it as bright as daylight. A dozen of the long huts were already on fire. Incendiaries were showering down and others were igniting every minute. The explosions of bombs and guns merged into a deafening drumfire.

Gregory was nearly through the cluster of trees. At the side of the road, less than a hundred yards away, he suddenly saw a figure that had previously been hidden by them. Against the

glare of the blazing camp there could be no mistaking the
solitary, broad-shouldered man who was standing quite still
watching its destruction. With infinite relief, Gregory staggered
to a stop. Then, with all the remaining strength of his lungs,
he yelled:

'Stefan! Stefan! For God's sake take cover.'

Kuporovitch did not turn and through the roar of the explosions it seemed unlikely that he could have heard. Starting
to run again, Gregory gave another shout.

At that moment there came a blinding flash, another and
another, as a stick of bombs straddled the coppice. The trees
to either side of the road swayed and crumpled. Gregory
glimpsed one as, uprooted by the blast, it toppled and fell.
There was no escape. It crashed directly on to him. One
moment he had been running, the next he was pinned to the
ground in the middle of the road. An intolerable pain shot
through his body. His eyes seemed to burst out of their sockets.
A terrible weight on his left leg held him captive. Even as he
strove to lift his hands they flopped back slack and useless.
Everything about him had gone black. The crashing of bombs
and roar of guns now sounded distant, as though his ears
had suddenly been plugged with cotton wool.

Through a mist of pain a thought flashed into his brain. It
was the 17th of August. An 8 day in the 8th month. Malacou
had warned him that any such day, in conjunction with his
birth number, 4, would prove highly dangerous to him,
and particularly so in his association with Kuporovitch. Yet
he had ignored that warning and been brought to the fatal
date on account of the Russian's having to be a day late in
coming on his fortnightly forty-eight-hour leave. Malacou
had also told Gregory that he might die in the hour of his
triumph.

This, then, was it! He had had a good run for his money
and Peenemünde was being destroyed. But he had come to the
end of the road. His agony then seeped away as he slipped
into total unconsciousness.

8

Sentenced for Life

WHEN Gregory came to he was at first conscious only of the
agony that racked his body. Vaguely he realized that he was
being carried and that at every step his bearer took an intolerable spasm of pain shot from the region of his hip up
towards his heart. He began to whimper and, indistinctly, he
heard a voice speaking to him. But he had been temporarily
deafened by the nearby explosion of the bomb that had brought
the tree down upon him. He wanted to implore the man who
was carrying him to stop and put him down, but he could not
formulate the words. The stabbing pain increased with every
step and again he fainted.

The next time he became semi-conscious it slowly penetrated
his thoughts that he was lying in a shallow ditch and that
someone was heaping earth upon him. He felt certain then that
he really must be dead and that whoever had found him was
giving him a perfunctory burial. Knowing that anyone might
lose a limb yet still feel an ache in it, he told himself that agony
from wounds that a body received before death must continue
for a time in the consciousness of the spirit that had departed
from it. Resigning himself to that conclusion, he lay still and
prayed that it might not be very long before he was relieved
of the ghastly throbbing that racked him. After a while the
pain subsided as his mind again blacked out.

When, once again, his brain began to stir, his eyes flickered
open and he saw that it was full daylight. His still pain-racked
body had a weight upon it, as though he were lying beneath a
dozen blankets, but his face was not covered and, as with
lacklustre eyes he lay gazing upwards, he saw the branches
and tops of trees.

Suddenly his mind cleared. He recalled that it was a tree that had felled him. The events of the previous night flooded back: his desperate race to stop Kuporovitch from entering the camp, the Experimental Station going up in flames. He no longer supposed himself to be dead, and the sight of the trees about him led him to assume that he was still in the coppice where he had been struck down. It seemed that some-one must have found his unconscious body, carried it to a ditch and cast a light covering of earth over it. Yet why had they not covered his face? That puzzled him; but the gnawing pain in his thigh prevented him from concentrating on the question.

For a long while he lay comatose. Then he roused again. The thought entered his mind that, although hundreds of people must have been killed in the raid, sooner or later the soldiers of the guard who had chased and found him would return to bury him properly. He must not fall into their hands. Somehow he must get away from the coppice before they came back to it.

Gritting his teeth he tried to sit up. But the pain became too agonizing and he fell back. After a time he succeeded in turning over. His arms and right leg were still sound; his left leg a dead weight, red-hot and throbbing madly. Clutching a tree root, he levered himself up on his good knee, hauling his body out from under the heap of leaves and top soil. Foot by foot, and fainting twice on the way, he managed to drag himself some twenty feet, to the side of the coppice nearest which the trees ended.

After lying there a long while he recovered sufficiently from his efforts to raise himself on his elbows and look about him. In the near distance he saw a village from the middle of which rose a church spire. To his amazement he recognized the spire as that of the church in Kröslin.

How he had got back to the mainland side of the creek he could not imagine. No guard would have brought his pre-sumably dead body there. Perhaps he had only dreamed that he had been carried for some distance, and his subconscious will to survive had given him the strength to stagger back through the screen of trees and, undetected owing to the confusion caused by the raid, get across the creek. Yet to have done that with a smashed leg seemed impossible.

For a time his pain-racked mind rejected the problem; then as the church spires in Peenemünde and Kröslin looked much alike, he decided that it must be that of the former, but from an angle at which he had not previously seen it.

Throughout the day there were long periods during which his mind blacked out entirely. During others he strove vainly through a mist of pain to think of steps he might take which would give him some chance of survival; for he felt certain that unless he could secure help, or somebody found him, he would die there.

Twilight came and, eventually, darkness. Hours afterward, as it seemed to him, he caught sight of the beam of a torch flickering among the trees. For a long time past his sufferings had been added to by a terrible thirst. Now, resigned to falling into the hands of the enemy as the only possibility of receiving relief, he called feebly for help.

Footsteps came hurrying towards him, then a voice that he did not recognize cried in German:

'Here he is! Bring along the coffin.'

As the man spoke he thrust both his hands under Gregory's shoulders and began to pull him up. The pain caused by his being lifted was so excruciating that he fainted.

When he came round he was submerged in complete darkness. Now his memory of previous events returned immediately. The man who had found him had called to someone else to bring a coffin. By feeling about with his hands he realized that he was lying in one; then, with a gasp of relief, that he had not yet been buried, for the coffin was jolting and evidently being taken somewhere.

Panic seized him. His having called for help had shown that he was not dead. Yet the fiends of the Gestapo were capable of anything. Perhaps they meant to lower him into a grave while still alive. Frantically, with clenched fists, ignoring the increase of pain it caused him, he began to hammer on the coffin lid and plead to be let out.

The coffin lid was not nailed down, so lifted a little as he pounded on it. But his cries were feeble and were not heard. His effort caused him to swoon, but he soon came round and frantic thoughts again seethed in his brain. Perhaps, since he had fainted when half-lifted, the man had thought that he was already *in extremis* and had then died. If so, he was probably being taken to a cemetery for proper interment. But why should the Nazis trouble to do that with his body when, as the result of the bombing, they must have so many of their own dead to look to?

So far, during his periods of semi-consciousness, he had been thinking of himself as an Englishman and British agent. Now it occurred to him that he must still be wearing the uniform of a German Major, and there was no reason to suppose that the men who had found him should believe him to be anything else. If that were so they would regard him as one of their own casualties and, most probably, were about to give him a respectable burial. There was, then, still a chance that when they reached their journey's end he might get himself taken to hospital.

Hopes and fears continued alternately to agitate his bemused mind. The rocking and jolting of the coffin had the same effect as if someone were constantly pummelling his injured thigh and, crazed by pain, his mind wandered from the present to scenes of the past.

After what seemed an eternity the vehicle on which he was came to a standstill. He caught the sound of footsteps on boards near the coffin and the lid was taken off. Dimly he realized that it was still night, for a torch was shone down into his face, blinding him. It had been very hot in the coffin and, as he felt the cool air on his face, he knew that it was damp with sweat; so he must be running a high fever. A hand was eased into his tunic to feel his heart, then a gruff voice said:

'Holy Virgin be praised! He has survived the journey.'

In normal circumstances he would have been certain that it was Kuporovitch who had spoken; but his last glimpse of his friend had been in silhouette against the glare of the burning camp on Usedom, so he believed himself to be the victim of hallucination. His right arm was lifted. By the light of the torch he saw that the sleeve of his tunic had been cut away. He felt the jab of a hypodermic needle and in another few moments lapsed back into unconsciousness.

For a long while, each time he came out of his drug-induced stupor, he dimly realized that he was shouting in delirium, then the kindly needle sent him off again. When at last he opened his eyes with a clear mind he gradually took in the fact that he was in bed in a vaulted stone-walled chamber. As he feebly raised a hand he heard a movement beside him, then Kuporovitch's face came into view above his.

'So, my poor friend, you are conscious once more,' murmured the Russian. 'St. Nicholas and all the Saints be thanked. For the past week I have feared you would die, but now you will turn the corner.'

Gregory strove to reply but could only mumble, and the excruciating pain again shot up from his thigh to his heart. Kuporovitch gently raised his head, gave him a soothing drink, then, with another injection, sent him off.

During the three days that followed he awoke several times to lucid intervals, his powers of comprehension increasing with each. On every occasion he found Kuporovitch beside him and gradually learned from him what had taken place after the great raid on the fatal 17th August.

His friend had heard his last shout, turned and seen him struck down by the falling tree. Only the Russian's great strength had enabled him to lift the splintered trunk from Gregory's body. Finding that he was still alive, Kuporovitch had carried him back up the road, then left it and entered the belt of trees that screened the interior of the island from the creek. The confusion resulting from the raid, and the fact that the arc lights had been switched off, had enabled him to get Gregory through the wire fence unobserved. By a dispensation of Providence it had been low water in the creek, so he had been able to cross it by the nearest ford. On his early reconnaissance of the mainland bank one of the places he had marked down as an emergency hideout had been a group of trees not far from Kröslin. Almost exhausted, he had got Gregory there, then taken an hour to recover from his terrible exertions and consider their situation.

His first idea had been to walk into Wolgast and get help, but it had suddenly struck him that Gregory must have left his boat on the far side of the creek, so in the morning it was certain to be discovered. Sooner or later the wireless would be found in it. When that happened the Germans would swiftly put two and two together. They would jump to it that Major Bodenstein and his servant, Janos Sabinov, had been spies and it was messages sent by them that had brought about the raid on Peenemünde. The whole police network in northern Pomerania would then start buzzing like a hornets' nest with imperative orders to hunt them down and, if Gregory were in a hospital, he would promptly fall into the hands of the Gestapo. Yet with him lying at death's door it was out of the question to remain in hiding and hope later to slip safely out of the district.

Kuporovitch had then decided that the only hope for Gregory was to leave him there and try to get help from Sassen; so, the better to conceal him from any passer-by, before setting off he had partially buried him.

On reaching Wolgast he had found that the marshalling yard there had also been bombed and that part of the town was in flames. Skirting it he had reached the road to Greifswald and after a while got a lift in a lorry that took him through the barrier and to the town. From Greifswald he had somehow managed to walk the seven miles to Sassen, arriving there at seven o'clock in the morning. Taking great precautions against being seen by anyone, he had gone to the ruined Castle. There he had found Malacou up and, by his own mysterious means, already acquainted with a general outline of the situation.

The doctor had given him a potent draught that had temporarily restored him, and they had consulted on what best to do. Their decision had been that the following night Kuporovitch should accompany Willi von Altern in the lorry back to the coppice near Kröslin and pick up Gregory. Owing to the chaos caused by the raid, the Russian thought it unlikely that the wireless would be discovered during the course of the day. Unless it was, the hunt for them would not start immediately so his pass for going to and fro through the barrier would still be good that night, but he had been quick to see that to the plan there was another danger. Although Willi was half-witted, he might later give away having brought Gregory back to Sassen.

Malacou had got over that hurdle by saying that people whose brains were in such a state were very easy subjects to hypnotize; so he would send for Willi and while talking to him about some farm matter put him under. He could then be made to forget permanently everything that took place during the next twenty-four hours.

There remained the problem of getting Gregory back to Sassen through the barrier, as it would have later proved their undoing if it were recorded at the guard post there that Major Bodenstein, suffering from wounds that made him incapable of escaping from the district, had been brought out in the Sassen lorry. That problem had also been solved by Malacou thinking of the coffin. For a dead body no pass would be required and, well lined, a coffin would serve just as well as a stretcher. He had added that Willi while under hypnosis could be made to knock up a rough one during that evening.

Their plan being settled, Kuporovitch had fallen into a sleep of exhaustion. In the evening the doctor roused him for a hearty meal and gave him morphia and a hypodermic to take with him. After dark he had set off with Willi. At the barrier he had had some anxious moments, but all had gone well. On reaching the coppice he had been terribly afraid that he would find Gregory dead and, on finding him gone from the shallow grave, had feared that he must have been stumbled upon and carried away by the Germans.

But Willi had heard Gregory's cry for help so had been the first to reach him and had foolishly tried to lift him up before Kuporovitch could give him an injection. That its effects had worn off during the latter part of their journey, Malacou said later, must have been due to the acuteness of his pain having pierced his consciousness; but otherwise everything had gone according to plan.

In the early hours of the morning they had cut off his clothes in the room in the ruin now used as a kitchen, and on the table there his terrible wound had been cleaned and bandaged up by the doctor. They had then carried him to an upstairs room, the roof of which was still sound, and Kuporovitch had remained there with him ever since.

Gregory also learned that the raid on Peenemünde had

proved an outstanding success. Hauff had let it out to Khurrem
that the Germans estimated that the better part of six hundred
bombers had been employed in the raid. They had come in
accompanied by a force of Mosquitoes that had bombed Berlin
and the Germans had been deceived into thinking that the
whole air fleet had dropped its bombs there. But, a little short
of the capital, the Lancasters had swung north, passed over
Rügen island, then come in from the sea and swooped on
Peenemünde, coming down to eight thousand feet to make
certain of their targets. The German night fighters had inter-
cepted them on the way back and had shot down forty
aircraft, but the havoc caused by the raid had been terrible.
Many hundreds of the labour force in the crowded hutments
had been wiped out or burned to death, scores of German
technicians had been killed or wounded, the whole Station was
a shambles and it would be impossible to resume work there
for many months.

About Hauff himself there was also news. On the night of
the raid his wife had died. His account of the matter was that
the sound of the distant raid had reached him just as he was
going to bed. Looking out of a window he had seen the fierce
glow in the sky and realized that Peenemünde was being
attacked; so he had gone downstairs, got out his car and
driven into Greifswald in case his S.S. unit there should be
required to give help in the emergency. When he had got home
the following morning he had found his wife at the bottom of
the stairs with her neck broken.

Normally, being a chronic invalid, she rarely left her room;
but it was assumed that, frightened by the roar overhead of the
returning aircraft, and the firing of an anti-aircraft battery
stationed not far away, she had thought she would be safer on
the ground floor of the farm or, perhaps, had gone down to
make herself a cup of coffee, but had tripped at the top of the
stairs and fallen to her death.

Recalling what Khurrem had told him about Hauff's designs
on herself and the Sassen estate, Gregory thought it by no
means improbable that the Sturmbahnführer had suddenly
decided that the raid provided a good opportunity for him to
rid himself of his unwanted wife. However, Kuporovitch

went on to say that but for Hauff they might by now be in the clutches of the Gestapo.

On the third day after the raid the wireless had been found in Gregory's boat, with the anticipated results. A description of them both had been issued and a big reward offered for their capture. Oberführer Langbahn had arrived at the Manor with a carload of his S.D. thugs and everyone there had had to submit to hours of questioning.

The farm people could say only that they had had no reason whatever to suspect that Major Bodenstein was not a genuine Rhinelander or his servant a simple pro-German *hilfsfreiwilliger* from some part of Czechoslovakia. Willi stated that owing to his war injuries his memory had become extremely faulty but he could recall nothing suspicious about the two men. Malacou had sworn that Gregory had shown all the symptoms of a man afflicted with heart trouble, Khurrem had declared that he must have undoubtedly known her late husband when he was Military Attaché in Turkey as otherwise he could not possibly have imposed upon her; and all concerned indignantly repudiated the suggestion that they had knowingly harboured enemies of the Reich.

Nevertheless, the angry Oberführer would have had them carted off to a concentration camp had not Hauff been present and seen his plan for marrying Khurrem about to be ruined. He had swiftly intervened and pleaded with his superior. Knowing Khurrem so well, and of her father's voluntary work at the clinic, he was able to vouch for their patriotism and his offer to be personally accountable for their future activities had been accepted.

No-one on the farm, of course, had the least reason to suspect that Gregory and Kuporovitch had returned to Sassen and were living in the ruin; so they could now consider themselves safe there until Gregory was fit enough to leave.

When he asked Kuporovitch if he had any idea when that might be possible the Russian sadly shook his head. 'Alas, my poor friend, it will be many weeks; perhaps months. Every day Malacou comes up here to see you and dress your wounds. He does so always at times when he knows you to be unconscious from the dope he gives you. But his report on you fills

me with distress. The tree-trunk that struck you down fractured your left thigh and it is a compound fracture. He thinks
that there is little chance of your regaining the full use of that
leg until after Christmas.'

Gregory gave a heavy sigh. 'I suppose I'm lucky to be alive;
and that I am is certainly due to your courage and loyalty,
Stefan. But Christmas is four months off; so you mustn't
remain here all that time. Malacou will look after me; so
you've no need to worry that you won't be leaving me in good
hands. You must return to England and give them the good
news of what our bombers did to Peenemünde.'

Kuporovitch laughed. 'You are becoming delirious again,
dear friend. Reconnaissance 'planes will tell them that better
than I could; and wild horses could not drag me from your
side. Come now, it is time for me to give you another injection
and so relieve your pain.'

It was their first long conversation and it had taken a lot out
of Gregory. For some days past the acute pain that had
caused him to groan with every movement had subsided to a
dull ache, but it was nagging at him badly now, so he submitted
without argument.

The next day Malacou came up to see him during one of his
spells of full consciousness. For a while they talked of the raid
and the events that had followed it. Then Gregory asked the
doctor about his prospects.

Malacou replied gravely, 'Your leg was completely crushed;
so it will be a long time before you can get about again. Most
fortunately there was no indication of gangrene setting in, so
the question of trying to save your life by amputation did not
arise. You are over the worst now and should soon be able
to consider yourself convalescent. But you must be very patient
and put your faith in me.

'Owing to my studies of the Microcosm, the human body is,
to me, an open book. I need no X-rays to inform me of the
exact extent of your injuries; and how, in relation to the
Macrocosm, the most favourable influences may be brought
to bear on their alleviation. Each part of the body comes under
the influence of one of the signs of the Zodiac. The thighs are
the province of Sagittarius—the Archer—and by correlating

the hours in which I treat you with those when that sign is in the ascendant we shall ensure your full recovery.

'But I must warn you of one thing. I have never practised more than minor surgery, so I could not undertake to operate upon you. Yet there is no way of restoring your leg to near normal except by an operation. It would, too, have to be a major one, as your femur is fractured in several places. It should be reset by an expert and strengthened with plating; but, placed as we are, there is no competent surgeon whom I could call in without the certainty that it would lead to you and all of us being arrested by the Gestapo.'

Having contemplated this most unpleasant piece of information for a few seconds, Gregory asked, 'When my leg has healed will it hamper me very much in getting about?'

'I fear it will. For many weeks it will bear no weight; so you will have to use crutches. Later, well . . .' Malacou sighed, '. . . it would be no kindness to give you false hopes about the future. You will always have a limp—and a bad one. Your left leg will be three or four inches shorter than your right. Still worse, it will be twisted with the knee turned a little outward. These distortions will, in due course, affect your spine, so that when standing up you will be bent forward and sideways.'

Gregory gave a sudden bitter laugh. 'So I'm to become a human crab, eh?'

The doctor nodded. 'I'll not dispute your comparison. But, remember, you are very lucky to be alive.'

'So I gather. And I certainly agree that to call in a German sawbones would be asking for all of us to be lined up opposite a firing-squad—or worse. Well, there it is. I suppose I'll have to make up my mind to becoming an unsightly cripple.'

They fell silent for a moment, then Malacou said, 'One other thing. For the past eleven days I've been drugging you very heavily so that you should remain unconscious when I dressed your wound. But now you are over the worst I must reduce the size of the injections. That means I shall have to cause you considerable suffering; unless, that is, you are willing to agree to my putting you under hypnosis.'

Gregory considered the suggestion for a moment, then he

shook his head. 'Thanks, Doctor, but I've always had a prejudice against surrendering my will to anyone, so I think I'll put up with the pain.'

Malacou shrugged. 'Just as you wish. But think it over. Hypnosis is now recognized by the medical profession as perfectly legitimate treatment; and the less you suffer the quicker your recovery will be. You can always change your mind.'

Kuporovitch rarely left Gregory's side and had stood silently by listening to the conversation. When the doctor had gone the Russian did his best to console his friend for the sentence that had been passed upon him. But there was little he could say to lighten Gregory's gloom.

On the three days that followed the injections were reduced; so that on the fourth, when Malacou dressed Gregory's wound, he was not fully under. With the further reduction of the drug he remained conscious through those gruelling sessions, and woke each day to spend hours dreading them. But in other respects he steadily gained ground. The hunchback Tarik was an excellent cook and, tempted by the attractive little dishes he produced, Gregory's appetite greatly improved. He also became able to talk without each breath he drew hurting and, for short periods, he managed to take his mind off his wretched situation by reading for a while books that the doctor brought him.

It was on September 7th that Kuporovitch sprang a sudden unwelcome surprise on him. That evening the Russian said, 'Dear friend, I have been thinking. Now that three weeks have elapsed since your calamity there is no longer any fear of your having a relapse. While your life was in danger you know well that nothing would have induced me to leave you. But you will have to remain here for a long time yet. You are safe here and well looked after. Others will perform for you the small services that are all you now require; so would you think very badly of me if I attempted to make my way home?'

'Of course not, Stefan,' Gregory replied, endeavouring to force a smile. 'No-one could have a more loyal friend. Had you not stuck to me on that ghastly night I'd be a rotting corpse by now. The hunchback will do all the chores that you've been doing and I've lots to read. Naturally, I'll miss you terribly;

but it would be absurd for you to remain here kicking your heels for another three months or more. Of course you must go home. In a way I'm glad you have decided to, because it's three weeks since we've been able to communicate with London, and Erika and Madeleine, not to mention dear old Pellinore, must be getting very worried about not hearing from us. Have you thought of any plan yet for getting out of this damned country?'

'No,' Kuporovitch shook his head, 'I wished to obtain your agreement first; then I thought we might talk it over with Malacou.'

'You're right. He's a wily old bird. I'm sure he will produce some good ideas that will help you to evade trouble on your journey.'

For some while they discussed the project, then Kuporovitch settled Gregory down for the night, undressed and got into the bed that had been fixed up for him in one corner of the room.

Now that Gregory was being given only a sedative at night, when its first effect had worn off he was subject to long periods of wakefulness. That night he lay awake for hours, thinking of Kuporovitch's imminent departure. He knew well enough that it was quite one thing to display high courage, exceptional endurance and devotion to a comrade during periods of emergency; and quite another to continue for weeks on end, cooped up, bored to tears and sticking it only because that seemed to be the right thing to do. So he felt that he could not blame his friend for leaving him, but he knew that when the lovable and ever-cheerful Russian had gone a desperate loneliness would be added to his other miseries.

Next day, when Malacou came to dress Gregory's wound, Kuporovitch told the doctor of his decision. Instantly the tall, dark-faced master of the ruin swung round upon the Russian. His black eyes flashed, his big, hooked nose stood out like an eagle's beak as he thrust forward his head and his full red lips trembled with anger.

'You'll do nothing of the kind,' he declared harshly. 'You must be mad even to think of such a thing. Do you wish to have us all stripped and bleeding in one of the Gestapo torture

chambers? Three months here has made your German fairly
fluent. But you could never pass as a German. And the papers
you brought with you are now your death warrant. You'd not
get twenty miles before you were halted and asked to give an
account of yourself. Within a matter of hours they would be
flogging you with their steel rods and pulling out your toe-nails.
No-one can stand up to that sort of thing. Despite yourself,
you would give us all away. No! No! You will put this crazy idea
out of your head and remain here looking after our invalid.'

It had already occurred to Gregory that if Kuporovitch
were caught he might bring disaster on them all, but he had
not wished to appear to be taking advantage of mentioning such
a possibility as a means of dissuading his friend from leaving
him. Now he remained silent; but he could not help feeling a
reaction of selfish pleasure when the Russian looked uncomfortably at the ground and muttered:

'Pardon me. I had not thought of that. I see now that I
must abandon the idea.'

The next three days were uneventful. Sweating and moaning,
Gregory submitted to the doctor's ministrations. Kuporovitch
continued to bring up his meals, wash him and perform the
functions of a nurse. For the rest of the time he sat on his own
bed in the corner, talking a little, reading a little and apparently
resigned at having had to give up his project of trying to get
home.

On the morning of Saturday the 11th, Gregory awoke about
seven o'clock and saw that Kuporovitch's bed was empty.
To that he paid no special heed, assuming that his friend had
left the room for some normal purpose. Ten minutes later
Malacou burst in, gave one look at the Russian's empty bed,
then lifted his hands, wrung them and wailed:

'I knew it! The moment I awoke, I knew it! He is gone! He
is not downstairs; he is not here! Iblis defend us from this
madman. He will be caught! He will betray us. What are we to
do? Oh, what are we to do?'

For the first time since they had met Gregory found himself
regarding Malacou with a faint contempt. He felt no doubt
that the doctor was right and that during the night Kuporovitch, ignoring the danger into which he might bring them, had

slipped away. But nothing could now bring him back. The doctor's loss of control seemed lamentable and his outburst entirely futile.

As Gregory lay looking up at the suddenly haggard face of the occultist he felt a little sorry for him, but he was far more grieved for a different reason. He took it hard that his friend had not told him of his secret intention; nor even left a written message near his pillow, bidding him good-bye.

9

Devil's Work in the Ruin

FOR some minutes Malacou continued to wring his hands and lament, crying:

'That accursed Russian will betray us. I know it! I know it! Those black fiends will come and drag us all to the slaughter. They'll strip us of our clothes and hang us up by our testicles. They'll shave Khurrem's head and thrust a red-hot poker into her. Oh, woe is me; woe is me! Was it not enough that I should be born one of the afflicted race? Have I not forsworn Jehovah? Where have I left the Path that this chastisement should come upon me?'

Lifting himself painfully into a sitting position, Gregory shouted:

'Stop that! Pull yourself together, man! It will be time enough to start squealing when the Gestapo use their rubber truncheons on you. They've not got us yet.'

Malacou abruptly ceased his wailing, stared at him and muttered, 'You are right. The thought of abandoning all the aids to my work here breaks my heart. But I must make preparations to leave Sassen at the earliest possible moment. If I can reach Poland I'll have little to fear. I still have many friends there who will aid me. These Nazi swine cannot know that I lived there before the war. I still own a house in the town of Ostroleka, north-east of Warsaw. In the country districts many thousands of Jews have been left their liberty, because the Germans cannot afford to deprive themselves of the produce they grow; and my Turkish passport will protect me from molestation.'

Gregory's heart gave a sudden lurch. Obviously Malacou would not jeopardize his flight by taking with him a stretcher

case and at that a man whom the Gestapo must still be hunting
high and low. After a moment he asked, 'Do you then intend
to abandon me?'

The doctor hunched his shoulders and spread out his hands.
'What else can I do? After all, it is you who have brought this
terrible situation upon Khurrem and myself.'

'That is not true!' Gregory snapped back. 'You brought it
on yourself by having Khurrem send that message about
Peenemünde to Sweden.'

'Well, perhaps. But I must have been temporarily out of
my wits to do so. I succumbed to the temptation to strike a
blow against the tormentors of my race, and see where it has
landed me.'

'Damn it, man! How can you stand there now and bleat to
me that the risk you must have known you were taking was
not worth while? Between us we have succeeded beyond our
wildest hopes. Tens of thousands of your people have died
without the chance to avenge themselves on a single Nazi. If
we have to give our lives that's a small price to pay for the
destruction of Peenemünde.'

'But I do not want to die,' Malacou wailed, beginning to
wring his hands again. 'I have work to do; work of great
importance. That I must leave you here distresses me greatly.
But why should I stay here to be tortured and murdered with
you when I still have a chance to escape?'

As Gregory could not yet even move from his bed he needed
no telling that his only possible chance of saving his own life
lay in persuading the doctor to remain at Sassen. If Malacou
left it was certain that he would take Tarik, as well as
Khurrem, with him. That meant that if Kuporovitch succeeded
in getting away and the Nazis did not arrive to find the long-
sought Major Bodenstein abandoned there, he would suffer a
lingering death from thirst and starvation. He wondered
grimly how Kuporovitch would feel about it if he ever learned
the terrible fate that had overtaken his friend as a result of his
decision to try to get back to England. Knowing that he was
fighting for his life, Gregory racked his wits for a way to make
Malacou change his mind. Suddenly one came to him and he
said:

'If you leave me here you are going to die anyhow. I'll
see to that. By telling me of your plan to go to Poland you've
played into my hands. Directly the Gestapo boys get here I'll
tell them where you've gone.'

Malacou's dark face paled. 'No! No!' he gasped. 'You
wouldn't do that. Think of all I have done for you.'

'What you've done won't cut much ice if you leave me here
to die of starvation.'

A sudden evil gleam showed in the doctor's black eyes and
he shook his head. 'You forget that you are at my mercy.
I'd have no difficulty in seeing to it that you were dead before
the Nazis got here.'

At this checkmating of his threat Gregory drew in a sharp
breath. Then he exclaimed, 'So you'd go to those lengths,
eh? To save yourself you'd even murder a man who is your
ally?'

For a moment Malacou continued to glower at him, then
he muttered, 'To do so will save you from torture; and, as you
hold this threat over me, I see no alternative.'

'There is an alternative,' Gregory retorted with assurance.
'All this time you have been taking it for granted that Kuporovitch will be caught. But if he is not you have nothing to fear.
And unless he's very unlucky I've little doubt that he'll succeed
in getting away.'

'You cannot really believe that.'

'I do. His mild, happy-go-lucky nature is very deceptive.
I've worked with him for months in Paris and other places,
right under the noses of the Nazis. He is as cunning as a weasel,
up to a hundred tricks and completely ruthless. If anyone gets
in his way he'll kill him without the slightest compunction,
and he possesses remarkable endurance. You have only to
recall his extraordinary feat of getting me away from Peenemünde.'

'You may be right, but I dare not risk it.'

Suddenly an inspiration came to Gregory and he said,
'Listen. Before you set about murdering me, or exciting comment at the Manor by making arrangements for your flight,
why not go downstairs and consult the oracles? You can't
have lost your faith in the stars and that horoscope of Kuporo-

vitch that you drew up. Surely if there really is any basis for your beliefs you could find out what his chances are.'

Slowly Malacou nodded. 'Now you speak sound sense. There are many reasons for my wishing to remain here if I can do so in safety.' Turning, he picked up from the bed a pair of pyjamas he had lent the Russian and added, 'I can psychometrize these. Together with his horoscope that should tell me what we want to know.'

As he left the room Gregory relaxed on his bed with a sigh of relief. Yet he knew that he was still under suspended sentence of death. His thigh began to pain him, but his mind was so filled with apprehension that he was fully conscious of the throbbing only now and then. An hour dragged by and the better part of another; then Malacou entered the room again.

His dark, hooded eyes now looked tired from the efforts that he had made to concentrate, but his face was no longer grey with fear. Passing a hand wearily over his thick black grey-flecked hair, he said in a toneless voice:

'I have done it. And the omens are favourable—very favourable. Today is the 11th and he could not have chosen a more propitious date. Not only is he ruled by the 2, but he was born on an 11th. Moreover, his two best days of the week are Sunday and Monday; therefore astral influences should continue to protect him tomorrow and the day after. His horoscope bears out what you say about his endurance, courage and resource; so with three fortunate days before him there is very good reason for hoping that he will get away from the district without accident. But probably not without a fight. I saw newly spilled blood in connection with him; and in some way he becomes involved with a servant of Mercury—perhaps a postman—but in what way I could not determine.'

'Then,' Gregory asked eagerly, 'you are prepared to stay here?'

'Yes. For me to leave Sassen now would be to fly in the face of the omens. My own stars predict an uneventful period for me for some months to come. Besides, I have re-examined your horoscope and it is now much clearer to me. We are destined to work together in the future and you will be the means of saving me, probably from death.'

'I am delighted to hear it,' Gregory remarked with uncon-
cealed sarcasm. 'Perhaps, then, you will set about giving me my
daily dose of hell by redressing my leg, for I couldn't save a
rabbit from a snare as long as I remain like this.'

Malacou shrugged. 'You have cause to bear umbrage against
me for my recent conduct. But I ask you to remember that I
am endowed with very different qualities from yourself. You
are a man of action, whereas I am a contemplative with an
unusually vivid imagination. People like myself become
frightened easily and liable to be panicked into taking any
steps which they think may save them from physical pain. You
have great fortitude, whereas I——'

'God knows I need it,' Gregory cut in bitterly. 'However
vivid your imagination may be, I doubt if you can realize the
gyp it gives me every time you treat my wound.'

'I have a very good idea of it,' the doctor replied seriously,
'and to show you that I am not altogether a coward I will,
if you like, actually experience it.'

'How can you?'

'By taking your pain upon myself. You must have heard of
that being done by psychic people who are also good Samari-
tans?'

'Yes, I have,' Gregory agreed. 'Very well, then. You owe me
something for the scare you gave me two hours ago. We'll call
it quits and I'll try to forget about that if you can do your stuff
on my leg without causing me any pain.'

Rolling down the sheets, Malacou set about his daily
ministrations. As he removed the bandages Gregory, to his
amazement, felt only a slightly increased throbbing, but the
occultist began to groan. Soon he was sweating profusely.
Now and then he closed his eyes and, breathing heavily, had
to stop. Twice his thick red lips quivered in an abrupt cry. By
the time he had done his face was again haggard and as he
stepped away from the bedside tears were running down his
furrowed cheeks.

Collapsing in a chair he sat there for a few minutes panting
and mopping his face. When he had recovered a little Gregory
said, 'I'm grateful to you for that. How I wish to God someone
could take my pain every day.'

Malacou grunted. 'For accepting it you have only yourself to blame. I told you a fortnight ago that it could be absorbed into your unconscious if you would allow me to hypnotize you.'

'And I refused.'

'To persist in doing so surprises me in a man of your intelligence. Do you not see how illogical it is to reject this method of killing pain, while being perfectly willing to let me inject you with pain-killing drugs? You would not refuse to be anaesthetized either, if you had to undergo an operation, would you?'

'That's true,' Gregory said slowly, 'but you are not an ordinary doctor, and Kuporovitch was convinced that you had entered into a pact with the Devil. Add to that, barely half an hour ago, you forswore your God in front of me. I'm pretty sceptical about that sort of thing myself, but——'

'The Russian thinking that does not surprise me,' Malacou broke in. 'They are a backward race and still greatly influenced by superstition. He, too, would be particularly imbued with such ideas, because he is subject to the Moon. Such people readily attribute every happening to the intervention of Christ or Satan. To suppose that is absurd, as people in Western Europe have come to recognize. As for my denying Jehovah, I no longer subscribe to the Jewish faith. It was only like a Protestant exclaiming "To hell with the Pope". Anyhow, you at least appear to have an open mind on the matter, so I will bring you some books on hypnotism to read; then you will see for yourself that no question of good or evil enters into it.'

For several days, in spite of the occultist's favourable prognostications about Kuporovitch, Gregory continued to be extremely anxious about him, but by the Wednesday it seemed fairly certain that he had got away safely and by that time would have succeeded in establishing for himself a new identity.

About the latter possibility one matter gave both Gregory and Malacou food for speculation. It was that the village postman had also disappeared. He was an elderly dug-out who had returned to duty on account of the war, a widower and lived alone. He had last been seen on Friday evening working in his garden and when he had not turned up at the village post office on Saturday morning it had been supposed that he was ill; so a girl had been sent out to do his round. As there was no delivery on Sunday, no-one had worried about his absence until Monday morning. The police had then been informed and had searched his cottage, but could find no clue to his disappearance; and no-one could suggest any reason why he might suddenly have decided to leave Sassen.

In addition to cooking and bringing up Gregory's meals, Tarik had taken Kuporovitch's place in looking after him and now helped him with certain exercises the doctor had prescribed to keep his circulation going. As he had soon learned, the hunchback always either communicated in silence with his master or spoke Yiddish to him. Apparently he knew no other language, so Gregory had to indicate his wants by signs and was unable to find out whether under the man's bald cranium there lay the mind of a simple, unfortunate being or a sinister personality.

Khurrem had already visited the invalid several times and now she came to see him more frequently. But she was still obviously oppressed by her secret worries, so made anything but a cheerful companion. Gregory felt sure that her visits were due only to her wish to show appreciation of his having offered to help her if she would confide in him, but she came no nearer doing so. In consequence, when their stilted conversations lapsed, and she said that she ought to get back to the farm, he never sought to detain her.

The result was that he now spent many hours each day alone, and as pain often kept him awake at nights he became subject to terrible fits of depression about his future as a cripple. His only escape lay in reading. Before the end of the week he had got through several books in German on hypnotism and J. Milne Bramwell's great opus on the subject in English.

When, in due course, Malacou asked him how he was getting on with his reading, he replied, 'I have learned quite enough to convince me that hypnotism is simply an extension of the powers of the human brain and owes nothing to the supernatural.'

The doctor showed his long teeth in a smile. 'Yet you will agree that anyone who practised it a few hundred years ago would have been credited with supernatural powers?'

'Yes, I don't doubt that they would.'

'There, then, you have the explanation of all these mysteries. *Supernatural* is simply a word to express any happening that lies beyond our present comprehension and *magic* the procuring of a result normally regarded as impossible when judged by the accepted laws of cause and effect. As more and more natural laws receive recognition, the *magic* of yesterday becomes the *science* of today.'

'That sounds perfectly reasonable; but do you suggest, then, that contrary to popular belief magic never entails calling upon the forces of evil?'

'I would not say that, although, of course, from the beginning of time people have differed about what is *good* and what is *evil*. There are laws governing the *material* plane and laws governing the *spiritual* plane. During the past two hundred years many of the former have been harnessed to the great benefit of mankind—electricity, for example; and the modern wizards we term *scientists* take credit for new discoveries every day. But the greater part of the laws governing the spiritual plane they still refuse to recognize or investigate. To apply such laws requires the development of a person's higher being so that he is in rapport with powers that enable him to bring about that which he wishes to achieve.'

'I see. But as spiritual powers are either of God or the Devil, that must entail becoming a priest of sorts to one or the other.'

'Not necessarily. Everyone has spiritual powers within himself. A knowledge of them enables an occultist to use certain unseen forces for his own ends without attracting to himself either good or evil. Prolonged study of these mysteries has enabled me to do so.'

'Then why did you not use yours to ensure Kuporovitch's getting away safely?' Gregory asked shrewdly.

'Because my command of the unseen forces is strictly limited. Just as scientists are still only on the fringe of discovering the laws that govern the material universe, so modern occultists are still only gradually obtaining knowledge of the laws that govern the realm of the spirit. The ancients knew far more of them than we do; but when their civilizations were overrun by barbarians that knowledge was lost. We are regaining it only a little at a time by deep thought and patient experiment.'

'Your contention is, then, that such people as yourself are, in a way, scientists and that evil plays no part in occult operations.'

Malacou shrugged. 'It need not do so. Naturally the supreme powers lie at the root of all things. I was seeking only to assure you that certain results that you would term "miraculous" can be achieved without calling for help upon either good or evil forces. There are ten grades of occultists, ranging from Neophyte to Ipisissimus. Only those holding the three highest ranks have passed the Abyss and so irrevocably committed themselves to follow either the Right Hand or Left Hand Path. I am no more than a Practicus, so still engaged in mastering the mysteries of the Qabalah. However, while in the lower grades I achieved entry to the Astral Plane and complete success in Asana and Paranayama, which enables me to perform many minor magics.'

'And you claim that your success in such practices owes nothing to evil forces?'

'I do. Surely you do not suppose that every clairvoyant, thought-reader, hypnotist and pain-taker has entered into a pact with Satan?'

'No; of course not.'

'Then why be so frightened and continue to put up with your pain when by hypnotizing you I could relieve you of it?'

For several minutes Gregory remained silent. All things considered, he decided that Malacou had made his case; so at length he said:

'Very well, then. Life will be a lot pleasanter for me if I don't have to lie here for hours dreading these daily ordeals. Let's start tomorrow.'

When Malacou came up next morning he was wearing an elastic band round his head, from the centre of which, above his forehead, there rose a circular metal mirror of the kind that doctors use for reflecting light down a patient's throat. Sitting down opposite Gregory, he told him to keep his eyes on the metal disc and to open his mind by not allowing it to follow any chain of thought.

Having taken a decision, it was against Gregory's nature to adopt half-measures in carrying it out; so he fixed his gaze steadily on the disc and as each thought drifted into his mind promptly dismissed it. As he stared at the bright metal it seemed gradually to increase in size until its light blotted out everything else and he had the sensation of being drawn towards it. Surprisingly soon he felt drowsy, his eyelids flickered a few times then fell; yet through them he was aware of a strong, rosy glow. He then felt his hand lifted and was vaguely surprised that when left unsupported his arm remained up in the air at right-angles to his body without his exerting the least effort. After that his mind became blank.

When he recovered his faculties he was again lying back in bed and Malacou was looking down on him. With a smile the doctor said, 'By offering no resistance you made things easy for me. You were under for half an hour and did not make so much as a murmur. What is more I was able to lift you up and turn you round so that for a while both your legs were dangling over the side of the bed and the blood could flow more freely into them.'

Gregory returned his smile. 'I didn't feel a thing. What a blessed relief to know that I haven't to suffer any more when you do my dressings. I'm very grateful to you, Doctor.'

Since Gregory and Kuporovitch had returned from Peenemünde Malacou had, from time to time, brought them up news of the progress of the war as given out on the German radio. For the first fortnight Gregory had been too ill to take in much that had happened, but he gradually caught up with events. Two days after he had been struck down the Allies had completed their conquest of Sicily; and on September 3rd they had gone into the toe of Italy.

This news amazed and appalled him. It had seemed so obvious that the German forces in Sicily would withdraw to the great natural bastion of Mount Etna on the north-east corner of the island and that, although they could be boxed in there, it would take many weeks, or even months, before they could be finally subdued; so the enemy would have all that time to bring up reinforcements and prepare defensive positions across the straits in the south of Italy. And eight weeks had elapsed between the first landing in Sicily and this on the mainland. That meant for certain that the Allies must meet with fierce opposition and could have little hope of making a swift deep penetration, as could have been the case had they landed further north.

Four or five days after the Allies had crossed the Straits of Messina the Italians had broadcast an announcement that they had signed an armistice. At first it looked as if the Italian surrender would make the occupation of the country comparatively easy. But that had not proved at all the case. Instead of withdrawing the Germans had continued to hold the strong defensive positions they had prepared, and had found little difficulty in tying down Montgomery's invading troops in the toe of the peninsula.

A few days later, the Germans had made themselves masters of Rome, then, by a brilliant exploit, snatched Mussolini in an aircraft from a high plateau on which he had been held prisoner and set him up as the head of a new Fascist Government in the north, on Lake Garda.

Belatedly, the Allies had attempted to outflank the Germans in the south by a landing at Salerno, but had failed to achieve their object. Kesselring had reacted with amazing speed and not only hemmed in their new bridgehead but looked like driving them back into the sea. Their fate still hung in the balance; and Gregory could only pray that this ill-conceived campaign—so different from any of the proposals put forward by the British Joint Planning Staff early that year—would not bring a series of bloodbaths and disasters to the Allied Armies.

For three days Malacou continued to come each morning and dress his wound, while he remained in oblivion. On the fourth, soon after waking, he got a strong impression that the doctor would not come in the morning but in the afternoon; and that proved to be the case. When he remarked on it, Malacou smiled and said:

'This is excellent. My delay in coming to you was deliberate. I sent out that thought and you received it.'

At that Gregory felt slight alarm and replied quickly, 'If my allowing you to hypnotize me is going to lead to your dominating my mind I'd prefer to put up with the pain.'

Malacou shook his head. 'The transference of thoughts between two people does not lead to one dominating the other. It is an equal partnership. To prove that, I suggest that now we have achieved some small degree of rapport you should try to convey a thought to me. Tomorrow I will not come to you until you send for me.'

Gregory agreed to try out this intriguing experiment and, sure enough, having waited until midday next day, when he had been concentrating hard for some ten minutes on willing the doctor to come to him, Malacou, smiling with satisfaction, appeared.

Sitting down, he said, 'I will tell you now why I am anxious that we should develop telepathy between us. The stars, as I told you some while ago, foretell that at some future time we shall again work together against the accursed Nazis. When that time comes, being able to communicate our thoughts to one another while at a distance could prove of inestimable value.'

It was impossible to dispute the immense benefit that two secret agents would derive from such an unusual advantage; so, after a moment's thought, Gregory said that he was willing to practise tuning his mind in to Malacou's. They then agreed that Gregory should memorize and transfer to the doctor certain passages from the books he was reading, and that in future the doctor should endeavour to convey the radio bulletins to him by telepathy.

During the week that followed they had numerous failures, some partial successes and sufficient complete transferences to encourage them. Towards the end of the week it was clear that the rapport between them had become much stronger. Through it Gregory learned that the Germans were no longer boasting that they would annihilate the Allied force that had been clinging to the beachhead at Salerno; but, as against that, they had captured Rhodes, and as long as they held that bastion adjacent to the Turkish coast it was clear that Churchill's hope of bringing Turkey into the war on the side of the Allies must remain frustrated.

Gregory regarded that development as a major set-back, but towards the end of the month Malacou predicted that events would soon take a turn in favour of the Allies; and he proved correct. The Russians again surged forward and captured Smolensk; then on October 2nd the Germans admitted that their forces in Italy had made a 'strategic' withdrawal and allowed the American Fifth Army to enter Naples.

It was on the following day that Gregory said to Malacou, 'I've no wish that this game we are playing should lead to my prying into your private affairs, but yesterday when I first established rapport with you I got the impression that you were worrying about Khurrem. It's some days since she has paid me a visit. Is she, by any chance, ill?'

'No; but you were right,' Malacou replied gravely. 'I am greatly worried about her. As you may recall, Herman Hauff's wife was found dead the night after the raid on Peenemünde. That is now six weeks ago, and he has asked Khurrem to marry him.'

'I see,' said Gregory thoughtfully. 'It's a pity that he is a Nazi; and, perhaps, a wife-murderer into the bargain. In the circumstances her dislike of the idea of taking him for a husband is very understandable. But to marry again is just what she needs to pull her together.'

Malacou rounded on him with blazing eyes and cried, 'My daughter is everything to me. I'd rather see her dead first.'

A little startled by the doctor's outburst, Gregory said no more; but as the days went by he sensed that Malacou was becoming increasingly uneasy. However, towards the middle of October it transpired that it was not only about Khurrem's situation that he was worrying. After he had treated Gregory on the 15th he said:

'For some days I have been greatly concerned by new portents that have arisen. I feel convinced that some revolutionary change is shortly to occur in your situation. It will not be harmful to you; but a new influence that is extremely potent is about to make itself felt here and it will be adverse to the rapport we have succeeded in establishing between us.'

More he could not say and Gregory's speculations got him nowhere; but very early on the morning of the 17th the prediction was fulfilled in a manner that he could not possibly have anticipated. While it was still dark he awoke to find Malacou bending over him. In a hoarse voice the occultist said:

'The stars never lie. Kuporovitch has returned. He has dyed his hair black, thinned out his eyebrows and grown a moustache; so for a moment I did not recognize him. He comes from Sweden and with him he has brought a surgeon and a nurse.'

Gregory's mind flamed with sudden hope. 'You mean . . . you mean to operate on me and put my leg right?'

'That is what they hope to do, but it is not possible to assess the chances until the doctor has examined you.'

'Then bring him up, man! Bring him up so that he can have a look at my leg.'

'No, you must be patient for a while. He is an elderly man and they have all walked here from Grimmen, carrying their luggage. He has declared that he must sleep for a few hours before making his examination.'

'But Stefan! Kuporovitch! He would think nothing of such a midnight tramp. Bring him to me so that I can thank him. My dear, loyal friend. How could I ever have imagined for one moment that he would have left me for selfish ends?'

'He and the nurse are both eager to see you. I left them refreshing themselves with a glass of wine while I came up to tell you of this strange turn in your fortunes. I will go down and fetch them.'

Five minutes later a woman in nurse's uniform entered the room. Her hair was hidden under her cap and in the dim light for a moment Gregory could not make out her features. Then his heart gave a bound. For a few seconds he thought his imagination was deceiving him. But as she smiled he knew it was no illusion. She was his beloved Erika.

Next moment she was kneeling by his bed, her arms round him, her cheek pressed to his, sobbing with happiness. Taking her lovely face between his hands, he kissed her again and again until they were both breathless. When at last she knelt back he saw Kuporovitch standing on the other side of the bed. Seizing the smiling Russian's hand he pressed it and cried:

'Stefan, you old devil! How can I ever thank you for this? I've no words to express what I feel. But how did you ever manage it? That you should have succeeded in getting back to me bringing Erika and a surgeon is little short of a miracle.'

The Russian shrugged. 'Dear friend, where there's a will there's a way; and Sir Pellinore smoothed out most of our difficulties. I could not allow you to become a cripple for life if there were any possible means of saving you from such a fate. When I succeeded in reaching England Sir Pellinore agreed that no effort must be spared to bring you aid. Erika insisted on coming too. To improve her capabilities as a nurse, until we could leave England she spent eighteen hours a day watching surgeons at work in operating theatres. Sir Pellinore arranged for us to be flown out to Sweden in a Mosquito and, no matter how, enabled us to enter Germany with Swedish passports. The rest was easy.'

'But this surgeon? If it should come out that he came here to operate on a man who is in hiding from the Gestapo the Germans will have no mercy on him. He must know that. How did you persuade him to take such a risk?'

Erika wiped the tears of happiness from her blue eyes and laughed. 'Money, darling; money. Sir Pellinore gave me a cheque for ten thousand pounds and through contacts in Sweden we induced one of the best surgeons in Stockholm, a Dr. Zetterberg, to run the risk for this colossal fee.' Turning, she looked up at Malacou and added, 'We felt sure that if we could get here safely, and in the middle of the night, you would agree to conceal us all in your castle.'

Malacou had stood silently by taking in most of what had been said, as, although he did not speak English, he knew enough to understand it. Now he bowed to Erika and said:

'*Gnädige Frau*, naturally I wish to do all I can to help you. But what you ask presents certain difficulties. This old ruin has few habitable rooms. Mr. Kuporovitch could again sleep on a bed in the corner here, but there is nowhere where I could accommodate yourself and Dr. Zetterberg for any length of time. And it would be much too great a risk for you both to live in the manor house. There is, too, the question of food. While Mr. Kuporovitch was here, Mr. Sallust was on a very light diet, so for all practical purposes I had only one extra to feed. But now he is eating well again, and to have enough food sent for four of you in would be certain to arouse unwelcome comment.'

After some discussion Malacou agreed that for a few nights they would manage somehow, then he and Kuporovitch left Erika and Gregory to delight in their reunion.

Soon after midday Dr. Zetterberg came up to make his examination. He was a tall, thin, grey-haired man with bright blue eyes and a pleasant smile. After a brief survey of Gregory's wound he turned to Malacou and said:

'As I was led to suppose, this is going to be an extremely difficult operation. I would not have consented to come here without my own anaesthetist, but Mr. Kuporovitch told me he felt confident that you, Doctor, would be capable of administering an anaesthetic without endangering our patient. Is that so?'

Malacou nodded, 'I have given anaesthetics on a number of occasions, but as I am an expert hypnotist I would greatly prefer to put him under deep hypnosis.'

Dr. Zetterberg frowned. 'To rely on hypnotism to perform an operation of this kind would be most unusual. I hardly think——'

Gregory quickly cut in, 'Dr. Malacou has been using hypnosis while dressing my wound and I haven't felt a thing. May I suggest that he should put me under while you make your examination. Then you could judge his powers for yourself.'

To that Zetterberg agreed and, on finding that Gregory did not even flinch however roughly the wound was handled, he somewhat reluctantly consented to Malacou's proposal. He said that twenty-four hours would be needed to prepare Gregory, and that as the shock to the patient's system would be serious he intended to remain on there for at least four days or perhaps a week.

Malacou then told them of the arrangements on which he had decided after talking with Khurrem. Kuporovitch was to share Gregory's room, a bed was to be made up for Dr. Zetterberg in the library and, as Erika would be staying on after the doctor left, she was to live in the manor house.

At that Gregory took alarm for Erika's safety, but Malacou reassured him. Her passport described her as Frau Selma Bjornsen. Khurrem was giving out to the servants that an old friend of hers from Sweden was coming to stay with her for some weeks and the train by which she was arriving would not reach Grimmen till late that evening. As it was now dark early Khurrem could leave the house in her truck about six o'clock, but instead of driving in to Grimmen she would pick Erika up outside the ruin soon after seven and take her to the Manor in time for the evening meal.

Usually Gregory slept for a good part of the afternoon, but that day he was far too excited to think of sleep and Erika sat with him until it was time for her to leave. Kuporovitch then took her place and told Gregory about his escape.

He had made his way without difficulty to Kiel, stowed away in a small coastal steamer that plied up and down the Little Belt and, in seaman's clothes that he had stolen from a locker, slipped ashore after dark at the little port of Aabenraa, in Denmark.

Being one of the smallest countries in Europe, Denmark had been able to offer only a token resistance to the Germans when they had invaded it in 1939. Its population was by habit law-abiding and, strategically, the peninsula could be ruled out as a base for an Allied invasion; so the Nazis anticipated no trouble there. Having taken over its military establishments and put in representatives empowered to squeeze the country as far as possible of its natural products, they had, thereafter, left it more or less to run itself. Perforce, in major matters, the Danes did what they were told; but, having centuries of tradition as a free people, they bitterly resented the overlordship that had been thrust upon them. In consequence, whenever possible both police and people wilfully obstructed the Germans in their searches for Jews who had fled from Germany, escaped prisoners of war and deserters.

In crossing to the west coast Kuporovitch had avoided all towns and inns, and it was as a deserter that he had posed at the lonely farms at which he had taken shelter. His story had been that he was a Latvian seaman whom the Nazis had forced to serve in one of the auxiliary vessels of their Baltic Fleet, but when his ship had put into Kiel for a refit he had managed to get away, and he was now hoping to get employment in a North Sea fishing trawler till the war was over.

On reaching Esbjerg he had gone north from the city for a few miles to the village of Hierting, and there taken lodgings with a pretty young widow. Quite soon they had been on such intimate terms that he had felt it safe to confide the truth to her. In all the occupied countries, as long as the Germans were gaining victories resistance had been almost negligible and confined to acts of defiance by brave individuals here and there; but when the tide began to turn, bringing hopes of freedom, resistance groups had sprung up in them all and soon coalesced into powerful secret organizations. After cautious probing among her friends, Kuporovitch's pretty widow had succeeded in putting him in touch with a local group leader. A fortnight later he had been got away in a fishing trawler that had escaped from the German guard-boat in a fog, and had landed at Hull.

Having congratulated him on his exploits, Gregory asked casually, 'And what did you do with the village postman?'

Kuporovitch sadly shook his head. 'Ah, dear friend, that was a most distressing business. I realized, of course, that he was certain to be missed. But he was quite old, you know. Life could not have held much more for him. And, after all, had we met on a battlefield in the first great war when he, too, was no doubt a soldier, I should almost certainly have killed him then. Let us look upon it that the good God saw fit to grant him an extra twenty-five years of life. You see, I had to have his uniform, his bicycle and his letter sack. No policeman ever asks to see a postman's papers. But let us say no more about it; the subject is a painful one to me.'

Gregory refrained from comment. Every hour of every day the Nazis were doing far worse things than rob old men of the last few years of their lives, and he felt that it was not for him to call in question any act that might help to strangle the hydra-headed monster that Hitler had created. The great thing was that Kuporovitch had both got away and had brought him the aid which might enable both of them to fight another day.

After a moment the Russian went on, 'There is one thing I

must tell you. When I left you before it was to bring you help. Now, when Dr. Zetterberg goes, I intend to leave again with him.'

'But Stefan!' Gregory exclaimed, 'what about Erika? I'm not thinking of myself but if there is trouble I'm in no state to protect her.'

'*C'est vrai; c'est vrai,*' Kuporovitch nodded. 'I thought long about that. But she is a German, so knows the ropes in this country, and she is as agile-minded as either of us. She should be safe here at Sassen and with the Swedish passport she is carrying she could return to Sweden without difficulty at any time she wishes. I have discussed the matter with her and she insists that I should go. You see, after this operation it will be many weeks before you are fit to travel; and, although I play pleasant games with other women, I adore my little Madeleine. Early in January she is going to have a baby, and I must not risk not being with her at such a time.'

'Of course you mustn't,' Gregory agreed immediately. Then he laughed. 'Somehow, Stefan, I've never thought of you as a father. But I'm sure you'll make a good one. Congratulations and the very best of luck. Don't worry about Erika and myself; we have little to fear as long as we remain at Sassen. And give my fondest love to Madeleine. Tell her I'll be thinking of her.'

Kuporovitch stroked the little moustache he had grown, then produced a cardboard folder from his pocket. '*Merci, mon vieux.* As you say, you should be safe while here. The Jew's life hangs on his protecting you from discovery. And although I dislike and fear the man, and was most unhappy to find that you had allowed him to hypnotize you, I respect his knowledge and shrewdness. But when your leg is sound enough for you to walk you've got to get home; and I've thought of that. Here is a Swedish passport. Assuming you will return with Erika we had it made out in the name of Gunnar Bjornsen; so that you could pass as her husband.'

'Stefan, you think of everything,' Gregory smiled, taking the passport and putting it with his wallet in the drawer of a little bedside table that had been found for him. 'For what you have done for me I'll never be able to repay you.'

The Russian shrugged. '*Parbleu!* Think nothing of it. I know that you would have done as much for me.'

On the following afternoon a stout trestle table was brought in. Gregory was lifted on to it, Malacou put him into a deep trance and the operation was performed. His thigh bone had been so badly crushed that it proved even more complicated than the Swedish surgeon had expected and the patient had to be kept under for four hours before the operation was completed. Dr. Zetterberg was grey-faced and sweating when he handed his blood-stained rubber gloves to Erika and said:

'If his system survives the shock, in time he should regain the full use of his leg. He will limp, of course; but the degree of his limp will depend on how soon he puts weight upon his leg. He will be well advised if he refrains from attempting to walk without crutches for at least two months.'

For three days Malacou allowed Gregory to emerge from hypnosis only for brief intervals. Each time after doing so he soon ran a high temperature, and it was evident that he was hovering between life and death. On the evening of the fourth day Malacou brought up a copy of the Sephirotic Tree on ancient parchment and, while Kuporovitch watched him with extreme antipathy and Dr. Zetterberg with ill-concealed cynicism, he hung it up over the head of Gregory's bed. Erika remained in the background, her fine features drawn with anxiety, but her expression noncommittal.

This diagrammatic representation of the mysteries of the Cabbala consisted of a diamond-shaped framework carrying ten circles in each of which were inscribed Hebrew characters. Pointing at it, Malacou said:

'Behold the Key to all Power, from the Beginning unto the End, as it is Now and shall Be for Evermore. The symbols in the lowest circles represent the Kingdom and the Foundation. Those above, Honour and Virtue. Proceeding upwards, Glory, Dominion, Grace, Intelligence, Wisdom and, finally, the Crown. By these I shall conjure the entities untrammelled by flesh to spare our brother to us.'

Exchanging glances of embarrassment Kuporovitch and the Swede withdrew, but as Malacou began to genuflect in front of the Tree and murmur Hebraic incantations Erika knelt down. The first great love of her life had been a charming, gifted and highly intelligent Jewish millionaire, and she had come to respect his beliefs. It was his having been taken to a concentration camp that had caused her to denounce the Nazis publicly and she would have shared his fate had she not been the daughter of a Bavarian General and a friend of Goering, whose influence had saved her.

The following morning there could be no doubt that Gregory had taken a turn for the better. He was no longer sweating and his temperature had dropped to near normal. On the sixth day after the operation the surgeon expressed himself as satisfied with Gregory's state and he was sufficiently recovered to say good-bye to his loyal friend Kuporovitch. After dark that evening Khurrem drove the Russian and Dr. Zetterberg to Grimmen.

Before the operation Gregory had been putting on weight, but it had taken a lot out of him, so for the next fortnight he was again in a very low state and made only slow progress.

For appearances' sake Erika had to pass a good part of her time with Khurrem, but the pretence of going in the afternoons for long, solitary walks enabled her to spend a few hours every day with Gregory. During them she often read to him and always brought him such war news as came in. The Russians were still advancing and had taken Kiev, but the Allies were making little progress against the tough resistance of the Germans in southern Italy.

Sometimes they talked of Khurrem and her unhappy state. She was still drinking heavily and Herman Hauff continued to press her to become engaged to him. It was Erika's opinion that Khurrem might have agreed had it not been for her father. The mutual interest Khurrem and Hauff shared in running the farm efficiently made a bond between them and there was no proof that Hauff really had murdered his wife. Admittedly he was a Nazi, but in other respects he was not a bad fellow and, as Erika pointed out, Khurrem's husband had also been a Nazi.

She was also inclined to believe that, quite apart from the question of Hauff, Khurrem's unhappiness was in some way due to her relations with her father. He unquestionably dominated her completely, yet he made no attempt to stop her drinking. Erika was convinced too that in spite of all that Malacou was doing for Gregory his influence was a sinister one, and although she tried to conceal it, she found it difficult to hide her growing aversion to him.

Her instinctive feeling that Malacou was an evil man caused her to worry about his hypnotizing Gregory when dressing his wound, and she tried to dissuade him from continuing to practise thought transference with the doctor. But by that time Gregory had developed the power to an extent that enabled him even to hold short conversations with Malacou by telepathy; and he was so fascinated by his progress that he would not agree to give up these intriguing sessions.

By mid-November he was again able to sit up and his new wounds had healed sufficiently for Erika to massage his sadly wasted limb. During that week, too, his general health showed a sudden marked improvement. Malacou told him that this was because the Earth was about to enter the Sign of the Zodiac ruled by Sagittarius, which ran from the 21st November to the 20th December, and was especially favourable to all matters concerning the thighs and legs.

Ever since Gregory had sufficiently recovered from his operation to enjoy his periods of consciousness the sight of Erika had re-aroused in him the emotions natural to a lover and she had eagerly returned his endearments; although owing to his state, they had had to confine themselves to kisses and caresses. But by November 25th his urge to make love to her again in the fullest sense had become so strong that he pleaded with her to let him.

At first she would not hear of it; but for the next few days he continued to beg her to undress and lie down with him, swearing that he would remain quite still, so that he should not strain his leg, and leave it to her to play the man's part.

Tempted as she was to agree she protested that, although by exercising great care she would not harm him, she positively dared not from fear that Malacou might suddenly come in and surprise them. Promptly, he assured her that his telepathic faculties would give him ample warning of the doctor's approach.

At that she shook her golden head and laughed, 'No, no, my darling. You cannot persuade me that while locked with me in love's embrace your mind would be capable of also keeping cave for Malacou. If we are again to take full joy of one another it must be at night when there is no chance of our being disturbed.'

'But how can we?' he frowned. 'Even if you could get away undetected from the Manor there is only one door to this ruin and it's always locked. To ask Malacou for a key would give the game away.'

After a moment she said, 'Everyone at the Manor is in bed and sound asleep well before midnight; so no-one would know if I crept downstairs and let myself out. And as this is a ruin I'm sure there must be other ways of getting into it than by the door. It is Malacou's day at the clinic tomorrow, so I'll take the opportunity to explore.'

On the following afternoon, when she came to him, her big blue eyes were bright with excitement and she said at once, 'I've found a way in. At the head of the stairs outside this room there is another door. It leads out on to a lead walk parallel to the roof of the Castle chapel. Stefan told me that while he was cooped up here with you after you got away from Peenemünde he used to take his exercise there, because one can't be seen from below. At the far end of the walkway there is a gap in the battlement and its fallen stones form a big pile on the ground. From the ground to the leads is only about fifteen feet and I was always good at climbing, I'm sure I could scramble up it and come to you that way. Oh, darling, just think of it! I can hardly wait. I'll come to you tonight.'

With many kisses Gregory urged her to be careful. Then when she had left him he did his utmost to concentrate on a book, so as to lessen the likelihood of Malacou picking up his thoughts of the promised joys to come.

For him the evening positively crawled by and after he had turned down the incandescent burner beside his bed he found it impossible to keep his mind from forming pictures of Erika's lovely form.

It was with good reason that before she was out of her teens she had become known as 'The Beautiful Erika von Epp', for it was not her oval face alone, with its smooth forehead crowned by waves of true golden hair, her great laughing eyes and rich, full lips that made her a living masterpiece of art; from small feet and ankles her long legs curved up to splendidly rounded hips and above her narrow waist her torso blossomed into two firm, smooth domes that stood proudly out so that they would have fitted perfectly into outsized old-fashioned champagne glasses.

At last, soon after midnight, the door creaked slightly and she slipped into the room. When he turned up the light he saw that she was wearing only a warm, belted, camel hair coat over her nightdress. She was still panting slightly from her climb, but looked all the more lovely with her hair dishevelled. Her eyes were liquid and sparkling; her cheeks rosy with excitement. Smiling at him she slipped off her coat, then, stooping quickly, took the hem of her night-dress in both hands and pulled it off over her head.

He shut his eyes then opened them again and breathed, 'If this were my first sight of you I'd think Venus had come to earth again.'

Kicking off her shoes, she ran to him crying, 'Think of me as Venus, then, and I'll transport you to heaven. Oh, darling, it's been so long! You can't think how terribly I've wanted you!'

'And I you!' his voice came huskily as he stretched out his strong arms to her.

Throwing herself on her knees beside his bed, she put her hands on his biceps and checked his movement. 'Oh, be careful! For God's sake be careful! You swore you would lie still and let me love you. You've stormed the gates of paradise often enough in the past. This time they'll open for you, but oh, so very gently.'

Raising her chin she opened her mouth and offered it for his kiss. He took her face between his hands and drew her lips down on his. Her breath began to come quickly and she closed her eyes. Then as he released her she rolled back the sheet and lay down with him on his sound side. Leaning over she kissed him again and again while his hands caressed her body. When they could restrain themselves no longer she knelt up and, as she had promised, transported him to heaven.

Next day he awaited her coming with some anxiety. But all had gone well; she had accomplished her downward climb without accident and got back to her room without disturbing anyone. After long kisses and talking over the delights of their midnight encounter she said:

'I've news for you, and rather disturbing news at that. Khurrem told me this morning that she has promised to marry Herman Hauff; but only because he forced the issue. Apparently, after the Peenemünde raid, when the Gestapo were hunting for you and Stefan, as you had both stayed here before moving to Wolgast, they came here and would have arrested Khurrem and her father had not Hauff used his influence to protect them. Yesterday he threatened that if she wouldn't become engaged to him he would withdraw his protection and report that he had overheard them saying the sort of things that people aren't allowed to say about Hitler.'

Gregory frowned. 'What swine these Nazis are. Poor woman, I'm sorry for her.'

As Erika lit a cigarette she gave a slight shrug. 'I don't know. She doesn't love him, of course, but I think it's rather a relief to her that matters have come to a head. It's telling her father that she's dreading. Quite apart from his antipathy to the idea of her marrying an S.S. man, I'm sure that he wants to keep her to himself. It's certain he will be furious.'

'I don't doubt it. But after blowing his top he'll have to agree. Physically he is a coward, and he told me himself he'd even commit murder rather than be hauled off to a concentration camp. Did she go so far as actually to settle on a date for their wedding?'

'No; but Hauff insists that it should be before the New Year, and that's not much more than four weeks from now.'

When Gregory asked Erika to come to him again that night she firmly refused, giving as her reason that too much excitement was certain to be bad for him, and that the sooner he could build up his strength the sooner they would be able to get away. For some while they argued, but she remained adamant and told him that for the time being, at least, he must remain content with her coming to him twice a week.

Malacou paid his usual visit to Gregory next morning and,

although he said nothing about Khurrem, it was evident from his manner that she had told him of her engagement. However, with him he had brought Tarik, who was carrying a pair of crutches and a sling. Between them they got Gregory up and supported him while he tried the crutches out. On this first occasion, having been bed-bound for so long, he could hardly stand alone, but the following two days he managed a few faltering steps.

During these trials the doctor continued to look black and sullen, but Gregory paid little heed to this moodiness because he was so entranced at the prospect of being able to walk once more and, between whiles, with joyful thoughts that on the fourth night from her first visit Erika had promised to come to him again.

That evening after Gregory had had his meal and Tarik had taken away his tray, knowing that Malacou's mind would be fully occupied with his worry over Khurrem, he turned down his light, lay back and let his imagination have free play anticipating the joys of the coming night.

Soon after midnight he was roused from his semi-dreaming state by the sound of hurried footsteps outside and next moment his door was flung open. Recalling the caution Erika had used on her first visit, he feared for a moment that something had gone wrong and it might be someone else. Hastily he levered himself up in bed and turned up the light. Framed in the open doorway Erika was standing. But she was trembling violently, her eyes were wide and staring and her face was drained of blood.

'Darling!' he cried, 'what on earth's the matter? You look as if you'd seen a ghost.'

'No!' she gasped. 'No; but something worse. When . . . when I climbed up on to the walkway I saw chinks of light coming through the chapel roof. I . . . I clambered over on to it and knelt down near a rent to see what was going on. Oh, Gregory, a Black Mass was being held there. Or, at least, its Jewish equivalent. Instead of a cross, the Sephirotic Tree had been nailed up above the altar. To either side there were Hebrew candlesticks with seven branches and the candles in them were black. Malacou and Khurrem were there wearing robes covered with the signs of the Zodiac, and Tarik was standing to one side swinging a censer.'

For a moment she broke off to get her breath then, her voice rising to an hysterical note, she cried, 'After I'd watched for a few minutes Malacou stopped chanting. Khurrem got up from her knees. They both stripped off their robes. They had nothing on beneath them and stood there naked. Then . . . then, he picked her up and seemed to be offering her to the spirit of Evil. And . . . and then he had her on the altar. His own daughter, Gregory! His own daughter!'

10

Battle of Wills

GREGORY stared at Erika in horror. For a moment he was at a loss for words, then he exclaimed, 'It almost passes belief that a man could do such a thing.'

'It's true!' she cried. 'Every word I've said. I saw it with my own eyes.' Then, bursting into tears, she threw herself down beside him.

Putting his arms about her shoulders, he strove to comfort her. 'There, there, my sweet. To have witnessed such a scene must have upset you terribly. But at least we now know where we stand. Stefan was right. Malacou really is a disciple of the Devil.'

'But incest!' Erika sobbed. 'The sight of them locked together naked on that altar almost made me sick. It was revolting—utterly horrible.'

'Dearest, I can imagine how you must have felt; but I suppose Satanists stick at nothing. Probably the more evil the things they do, the more power they draw down to themselves from Satan. One can only pity Khurrem. She is completely dominated by him. And this explains the wretched state she's in: her long silences and heavy drinking. I don't suppose it is the first time this has happened. No doubt she's still good at heart and loathes having to give herself to her father, but he compels her to.'

Still sobbing, Erika nodded. 'I . . . I'm sure you're right. People whose consciences are troubling them often try . . . try to drown their thoughts in drink. But how awful for her, darling; how awful for her to . . . to have to let him make use of her body. Somehow we must help her to escape from him.'

For a moment Gregory remained silent, then he said, 'Listen, my sweet. However much you may feel the urge to try to help her you must make no attempt to do so; anyhow, for the present. I'm helpless here. Until I can stand on my feet again and give a good account of myself we'll both remain in Malacou's power. You've got to do your damnedest to act naturally tomorrow with both of them, and for the time being try to put out of your mind what you saw.'

Suddenly she jerked herself away from him, her eyes distended, her expression again one of terror. 'But, darling, I thought I told you. They know I saw them.'

'What!' he exclaimed. 'No! How could they?'

'When I was kneeling on the roof of the chapel looking down at them my knees were on one beam and my hands on another. As I moved to get up I slipped. By then my hands were off the beam. One of them landed on a plank and it was rotten. Part of it snapped off and fell. For a moment I remained there petrified. They both stopped . . . stopped what they were doing and looked up. They must have known that it was I who was spying on them. Who else could it have been?'

'It might have been a tramp who'd climbed up there hoping to find a way into the ruin to get a night's shelter,' Gregory suggested. But even as he spoke he knew that he was fooling himself. Malacou's highly developed sixth sense would have told him that it was Erika who was up on the roof.

'No, that won't wash,' he conceded quickly. 'This is bad, my darling; very bad. But we mustn't take too black a view. Malacou knows that we are in no position to make trouble for him, and there's a chance that he may be too ashamed of himself to mention it. Anyhow, we must pretend that we know nothing of this, then he may think that you did not actually see what he was doing and supposed him only to be engaged in some occult ceremony. For us the really important thing is that we should keep clear of the Nazis; and that goes for him, too. He can't throw us out without incriminating himself; so he's got to keep us here until I'm fit to move under my own steam. Our best course will be to ignore the whole thing and we'll hope that he and Khurrem will, too.'

After a while Erika agreed to do her best to act naturally with them both the next day; then she crept into bed with

Gregory and lay for a long time with his arm about her. There could be no question now of their making love; only of her drawing sufficient strength from him to face the return journey past the chapel roof. In the early hours of the morning, when it seemed certain that the hideous ritual was long past its culmination and the chapel would again be deserted, she summoned up her courage to kiss him a belated good-night and set off on her way back to the Manor.

At his usual hour next morning Malacou came to Gregory's room. There were pouches under his eyes and his dark face seemed more heavily lined than usual. Sitting down he said at once:

'Before the arrival of your friends I told you that a new influence was about to make itself felt here and that it would be adverse to the rapport we had succeeded in establishing between us. When Kuporovitch reappeared I thought he would be the cause of it, but in that I was wrong. It is the woman whom you have made your mistress who has come between us, and I will not tolerate her presence here. She must leave tonight.'

That Malacou might make such a demand had never occurred to Gregory. Frantically he sought in his mind for a way to avert such a blow but, caught off his guard, he cried angrily, 'You lecherous blackguard! This is because she found you out, eh?'

The doctor nodded. 'She has brought this on herself. She saw things she was not meant to see.'

'She did, indeed! And for you to embrace your daughter carnally is against the laws of God and man. We know you now for what you are—a Satanist. With her you performed a Black Mass. You can't deny it.'

'I do not seek to. But desperate situations require desperate remedies. Every Black Mass, as you term it, is said with an intention. Although I have said nothing of it, you know the situation that has arisen between Khurrem and Hauff. He has to die; and the ceremony I performed was with that intention.'

For a moment Gregory considered this explanation, then he said, 'I know you are bitterly opposed to her marrying Hauff; although I've reason to suppose that she is not altogether unwilling. That makes things infinitely worse. And to have forced her to commit incest with you in the hope of getting rid of him is utterly unforgivable. Rather than perform such an abominable act surely you could have overcome your prejudice against him as a German and a Nazi. You did so in the case of von Altern. In fact you told me that you favoured the match and actually bought him for her.'

Malacou passed a hand wearily over his black, grey-flecked hair. Then he gave a slight shrug and said, less aggressively, 'That was entirely different. Perhaps you will understand me better if I tell you that I have loved only two women in my life: my wife and Khurrem.

'I married my wife when she was sixteen; at sixteen Khurrem had become the image of her dead mother. Condemn me if you will, but at that age I seduced her. She was not unwilling, for she thought more highly of me than of other men. For ten years we were completely happy and our relationship had nothing at all to do with Satanism. Then she met von Altern and fell desperately in love with him. I loved her dearly, so gave way to her pleading and arranged for her to marry him.

'A few years later came the war and I left Poland to live here. Von Altern's military duties had already taken him away. Khurrem is passionate by nature and she was then at an age when women feel their greatest desire for sexual satisfaction, so I soon persuaded her to play again the part of a wife to me. By that time I had progressed far in my occult studies and I needed a woman's aid. At first she was reluctant, so I hypnotized her and in that way made her give herself to me as the culmination of an occult operation. But such ceremonies are far more effective if the woman is conscious of the part she plays and is willing. As time went on I lightened the state of hypnosis under which I took her, until from habit she accepted the role that fate had decreed for her. From that time onward, on certain favourable days each month, I have been able to continue my enjoyment of her with the advancement of my occult activities. It is thus that the present state of things has come about.'

Frowning, Gregory listened to this appalling story, then he said, 'You have made her, then, your chattel; and, like yourself, a servant of the Devil.'

'You may term her that,' Malacou retorted defiantly, 'but she is also my love, and I will not be robbed of her. I will allow nothing, nothing to come between us. That is why Hauff has to die; and your woman, who would try to part us, must go.'

'No, no!' Gregory protested. 'I can't possibly do without her.'

'Tarik and I looked after you when neither she nor Kuporovitch was here and now that you are in a much better state it will be even easier for us to do so.'

'Maybe! But God knows I've spent weeks enough alone here for hours on end. I need her companionship.'

'You will have to do without it.'

'Why the hell should I?'

'Because her continued presence would interfere with the development of the psychic link between us.'

'There will be no further link. I'll see to that. Nothing will induce me to lend myself again to these practices. I'll not have you lead me to become a servant of Satan.'

Malacou's eyes flashed and his voice was firm. 'That need not follow; but you will obey my wishes. And it is my wish that when Frau Bjornsen comes to see you this afternoon you should tell her that she must leave Sassen tonight.'

'She will refuse. She'll tell you to go to hell where you belong.'

'She will not refuse. And unless she prefers to risk bringing the Gestapo here she will leave the Manor without making a scene. Remember, you are still a helpless cripple, so completely in my power. If I wish I could starve you into sending her away. But I do not want to impede your recovery. Instead, I shall have it conveyed to Herman Hauff that she is an anti-Nazi and is saying things detrimental to the regime. He will then have her deported.'

Gregory knew he was cornered. If he allowed Erika to resist and Malacou had her denounced her papers would be very strictly examined; then, should there be the least flaw in them, that might lead her into desperate trouble; whereas if she presented them herself at the frontier there was little to fear. Besides, even if they took the risk of ignoring his threat, in the

belief that he would be most loath to draw the attention of the
Gestapo to anyone who had stayed as a guest at Sassen, how
could they possibly carry on a war against him when he had
so many means of bringing pressure on them?

'Very well, then,' he agreed angrily; 'since you insist, I'll
tell her she must leave.'

That afternoon proved one of the bitterest he ever remembered. For three hours he and Erika tried to think of a way in
which they could get the better of the Satanist and force him
to rescind his demand, but in vain. At length, tearfully and in
great distress, they parted, Erika having promised to let Gregory
know the moment she arrived safely in Sweden, by means of a
message of thanks sent to her hostess.

For the next forty-eight hours Gregory got little sleep, both
from worrying about Erika's safety and about his own position;
for Malacou did not come to see him, and speculating on the
Satanist's possible powers made him most uneasy. But on the
second evening the doctor reappeared and brought with him a
telegram addressed to Khurrem. It had been handed in the
previous afternoon at Trelleborg and ran: *Rotten crossing but
soon over many thanks for generous hospitality. Selma.*

When Gregory had seen it Malacou sat down and said,
'For the past week I have been able to spare little thought
for you, owing to my preoccupation with this affair of Khurrem's; but now I am capable of concentrating again on other
matters. Now you know that Frau Bjornsen has arrived safely
in Sweden your mind should also be free from anxiety.
Therefore, let us talk.'

'I have nothing to say to you,' Gregory replied quietly. 'The
only thing I intend to concentrate on is getting well, so that I
can relieve you of my presence as soon as possible.'

'In that you are mistaken,' the doctor told him with equal
quietness. 'For our future relationship it is of the first importance that we should further develop the telepathic faculties
that we have established between us.'

'There will be no future relationship. When I leave this place
I hope never to set eyes on you again; and if I do I shall avoid
you like the plague.'

'In that you are again mistaken. You cannot avoid your

destiny and it is written in the stars that we shall be brought together. For some time past it has no longer been necessary for me to hypnotize you while attending to your leg. But if you refuse to co-operate with me I shall be forced to resume the practice and so compel your obedience.'

'I won't let you!' Gregory burst out. 'I did before, but now I'll resist you with all the force of my will. And you'll find it stronger than yours.'

Malacou closed his eyes and bent his head, then remained silent. Two minutes later Tarik came into the room and the doctor spoke to him in Yiddish. The hunchback advanced on Gregory. Bracing himself, he shouted at Malacou, 'Call him off. If he lays hands on me I'll strangle him.'

'Should you try, you would be more of a fool than I take you for,' remarked the doctor. 'Tarik is very strong and if you struggle it is certain that you will re-break your leg.'

Gregory knew that to be true. Confronted with this awful dilemma, he let Tarik get behind him as he sat up in bed and place his hands firmly on both sides of his face; but he closed his eyes tightly and forced down his head. Tarik slowly pulled it up again and, although Gregory grabbed his wrists and pulled upon them, he found it impossible, without straining his body, to exert enough strength to break the grip.

While the hunchback held his head in that position, although Gregory's eyes were closed, he knew that Malacou was staring at him with intense concentration. With all the strength of his will he strove to fight off the Satanist's influence, and the word-less battle continued for nearly twenty minutes. Then, at last, Gregory felt his mind slipping and went under.

When he emerged from his trance Malacou was smiling, and said to him, 'You have been under for only a few minutes as it is not my intention to take advantage of you if you will only be reasonable. I did as I did just now only to show you that I can dominate your mind whenever I wish. But it would be a foolish waste of time to enter on these struggles every day. Listen now to what I have to say and when you have heard me out I hope you will prove more amenable.

'I admit to having misled you when I implied that as an occultist I had not Passed the Abyss. I am an Adept, although

not a very advanced one, and there are still many limitations
to my powers. But when I told you that many minor magics
can be performed without any commitment to evil I was not
lying. That is the case with fortune-telling, while to consult the
stars is no more harmful than endeavouring to envisage a
country unknown to one by studying a map. We come now to
affecting others by means of occult power.

'Whether you agree or not that witches and wizards can
cast spells and destroy the health of people against whom they
have a grudge, I think you will agree that certain holy persons
of all religions have performed what we call "miracles".

'Such powers are derived through the practitioner drawing
down to himself unseen forces that inhabit the spirit world.
These forces are either Good or Evil and making use of them
is termed either White Magic or Black Magic. For major
operations it is necessary to call directly on the aid of either
God or the Devil. The Saints could not have performed their
miracles without praying for help to their Divinity, and I could
not hope that Herman Hauff will die had I not appealed to the
Lord of this World to destroy him for me.'

'You admit, then,' Gregory broke in, 'that you are a wor-
shipper of the Devil?'

Malacou nodded. 'Yes, I have chosen to follow the Left
Hand Path; because in no other way could I achieve my desires.
But whether an act of magic is Black or White depends on the
intention of the occultist who performs it. If it is undertaken
for selfish ends, as was the case with the ceremony I performed
to remove the menace to my happiness in the person of Hauff,
it is Black. But if it is undertaken for unselfish ends it is White.

'You do not stand in my path in any way. On the contrary,
we have the same hatred for the Nazis and wish to bring about
their ruin. Moreover, you must agree that in receiving you here
in the first place, and for many weeks giving you the shelter of
my home while you recover from your injuries, I have taken
considerable risks on your behalf. There is, too, my conviction
that we are destined to work together in the future and that
you will save my life.

'All this adds up to the fact that you have no possible cause
to fear ill from me. Such minor magics as I have performed in

connection with you have all been White. That I have used Black Magic for other purposes has no bearing on the matter. I do not expect you to approve of that any more than if you had found me out to be a sadist or a blackmailer. But I do ask that you should endeavour to put out of your mind, as far as possible, your knowledge that at times I perform acts of which you highly disapprove; and, in all other matters, regard me as your ally. Have I made myself clear?'

Slowly Gregory nodded. He felt that Malacou had made a big point by implying that while working against the Nazis he would not have rejected the help of any ordinary crook, and he could not dispute the fact that he owed his escape from death at their hands to the sanctuary that the doctor had afforded him. It had to be faced, too, that if he refused to comply with Malacou's wishes the doctor had already proved that he could force him to under hypnosis. Mentally reserving to himself the right to oppose any act of Malacou's towards himself that he considered suspect, he said:

'All right, then. Provided we keep off the subject of Satanism, I'm willing to renew practising our telepathic communications.'

Having taken his decision he again entered on this mental activity, at first cautiously, then, when he found no harm came of it, with goodwill. As the December days progressed he was able to tell the doctor about the patients he had treated on his days at the clinic, while Malacou could always tell him what books he had been reading and how his attempts at walking were progressing. He was fast regaining his strength and with the aid of crutches could now propel himself not only about his room but up and down the walkway outside on the roof along which Erika had come on her two visits to him.

Shortly before Christmas he decided that in another week or so he would be fit enough to make a bid to get home. He was by then able to put his left foot to the ground and bear a little weight on it; and, although it might yet be a considerable time before he could dispense with a crutch, he saw that as no bar to his making the journey. At the prospect his mind naturally turned more and more frequently to happy thoughts of exchanging his dreary life in the old ruin for the joys of being with Erika and back at his comfortable flat in London. So he was not at all surprised when, on Christmas Eve, Malacou said to him:

'Several times recently I have picked up your thoughts about leaving here.'

'Yes,' Gregory agreed. 'I can already manage to dress without help in the clothes you procured for me to take my walks along the roof, and in about a week I shall be fully fit to travel on my own. I shall, of course, go by the route that Frau Bjornsen took; from Grimmen along the coast to Sassnitz, then cross by the ferry boat to Trelleborg. When I reach Stockholm I may have to wait about a bit until I can get back to England by one of the Mosquitoes they send over with despatches for the British Embassy, but I expect one comes in about once a week. The only tricky part will be getting from here to Grimmen. But I take it you could hypnotize Willi again, so that he can run me in by the lorry and have no memory afterwards of having made the trip.'

Malacou shook his head. 'I fear that what you propose is out of the question.'

'Why?' asked Gregory quickly. 'Has anything happened to Willi?'

'No. It is simply that I have no intention of allowing you to leave here.'

'What the devil do you mean?'

'What I say. I have already told you more than once of my conviction that our fates are linked. Some months hence I shall enter a period of great danger. In fact, the stars foretell my death, unless it can be averted by a person whose horoscope is very similar to yours. The horoscopes of individuals vary even more than do their fingerprints, so the chances of anyone else capable of saving me being at hand when this crisis arises are extremely remote. If I allow you to return to England I cannot see you risking your life by coming back to this part of Germany as long as the war continues. Therefore, my own life depends on my keeping you here.'

'In that you're wrong,' Gregory snapped angrily. 'Even if you can succeed in detaining me as a prisoner—and that I doubt once I've got back the full use of my leg—when you are faced with death I swear I'll not lift a finger to save you.'

'Oh yes you will. The circumstances in which I shall be in dire peril are still hidden from me. But when the time comes you will be just as much a plaything of fate as myself. Your stars will compel you to act in my defence.'

'Damn you!' Gregory shouted. 'I'll force you to let me go. Now that I'm stronger I'll no longer allow you to dictate to me. Good always triumphs over evil. I'll break that evil will of yours. Come on! I challenge you.'

As he spoke he looked straight into Malacou's eyes. The doctor closed his for a moment, then opened them again and returned Gregory's stare. For what seemed an endless time to Gregory he strove with all his mind to overcome that of his adversary, but the dark, hooded eyes into which he was gazing remained unwinking and gradually seemed to grow larger. At length he could see nothing else and felt his concentration weakening. He knew then that he was beaten and, with a cry of despair, lowered himself with bowed head on to the side of his bed.

Sentenced again to spend further months as a prisoner, the bitterness of his thoughts on Christmas Day were exceeded only by those on the afternoon that Malacou had forced him to part with Erika. Now that he was nearly fit to travel the frustration he felt at being held against his will was overwhelming, and it kept him awake for the best part of the night. But next morning his thoughts were temporarily distracted from his miserable situation by a new event.

Malacou burst in upon him, his eyes bright with excitement and so agitated with delight that he could hardly speak. As Gregory stared at him, he gasped out, 'Praise be to Iblis! He has hearkened to his servant. Hauff is dead!'

'Dead!' Gregory exclaimed. 'Is he really?' For he had never seriously credited the Satanist's belief that his abominable ceremony would have the desired end. 'What happened? How did he die?'

'He was in that powerful car of his. He always drove it like a maniac, without a thought that he might kill someone. And now he's killed himself. I'm told he went in to a *Weihnachtsfest* party in Greifswald yesterday and I've no doubt he got drunk. When he was driving home in the early hours this morning he crashed into a farm wagon. His car was smashed to pieces and he died from his injuries shortly afterwards.'

'Well, that's that.' Gregory relaxed on his bed. 'You've got your wish, but as there's a living God you'll have to pay for it when the time comes to settle all accounts.'

'Maybe, maybe,' the Satanist muttered, his expression suddenly changing to one of fear. 'But Khurrem is mine! Khurrem is mine! No-one can now take her from me.'

'I wouldn't be too certain of that,' Gregory remarked cynically. 'She'd be very attractive if she cleaned herself up and, remember, she is an heiress. Some other chap may get the idea that he'd like to take her on and become the master of Sassen.'

Malacou shook his head. 'No, no. If that were likely I'd have read it in the stars. She must now go through a black patch; a very black patch. But no other man is coming into her life.'

Snow fell next day and for some days afterwards Gregory had to give up his exercise on the roof from fear of slipping as, even when Tarik had swept a path along the walkway for him, temporary thaws brought down little avalanches which continued to make it dangerous. But every day he now spent several hours exercising in his room with most satisfactory results. Meanwhile he cudgelled his brain for a way to outwit Malacou, but, resourceful though he was, he could think of no safe way of getting into Grimmen unless he could persuade the Satanist to hypnotize Willi.

Another week had dragged by when, on the afternoon of New Year's Eve, much to his surprise, Khurrem paid him a visit. Understandably, she had not done so since Erika had seen her lying naked on the altar of the chapel *in flagrante delicto* with her father and, as she came in, Gregory wondered how she had managed to overcome her embarrassment at facing him again.

Looking at her, he recalled her father's having said that she was due to go through a very bad period, for her condition had greatly deteriorated since he had last seen her. The fine grey eyes that at times lit up her face were dull and had big black shadows beneath them. Her red hair had obviously not been properly done for several days, her long face looked thinner than ever and her cheeks were furrowed.

Gregory's first thought was that he might possibly be able to make use of her in some plan to escape but, even if she could be persuaded to drive him into Grimmen, as Malacou had the power to read both her thoughts and his, it seemed certain that the Satanist would gain knowledge of their intentions and take steps to frustrate them.

As he reluctantly dismissed the idea, she produced a letter and said, 'Mr. Sallust, you are an upright man and the only person here whom I can trust. I know that you must think very badly of me, but if you knew the story of my life I think you might pity rather than despise me. At least I feel sure you will not refuse to do me a small service. I want you to keep this letter until tomorrow morning; then open and read it, and afterwards give it to my father.'

'Certainly I'll do that,' he replied, taking the letter. 'I'm afraid you have been going through a very bad time. If there is any other way in which I can help you, please tell me. It is not for any of us to sit in judgement on others, so whatever you care to say to me you need have no fear that I'll make any comment that will hurt you.'

'No,' she said sadly. 'If I had married Herman Hauff things might have turned out better for me, but there is nothing anyone can do to help me now. You'll promise, though, not to open my letter until tomorrow morning, won't you?'

'Yes, I promise,' he said gravely.

At that she began to walk towards the door, but on reaching it she turned and said, 'I shan't be seeing you again. I'm going away. But that's in the letter, so you mustn't tell my father. I'm frightened of him. But you need not be, because you have great courage. You will get away, too. My occult sense tells me that. I shan't go far at first, so I'll be thinking of you and trying to help you. When you get back to England give my . . . my love to your beautiful lady. She, too, was kind to me.'

When Khurrem had gone Gregory sat on the edge of his bed thinking for a long time about her. Knowing how tragic her life had been, he felt that she was more sinned against than sinning, so was deeply sorry for her. By her decision to break away from her evil father she had shown more guts than Gregory would have expected, and he found himself smiling wryly at the fury Malacou would be in next morning when he learned that she had left him.

In consequence, he felt no surprise when the Satanist roused him from sleep by again bursting in on him early on New Year's Day. Malacou's face was haggard and his eyes wild. He seemed utterly distraught as he stood for a moment staring down at Gregory. Suddenly he gave a wailing cry, then gasped:

'Woe is me! Woe is me! My Master has betrayed me. Khurrem is dead! Khurrem is dead!'

Pulling himself up in bed, Gregory cried, 'Good God! I knew she intended to leave you but not . . . not that way.'

'She asked for death,' Malacou wailed. 'She has taken her own life. Immediately I woke I knew that something terrible had happened. I hurried over to the Manor. And there she was. Dead! Dead with an empty bottle of sleeping tablets still clutched in her hand. Oh, woe is me! Woe is me! I am undone and desolated. I loved her beyond bearing and she is now gone from me.'

Gregory had put Khurrem's letter beneath his pillow. Fishing it out, he opened it and read the spiky handwriting, which ran:

I can stand no more, so I have decided to take my life. My regret at Herman Hauff's death plays no part in this. I did not love him, but as his wife might again have found some peace of mind. I did not hate my father for what he did to me when I was sixteen and the guilt for allowing him to continue as my lover was as much mine as his. But more recently he has used my body for his abominable rites. The thought of what may result from this haunts me with terror. His caresses have become loathsome to me, and for having forced me to become a hand-maiden of evil I can never forgive him. To his other sins must be added his driving me to put an end to my earthly being. May he meet with his deserts in the Hell that he deserves and may the Lord God of Israel have mercy on my wretched spirit.

Khurrem von Altern

Having read this terrible missive, Gregory said gravely, 'Khurrem left this with me yesterday afternoon. She told me to read it this morning, then give it to you.'

Malacou took the letter and his thick red lips moved slowly as he read it through. When he had taken in its contents he let it flutter to the floor. Then falling on his knees he began to moan and bang his forehead on the ground.

Suddenly Gregory felt impelled to look away from him towards the door. His eyes dilated, for he could have sworn that for a moment Khurrem was standing there. She was pointing at her father and her soundless words rang through Gregory's brain like a trumpet call.

'Now! Now! His mind is distraught. He cannot resist you. Now is your chance to defeat him.'

Instantly he seized his crutch, slipped out of bed and stood over Malacou. Still on his knees, wringing his hands and tearing at his hair, the Satanist wailed, 'I have lost her! I am accursed! Oh, woe is me! What shall I do? Oh, what shall I do?'

'I will tell you,' Gregory shouted at him.

Ceasing his cries, Malacou stared up at the figure towering over him.

'You will go downstairs and fetch that drawing of the Sephirotic Tree,' Gregory said firmly.

'You . . . you have thought of some way to help me,' Malacou stammered. 'Yes, yes; the stars have declared you to be my friend and guardian.' Staggering to his feet, he lurched out of the room. Two minutes later he came running back, clutching the ancient parchment.

'Now,' Gregory commanded, 'tear it up.'

Malacou's eyes filled with amazement, then they flickered. He shuddered, his hands trembled and from his mouth saliva ran down his chin. 'No!' he panted. 'No! I cannot. It is a sacred document.'

'You must,' Gregory cried harshly. 'You must! Only by recanting from evil can you hope to escape the curse that Khurrem has put upon you.'

For a long moment the eyes of both of them remained locked in silent battle. Gregory was praying frantically, 'O Lord, help me to overcome him! Dear Lord, help me to overcome him!' Suddenly his body responded to a divine command. Placing the foot of his injured leg firmly on the ground, he threw away his crutch.

He did not fall or even need to ease the weight his foot had taken, but remained drawn to his full height glowering at Malacou. At the sight of his action the Satanist wilted. His eyes fell and with shaking hands he tore the parchment from top to bottom.

That evening, the 1st of January 1944, Gregory left Sassen. On the 25th of the month he landed safely in England.

11

The Great Strategic Blunder

FIVE hours after Gregory landed in England he was sitting in the lofty book-lined room that had been the scene of the beginnings and ends of all his secret missions. It looked out from the back of Carlton House Terrace to the Admiralty, the Foreign Office and the other massive buildings in which throbbed the heart of Britain's war machine. The fact that it was raining did not depress him in the least.

Beside him on a small table were the remains of a pile of foie gras sandwiches off which he had been making a second breakfast, and nearby stood an ice-bucket in which reposed a magnum of his favourite *Louis Roederer 1928*. From it his silver tankard was being filled for the second time by his old friend and patron, Sir Pellinore Gwaine-Cust.

Sir Pellinore was well over seventy, but the only indication of his age was the snowy whiteness of his hair, his bushy eyebrows and luxuriant moustache. His startlingly vivid blue eyes were as bright as ever, he stood six feet four in his socks and, as a person, was one of those remarkable products that seem peculiar to Britain.

In his youth he had been a subaltern in a crack cavalry regiment and during the Boer War he had won a well-deserved V.C. A few years later his ill-luck at some of the little baccarat parties given by friends of his for King Edward VII, and his generosity towards certain ladies of the Gaiety chorus, made it necessary for him to leave the Army and he had accepted a seat on the Board of a small merchant bank.

His acquaintances thought of him as a handsome fellow, with an eye for a horse or a pretty woman and an infinite capacity for vintage port, but with very little brain—an illusion which he still did his utmost to maintain—so the directorship had been offered him solely on account of his social connections. To the surprise of those concerned he had taken to business like a duck to water.

Other directorships had followed. By 1914 he was already a power in the City. After the war he had refused a peerage on the grounds that there had been a Gwaine-Cust at Gwaine Meads for so many centuries that if he changed his name his tenants would think he had sold the place. Foresight had enabled him to bring his companies through the slump of the thirties and he emerged from it immensely rich.

Although his name was hardly known to the general public, it had long been respected in Government circles. To his great mansion in Carlton House Terrace, Ambassadors, Generals and Cabinet Ministers often came to consult him privately on their problems, and they rarely left without having drawn new strength from his boundless vitality and shrewd common sense.

Gregory had just finished giving an account of events at Sassen since Erika had been forced to leave him there and of his final battle of wills with Malacou. Sir Pellinore towered over him, still grasping the neck of the magnum with a hand the size of a small leg of mutton. As he dropped the bottle back into the ice-bucket he boomed:

'Well, I'll be jiggered! So you forced the Malacoo feller to recant, eh? Made him swallow his own hell-broth. Shows how mistaken one can be. You're the last man I'd ever have expected to play the part of a sky-pilot. It's clear you've missed your vocation.'

'Thanks,' Gregory laughed, 'but I don't think I'd fancy myself in a dog-collar.'

'Perhaps you're right. Might spoil your sport with the gals, eh?'

'You're thinking of yourself,' Gregory twitted him. 'Erika's the only woman in my life and——'

'And I'm the Grand Cham of Tartary,' Sir Pellinore cut in. 'How about that Hungarian wench you brought back with you from your last trip? The Baroness Tuposo—no, Trombolo or some such outlandish name. By Jove, what a smasher she was!' The elderly Baronet's bright blue eyes glittered at the memory. 'If I'd been ten years younger I'd have taken her off you and smacked her bottom myself.'

'I've no doubt you would. But Sabine was the last flutter of my murky past and the less said about her the better, because Erika should be here shortly.'

'You telephoned her from the R.A.F. station then. That's good. Seein' the mucker I made by bringing her down hot-foot from Gwaine Meads last time you got home, I didn't like to risk it. Thought you might bring back one of those blonde bombshells they export from Sweden.'

'That was considerate of you. God knows I was stuck there long enough to have acquired a harem.'

'Yes. Sorry about that. But I gather from General Gubbie it's always the same with these S.O.E. jobs. When they want one of their cloak-and-dagger Johnnies to thrust a spanner in the Nazi works they can get him sent out overnight; but when he's singed what there is of the house-painter feller's moustache, they leave their chap sittin' on his backside till Doomsday.'

'It was all to the good, really. Naturally, I wanted to get home; but the people at our Embassy could not have been kinder and I benefited a lot from being under Dr. Zetterberg for the best part of a month. It was far from pleasant having to lie on my back again for most of the time with a damn' great weight attached to my foot, but there wasn't the temptation to kick over the traces that there would have been here.'

'How is your leg?'

'Far better than I could ever have expected. Thanks to your having tempted Zetterberg with that staggering fee to risk his neck by going into Germany, I'll not have to spend the rest of my life as an unwieldy cripple. I only wish there were some way in which I could repay your princely generosity.'

'Nonsense,' Sir Pellinore responded gruffly. 'Seein' you here on your two feet does that. The money was a bagatelle. You must know that I'm lousy with the stuff. But tell me more about this Maluku feller. If Erika hadn't vouched for it I'd never have believed in such goin's on. It's straight out of the Dark Ages.'

Gregory sighed. 'Neither would I if I hadn't come up against it myself. But one can't laugh at the fact that I was struck down on a day that he predicted would, in connection with Stefan, hold the maximum danger for me.'

'That might have been coincidence.'

'Not if you take into consideration all the lucky breaks we had on the days he said would be favourable to us; and Hauff's death. It was that which finally convinced me that he really was in league with the Devil.'

'Umph! Erika told me about that. Rollin' his own daughter in the hay. What a thing to do! Takes a lot to shock me, but there are limits. Can't see much fun in having a woman on a stone slab, either. Still, that's beside the point. If it wasn't that Erika swears she saw the two of them having an upsy-daisy I'd put the whole thing down to your having been round the bend for a while owin' to the pain you were suffering.'

'You can count that out. I was cooped up with him in that ruin for over four months and for most of that time I was as sane as you are. What is more, although we are now separated by hundreds of miles of land and sea, I still get his vibrations and know what is happening to him.'

'God bless my soul!' Sir Pellinore gulped down a great draught of champagne. 'You can't really mean that?'

'I do. His killing of Hauff led to Khurrem's committing suicide, and that has landed him in one hell of a mess. I always thought it a bit odd that on Ulrich von Altern's death the Sassen estate did not pass to his brother Willi. It probably did but, as Willi was a nut, the odds are that he wouldn't have realized it; and Malacou managed to fix things so that the von Altern lawyers would agree to Khurrem running the place for him. Anyhow, now Khurrem is dead her papa is up against it. The family have muscled in and a distant cousin named Gottlob is creating trouble. He is next in line to Willi and, on the plea that Willi is not all there, he is trying to get a court order that will make him Willi's guardian and enable him to take over Sassen. As the family has never had much time for their Turkish relations by marriage, it means that if Gottlob wins his case Malacou will be out on his ear.'

'Devil take me! You can't possibly know all that through thought transference.'

Gregory smiled. 'I wouldn't call on the Devil if I were you. It looks to me as though this is his pay-off to Malacou for my having made him rat on his Infernal Master. But I am certain that is what is going on.'

'Bosh, my boy! Bosh! You must be loony. You dreamed it.'

'In a way, perhaps. But they are waking dreams. I get them at odd times every day and I feel as though I were talking to Malacou just as I am to you.'

Sir Pellinore's slightly protuberant blue eyes took on a thoughtful look. Brushing up his white moustache, he said, 'For God's sake forget this nonsense. It was understandable while you were being hypnotized by this Malodo blackguard. But not now. What are your plans?'

'My limp is no bar to my returning to duty, but I reckon I've earned a spot of leave; so I mean to go back to Gwaine Meads with Erika for a month or so. After that I take it there will be no difficulty about my again resuming my old job in the Cabinet War Room?'

'None whatever. It was agreed it should be a permanent appointment and a stand-in employed whenever I wanted you seconded for special service.'

'That's O.K., then. And we won't be wanting any more stand-ins. Odd though it may seem, I've seen quite enough of the Nazis at close quarters. I'd rather remain here sticking pins in maps till the end of the war.'

Sir Pellinore bellowed with laughter. 'Got cold feet at last, eh? But you're making a big mistake, my boy. You'd be safer in Berlin than London once the house-painter feller gets going with his secret weapon.'

Gregory looked up quickly. 'I thought that had been sorted out by the raid on Peenemünde.'

'Yes and no.' Frowning slightly, the Baronet stood up and refilled their tankards. 'You and that Russian crony of yours enabled the R.A.F. to do a splendid job. The raid set the wurst-eaters back a good six months. Apart from blowing the place to merry hell we've learned that all the blueprints they had ready to send out to factories were destroyed. But that was back in August; and, of course, the backroom boys who escaped the slaughter got away with the designs still in their bristle-brush heads. Intelligence recently reported that they've been at it again for some while in the Hartz Mountains.'

'But that's hundreds of miles from the sea. They can't be going to complete their tests with the long-range rockets right in the middle of their own country?'

'No. Our guess is that Peenemünde goin' up in smoke took the heart out of them about that idea. Probably hadn't got far enough with it for it to be worth while starting again. Looks as if they're concentratin' on the little fellers that have got wings. Pilotless aircraft they call 'em. Anyhow, they are beaverin' away in underground workshops this time and there's no way we can smoke 'em out. R.A.F. might as well go lookin' for whales in the North Sea as try to pinpoint these ant-nests among all those miles of Christmas trees. They've been pushin' ahead with launching sites across the Channel, too. In December it was reported that they were workin' on about seventy of them. That side of it the R.A.F. is doing its best to tackle. In spite of the hundreds of anti-aircraft guns protectin' 'em, a lot of them have been knocked out. But plenty more are being built; so come the spring we must expect trouble.'

'It's still possible that poor old London may take it on the chin, then?'

Sir Pellinore shook his white head. 'Won't be as bad as that. I was only pulling your leg when I said you'd be safer in Berlin than in London. And you're dead right about staying put here now you have got back. You've done more to make the sauerkrauters spit blood than any other dozen agents already; so it's England, Home and Beauty for you from now on. I'll not have our people send you out again, however hard they press me. As for these robot aircraft, I feel pretty certain we can cock a snook at them. Everything points to their not being able to carry more explosive than a medium-sized bomb, and there'll be a limit to the number they can make. Odds are that half of 'em will go off course and those that do get here won't make things anywhere near as bad as they were in the Blitz. Given a bit of luck we may even have put the Nazis out of business before they are ready to start lobbing the damn' things over here.'

'For those words of comfort, many thanks. Now let's have the lowdown on how the war is really going.'

'Makes me see red even to think about it.'

'Oh, come!' Gregory protested. 'We've been on the up and up for a year past now. Jack Slessor got on top of the U-boat menace last spring. The R.A.F. is bombing hell out of the German cities. The Yanks must be over here by the million by this time, and since the old Russian steam-roller really got moving the German Army, good as it is, has proved incapable of stopping it.'

'Stoppin' the thousands of tanks we've sent them, you mean,' glowered the Baronet. 'Mind, I'm not belittling the guts the Ruskies have shown; but they couldn't have socked the wurst-eaters the way they have if it hadn't been for the colossal amount of fighting gear we've sent them by way of Murmansk. And what those Arctic convoys cost us! It's sheer murder. Our Navy is too stretched to give them much protection. Goin' round Norway they have to run the gauntlet of the Luftwaffe and the U-boats and German surface vessels into the bargain.'

'Yes, that must be pretty grim.'

'Grim! I should say so. Our poor lads are half frozen for most of the time, and bombed, shelled and torpedoed for the rest. No chance of bein' picked up either if your ship goes down. Two minutes in those icy waters and you're a deader. It's the Red Duster and the White Ensign we've got to thank for the Russian victories. Of course the public knows next to nothing about that, so the only credit we've been able to claim was the sinking of the *Scharnhorst* on Christmas Day. Admiral Fisher caught her sneakin' up on a convoy and blew her to smithereens.'

'Well done he. But even if we are largely responsible for Uncle Joe's big come-back and it's costing us a lot of lives, I can't see why you are so pessimistic about the war situation in general.'

'Ever looked at the map of Italy?'

'Yes; and of course we've got ourselves bogged down there.'

'You've said it. But, infinitely worse, we've chosen the worst

conceivable place to launch a campaign against Axis-held
southern Europe. We're not only bogged down now, but when
we do break out the territory is so much in favour of the
enemy that we're goin' to be bogged down again and again,
the whole way up Italy.

'Once we had North Africa the game was in our hands. But
we threw away all our trumps. Those damn' fool Americans
vetoed Churchill's plan for going into the Balkans, where the
Greeks and Yugoslavs would have risen to a man and slit the
throats of the German garrisons. We could have driven straight
up to Budapest then and had the Hungarians with us, too.
Joined up with the Russians, saved ourselves from this murderous business of the Arctic convoys and encircled the southern
flank of the German Army in the East.'

Sir Pellinore swallowed another gulp of champagne and
went on angrily, 'To have missed that chance was bad enough,
but since the Yanks wouldn't have it from fear that after the
war Central Europe would become a sphere of British influence
we might at least have done better than go into Italy by the
basement.'

'I couldn't agree more,' Gregory said quickly. 'And if the
intention was not limited to relieving Malta and making the
Med reasonably safe for Allied shipping, but later to invade
the Italian mainland, we ought never to have gone into Sicily
at all. We should have done it via Sardinia and the Gulf of
Leghorn.'

'Of course. Mountbatten was for that, Cunningham was for
it; and it would have been their responsiblity to get the troops
ashore. Portal and Pug Ismay inclined that way, too; and in the
early days, when the pros and cons of Sicily and Sardinia were
discussed, Churchill had said that he could see no sense in
climbing up the leg of Italy like a harvest bug. From the
beginning the Joint Planning Staff had been all for Sardinia
and at the Casablanca Conference, when the matter was finally
decided, they staged a revolt. But Alan Brooke wouldn't have
it. He'd always favoured Sicily and at the last conference
in Washington he'd persuaded the Americans to accept his
choice. At Casablanca he fought the others tooth and nail. He
flatly refused to go back to the Americans and reopen the

question. Said they would get the idea that the British didn't know their own minds.'[1]

'What!' Gregory exclaimed. 'You can't really mean that he forced the issue upon which the whole course of the war and thousands of British lives depended simply to avoid having to confess to the Americans that his colleagues were against him and he might be wrong.'

'That's what it amounted to.'

'Why didn't Churchill intervene?'

Sir Pellinore shook his head. 'He never does. He produces some very good ideas and some very dangerous ones. He never stops gingering up his Chiefs of Staff to use everything we've got against the enemy. But he sticks to protocol like a leech. Can't blame him for that. Duty of a Prime Minister to accept the decisions of his military advisers. How at times he resists the temptation to override them I can't think. But he never abuses his position. As spokesman for the Chiefs of Staff, Alan Brooke had sold him this one about going into Sicily before they left London. And he has great faith in "Brookie", so that was that.'

'What a shocking business!'

'And look where Alan Brooke's pigheadedness has landed us. Etna commands the whole of north-eastern Sicily. Any fool could have foreseen that the wurst-eaters would dig in on its slopes and hold us up there while they reinforced southern Italy. Naturally, by the time Montgomery did throw them out they were ready for us and able to give us a bloody nose when we landed—and another at Salerno. And why Salerno, in God's name? If we'd gone in further up at Anzio we'd have had Rome for the askin'! The Italians had surrendered and could hardly wait to come over to us so as to get their own back on Musso's Nazi pals who have been kicking them round for so long. But rather than take a justified risk we missed the boat again; and as we failed to show the flag the Eyeties knuckled under.'

Gregory nodded. 'Yes, we ought to have made the Anzio landing in September instead of last week. How are things going there?'

1. Historical note: See Arthur Bryant's *Turn of the Tide*, based on the war diaries of Field Marshal Viscount Alanbrooke, pages 557–8.

'They're not. The whole Italian campaign is one hell of a mess. What's more the Generals have landed themselves with just the sort of party they always swore they would avoid. All of them were junior officers in the First World War. Fought at Loos, Ypres and that other bloodbath, the Somme. Never again, they said; never again will we expose troops to wholesale slaughter. And Churchill laid it down that whenever a battle looked like becoming a sloggin' match it was to be broken off. Then what happens? The Army is sent to fight its way up Italy. Two-thirds of the country's rugged mountains and rushing rivers. No room for manœuvre. Poor devils have got to fight for every yard of ground and are held for weeks while being shelled to blazes in the same position.

'It's more than six months now since this crazy business started with our landings in Sicily. The wurst-eaters have had all that time to fortify their Gustav Line along the Grigliano and Rapido rivers. The whole thing is stiff with steel and concrete pill-boxes and they've got us pinned down there. In the centre of the line there's a damn' great mountain with the monastery of Cassino on top. No getting round it. The place has got to be taken by assault and the fighting there now is just about as bloody as it was at Passchendaele. The only solution was a landing at Anzio. If it had come off we should have outflanked the whole German line. But it hasn't, because a bun-headed American General was given command and he's bungled the whole job.'

Gregory raised his eyebrows. 'Tell me more. I haven't heard a thing about this.'

'Neither, thank God, has the British public as yet, else they'd be yellin' for his head on a pole. He's a feller named Lucas. The great battle launched at Cassino on the 12th was to draw down all the enemy reserves from central Italy; and it did the trick. What is more our deception people did a splendid job. They foxed the wurst-eaters completely and handed Anzio to Lucas on a plate. His troops got ashore with hardly a shot fired. By midnight he had landed thirty-six thousand men and three thousand vehicles. Our Guards Division, bless 'em, was in the van and ran true to form. They penetrated sixteen miles inland. Sixteen miles! And they cut the road between Rome and Cassino. Then, what does this moron do? He thinks he'd like to wait for his armoured corps in case there might be a battle. So he recalls all his advance troops back to the beach and makes them sit there for two days. Two days, mark you! And for all that time the road to Rome was open. The Italians have informed us since that the Germans had sent every man jack they had up to Cassino and a single mechanized battalion could have seized the city.'

Grabbing the neck of the magnum, the Baronet picked it up. Then, seeing that it was empty, he thrust it back and rang the bell. Still scowling, he muttered, 'I've always said that the one thing wrong with a magnum is that it holds too much for one and not enough for two. We'll open another to keep us going till lunch.'

'That's fine by me,' Gregory agreed, 'I haven't tasted the real stuff for eight months. But what a shocking story. What's the position now?'

'Owing to Lucas's bungling, he got himself boxed in and darn near chucked back into the sea. Must give it to the sauerkrauters that they know how to meet a crisis. God only knows where they found them, but they rushed up about twenty thousand men. On the third day it was touch and go. But Alex went in himself. Saw every Brigadier in the outfit personally and restored the situation. Battle at Cassino couldn't be broken off, of course. And the Anzio beach-head averages only four miles in depth, with our people thick as flies on it, taking casualties from every shell that comes over. So now we've got two bloodbaths on our hands.'

'And to think how different things might be if only we had gone into Sardinia.'

'Yes, we'd be in the valley of the Piave by now and at far less cost. Alex would have been preparing for a drive in the spring by the route through the Julian Alps that Napoleon took. By summer we'd be in Munich and Vienna. Would have saved us from the immense task of preparing for a Second Front, too; and all the risks entailed by buttin' our heads against the house-painter feller's Atlantic Wall. But we haven't even got Rome yet so I would put my shirt on it that the historians will assess Alan Brooke's having pushed us into going into Europe by way of Sicily as about the biggest strategic blunder of all time.'

'An invasion of the Continent from England is definitely on, then?'

'Yes. Roosevelt and Churchill gave Uncle Joe their word on that at Teheran. I don't have to tell you to keep a still tongue in your head. Anyhow, you'll pick up all the lowdown about it when you get back to the War Room. It's scheduled for the first week in May and detailed plannin' for it is going ahead full steam now. As you may know, Oliver Stanley and his Future Planners did all the ground work as far back as early '42, and the pot's been kept bubbling ever since. Churchill's never been keen on it because it's against all sense to attack a powerful enemy at his point of greatest strength. He's always favoured using our seapower to go in through the Balkans. Dead right too. We could have taken our pick of a thousand miles of coast where the enemy's very thinly spread and so far from home that it would take him weeks to build up a front. But the Americans have been all for a cross-Channel show from the word go. Our people had all they could do to stall them off from getting themselves and us a bloody nose last year. We had to agree, though, to rev up the planning. About the time you went to Germany, General Morgan was appointed top boy of a show called C.O.S.S.A.C. with a big combined staff and they've been at it hammer and tongs ever since working out the nuts and bolts needed for the job. So when you go back you'll hear talk of nothing but Mulberries and landin' craft.'

'Who's going to command the big show?'

'Eisenhower.'

'What do you think of him?'

'Grand chap. Mind, he has yet to prove his abilities as a General. Alex ran the show for him in North Africa. But as a person you couldn't have a better. He has buckets of charm, has the sense to listen to what other people have to say and is determined that there shall be no jealous bickering. He's told his own staff that if any of them don't get on with the British they'll get a ticket for the first ship home.'

'Oh come, now,' Gregory smiled, 'you can't really mean that you approve of one of our Allies?'

'What's that? Insolent young devil! Nonsense! I've never said a thing against the Americans. Splendid fellers. Their generosity is boundless and if you don't lay the law down to them they're eager to learn. Fight like tigers, too, once they've been shown how. It isn't their fault that most of their top men have nothing but sawdust in their heads.'

At that moment the door opened and Erika was shown in by the parlourmaid, who also brought the second magnum. With cries of joy, the lovers embraced while Sir Pellinore opened the champagne and soon Gregory was telling Erika of his escape from Malacou.

Stefan Kuporovitch arrived shortly afterwards. Twelve days earlier his wife had presented him with a son; so Gregory had got back in time to act in person as one of the boy's godfathers, Sir Pellinore having agreed to be the other, while Erika was to be godmother. In due course the four of them enjoyed a lunch that few restaurants could have provided in the fifth year of the war, and with the dessert they drank a bottle of Imperial Tokay to the health of Madeleine and the small Gregory Pellinore Kuporovitch.

The following day Gregory saw a specialist who said that Dr. Zetterberg had done a splendid job on his leg and that, although he might suffer some pain from it from time to time if he overtaxed it, in another few months it should serve him as well as the one that had not been injured. It would, however, always be about half an inch shorter than the other.

In order to correct that he went to Lobbs in St. James's Street and ordered himself several pairs of shoes, the sole and heel of the left one of each pair to be half an inch thicker than the right, so that when he wore them his limp would not be noticeable. After three days in London he returned with Erika to Gwaine Meads.

The greater part of the lovely old house had been lent by Sir Pellinore to the R.A.F. as a hospital, but he had retained one wing to which he sent a few special guests who needed a quiet time to recover from particularly arduous service in the war. Gregory always stayed there after his missions and Erika had lived there permanently since she had escaped from the Continent. Although in the early months of the war she had trained as a nurse, she greatly preferred administrative work; so she had taken on the job of supervising the non-medical staff, dealing with rations, arranging recreations for the patients and other such tasks. Madeleine, having been a professional nurse in France before her marriage, had worked there up till Christmas as a Sister and was soon to resume part-time duty.

Early in February Kuporovitch took a fortnight's leave from his job of translating Russian documents in the War Office, and on his first Sunday at Gwaine Meads the baby was christened in the local church. Sir Pellinore came up for the ceremony and presented his godson with a gold-and-coral rattle and a cheque for a thousand pounds, then he ordered up from the cellars champagne for the whole staff of the hospital and its patients.

After their generous host had departed the following morning for London the four friends settled down to as pleasant a time as was possible in view of the bitter winter weather. Several days of snow and sleet, followed by biting winds, kept them largely to the house and, as none of them was a keen bridge player, to amuse themselves they resorted to various pastimes such as bezique, dominoes, Monopoly and guessing games.

In mid-March, a shade regretfully yet eager to be again in the swim of things, Gregory returned to London and once more put on the uniform of a Wing Commander. Both his uniforms dated from August 1942, so he thought it time he had another. When he was measured for it at Anderson and Sheppard's he told his cutter that he was in no hurry for it, as he did not mean to use it until he next went on leave. To order it proved a waste of money, for he never went on leave again.

12

The New Menace

GREGORY'S colleagues in the War Room were mainly other Wing Commanders, Lieutenant-Colonels and Commanders R.N., all middle-aged or elderly men specially selected from the host of officers who had served in the First World War and had been eager to serve again. As they were all intelligent and charming people the War Room could be described as a 'happy ship'. They welcomed Gregory back with drinks in the tiny mess and invitations to lunch at their clubs, but were much too discreet to ask him where he had been during the past ten months.

Neither did any of them go out of their way to pass on to him such information as they had picked up about the plans for 'Overlord'—the codeword for the coming invasion of the Continent—but from conversations with senior officers and Cabinet Ministers who looked in at the War Room late at night, and usually seemed to assume that only very special secrets were kept from its staff, Gregory soon had a very good idea of what was going on and he discussed such matters with Sir Pellinore, who was always extremely well informed.

They had resumed their arrangement that Gregory should have supper with the elderly Baronet every Sunday evening. Like everyone else, Sir Pellinore's household was subject to rationing, but he had tackled that problem with his usual vigour and every week had sent up from Gwaine Meads supplies of non-rationed items, such as poultry, turkey eggs for omelettes and home-smoked eels. So after meals that were treats to Gregory they retired to the library and, stimulating their minds with ample potations of pre-1914 Kümmel and old brandy, reviewed every aspect of the war.

Sir Pellinore continued to deplore the fact that as the Americans had more men and more money they were in a position to dictate how the Allies' forces should be employed. Among their major stupidities he counted their flat refusal, in spite of Churchill's most desperate pleas, to spare a single Brigade to take over Rhodes from the Italians before the Germans had a chance to get there; thus having ruined our excellent prospects of persuading Turkey to enter the war as our allies.

The reason the Americans gave was that they needed every man they could lay hands on, not alone for the cross-Channel operation but to stage a subsidiary invasion of the south of France. And for this project they also intended to rob General Alexander of the best Divisions from his Army in Italy.

In the meantime things were going no better there. With a resolution that could only be admired, the Germans were obeying their Führer's order that there should be no withdrawal. They had clamped down like a vice on the country and terrorized the Italians into continuing to keep the railways and their supply services going. Meanwhile, the Anzio beach-head continued to be boxed in.

After the great battle for Cassino in January there was a temporary lull. But it had flared up again in mid-February and, although the American General Mark Clark had the historic monastery reduced to ruins by bombing, that got the Allies no further.

On the 16th of the month the enemy made a ferocious assault on the Anzio bridgehead and it was again touch and go whether the seventy thousand men now crammed in there were to be driven into the sea. They succeeded in clinging on to their few miles of Italian soil, but only at the cost of terrible casualties. In mid-March there came the third great battle for Cassino, but the Germans held the heights and the Allies were again driven back with fearful losses. Strategy had gone by the board, the Allies were now paying an appalling price for entering Europe by way of Sicily and the Italian campaign had degenerated into the same ghastly war of attrition and futile sacrifice of life that had been waged for so long by the bone-headed Generals of the First World War on the Western Front.

Each time Sir Pellinore and Gregory met, after deploring the situation in Italy the Baronet asked gruffly, 'Got yourself out of this habit of thinking about that Black Magician feller yet?'

But Gregory always had to shake his head and say, 'No. Whenever I'm at a loose end for a few minutes during the daytime, or when I wake in the mornings or am dropping off to sleep at night, he still comes through. I just can't help it. And, to be honest, in a way I don't want to. To know what's happening to him holds an extraordinary fascination.'

Through these occult communications he was convinced that in March Gottlob von Altern had succeeded in obtaining a court order to become Willi's guardian and take over the Sassen property. Malacou had then tried to come to an arrangement with Gottlob to retain the ruined Castle as a tenant. This had looked like going through, but, early in April, Malacou had found himself in further trouble. Gottlob's accountants had been going into the financial transactions at Sassen since Ulrich von Altern's death and unearthed the fact that Malacou had sold several of the outlying farms for a very considerable sum. When called on to repay the money he had been unable to do so because, although it was still unknown to the lawyers, believing that Germany was certain to be defeated and the mark become almost worthless, he had smuggled the money out to Sweden.

To get it back soon enough to satisfy the von Altern lawyers would have entailed a big risk of the authorities finding out what he had done and such currency offences were punishable by a heavy prison sentence. His efforts to secure time to pay had been unavailing and a fortnight later he had learned by his own mysterious means that a writ had been issued against him, charging him with having defrauded Willi. Knowing the verdict must go against him and that he would be sent to prison, he had decided on flight. With Tarik he had driven by night over the Polish border and, after various subterfuges to avoid being traced, had reached his house at Ostroleka.

As the spring advanced the preparations for 'Overlord' increased in tempo. The work to be undertaken was immense. Hundreds of trains had to be earmarked for carrying troops and stores to ports, roads widened, camps built, hards constructed in the estuaries of rivers for embarking into the many types of landing craft, shipping brought from all over the world and concealed, as far as possible, in the northern ports, Mulberry harbours made and camouflaged, thousands of maps printed, innumerable measures taken to deceive the enemy about the date and place of the landings and scores of conferences held. Yet, in spite of everyone concerned working day and night, D-Day had to be postponed from May to June.

While all this was going on the enemy was also extremely active. Although he still had no idea when and where the invasion would come, such vast preparations for it could not altogether be concealed. In consequence, from Norway right down to Biarritz, thousands of forced-labour gangs were at work strengthening the Atlantic Wall.

With grim determination, too, the Germans continued to press on the preparations to launch Hitler's great hope—the secret weapon. Owing to raid after raid by the R.A.F., they had been forced to abandon work on the big launching sites on the French coast first spotted by our reconnaissance aircraft. But they had since developed a smaller type which was much harder to find. Many of these were also destroyed, but hardly a day passed without new ones being discovered.

It was one night early in May that Sir Pellinore asked Gregory, 'If "Overlord" is successful what do you reckon the chances are of the house-painter feller throwin' in the sponge shortly afterwards?'

'None,' replied Gregory promptly. 'Hitler is a maniac and will fight to the last ditch.'

'That's my bet. But how about the German Army? D'you think that if they get a good lickin' in Normandy they'll rat on him?'

'I doubt it. They would probably like to; but it's not in the nature of the Germans to defy a master. I should say the only chance of a sudden collapse is if someone bumps Hitler off.'

'That's my view, too,' Sir Pellinore agreed gloomily. 'Then if the war goes on into the autumn, it looks as if we'll have to face up to those bloody great rockets.'

'But I thought that after Peenemünde they had abandoned work on them.'

'So did we all. But we've recently had it through from the Polish Underground that they didn't. Seems the swine got goin' again on 'em as soon as they could up on the Polish marshes. New place is north-east of Warsaw and out of range of our bombers, so there's damn' all we can do about it.'

Soon afterwards Gregory had confirmation of Sir Pellinore's unpleasant news. The new menace and its possible consequences began to be hinted at in uneasy whispers by his colleagues in the War Room. Then a week later, when lunching with an old friend of his—who had been a Cadet with him in H.M.S. *Worcester* and, since 1941, had worked in the Deception Section of the Joint Planning Staff—he cautiously led up to the subject.

The other Wing Commander made a grimace and said, 'As it is not a plan, there's no reason I shouldn't tell you what I know about it; although, of course, everything possible will be done to keep it from the public, so as to avoid a panic. There's no doubt about it that Jerry is banging off these things in Poland, and that in a few months' time we may get them here. The high-ups are fairly peeing their pants at the thought of what may happen to London.'

'Has anyone found out yet exactly how much damage they will do?' Gregory asked.

'Yes. There is quite a useful Underground in Poland, and I gather we've received a pretty accurate picture of these things from them. I was representing my little party only yesterday at a high-power meeting. It was called by the Home Office to discuss re-evacuating London and that sort of thing. Sir Findlater Stewart took the chair. He said that these rockets each weigh seventy tons and have a twenty-ton warhead. Just think of what that means.'

Gregory nodded. 'I heard that when I was in Switzerland, a long while ago, at the time they had only got them on the drawing board and I could hardly credit it.'

'Well, that's not far off the estimate our people made from the photographs taken over Peenemünde; and now we know it for a fact. What is more, the boffins have worked it out that

each one that lands on a densely populated area will turn
a quarter of a square mile into rubble, kill four thousand
people and cause a further ten thousand casualties.'

'God, how awful!'

'Have another Kümmel,' said the Deception Planner.

'Thanks,' murmured Gregory, 'I need it.'

That day Gregory was not due on duty in the War Room
until ten o'clock in the evening, so after lunch he went down
to his flat in Gloucester Road and slept through the rest of
the afternoon. As he gradually came out of his slumber he remained temporarily unconscious of his surroundings, but
could see Malacou quite distinctly. The occultist was in a
smallish room that had good but old-fashioned furniture. In
his subconscious Gregory had seen the room several times
before and knew it to be Malacou's study in his old house at
Ostroleka.

With him there were two men of the *Totenkopf S.S.*, and it
was clear that he was in trouble. But it was not in connection
with the money of which he had defrauded the von Alterns,
otherwise the men would have been *Staatspolizei*. These were
members of a special organization known as *Einsatzgruppen*,
composed of criminals and fanatics embodied by Himmler for
the purpose of exterminating the Jews. One of them held
Malacou's passport and was questioning him closely about it.
Clearly they believed him to be a Jew and on that account he
was in grave danger of being taken off to a concentration
camp.

From previous telepathic communications Gregory had
received during the past six weeks he already knew the background of the situation. Malacou had proved wrong in his
assumption that, owing to the great number of Jews in Poland
and the German's need of the crops they grew, the majority
of them had been left at liberty. Earlier that had been the case
and it was only the Jews in Germany who had been sacrificed
to the Nazi ideology. But both Hitler and Himmler were so
obsessed with the idea that the Jews were the deadly enemies
of the whole human race that in 1943 Hitler had agreed to let
Himmler apply his 'final Solution of the Problem' to every
territory over which the Swastika flew.

For many months past a systematic round-up of the Jews had been operating, not only in Poland but in France, Belgium, Holland and even countries as distant as Yugoslavia and Bulgaria. As they were too numerous in Central Europe to be dealt with at once individually they had, at first, simply been herded into ghettos in the larger cities. Then concentration camps with gas chambers had been constructed and staffed with Himmler's *Einsatzgruppen*. To these the Jews were now being moved in batches and tens of thousands of them had already been liquidated.

In consequence, when Malacou arrived in Ostroleka he had found that all his relatives were either dead or confined to the Warsaw ghetto. Extremely uneasy in mind, but not knowing where else to go and protected by his Turkish passport, he had settled down there and had been living very quietly. But evidently someone who knew he had been born there a Jew, and had a grudge against him, had given him away.

Although Gregory had no cause at all to love Malacou, he could not now help feeling sorry for him and was very relieved when the Nazis, having found that his passport was in order, decided not to arrest him until further enquiries had been made into his past.

In the Cabinet War Room on nights when there was no special activity it was customary at about two o'clock in the morning for the four duty officers to lower the lights and doze beside their telephones. That night, soon after Gregory had settled down, he seemed to be watching Malacou. The occultist was now outside his tall, narrow-gabled house in the small town street. With Tarik's help he was loading food into an old-fashioned pony trap; and soon after, with Malacou loudly lamenting as he drove off, it clattered away into the night. From this it was evident that he thought it too dangerous to await the results of the threatened investigation and had decided to leave Ostroleka while he still had the chance.

During the fortnight that followed Gregory caught several glimpses of the fugitives. For a week they hid in the depths of a wood, then when he next saw them they were following a narrow track that wound between tall forests of reeds in a desolate area of marsh. Both of them were bowed under huge bundles strapped to their shoulders, so evidently they had had to abandon the pony and trap. Two days later he saw them again, now installed in a cottage in the middle of the marshes. It was sparsely furnished but had obviously been abandoned for some time, as they were patching a hole in the roof, through which water had seeped leaving stains on a dresser in the living room. He gained the impression that it was a shooting lodge which in happier times had been used for duck shoots by the owner of some manor house in the vicinity and, owing to its isolated situation, it looked as if Malacou could hope to remain there in safety.

On May 11th a new offensive was launched against the Gustav Line and for the following week the battle in southern Italy again raged with maximum intensity. Then, on the 23rd, the Allies at last succeeded in breaking out of the Anzio bridgehead; but D-Day was just approaching and all thought in the Cabinet Offices was concentrated on the final preparations for it. Quite unexpectedly, Gregory became involved in them when Air Chief Marshal Sir Richard Peck rang him up and asked him to come up to his office in the Air Ministry.

Richard Peck had for some time past held the post of Assistant Chief of Air Staff (G). This entailed handling all the problems that the other Air Chiefs had neither the time nor the inclination to tackle. One job he had taken on of his own initiative was to make himself the Overlord of Air Ministry Press Relations and, one day when lunching with him at a corner table that was always reserved for him at Quaglino's, Gregory had happened to mention that for several years he had earned his living as a foreign correspondent. It was on that account that the Air Chief Marshal had sent for him. Having given Gregory a cigarette, he said:

'Our American friends are extremely generous with their money but by no means so generous about their tributes to the part we are playing in the war. Reading their papers every day, as I do, one would get the impression that Britain has become no more than a base for Uncle Sam's gallant boys to pitch into the Germans. Later, of course, there will be many more American troops fighting on the Continent than there will be British, because their reserves of manpower are much greater than ours. But for Operation "Neptune" the actual landings will be about fifty-fifty. What is more the success or failure of the operation depends entirely on us, because it's the British Navy that's got to put the troops ashore. Even so, you can take it from me that our chaps won't get more than a tiny paragraph in the American dailies. And then it will be on the lines, "poor old Britain is pretty exhausted after the tough time she's been through but she helped us all she could".

'Now I want the American people to know the truth and there is one way I can do it. We don't stand a hope with the dailies, but we can get signed articles by writers of repute into the weeklies and glossy magazines. To do that I've combed the R.A.F. for well-known authors and others and had them seconded to me for the few days that count to act as temporary war correspondents who will cover the landings. I've got Terence Rattigan, Dennis Wheatley, Christopher Hollis, Hugh Clevely and a score of others and I'm sure you would write a really lively report, so I'd like to have you, too. Are you willing to play?'

'Certainly,' Gregory agreed at once. 'If Brigadier Jacob will release me from the War Room there's nothing I'd like better than to fly over the beaches.'

The Air Chief Marshal shook his head. 'No. In your case that's not on. The same applies to Wheatley. General Ismay has already ruled that no-one employed in the Cabinet Offices must be exposed to the risk of being shot down. They know too much. If they fell into the hands of the enemy and had their thumbs screwed off they might give things away. But don't let that worry you. There will be so much smoke going up from shells and bombs that you wouldn't be able to see the coast of Normandy anyhow. I have a much more interesting assignment for you. I want you to go down to Harwell and see General Gale take off with the 6th Airborne Division. That will be the spearhead of the invasion.'

13

Portrait of a Born General

As a result of his conversation with Sir Richard Peck, on the
sunny morning of June 3rd Gregory left London in an Air
Ministry car. Owing to the rationing of petrol the Great West
Road was almost empty, so the car soon reached Maiden-
head. In peacetime the river there would have been gay with
picnic parties in punts and launches, but it was now still and
deserted. The car sped on past the even lovelier reaches of the
upper Thames, then across downlands until over the horizon
there appeared the widely spaced hangars of Harwell Aero-
drome.

It was a peacetime R.A.F. station with well-designed buildings and commodious quarters, but as it was now also the
headquarters of the 6th Airborne Division it was crowded with
soldiers as well as airmen. Gregory reported to the Adjutant
who took him to the mess, where within half an hour he had
made a dozen new friends.

Among them was Wing Commander Macnamara, whose
aircraft was to tow the glider that would take General Richard
Gale to France, and the Station Commander, Group Captain
Surplice, who his officers united in saying was the finest C.O.
under whom they had ever served. Squadron Leader Pound,
a veteran of the First World War and Principal Administrative
Officer, then took Gregory to the Briefing Room.

There, behind a locked door with an armed sentry on guard
and blacked-out windows, another beribboned veteran was
preparing the maps from which the air crews would be briefed
when the signal came through that the 'party' was definitely
on. Then at six o'clock the visitor was taken on a tour of the
great airfield with its broad runways and scores of parked

aircraft and gliders. They were wearing their war-paint: special recognition signs painted on only the night before, after the camp had been 'sealed'. No-one who now entered it would be permitted to leave or write or telephone from it until the invasion had taken place.

After the drive round, Major Griffiths, who was to pilot the General's glider, took Gregory up for a twenty-minute flight in it. There was a stiff wind so it was a little bumpy, but that did not worry him. The roar from Macnamara's towing aircraft came plainly back to them; then, as he cast off, there came a sudden silence and a few minutes later they glided safely back on to a runway.

Next Gregory attended a preliminary briefing. It took the form of a colour film showing a part of France. For those in the long, darkened room it was just as though they were seated in a huge aircraft flying over the country shown in the film. Again and again they seemed to be carried over the German-held beaches to the fields on which the paratroops were to be dropped and the gliders come down, while the commentator pointed out the principal landmarks by which the pilots could identify their objectives.

Back in the big mess Gregory found it now packed to capacity with equal numbers of officers in khaki and Air Force blue. They all looked wonderfully fit and their morale was terrific. Macnamara introduced him to General Gale, a huge man with a ready laugh, shrewd eyes, a bristling moustache and a bulldog chin.

They soon discovered that they were the same age. 'And a damn' good vintage, too,' said the General.

An officer asked the General what weapon he was going to take for the battle. He roared with laughter. 'Weapon! What the hell do I want with a weapon? If I have the luck to get near any of those so-and-sos I'll use my boot to kick them in the guts.'

After dinner Gregory drank and laughed with a score of officers; then, as they drifted off to bed, he stayed up for another hour talking to General Gale alone. Among other things they discussed the qualities that make a good leader, and the General said:

'Efficiency; that's the only thing that counts. If the men know that you really know your job, they'll follow you blindly anywhere.'

Gregory did not agree. He argued that efficiency might be nine-tenths of the game, but the last tenth was personality. To make his point he instanced that his companion was wearing light grey jodhpurs instead of battle-dress.

'What's that got to do with it?' the General wanted to know. 'I wear the damned things because they're comfortable and I hate the feel of that beastly khaki serge.'

'Exactly,' Gregory laughed. 'Most people would be shy about dressing differently, but you don't care a hoot. You've the courage of your convictions and if you have them about clothes you must also have them about running your show.'

When they at last went to bed they were a little worried about the weather, but they knew that a postponement of the operation would not even be considered unless it became exceptionally bad. That Saturday night hundreds of ships were already moving to their concentration points, so the security of the whole operation might be jeopardized if the invasion were put off even for a single day.

In the morning the weather had worsened. Nevertheless a Wing Commander Bangey took Gregory up for a flight in one of the paratroop-dropping aircraft. They did a practice run over a diagonal road that had a certain similarity to a road in the target area and the crew went through the exact drill they would follow when they were dropped in France.

Then, when Gregory got back, the blow fell. At 11.30 the Station Commander sent for him to tell him that the operation would not take place that night.

Both Gregory and General Gale were utterly appalled. They were the only people on the station who realized the full implications of a postponement. There were now over four thousand ships which had moved up in the night and many thousands of smaller craft massed round the Isle of Wight. The enemy had only to send over one recce plane and he would learn that the invasion was just about to start. That would give him twenty-four hours in which to rush additional troops to the French coast and when our troops landed they would find every gun manned.

Worse, the Germans might send their whole bomber force over that Sunday night to the Solent and if they did it must result in the most ghastly massacre among our close-berthed stationary shipping.

Fortunately, no more than a dozen people on the station knew the date that had been decided for D-Day, so remained unaware of the postponement and the terrible consequences that might arise from it. They knew only that, the camp having been sealed, D-Day must be imminent, and their joy was unbounded at the thought of at last being able to put into real use the drills they had practised for so long.

In consequence that night the crowded mess was a scene of even greater excitement and mirth. Both soldiers and airmen were offering long odds that within a week of the invasion the enemy would collapse and the war be over, but finding few takers. About nine o'clock a sing-song started. The station doctor, Squadron Leader Evan Jones, produced his accordion and they made the rafters ring with all the old favourites, from 'She was poor but she was honest' to 'Auld Lang Syne'. Then three-quarters of an hour after midnight Gregory learned from the General's A.D.C. that a signal had just come in. The great decision had been taken. The following night the show was definitely on.

The morning of Monday June 5th passed quietly. Very few people knew as yet that this was D minus 1. But at lunch-time the whispered word went round, 'Final briefing at three o'clock.'

For the past week the Italian campaign had become the forgotten front, but while Gregory was still at lunch it was suddenly announced that General Alexander had captured Rome. An outburst of cheering greeted this splendid news and Gregory was particularly delighted, because everybody in the War Cabinet Offices regarded 'Alex' as by far the best of our Generals, and that his triumph should not have been spoilt by coming after D-Day was a most happy occurrence.

In the afternoon there were three briefings, each taking an hour, for the three separate but co-ordinated operations.

Major-General Crawford, the Director of Air Operations War Office, had arrived from London and with him was Air Vice-Marshal Hollinghurst, the A.O.C. of the Group. Group Captain Surplice opened the proceedings by reading Orders of the Day from General Eisenhower and the Air Commander-in-Chief, Sir Trafford Leigh-Mallory. Then, having run through the general lay-out, he asked General Gale to describe the part his Division was to play.

The General said that his task was to protect the left flank of the Allied Armies. To achieve this three landings would be made to the east of the River Orne. It was imperative that a large fortified battery that enfiladed the assault beaches should be silenced. One of the first parties to land would raid a small château and seize a car known to be in its garage. Two para-troopers, both Austrians, would drive the car hell-for-leather towards the steel gates of the emplacement, shouting in German, 'Open the gates! Open the gates! The invasion has started.'

The Germans would have heard the aircraft overhead, so it was hoped that they would open up; then the paratroopers would hurl bombs through which would make it impossible to close the gates again. It was a suicide job and might not come off. To make certain of silencing the battery, the General intended to crash-land three gliders across the fort's concrete and barbed-wired surrounding ditch.

The other two parties were to seize two adjacent bridges about five miles from the coast, one of which crossed the Orne and the other a canal running parallel to it. He then meant to establish his battle H.Q. between the two seized bridges and infest with his men all the territory to the west in order to delay an attack against the British flank. Then when the attack came, as come it must, he would fight with his back to the double water line.

As Gregory listened he was thrilled by the thought that this was no academic lecture, no Staff College exercise, but the real thing. That was brought even more sharply home a few minutes later as the General went on to say that the 21st Panzer Division would be at them pretty soon, so he would need every anti-tank gun he could get in and need them pretty badly. Then, as though it had only just occurred to him, he

added, 'As a matter of fact we shall want them tomorrow.'
At that a roar of laughter went up from the packed benches.

Other briefings followed: by the Station Commander, the
Signals Officer, the Secret Devices Expert and the Meteoro-
logical Officer. The last predicted clear skies under two thous-
and feet and broken cloud above which would let enough
moonlight through for the pilots to pick up their dropping
zones without difficulty.

At dinner that night Gregory looked down the lines of young
faces. All of them were flushed with excitement, eager and
merry. Not one of them seemed conscious of the fact that this
might be the last meal he would ever eat; and Gregory thought
how proud their parents and friends would be if they could
see them.

Before leaving London he had looted Sir Pellinore's cellar
of a few bottles of one of the finest hocks in the world—
*Ruppertsberg Hoheburg Gewürztramminer feinste Edelbeer-
auslese 1920.* At his suggestion General Gale asked General
Crawford, Air Vice-Marshal Hollinghurst, Wing Commander Macnamara and his A.D.C. to help drink them to an
Allied victory.

As they drank the fine wine they talked of the coming
battle, but Gregory's thoughts were temporarily elsewhere.
They had gone back to that other fine hock of the same
vintage that he had drunk with Malacou the first night they
met at Sassen; and he found himself once more overlooking
the occultist.

Malacou and Tarik were still in their lonely cottage and had
made themselves very comfortable. The former had succeeded
in bringing his astrological gear with him and was seated at
the table in the living room working on some problem. A
third man was present: a tall, lean fellow dressed in rough
clothes but with a fine-featured intelligent face. On Malacou
becoming aware of Gregory's ethereal presence he broke off
his work to communicate that they had no fears for the
moment, and that their companion was a Polish engineer,
also in hiding from the Nazis, who had recently taken refuge
with them.

At ten o'clock Group Captain Surplice came into the mess

and carried Gregory off with him. First, in his car they made a
complete tour of the airfield, but everything was in perfect
order and there was no need for even one last-minute instruction. Then they went to the Watch Tower, to within a few
yards of which every aircraft had to taxi up before receiving
the signal to take off. The weather was still far from good, but
it had improved a little and there were breaks in the clouds
so that the late summer twilight faded almost imperceptibly
into moonlight.

The first wave consisted of fourteen aircraft carrying para-
troopers, followed by four aircraft towing gliders containing
special material needed as soon as possible after the paratroops had landed. The wave was led by Wing Commander
Bangley, and with him as a passenger went Air Vice-Marshal
Hollinghurst. He had been forbidden to go, but 'Holly', as
this plump, dynamic little man was affectionately called by
his subordinates, declared that only being handcuffed and
locked up would stop him from witnessing the fine show his
boys would put up after their many months of training.

At three minutes past eleven precisely the first aircraft took
off. The others followed at thirty-second intervals. A Wing
Commander standing beside Gregory timed them with a watch.
Not a single aircraft was early or late by a split second.

There now came a period of waiting, as the second wave
was not due to start until 1.50 a.m. During it Air Chief Marshal
Sir Trafford Leigh-Mallory flew in. Hurried explanations had to
be thought up to account for 'Holly's' absence. Someone said
he thought he was at the Signals Office, but he could not be
found and, fortunately, his C.-in-C. had to take off again to
continue his round of inspections.

Midnight came, but somehow it did not seem to Gregory
to be the beginning of the long-awaited D-Day. For him and
his companions that had started hours ago. Accompanied by
Surplice he walked along to General Gale's glider so as to
spend this last three-quarters of an hour with him. The General
had just returned from a visit to his men before they left
their tented camp, where he had been drinking good English
beer with them, and they were still cheering him to the echo
as he came on to the airfield.

To ease the suspense of these last minutes Gregory started telling bawdy stories; the others joined in and laughed a lot. The General looked a more massive figure than ever now that the many pockets of his special kit were stuffed with maps and the dozens of other things he would need when he landed in France; but he was still wearing his light grey jodhpurs.

'What about your Mae West, sir?' one of his officers asked.

'Oh, I can put that on later if I have to,' he protested.

'Might be a bit tricky then, sir,' the officer persisted.

Turning to Gregory the General said, 'I'm supposed to be commanding this damn' Division, yet look how these fellows bully me. All right; I'll put it on if you like.'

About six people then tried to help him into it and one of them said, 'The tapes should go as high up under your arms as possible, sir.'

He burbled with laughter again. 'I know what you're up to. If we fall in the sea you want my head to go under and my bottom left sticking up in the air.' Then a moment later he slapped his broad chest and exclaimed, 'Good God, look at me! I must look like Henry VIII.'

His jest was not without point and some minutes earlier Gregory had noticed that painted on the side of the glider was the name of another English King—Richard the First. That, the A.D.C. had said, was because Richard Gale was to be the first British General to land in France by many hours, but the unintended parallel struck Gregory most forcibly. The great Crusader, Richard Cœur-de-Lion, had been physically just such another big man as the General who now towered over the little group standing round him, and this modern lion-hearted Richard was about to lead another Crusade against far more evil men than the Saracens who had then occupied Jerusalem.

The last little scene before he emplaned was another of those jests which delight true British fighting men when about to go into battle. A few mornings earlier, on finding that there was golden syrup for breakfast, the General had exclaimed, 'By Jove! I love golden syrup and I haven't seen any for years.' So now Surplice, who had been his official host, presented him with a tin to take to France with him.

A few minutes later Gregory returned with the Station Commander to the Watch Tower. The signal was given and the twenty-five gliders, towed by Albemarles, began to move off. They were led by Macnamara in S for Sugar, towing Richard the First and his personal staff. With the regularity of clockwork they took off at the rate of one a minute and lifted gently to disappear in the night sky.

The aircraft in the first wave were now due back; so Gregory and his host hurried over to the Briefing Room, hardly able to contain their impatience to learn if all had gone well. At last the first pilot and his crew came in. He said that, in spite of a sudden worsening of the weather, he had dropped his parachutists right on the spot at seventeen and a half minutes past midnight. But he seemed a little disappointed. Asked by Surplice why he was looking so glum, he replied:

'Well, sir, it might have been one of the practice droppings we've carred out so often here. It was quite dark, no flak, nothing to see, no excitement. In fact it's difficult to believe that we've had anything to do with opening up the Second Front.'

To Gregory that was the best possible news. It meant that his friends in the Deception Section had achieved an almost unbelievable triumph. The enemy could have known neither the date nor place of the expected assault. General Montgomery had been given the dream of all Commanders when opening a great battle: complete tactical surprise. Our losses during the landings a few hours hence would now be only a tithe of what they would have been against an alerted opposition.

As other pilots came in this splendid news was confirmed. Only the later comers had seen anything. Not till after they had dropped their parachutists had some enemy batteries opened up with light flak. Then 'Holly', safely returned, said that he had seen the synchronized attack by heavy bombers on the fortified battery—a last attempt to destroy it by pinpoint bombing. All who had seen the terrific explosions by which the redoubt had been lit up agreed that very few of its German garrison of one hundred and eight could still be alive or in any state to lay a gun.

But then, to discount this excellent beginning, a little group of face-blackened paratroopers came in. Their team had included their Brigade Major and it was he who was to lead the way down. He was a big man and had got stuck in the hatch; they could not push him through or pull him out. The pilot had taken the aircraft out to sea and ran it up and down the coast for half an hour, but the Major's men could not get him either in or out. At length he had lost consciousness, so it had been decided that the only thing to do was to return to England. Only after the aircraft had landed had they succeeded in getting him free. The pilot pleaded desperately to be allowed to make a second run so that at least the others might join in the battle, but Surplice would not let him. The air over the whole Channel was now alive with aircraft on exactly timed and carefully planned routes; so for a lone 'plane to attempt to pass through them would have been much too dangerous.

Worse was to come. A pale-faced young pilot entered the room and came up to his Station Commander. 'I'm sorry, sir,' he reported. 'I don't know what to say, but my string broke. We lost our glider about three miles from the French coast.'

Surplice laid his hand on the boy's shoulder. 'I'm sure it wasn't your fault. Tell me what happened.'

'Well, sir, it was those bloody Met. men who let us down. Our orders were to drop the gliders off at sixteen hundred feet. But there was cloud down to eight hundred and no moon coming through. It was as black as pitch. I went down as low as I dared to try to get in the clear but in the darkness the glider must have lost my tail light and have become unmanageable. With him trailing wild, the strain snapped the tow-rope. There was nothing we could do about it.'

It was estimated that the glider might have had enough height to make the beach or, at least, shallow water. But it was certain that the load of stores it carried would never reach the leading paratroops for their urgent operations.

A few minutes later a second tug pilot came in. The same sad story. Low cloud several miles before he had reached the French coast, the following glider suddenly losing control and its tow-rope snapping. The third and fourth pilots arrived, white-faced and shaken. They, too, had lost their gliders out over the sea.

The Briefing Room was now crowded with returned air crews drinking tea and munching hot scones while waiting to make their detailed reports to the Intelligence Officers. But they spoke in low voices. Whispered word of the bad news had gone round and the atmosphere was one of gloom.

It was now about a quarter to three in the morning, and the next two hours were grim. Gregory, having no duties to perform, had accepted the many drinks pressed upon him during the long evening. It had turned cold and misty and he felt stale from the amount of liquor he had consumed. He would have given a lot to go back to the mess and brace himself up a little with a brandy and soda; but he did not like to suggest it.

With Surplice, Squadron Leader Pound, the little Welsh doctor and a few others, he stood miserably about waiting fearfully for news. If all four of the first flight of gliders had gone into the 'drink' what chance had General Gale and his string of twenty-five and all the other flights that had headed for the same area with the rest of the Airborne Division from other stations in the Group?

Dozens of those young daredevils who had been drinking so cheerfully in the mess only a few hours before were now almost certainly dead, and others, weighed down by their heavy equipment, must be swimming desperately for their lives in the cold waters of the Channel. Hundreds more might be crashing and drowning while Gregory and his companions stood miserably waiting for news.

If the General and a large part of the Airborne Division were lost their task would remain unaccomplished and the left flank of the British Army would then be left open to attack. There were hours to go yet before the first seaborne troops were due to splash their way ashore, and the Germans must now have known for over three hours that the invasion had really started. If the airborne operation failed the enemy would counter-attack the open beaches in the morning and quite possibly hurl our troops back into the sea, rendering the whole vast plan for liberating Europe a complete failure. The strain of waiting for news was appalling, and for Gregory, so used to action, so unused to patient vigil, it was a positive agony.

At last, soon after half past four, they heard the drone of aircraft. The tugs of the second wave were returning. At a quarter to five the first air crew came in. The Briefing Room was now still with a breathless silence. Scores of anxious eyes searched the faces of the newcomers for a verdict. They looked about them in surprise at this tense reception. Then they reported. The cloud had lifted and they had cast off their gliders dead on the mark.

Crew after crew appeared with the same glad tidings. When Macnamara came in there was a rush towards him. He was smiling, laughing. He had put General Gale down at half past two exactly at the place where he had planned to land. Soon afterward it was known that not a single glider in the second wave had been lost.

Douglas Warth, an official war reporter, had gone over with the first wave of paratroops. Since his return he had been waiting only to learn what had happened to General Gale and the others. Three days ago, that now seemed like a week, he had come down in a jeep, and he offered to take Gregory back to London in it.

Gregory gladly accepted. As he was saying good-bye to Surplice and thanking him for his kindness, the Chief Intelligence Officer came up with a message from the Control Room; he said, 'All aircraft safely landed, sir, and no casualties.'

Beaming with delight, Gregory congratulated the Station Commander and shook hands with several other new friends he had made during those never-to-be-forgotten days. He then collected his kit and accompanied Warth to the jeep. No longer tired but filled with elation they drove through the summer dawn, with birds singing in the hedgerows, back to London.

By seven o'clock he was in the Cabinet Offices War Room and got the broader picture. Of the two hundred and eighty-six aircraft despatched to land the Airborne Division only eight had failed to return and the glider losses had been far fewer than anticipated. A few hours later he learned that

General Gale had landed without accident and, achieving complete surprise, had secured the two bridges that were his principal objective. That night Gregory listened with Sir Pellinore to one of the finest broadcasts delivered in the war. It was given by the King and in well-informed circles it was known that His Majesty had written every word of it himself. Then they drank a health to George VI and Richard the First.

D-Day and its terrible hazards were, at last, over; but the war was still a long way from being won, and a week later it entered a new phase. On the night of June 12th/13th the first pilotless aircraft descended on London. As had been anticipated its warhead was no bigger than an average-sized bomb; so, after the first excitement, the public proceeded to settle down and grin and bear this new affliction; although they proved to be disconcerting things, as they had a nasty habit of suddenly turning round and coming down in a place where they were not expected. But a high proportion of them were prevented from reaching London by fighter aircraft, Ack-ack and the balloon barrages. The foremost thought in most people's minds was still joy that the invasion had at last taken place, and that 'Monty' was now safely established in Normandy with a bridgehead deep enough for there to be little fear that our men would be driven back into the sea. So the general feeling was that the buzz-bombs were only a temporary annoyance which might soon be brought to an end by the Germans throwing in their hand.

Throughout June Malacou's communications to Gregory continued, and he soon became aware that the occultist's thoughts were now mainly engaged by a new interest. The Polish engineer was a member of the Underground and the cottage in which they were living was on the new experimental range being used to test the giant rockets. The firing point for the rockets was a good twenty miles away from the cottage so most of them sailed high overhead, but now and again one came down prematurely and fell in the marshes.

The Pole was the leader of a group spread widely over the countryside and its members spent some of their time making notes of the number of rockets fired, how many of them were duds and where those duds fell. But the group had no wireless or any other means of communicating their information to London, as they had started up independently and were not in touch with the main Polish Underground. In addition to charting the rockets they went out at night and committed various acts of sabotage, such as tearing up sections of railway line and destroying small bridges. To aid these exploits Malacou was again busy with his astrological studies in order to be able to predict for his new friends the most favourable nights for them to undertake their clandestine activities.

Sir Pellinore had now come to the conclusion that as Gregory was obviously sane there must be a genuine foundation for the telepathic communication he was receiving; and when Gregory told him about the Pole's plotting of the rockets he was greatly interested. The anxiety about them in high quarters, far from dying down, had considerably increased. Thousands of tents were being manufactured to house the refugees who would be driven out of London and great dumps of medical stores and tinned food were being accumulated secretly at various places in the Home Counties. Plans were being made to deceive the public who were not in the immediate area of the first mighty explosion as to its cause, so that they should not panic, and arrangements were being made for the immediate evacuation of hospitals, children and pregnant mothers in the Metropolitan area.

By early July public morale was beginning to decline again. The V.1's were starting to get on people's nerves and the destruction caused by them had become considerable. Moreover, matters were not going anything like as well in France as had been expected. Most fortunately, the Deception Plans were continuing to function admirably. By the creation of a mock army in Kent, and other measures, Hitler continued to be convinced that the Normandy landings were only a feint, and that the main assault against his Fortress Europa was due to be launched at any moment across the narrows into the Pas de Calais. In consequence, he flatly refused the pleas of his Generals to allow the Armoured Divisions there to be brought south against the Normandy beach-head.

Yet, in spite of this, Montgomery was making no progress. He had informed the Chiefs of Staff that his object was to draw the Germans down on the positions he held and then destroy them. But it had been expected that a month after their landing the Allies would be well into France and, possibly, across the Seine. So far he had not even captured Caen; and to those who had originally planned it, the Second Front was proving a grievous disappointment.

On July 16th Gregory was on day duty, so he went to bed in his flat at his normal hour, which was about eleven o'clock. But he found that he could neither concentrate on his book nor, when he put out the light, get to sleep, because Malacou was in a great state of excitement and his thoughts were coming through with exceptional clarity.

In addition to keeping a careful record of the performance of the rockets, the Polish Resistance leader had been seeking to get at and examine one of them. To do so was far from easy; because, whenever there were firing trials, the Germans stationed little squads of their men over many square miles of the marshland and when a rocket came down prematurely their job was to locate and dismantle it as soon as possible.

Two days ago a rocket had gone wild and fallen miles away from the marshes, on the bank of the river Bug. No German patrol had been anywhere near and some Poles had rolled the rocket down the bank into the river; so that when the Germans reached the locality they had failed to find it. The previous night the Poles had retrieved the rocket from the river and hidden it among the reeds, then sent word to the engineer who was living with Malacou. That night he had gone off to join them and they were now working like demons to dismantle the tail of the rocket, which contained its mechanism. Malacou meanwhile was still in his cottage and a prey to fearful anxiety lest the Germans should catch the Pole and his companions either while working on it or, still worse, when they brought the pieces they secured to his dwelling, where they intended to hide them in the woodshed.

Eventually Gregory dropped off to sleep, but he woke next morning with the knowledge that the job had been completed without mishap and that the Polish engineer was now in possession of a complete set of the parts that made the rocket work.

After lunch that day Gregory walked across the Horse Guards and looked in on Sir Pellinore. When he retailed what he believed to have happened the elderly Baronet's blue eyes popped. Jerking forward in his chair he slapped a long leg encased in a pin-striped trouser with a mighty thud and cried:

'By Jove! If only we could get hold of those bits and pieces! Might be the savin' of London! I was talkin' to Lindemann the other day. Seems we're working on a device now that'll explode shells and bombs in mid-air. What these science wizards will get up to next, God knows. Still, the Prof. says it's perfectly possible. Got to make one box of tricks to set off the other, though. But if the boffins knew how these rockets worked we might blow 'em up while they were still sailin' over mid-Channel.'

'If that's so,' Gregory said, 'we ought to do our utmost to collect the mechanism that this Polish engineer has secured. And, of course, to let us have it is the reason he risked his neck to get it. But how we could set about that I don't see.'

'I do,' replied Sir Pellinore promptly. 'Our bombers haven't the range to reach Poland. But lighter aircraft fitted with extra fuel tanks can. S.O.E. are sending one or two in every week now to drop supplies for the Polish Underground. I'll have a talk with Gubbie about this.'

'By all means do. But I doubt if that will get us anywhere. Even if General Gubbins can be persuaded that I am in telepathic communication with a man hundreds of miles from England, and is willing to send an aircraft to collect this stuff, I couldn't tell him where to send it. I've only the vaguest idea where this place is. It can't be many miles from Ostroleka, where Malacou had his house; I'm sure of that. And the cottage is situated near a stretch of broad very winding river from which tributaries make forks some miles on either side of the cottage. But there are any number of rivers in that part of Poland and I couldn't possibly describe it well enough for a pilot to identify.'

'But you . . . No.' Sir Pellinore hastily hauled himself to his feet. 'Forget it, Gregory. Odds are it's all moonshine.'

'It's not moonshine,' Gregory replied uneasily. 'And I'll not be allowed to forget it. I'm certain of that. As sure as God made little apples Malacou will be coming through to me again and urging me to think of some way of getting those bits of mechanism to England.'

His prediction proved right. That night Malacou ceaselessly bombarded Gregory with his thoughts. He declared that the prize the Poles had secured was invaluable. His friend the engineer had managed to get away with the whole works and now knew how the rockets functioned. It was imperative that an aircraft be sent to pick him up and fly him with the mechanism to England. Then the rockets could also be made in Britain and Hitler would derive no overwhelming advantage by having sole possession of his secret weapon. The nearest village to the cottage was Rózan, and westward from it there ran a long stretch of good straight road along which there was never any traffic at night; so an aircraft could land on it. Gregory had only to let him know the night the aircraft would come in and they would be waiting for it. Three-quarters of an hour would be enough to load the stuff on to the 'plane. In that desolate area the risk of the Germans arriving on the scene while they were doing so was negligible. The aircraft could then take off again for England.

In the morning, still tired after his restless night and far from happy, Gregory telephoned the War Room to say he had an urgent matter to deal with so would not be in till midday. Then he went to Sir Pellinore. They had a lengthy talk, at the end of which with a heavy sigh the elderly Baronet rang up General Gubbins. Half an hour later, in Sir Pellinore's Rolls, they drove to Baker Street.

The little General, dapper as ever in the Bedford Cord riding breeches and well-polished field boots he affected, listened noncommittally to what they had to say, then he said:

'Of course telepathy has been scientifically proved, so it's pointless to argue about that; although I find it very difficult to believe that it could be maintained between two people continuously and over such a great distance. Frankly, I'd turn this proposition down flat had it to do with anything other than the rocket. But to find means of protecting ourselves from that is now an all-time high priority.

'It's not only London we have to think of; though God knows

the results it may have here are too ghastly to contemplate. It's the invasion ports as well. Monty is blazing off thousands of rounds every day. If the ports that are supplying him with shells and hundreds of other items could be rendered unusable, even for a week, he would be a dead duck. The beach-head he is holding is still narrow enough in all conscience and deprived of ammunition he could not possibly stop the Boche from driving his whole Army back into the Channel.

'In view of all that is at stake I'd be prepared to send an aircraft on a sortie to the moon if there were the least chance of its bringing back information which might scotch these hellish rockets. The devil of it is, though, that we have no down-to-earth means of communicating with these people. Since we can't arrange with them to put out recognition signals and be ready to receive our aircraft on a certain night, there can be no hope of such an operation succeeding. No pilot could even find the place.'

'No,' Gregory agreed heavily, 'but given moonlight I'm certain I could tell the pilot where to land; and it happens to be my bad luck that I am the only person capable of making the necessary arrangements with Malacou. I swore I'd never again set foot on German-held territory until the war was over, but on those two counts I see no alternative. I'll have to guide the pilot in and pick up the mechanism of the rocket myself.'

14

The Best-laid Schemes of Mice and Men . . .'

WHEN they began to discuss the operation the first thing Gregory learned was that he would have to make the flight from Brindisi in Italy. There was not much difference in the actual distance flying east from Suffolk or north from Brindisi to central Poland; but the latter route was preferable because an aircraft taking it ran less risk of encountering flak or enemy night fighters. All operations for dropping arms and supplies to Resistance groups in Poland, Czechoslovakia and Yugoslavia, as well as northern Italy which was still held by the enemy, were carried out by special squadrons under the command of Air Marshal Sir William Elliot, C.-in-C. Adriatic, whose headquarters were at Bari.

For there to be any chance at all of this hazardous operation succeeding it would be necessary to undertake it on a night when reasonable weather over Poland could be predicted and during the period of maximum moonlight which, that month, ran from the 23rd to the 29th. So it was agreed that Gregory should leave England on the 21st. Sir Pellinore telephoned Brigadier Jacob and arranged that Gregory should be relieved of his duties in the Cabinet War Room right away, then he telephoned Erika and asked her to come down to London on the afternoon train.

When they left General Gubbins's office Gregory went straight down to Gloucester Road, told the faithful Rudd that he was off on his travels again, then packed a bag and took a taxi up to Carlton House Terrace. Erika joined him that evening and when he broke the news to her about his new mission she did her best to hide her distress. He endeavoured to reassure her by stressing the fact that aircraft sent on such missions nearly always returned safely; and that, apart from the flight, he would be in danger only for an hour or so while picking up the parts of the V.2, and should be back in England within ten days of setting off. So during the next three days they did their best to forget this new peril he was about to face.

But that was far from easy, as he had to spend long periods endeavouring to secure from Malacou more precise information about the situation of the cottage and make arrangements with him for the landing.

After several such sessions Gregory was as satisfied as he could be in the circumstances. The cottage lay about twelve miles to the north-east of a fair-sized town named Pultusk, and this, together with the conformation of the rivers, should enable him to identify the second-class road from Rózan on which the aircraft was to land, provided there was a fair degree of moonlight. But the arrangements for the pick-up had to be left distinctly vague.

Although the road was hardly ever used at night, owing to the sabotage operations carried out by the Poles, S.D. men on motor-cycles patrolled a main road that was not far distant to the west; so to put out flares to guide the aircraft in would entail much too great a risk. Moreover, as Gregory could not specify the night on which the landing was to be made until shortly before the aircraft took off, at such short notice it would not be possible to muster a number of Polish partisans to help carry the heavy cases containing the rocket mechanism from the cottage to the 'plane, but between them they should be able to do the job in an hour at most; and on every evening from the 23rd Malacou would keep his mind free to receive a message from Gregory that he was on his way.

On Friday the 21st Gregory said his good-byes to Erika and Sir Pellinore. Both of them had an instinctive distrust of Malacou, so urged Gregory to exercise the greatest caution in his dealings with him and to run no unnecessary risks. To that he replied that in this affair Malacou was acting only as a medium for the Polish engineer, in whom they had every reason to have faith; and that as far as risks were concerned, if there were any signs that the aircraft might be caught while on the ground it would not land.

He left London by train for St. Evill in Cornwall. A Flight Sergeant met him on the platform and drove him to the R.A.F. Station. There he reported to the Station Commander, who took him to the mess for drinks and a meal. An hour and a half later he was on his way. After flying far out into the Atlantic the aircraft turned south-west and, without seeing any signs of enemy activity, landed him at Gibraltar. There he spent a few hours, then went on in another aircraft across the sunny waters of the western Mediterranean to arrive at Brindisi on the Adriatic shortly before midday on the 23rd.

A Group Captain took charge of him and it soon emerged that, like Gregory, as a young man his host had been a subaltern at the end of the First World War; so over drinks in the mess they began swapping reminiscences and got on famously. Later, when they discussed the forthcoming operation, the Group Captain told him that the worst headache to be faced was that it was still high summer. Aircraft dropping supplies for Resistance groups in Yugoslavia, or even Czechoslovakia, could leave after dark and return before dawn; but a trip to central Poland meant a five-hour flight each way and, allowing an hour for the pick-up, that meant that the aircraft could not leave Brindisi much after seven o'clock; so it would still be light enough for it to be spotted by German fighters when it passed over the northern Adriatic.

A Dakota with additional fuel tanks had been laid on for the job, and at a conference next day it was decided to guard against possible interception by sending a Liberator to escort it on the first part of its journey. At the conference Gregory met the crew of the Dakota that was to fly him in. The Captain of the aircraft was Wing Commander Frencombe of No. 267 Squadron, the pilot Flight Lieutenant Culliford, the navigator Flight Lieutenant Williams, the W/T operator Flight Sergeant Appleby, and a Polish Flying Officer, K. Szaajer, from the Polish Flight had been seconded to act as interpreter if necessary.

Everything had been made ready to carry out the operation that night but the Met. report was unfavourable, so with keyed-up nerves they waited to see if the next day would bring an improvement. It did, so on the evening of the 25th they made their final preparations. Soon after seven o'clock they went out on to the airfield. A last check-up was made on the Dakota KG.447 then, clad in windproof clothing and wrapped in rugs to keep them as warm as possible during their long cold journey, at 19.37 hours they took off.

While over the Adriatic they were spotted by German patrol-boats that carried anti-aircraft guns, but were flying sufficiently high to escape the flak that was loosed off at them. By half past eight they were over Yugoslavia and a little before ten o'clock when they were approaching Budapest, darkness having fallen, their escorting Liberator turned back and left them. With a steady hum the Dakota soughed on over Hungary and Czechoslovakia.

For a good part of the flight Gregory slept, then half an hour after midnight Flight Lieutenant Williams roused him to tell him that they were approaching their destination. The aircraft was steadily coming down from the great height at which it had been flying, so he took off his oxygen mask and went forward into the cockpit.

To check the features of the country far below with the map was anything but easy, as there were patches of drifting cloud that now and then obscured the moon for up to two minutes at a time, and when the moonlight did glint on water the whole of the area to the north-east of Warsaw was so intersected by the rivers Liwiec, Bug and Narew, with their many tributaries, that Gregory began to fear that he would not be able to identify the two forks between which lay Malacou's cottage.

For some fifteen minutes he and Williams peered down, sweeping the landscape with powerful night glasses, then the Flight Lieutenant said, 'We've overshot it. We must have by now,' and told the pilot to turn back.

The aircraft heeled over as Culliford brought her round. Just as he straightened out a pair of searchlights suddenly came into action away to the west and in wide arcs began to sweep the sky. As the Captain of the aircraft muttered a curse another pair opened up to the south, then a third pair almost immediately below them. It was evident that the German listening posts had picked up the sound of their engines.

The pilot banked the aircraft, then put her into a steep

dive. As Gregory righted himself from a lurch Williams shouted to reassure him. 'Our trips over Poland are so infrequent that there's a good chance they'll take us for one of theirs that has got off course. Unless they catch us in a beam and identify us as an enemy they won't shoot.'

Culliford had brought the aircraft down to five hundred feet, so it was now well below the angle at which the searchlights were sweeping. Two minutes later Gregory heard Malacou's voice as clearly as though he had been in the 'plane, calling, 'Here! Here! Come down! Come down!'

Staring earthward he suddenly recognized the bend in the big river near which the cottage lay, then the road to Rózan some way to the north of it. Putting one hand quickly on the pilot's shoulder, he pointed downward with the other. Culliford nodded, turned the aircraft in a wide sweep and shut off his engine. Slowly she sank, then, bumping only slightly, taxied to a halt on the long straight road that ran through the marshes.

Gregory, Williams and Szaajer scrambled out and looked quickly about them. A cloud had just obscured the moon again, but next moment they spotted a torch being flashed at intervals some quarter of a mile away. While the three of them ran towards it the others remained in the aircraft so that if need be it could make a quick getaway.

As they approached, the flashes from the torch ceased and they all drew their pistols in case they were walking into a trap. But Gregory went forward confidently, because for several hours past, except during his sleep in the aircraft, he had been concentrating on letting Malacou know that the pick-up was to be that night, and the occultist's clear call to him, only five minutes earlier, confirmed that his telepathic communication had been received.

The moon suddenly came out again and two figures emerged from a patch of tall reeds at the roadside. Malacou stepped forward and cried joyfully, 'Mr. Sallust, I knew that I could not be mistaken, and that you were on your way. It is a great relief that you have got here safely.' He then introduced his companion as the Polish engineer Mr. Kocjan.

When Gregory had introduced the others Kocjan, also speaking German, pointed at the searchlight beams and said quickly, 'Now that they have lost the sound of your engines they will know that the 'plane must have come down, and may suspect that it is British. It might have landed several miles from here, so there is no cause for panic. But, all the same, we must not lose a moment. Come; follow me.'

Turning, he led them at a loping run along a winding path fringed by tall fields of reeds and occasional patches of water. Ten minutes later they reached the cottage.

The windows were blacked-out, but an oil lamp was burning in the living room and Gregory saw that two men dressed in rough farm clothes were silently waiting there. As they came to their feet, Kocjan said:

'These are two of my brave fellows. There are many packages to carry to the 'plane so I wish I could have collected more men, but this was the best I could do at such short notice.'

Malacou, still breathing heavily from having had to run, stepped over to the stove and said, 'I thought that after your long flight you would be half frozen; so I have here some soup for you.' Pouring the steaming liquid into three bowls, he handed them to Gregory, Williams and Szaajer.

'It's very welcome,' Gregory smiled, and Szaajer broke off a conversation he had started with the two farm workers to bow his thanks. But Kocjan said abruptly, 'Drink quickly, please. We shall need every hand.' Then he signed to his helpers and they followed him out of the room.

While Gregory sipped at the scalding soup, Malacou confirmed in words the misfortunes that had befallen him during the past six months, giving a brief version of the thoughts he had conveyed by telepathy. As soon as they had finished he led them outside and round to a woodshed at the back of the cottage. It was lit by another oil lamp and Gregory saw that the two farm workers had already left with a first load. But Kocjan was there and the hunchback Tarik, who was helping him load a packing case on to a low, two-wheeled truck. Beyond them lay a pile of at least a score of roughly made crates and bundles. As Gregory's glance fell on them, he exclaimed uneasily in German:

'Good God, what a mass of stuff! If all that pile contains metal parts they must weigh a ton.'

'No, nothing like it,' grunted the Pole. 'It is the awkward shape of many pieces that makes them appear so bulky, and several of the cases contain documents we succeeded in stealing in a raid we made on a German headquarters. They may prove valuable, although not in the class of the rocket. We managed to prise off the tail, so have the whole works and have reason to be proud of our achievement.'

'You certainly have,' Gregory agreed. 'I'm only wondering if the aircraft can take it all. She's fitted with additional fuel tanks, of course; but she needs every gallon for her fourteen-hundred-mile flight here and back.' Then he turned to Williams and asked him in English what he thought.

The Flight Lieutenant shrugged. 'We have room enough for it, but there's more of it than I expected. If he is right about the pieces not weighing a great deal we'll make it.'

'Come now! You waste time talking,' cut in the Pole angrily. 'Do you not realize that those S.D. swine are now out hunting for us? Every moment counts. Grab anything you can lift, all of you, and hurry with it to the aircraft.'

The crate was now on the trolley and, at a stumbling run, he set off with it. The other four picked up loads and followed him. As Gregory staggered along with a big box balanced on his shoulder, he saw that the searchlight beams no longer raked the sky. That fact confirmed the Polish leader's statement that the enemy knew the 'plane must have landed and now had their patrols out searching for it on the ground.

Ten minutes later they reached the aircraft. Culliford had taxied it up as near as he could get to the path between the reeds, then turned it round ready to take off. The farm workers had already stowed their first loads in her and were about to return for others. Altogether they made a party of eight, but they all had to make two more trips before they had cleared the woodshed. By then, as the result of Gregory's exertions, his bad leg was beginning to pain him; and the aircraft had been on the ground for an hour and ten minutes.

By the time the last package had been stowed clouds had piled up so that the sky was three-quarters overcast, and Wing Commander Frencombe was a little worried that his pilot might not be able to keep to the road during the run-up for the take-off. He then suggested that the two farm hands should be given torches and asked to take up positions on either side of the road some way ahead of the aircraft. Szaajer translated the request and the two men agreed. They then said good-bye to their leader and the Polish Flying Officer went off with them in the direction of Rózan to show them exactly where they should stand.

Seeing that it would be some minutes before Szaajer returned, Gregory walked a little way along a path among the reeds to relieve himself from a pain in the stomach that he had been feeling during the past half-hour. Kocjan meanwhile climbed into the aircraft and Williams followed him. A minute later Gregory caught the sound of voices raised in an altercation. Then Frencombe shouted to him:

'Sallust, where are you! Your friend wants us to take him and his servant back with us. That wasn't in the understanding, was it?'

'No,' Gregory shouted back. 'Certainly not. I'll be with you in a minute.' Hastily he pulled up his trousers and ran towards the 'plane. On emerging from the reeds he saw that Malacou was half in and half out of the hatch, and clinging to it, while Tarik stood just below him.

Suddenly there came a shout from Szaajer, who by then was three hundred yards up the road. 'Take off! Take off! *Die Sicherheitspolizei* are coming.'

Under the wing of the aircraft Gregory glimpsed distant headlights approaching swiftly from the direction of Rózan and caught the roar of motor-cycle engines. In a mixture of German and French Malacou was pleading desperately with Frencombe, who was barring his way into the aircraft.

'Please! Please! You must take us! You must! This country is accursed. You cannot deny me the chance to leave it.'

'I can't,' Frencombe shouted at him. 'It was agreed that we should pick up Mr. Kocjan, because he's found out all about the rocket's mechanism. But no-one else. We've all the weight we can carry as it is. Let go, damn' you, so that Sallust can come aboard.'

The duty of the Captain of the aircraft was to save it at any cost from falling into the hands of the enemy. Its engine was already ticking over and next moment he snapped an order to his pilot. The engines burst into a roar and the Dakota began to quiver. Thrusting Tarik aside Gregory seized Malacou by the legs and dragged him from the hatch. They fell together in a heap.

As Gregory staggered to his feet, Frencombe cried, 'Come on! Come on! Quick!', then leant from the hatch and stretched out a hand to help him up. But Tarik, seeing his master attacked, gave an angry grunt, charged Gregory and grappled with him. It was no time for half-measures and, knowing the Turk's strength, Gregory kneed him hard in the groin. With another grunt, Tarik released his hold and doubled up.

By then the aircraft had begun to move. Swinging round, Gregory ran beside it. His bad leg began to give him gyp, but he was only a few feet behind the still-open hatch and Frencombe was yelling encouragement to him. As the Dakota bumped along the road its pace increased, but Gregory put on a desperate spurt and succeeded in clutching the lower rim of the hatch. For one wild minute he was dragged along while Frencombe knelt down to grasp his wrist. But just as their hands met the aircraft lifted. The force of the slipstream against which Gregory had been battling proved too great. His aching fingers lost their precarious hold. He fell to the road and rolled over and over into the reeds.

The roar of the aircraft's engines had drowned that of the approaching motor-cycles, but as it soared away he heard a burst of Sten-gun fire. Half stunned, he lay where he had rolled, partly submerged in shallow muddy water, wondering if the S.D. men had seen him. Excited shouts in German came from some fifty yards away, then the sounds of the motor-cycle engines and more shots, but they seemed further off, and gradually the purring receded into the distance. Crawling out of the marsh he looked about him.

The moon had come out again, but the aircraft had disappeared and the road was empty. He realized that after shooting at the Dakota as she took off the S.D. men must have turned their machines about, pursued her as far as they could, still firing, and by now were searching for Szaajer and the two farm hands, whom they must have seen in their headlights.

For the wretched position in which he found himself his only consolation was that there was now a good hope that the Dakota with its precious cargo would get home safely.[1]

Walking back to the place where he had left Malacou, he called to him at first softly then louder. He received no reply so it was evident that while he was still hiding among the reeds Malacou, Tarik, Szaajer and the two farm hands had all made off into the marshes and were now well away from the road.

Crossing it, he made his way some distance along the path that led to the cottage then, in a well-sheltered spot, sat down to consider his position.

It could hardly have been worse. He had had no chance to ask Frencombe to return and pick him up the following night, or on the next when conditions were suitable. Yet, as he thought of that, he decided that even if he had it was unlikely that the Wing Commander would have agreed. Now that the Germans in that area had been alerted it was certain that they would keep a sharp look-out for further landings; so for Frencombe to return would have meant the crew running their heads into a noose. Grimly, Gregory faced the fact that he was stuck there and would have to make his way home by whatever way he could.

Suddenly it crossed his mind that it was now early morning on the 26th, a derivative of the fatal 8 which Malacou had declared to be so unlucky for him. It was on the 17th, another 8, eleven months before, that he had been overtaken by disaster at Peenemünde. His evil number had caught up with him again, but he strove to ignore this unlucky omen and again to regard his situation objectively.

When he had set out he had known there was a risk that the aircraft might be shot down or that they might be surprised while loading the parts of the rocket into it, but he had never visualized himself being left stranded in Poland, and although he could pass anywhere as a German he could not do so as a Pole. He had not even a smattering of the language; so his only

1. Historical note: In this way a V.2 mechanism was brought to England, but the gallant Polish engineer who secured it returned to Poland where he was caught by the Gestapo and executed on August 19th of that year.

asset was that, under the roomy flying kit that he had left in
the aircraft, he had been wearing old but good-quality country
clothes in which he would be inconspicuous.

Two things caused him special anxiety. The first was that
the Germans would be scouring the district for anyone who
might have landed from the aircraft and, if challenged, he had
no papers to show; neither was there any means of transport by
which he could get out of the danger area while it was still
dark. The second was even more serious. As it had not even
crossed his mind that he might be left behind he had not
brought any Polish money with him. For that omission he
cursed himself roundly, as he felt that he should at least have
foreseen that the aircraft might be shot down and, if he survived, find himself in more or less his present situation.

His mind naturally turned to Malacou. Placing himself in
the occultist's shoes, he tried to divine how the middle-aged
Jew would react to his near escape from capture. It seemed
probable that he was still hiding somewhere not far off in the
marshes. But he could not remain there indefinitely. He would
have either to resume his unhappy search for a new refuge or
return to his cottage and, when the S.D. men paid it a visit,
as they certainly would, trust in his ability to persuade them
that he knew nothing about the Polish Resistance group or the
landing of the aircraft.

Even if he made use of the rest of the night to put as great a
distance as possible between himself and his cottage he could
not get far on foot; so there was still a chance that he would be
picked up next day. And if he were the very fact of his flight
would be taken as proof of his guilt. Therefore it seemed he
would stand a better chance if he stayed put and gambled on
being able to bluff things out. If he had decided to take that
line it followed that the sooner he got back to his cottage the
better, so that he would be in bed and, apparently, asleep
when the S.D. men arrived.

It then occurred to Gregory that somewhere in the cottage
Malacou would almost certainly have hidden a considerable
sum of money against an emergency and it was money, above
all else, that he himself needed at the moment. If Malacou was
there he could be persuaded to part with some of it; if not,

the place could be ransacked until it was found. As against that, going to the cottage would entail a certain degree of danger, as the S.D. men might already be there or come on the scene while the money was being searched for. But after weighing the pros and cons for a few moments Gregory decided to risk that.

Getting to his feet, he set off along the path. At intervals other paths led off from it, and for a while he feared he would lose his way. But he had made the trip three times that night, so only once got off the right track. Shortly after having got back on to it, he caught sight of the roof of the cottage silhouetted against the night sky.

Cautiously he approached it. The door stood open and a faint light from it dimly lessened the surrounding gloom. It seemed unlikely that Malacou would have left the door open, so the inference was that the S.D. men had already visited the place and either found it empty or carried him off. Still treading with great care, although he now believed the cottage to be deserted, Gregory continued to advance and stepped into the small, square hall. The light was coming from an inch-wide crack down the edge of the living-room door, which had been left ajar. Just as he was about to push it open he heard a gruff voice say in German:

'Talk, you Jewish pig, or it will be the worse for you.'

For an instant Gregory remained standing with his hand raised, as if frozen. Only by the man speaking at that moment had he been saved from blundering in and almost certainly being shot down. The scene being enacted in the room leapt to his mind as clearly as if he could see it through the door. The S.D. men had caught Malacou there and were questioning him. Next minute the occultist's voice came in a tremulous whine:

'I tell you I know nothing. I was about to go go bed. I swear it!'

'At three o'clock in the morning?' sneered the German. 'You lie! You had just . . .'

Gregory lost the rest of the sentence. With infinite caution he had stepped back. Turning, he stole away in the direction from which he had come. The snatch of conversation he had

overheard made it clear that the S.D. men had arrived before
Malacou had had time to get his clothes off. The irony of it
was that he often stayed up until the small hours making involved calculations from his astral charts and pondering over
occult operations. But the Nazis would never believe that.
And they would now treat his Turkish passport as so much
waste paper. They would haul him off to a concentration
camp and beat the truth out of him with steel rods. He would be
lucky if he escaped the gas chamber. Gregory could only pity
him, for he was far from owing him anything; and any attempt
to rescue him would have meant a more than fifty-fifty chance
of being killed himself.

Next moment, struck by a sudden thought, he pulled up.
The S.D. men's motor-cycles must be somewhere nearby.
Turning about, he padded softly round to the back of the
building. There, propped up on their stands and with lights
out, at the entrance to a dirt track road that presumably led
to Rózan, stood the two machines. His heart suddenly lifted.
One, at least, of his urgent problems had been solved. He had
only to sabotage one of the machines, then ride off on the
other, to be well clear of the district before dawn.

As he took another step forward a terrified shout came from
the cottage. At the sound he halted again. He was standing
within two feet of a clapboard wall that formed the far side
of the living room and could well imagine what must now be
happening in there.

Setting his mouth grimly, he advanced towards the nearer
motor-cycle, thinking as he did so that it might just as easily
have been himself who was being beaten up. Had it been,
Malacou, with his dread of physical violence, would certainly
not have attempted to rescue him. No; it was bad enough that
his contact with the occultist had led to his becoming stranded
and penniless many hundreds of miles from any escape route
to a neutral country. He would need all the resource and
stamina he possessed to keep clear of trouble himself.

When he was within six feet of the machine, a piercing scream
rang out. Again he halted in his tracks. That hideous sound
could mean only one thing. Those swinish Germans were not
merely beating up the unfortunate Jew; they had started in to

wring a confession from him. Gregory's stomach seemed to turn over. Yet, horrible as was the mental picture of Malacou being tortured, he steeled himself to ignore it.

Another scream echoed through the silent night. A cold sweat broke out on Gregory's forehead. He was seized by a fit of nausea and closed his eyes. A moment later he told himself that the ghastly treatment now being meted out to Malacou could be no worse than that inflicted on hundreds of other people in the countries over which the beast named Hitler ruled. After a few seconds he opened his eyes and had got hold of himself again. With renewed resolution he advanced to the motor-cycle and knelt down beside it with the intention of removing the sparking plug. As he reached out for the leather toolbag behind the saddle he realized that his hands were slimy with sweat and trembling so much that he could not undo its buckle.

Scream after scream came from the cottage. Gregory was shaken by a shudder. In a hoarse voice he let out an unprintable Italian oath that he used only at times of extreme distress. Then he began to curse Malacou. The occultist had been no more to him than a chance acquaintance met with in the course of a secret mission. He was a practitioner of bestial rites, had forced his daughter to commit incest with him and had driven her to suicide. He had robbed the von Alterns and by his evil machinations brought about Herman Hauff's death. He had held Gregory at Sassen against his will and to protect himself had even been prepared to murder him rather than let him fall alive into the hands of the Nazis. Lastly, that very night it had been his attempt to get away from Poland that had landed Gregory in this wretched situation. Few people could have less claim to Gregory's pity, let alone by his misfortune saddle him with the moral responsibility of attempting his rescue at the peril of his own life.

Frantic to get away and be done with this nightmare episode, Gregory continued to fumble with the tool satchel. He got the buckle undone but his sweaty fingers could not find the spanner needed to unscrew the sparking plug. Yet to ride off on one machine and leave the other still capable of functioning would, he knew, immensely reduce his chances of evading capture.

As he knelt there Malacou's whimpering cries continued to come clearly to him. Punctuated by brief intervals during which even his choking gasps for breath could be faintly heard, he gave tongue to imprecations, long-drawn-out groans and gabbled pleading. Gregory's hands dropped to his sides and he stood up. However evil and worthless the man who was being tortured, he could stand it no longer.

Yet his sudden decision to intervene, whatever the cost to himself, did not prevent him from exercising his habitual caution. Planting each foot carefully, so that its crunch was barely audible, he walked round the house. When he reached the front door he got out and cocked his automatic. Stepping softly into the hall, he peered through the inch-wide crack between the door-jamb and the living-room door. The sight that he glimpsed through it did not surprise him. It served only to harden his cold rage against those thousands of Germans whom Hitler had turned into beasts more ferocious and pitiless than any to be met with in the wildest jungle.

Although to him it had seemed an age, probably less than two minutes had elapsed since he had heard Malacou's first screams; so the wretched man had not yet fainted from the agony to which he was being subjected. One square-faced blond young brute was holding the Jew's arms pinioned behind his back, while the other, who had his back to Gregory, was holding a cigarette lighter under Malacou's chin.

With his left hand Gregory thrust the door wide open. Lifting his right, he shot the nearer Nazi through the back of the head. In a second the tableau dissolved into a mass of whirling arms and legs. The head of the shot man jerked forward and spurted blood. Then he crashed to the floor. The other thug released Malacou and grabbed for his gun. Malacou, maddened by pain, his eyes starting from his head, heaved himself forward, tripped on the fallen Nazi then cannoned into Gregory. At the moment they collided Gregory fired his second shot. The man who had been holding Malacou had his pistol out but had not had time to take aim. To escape Gregory's shot he flung himself sideways, crashed heavily into a dresser at that side of the room, failed to recover his balance and fell sprawling on top of his dead comrade.

For a moment Gregory had been in complete command of the situation. But only for a moment. Malacou's blind charge to get through the door and escape had thrown him, too, off balance. Just as he fired, Malacou, with arms flung wide, had come hurtling at him. His pistol hand was knocked up and sideways. With a sickening thud it hit the door-jamb, breaking the skin of his knuckles. He gave a gasp of pain and the pistol dropped from his nerveless fingers.

Malacou, bellowing with fear and pain, ducked beneath his outstretched arm, brushed past him and, still howling, dashed through the front door out into the darkness. Even as Gregory cursed the Jew his eyes remained fixed on the surviving Nazi. He had scrambled to his knees and still held his gun. Before he could lift it Gregory leapt forward and kicked him in the face.

With a yelp he went over backwards. His pistol exploded and the bullet brought some of the china crashing down from the dresser. Losing not a second Gregory stepped over the body of the man he had shot and, as the other Nazi came up on his knees, kicked him in the crotch. From his bleeding mouth there issued an agonized wail, his eyes seemed about to start from his head, he dropped his gun, clutched at his testicles and bent right forward. Berserk with hatred for these blond beasts that Hitler had let loose upon the world, Gregory kicked the man's head with his heavy shoe then, after he had slid to the floor, kicked it again and again until it was a mass of blood with the temple stove in and he was undoubtedly dead.

When Gregory at last ceased kicking a sudden silence descended on the cottage. Breathing hard from his exertions he stood there surveying the shambles about him. Gradually, as he sucked the bleeding knuckles of his right hand, his frenzy subsided. He felt no compunction for what he had done; only a sense of relief that he had emerged victorious and without serious injury from such a violent and uneven conflict. Walking to the door he shouted for Malacou, but there came no reply. Evidently the pain-crazed Jew had made off in the darkness and was hiding somewhere in the marshes. In view of what had taken place in the cottage it now seemed unlikely that he would again risk returning to it.

As Gregory stood there in the open doorway he suddenly recalled the foreknowledge about which the occultist had been so greatly concerned when at Sassen. His stars had foretold that at about this time in 1944 he would be in grave danger of death, but would be saved by Gregory. At the thought Gregory grinned wryly. The prophecy had come true. All against his better judgement he had found himself compelled to rescue Malacou. But whether, now that he was again on the run, he would succeed in evading capture was quite another matter. Whether he did or not meant nothing to Gregory. Brushing the Jew from his mind, he turned back into the cottage to deal with matters there.

He thought it unlikely that the two dead S.D. men would be missed until early in the morning, when they would be due to report before going off duty. Soon afterwards the country would be scoured for them and all lonely buildings in the area searched. But the longer the time that elapsed before their bodies were discovered the longer it would be before they were known to be dead, and a general call sent out giving the numbers of their motor-cycles with urgent orders to arrest anyone found using one of them. Therefore, Gregory reasoned, if he put in an hour's hard work now, removing all signs of the struggle from the cottage and hiding the bodies in the marshes, he might delay for several hours the whole countryside becoming alive with police and troops on the look-out for him.

He stood for a moment looking down on the two dead men, then ran quickly through their pockets, taking their wallets and loose change. They were much of a size and he judged both to be an inch or two taller than himself. The man whom he had shot through the back of the head had blood all over his tunic; the other, although badly battered about the face and head, had bled comparatively little. Choosing the latter, Gregory set about the grim task of stripping him of his uniform. When he had got it off he dragged the body in a fireman's lift up across his shoulders. Bent nearly double under the weight, he carried it about fifty yards along the path by which he had come to the cottage, then for a further fifteen along a side turning on one side of which water glistened faintly between tall patches of reeds. After pausing for a minute to regain his breath, he exerted all his strength and heaved the body as far into the reeds as he could.

Returning, he collected a torch that had been part of the man's equipment and a big jug from the living-room dresser, then went round to examine the two motor-cycles. The tanks of both were well over half full, so he drew off enough from one to fill the other, then wheeled the partly empty one round to the front of the cottage. Leaving it there on its stand, he carried out the second body and sprawled it across the machine. Having satisfied himself that it would not fall off, he wheeled the motor-cycle with its gruesome load down to the place where he had thrown the first body into the water. Another heave and the second body followed the first. Upending the motor-cycle so that only the back wheel touched the ground he ran that into the water as far as he dared then let it crash down on top of the two bodies.

As the splash resounded he stood back gasping to survey his handiwork. The mudguard and part of the rear wheel of the machine still showed above the water, but there was nothing he could do about that. Anyone passing there in daylight could hardly fail to notice the partially submerged motor-cycle but only a small patch of reeds had been broken down and the marshes covered a wide area, so it might be several days before the bodies were found; and Gregory's purpose would be served if the S.D. men's fate remained uncertain for twenty-four hours.

His exertions had tired him terribly and his leg was paining him badly again, but he had now completed the most laborious part of the task he had set himself. Mopping the sweat from his forehead, he returned to the cottage at a slow walk. In a corner cupboard of the living room he found a bottle of Polish Cherry Liqueur and poured himself a good tot. It was poor stuff, made from potato spirit, and he needed no warming up, but it lent him new vigour for his further activities.

Lighting the oil stove he put a saucepan of water on to boil. While it was heating up he collected the pieces of broken china and hid them above the eyeline on the top of the dresser, then changed into the uniform of the S.D. man whom he had stripped. Under one of the beds in the bedroom he found a suitcase and a hold-all. The latter being better suited to his purpose, he packed his own clothes in it, adding to them shaving and washing things that had belonged to either the Pole or Malacou, a soft Tyrolese hat with a feather in the band and such oddments of food as he found in the larder.

By that time the water was boiling. With a bucket and sponge he got down on his knees and, blessing the fact that the floorboards were covered with cheap linoleum, cleaned up the spilt blood. That done, he set about hunting for the reserve of money that he felt sure Malacou would have hidden somewhere about the cottage. Taking care to disturb things as little as possible, he searched every drawer and cupboard, looked behind the books in a small bookcase and for a loose brick in the hearth, then with a smooth skewer from the kitchen he prodded the pillows and mattresses, hoping to hear the rustle of bank notes. He had no luck, except in finding a map of Poland that would prove useful.

As a last resort he went through to a small slip room which he guessed had been occupied by Tarik. While hurriedly running through the hunchback's few poor belongings he wondered what had become of him; but could only assume that after they had all been surprised on the road either he had not returned to the cottage or, if he had, on the arrival of the S.D. men he had panicked and fled. Either way, it seemed a fair bet that, like Malacou, he was somewhere out on the marshes. Owing to the strong psychic bond that linked them, it seemed probable that by this time he had found his master and was striving to comfort him after the ordeal through which he had passed.

Gregory's search of Tarik's room did not yield even a few Polish *kopecs* or German *Pfennige* and a glance at his watch showed him that it was now nearly half past three; so he decided that he must abandon his hunt for any hoard that Malacou might have concealed in the cottage. That there was a round sum of money hidden there somewhere he would have bet his last shilling; but it now seemed certain that it had been secreted under the floorboards or somewhere in the thatch of the roof, and he could not possibly give the time to such thorough explorations.

Swiftly checking through the money he had taken from the two Nazis he found it amounted to eighty-four *Reichsmarks* and seven *Pfennige*, together with a few small-denomination Polish notes for which he had no use. That was the equivalent of about £7 10*s*. in English money; so would keep him only for a few days and was hopelessly inadequate for any attempt to get out of German-held territory. But it was better than nothing.

Still furious that his prospects of eluding his enemies should be so heavily handicapped by his failure to find Malacou's hoard, he quickly set the living-room furniture to rights so that no-one entering it would now have grounds for suspecting that a fight to the death had recently taken place there. Then he put out the oil lamp and, closing the front door behind him, went round to the back of the building.

At intervals, between his most strenuous exertions during the past hour, he had been trying to make up his mind on the best course to pursue. Lacking a solid sum to offer as a bribe, he felt certain that he had very little chance of persuading a skipper in one of the Baltic ports to run him over to Sweden. For a while he had contemplated the route Kuporovitch had taken, from Kiel up the Little Belt and across Denmark; but Kiel was over five hundred miles away and lack of money would again prove an obstacle almost impossible to overcome. The frontier of Switzerland was still more distant, and that of Spain obviously out of the question.

The more he thought about it, the more convinced he became that money was the key to his problem. Without ready cash to distribute as need be he was like a boxer who has been handcuffed. Somehow he had to have funds, and considerable funds at that. But how could he possibly secure them? Not by remaining in the countryside. That was evident. Trees that grow golden apples flourish only in towns. They were banks, prosperous businesses and rich people who had big money and could be persuaded or tricked into parting with a wad of it.

He must, then, make for a city. And there was another advantage in that. Once the hunt was up the roads would all be scanned for him and the stolen motor-cycle, whereas in a city he would be able to lose himself in the crowds. But to go to

Warsaw was no good, or to any other Polish city, since he could not speak Polish and he must get out of Poland as soon as possible. Czechoslovakia was no good either. To establish a new identity that would hold water he must get into Germany.

His mind ranged over the map which from long study he was able to visualize easily. In the north one city stood out beyond all others. It was the German capital.

For a moment Gregory shied away from the idea of endeavouring to seek safety in the heart of the Nazi Reich, for in it were concentrated the headquarters of every police organization that played a part in controlling Hitler's empire. Then an episode in a story he had read many years before recurred to him. It was by that great short-story writer C. E. Montague, and opened with the small son of a British Ambassador playing in an Embassy garden. He had been given a tortoise and his nurse said that beyond all things to eat tortoises loved cockroaches. A cockroach was procured, presumably from the Embassy kitchen, and set down in front of the tortoise like an early Christian before a lion. Realizing its peril, the cockroach lost not a second but leapt into the armpit of the tortoise, thus making it impossible for the tortoise to snap it up.

Having strapped the hold-all containing his clothes on to the motor-cycle behind the saddle, Gregory kicked the starter, mounted the machine and set off for Berlin.

15

The Armpit of the Tortoise

THE track ran north-east and after bumping along it for a mile and a half he found that it came out on the road to Rózan. Turning west he increased his speed and two minutes later passed the place where the aircraft had landed. A few miles further on he struck the oroad main road where it made a sharp angle. During the past week he had imprinted on his mind a map of the area, so he knew that the left-hand fork led south to Pultusk and Warsaw. Thinking it wise to keep well away from the more highly populated area round the capital, he swung right and, now that his powerful machine had a good surface to move on, roared away to the north.

After about six miles he passed through a silent village, and another twelve brought him to a small town that he decided must be Przasnysz. There the trunk road continued straight on through the market square but, feeling that he was now sufficiently far north of Warsaw, he took a side turning that led west.

Now that he was over thirty miles away from Malacou's cottage he was entering territory that he had not memorized; so a little way outside the town he pulled up, got out the map he had found at the cottage, shone his torch on it and spent some minutes studying it for the best route to take. He saw that the second-class road he was now on wound about considerably, but its general direction was westward and in a little over twenty miles would bring him to the town of Mlawa. From there it curved north-west through two villages, then ran west again to the railway junction of Brodnica.

When he reached Mlawa the summer dawn was breaking and there were lights in the windows of some of the houses, but no-one was yet about. A church clock struck five as he passed on his way out of the town. For the next hour he still met no traffic, but from some of the farms men and women were trudging off to work. At about half past six he entered Brodnica. There were a few people in the streets and a Polish policeman on duty in the square; but after a hasty glance at him everyone looked quickly away, afraid, he guessed, that he might see in their eyes the hatred they had for everyone in the uniform he was wearing.

From Brodnica he took the road to the provincial city of Turum, which lay another forty miles away to the south-west. Owing to petrol rationing the road continued to be free of traffic except for an occasional farmer's cart, but by the time he was half-way to Turum he was feeling very tired. A little less than twelve hours had elapsed since he had left Brindisi in the aircraft, and he had slept for a good part of the flight, but the past five hours had put a great strain upon him. Although it was eleven months since his leg had been smashed it continued to be a disability when used in strenuous exertions. Disposing of the two S.D. men's bodies had taken a lot out of him and between half past three and seven o'clock he had covered over a hundred and ten miles.

He would have given a lot to lie up for a few hours somewhere that side of Turum, but he felt it imperative to take the utmost advantage of the lead he had secured; so he made up his mind to keep going until he had passed through the provincial city. He reached its outskirts about seven-thirty. By now, although it was most unlikely that the bodies of the S.D. men would have yet been found, it was possible that their failure to report had led to a general call being put out for them; so, as a precaution against the number of his motor-cycle being noted, instead of going through the city centre, where it was certain that traffic policemen would be on duty, he turned off to the right and made a wide detour through the suburbs until he got on to the main highway that led to the city of Bydgoszcz.

As soon as he was clear of Turum he began to look about for a suitable place to lie up during the day; but, as so often happens when looking for a good place to picnic, his luck was out. The country was as flat as a pancake and open fields stretched away on both sides of the road as far as the eye could see. With faultless rhythm the machine carried him on mile after mile until he was so weary that he feared that he would not be able to control it for much longer, and it was not until he was within twelve miles of Bydgoszcz that he drew near a wood that would serve his purpose.

Slowing down, he turned off up a track through the trees, then began to look about for a place where he might hope to sleep for a few hours without anyone coming upon him.

Several hundred yards from the road he reached a wooden bridge over a small stream. Having dismounted and scrambled down to the water's edge he found that there was just enough room to conceal the motor-cycle under the bridge on one bank and for him to stretch out and sleep on the other. To get the heavy machine down and into its temporary garage took all his remaining strength. Straining and cursing, he managed it; then unrolled the hold-all to lie upon and used the country clothes in which he had flown out from England as a pillow.

In the five hours since he had left Malacou's cottage he reckoned that he had covered some hundred and sixty miles, so he was well out of the danger area and felt he could consider himself extremely lucky. His main worry for the moment was the thought of Erika's distress when she learned that he had not returned with the aircraft. At the moment, as it was half past eight, he thought it certain that she would be awake. Visualizing her in bed at Gwaine Meads, he thought of her with love and longing; but he was so exhausted that after a few moments he fell fast asleep.

When he awoke a glance at his watch showed him that it was getting on for four o'clock in the afternoon, so he had slept for over seven hours. Although he felt much refreshed his bad leg was very stiff, and it was not until he had exercised it gently for some minutes that he turned his thoughts to other matters. Anxious as he was to put more miles between himself and Rózan, he decided that, now the hunt must be up for the missing men, it would be wiser not to make another start until dusk had fallen; for after dark there would be much less likelihood of a policeman chancing to notice the number on the motor-cycle and connecting it with any call that had gone out.

He felt ravenously hungry but the only food he had found in the cottage larder was the half of a small wild duck, a lump of sausage, a thin wedge of cheese and a loaf of rye bread. Putting aside the duck and cheese for his dinner, he slowly masticated some of the coarse bread and sausage then made a more thorough examination of the two S.D. men's wallets. Both contained permits to buy petrol, but he knew that if he produced one of them at a garage the number on the card would be entered in a book and he would have to sign for the petrol in the name of the man to whom it had been issued. Sooner or later such a forgery would be discovered, giving away the direction in which the stolen machine had been driven, and enabling the garage man to give a description of him and that might prove his undoing. His strongest card was that although every effort would be made to trace the machine, unless Malacou was caught and squealed the police could not have the faintest idea what the person who had made off on it was like. To protect this most valuable anonymity he decided not to use either of the permits unless all other ways of securing a further supply of petrol failed.

In both wallets there were also identity cards, but to have made use of one of them would have been acutely dangerous, as the names of the missing men would, anyway for the next few days, be in the minds of every policeman in north Germany. However, as he was wearing the uniform of an S.D. trooper no-one, other than an S.D. officer, had the authority to challenge him, and it was very unlikely that he would run into one until he reached Berlin. In the capital, though, as the badges he was wearing would show that he belonged to a formation stationed in occupied Poland, he might well be challenged and if he were the fat would be in the fire.

This thought made him wonder if it would not be wisest to put on his civilian clothes while he had the chance, but the uniform was such an excellent protection from any form of interference while on the road that he decided not to change out of it as yet.

As he had nothing else with which to occupy himself, the

next few hours seemed interminable. He thought a lot of
Erika, wondered what had happened to Malacou and cursed
the day he had met him; then speculated on possible ways of
obtaining money when he reached Berlin, but gave that up as
futile for the present.

At length the shadows began to fall. Still hungry after his
last unsatisfactory meal he ate the rest of the rye bread and
every shred of the duck, then set about the job of getting the
motor-cycle up the steep bank of the stream. Slipping, holding,
cursing, it took him a good ten minutes, and when he did get
the heavy machine on to the level he had to sit down for a
while to recover from his efforts. Then, kicking the engine into
life, he wheeled it, just ticking over, to within twenty feet of the
road. Having made certain that nothing was approaching from
either direction, he mounted it and set off.

He still had another twelve miles to go to Bydgoszcz and
the petrol in his tank was getting very low, so he was
uneasily aware that somehow, soon, he would have to get it
filled up. Slowing down at two villages through which he passed,
he kept a sharp look-out for a possible source of supply but,
apart from garages, failed to find one. By that time he was
nearing Bydgoszcz and was getting worried; so when, outside a
fair-sized villa on the outskirts of the town, he saw a car, he
pulled up beside it, dismounted and sounded the klaxon.

After a few minutes a short plump, elderly man came out of
the house, walked down the garden path and asked him in
German what he wanted. In the harsh, dictatorial voice habitual
to S.D. thugs, Gregory said that he had run right out of petrol
and must have some. The man suggested that he should go on
into the town and, as it was only a little after nine o'clock,
knock up a garage. Gregory replied that his tank was almost
drained, that he was on urgent duty and could not afford the
delay should his machine fail before he reached the pump.
The man protested that he was a doctor and about to visit
a bad case at a farm some miles away, so could not spare any
petrol. Gregory said he could not help that. Petrol he must
have, and at once. He would give the doctor a chit to secure
more, but unless he met the demand he would find himself in
trouble.

Under the threat the doctor quailed, became ingratiatingly polite and hurried back to the house to fetch a piece of rubber tubing. While he was absent Gregory took from the breast pocket of his uniform a notebook and fountain pen and scribbled on one of the pages: *Commandeered from Herr Doktor ——, seventeen litres of petrol for urgent requirements,* then signed it: *Albrecht Schmidt, No. 4785 Sicherheitsdienst.* Ten minutes later the petrol had been siphoned from the tank of the doctor's car into the tank of the motor-cycle and Gregory had filled in the doctor's name on the chit.

During this transaction Gregory kept the peak of his uniform cap pulled well down over his eyes and, the light from the headlamps by which it had been carried out having been well below the level of his face, he felt sure that the plump doctor, if ever called on to give a description of him, would be able to give only a very vague one. With an abrupt word of thanks, he set off again to go through Bydgoszcz.

By luck he found a bypass that took him round it to the entrance of an autobahn signposted 'Berlin'. He roared along it for sixty miles. Then it joined the Danzig-Berlin highway with a signpost that said 'Berlin 160 Kilometres'. Down it he continued to let the powerful machine rip, and when he had covered three-quarters of the distance he could see a glow in the sky ahead that was evidently over Berlin.

As he drew nearer he realized that an air-raid was in progress. The glow was from fires and the scores of searchlights that swept the sky. A myriad tiny sparks flickered at the extremities of the beams as hundreds of anti-aircraft shells exploded, and in the distance he caught the continuous rumble made by the crashing of the bombs. By the time he neared the end of the autobahn the raid was over and only a lurid glare from raging fires lit the sky.

By then it was half past one in the morning. Slowing down, he looked out for a suitable spot in which to abandon the motor-cycle. Not finding one he took a side turning to the north along which, interspersed among fields, back lots and orchards, there were small factories and short rows of small houses. A mile or so along it he came to a humpbacked bridge beneath which ran a railway culvert.

Pulling up at the side of the road he took a screwdriver from the tool kit, removed the number plates from the machine and put them in his pockets. Then, making certain that no-one was about, he wheeled the motor-cycle some distance off the road, unstrapped the hold-all and pushed the machine over the brick edge of the culvert, so that it crashed on to the railway line fifteen feet below. Pleased by the thought that the next train that passed would render Germany the poorer by one powerful motor-cycle and that, with luck, it might even derail itself, he picked up the hold-all and returned to the road. Five minutes later he threw the number plates into a deep ditch which was screened by a fine crop of nettles.

He now felt very tired and after half an hour's tramp through the blacked-out deserted streets of the suburb he was limping again. But about two o'clock he came upon the sort of place for which he was looking. It was an unpretentious inn, somewhat older than the majority of the buildings in the neighbourhood, with a tea garden beside it and large enough to have eight or ten bedrooms.

Several minutes of ringing and knocking roused and brought down the landlord, a very fat, elderly man with a patch over one eye, wearing a threadbare dressing gown. After giving him a Nazi salute and a loud '*Heil Hitler*', Gregory said in a disgruntled voice:

'I'm on leave from Hamburg. My girl lives in this neighbourhood and I'd planned to spend my leave with her. But she left her digs two days ago and her letter telling me where she's moved to must have missed me. Her bloody landlady either doesn't know or won't tell me on account of a quarrel they had, and I've spent half the night trying to trace her without any luck. I'll find her tomorrow through mutual friends, but I've been up since five this morning, so I want a room to sleep in.'

The landlord shook his head. 'I'm sorry, *Herr Reiter*, I'd be pleased to oblige you. But the bombing has destroyed so many people's homes that every room I've got is taken.'

'*Teufel nochmal!*' Gregory groaned. 'What hellish luck. Still, it can't be helped. As I'm nearly out on my feet I'll doss down on a sofa in your lounge.'

To that the landlord readily agreed, ushered him in and

locked up again. As they passed through the saloon bar
Gregory noticed two glass covers with *Brötchen* under them
and a jar of biscuits. Announcing that he would have a snack
before going to sleep he asked the man to fix him a double
brandy and Apollinaris.

While Gregory munched and drank they carried on a
desultory conversation. The landlord asked how things were
in Hamburg and Gregory told him that the bombing had been
perfectly bloody. His companion replied that the bombing had
been perfectly bloody in Berlin, too. Then, obviously for
Gregory's benefit, he endeavoured, not very successfully, to
say how convinced he was that the Allies would soon be driven
out of France and the war brought to a victorious conclusion
by the Führer's 'Secret Weapons'.

Having eaten his fill Gregory asked the man what he owed
him, then took out his wallet and paid. As he did so he fixed
the landlord with a steady stare, silently daring him to ask for
a ration slip. To ignore regulations of that kind would, he
knew, be in keeping with his role as an S.D. trooper, and the
man accepted his abuse of his uniform without comment.
Eager to please, he offered to find a rug for Gregory to wrap
himself in, but the night was warm, so Gregory told him not
to bother. Five minutes later he had stretched out on a sofa in
the inn parlour and the landlord was on his way back to bed.

As an old soldier Gregory possessed the ability to wake near
any hour on which he had set his mind and before he dropped
off he set his mental alarm clock for half past five. Rousing at
that hour he felt stale and shivery, but he found the cloakroom
and a wash revived him. In there he also shaved in cold water
and changed from the uniform into his own clothes, packing
the uniform into the hold-all; but he stowed the shaving kit
into one of his pockets.

In the bar, on the old principle that when in enemy territory
one should live off the land, he helped himself to a pint flagon
of *Branntwein* and stuffed his pockets with as many *Brötchen*
and biscuits as he could get into them. Then, shortly before six
o'clock, still carrying the hold-all, he quietly let himself out of
the front door.

He had entered the capital from the north-east, and although he knew the centre of the city well his knowledge of the metropolitan area was only rudimentary. He was aware that its equivalent to London's East End lay in Moabit and Charlottenburg, and that the rich lived further out to the south and west, mainly in the exclusive suburb of Dahlem or on pleasant properties along the east bank of a long stretch of water known as the Havel, at the extremity of which lay Potsdam. But of Berlin north of the River Spree he knew nothing so, taking the sun for a guide, he headed south.

Now that daylight had come he found his surroundings more than ever depressing. Unlike the English and the Dutch, the Germans have never been keen gardeners so, although it was high summer, there was hardly a flower to be seen in front of the long rows of small houses and blocks of workers' flats. Here and there along the road there was a factory, to which men and women were now cycling up in droves to start on the day shift, or a line of still-closed shops. Every few hundred yards buildings had been reduced to rubble by the bombing, and several times he had to turn down a side street because the main road was closed owing to time bombs dropped in a recent raid.

Whenever he had to turn off course he veered to the west and, after a time, found himself in the broad Friedrichstrasse. Proceeding down it, he reached the bridge over the Spree. In the middle of the bridge he halted, put his hold-all on the stone coping and stood there for a while looking down at the river. As is always the case on a city bridge, several other loungers were doing the same thing. Having stood there for a few minutes, he made a gesture as though to take up the hold-all, but knocked it off the parapet. As it hurtled downwards and splashed into the river there came excited cries from the nearest bystanders. Gregory leaned over and stared down in apparent consternation. A few people moved up and commiserated with him. But there was nothing to be done. The hold-all had already sunk, and there was no possibility of its recovery.

With a glum face, which concealed his inward satisfaction, he turned away. He had now disposed of everything which could connect him with the affair at Malacou's cottage.

So far, so good. But he was still faced with two far more difficult problems—how to reach and cross a neutral frontier and, more difficult still, how to acquire the money to reach one.

Walking on, he came to the Unter den Linden, with its imposing blocks and three lines of fine trees. He found it sadly altered since he had last seen it in the winter of 1939. Bomb blast had torn great gaps in the trees, every few hundred yards there were railed-off craters, and during four and a half years of war the paint had peeled from the handsome buildings that lined it. Many of them had collapsed as a result of the air-raids, or had been burnt out.

Turning west, he decided to make a short tour of the principal streets in order to refresh his memory of the geography of the city. Strolling down the Wilhelmstrasse, he saw that Goebbels' Ministry, the Reich Chancellery and the huge block formed by Goering's Air Ministry all had chunks out of their upper storeys due to bombs. Had he still been wearing his stolen S.D. uniform he would never have dared to turn into the Albrecht Strasse, as in it was the H.Q. of the Gestapo, and from it officers were constantly coming and going, one of whom might have challenged him. But now that he was again in civilian clothes, with nothing to distinguish him from other ordinary Berliners, he passed the building with impunity, wondering only where his old enemy Gruppenführer Grauber was at that moment.

By way of the Potsdamer Platz and the Hermann Goering Strasse he made his way back to the Linden where it ended at the Brandenburg Gate. Beyond it to the east lay the Tiergarten. That, too, was pockmarked by bomb craters with, between them, a veritable forest of long-barrelled ack-ack guns and batteries of searchlights. In a part of it in which the public were still allowed to walk, he sat down on a bench to consider his extremely worrying situation.

In Berlin every man and woman was an enemy. There was no-one from whom he could borrow money or secure any other form of help, and however carefully he endeavoured to conserve the small store of marks he had taken from the S.D. men's wallets they must be exhausted in the course of a few days. It therefore seemed that his only means of obtaining

funds was by robbery. Although he was armed he decided that
to attempt a bank hold-up would be too risky, while if he tried
burgling a private house it was very unlikely that he would find
in it the sort of sum he needed in ready money.

It then occurred to him that the cash desk in a smart
restaurant such as Horcher's, or in the dining room of a big
hotel, would be certain to contain a fat wad of notes, particularly after dinner; and that he would have a much better
chance of getting away with it than by trying to rob a bank. The
Adlon was not far off, so he stood up with the intention of
paying it a visit and spying out the land.

The buildings on either side of the great luxury hotel had
been blitzed, but it appeared to have escaped damage. He felt
a little dubious about going into this famous haunt of
Germany's aristocracy and millionaires, dressed in old country
clothes; but the war had brought about as great a deterioration
in Berlin's social life as the Allies' bombs had on the appearance
of the city. Prostitutes and profiteers now rubbed shoulders
with the old *haut monde* and many people who had been
bombed out, having lost their wardrobes, were reduced to
wearing any clothes they could pick up on the Black Market.
So, as he entered the big foyer, he was pleased to find that
among the motley throng moving about its business there he
was not at all conspicuous.

By then it was the pre-lunch hour so dozens of people were
arriving to join friends for cocktails. Walking through to the
entrance to the restaurant he saw that a woman was seated at
the cash desk and that it consisted of a wooden box the upper
part of which was enclosed by plate-glass screens. That did not
look very promising as it would be far from easy to grab the
money through the low aperture in the front of the box.
However, there were many hours yet to go before nightfall, so
plenty of time for him to reconnoitre other places in one of
which it seemed certain a snatch and run would prove easier,
and it occurred to him that might be the case in the bar.

On entering it he felt that he deserved a drink and that to
have it in these pleasant surroundings would be worth the extra
cost so, damning the expense, he ordered a large champagne
cocktail. Sitting up at the bar, he turned on his stool and ran

his eye over the many pretty women and their escorts who were having drinks at the little tables on the other side of the room. Suddenly his heart gave a bound. A slim young woman seated with her back to him had her hair dressed high, with a few delicious little dark curls on the nape of the neck, and he had many times kissed just such curls on the neck of Sabine Tuzolto.

Could it be? She looked the right height. If so . . . Quickly, he picked up his drink and carried it to a place further along the bar. From his new position he could see the girl's face in one of the big gilt-framed mirrors on the opposite wall. At a glance he saw that her features bore no resemblance to Sabine's, and he was conscious of a sharp stab of disappointment. But her having called Sabine to mind gave him an idea.

Although Sabine was Hungarian and her home was in Budapest, since she had become Ribbentrop's girl friend she had spent a great part of her time with him in Berlin. If she was still the Nazi Foreign Minister's mistress it was possible that she was in Berlin now. Yet, even should she be, Gregory was by no means certain that he could count her a friend.

As he drank his cocktail, his mind shuttled back and forth recalling episodes from the two periods in which they had been lovers, and speculating on what her present feelings towards him might be.

He had first seen her one night in 1936 at the Casino in Deauville,[1] a supremely beautiful girl just turned twenty. Her companion had been the head of an international smuggling ring and he had been making use of Sabine in his nefarious activities. She would have been arrested and sent to prison with others of the gang had not Gregory later got her out of England. He had taken her back to Budapest and there, for several joyous weeks, she had willingly rewarded him by becoming his mistress.

His mind moved on to those hectic weeks he had spent in Budapest in the summer of 1942; to how Sabine had saved him from his enemies and returned with him to England; to the way she had fooled him and, when in London, spied for the Nazis, got caught and been arrested.

1. See *Contraband*.

When she was a prisoner in the Tower of London it had seemed near impossible to get her out. But by an intrigue with the Moldavian Military Attaché, Colonel Kasdar, Gregory had enabled her to escape and return to Germany. And he had done so without laying himself open to any charge for he, in his turn, had fooled and made use of her.

The convoys carrying the Allied troops for 'Torch' were already on their way to North Africa. With the connivance of the Deception Planners he had sent her back to Ribbentrop with false information about the objective of the expedition. Later it had been learned through secret channels that the information she took back had duly reached Hitler, and had so fully corroborated all the other measures already taken to fool the Germans that the deception plan had proved a complete success.

Believing that the 'Torch' convoys were making for the east coast of Sicily, so would have to pass through the narrow Straits of Bon on the afternoon of Sunday November 9th, Kesselring had grounded his air force the previous day, when the convoys were within range, intending to blitz them with maximum effect on the Sunday. But at midnight the convoys had turned back and at dawn on the 8th landed their troops in Oran and Algiers without the loss of a single ship.

As Gregory toyed with his champagne cocktail and thought of all this, he wondered what Sabine's reactions would be if she were in Berlin and he could find her.

Since the Nazis had shot so many W.A.A.F.s and other courageous women who had parachuted into German-occupied territory the British authorities had decided to put chivalrous scruples behind them and have Sabine shot. As he had got her out of the Tower she owed her life to him; while by having enabled him to escape from Budapest he owed his life to her. That cancelled out. But in order to save her he had had to deceive her so that she in turn would deceive Hitler; and how she had come out of that he had no idea.

It was quite probable that on discovering that he had been fooled Hitler had been furious with Ribbentrop and Ribbentrop furious with her for having led him to communicate false information to his Führer. The odds were, therefore, that she had been through a very sticky time and if she realized that Gregory had deliberately lied to her there was a risk that her resentment might be so intense that she would hand him over to the Gestapo. As against that, in this great city filled with enemies she was the only person who might, for old times' sake, be persuaded to befriend him; so he decided to try to seek her out.

Finishing his drink, he went to the row of telephone booths and looked in a directory for the name Tuzolto. As he had feared, it was not in the book. The only other way of tracing her, if she was in Berlin, was through Ribbentrop; but to ring up the Minister was out of the question. All the same, Gregory looked up Ribbentrop's private number, found that he still lived in the suburb of Dahlem, and made a note of the address.

Leaving the Adlon he went back to the Tiergarten, sat down on a bench and made a scratch meal off some of the now mangled *Brötchen* and crumbled biscuits that he had hastily pushed into his pockets early that morning.

At about half past one he walked to the nearest tram halt and asked a woman standing near him if a tram went out to Dahlem.

'No,' she replied, 'you would have done better to go to the Potsdamer Bahenhoff and take an electric as far as the Grunewald; but these days there's always a chance that the line is blocked and they're not running. You'd best now take the next Potsdam tram and get off at the Round-point in the wood. The conductor will tell you.'

A few minutes later Gregory forced his way on to a crowded tram. It followed the main artery west towards Charlotten-burg. As it clanged its way into the workers' quarter he was amazed to see on both sides of the highway the havoc that bombs had wrought. Whole rows of buildings had been rendered uninhabitable. Many had been reduced to piles of debris, others gaped open with tottering, shored-up walls rearing skyward. It seemed impossible that anyone could have survived in what must have been such a hell of explosions, flame and collapsing houses. Yet the pavements were swarming with ill-clad, glum-looking people.

After traversing two miles of this nightmare area the tram

turned south-west and entered a slightly more prosperous neighbourhood. Here, too, there was much evidence of the air-raids and at one point the passengers had to leave the tram because the road was blocked. But after walking a few hundred yards they boarded another tram which carried them into better suburbs on the edge of the Spandau Forest. In due course they reached the Round-point. The woman conductor told Gregory to take the road to the east and that there was no tramway to Dahlem, but he might get a 'bus if he waited long enough.

Deciding to walk, he set off along a road lined with houses standing in their own gardens. Half an hour later he arrived in the leafy side road he was seeking and another two hundred paces brought him to the gate to Ribbentrop's villa.

It was a commodious monstrosity typical of those built by wealthy industrialists in Victorian times. That Ribbentrop had not left it after his rise to power for some more spacious and imposing mansion showed that he had neither the taste nor ostentation of Goering; but he would naturally do his public entertaining at the Foreign Office and, Gregory suspected, probably continued to make the villa his home for sentimental reasons, as it had been the scene of many momentous meetings during the rise of the Nazi Party.

Gregory regarded it with interest, recalling what he had heard about the place. Ribbentrop had been one of the very few of Hitler's early adherents who had money; or, rather, his wife had, for he had married Anneliese Henkel, the heiress of the great German Sparkling Wine House, of which he had been an employee. Hitler had often stayed with the couple in this Dahlem villa and as he understood no language other than German, Ribbentrop, who was fluent in both French and English, habitually read out to him translations of the political articles in the leading foreign Press. It was their long discussions after having read these articles that had convinced Hitler that Ribbentrop was another Bismarck, and later led to his appointment as Ambassador to Britain, then as Foreign Minister of the Third Reich.

As Gregory stood there he thought how differently things might have gone had those intimate talks never taken place. It was Ribbentrop who had convinced Hitler, in spite of the strenuous, contrary opinions expressed by the professional diplomats and by Goering and the General Staff, that the British people had become entirely decadent and that there was not the least likelihood of their Government going to war on behalf of Poland. That he had proved completely wrong had not shaken Hitler's faith in him; for, even to himself, the egomaniacal Dictator would never admit that his judgement had been at fault; so it was the vain, self-opinionated, ex-wine-salesman who had been mainly responsible for bringing about the war, and who continued to lord it at the Foreign Office.

Pushing open the side gate, Gregory walked up a path that led to the back entrance of the villa and rang the bell. It was answered by a kitchen maid, of whom he asked if he could have a word with the Herr Reichsaussenminister's valet. She told him to wait and after a few minutes an elderly fat-faced man came to the door. Departing a little from his normally impeccable German, Gregory said to him:

'Forgive me for troubling you, *mein Herr*, but I am a Hungarian, recently arrived from Budapest. My mother was the nurse of the Frau Baronin Tuzolto and I have messages for her. But I have not her address and she is not in the telephone book. My mother told me that she is a close friend of the Herr Reichsaussenminister; so it occurred to me that someone in his household might be able to help me.'

The fat-faced man grinned. 'Yes, she was a friend of his and as lush a piece as anyone could find to go to bed with; but I don't think he sees much of her now. She never comes here, of course. The missus wouldn't have stood for that. The boss installed her in a nice little villa he owns on Schlachten Insel, just at the entrance to the Wannsee. Used to use it for boating parties when times were better. For all I know she's still there. Anyway, you could go there and enquire. That's the best I can do for you.'

Having learned that the place was called the Villa Seeaussicht and the best way to get to it, Gregory thanked the man profusely and turned away. From Dahlem he walked back to the Round-point, from there he took a tram a further two

miles along the road to Potsdam, then walked again down a
side road through the woods to the Havel.

At that point the fifteen-mile-long lake was a good mile and
a half wide and he saw that Schlachten Island projected from
near the shore on which he stood, about three-quarters of a
mile into it. Crossing a short causeway to the island, he found
that there were several properties on it and that the Villa
Seeaussicht was on the south shore; so evidently derived its
name from having a splendid view right down the broad arm
of the Havel known as the Wannsee.

Framed in trees, the villa stood about fifty yards back from
the road. To one side there was a separate building, obviously
a big garage with rooms for a chauffeur above, but it was shut
and no car stood outside it. The villa itself had three storeys
and its size suggested that it was about a ten-room house.
Muslin curtains in the upper windows implied that it was
occupied, but in the drowsy heat of the summer afternoon no-
one was about; so Gregory felt that he could carry out a
reconnaissance without much fear of being seen.

Being so doubtful about the sort of reception Sabine would
accord him—if, indeed, she was still living there—he was most
anxious to avoid presenting himself in circumstances which
might prejudice the results of their meeting. For that it was
essential that he should come upon her unannounced and alone,
so that should she prove willing to help him there would be a
chance for her to hide him there temporarily without any
servant being aware of his presence or, should she at first
prove hostile, he would at least have a chance of talking her
round before she gave him away in front of any third party.

Entering a side gate he stepped into a shrubbery, then made
his way along a narrow passage behind the garage to a small
yard. Beyond the yard there was another shrubbery, under
cover of which he continued to advance. From between the
bushes he could now see that the back of the villa looked out
on to a pleasant lawn that ran down to the water and that at
one side of its extremity there stood a low boat house. He saw,
too, that about half-way down the lawn, on his side of it, there
was a swing hammock with a striped canopy. As the hammock
was end on to him he could not see if anyone was in it; but a

book lying on the ground and a garden table nearby, with a glass
on it, suggested there might be. Treading with great caution
he reached the back of the deep hammock and, holding his
breath, peered over the edge. His heart gave a bound. Sabine
was lying there asleep.

So his luck was in. He had sought and found her. But was
finding her really good luck, he wondered, as he gazed down
at this lovely wanton creature who had been the mistress of
both himself and Ribbentrop. From what the fat-faced valet
in Dahlem had said it seemed that Ribbentrop had cast her off.
If that had been due to the false information with which he,
Gregory, had sent her back to Germany, she might seize
eagerly on the chance to revenge herself. And there was another
thing. If he could succeed in explaining away his having lied
to her, and she ranked the safety of her old lover above her
duty as a Nazi, her welcome might prove almost as dangerous
as her enmity. He knew her amorous nature too well to suppose
that, should she agree to hide him, she would not expect him
to go to bed with her again. And he was most loath to be
unfaithful to Erika. Yet in Sabine lay his only hope of getting
safely out of Germany.

16

The Lovely Wanton

SABINE was dressed in a light summer frock, and for a few moments Gregory stood there admiring her slim figure and the perfection of her features. She was now about twenty-eight and had changed little since he had first known her. A few tiny laughter wrinkles showed at the corners of her mouth and her hips and bust were slightly larger, but her magnolia-petal skin remained unblemished and a splendid foil to the dark hair that grew down so attractively into her smooth forehead as a widow's peak. Her mouth was a little open and showed a glimpse of her small, even teeth; her lips had always been a bright red, which he knew owed little to lipstick, and her dark eyelashes curled up making delightful fans on her cheeks.

Stepping back out of sight, in a clear voice he spoke one of the few sentences in Hungarian that he knew: 'Holy Virgin, we believe that without sin thou didst conceive.' It was the first line of a couplet he had heard her say a score of times before they had gone to bed together.

Suddenly there was a stir in the hammock. As Sabine sat up he ducked down behind it. With a low laugh she completed the couplet, 'And now we pray, in thee believing, that we may sin without conceiving.' Then she cried, 'Come out from behind there, whoever you are.'

Putting his head up above the back edge of the hammock, he grinned at her.

'Gregory!' she exclaimed, her black eyes going round with amazement.

'Then I'm not the only one who has heard you say your little prayer,' he laughed.

'Goodness, no,' she laughed back. 'But I thought you must

be one of my old Hungarian boy friends. What in the world are
you doing here?'

'Oh, I'm in Berlin to destroy the Third Reich and put an end
to the war,' he replied lightly.

'I wish to God you could,' she said with sudden seriousness.
'The air-raids have become simply ghastly. Every night I go to
bed expecting to be blown to pieces before morning. But,
honestly; how do you come to be in Berlin?'

'The usual way. I caught an aircraft and was dropped by
parachute.'

She frowned. 'You've come as a spy, then? After you got me
out of the Tower and failed to get away yourself it was certain
you would be arrested. I thought, perhaps, that you'd escaped
from prison and managed to get here as a refugee. You told
me that if your plan failed you would be finished with the
British and try to get to Ireland.'

'It didn't fail, as far as you were concerned,' he said quickly.
'But, of course, I was arrested. They gave me a whacking great
prison sentence; so I've had a very thin time these past eighteen
months. I'm only out now on what you might call ticket-of-
leave. Sent here to spy for England.'

As he told the lies he had prepared should he succeed in
finding her, he watched her expression intently. For now was
the critical moment. To his immense relief the frown left her
face and, shaking her head, she said, 'So you've been in prison
on my account. You poor darling. But come round here and
tell me about it.'

'I'd better not,' he replied. 'I might be seen from the house
and I'm on the run, remember. I knew I could trust you, but for
both our sakes we mustn't be seen together.'

She shrugged. 'You needn't worry. In the daytime I'm all
alone here except for my maid Trudi; and it's her afternoon
and evening off.'

Reassured, Gregory came round from behind the hammock
and sat down beside her. With a smile, he said, 'You wouldn't
be you, my sweet, if you didn't have company at nights. Is it
still Ribb, or have you another boy friend?'

'I still see Ribb at times, but not often these days. He lets me
stay on here, though, and my present boy friend, if you can call

the old so-and-so that, was provided by him. He's a once-a-weeker. Think of that, as a contrast to yourself, my dear, and those wonderful first weeks we spent together in Budapest.'

Of them Gregory needed no reminding. As her dark eyes, full of wickedness, caught his he could see her again lying naked and laughing on a bed, shaking her hair back a little breathlessly as she reached for a glass of champagne. This disclosure made him more uneasy than ever; for, since Sabine had such an unsatisfactory lover, he felt certain now that if she did let him stay there she would look on him as a heaven-sent outlet for her amorous propensities. As he was wondering how he could deal with such a situation, she said:

'You'd never guess who my present boy friend is.'

'Without a clue, how can I?'

'Oh, he's an old friend of yours; at least, a sort of connection —er, by marriage.'

'But I'm not married.'

'No, but there's that lovely blonde that got so het-up when she learned about our trip together down the Danube. You told me in London that for a long time past you had looked on her as your wife.'

'What, Erika? But I've never met any of her relations.'

Sabine's big, dark eyes twinkled with amusement. 'You've met her husband.'

'Kurt von Osterberg! My God, you can't mean . . .?'

'I do. He has been living here with me for the past three months.'

'But damn it! He must be nearly sixty and . . .'

'Don't I know it, my dear. And I shouldn't think he ever was much good between the sheets. But there it is. I'm saddled with him and trying to make the best of it.'

'But in God's name why?' Gregory stared at her in amazement. 'You're as lovely as ever you were, and could take your pick of a hundred lovers. Von Osterberg hasn't even got any money. Erika married him only because it meant so much to her dying father that she should rehabilitate herself in the eyes of the aristocracy after her affaire with Hugo Falkenstein; and she picked Kurt because she knew that if she financed his scientific experiments with a part of the millions Falkenstein left her he would raise no objections to her having boy friends.'

Sabine made a little face. 'My dear, for getting me out of the Tower you say you had to pay by being sent to prison. After I got back here I had to pay in another way, because the information you gave Colonel Kasdar was false.'

'I know; but I didn't realize that till afterwards,' Gregory lied smoothly. 'As I told you, I was never a Planner myself, only one of the bodies in the Cabinet War Room who stuck pins in maps. I thought that I'd passed the right dope to Kasdar for you to take back, but my pal on the Planning Staff had sold me the Deception Plan.'

'Is that the truth?' she asked, a shade suspiciously.

'Of course,' he replied, without blinking an eyelid. 'Kasdar's price for getting you away in a Moldavian ship was that I should get him the objectives of Operation "Torch"; so that by passing them on to the Nazis he would stand well with them when they had won the war and Hitler took over all the little neutrals that had stayed on the fence. He was pretty well informed about most things, so I didn't dare try to trick him. If he'd found me out he would have ditched us both.'

'Well, I'll take your word for it. There are times when even Ribb doesn't know what the Führer has really decided. He's often told me that so many different versions about our next moves are put out by Bormann and Keitel that he is led to believe one thing and Goering and Himmler others. I suppose in Churchill's headquarters it's much the same. Of course, I couldn't help suspecting you, but I did think you might have been fooled yourself.'

Gregory suppressed a sigh of relief at having got over that nasty fence. But she was going on:

'All the same, you landed me in a pretty mess. As your information tallied with so much else they'd had, the Führer didn't take it out of Ribb; but Ribb did out of me because he had given himself a lot of kudos from having had in me a first-class spy who had done better than any of Admiral Canaris's people or Himmler's. As soon as it emerged that I'd been fooled the fat was in the fire. Himmler came back at Ribb and raked up his man Grauber's report about you and me in

Budapest. They swore I'd deceived Ribb deliberately and demanded that I should be handed over as a British agent.'

'My dear, I *am* sorry!' exclaimed Gregory, with genuine feeling.

'And well you may be,' she said, frowning at the memory. 'For a few days I was scared stiff. But Ribb saved my bacon. By sheer luck one of his agents had just turned in information that Marshal Weygand was contemplating a break with Pétain and planning to make himself Chief of a separate French State in North Africa, then bring it over to the Allies. Ribb said I had got it for him in London. Weygand was arrested before he could leave France and evidence was found that he meant to play traitor. That evened up the score against the black I'd put up and enabled Ribb to claim that I was on the level. But to keep Himmler and Co. quiet I had to keep the pot boiling.'

'How d'you mean?'

'The Gestapo were still so suspicious of me that Ribb had to show my Nazi zeal by using me in other ways. He made it obvious in public that he had dropped me as a mistress, so it should appear that I was no longer in favour with the Nazis, then he arranged for me to get to know various people who were believed to be plotting against the Führer. The first group was a Professor of Philosophy named Kurt Huber and a couple named Scholl. It wasn't difficult to fool the old boy and I got hold of some of his papers.'

'Do you mean that you turned them in?' Gregory asked, with difficulty concealing how shocked he felt.

Sabine lit a cigarette and nodded. 'Of course. I could only enable Ribb to keep me out of a concentration camp by showing willing, and they were, as near as makes no difference, Communists. That's the one thing Hitler and I think the same about. All Communists are poison and the sooner they are eliminated the better.'

Gregory knew her views about that from the past too well to argue the matter; and as he considered Communism to be as much a menace to civilization as the Nazis he only asked, 'What then?'

'Later I was given the Kreisau Circle to tackle. The group takes its name from the Silesian estate of Count Helmuth von

Moltke, because he and Count Peter Yorck and others used to meet and plot there. But they came quite frequently to Berlin. They were intellectuals who started off as Socialists, but they went Communist, too, and were trying to sell us out to the Russians. That little coup put me in the clear. And when Ribb gave Himmler the information I'd obtained about them even that big fat slob had to admit that his suspicions of me had been unfounded.'

'Well, you've been a busy girl,' Gregory smiled.

'Busy in a way I don't like,' she retorted. 'There have been others, too, that I've failed to get anything on. And I prefer to pick the men I go to bed with. Still, it's better than having to eat offal in a concentration camp and being had by three or four Nazi thugs every night.'

'How about von Osterberg?' Gregory enquired. 'I'd bet my last cent that he is not a Communist.'

'Oh no. That's quite a different kettle of fish. But the aristocracy and most of the Generals have always been anti-Hitler. On and off for years they have been plotting to kill him, and since the Allies landed in France it's been brewing up again. Kurt is in it. I'm certain of that. He has been working for years on these Secret Weapons, and for the past year or more he has been the top boy at an underground laboratory near Potsdam. As that's not far from here Ribb thought it would be a good idea for me to play around with him, then when he was bombed out of his flat suggest that he should come to live here. Reluctantly I obliged. He was terribly flattered, of course, that anyone like myself should take an interest in him, so he fell for me like a ripe plum. I'm really like a mother to him and he gives me very little trouble.'

'Still, that must be pretty dull for you,' Gregory grinned at her. 'And what a shocking waste of the very best fissionable material.' Next second he was cursing himself for what he had said. If he remained there she was going to prove a terrible enough temptation without his leading her on.

'Don't worry,' she smiled back. 'Kurt is away for a few nights now and then; and there are the afternoons. I'm sure those old Viennese psychologists would approve my methods. The Führer has said that it's our duty to entertain our heroes on leave from the front, so I stave off getting any complex about suffering from night starvation by playing fairy god-mother to a variety of young men.'

'I hope you haven't become altogether promiscuous,' Gregory remarked.

'No. Hardly that. But you know well enough that I've never been exactly frigid. And I dare not take a regular lover for fear of complications. Even with the bombing there are still parties. In fact, more hectic ones than ever. Now we're all so afraid that every night will be our last, half the women in Berlin have become like alley cats. They're half drunk most of the time and will go with any man who asks them. People aren't even shocked now when they go into their hostess's bedroom and find a couple on the bed. I have only to go to a party to be besieged by a dozen applicants; and if I feel that way I make a date, or see the night out with the man I like best.'

'But, reverting to von Osterberg, how extraordinary that, of all people, you should have had to take on Erika's husband.'

Sabine shrugged. 'I don't see anything very strange about that. As far as we know these plotters are quite a small clique, and he just happens to be one of them. You're not jealous, are you? After all, you've been hitting it up with the poor man's wife.'

'Good lord, no. Why should I worry? I've got the best part of the bargain.'

'That's not very complimentary.'

'I meant that as far as this foursome is concerned I'm more fortunate than you are,' he amended hastily.

'Foursome!' Sabine repeated with a sudden laugh. 'In the old days, if only Kurt were younger and more attractive, we might have had one. In Budapest it was quite a thing for two couples to go off to some place in the country for the weekend and for the husbands to swop wives or mistresses, then finish up by all playing games together. When it came to a free-for-all I bet I would have made Erika jealous before I'd finished with you.'

Gregory shook his head. 'My dear, you are incorrigible, and the most lovely piece of wickedness. But such a situation is never likely to arise, and I'd like to talk about the present. As

I've told you, I'm on the run. Not actually being hunted at the moment, but I've no papers, no ration card and very little money. I had all these things, of course, but my wallet was stolen while I was sleeping in an air-raid shelter last night; so I'm really up against it. For old times' sake, would you be willing to hide me for a while?'

Her face remained expressionless as she replied, 'I don't know. I've my own skin to think of. You admit that you are here as a spy. I ought to say "Yes", then when you are asleep do a Delilah on you and send for the police.'

'I'm sure you wouldn't do that,' he smiled; then added seriously, 'Besides, if you did, I'm armed and agile; so it could only result in several people getting killed.'

'Including me, if you had the chance?'

'No. I couldn't do that after what we've been to one another. Not even if it meant the difference between my getting away and being captured.'

'I believe you mean that,' she said quietly. 'So you win. We've both risked being put on the spot for one another before, so we'll risk it again. But tell me what you're really up to here. Not this nonsense about stopping the war single-handed.'

'It's quite simple. In London they know that the air-raids must have hit Berlin pretty badly, but not how badly. Air-reconnaissance photographs give a general idea, but no more; and for months past the Allies haven't had an agent here worthy of the name. For eye-witness reports of conditions in the industrial districts and actual buildings of importance destroyed they've had to rely on the accounts of neutral diplomats who have refused to stick it here any longer and returned to their own countries; and, of course, by the time they reach London such reports are weeks out of date. To come here and find out is a pretty tough assignment, but the chaps who run that sort of thing knew that I know Berlin and can pass anywhere as a German; so they came to me in prison and offered to annul the remainder of my sentence if I'd take this trip and come back with the goods.'

'You want me to hide you, then, while you spend a week or so checking up on the damage that's been done to the city?'

'No. I've seen quite enough already to put in the sort of

report that will satisfy them. My problem now is to get home. With my wallet I lost the coded names and addresses of two neutrals living in Berlin who, I was told, might help me in an emergency, as well as my forged identity papers and money; so I'm stranded. What I want you to do if you possibly can is to get other papers for me and some cash; so that I can make my way to a neutral frontier.'

'I can let you have all the money you need,' Sabine replied; then she added with a worried frown, 'But to get identity papers for you is going to be far from easy.'

'Money is more than half the battle,' said Gregory quickly. 'For a good round sum I might be able to buy a passport from some minor official in a neutral Embassy; but to find such a man would take time and I don't want to embarrass you with my presence for longer than I can help. Another possibility would be for me to hang about in a well-populated district while an air-raid is in progress and hope to find someone just killed, then take his papers.'

Sabine shook her dark head so that her hair shimmered in the sunshine. 'No. To approach anyone on the staff of an Embassy is too great a risk. He might agree to get you what you want, then when you went to collect it turn you in to the police. But your second suggestion has given me an idea. People are brought home dead or dying every night. Their wives or relatives are then left with their papers. I've known several women who've lost their menfolk in the last few months. I could go to see them and sound them out. I might be able to get a set of papers for you that way.'

'Bless you, my dear. I'll never be able to repay you.'

She patted his hand. 'Dear Gregory, you never know. These days we're all living on the edge of a volcano. If I do survive the war I'll probably find myself penniless. If so, I'm sure I could count on you to see me through to better times.'

'Of course you could. Now about hiding me. Where do you suggest that I lie low? How about the rooms over the garage?'

'Yes, they are furnished and empty. My car's still there, but I had to get rid of my chauffeur over a year ago when it became impossible for even people like me to get petrol. We all go about on bicycles now. I see no reason, though, why you shouldn't occupy one of the top bedrooms in the house. Kurt never goes up there and it would be more convenient for Trudi to bring you your meals.'

'Are you absolutely certain you can trust her?'

'Yes. I shall simply tell her that you are in trouble with the Nazis. That will be quite enough. She is Hungarian but her mother was a Jewess. And what those fiends are doing to the Jews in Budapest is beyond belief. Hitler is positively obsessed by his fanatical determination to exterminate the whole Jewish race. Ribb told me it was that much more than strategic considerations that led to his taking over Hungary. There were more than a million Jews in Budapest alone; mostly good honest people who ran all our industries and commerce for us. I gather it was the sweeping advance of the Soviet Armies that decided Hitler to go into Hungary and kill all the Jews while he had the chance; and Himmler, who from the beginning has made race-purity his overruling passion, urged him to it. They sent a man named Adolf Eichmann there. He is the head of what is termed the "Office of Jewish Emigration", but it would be better styled "The Office of Wholesale Murder".'

'He is the brute who drove all the Jews in Poland into ghettos, then systematically slaughtered them, isn't he?'

'That's the man, and as his *Einsatzgruppen* could not shoot the poor devils quickly enough he invented the gas chamber. They sent him to Budapest in March and he made his head-quarters the Majestic Hotel. The hordes of Jews rounded up were so enormous that they overflowed the ghettos; so thousands and thousands of them were packed into cattle trucks, ninety to a truck—can you imagine it?—to be sent to Germany. But only a handful ever got here. The trains were shunted on to sidings and the people in them left to starve to death.'

'God, how appalling!'

'Isn't it? And no-one can stop it. The Generals try to when they get the least chance; but Bormann's Gauleiters have the power to overrule them. It's said now that Himmler's ape-men have murdered over four million Jews.'

Gregory shook his head. 'After all, there are great numbers of decent Germans. One would think they'd get together and stage some sort of protest at such hideous barbarity.'

'They daren't. Everyone knows what is going on, of course, and about the tortures that are inflicted on the prisoners in the concentration camps. But no-one mentions these horrors above a whisper. They'd pay for it with their lives if they did. But let's get off this frightful subject and go across to the house.'

The interior of the villa was much as Gregory had expected: a flight of stairs led straight up from the hall; on one side was a drawing room that ran the whole length of the house, with a bay window looking towards the road and French windows leading on to the garden at its other end; off it, beyond a velvet curtain, there was a small writing room; on the other side of the hall was a dining room and, in rear of it, the kitchen.

Up on the top floor Sabine showed Gregory the room he was to occupy. It was comfortably furnished and, she said, had been used by her manservant when she had had one. Trudi's room and two others were on the same floor, but there was no bathroom; so Sabine told him he would have to wait until Kurt had gone to his laboratory then use the one on the first floor.

Down there she showed him her luxuriously furnished bedroom, which was as big as the drawing room, and off it, above the back hall, was the bathroom. Beyond that lay a dressing room and the best spare bedroom, in which von Osterberg usually slept. As they came out of the bathroom she smiled, and said:

'Kurt goes off to his work every morning at half past eight. Trudi will bring you up your breakfast as soon as he has gone. I don't usually get up till ten o'clock or later; so perhaps when you've had your bath you would like to come and keep me company?'

Her smile made the implications of this invitation quite unmistakable, and Gregory knew that, although he had found sanctuary, he had come to the edge of a precipice.

17

A Nation in the Toils

GREGORY made no immediate reply. The thin laughter lines on either side of his mouth deepened in the suggestion of a smile. Yet, had Sabine known it, this half-smile was not one of pleasurable anticipation; it was caused by a quirk of cynical humour at a thought that had suddenly flashed into his mind.

He was thinking again of the cockroach and the armpit of the tortoise. To escape from that devouring beast the Gestapo by jumping into the bed of one of the loveliest ladies in Berlin surely transcended any other possible way of emulating that life-saving feat. It could happen only to one dearly beloved by the gods.

She had no need to remind him of the sensual delights her slim white body had to offer. During the last half-hour her full red lips, big liquid eyes, shining hair, the scent she used, her every movement, had brought back to him a score of memories of their nights together in Budapest and on the Danube.

Yet in the story the cockroach had been compared to an early Christian set before a lion. And in a sense that, too, applied. Early Christians had made a fetish of chastity and out of love for Erika he had sworn to himself that while away from her he would remain chaste.

Since getting away from Poland he had several times concentrated hard on trying to let her know by thought transference that he had not been captured and was uninjured; and twice he had felt a response which led him to believe that she was praying for his safety. That she should, by astral means, pick up the knowledge that he was again with Sabine did not seem remotely possible. But she might well get the feeling that he was lying in the embrace of some other woman, and that would make her acutely miserable. Damnably alluring as Sabine was, he knew that he would be guilty of true evil if he risked adding such thoughts to the intense distress that must be afflicting Erika on his account.

As he sought desperately for a way to evade the issue, Sabine said sharply, 'You're looking very glum all of a sudden. Is it that you no longer find me attractive, or have you become impotent?'

Her last words suddenly brought inspiration to him. Looking down, he sadly shook his head and asked, 'Have you not noticed my limp?'

'Well, yes,' she admitted. 'It did strike me that you were limping a little as we crossed the lawn. I thought that maybe you'd just hurt your foot.'

With a heavy sigh he lifted his left leg and showed her the extra half-inch of leather on the sole of his shoe. Then he said, 'Berlin's not the only place that has air-raids. We have them in London, too. About six months ago when I was in Brixton Prison a bomb fell on it. My left leg was shattered and I was lucky to escape with my life. On my hip and thigh there are the most ghastly wounds. But they are healed now, so that's not the worst of it. A piece of flying debris struck me between the legs and carried away the most precious half-inch of flesh a man has on his body.'

'Oh, you poor darling!' she cried, putting her arms round his neck. 'How absolutely frightful for you! What an awful thing to happen. Then you'll never . . . never be able to make love again?'

In the past they had always bathed together. Suddenly it struck him that as he was to use her bathroom she might quite possibly walk in on him next morning and, seeing him naked, realize that in spite of his scarred leg he had lied to her. Swiftly he hedged and said:

'No. Thank God, it's not as bad as that. The surgeons did a wonderful job of grafting and at least I benefited by being for four months in the prison hospital instead of in a cell; though the pain of the dressings was ghastly. You'd hardly notice anything, but before I left England my doctor said that my

only chance of not destroying the good job they've done is
to continue to count myself out of court for some time to
come. Anyhow, for another month or two. For this to have
happened and then for me to find you again is the shabbiest
trick the Devil has ever played me. But there it is, my sweet;
I'm no good to you.'

'Oh dear, what a tragic disappointment,' she said unhappily.
'And from the moment you popped up from behind my
hammock my mind's been full of all the lovely games we used
to play. Still, it's much worse for you and we must just try not
to think about it.' Kissing him lightly, she added, 'Let's go
upstairs again and get your room ready.'

Together they made up the bed and Sabine dug out for him
a flowered silk dressing gown, pyjamas and other things that
Ribbentrop had kept there for his visits. Then they went down
to select cold food from the larder for his supper. Gregory
was surprised to see half a game pie, a salmon trout, the
remains of a ham, an *Apfelstrudel*, a block of Gruyère cheese
and a variety of fresh fruit, as well as white rolls, a dozen eggs
and a big slab of butter.

'By Jove!' he laughed. 'In spite of rationing you manage to
do yourself jolly well. In London we now get only two eggs a
month, a scrape of butter, a few rashers of bacon and a chop
a week to eke out things like soya-bean sausage and the sort
of fish one used to give the cat.'

'Really!' She looked at him in astonishment. 'Surely you
have a Black Market?'

'We have. But only spivs and shysters use it. All patriotic
citizens who are determined to win the war refuse to encourage
that sort of thing.'

She shrugged. 'It's different here. You can still get pretty
well anything you want if you've the money to pay for it, and
everyone's so utterly sick of the war that they don't feel
patriotic any longer. Most of us fear we haven't long to live,
so to hell with rationing. Help yourself to as much as you want,
but don't take the salmon trout. Kurt had it sent to him by a
friend, and if part of it's gone he'll ask questions.'

While Gregory filled a tray high with good things she went
down to the cellar and brought up for him a bottle of hock.

By then nearly two hours had gone since his arrival at the villa, and when she had helped him carry the things upstairs she said, 'It's close on six o'clock and Kurt will be back soon; so I must leave you.'

Taking her in his arms, he kissed her. Then, as her full soft lips melted into his, he drew away and said, 'Although I'm on the run I wouldn't have missed today for anything. How I wish . . . but there it is, my sweet. A million, million thanks. See you in the morning.'

As soon as she had left him he felt suddenly overwhelmed with tiredness. It was now Tuesday evening and since waking in Bari the previous Sunday morning he had had barely twelve hours' sleep, and none of that with his clothes off. Undressing slowly, he got into bed, and only hunger impelled him to eat his excellent supper. When he had done he put the tray aside, thought for a moment of his luck in having found Sabine and her generosity in taking a considerable risk to hide him; then instantly fell asleep.

When he roused next morning a grey daylight was filtering into the room, so he turned over and dozed again until there was a soft knock on the door. On his calling '*Herein*', Trudi appeared with his breakfast.

She was a short plump girl with dark hair, a fresh complexion and quick, boot-button eyes. Bobbing to him, she smiled and gave him the traditional greeting, '*Küss die Hand, mein Herr*', then set the tray down on the bed.

To establish good relations he talked to her for some minutes about the old days in Budapest, and the unutterable evil that Hitler had recently brought upon that lovely city. Then, having told him the *Herr Graf* had left and the *gnädige Frau Baronin* would like to see him when he had had his bath, she bustled away.

Greatly refreshed by his long sleep Gregory tucked into the big plate of ham and eggs, ate two fresh peaches and lapped up the coffee, which he guessed must have come via the Black Market from Turkey. By nine o'clock he was having a most welcome bath and soon after, clad in Ribbentrop's dressing gown, he went in to Sabine.

She was sitting up in bed. He thought that she looked

absolutely adorable and for a moment cursed himself as a fool for the puritanical scruples that had denied him the delight of getting in beside her and smothering her flower-like face with kisses. With an effort he got a hold on himself, kissed her good morning and perched himself on the side of her big bed.

Smiling, she returned his kiss then sighed and said, 'Oh God, how I hate this war. Just to think what a bomb has done to you and robbed us of. And the even worse things that have happened to such thousands of other people. May that filthy little Austrian that brought it on us rot in hell for all eternity.'

'You seem to have changed your views quite a lot since last we met,' Gregory grinned. 'Two summers ago when we talked of these things in Budapest you were a hundred per cent pro-Nazi.'

'Yes,' she admitted. 'But look what the Communists did to Hungary after the First World War. Those gutter-bred swine robbed families like mine of everything we had, and did their utmost to degrade everyone to their own filthy level. You British, with your stupid, pale-pink Liberalism, made no effort to stop them. Neither did the French. The only people who had the guts to stand up to them were the Italians and the Germans. Naturally, as German influence was so strong in Hungary I became a Nazi. What sensible person wouldn't have? But I'm not a Nazi now. They've made themselves untouchables. Say that I'm a Fascist, if you like. But I'm not a Nazi.'

Gregory nodded. 'There's a lot to be said for the Fascists. Old Mussolini did a great job in cleaning up Italy. If only he'd stayed neutral he'd be on the top of the world today and Italy positively bulging with money made out of both sides during the war. That he got *folie de grandeur* and thought that with Hitler's help he could become a modern Roman Emperor, ruling the whole Mediterranean, was one of the greatest tragedies of our time. Little Franco, too, has done a great job of work in Spain. What is more he has had the sense to keep his country out of the war, so given it a real chance to recover. Why people should cavil at him for having put the Moscow-inspired agitators and saboteurs behind bars I could never see. If he'd run his country on the lines the idiot British and French intellectuals and those crazy Americans would have liked to see, by this time Spain would have had a Communist Government. Quite a useful card for the war against Hitler. But what about afterwards, with Russian bombers based there only two hours' flight from London and Paris? Some people simply can't be dissuaded from trying to cut off their noses to spite their faces. But all this is beside the point. You say you're no longer a Nazi; but you're still working for them.'

'Up to a point,' she agreed thoughtfully. 'I'd still turn in these dirty little Marxists who'd like to see Germany a Soviet Republic, whenever I could get the goods on them. But I've never yet given information about those of our own kind who would like to see Hitler as an ugly corpse.'

'Are there many people who feel that way?' he asked.

'Quite a few. Of course millions of ordinary people must wish him dead simply because they believe it would bring about an end to the war. Although it's amazing how many of them, and, I gather, particularly the troops at the front who don't suffer from the bombing, still believe in him. They get nothing but Goebbels' propaganda, and day after day he plugs away about the Secret Weapons that are yet going to get Germany out of her mess. You may not know it, but London has already been destroyed by the buzz-bombs, the invasion ports soon will be and the long-range rockets are going to send New York up in flames. Only the upper crust know that to be poppy-cock, and the middle classes doubt it but the great majority believe it to be gospel. That's what keeps them going. That and fear of the Russians.'

'What sort of people are the few you mentioned? I mean, those who would take a hand in putting an end to Hitler if they had the chance?'

'They are a very mixed bag, most of whom wouldn't see eye to eye in anything else at all. There is every sort of group ranging from Communists to the old aristocracy who'd like to see a Kaiser on the throne again; the old Trade Union laddies, Social Democrat ex-Deputies, priests of both the Roman Catholic and Lutheran faiths, high-up Civil Servants, ex-Diplomats, Generals of the Wehrmacht: the lot.'

'Then since leaders in every sphere feel that way and are

prepared to sink their differences to achieve this one end they must form a very powerful group of conspirators.'

'They're not. All the civilians showed their colours too clearly before the war. Hitler dismissed them from their posts ages ago, and although they've been left free they are constantly watched by the Gestapo. I'm speaking now of men like the Socialist leaders Julius Leber and Wilhelm Leuschner, Dr. Karl Goerdeler the ex-Mayor of Liepzig, the ex-Ambassadors Ulrich von Hassell and Count Werner von der Schulenburg, the former Prussian Finance Minister, Popitz, and the former President of the Reichsbank, Dr. Schacht. I've good reason to believe that a lot of them are in touch with one another; but if they do meet it is at night in cellars of bombed-out buildings. If one of them so much as raised a finger in any public act he and his whole family would find themselves in a torture chamber.'

'Yes; I realize that there's not much the civilians can do until they are given a lead, but that doesn't apply to the Generals.'

'You think that just because they command great bodies of men, but in reality they hold only the shadow of power. Hitler's always known that the Generals were secretly against him. Although he could not do without them, soon after he came to power himself he set about putting shackles on them. The von Blomberg affair provided him with a lucky break for a first step towards that.'

'You mean when the Field Marshal married his typist and she turned out to have been a prostitute?'

'That's right. Before that Hitler was only technically Supreme Chief of the Armed Forces, but when Himmler produced the photographs of Blomberg's wife posing in the nude for dirty pictures, and he was sacked, Hitler took over his job as Minister for War and has kept it ever since. Keitel more or less took over Blomberg's work, but he's really only Hitler's mouthpiece at the War Office, and a vain, weak toady at that. Then there was the scandalous affair of von Fritsch.'

'He was kicked out for being a pansy, wasn't he?'

'No; it was because he opposed Hitler. The evidence Himmler produced about him was composed of lies from beginning to end. Although Hitler had it suppressed, it came out afterwards that the evidence concerned a man named Frish. At a Court of Honour even Goering stood up for von Fritsch, but he was sacked all the same. As Commander-in-Chief of the Wehrmacht, he was succeeded by von Brauchitsch. After the failure of the Russian offensive in 1941 he quarrelled violently with Hitler about how to retrieve the situation, so that winter he, also, was sacked. Then, instead of appointing another C.-in-C. to succeed him, Hitler took that job on himself as well. So from 1942 he has had the whole Wehrmacht in his pocket.'

'But the Chief of Staff and the Army Group Commanders must still have enormous powers.'

'They haven't. General Beck was said to be the best of the German Generals in pre-war days; but he was violently opposed to Hitler's plans for making war, so he was pushed out in '38. Hitler put Halder in his place, and he was pretty subservient. But even he couldn't stick the mess Hitler's orders were making of the Russian front so he resigned in the autumn of '42. Jodl stepped into his shoes, but he's only allowed to advise Hitler on planning and strategy. As for the Army Group Commanders, they last only as long as they carry out Hitler's crazy orders. Von Rundstedt is a really great soldier. He commanded the breakthrough that put France out of the war, but in 1941 he refused to accept some insane plan of Hitler's, so Hitler threw him out.'

'He was recalled, though, and is C.-in-C. West at the moment.'

'About that you are wrong. He was recalled as the only General thought capable of stemming the invasion. Hitler promised him a free hand, but interfered all the same. I gather that ten days ago there was a blood row. Anyhow, von Rundstedt is out again and has been replaced by von Kluge. Von Manstein is another of the big brains. He has twice refused to have his Army massacred by trying to carry out Corporal Hitler's ideas and resigned, and twice has been recalled. It's the same with all the rest of them. They don't know from one day to the next how long they will be left in their commands, or what precautions Hitler has taken to suppress a *Putsch* with Himmler's S.S. Divisions; and they are

under strict orders not to communicate with one another. If
only one of them had the guts to turn his Army round and
march on Berlin I haven't a doubt the others would join him
and Hitler's goose be cooked. But as none of them knows
what's going on except in his own H.Q., none of them dare
take the risk.'

'I suppose each one of them is waiting for a move by the
next chap higher up.'

'That's it. They've been brought up that way from their
cradles.'

Suddenly Sabine threw the bedclothes back and, for a
moment, lay fully revealed through her transparent nightie.
Thrusting her bare legs out of bed, she said, 'But if I'm to try to
get you some papers I mustn't stay here all day. I must go into
Berlin and see a few likely people.'

Gregory felt his heart begin to pound and his mouth go dry.
Hard put to it to keep his face expressionless, he wondered how
long he would be able to resist temptation if she continued to
display herself to him like this. Uneasily he recalled having
told her that it was six months since he had been wounded and
only another month or so was needed for his complete recovery,
so . . . Quickly he picked up her flimsy dressing gown and
draped it over her shoulders; then asked in a slightly hoarse
voice, 'When do you expect to get back?'

She turned round and looked up at him a little uncertainly.
'Well, the truth is that I have a date for three o'clock this
afternoon with a young Panzer Captain at an apartment he's
been lent. Of course, darling, if you were your old self . . . But
as things are . . . He's a nice boy and his leave ends at
midnight. I wouldn't like to disappoint him. You do understand, don't you?'

He smiled down into the flower-like face with the big dark
eyes, rich mouth and magnolia-petal skin. 'Of course I do.
You won't be back till the small hours, then.'

'Oh yes I shall. I only go to evening parties in Berlin, or stay
out late, during the dark periods of the moon, when the R.A.F.
don't put on the worst air-raids. I shall be back by about seven,
but Kurt gets home soon after six; so I shan't see you till
tomorrow morning.'

As she slipped on her mules, he gave her a pat on the behind. 'Very well. Have a good time. I'll be thinking of you. Perhaps, though, in the circumstances, I'd better not.'

'No. It would be bad for you to give yourself ideas. Get a good book and bury yourself in it. There are lots downstairs. Trudi will get your lunch and bring your supper up to your room.'

When he had seen her off to Berlin he went through the drawing room to the little writing room. It held only a desk and two chairs, but the walls were lined with books. Ignoring them for the moment, he began going through the papers in the desk, just on the off-chance that he might learn something more about the people who were plotting against Hitler. As he had expected, there were only bills, personal letters and, to him, indecipherable mathematical jottings. He felt pretty sure that if von Osterberg kept anything to do with the conspiracy there Sabine would have known of it and, as she had talked so freely about the affair, would have told him. Having put each batch of papers back exactly as he had found them, he selected three books then adjusted the others on the shelves so that the gaps should not show.

As it was a lovely summer day he would have liked to go out and sit in the garden but decided that he must not risk being seen by any of Sabine's neighbours. For the same reason he thought it best not to remain downstairs, in case some inquisitive person happened to catch sight of him through the drawing-room window. So he retired to his bedroom, made himself comfortable with a book, tried to keep the alluring Sabine's activities out of his mind and spent the rest of the day there.

The previous night's air-raid had been a minor one and, owing to his exhausted state, he had slept through it. But that night he woke soon after midnight to the thunder of scores of big bombers roaring overhead. Sabine had told him that during air-raids she, von Osterberg and Trudi went down to the cellar, but for him to join them was out of the question. Although he hated raids he was not unduly scared, for he knew that the moonlight glinting on the long stretch of the Havel must give the bombers their direction, and they would not

waste bombs on the scattered private houses round the
southern end of it when they had only five or six more miles
to fly to drop their loads on central Berlin. Nevertheless, for
over an hour all hell seemed to have been let loose. At times
the explosions merged into a continuous distant roar, hundreds
of ack-ack guns were in constant action, at times pieces of their
shells rattled down on the roof and now and again when a
bomb fell nearer the house shuddered.

After he had breakfasted and bathed next morning he went
in to see Sabine. She told him at once that her luck had been
out the previous day. Her two best hopes of securing papers for
him had both left Berlin, and the Panzer Captain had proved
disappointing. About the latter's performance, to Gregory's
considerable discomfiture she went into details; so as soon as
he could he changed the conversation.

Asked about her plans for the day, she said, 'There's a
woman I know who's just lost her son. He'd been seriously
wounded at the front so was given a job in Goebbels' office,
but he died from further wounds in an air-raid about a week
ago. She may have his papers and be prepared to part with
them. Anyway, I'm going to have a snack lunch with her
today. But I've nothing after that; so I'll be back about half
past three and we'll spend the rest of the afternoon together.'

While she was out Gregory again spent the time in his room
and on her return she came up to him. But she had had no luck.
Her friend had returned all her son's papers to the Propaganda
Bureau. At midday it had clouded over and it was now raining
on and off; so the garden being ruled out Sabine said they
would be more comfortable sitting in the drawing room.

Down there they talked for a time of the happy days they
had spent in Budapest; then Gregory led the conversation back
to the conspiracy. 'Do you think,' he asked, 'if one of these
people managed to assassinate Hitler that the Generals would
succeed in getting the better of the other Nazis and take over?'

She shrugged. 'The question doesn't arise, because no-one
will succeed in assassinating Hitler. He knows that there are
quite a number of people who would willingly give their lives
to kill him, so the precautions he takes to protect himself are
quite extraordinary. Surrounding his headquarters at Rasten-

burg there are three rings of check points; so no civilian stands a hope in hell of getting through them all. His staff are all hand-picked as one hundred per cent pro-Nazi, and the duty officers who report to him there have all been most carefully vetted.'

'But he must leave his H.Q. at times.'

'He does, but only very infrequently. Some time ago he was persuaded with great difficulty to go on a visit to the Eastern Front, and they nearly got him there. Apparently someone asked the pilot of his aircraft to take a parcel said to contain two bottles of brandy back to a friend at the base. Actually, it contained a bomb, but the bomb failed to go off.'

'Did he find out about that?'

'No; luckily for the conspirators, because they managed to retrieve the parcel at the other end. Hitler does seem to be gifted with a sort of sixth sense, though. He has flatly refused to leave his H.Q. again.'

'I take it that Kurt told you about this?'

'Yes; and lots more. He says Hitler is incredibly suspicious and remarkably difficult to get at. He arranges all functions at which he still has to make a personal appearance for a given day, then cancels them at the very last moment. Sometimes he does that two or three times, then lays the party on at an hour's notice. Deliberately, of course, so that anyone who has planned to have a crack at him has his arrangements thrown out of gear and misses the chance.'

'Do you turn in to Ribb all you get out of Kurt?' Gregory asked.

She shook her head. 'Oh no. If he were a pro-Communist trying to arrange a pact with Russia I would. But, as I've told you, I'd be delighted to see Hitler dead; providing the right people do the job and are ready to take over.'

'Say someone did kill Hitler, what chance do you think von Osterberg and his pals have of establishing the sort of set-up you'd like to see?'

'Very little. They'd have to get the better of the S.S. troops in Berlin, and that wouldn't be easy for them these days. Before the war, and for some time after it started, Himmler's people couldn't have done much against the Army. For some

reason that I've never understood Hitler would allow him to
raise only a few battalions of Nazi troops. Those he took in
were most carefully selected. They all had to produce evidence
of Aryan descent for three generations on both sides and
measure up to the highest physical standards. The original S.S.
was quite something: an élite corps of blond young blackguards
who believed that Hitler was God and Himmler his Prophet,
and would shoot a Jew as soon as look at him. But all that is
altered now.'

Gregory nodded. 'I thought that must be so, from the number
of S.S. Divisions now fighting on the battle fronts. So many
could not possibly have been put into the field without a serious
dilution of the original hand-picked specimens of Nazi
frightfulness.'

'Yes, that's what happened. The more Hitler became
convinced that the Army Chiefs were letting him down, the
more he turned to "the faithful Heinrich" and allowed him to
create a bigger and bigger private Nazi Army. Ever since
Himmler got himself in with Hitler he's spent most of his time
intriguing to get greater power into his hands; so once he got
the green light from his boss nothing could stop him. He
started recruiting left, right and centre. Not only Germans,
but Frenchmen, Belgians, Dutch, Scandinavians and even
Mohammedans from Yugoslavia. Today there are at least a
million men under his orders. They wear the uniforms of
soldiers but are completely independent of the Wehrmacht.
They take orders from the Generals only when they are in the
battle line, and their Divisional Commanders have the right
even to ignore those if they don't like them.'

'You feel then that these Nazi troops are numerous enough
to defeat the units of a regular army if one of the Generals
launched a *Putsch* against Hitler?'

'In Berlin they are. One evening Kurt told me quite a lot
about that. In the city the Army has nothing but a Guard
Battalion and a few details at the War Office. Of course, they
could call on the troops and cadets in the Training Centres
outside the capital. But it would take them several hours to
get there. Meanwhile, unless they lost their heads, the
Commanders of Himmler's S.S. troops would not just sit

about waiting to be mopped up. And there are plenty of them in the S.S. barracks. Many more than enough to put down a revolt by the Army before the Generals could bring in other units.'

'Then it seems that no General in the War Office would risk starting anything, even if he learned that some pal of his had succeeded in bumping off Hitler?'

Sabine shook her head again. 'No, and any hope of Hitler being bumped off is only wishful thinking. He is far too careful of himself. What is more, it's my belief that he's under the protection of the Devil. Until the Russians or the Allies reach Berlin I'd bet any money that no-one will ever get him.'

At that moment they heard the front gate slam. Glancing swiftly out of the bay window they saw von Osterberg propping his bicycle up against the fence.

'It's Kurt!' Sabine exclaimed in alarm. 'What can have brought him home so early? Quick! For God's sake, hide yourself.'

Von Osterberg was already running up the garden path. Had Gregory crossed the room he would have been bound to be seen by the Count through the window, or have run into him in the hall. There was only one thing for it. He dived through the velvet curtains at the entrance to the little writing room and pulled them to behind him.

For a moment he stood there, wondering if he could get out through one of the windows without being heard. Then through the curtains behind him he heard von Osterberg burst into the drawing room and cry:

'We are free! Free! Hitler is dead! Hitler is dead!'

18

The Great Conspiracy

GREGORY had his hand stretched out towards one of the windows in the little room. But at the Count's cry he remained transfixed.

Sabine's voice came through the velvet curtains, 'Hitler dead! No! How? Surely no-one could have got into his headquarters and shot him. A stroke?'

'No. It was a bomb. At least I think so. No details are known yet. But he's dead. He must be. The codeword *Walküre* has been sent out. That makes it certain. I received it in my office twenty minutes ago, and I left at once to let you know.'

'You were in the plot, then?'

'Yes. Several times recently arrangements have been made to assassinate the swine, but they couldn't be carried through because of his habit of altering his day's schedule at the last moment. There were difficulties about the bomb, too. Our German fuses hiss when they are started, so a package containing one would attract attention. But British fuses are worked by acid. They are started by breaking a glass capsule containing the acid and in a given time it eats through a wire. That's how I was brought into it. In my laboratory I have captured explosives as well as our own with which to experiment. I supplied the fuses. But they meant to get him this time, anyhow. If the bomb didn't go off it was intended to shoot him.'

'Kurt, I think you might have told me about this.' Sabine's voice sounded a trifle peevish.

'My dear, I couldn't,' he replied apologetically. 'All of us took an oath of secrecy. And I was never in the inner ring; so

I didn't know that another attempt was to be made today or who the gallant fellow is that did this splendid deed. But what's that matter? We're free! Free from that gutter-bred monster at last!'

'How about the others, though?' Sabine asked. 'Himmler? Goebbels? Goering? They won't give in without making a fight for it.'

'Don't worry. They'll be taken care of. That was the object of sending out the codeword *Walküre*. By now the Generals who are in this will have taken over at the War Office. The Guard Battalion will be in possession of key points like the Broadcasting Station, and troops from the Tank and Artillery Schools will be marching on Berlin.'

'Who is responsible for the *Putsch*?'

'Colonel-General Ludwig Beck; and he has the support of many others who refused to kowtow to Hitler: Field Marshal von Witzleben, who is to become Commander-in-Chief of the Armed Forces; Halder, who'll probably be chosen as Chief of the General Staff; Hoeppner, Olbricht, Fellgiebel, Oster, Hase, Wagner and Admiral Canaris. A number of our ablest younger officers are in it too: Merz von Quirnheim, Claus Schenk von Stauffenberg, Fabian von Schlabrendorff and Henning von Tresckow. It was he who put the bomb in Hitler's 'plane when he went to the Eastern front, though, of course, I couldn't tell you so at the time. Both the Police Chiefs, Count Helldorf and Artur Nebe, are with us; and several of the Army Commanders at the fronts, Von Kluge and Rommel among them. As Military Governors in France and Belgium, Stuelpnagel and Falkenhausen have promised to arrest all the Nazis in Paris and Brussels. Everything has been thought of. We have nothing to fear.'

Gregory had turned and taken a silent step back towards the curtains. Peering through the narrow gap between them while von Osterberg reeled off this impressive list of names, he took stock of the aristocrat-scientist who was still Erika's husband. It was two and a half years since he had seen the Count and in that time von Osterberg had aged considerably. He was of medium height, thin and his hair had turned nearly white. He looked a good sixty, but he was still a handsome man, apart from a scar that seamed the left side of his face from eyebrow to chin. Gregory had given him that for his cowardice in succumbing to pressure from the Gestapo and luring Erika back into Germany so that she might be held as a hostage for her English lover.

Hurriedly von Osterberg was going on, 'Beck is to be the new German Head of State; but only temporarily till we have the situation well in hand and have come to terms with the Anglo-Americans to help us stave off a Russian invasion. In spite of that fool Roosevelt having made it so difficult for us to negotiate by his announcement at Casablanca about insisting on "unconditional surrender", they can't refuse to treat us reasonably now we've got rid of the Nazis. And the last thing they want is to have Germany, Austria and Hungary fall into the hands of the Communists. But we're all against a permanent military dictatorship. As soon as we have cleared up the mess Karl Goerdeler will take over from Beck and form a coalition government, including the Socialist leaders as well as Popitz, Schacht, Donhanyi, von Hassell and our other friends. Then there will be free elections again. But I'll be able to tell you more late tonight or tomorrow morning. I only looked in just to give you the great news. I'm on my way into Berlin to find out how things are going.'

Giving Sabine a perfunctory kiss on the cheek, her elderly lover hurried out into the hall. Caution demanded that Gregory should remain where he was until the Count was well clear of the house. But no sooner had his footsteps sounded running down the garden path than Sabine stepped swiftly across the room and took down a gilt-framed oil-painting from the wall. It had concealed a small cupboard. Opening it, she grabbed up a telephone receiver and after a moment said into it:

'I want Herr von Weizsaecker. Urgently! Urgently! Highest priority. This is number forty-three speaking.'

The garden gate had slammed so Gregory came back into the room and said, 'This is tremendous news. But what are you up to?'

Impatiently she waved to him to be silent, then spoke into the telephone again. 'Is that you, Ernst? Put me through to the

Reichsaussenminister. At once! At once! It's desperately important!'

'Hey!' Gregory cried. 'Are you trying to sabotage the plot?'

Her dark eyes flashing, she covered the receiver with her hand and almost snarled at him, 'Of course not. I couldn't now, even if I would. This is a private matter.'

Speaking again into the telephone, she said, 'What! He is at his headquarters in East Prussia: Schloss Steinort? Then get on to him at once. Don't lose a moment. Tell him I've just learned that the Führer is dead. Blown up by a bomb or something; and that the Generals have seized control in Berlin. Tell him to look out for himself.'

Panting slightly she hung up, shut the door of the secret cupboard, shook back her dark hair and said to Gregory, 'That's the private line to the Foreign Office that Ribb had installed for his use when he was staying here. I haven't used it for ages. Thank God it hadn't been cut in an air-raid. As far as I'm concerned Hitler can rot in hell. So can most of the other Nazis. But I had to give Ribb a chance to get away. After all, he's an old friend and has always treated me very decently.'

Gregory was in no position to quarrel with these sentiments. In fact he felt admiration for the decision and swiftness with which she had acted. Smiling now, he said, 'Of course you're right. Your warning should enable him to take a 'plane to Sweden before the Army boys get him. It's a bit of luck for him, though, that instead of being in Berlin he is somewhere miles away in the country.'

She shrugged. 'I thought it almost certain that he would be. Since the air-raids became so bad all the top Nazis spend most of their time at comfortable headquarters up in East Prussia. They not only escape the bombs but have the advantage of being near Hitler's funk hole in the woods near Rastenburg. He's always fancied himself as the Big Bad Wolf, and often goes about humming the childish ditty; so they call it the *Wolfsschanze*.'

'Well, he won't go about singing "Who's afraid of the Big Bad Wolf" any more,' Gregory grinned. 'So I think that calls for a celebration.'

Relaxing, she smiled back at him. 'How right you are. Let's go down to the cellar and bring up the best bottle in it.'

He followed her down to find that the wine cellar was larger than he would have expected in a villa of that size and had been well stocked by Ribbentrop. They chose a magnum of Pol Roger '28 for themselves and a bottle of Tokay for Trudi. When Sabine took the bottle into the kitchen and told her the news she broke down and wept for joy. Opening the magnum they insisted on her having a glass from it with them to drink to a happier Europe. Then they took the magnum into the drawing room and excitedly speculated on the results of the *Putsch*.

By half past seven they had finished the magnum, so got up another then went out to the larder and collected a cold supper. About half past nine they were both feeling on top of the world from the amount of champagne they had drunk. Stretching her arms up over her head, Sabine lay back in her armchair and said with a sigh:

'Oh, darling, how I wish you could carry me up to bed so that we could really celebrate. Is it quite impossible?'

Gregory felt that if any circumstances could ever excuse his being unfaithful to Erika these were they. The war was as good as over, and he had lived through it. Even should the police question and arrest him he now had little to fear. By tomorrow the Gestapo would be hunted men and their torture chambers being hastily dismantled so that as little evidence of German atrocities as possible would fall into the hands of the victorious Allies. The Police would do no more than lock him up until arrangements could be made for the repatriation of prisoners of war, and the Allies would lose little time about that. If ever there were a night that called for more champagne and finishing up in bed with a lovely girl, this was it.

Sabine stood up. Her eyes were moist and shining as she impulsively seized his hand and cried, 'Come on! It's six months since you received your wound. You said you had only a few weeks to go to be completely fit again. A few weeks couldn't make all that difference.'

As he resisted her pull on his hand, she perched herself on his lap, flung an arm round his neck and glued her mouth to his. Her dark hair brushed his cheek and her heavy scent came to him in waves. He felt his senses swimming. Breaking their kiss, she threw back her head and pulled at him again. 'Darling, I want you terribly! Take me upstairs! Take me upstairs and love me like you used to do.'

'No!' he gasped, pushing her from him. 'I can't! It's not fair to ask me. Would you, if just for the sake of tonight you might ruin your chances of ever being able to make love again?'

For a moment she was silent, then she gave a heavy sigh. 'No. You're right. I'm sorry, my dear. It was beastly of me to try to make you.'

With a surge of relief he shut his eyes. Opening them again, he said, 'I'm sorry. Terribly sorry. But we ought to go upstairs all the same. There's no telling when Kurt will be back, and he mustn't find me here. In spite of the *Putsch*, that would be disastrous. His hatred for both myself and Erika knows no limit. He is proud as Lucifer, and that his Countess should have left him for a British agent while our countries were at war made him see so red that he even lent himself to helping the Gestapo to trap her. It was I who gave him that ghastly scar before going into Germany to rescue her. And, of course, by coming to England she was posted as an enemy of the Reich, so her fortune was confiscated, and he lost the use of her money. For all this he'd jump at the chance of being revenged on me. Even if the Gestapo's got its hands full he could call in the Police and at a time of crisis like this that could still have most unpleasant consequences.'

'We'll go up to your room, then,' she agreed. 'I'll tell Trudi to stay down here and she will warn us when she hears Kurt come in at the gate.'

The second magnum was nearly empty, so they collected a third from the cellar, with the idea that even if they couldn't make love they could get tight. Upstairs Sabine made no further attempt to seduce him and they talked about the war, speculating on whether in a few days it would be finished altogether, or if the Anglo-Americans would accept the German plan for joining them in fighting the Russians; and a score of other matters.

At midnight there was the usual air-raid, but no bombs fell

near; and by then they were too full of good wine to take much notice of it. Then about one o'clock Trudi came bursting into the room, to say that von Osterberg was by now in the hall and would be coming up at any moment expecting to find her mistress in bed.

Hastily kissing Gregory good night, Sabine said to him, 'It's most unlikely that Kurt will go to his laboratory as usual tomorrow morning; so you'd better stay up here. I'll sneak up and let you know what's been happening at the first chance I get.' Then she fled downstairs.

Elated as Gregory was by the day's events, his share of the two and a half magnums had made him drowsy; so once in bed he soon dropped off to sleep. But half an hour later he was woken by the light going on and Sabine shaking him. The consternation in her face told him at once that something had gone terribly wrong. As he hoisted himself up on his pillows, she said quickly, 'The *Putsch* is a wash-out. Hitler's not dead after all. In Berlin the Generals made a mess of things and the Nazis are out gunning for them.'

'Oh hell!' he muttered as he gathered his wits together. 'What filthy luck. But tell me more. Where's Kurt? Has he cleared out and made a bolt for it?'

'No. He has nowhere to bolt to where they couldn't lay him by the heels if they go after him. He is hoping he won't be implicated; but at the moment he's in the cellar shivering with funk as though he had an ague. He means to sleep down there and remain in hiding until we know more about what's going on. If the Gestapo come on the scene I'm to tell them that he hasn't been home since yesterday morning, in the hope that they'll think he's made off to the country. They'll have so many bigger fish to fry that if they don't find him here they may not bother about him—anyway for the time being. Then, in a few days' time when things have quietened down, if they haven't been back and made a thorough search of the house he'll be able to assume that no-one has given him away, and screw up his courage to come out again.'

Gregory gave a not very cheerful laugh.

'There's nothing funny about it,' she said severely.

'No; I suppose not. But the thought that you are hiding two

boy friends now, one upstairs and one down, momentarily tickled my sense of humour. Tell me, though, what went wrong with the *Putsch*?'

'Move over, so that I can get into bed with you,' she said. 'I've got next to nothing on, and it's chilly standing here.'

As she wriggled down beside him he felt that he had no option but to put his arm round her. Then, as she laid her head on his shoulder and turned over towards him, her soft body moulded itself against his side. He shut his eyes and his heart began to hammer, but he fought a silent battle endeavouring to keep his mind on the *Putsch*. Fortunately for once Sabine's thoughts were not centred on amorous delights, but on events; so she began at once:

'The bomb went off all right, but either it wasn't powerful enough or Hitler wasn't near enough to it to get its full effect. Goebbels put out a broadcast about the attempt late this evening. But his account of the affair is certain to be a tissue of lies; so there's not much that's known for certain. The bomb was taken to the *Wolfsschanze* by Count Claus Schenck von Stauffenberg. He must be a terrifically gallant young man because he'd already been terribly wounded when he walked into a minefield. That cost him an eye, one hand and the use of all but two fingers of the other; so how he managed to do the job at all I can't imagine.

'Anyway, after the bomb went off he succeeded in getting to his 'plane and back to Rangsdorf, the airport outside Berlin, and he telephoned the War Office from there confirming a message that Hitler was dead that had been sent by one of his fellow conspirators at the *Wolfsschanze*. Beck and some of the other Generals in the plot had assembled at the War Office. Soon after they received the first message they arrested General Fromm, the Commander-in-Chief, Home Army, because he refused to play, and issued their codeword, *Walküre*. I gather that for cover purposes it was to be used for an exercise that would bring the troops at the training depots outside Berlin into the city, in the event of a revolt by the thousands of half-starved foreign workers here. But early in the evening things started to go wrong.

'Fortunately Kurt met a friend outside the War Office and

they didn't actually go into the building. Instead, they decided to go off and join another group of the conspirators who had assembled in a private apartment not far off. So from that point on I know only what Kurt managed to pick up and the bits in Goebbels' broadcast that sound like facts. Apparently a Major Remer, who commanded the Guard Battalion, became suspicious about the orders he had received, so went to Goebbels. That put the fat in the fire, and the troops from outside Berlin failed to turn up. About the same time General Fromm learned that Hitler was still alive; so he arrested the Generals who had arrested him, and a lot of people were shot.'

Gregory sighed. 'What a tragic mess. If only the plot hadn't failed the war might have been over in a week; but now I suppose it will drag on for months, anyway until the Allies have occupied the Ruhr and crossed the Rhine.' After a moment he added thoughtfully, 'I don't wonder Kurt is scared out of his wits. Tell me, though, do you care much whether he lives or dies?'

'Oh, I'd hate him to be caught,' Sabine replied at once. 'Although he's no good as a lover, I'm quite fond of him in a way. I've always got on well with elderly men who are well bred and intelligent. They're much more cosy to live with. Young men are always making jealous scenes and should be kept strictly for one's bed. That is, except for a few very special men, like you, darling. I'm sure I must have told you how I adored my husband, Kaleman, and when I married him he was more than twice my age. I don't love Kurt, of course, but short of having the Gestapo take me to pieces I'd do anything I could to save him.'

For a moment Gregory considered the situation. It was in his own interests that von Osterberg should die, as that would free Erika. But, even so, the thought of any man whimpering in a torture chamber when there was a chance of preventing it was intolerable, so he said:

'If you want to save him you've got to get him back to his own bed and out of the house at the usual time tomorrow morning. Should the Gestapo find out that he was involved in the plot his goose would be cooked anyhow. But they may not.

In any case they will be buzzing round like a swarm of wasps, checking up on everyone they think might have been even remotely connected with the conspiracy, and it is certain that a man in Kurt's position will be on their list of suspects. Therefore his only chance is to act normally. If they come here at night they must find him in bed. Any story by you that he has simply disappeared would start an immediate hunt for him. Still more important, he must go to his laboratory and carry on as usual. If he doesn't his absence will be reported, and that's certain to be taken as a confession of complicity. Then when they come here and dig him out he won't stand an earthly.'

Quickly, Sabine drew away from Gregory and sat up. 'You're right, darling! Absolutely right! I'll go down at once and make him see the sense of what you've said.' As she jumped out of bed, Gregory caught another whiff of her exotic scent. Then she pulled on her dressing gown and ran from the room.

Next morning it was Sabine who brought up Gregory's breakfast. As she set the tray down she told him that Kurt had taken the advice she had given him and, fortified by a stiff brandy against awful forebodings, had just gone off to his laboratory. She added that, as soon as she had dressed, she meant to go into Berlin to find out all she could about what was happening.

It was not until after five that she got back and came upstairs to tell him the result of her reconnaissance. The wildest rumours were flying about, but there could be no doubt that the *Putsch* had failed utterly. Several people near Hitler had been killed but he had escaped with minor injuries. Beck had committed suicide, von Stauffenberg and several others had been shot, and the Gestapo were arresting people left, right and centre.

For a time they discussed various versions of the affair, then, when it neared six o'clock, Sabine went downstairs filled with anxiety to know whether von Osterberg would return. The room Gregory occupied looked out on the road so, from behind a curtain, he too kept watch. Soon after six the Count pedalled up, then with sagging shoulders walked up the garden path. From his return it was clear that the Gestapo did not yet know that he had been among the conspirators; but there was

still a very worrying possibility that, under torture, one of
those who had been arrested would give him away.

However the next day, Saturday, he again returned safely
but in time for lunch; and the dreaded visit from the Gestapo
did not take place that day nor on the Sunday. From fear that
he was being watched and if he happened to meet some friend
who was already known to have been involved it might later
be used against him, von Osterberg refused to leave the house;
so Gregory spent a very dull weekend confined to his room.
Trudi managed to smuggle up food hidden in a basket for him,
but he did not see Sabine for even a few moments.

Most of the time he spent in reading and sleeping; but now
that the first excitement about the attempt on Hitler had died
down he felt better able to concentrate on trying to reassure
Erika that he was safe. In that he felt he had succeeded, as
twice he got distinct impressions of her at Gwaine Meads,
thinking of and praying for him; and this strengthened his
resolution against being lured by Sabine into agreeing to chance
a set-back to his supposed affliction should she again become
too loving when with him.

By Sunday night it was six days since he had parted from
Malacou and after getting away from Poland he had not given
the occultist a thought. But that evening he saw Malacou
again clearly. With his shoes off, and looking utterly miserable,
he was sitting under a hedge eating raw carrots. It looked as
though during the past week he had become a tramp and had
walked a considerable distance, but whether he was still in
Poland or had come west into Germany Gregory could not
tell. However, he was aware that Malacou's misery was not
caused only by his own wretched fate; he was grieving for
Tarik, who was dead. The hunchback had panicked and run
from the cottage in an endeavour to escape when the two S.D.
men had arrived there. As he had ignored their shouts to halt,
one of them had shot him in the back. Owing to the darkness
Gregory had not seen his body, but Malacou had found it
later.

Regarding Malacou as an unsavoury episode in his life that
was now closed, Gregory thought how lucky he was to be in
such comfortable quarters instead of, as he might well have

been, eating carrots in a field; then he dismissed the unfortunate Jew from his mind.

On Monday von Osterberg went to work again and Sabine made another trip to Berlin, both to secure what news she could and try other people of her acquaintance in the hope of securing papers for Gregory. Tuesday, Wednesday and Thursday passed in a similar manner and, as no move by the Gestapo had been made against the Count, it began to look as if he was going to escape the fate that had befallen many of his friends. Sabine continued to have no luck about papers, but every afternoon she returned from her expeditions an hour or more before von Osterberg was due back and was able to give Gregory more and more details about the plot that she had picked up from friends in high places. So, by the end of the week, he had a pretty accurate picture of the development of the conspiracy from its beginning to its disastrous outcome.

As he was aware the Army Chiefs, being convinced that Germany was in no state to face another war, had strenuously opposed Hitler's plans, both for breaking the Versailles Treaty by re-militarizing the Rhine Zone and for going into Austria. That he had pulled off both coups successfully, against their advice, had greatly weakened the Generals' position; but when he told them that he intended to annex the Sudetenland, they had decided the time had come when no more risks could be taken, and had made plans to eliminate him. At that time their power was still considerable, so they certainly could have done so. But the ground had been cut from beneath their feet by Munich. Chamberlain and Daladier gave Hitler everything he asked. After three such bloodless triumphs Hitler became more than ever the idol of the German people. However dangerous the Generals knew him to be they positively dare not pull him from his perch, for it would have brought upon them the outraged anger of the whole nation.

In the case of Poland they could do no more than bleat a warning. Again he ignored it and, glumly apprehensive, they entered on the war with all the efficiency for which their caste had long been famous. Poland was finished in a fortnight, but the campaign had necessitated leaving Germany's western frontier almost naked. They thanked their gods that France showed no disposition to launch an immediate offensive, but were convinced she would launch one in the spring; and the German Army was then weaker than that of France. Again, they had decided that they must eliminate Hitler before they had a full-scale world war on their hands. The result had been the Munich bomb plot in November 1939, in which Hitler had narrowly escaped being blown up. About that Gregory had needed no telling, as he had been involved in it himself.

In the spring there had followed the staggering series of *Blitzkriege* by which Hitler had made himself the Overlord of Denmark, Norway, Holland, Belgium and France. The Generals had been amazed by their own successes but happily accepted them and, much as they continued to dislike 'Corporal' Hitler, felt that there could no longer be any question of getting rid of him.

The following year had seen further German triumphs in the Balkans and the great drive into Russia. Over the latter they had always shaken their heads, and by the winter their forebodings were proving only too well justified. But in the meantime their wings had been clipped. Many of them had been sacked for opposing Hitler's 'inspired' strategy; others were separated by many hundreds of miles and had been forbidden to communicate with one another.

So it had not been until disaster after disaster on the Russian front that a common desperation had driven a number of General Staff officers to risk a series of secret meetings and, in partial collaboration with members of the civilian Resistance groups, again plan to depose or kill Germany's Evil Genius.

They were still hampered by the fact that every officer and man had personally sworn allegiance to Hitler and that, owing to Goebbels' propaganda, millions of Germans still had complete faith in him. But it appeared certain that the Allies were about to invade Europe; so it had been decided that, psychologically, that would be the moment when the German troops and people would most readily accept the overthrow of the Nazi regime.

In consequence, from mid-June the most determined group had begun to make definite plans. The handsome but sadly disfigured young Colonel Count von Stauffenberg had recently been appointed Chief of Staff to the Replacement Army. In this capacity it was one of his duties to report at Hitler's morning conferences on troop units ready to be despatched to the battle fronts. A satisfactory bomb having been made ready, he volunteered to take it in his brief-case to one of these conferences and leave it there, so that it would, blow Hitler up.

However, it was decided by the plotters that it was essential to eliminate Goering and Himmler from the succession at the same time, so they must both be present when the attempt was made. Hitler was then at Berchtesgaden in the Obersalzberg and it was learned that on July 11th Goering and Himmler would be there too. On that date von Stauffenberg took his bomb to the conference, but it transpired that although Goering was present Himmler was not, so the Count returned with the bomb still in his brief-case.

On the 15th he again took his bomb to a Führer conference at Berchtesgaden, but neither Goering nor Himmler attended it; so again he refrained from setting the fuse of the bomb going.

These abortive attempts had dangerous repercussions for, believing Hitler's death to be imminent, Stauffenberg's confederates in Berlin had twice set the machinery to work for bringing troops into the capital. This had to be laughed off as an exercise against the possibility of a revolt by the foreign workers. But such an excuse would not be accepted again. Therefore it was decided that Stauffenberg must go through with his next attempt whatever the circumstances, even if Goering and Himmler could not be sent in pieces to another world with their Führer.

By the 20th Hitler had moved from Berchtesgaden to the *Wolfsschanze* in East Prussia; so it was there that von Stauffenberg flew with his brief-case containing the bomb. But the stars were against him. Owing to a fault in the ventilation system of the concrete cellar in which Hitler habitually held his midday conferences, it was held instead above ground in a long flimsy wooden hut.

Having made his report, von Stauffenberg, who was sitting next to Hitler, excused himself to go out of the hut to telephone, leaving his brief-case resting against the leg of Hitler's chair. The bomb went off, the hut was shattered and, feeling certain that Hitler was dead, von Stauffenberg jumped into a car that his A.D.C., von Haften, had ready for him. Owing to his agitation the courageous Count had left his hat and gloves on the conference table. In spite of his being improperly dressed they got past the three check points, although only through the last after having their names taken and von Stauffenberg exercising his authority as a Colonel to overawe the well-disciplined guard who had taken alarm at the sound of the explosion. They then emplaned for their two and a half hours' flight back to Berlin.

Meanwhile Beck and the other Generals had begun to play their parts in the capital. General Fellgiebel, who was in the plot and responsible for communications at the *Wolfsschanze*, had actually seen his Führer blown through the side of the wooden hut; so he immediately put through a call to Berlin to say that the attempt had succeeded. On receiving it General Olbricht, the Chief of Staff of the Home Army, issued the codeword *Walküre*, then went to his C.-in-C., General Fromm, and told him that Hitler had been assassinated.

Fromm refused to believe it. Yet all might still have been well had not Fellgiebel suddenly got cold feet. Instead of permanently sabotaging the telephone exchange at the *Wolfsschanze* after putting through his call, as had been intended, on being warned that he was watched he left the exchange undamaged.

To convince Fromm that Hitler was dead, Olbricht offered to telephone the *Wolfsschanze* expecting the line to be useless. Instead he got straight on to Keitel, who assured Fromm that the Führer was still alive.

At that, Fromm refused to play; so Beck, who had by then arrived, arrested him and put him in another room with a junior officer to stand guard over him. General von Hase had also arrived and, as Commander of the troops in Berlin, ordered the Guard Battalion to surround the Government quarter. Then, apparently, the conspirators simply sat back and waited for the dynamic von Stauffenberg to join them.

It so happened that a Major Otto Remer, who had recently

been posted as C.O. of the Guard Battalion, was a convinced Nazi. Even so, he would probably have carried out the orders of his Army superiors but for another piece of ill luck that befell the conspirators. Hitler's faith in the loyalty of the Army had deteriorated to the point of taking a leaf out of the Russians' book, and attaching Political Commissars to all formations. His nominee with the Guard Battalion was a Lieutenant Hagen, previously employed in Goebbels' Ministry. Hagen queried the order and persuaded Remer to let him go with it to Goebbels and, instead of arresting him, consult him about it.

Hagen found that Goebbels had already heard about the attempt on his Führer's life over the still-open telephone line from the *Wolfsschanze*. Believing the Generals to have seized Berlin, he was down in a cellar under his Ministry holding a pistol and contemplating blowing out his brains. On Hagen's arrival he realized that there was still a chance of defeating the *Putsch* and sent him to fetch Major Remer.

By then Remer's men had surrounded the War Office, but he did not like to go in. The tanks had also arrived from the Training Depot, but their Commander had queried his orders with his Chief, General Guderian, who happened to have a jealous hatred of most of the other Generals and was inclined to be pro-Nazi. He told his subordinate that, although he was to carry out Exercise *Walküre*, in no circumstances was he to use his tanks against S.S. troops or Government buildings.

Von Stauffenberg reached the War Office at about five o'clock, to find that in the past three hours little had been done. The new Commander-in-Chief designate, Field Marshal von Witzleben, had belatedly turned up with his uniform in a suitcase, but finding Remer's troops round the War Office instead of attacking the Gestapo headquarters, and the tanks under orders not to help in the *Putsch*, he had got cold feet and had gone home again; while none of the others knew quite what to do.

After an interval of indecision on both sides Remer decided to obey Goebbels' summons. By then Goebbels had been on to the *Wolfsschanze* and had learned the truth about what had happened there.

The bomb had gone off at eighteen minutes to one. It was believed that a Colonel Brandt, who had been seated on the other side of Hitler from von Stauffenberg, had pushed the brief-case further under the heavy table, thus somewhat reducing the effect of the explosion. But, in any case, had the conference been held as usual, in the concrete bunker, everyone there would have been killed. As it was, two Generals, Brandt and Hitler's stenographer received mortal wounds, and several others, including Colonel-General Jodl, were seriously injured. Hitler escaped only because a minute before the explosion he had left his seat at the table to walk to the far end of the room and look at a wall map. Nevertheless the whole flimsy building had been disintegrated by the blast, and all of them were blown through the roof or walls, Hitler landing burnt, bruised and without his trousers.

Remer had been ordered to arrest Goebbels but still felt uncertain which side to take; so Goebbels picked up the telephone and put him on direct to Hitler. To his amazement, his Führer immediately placed him, a Major, in full command of all the troops in Berlin for the next twenty-four hours, and told him to arrest anyone, whatever his rank, who opposed his orders. Hitler then ordered Goebbels to get out a broadcast as swiftly as possible, attributing the attempt to a small group of fanatics and stating that he had come to no harm.

At about seven o'clock, to the consternation of the conspirators in the War Office, Goebbels made his broadcast. In the meantime von Stauffenberg had been frantically making long-distance calls to a number of Generals. Hitler's orders to hold every foot of ground were reversed. The Army in Courland was ordered to retreat at once from its dangerous position. Field Marshal von Kluge agreed to prepare to withdraw to the Rhine and gave orders that the bombardment of England with V.1's was to stop. Stuelpnagel in Paris and Falkenhausen in Brussels agreed to arrest all the Nazis in their commands; and soon after Goebbels put over his broadcast von Stauffenberg countered it with another, saying that it was a tissue of lies.

But it was by then too late. Dozens of junior officers not in the plot had arrived at the War Office. They demanded to know what was going on there; then, realizing that the *Putsch* now looked like being a failure, they decided to save their own skins by arresting the conspirators.

Fromm was released and took charge. Beck had a pistol and twice tried to blow his brains out, but only mutilated himself horribly, shooting out one eye, and had to be finished off by a sergeant. Von Stauffenberg alone put up a fight, but was overcome and at Fromm's orders, with Olbricht, von Quirnheim and von Haften, was shot at about midnight out in the courtyard.

So ended the ill-fated *Putsch* in Berlin.

19

Just Real Bad Luck

ON THAT afternoon of July 20th Mussolini, now reduced to puppet Dictator of Lombardy, was due to arrive on a visit to the *Wolfsschanze*. Hitler, slightly crippled in one arm and down his side, met his guest's train. There followed one of the Führer's two-hour-long tea parties at which the Duce and the senior members of his staff were present. By then all the Nazi leaders had arrived to condole with their master and congratulate him on his miraculous escape.

To the embarrassment of the Italians, the tea party developed into a slanging match. Goering roared insults at Himmler about the inefficiency of his police, Keitel vainly attempted to defend the Army as a whole while reviling the traitor Generals, Goebbels abused Ribbentrop who shouted indignantly, 'I will not be called Ribbentrop; my name is *von* Ribbentrop.'

During the earlier part of these proceedings Hitler remained silent, apparently in a delayed semi-stupor as the result of the shock he had sustained some hours earlier; but suddenly he came to life. Everyone else fell silent as, frothing at the mouth and with his eyes starting from his head, he began to rave.

While the white-coated footmen continued to move round with the teapots, pouring endless cups of tea, he carried on without ceasing for over an hour about how he, the most brilliant intellect in all German history, was being betrayed by a lot of hide-bound half-witted soldiers who would lose the war the next week if he ceased to tell them what to do; of how he had been spared by Providence to complete his task of purifying the world from the poison of the Jews, and how he would see to it that the traitors died by inches, and their wives and children and the decadent parents who had begotten such scum.

All this and much more Sabine retailed to Gregory, together with the names of soldiers, Civil Servants, Labour leaders and others who, day after day, were still being arrested by the Gestapo. But so far they continued to show no interest in von Osterberg.

It was on Friday afternoon that Sabine returned from Berlin with exciting news of a different kind. She had run into an old friend of hers who had recently returned to the capital after living for the past year in Munich. This lady's name was Paula von Proffin and before her marriage to a bank president, since dead, she had, like Sabine, been a model. Sabine described her as having a mouth like a letter-box but the most lovely eyes and, according to the report of lovers that they had had in common, she was 'simply terrific in bed'.

That she had possessed these attributes seemed just as well; for on the bank president's death it had emerged that he had been swindling his bank for years, so 'poor Paula' had been left to fend for herself as best she could. That best had been a succession of rich industrialists from whom, among other things, she had acquired several thousand pounds' worth of diamonds; and, on the side when the industrialists were out of the way, a variety of boy friends, mostly Cavalry officers, for whom she had a particular liking because she was an accomplished horsewoman. She had returned to the hell of Berlin only because an arms manufacturer, whose work kept him there, had offered to marry her.

Sabine had accompanied Paula back to the suite she was temporarily occupying at the Adlon and there, over the dry martinis, these two beauties had spent a happy hour swopping details about such luck as they had recently had in their favourite occupation. In due course Paula had related a most distressing experience that had befallen her about six weeks before in Munich.

She was then being kept in a handsome apartment by a maker of fire extinguishers named Bleicher who, owing to the air-raids, was positively rolling in money. One night at a party she had been introduced to Prince Hugo von Wittelsbach zu

Amberg-Sulzheim. The Prince's lack of chin was equalled only by his lack of money, but he was a physically fine specimen and Paula had felt flattered by the attentions of this connection of the Royal House of Bavaria. As Bleicher's business had taken him away from Munich that week Paula had consented to receive her new admirer the following afternoon in her apartment.

Prince Hugo's visit had terminated in a way that was to be expected and both parties had derived considerable pleasure from it. But the sequel had proved most unexpected and, as far as Paula was concerned, highly alarming. Next day the Prince had arrived with a suitcase and declared his intention of remaining with her permanently.

For three days and nights, between sessions of violent love-making, to which she confessed she had not submitted without enjoyment, she had begged the Prince to go home. But neither prayers, threats nor even the offer of a big sum of money would induce him to leave her; and, as he had taken her keys from her, she could not lock him out.

Moreover she had been extremely frightened for, as everybody knew, there was a strain of madness in the Wittelsbach family; and after twenty-four hours spent with Prince Hugo she felt no doubt at all that he had escaped being put under restraint only on account of his high standing as a Bavarian aristocrat.

On the third day Herr Bleicher had returned from his business trip. When he arrived at the door of Paula's apartment, happily anticipating a joyous reunion with his extremely expensive girl friend, she had pleaded illness and used every other excuse she could think of to persuade him to go away. But he had smelt a rat and forced his way through into her bedroom. There, it being a warm afternoon, he had come upon the receding-chinned but muscular Prince Hugo lying on Paula's bed, wearing only his monocle.

Excusably, perhaps, Bleicher had compared Paula to certain female dogs that exist only by scavenging in gutters. To this the Prince had taken exception; not on Paula's account, but because it implied that he, a scion of the Royal House of Bavaria, could conceivably have lowered himself to the point of frequenting a slum.

Shouting a refutation of the charge, and that to fight a duel with such an obviously low-born person as Bleicher was unthinkable, the Prince leapt naked from the bed, seized a knife from a tray that was on the bedside table and flung himself upon the fire-extinguisher merchant.

Fortunately it was a silver fruit knife, so not very sharp. But it was swiftly clear to Paula that murder would result unless her two lovers could be separated. Running from the apartment she had called on her neighbours for help and they had brought the Police. With difficulty the combatants had been pulled apart. Bleicher was cut and bruised but had suffered no serious injury and, having consigned Paula to the Devil, took himself off for good. But it had needed two policemen with the help of several bystanders to restrain Prince Hugo and get him down-stairs into a police van.

This latest demonstration of the Prince's unbalanced mind had led to his becoming an inmate of a discreetly run estab-lishment in which wealthy people with unpredictable mental-ities were looked after; and as far as Paula knew he was still there. The following day the Prince's clothes had been col-lected but, as a souvenir of her brief association with semi-royalty, Paula had retained the Prince's wallet, because it was embossed with the Prince's crest in platinum and small diamonds.

Asked by the quick-minded Sabine if the wallet had had anything in it Paula had shrugged and said, 'Only fifty marks and the sort of papers everyone has to carry these days.' She had then been persuaded to dig it out of her luggage.

Having concluded her account of this fortunate meeting Sabine opened her handbag and, with a happy laugh, presented Gregory with the Prince's wallet.

Quickly examining its contents, Gregory saw that, although Prince Hugo was ten years younger than himself, the descrip-tion of him was vague enough to get anyone who used it past a casual inspection, provided he was a little under six feet, of medium build and dark. Few people in Berlin could know about the episode that had taken place in Munich six weeks previously and, even had they done so, since then the Prince might well have been let out of the mental home in which he had been confined; so, with a little luck, his papers could prove for Gregory a passport to freedom.

When Sabine had finished the account of her coup it was getting on for six o'clock and, as von Osterberg could shortly be expected back, they had to postpone until the following morning discussing the best means for Gregory to leave Berlin.

By then, as he had been in hiding at the Villa Seeaussicht for ten days, habit had made him immune to temptation when seeing Sabine in her bedroom and since the night of the *Putsch* she had made no further attempt to seduce him; so after giving her a perfunctory kiss he perched himself on the side of her bed and they at once set about making plans.

He had already decided that his best chance of getting out of German-held territory lay in making for the Swiss frontier. He knew the Lake Constance district well, so thought he would have no great difficulty in stealing a boat one night on the German shore and crossing the lake under cover of darkness. But the main line from Berlin to the south ran through Munich, so there was just a chance that if there was an inspection of papers on the train, he might be called on to produce his in front of a fellow traveller who knew Prince Hugo von Wittelsbach zu Amberg-Sulzheim; and that could lead to his being denounced as an impostor.

Remote as this risk was, Gregory's natural caution made him loath to take it. Sabine then produced the idea that he should make the first stage of his journey in her car. Like most people who had cars laid up she had put by a secret store of petrol against an emergency and, after driving the car some distance from Berlin, Gregory could hand it over at a garage with sufficient petrol for a mechanic to drive it back to her. It was therefore agreed that he should drive the forty miles to Wittenberg, where there was a big railway junction, and from there take trains by a circuitous route to the Swiss border. There remained only the matter of money, with which Sabine had not yet provided him; so she got up at once to go into Berlin and cash a cheque for the sort of sum which would keep him going even if it was some weeks before he could get over the frontier.

It was half past twelve before she returned and gave him

the equivalent of about one hundred and fifty pounds in mostly high-denomination RM. notes. Having thanked her and promised to repay her as soon as that became possible, he stowed them away in the Prince's wallet; but, as it was a Saturday, it was by then too late for him to make a start that day. Neither could he do so the next, as von Osterberg would be in the house from lunchtime throughout the weekend, and it would not be possible to get the car out of the garage while he was about.

Resigning himself to another lonely Sunday, Gregory spent it up in his room, for most of the time reading by the open window. Owing to that, he was lucky enough to get a few minutes' warning when out of the blue the blow fell. At ten to four on the Sunday afternoon two cars roared up in front of the house and out of them jumped seven black-clad Gestapo men.

As they hurried up the path Gregory gave a swift glance round. He made his own bed each morning and Trudi had taken away the remains of his lunch; so there was nothing to show that anyone was occupying the room. Having envisaged such an emergency for the past week, he knew that his only chance of escaping capture lay in his getting up on to the roof. Running out on to the landing he shinned up the wooden ladder there, pushed open the trapdoor in the ceiling and emerged on the central gutter.

The trapdoor was nearer the back of the house than the front; so from above it he could see into the garden. It was just such another sunny afternoon as that on which he had come upon Sabine lying in the swing hammock, and she was lying there now. Von Osterberg was lounging nearby in a deckchair with a book on his lap. As Gregory took cover behind a chimney stack he saw them both jump to their feet, then the group of S.D. men hurrying towards them.

Next moment the Count had pulled a pistol from his pocket and put it to his head. There came a sharp report. Sabine screamed, von Osterberg collapsed in a heap with blood running over his face, and the Gestapo men closed round them.

It was obvious that the Count had chosen to take his own life rather than fall into the hands of his enemies; and as his death freed Erika Gregory could not repress a feeling of satisfaction at the thought that if he could get safely home he would, at last, be able to marry her. But there remained the 'if'; and should the Gestapo make a thorough search of the villa, as the odds were they would, his own number might well be up.

For a moment he contemplated dashing downstairs and attempting to make a bolt for it. But he felt certain that the drivers who had been left in the two cars would be armed. He was armed himself; but even if he could shoot his way past them, as the shooting would bring another seven gunmen hard on his heels his chances of getting clean away would be anything but rosy. Swiftly he dismissed the idea. The Gestapo had already got the man they had come for and, although it was to be expected that they would rummage through the rooms and cellar hoping to find his papers, they might not bother to look round the roof.

The risk being remote of anyone in the garden looking up and catching sight of the small part of Gregory not hidden by the chimney stack, every few moments he continued to snatch swift glances at the scene below. Using the deckchair as a stretcher, two of the Nazis carried the Count's body into the house, while another of them, holding Sabine by the arm, brought her, too, indoors. After that, for the best part of a quarter of an hour, that seemed infinitely longer to Gregory, nothing else happened to give him any idea what was going on.

Then he caught the sound of an engine and the clanging of a bell, both of which ceased nearby. Crawling to the front of the house, he saw that the Nazis had telephoned for an ambulance. A few minutes later von Osterberg was carried out to it. No sheet covered his body, so it seemed possible that he might not be dead. But the Gestapo was not accustomed to bother about such decencies; so Gregory thought that, even so, the Count probably was dead.

Silence fell again for a while. Then Gregory heard sounds of movement and the banging of doors immediately below. That told him that the Gestapo's search had brought them to the top floor of the house; so very shortly now his fate would be decided. Getting out his pistol, he cocked it and covered the trapdoor. If they attempted to come up on to the roof he could at least shoot down one or two of them; although he knew that would save him only temporarily, as the others would send for tall fire-ladders from which they could shoot at him simultaneously from several angles.

Breathing very quietly he remained crouching on the far side of the chimney stack. At length the sounds below ceased. For another five minutes, still taut with apprehension, he continued to stare at the trapdoor. Then he heard a motor engine start up. Leaving his post, he again crawled to a vantage point near the front of the house from which he could see down into the road. What he saw there greatly distressed him; but he had feared it might happen and there was nothing he could do about it. The Gestapo thugs were leaving and they were taking Sabine and Trudi with them.

When the two cars had driven off he opened the trapdoor and, still with his pistol in his hand, went softly down the ladder. In the brief sight of the cars, which was all he had had before they left, he had been unable to check the number of Nazis in them. Although he thought it unlikely, it was possible that one or more of them had remained behind to continue the search for von Osterberg's papers; and he was too old a hand to be caught napping.

With extreme caution, pausing every few minutes to listen, he eased his way downstairs, looking into each room on his way. In the occupied bedrooms several drawers had been left open, some of the Count's things and pieces of Sabine's lingerie lay scattered on the floors. The downstairs rooms had also been ransacked, but after padding softly round for ten minutes he had made sure that he was alone in the house.

Helping himself to a badly needed drink, he sat down and considered the situation. Although he was worried about Sabine he felt that he had no need to be desperately so. The warning she had telephoned to Ribbentrop on the afternoon of the *Putsch* must have reached him, and her generous impulse to give her ex-lover a chance to escape the conspirators should now pay her a handsome dividend. It was cast-iron evidence that she had not been in the plot; so Ribbentrop would continue to protect her. Much as Himmler hated his colleague at the Foreign Office, it seemed most unlikely that he would risk an open quarrel with him by taking to pieces a woman whom he knew to be acting as one of his colleague's agents and against whom there was no proof of guilt. All the odds were, then, that after they had made depositions at the Gestapo H.Q. about von Osterberg's comings and goings previous to July 20th she and Trudi would be released.

Just in case the Nazis for some reason paid a second visit to the house Gregory decided not to clear up the mess they had made. Later he got himself some supper and took it up to his room. After he had had his meal he sat at the open window, keeping a look-out for Sabine.

The shadows lengthened until it was fully dark, but she did not return. With gradually increasing apprehension he continued to sit there until shortly after midnight, when the nightly air-raid on Berlin started. When it had died down and there was still no sign of her he came to the conclusion that she would not now be back that night; so, as a precaution against being caught asleep, he collected cushions, pillows and blankets and, taking them up to the roof, made a bed for himself up there.

On the Monday morning he woke early and, after getting himself breakfast, again sat at his window, hoping that Sabine would appear. But by ten o'clock it seemed clear that the Gestapo intended to detain her; so he decided that he must do something about it.

Going downstairs, he went to the wall cupboard behind the picture, picked up the telephone receiver and jiggled the button. Almost at once a voice at the other end of the private line asked, 'Who is calling?'

'I'm speaking for number forty-three,' Gregory replied. 'I have a most urgent message for Herr von Weizsecker. Please put me on to him.'

'I regret,' said the voice, 'Herr von Weizsaecker is not here. He is at Schloss Steinort with the Herr Reichsaussenminister.'

'When will he be back?' Gregory asked.

There was a long pause, then the voice answered, 'It is thought this afternoon. But we cannot say for certain.'

Fearing that if he gave his message to an underling it might not get through, Gregory said, 'All right. I'll ring again this afternoon.' Then, considerably perturbed, he rang off.

Going out to the garage, he found that it had already been unlocked by the unwelcome visitors of the previous evening but, apparently, they had done no more than look round it. The low red sports Mercedes was still there chocked up, and as he looked at it he thought what a beautiful advertisement a photograph of it would make with Sabine at the wheel. To his relief, he also found her emergency store of petrol untouched. Keeping an ear open anxiously for anyone who might drive up to the villa, he spent the rest of the morning getting the car in order after its many months of being laid up. When he had finished the tanks were full to the brim with petrol and the engine purred like a dream.

By lunchtime Sabine had still not returned and he could only pray that the Gestapo had not yet started wielding their thin steel rods to disfigure her lovely body, and that of poor little Trudi, with a sickening criss-cross of agonizing red weals. Controlling his impatience as best he could, he waited until half past three then rang up on the private line again.

To his immense relief he was put through to Ernst von Weizsaecker. Refusing to give his name, he gave a brief account of what had taken place at the Villa Seeaussicht and urged him to lose not a moment in reporting the matter to the Herr Reichsaussenminister.

The Permanent Secretary did better. He said that on behalf of his chief he would intervene himself, and at once telephone Gestapo headquarters.

Having, to the best of his belief, saved Sabine and Trudi, Gregory was anxious to be on his way, but he would have liked to make certain that Sabine had been freed before he left. He also felt that if he did not set out till after dark fewer people would mentally register his having passed them as the driver of the conspicuous red Mercedes. There was no reason to suppose that their doing so would later have unfortunate consequences, but Gregory owed the fact that he was still alive to having never taken a risk that was avoidable, unless circumstances had made it absolutely necessary.

In due course he got himself a bottle of wine from the cellar and some cold food from the larder. He was just about to take it upstairs when the telephone from the public exchange began to ring. For a minute he stood listening to its insistent shrilling, then decided to answer it. He already had food and his few belongings stowed in the car, so if the call presaged trouble he could be off at a moment's notice. Picking up the receiver, he put his handkerchief over the mouthpiece so that it muffled his voice, and said, 'Hullo!'

It was Sabine who answered. 'If that's a Gestapo man you can look forward to being flayed by the Herr Reichsaussen-minister for daring to make a mess of my house. But if it's who I think it is I'm grateful to you for staying on in the hope of finding out what had happened to me. I've rung up to let you know that I've been released and come to no serious harm. That traitor von Osterberg tried to do himself in. But, like General Beck, he bungled it. Still, he made an awful mess of himself and is probably dead by now. They kept glaring lights on all night in my cell; so I'm feeling about all-in. Trudi and I are going to spend the night at the Adlon with Paula. We'll be back in the morning; but it's better that you should not wait for us. Good luck. See you sometime.'

'Thank God you are all right,' said Gregory. 'I'll get off then. A thousand thanks for everything. When our paths next cross you know you can count on me.'

By then it was half past seven. Immediately he had put down the receiver he hurried across to the garage. There was the possibility that the call might have been monitored and Himmler's people, still anxious to get something on Sabine, come along to find out to whom she had telephoned. Three minutes later he was at the wheel of the long, low car, heading for Potsdam.

It was disappointing that von Osterberg was not definitely dead; but there seemed a good chance that he might not survive his self-inflicted head wound. Putting the Count temporarily out of his mind, Gregory concentrated on the road ahead, while thanking his stars that, after nearly a fortnight of anxiety as a voluntary prisoner, he now had ample money and a good chance of making his way to freedom.

As he sped along the road that curved round the end of the Wannsee he had a sudden mental picture of Malacou. Now with bristling beard and dressed like a tramp, he was trudging

along a country road. The brief vision of the occultist called
to Gregory's mind that his lucky escape from capture by the
Gestapo the previous evening had taken place on a Sunday,
his most fortunate day of the week. Following this line of
thought, it suddenly came to him that today must be July 31st
and his birthday. Then that Malacou had told him that the 4,
being governed by Uranus, was unlucky and that he was protected from it only owing to his close association with the Sun.

When he passed through Potsdam that dangerous period for
motorists, semi-darkness, had come. As he entered the suburbs
of the bomb-stricken town he put out a hand to switch on his
headlights. Suddenly a girl ran out from the entrance to a
block of workers' dwellings. A man came running after her
shouting at her to stop. Evidently, in her anxiety to escape her
pursuer, she did not see Gregory's car, or thought she could get
across the road ahead of it. In an endeavour to avoid her he
swerved towards the pavement, but too late. His outer
mudguard caught her and, with a scream, she was sent flying
into the middle of the road.

Had Gregory been in England he would have pulled up
immediately, but he dared not stop to give particulars of
himself to the Police; and it was certain that the man who had
been running after her would do for her anything that was to
be done. After only a second's hesitation he let the powerful
car out to get away from the scene of the accident as soon as
he could.

But two hundred yards ahead there was a crossing. A
policeman was on duty there. He had seen what had occurred.
Stepping into the road, he signalled Gregory to halt. Ignoring
the signal Gregory drove straight at him. Only just in time he
jumped aside. Then Gregory caught the shrill note of his
whistle. Ahead a lorry was approaching. Grasping the situation, its driver swung his vehicle across the road. As it turned
Gregory saw that it was a great six-wheeler loaded with barrels
of beer. For him to crash into its side head-on at the pace he
was going would have been suicidal. Swerving again, he
mounted the pavement. Next moment the car hit a concrete
lamp post. There came the sound of screaming metal and
tinkling glass. Then he passed out.

20

No Escape

WHEN Gregory's eyes opened he was lying on his side. They took in the uniformed torso of a State policeman then, as his glance wavered round, another policeman standing a little further off against a background of whitewashed wall with notice-boards on it. That, and the memory of his recent crash, told him that he was in a police station. Behind him another man was doing something to his left arm, and he realized it must be a doctor patching him up.

Considering the speed at which the Mercedes had hit the lamp standard, he had come off very lightly. The muscles of his left arm had been strained, his ribs were badly bruised where the steering wheel of the car had caught them, and he had knocked himself out on the windscreen. When the doctor had bandaged his head and strapped up his arm they helped him to sit up and a police sergeant said:

'*Altesse*, it is my duty to charge you with driving dangerously and with ignoring the signals of a police officer to halt.'

For a moment, still being half dazed, Gregory was foxed at being addressed as 'Highness'; then it clicked home that the police must have the wallet and identity card he had been carrying, so took him for Prince Hugo von Wittelsbach zu Amberg-Sulzheim. With a slow nod he asked, 'The woman —the woman who ran out in front of my car. Is she . . . is she badly injured?'

The Sergeant shook his head. 'No. Fortunately, *Altesse*, she only strained her wrist and grazed one side of her face.'

Gregory sighed with relief. At least he would not be charged with manslaughter. But all the same he was in a nasty mess.

For the night he was put in a cell and the doctor gave him a sedative. At seven o'clock next morning he was brought breakfast and an hour later the doctor examined him, then pronounced him fit to appear in court. The Sergeant asked if he wished to send for his solicitor and he replied that he had not got one in Berlin, so would choose a lawyer to defend him when he was brought before a magistrate.

On waking he had felt sick with disappointment that when everything had been set fair for him to get away over the Swiss frontier this misfortune should have befallen him. But he tried to console himself with the thought that his case would be infinitely worse had he fallen into the hands of the Gestapo instead of those of the Civil Police.

At nine o'clock he was taken in a prison van to the Potsdam Law Courts. In a cell there a dapper little man came and introduced himself as Herr Rechtsgelehrter Juttner and deferentially offered his services. Clearly he was eager to have the chance to act as Counsel for a *Hochwohlgeborener* and, knowing the profound respect with which the German middle classes still regarded the old nobility, this suddenly brought home to Gregory the advantages of temporarily being a Prince. Putting on the haughty manner expected of him, he accepted the lawyer's offer and for some while they discussed the case.

Herr Juttner could not disguise the fact that it was a bad one, because Gregory might well have killed the policeman who had tried to stop him. There would also, he said, be two cases: one, the Reich against Gregory for dangerous driving, and another, private action, brought by the injured girl, Fräulein Elfrida Trott, for damages.

Now that Gregory's mind was again working at full speed he at once realized that the second could be the more dangerous to him. The first would be settled that morning; but a private action might not come on for some weeks. For that he would be expected to call in his Insurance Company, and that he could not do. Almost certainly, too, the Prince's relatives in Munich would get to hear of it. He would then be exposed as an impostor and the wrecked car would be traced to Sabine. An investigation would follow which, as they would be unable to meet and concoct a story to explain their association, was certain to land them both up to their necks in trouble.

Although the Prince's wallet had been taken from Gregory, he knew that he still had at his disposal the considerable sum in it; and, as Fräulein Trott's injuries were not serious, it occurred to him that she might be willing to settle out of court. Seeing his prospects of a second case slipping away from him, Herr Juttner somewhat reluctantly agreed to this; but she was waiting in another room to give evidence, so Gregory sent the lawyer off to see her. Ten minutes later he returned to report that she had accepted five hundred RM. as compensation.

That fence over, Gregory took the next one: that of dealing with the wrecked car. If it were left at the garage to which it presumably had been towed, unless something was done about it at once the police would ask for instructions about its disposal. To forestall their doing so Gregory asked Herr Juttner to deal with the matter as soon as the court hearing was over.

He said that the car belonged to the Baroness Tuzolto and, knowing her to be absent from her home, he had taken it without her knowledge or permission. Out of the money held temporarily by the police he asked Herr Juttner to pay the garage for returning the car to the Baroness. He then swore the lawyer to secrecy about the transaction, on the grounds that he had used an illegal store of petrol that the Baroness had had in her garage and wished to prevent her getting into trouble should that come out. Herr Juttner also agreed to convey to the Baroness the Prince's sincere apologies for having taken and wrecked her car, and say that as soon as he could he would pay her any compensation she might ask.

Gregory then enquired the lawyer's fee for all that he was to do for him and when Herr Juttner tentatively suggested seven hundred and fifty RM., the lordly Prince secured his complete allegiance by telling him that he should have a thousand. After Fräulein Trott, the garage and the lawyer had been paid, Gregory reckoned that would leave him only about three hundred RM. out of the sum Sabine had given him. But Juttner had been quite definite that he would not be able to get him off with a fine, and he knew that any balance of his money would not be returned to him until he left prison; so, for what he had achieved, he felt that the sixteen hundred or so marks had been well spent.

Soon after midday he was taken into court. There he pleaded guilty, offering as an excuse only that he had been desperately anxious to get back to Munich as soon as possible because a relative of his was lying dangerously ill there. Fräulein Trott, the man who had chased her out of the block of flats and the policeman whom Gregory had nearly run down gave their evidence. In view of the prisoner's rank the magistrate treated him with some deference; but said that the case was a serious one and that people in his position should set an example instead of committing such a flagrant breach of the law; then sentenced him to six months' detention.

Knowing that in Germany, unlike Britain, the authorities had a stranglehold over the Press, Gregory then expressed his contrition and asked that in order to spare his family the disgrace of his being sent to prison no account of the case should appear in the papers. To his great relief the magistrate agreed and gave the necessary instruction.

From the court he was removed to a cell in the Potsdam police barracks; and there for the rest of the day he contemplated his unpromising future. As a convict he considered his prospects of escape as far less good than if he were being sent to a prisoner-of-war camp. But at least he would be safe from the Gestapo—provided that his imposture as Prince Hugo was not discovered. And to maintain it, he had taken all the steps he possibly could.

On the Tuesday morning he was driven some twenty miles in a prison van and, on being let out, learned to his consternation that he had been taken to Sachsenhausen. He had expected to have to serve his sentence in a prison among ordinary criminals, which would have been bad enough; but Sachsenhausen was well known to be a concentration camp and he at once envisaged all the horrors that being confined in one called up.

To his surprise and relief, after the formalities of booking him in had been completed, he found that not only were his fears groundless but that his lot, anyway for the time being, was to be far better than any he could have expected. The camp consisted of several square miles of hutments surrounded by an open zone between high, barbed-wire fences. Within it there were many thousands of internees and, as a precaution against mass riots, it was divided into a great number of sections, one of which was known as the 'Political Bunker'. The inmates of it numbered only a few hundred and were termed '*Prominente*', because they were all people of standing who had been placed under restraint for a variety of reasons.

Some were awaiting trial, some were held only on suspicion that they were anti-Nazi and some were serving sentences of detention for anti-social activities; and Gregory had failed to appreciate that the magistrate had sentenced him not to imprisonment but to detention. For that, and for having been sent to serve his sentence among the *Prominente*, he had to thank the status he had acquired with his title; and before he went to sleep that night he was calling down blessings on Paula of the letter-box mouth, whose misadventure had provided this status for him.

He was allowed to continue wearing his own clothes, the guards were quite friendly, the food passable, the hut into which he was put clean and the wire-net bed he was given comfortable. The only hardship imposed was a prohibition against talking, and to enforce this guards kept the prisoners under observation both day and night. This constant surveillance convinced Gregory that escape was next to impossible, but he soon found that when out on exercise or in the wash-house neighbours managed to exchange whispered sentences.

By these means he learned that among the prisoners in his hut were Pastor Dietrich Bonhoeffer, Professor Edouard Jessen and General von Rabenau; while in other huts were Baron Karl von Guttenberg, Judge Hans von Dohnanyi, the Christian Democrat Deputies Adolf Reichwein and Theodore Haubach, Prince Philip of Hesse, who before quarrelling with Hitler had been a prominent Nazi, the Socialist leaders Julius Leber and Wilhelm Leuschner, Generals Stieff and Lindemann, Counts Moltke and Matuscha and many other distinguished Germans.

At first, on finding himself among such people, several of whom might know Prince Hugo, Gregory was greatly alarmed that his imposture would be discovered. But on arrival at the camp two pieces of cloth, each bearing the letter P and a number, had been sewn on to his coat and trousers, and after being for only a short time in the hut to which he was allotted he found that the guards always addressed the prisoners by their numbers. Thus, as Number 541, his identity was screened from his companions and he swiftly decided to keep it so by refusing to give them any information about himself. As most of them had something to hide and they all believed that stool-pigeons had been put in among them, when he replied to their whispered enquiries only by a shake of the head none of them showed any resentment; and soon he had made friends of several of them.

As is the case in all prisons a mysterious grapevine existed by which news of the outside world regularly trickled into the camp, and this was frequently augmented by new arrivals. A number of them, like many of the prisoners already there, had first been confined for some days in cells under the Gestapo headquarters in Berlin. All of these had been subjected to a greater or lesser degree of torture in an attempt to force them to admit their guilt and incriminate others. But they all maintained that they had managed to stand up to it; and that, although in its early stages the pain had seemed to become unbearable, there came a point at which the human mind could not only accept it but ignore it until relieved by unconsciousness.

Towards the middle of August the fate of the Generals in the 20th July plot became known. Field Marshal Witzleben, Generals Hoeppner, Fellgiebel, Hase, Thomas, and several officers of less senior rank had been dragged before a 'People's Court' and shamefully exhibited there, unshaven, in old clothes and without braces or belts, so that they had had to hold their trousers up. They had then been condemned to death. The manner of their death had been personally decreed in detail by the fiendish Hitler. They had been stripped nakèd, hanged, cut down and revived, then hung up again with butchers' meat hooks in their backs until they expired in agony.

General Fromm, too, had not escaped. In spite of his having endeavoured to save himself by ruining the conspiracy, he had shared the fate of the colleagues he had from cowardice refused to aid. Kaltenbrunner who, with the possible exception

of Grauber. was Himmler's most brutal-minded Lieutenant,
had seen to that, because he was furious that Fromm had had
von Stauffenberg and the other most active conspirators shot,
instead of simply arresting them and handing them over to be
tortured.

War news was also coming through. After over two months
on their Normandy beach-head without launching an offensive
the Allies had at last broken out. Towards the end of July the
Americans, under General Bradley, had driven through to
St. Loo on the coast of Brittany and simultaneously the
Canadians had made a determined assault up the Falaise road
against Caen. The Russians, meanwhile, had arrived at the
gates of Warsaw and, although they were the hereditary
enemies of the Poles, many thousands of Poles had risen in
rebellion at dawn on August 1st with the intention of anni-
hilating the German garrison and so enabling the Russians to
enter their city.

During this time, and particularly at night before going to
sleep, Gregory frequently concentrated his thoughts on Erika
and did his utmost to assure her that he was safe and well. At
times he seemed to get through and see her clearly at Gwaine
Meads; but she looked ill, and he knew that was from worrying
about him.

Once, in the third week of August, he spontaneously
contacted Malacou. The Jew was sitting in a prison cell.
Whereabouts Gregory had no idea, but it was clear that the
occultist had been caught. Yet he conveyed a strong impression
that he was not in the least worried about his situation. Why
that should be Gregory could not imagine, but he had no
doubt at all that his old associate was perfectly content to be
where he was.

At the end of the month there was an influx of new prisoners:
Dr. Karl Goerdeler, Ambassadors von Hassell and von der
Schulenburg, Admiral Canaris, General Hans Oster, the
Police Chiefs Count Helldorf and Artur Nebe, the ex-Finance
Minister Johannes Popitz and several others. All of them had
been arrested in the last week in July or early in August, on
suspicion of having been concerned in the plot to assassinate
Hitler. They had since been confined in the Gestapo head-

quarters, but no evidence against them being forthcoming they had now been sent to Sachsenhausen.

Gregory was particularly interested in Admiral Canaris, as he knew the little man to have been the pre-war head of the German Secret Service and to have continued in that capacity until the previous winter. Only then had Himmler's inordinate ambition to control everything he could lay his hands on enabled him to secure the Admiral's dismissal and absorb the old regular-officered Secret Service into the much greater Foreign Intelligence Department UA-1, that had been built up for him by his own man, Gruppenführer Grauber.

Rumour in the camp had it that Canaris had been anti-Hitler from the beginning, and had even deliberately withheld Intelligence because he wanted the Allies to win the war quickly so that Germany might escape the terrible punishment that was now being inflicted on her. It was said, too, that his second-in-command, General Oster, who had been kept on after the Admiral had been sacked, had stubbornly continued to thwart the Nazis whenever possible; so that either of them should still be alive was a miracle.

Early in September, further news of Germany's rapidly deteriorating situation percolated through the camp. In mid-August the Allies had made another landing in the South of France. Soon afterwards Bradley and Montgomery had succeeded in encircling and destroying a great part of the German Army in the West, in the neighbourhood of Falaise, while another American Army under General Patton had reached the Seine at Fontainebleau.

Then the 23rd of the month had proved a truly black day for Germany. King Michael of Rumania had carried out a *coup d'état*, disarmed the German troops in Rumania and gone over to the Allies. Simultaneously there had been a rising against the Germans in Slovakia and on General Le Clerc reaching Paris with an armoured spearhead the population of the French capital had risen and set about massacring its German garrison. A few days later the Finns, who, with extraordinary bravery, had for five years fought as Germany's ally and kept a large Russian Army occupied on their front, had at last thrown in the sponge and asked for an armistice.

It was clear that Hitler's 'Europa' was cracking right and left, if not yet in the centre. But Gregory's mind was by then more seriously occupied about his own situation. Admiral Canaris had been put in his hut and, being greatly interested in the little Admiral's career, Gregory had taken special pains to cultivate him. It had, however, transpired that, even while confined at Sachsenhausen, the ex-Chief of Abwehr Intelligence had special sources of information. One day when they were employed in their morning chore of cleaning out the hut, the Admiral had whispered:

'Number 541, I gather that you are on the camp register as Prince Hugo von Wittelsbach zu Amberg-Sulzheim. But I know you are not. Who are you?'

Rigid with alarm, Gregory had whispered back, 'You are right. But if it is found out who I am it will cost me my life; so I beg you to keep my imposture secret.'

Canaris had agreed but Gregory was badly scared. Since the Admiral had found him out others, less discreet, might do so. Moreover, the thought had never ceased to nag him that, sooner or later, the story of the false Prince Hugo's car smash would reach Munich, and an enquiry be set on foot that would lead to his detection. Escape, except in the event of some unforeseen circumstance, being out of the question, he decided that, somehow or other, he must rid himself of his dangerous identity.

To do so would be difficult, but it might be achieved if, owing to some mix-up among the prisoners, he could get himself transferred to another section of the camp under a different name. The only place in which such a mix-up might be stage-managed was the camp hospital and, as he was on the camp register as Prince Hugo, it occurred to him that he might get himself admitted by making use of the well-known strain of madness in the Wittelsbach family.

The following day, in pursuance of this plan, at the midday meal he poured his soup over his head. His companions showed surprise, while the guards only laughed. But he followed this up by a variety of eccentricities, including violent outbursts of speech in which he declared himself to be the King of Bavaria. Forty-eight hours later these tactics had the desired result and he was escorted, violently protesting, to the camp hospital.

There was no special hospital for the *Prominente* and that which served the whole camp was some distance from their quarters. Although it was a big building, with at least twenty wards, it could not have accommodated a tenth of the internees who should have been receiving hospital treatment.

By far the greater part of the prisoners were Jews, foreigners or middle-class Germans who had been arrested as socialists, pacifists or just for having been heard to grumble at the hardships brought about by the war. When, from malnutrition, tuberculosis, cancer or other diseases, these political prisoners became too weak to be any longer driven to work they were shot or left to die. Only those who were still strong enough to be useful, but had met with some accident temporarily incapacitating them, were sent to the hospital for treatment. The majority of its inmates were criminals who had received sentences and had been evacuated from the bombed-out prisons of Berlin to a special section of the camp. As Germans who were assumed to be politically 'clean' they were still protected by the old laws so, if seriously ill, sent in; but often not until they were at death's door. The two types could be distinguished on sight, for below their identification numbers on coat and trousers the political prisoners had triangles of red cloth, while the criminal prisoners had triangles of green.

In due course, an elderly overworked doctor gave Gregory a brief examination. As he had confined his violence to speech and had not attacked anyone, the doctor decided that he was not dangerous but inflicted with periodical fits of insanity; so would probably recover in the course of a few days, and sent him to an ordinary ward for observation.

He found, as he had expected, that manpower now being so short in Germany, the hospital was greatly understaffed and that conditions in it were appalling. There were no female nurses. The scant care given to the patients was by medical orderlies, all of whom were too badly crippled by old wounds to be sent back to the Front, and of these there was only one to each ward of forty beds. To assist him each had two 'trusties' who, helped by the inmates of the ward who were not bedridden, took round the food and kept the ward free of its worst filth.

The lack of supervision in this death house—for it was little
else—was most favourable to Gregory's project and he set
about it without delay, for his best chance of carrying it out
successfully lay in doing so before the hospital staff became
familiar with his features.

Being allowed to move freely about the ward he tried to put
the awful stench of the place out of his mind and spent the
afternoon going from bed to bed, finding out the circumstances
of the other occupants. Several of them were obviously dying
and it looked as if two or three of them would not last out the
night. One of these, wheezing terribly, said that his name was
Franz Protze and that he was a Lübeck lawyer who had been
sentenced to three years for having forged the will of one of his
clients. Having sympathized with him on his harsh fate,
Gregory moved on among the other beds until he had
completed the round of the ward. He then decided his purpose
would best be served by making use of the dying lawyer.

About six o'clock a doctor, who was himself a prisoner,
made the round of the ward; but he was evidently so inured to
being unable to cope with its perpetual horrors that he spoke
only briefly to a few of the patients, here and there handing out
a couple of aspirins and giving the others no more than a
glance. One man was found to be dead and the doctor told the
two trusties to remove his body. No night garments were
issued to the patients, so those in bed were all lying in their
soiled underclothes. The trusties unceremoniously stripped the
dead man and carried away his naked corpse.

When the doctor had gone bowls of bluish, heavily watered
milk and slices of bread with a smear of margarine were passed
round. Then, when darkness fell, to economize electricity, only
one low-power electric light was switched on, and those patients
who had been capable of moving about began to undress. The
crippled medical orderly also started to undress and it became
evident that he did night as well as day duty, occupying a bed
near the door. That gave Gregory some uneasiness, but he felt
that the chances were that, after their long day's work, the
orderly and the two trusties would all sleep soundly, so prove
no impediment to his plans.

By nine o'clock the ward had settled down for the night,

but Gregory felt sure that the doctors and other staff would still be about in their quarters for some time to come; so he controlled his impatience as best he could and lay listening to the grim symphony of groans, coughs, incoherent ramblings and occasional cries of pain that came from the other beds.

At length, about one in the morning, he got up; but, instead of dressing, he put on only his shoes, pulling his socks on over them to muffle the sound of his footsteps. Carrying his outer garments he crossed the ward to Protze's bed. The lawyer was scarcely breathing and did not open his eyes. Taking his coat and trousers from under the bed Gregory got into them, then left his own, carefully bundled up so that the identification numbers with their large P should not show, in place of those he had taken. Turning away, he stole like a shadow down the faintly lit ward, glided past the snoring orderly's bed, eased open the door, stepped out into the corridor and closed the door softly behind him.

When he had been brought to the hospital that morning he had seen that no sentries were posted outside it. That was not surprising, as comparatively few of the patients were in any condition to leave it and, even if they had, their chances of escape from the camp would have been no better than from one of its many sections. He was, therefore, fairly optimistic about getting away from the building provided he was not caught while leaving by a door or window.

Still moving like a shadow, he made his way down two passages then halted at a partly open door. As he peered in there was just light enough for him to see that the room was a kitchen. Slipping inside he gave a quick look round. On several long side tables there were stacks of food left ready for preparing the first meal of the day, among them ham, *Leberwurst* and apples, evidently intended for the staff. Having crammed his pockets with a selection of these he climbed up on one of the sinks, opened the window beyond it and climbed out. A quick look round showed him that no-one was about and he made off into the semi-darkness.

Had there been the least chance of escaping from the camp he would have made the attempt. But he was already convinced that to do so would be suicidal. The whole of the vast area that it covered was enclosed by two barbed-wire and electrified fences a hundred yards apart. The intervening space was floodlit by arc lamps and at intervals along it there were watch towers manned by sentries armed with light machine-guns. In addition, between the two fences a number of fierce Alsatian dogs were let loose every night; so even if a prisoner could have cut his way through the inner fence and the nearest sentries had been dozing, one or more of the dogs would have given the alarm and the escaper been riddled with bullets before he could reach the outer barrier.

Each section of the camp was also fenced off from its neighbours, but these fences were not electrified so could be got through without difficulty; and Gregory's immediate object was to get as far from the hospital as possible. During the next half hour he climbed through half a dozen fences and, while between them, kept as far as possible in the shadow of the huts. But there was little danger of his being caught, for no guards patrolled the interior of the camp at night because the brightly lit, well-guarded perimeter made escapes impossible.

Having put three-quarters of a mile between himself and the hospital, he found a tool shed in which the implements used by the slave labour in that section were stored at night. Groping about in it, he made himself a place to sit down with his back comfortably propped up then eagerly devoured the food he had taken from the kitchen. Replete from this unusually substantial meal he closed his eyes and fell into a doze.

When daylight came he remained where he was, praying that the next stage in his plan would prove equally successful. Sounds of the camp stirring into life filtered through to him then, at about seven o'clock, the shuffling of feet outside. A sharp order was given and a line of wretched, ragged prisoners filed in to collect picks and shovels. Some of them looked at him with dull, lacklustre eyes, but none of them spoke. A Capo, as the trusties selected as overseers were called, appeared, saw him sitting on the floor, yelled at him to get up and struck him with a whip. As he came to his feet one of the prisoners muttered, 'He's not one of our gang.'

The Capo went out and fetched an S.S. man who proceeded

to shout questions at Gregory. Passing a hand over his eyes to give the impression of being bemused, he told him that he did not know who he was or how he had got there, but he thought that he had been wandering about for most of the night.

As there were so many thousands of prisoners in the camp living under such appalling conditions, he felt confident that from time to time there must be cases in which the mental strain caused some of them to have blackouts and lose their memories. The result was as he had expected. The S.S. man gave him a kick, prodded him with a Sten gun, then marched him off to the camp headquarters. There, after a short wait, he was taken in to a lean, scar-faced Untersturmführer and his case reported.

Apparently in a daze, he stood there staring at the floor; but he knew that the next half-hour would decide the success or failure of his plan. By this time Franz Protze would almost certainly be dead. When the hospital orderlies removed his body to throw it into one of the common burial pits they would collect his clothes and turn them in at the camp clothing depot. With such deaths taking place every few hours it was most unlikely that anyone would notice that the number on the clothes was not that under which Protze had been admitted.

Gregory's bed would be found empty. But as he had gone in as a mental case there would not be anything very surprising about his having wandered off in the night. The headquarters would be notified, but he had not been in the hospital long enough for anyone there to give an accurate description of him. Where his danger lay was in his disappearance being connected with a man being found who had lost his memory. His hope was in the vastness of the camp and that as it was understaffed no serious effort would be made to trace him. Anxiously he waited to learn how the Gestapo officer would react to the report about him.

The number on Protze's clothes was E1076 and Gregory had made very certain that the triangles they bore were green, for had they been red to take them would have been the next best thing to signing his own death warrant. The Untersturm-führer wrote the number down on a slip of paper and sent an orderly with it to the camp registry. Gregory was marched to a corner of the room and ordered to stand there facing the wall.

He remained there for ten anxious minutes. The orderly then
returned and handed another slip of paper to his officer. After
a glance at it the Untersturmführer said to the guard, 'His
name is Protze, and he's serving a three-year sentence.'

Gregory held his breath. If the register also contained the
information that Protze had been admitted to hospital the
game was up. He would be sent back there and his imposture
discovered. But after a moment the officer added, 'Take him
back where he belongs.'

Although Gregory breathed again, he had other fences to
get over. When he arrived at Section E would the officer in
charge there, or one of the guards, have known E1076 well
enough by sight to declare that Gregory was not the prisoner
who had borne that number? He could only hope that with
so many deaths and the constant influx of new prisoners the
guards never bothered to look on the poor devils as
individuals.

A quarter of an hour later he was temporarily reassured.
The bull-necked Blockführer to whom he was handed over
gave him barely a glance, then said to the guard who had
brought him, 'Lost his memory, has he? Well, perhaps that's
lucky for the poor sod. You can't miss what you don't
remember, can you?'

Jerking his head towards a hut that had a large 6 painted in
white on the door, he added to Gregory, 'That's your hut,
No. 1076. Get inside and report to the Lagerältester.'

While a prisoner among the *Prominente*, Gregory had picked
up quite a lot about the organization of the camp outside that
privileged section. Only there were S.S. guards on duty night
and day. The many thousands of ordinary prisoners were
supervised and disciplined by trusties, the majority of whom
were habitual criminals. Under the orders of the S.S. Block-
führers, there were two types of these. Each hut, containing
about two hundred prisoners, was in charge of a Lagerältester
who tyrannized over its inmates and was responsible for their
good behaviour, while even tougher old lags, the Capos, ran
the working parties during the day.

Maintaining the vacant stare of a half-wit, Gregory went into
the hut and confronted the Lagerältester. He was a small

man with a mean, vicious face. On receiving no reply to his questions he slapped Gregory hard across the mouth. With iron self-control Gregory refrained from kicking the little brute in the crutch then strangling him, and remained there standing passively with drooping head. His restraint paid off. With a contemptuous shrug, the Lagerältester pointed to a bunk that had on it a blanket roll, a mess tin and a tin cup but, unlike the majority of the others, none of the few private possessions that the prisoners were allowed to retain.

Going to the bunk, Gregory put on the shelf above it his safety razor and the few other things he had been able to bring in his pockets. Meanwhile, he thanked his gods that the Lagerältester had either not familiarized himself with the faces of the two hundred men over whom he ruled or had assumed that Protze had died in hospital and his number been re-issued to a newcomer.

Two other men, both obviously so ill that had they been sent out to hard labour they would have collapsed, were in the hut scrubbing the floor, and Gregory was put to work with them. As he got down to it he took stock of his surroundings. Although the furnishings of the *Prominente's* huts were far from luxurious, those here were much inferior to them. The bunks were in three tiers instead of two, there were only benches instead of chairs and the narrow table in the centre did not look as though it would seat more than half the two hundred prisoners the hut was supposed to accommodate.

At midday he caught the trampling of feet and the prisoners came pouring in. Unlike the *Prominente* silence was not enforced upon them. A little group at once surrounded Gregory and asked him about himself, but he returned them only vague looks and stuck to his role of having lost his memory. The majority took no notice of him, their thoughts being centred on the meagre meal of coarse bread and thin soup that was brought in half cold from the cookhouse by some of their number. Although he was still replete from his midnight feast, in order not to arouse comment he entered the jostling crowd and secured his share.

The break lasted only half an hour, then the Capo came in and hustled the prisoners out. Gregory went with them as they

were marched to the northern end of the camp, where an
extension to it was being made, and set to work there digging
shallow foundations for a new row of hutments. From weeks
of underfeeding most of his companions were incapable of
sustained effort and from time to time the Capo lashed one of
them with his whip; but Gregory was still in good condition
so escaped such unpleasant attentions.

At five o'clock they were marched back to the hut, then ate
a meagre supper consisting of herb tea and a slice of bread with
a spoonful of jam apiece. Afterwards some of them talked in
groups or played games with small stones or bits of paper they
had collected; but most of them turned in, and by seven o'clock
they were all in their bunks.

Before dropping off to sleep Gregory lay for a while con-
gratulating himself on having pulled off a very risky venture.
Yet within a week he came near to regretting that he had not
continued to run the risk of impersonating Prince Hugo.

The fact that he had no longer to talk only in whispers was
small compensation for the loss of the other amenities he had
enjoyed as a *Prominente*. Conditions in the Criminal Section of
the camp were infinitely worse. The food consisted almost
entirely of slops: Linden tea twice a day and vegetable soup
with only a few pieces of meat in it. The bread ration was
strictly limited and their only solids were a few half-rotten pota-
toes in their skins or, three times a week, a small portion of
sausage. The liquid diet was not only insufficient and gave
many of them dysentery but also affected their bladders, forcing
them to get up to urinate two or three times every night. Added
to this they lived in constant dread of becoming the victims of
the spite of the Lagerältester or the Capo, the hut was squalid
and stank foully, and they were kept at their dreary task of
digging for the best part of twelve hours a day.

Yet Gregory's companions assured him that they lived like
princes compared with the tens of thousands of 'politicals' who
occupied the other sections of the camp. These poor wretches
had no bunks but slept, when they could, on palliasses filled
with rotten straw inadequate to their numbers; so that if one
of them got up in the night, he would find his place taken and
have to lie on the hard floor. For the least slackness they were

flogged unmercifully by their overseers; they were fed only on raw vegetables and stew made from half-rotten cabbages, potato peelings and consignments of food sent from all over Germany that had been condemned as unfit for human consumption. When too weak to work any longer they were shot or herded into the gas chambers and, daily, scores of them, driven to desperation, committed suicide by throwing themselves on to the perimeter fences which electrocuted them.

From time to time, as Gregory trudged out to work he passed gangs of these miserable beings forgotten by God. Gaunt-faced and terribly emaciated, their striped prison garments hanging loose about them, they staggered along to their daily labour of loading piles of rubble into trucks then pushing the trucks for a mile or more to the places where the rubble was required to make foundations. The sight of them brought to his mind the Zombies of Haiti who, it was said, had been drugged, buried alive, then dug up by the witch doctors and by a magical ceremony deprived of their minds; so that they afterwards laboured in the fields with no knowledge of whom they were or the lives they had led before they had been presumed dead and then buried. In the worst cases the simile was apt, for acute privation had robbed many of the political prisoners of the power any longer to think, and these glassy-eyed living skeletons were so numerous that a special word, 'Moslems', had been added to the camp argot to describe them.

As Gregory got on well with most people he soon established friendly relations with several of the men in his hut. They were a very mixed collection. Quite a number were educated men guilty of fraud, manslaughter, hoarding, sexual offences, blackmarketeering and so on; while others were professional criminals. A number of them were serving long sentences and had been inmates of the big Mobait Prison in Berlin, until its partial destruction by bombing had led to its being evacuated.

In two respects Gregory found their psychology interesting. Although in normal times most of them had been agnostics, uncertainty about whether in their present grim conditions their stamina would suffice for them to live out their sentences made all but a few of them turn to religion. It seemed that their only hope of survival now lay in the power of Jesus Christ to accept into His fold repentant sinners and, although there was no 'man of God' in the hut to lead them, Catholics, Lutherans, and even the unbaptized regularly joined together in prayer meetings.

The other interesting fact was that, although they were all normally patriotic Germans, they now longed for a speedy defeat of Germany as the only means of bringing the war to an end. Here, too, a mysterious grapevine operated, bringing news only a few days after major events of Allied victories that rejoiced the prisoners. How, Gregory could never discover, but at the end of the first week in September it was known in the camp that the Poles were still resisting the German garrison in Warsaw, that the Allied Army that had landed in the South of France had reached Lyons, and that the British had entered Brussels in triumph.

Soon after he had become No. E1076 he had another clear vision of Malacou. It was at about eleven o'clock in the morning. The occultist was standing in a Law Court with a warder on either side of him. On what charge he was being tried Gregory remained uncertain, but he had a strong impression that it had something to do with the von Altern estate.

At the evening roll-call on September 9th the prisoners had to make a show of rejoicing, as the Blockführer announced to them with delight that the Führer's long-promised decisive Secret Weapon was at last in operation. That morning the first long-range rocket had been successfully launched and landed on its target—the heart of London. As for months past Goebbels had been declaring that the Flying Bombs had reduced the British capital to ruins, the prisoners were not greatly impressed. Among themselves, they agreed that at worst this new weapon could now do no more than delay an Allied victory.

Their belief was strengthened by the continued advance of General Eisenhower's armies. By the middle of the month that from the south had advanced to Dijon, in the west the great port of Le Havre had been captured, and the main body of the Allies was pushing the Germans back to the Siegfried Line.

Some of Gregory's companions began to say that once the Siegfried Line was breached Hitler would surrender. Gregory doubted that but prayed for it, as he could think of no possible way to escape from the camp and an end to the war now seemed the only event which could lead to a termination of his present miserable existence.

Yet, only two mornings later, he was roused from his depression by a most unexpected happening. It brought him no nearer to securing his liberty, but at least gave him something new to think about.

Many of the prisoners were suffering from dysentery, so a latrine had been set up near the site on which they worked. It was no more than a trench with, parallel to it, a long stout pole on trestles over which the men could squat. From a distance the Capos kept an eye on the prisoners making use of it, to see that they did not shirk work by remaining there longer than necessary. But it was used by two other gangs working on the same site as Gregory's; so there were usually several men perched on the long pole at the same time, and by changing places in the row when the Capos were not looking it was sometimes possible to get a rest there of up to fifteen minutes.

Gregory had soon picked up this dodge and, on this occasion, had just moved down to squat again next to a hunched figure at one extreme end of the pole. He had been there only a moment when his neighbour said in a low voice:

'Greetings. I knew I should meet you here within a day or two, Herr Sallust.'

Experienced as Gregory was in controlling his reactions to sudden danger, to be identified in such a place was so utterly unexpected that the start he gave nearly sent him backward into the trench. Swinging round on the man who had addressed him, he found himself staring at Malacou.

21

A Strange Partnership

His eyes still wide with surprise, Gregory exclaimed, 'What the devil are you doing here?'

Malacou smiled. 'Like yourself, I am a convict. I have just started to serve a sentence of five years for having embezzled money from the von Altern estate.'

Gregory gave an abrupt laugh. 'So I was right. I saw you in court and thought it had something to do with the von Alterns. I knew, of course, that you had got away from Poland. But whatever induced you to return to your old haunts and risk being picked up by the civil police?'

'They didn't catch me. I went back to Greifswald deliberately, in order to give myself up.'

'In God's name, why?'

Malacou smiled again. 'The Germans are queer people. As Nazis, they deny their political opponents the protection of the laws and treat them like cattle, but at the same time they are born bureaucrats. Anyone found guilty of a civil offence is sent to prison, and even if he is known to be opposed to the regime the Gestapo would not dream of taking any action against him until he comes out. As you know, I am a Jew, and I look like one. After that terrifying affair at the cottage I would no longer have dared show my Turkish passport as a protection, and it is certain that I should have been hauled in on my appearance. That would have meant the gas chamber; so I gave myself up, counting on it that I would be tried and sentenced before the Gestapo office in Greifswald had had time enough to learn that I was wanted by their colleagues in Poland. It is not very pleasant here; but at least my life is safe and I shall outlive Hitler.'

'I see. Yes. That was certainly a clever move. At your age, though, I hope you are right that you will survive the rigours of this camp through the winter; for I'm convinced that Hitler will fight on to the last ditch.'

'He will. The stars foretell it. But also that I shall outlive him. Moreover, neither you nor I is fated to stay here until he dies. Before I gave myself up I hid for three days and nights in the ruined Schloss at Sassen. I had left most of my astrological impedimenta there and I slept for less than six hours. Through all the rest of that time I worked on foretelling the future course of the war, and on my horoscope and yours.'

'Why on mine?' Gregory asked.

'Because I already knew that our fates continued to be intertwined. You saved my life at the cottage, as I predicted; and in a new partnership we shall leave this place. It will mean our going into great danger, but we shall be given an opportunity to strike a mighty blow against the accursed Hitler.'

'Have you a plan then?'

'Alas, no. I know only that the rapport we have established between us will prove the key to this business, and that I must use to the utmost my powers as an occultist to make myself regarded by our captors as a special case. With that as my object, I have already made a start by reading the hands of several men in my hut and that of the fellow who is our guard. Palmistry is a sure lure to every kind of person.'

At that moment one of the Capos bellowed from about fifty yards away:

'You two at the end there! You've been long enough. Back to work now.'

'Meet me here again this afternoon,' Malacou said quickly. 'But leave it till about half past four. The guards always get slack towards the end of the work period.'

This totally unexpected meeting dissipated Gregory's depression and invigorated him as would have a sea breeze suddenly sweeping across a torrid desert. Malacou might be guilty of murder, incest and practising the Black Art, but his blood made him a deadly enemy of the Nazis and he possessed powers which, although their source might be evil, were granted to few. To co-operate with him might lead to freedom, and Gregory could hardly contain his impatience till their next meeting.

Immediately they were seated side by side on the pole above the unsavoury trench, the Satanist said, 'Your first step must be to get yourself transferred to my hut, so that we can talk whenever we wish and begin working together.'

'How will I do that?' Gregory enquired.

'Have you done any carpentry, bricklaying or plumbing?'

Gregory shook his head. 'No. I'm not much good at anything like that; although I suppose I could lay bricks after a little practice. Years ago I helped a friend with whom I was staying in the country to build some garden frames.'

'That will serve. Good craftsmen are rarely criminals. All the men doing such jobs on those new huts over there are amateurs. As you may know, before the war Himmler started a huge industrial concern known as D.E.S.T. It supplies bricks and cut stone for all Hitler's great architectural projects and is run entirely with slave labour. Sachsenhausen is one of D.E.S.T.'s largest depots and huge gangs are marched out every day to the brickfields. The whole of this camp was built by prisoners and an order was issued that those capable of doing technical jobs should receive better treatment and rations. All such prisoners in this section are in No. 1 hut and I got myself put in there as a carpenter. You have only to volunteer as a bricklayer and I'm sure you will be transferred to it.'

'I'll certainly apply to be.'

'Good. Now palmistry. Do you know anything about reading the human hand?'

'Nothing whatever.'

'That is a pity. Many people take it up for amusement at some time in their lives and I had hoped that would be the case with you. But no matter. You will soon learn.'

Gregory looked dubious. 'I shouldn't have thought that likely. Surely, to predict people's futures one must have a certain amount of occult power, and I'm not specially gifted in that way.'

'You do not have to be. Just as a doctor, having made a full examination of a body, can tell the patient's state of health and much of his past medical history, so a palmist who has learnt the meaning of the shape of the hands and the lines on the palms can speak with authority about a person's character, health, abilities, sexual powers and tell a great deal about his past.'

'But to foretell his future . . .'

'That, of course, is very different,' Malacou agreed. 'The future of everyone is written in the lines of their hands, but to interpret them accurately one must have clairvoyant powers and an ability to achieve rapport quickly with one's subject. In your case that is unnecessary. To these people here you can say the first thing that comes into your head, provided you do not predict for them any event in the near future which when it failed to occur would show you to be a false prophet. Once you have mastered the geography of the palm you will be able to tell them the things they are best at, how many times they have had relationships with women that amount to marriage or its equivalent, the number of children they have and much else. People are always amazed that by these means a stranger should be capable of uncovering what they know to be the truth about themselves, and the superstition inherent in human nature causes them to regard such a soothsayer with a special respect. It is that which I aim at for both of us.'

'I see the idea,' Gregory murmured, 'but not where it will get us.'

Before Malacou could reply one of the Capos shouted at them; so they had to pull up their trousers and rejoin their gangs.

About his ability to become a convincing palmist Gregory still had grave doubts, but he was confident that after some practice he could become a passable bricklayer. From the little experience he had had he knew that anyone, provided he was not in too great a hurry, could lay bricks accurately, and that if one did it day after day the speed at which one worked must soon improve. That evening he used his jam ration to bribe his Lagerältester to speak to their Blockführer and next morning, after roll-call, his transfer was effected.

Fortunately he was not called on to expose his very amateur status right away, as there were sufficient bricklayers already available for the work in hand; instead he was put on to carry

bricks and mix cement. But Malacou lost no time in starting
to teach him palmistry and the first evening they were together
he explained its rudiments.

The shape of the hands proclaimed their owner's nature;
short, thick hands were the lowest type and brutal, square ones
useful, knotty ones philosophic, conic ones artistic, very
slender ones idealistic. The three sections of the thumb from
the palm up, according to their construction, showed the
capacity for love, logic and will. The nails gave indication of
hereditary weaknesses; almond-shaped a tendency to lung
troubles, square ones towards bad circulation and diseases of
the heart, shell-shaped ones towards paralysis. Straight square
fingers gave practical ability, long pointed ones an artistic
temperament, very thin smooth ones psychic powers, those
with big knuckle joints a good brain for mathematics. The
first finger represented Jupiter—ambition, pride and a love of
power; the second Saturn—earnestness, prudence, a liking for
solitude and study; the third Apollo—imagination, grace of
mind and an appreciation of all things beautiful; the fourth
Mercury—quickness of thought, the gift of tongues and a
desire for change and travel. If one finger was a little long in
comparison with the others it indicated that the qualities of
the Planet it represented dominated the rest. The little mounts
at the base of the fingers if well developed reinforced the
strength of the Planets relative to that finger. Hairy hands
betrayed vanity; a thin dry palm, timidity; a thick soft one,
sensuality; one that was firm and elastic, energy and quickness
of intellect.

As Malacou explained, hands had an infinite variety and
before a judgement could be formed each characteristic had to
be weighed against the others; but that was not difficult after
a little practice. Generally, any special characteristic showed
plainly and most people had one. But the most fortunate had
no abnormality which indicated excess; the flesh of their hands
was resilient when pressed, their palms square and their fingers
long; giving them intellect and the vitality and practical
ability to put their gifts to good purpose.

Going on to the lines of the hand Malacou said that, with
the one exception of the Health Line, these at their best should

be long, clear and unbroken. From them one could gain additional information about the subject's character, the main events in his past and, without the aid of clairvoyance, something of his future; as, for example, liability to blindness or mental trouble and length of life.

Gregory found this all surprisingly easy to assimilate and on his second evening in hut No. 1, Malacou set him to work reading the hands of some of their companions. But, with some cunning, having already read these men's hands himself, he first tipped Gregory off about what he would find in their hands and what he should say to them. In consequence Gregory had only to confirm what his instructor had said while reaping the benefit of examining a number of hands; and as he did so he was again surprised to find how simple it was to assess people's major characteristics in this way.

He was, however, still puzzled by one thing, and afterwards he whispered to Malacou, 'As you can do this sort of thing far better than I can, why do you wish me to do it too?'

'Because the stars decree that you are to be my partner,' the occultist replied, 'and I have need of one. I am highly skilled in my special arts, but I lack the ability to put them to the best purpose. I need a resolute man like yourself to talk to others on my behalf, and with a practical mind to plan how we may best use my gifts to our advantage.'

'I see that,' Gregory agreed; 'but every plan should have an object. What is to be ours?'

Malacou shook his grizzled head. 'I don't quite know. I think mainly to impress those over us. If we could succeed in becoming soothsayers to the Commandant of the camp it is certain that we should be given better food and special privileges.'

For a few minutes Gregory thought this over, then he said, 'Just reading hands won't get us far. What we need is some startling prediction. You told me that while you were last at Sassen you consulted the stars on the course of the war. If you have real faith in the results of your endeavours could you not predict some major development that you expect to take place in the course of the next few weeks? A German victory somewhere would be best, although that seems unlikely.'

'That is an excellent thought,' Malacou smiled. 'In fact, it is just the sort of idea I hoped that you might produce. For your suggestion, it so happens that there are two things we might use. As the Russians have callously refused to go to the aid of those gallant Poles who rose against the Germans in Warsaw, I feel certain that very soon now they will have to surrender. The Germans will also achieve a triumph over the British, and that within the next few days. No news has yet trickled through about it, but at this moment there is a desperate battle going on in Holland, I think in connection with the bridges over the Scheldt, and the British will get the worst of it. Tomorrow I'll predict those two items to as many people as I can.'

'No,' said Gregory promptly. 'We can do better than that. We'll hold a séance in the evening and invite the Blockführer in to it. I will act as though I were putting you into a trance, you can mutter a few meaningless phrases of gibberish, then I'll pretend to interpret and announce your predictions. If only they are on the mark, that will really put up our stock.'

Malacou willingly agreed and the séance proved as successful as they could have hoped. Their fellow prisoners showed great interest and, although the Blockführer regarded the performance with cynical amusement, he was obviously intrigued.

The séance took place on September 20th. During it Gregory gave out a fuller account of Malacou's prediction. It concerned a great number of British parachutists being dropped too far behind the German lines for support from ground troops to reach them, so that they remained cut off and those of them who were not killed being forced to surrender.

Some days later the prediction was fulfilled by the failure of Montgomery's rash use of airborne troops at Arnhem. Then Goebbels announced in vindictive triumph that after many weeks of desperate resistance the Poles in Warsaw had surrendered and that, as saboteurs, those who survived were to be shot.

As Gregory had foreseen, this double achievement of Malacou's made a great impression on all who knew of it, and S.S. men from all over the camp began to come to the hut in the evenings to have their fortunes told. But there was no reaction from the Commandant.

Meanwhile Gregory found that his new situation had both

its advantages and disadvantages. He certainly fed better and lived in slightly greater comfort, but he found mixing cement and carrying hods of bricks for eleven hours a day so exhausting that he had difficulty in concentrating sufficiently in the evenings to do his best when reading hands.

Nevertheless, he drove himself to persevere with it and after a time became quite expert at reading character without having had any previous information from Malacou. He had, too, mastered the meaning of finer lines—little crosses, stars, squares, islands, offshoots and breaks—that indicated marriages, children, accidents, salaciousness, self-consciousness, a crooked mentality and other traits. On some points his subjects declared him to be wrong, but in the main they usually agreed that he was right about them; and he was interested to find that he could always do better with some guard or newcomer to the hut whom he had never previously seen than with a man whom he had come to know quite well and about whom he had formed an often erroneous impression from hearing what the man had said about himself.

With regard to the future, as a matter of principle both he and Malacou always endeavoured to cheer their subjects up by predicting their survival from the harsh life they led and better times ahead, with a safe return to wives who were remaining faithful to them and loved ones who had them constantly in their thoughts.

But one evening towards the middle of October Malacou took a very different line with one of the Capos. He told the man frankly that he was in grave danger of death by violence and, after obtaining from him his astrological numbers, that the third day hence could prove his fatal day unless he secured a release from duty. The man was one of the more brutal Capos and a cynic. He ignored the warning. On the third day one of the prisoners went mad, attacked him with a pickaxe and before he could protect himself had bashed in his skull.

As this prediction had been made in the hearing of two S.S. men who had come to have their fortunes told, it enormously enhanced Malacou's reputation as a seer; and from this episode there arose two developments.

It so happened that the man who had gone off his head was

a bricklayer. Next morning he had been first flogged then hung
from a portable gibbet in front of the whole section after roll-
call, after which Gregory had been given a trowel and ordered
to take the place on the building site of the dead man. Having
spent over three weeks as a labourer there Gregory had had
ample opportunity to watch the bricklayers at work so he found
no difficulty in putting up an adequate performance, and he was
extremely thankful for being given this more skilled but much
lighter task. Then, in the afternoon three days later, the Camp
Commandant sent for Malacou.

That evening the occultist gave Gregory an account of the
meeting. The Commandant was Oberführer Loehritz, a gutter-
bred brute with a rat-trap mouth and eyes like stones, who had
forced his way up to the rank of an S.S. Brigadier by the
ruthlessness with which, under Heydrich, he had cleaned up
the Jews and subversive elements in Czechoslovakia. Although
the slave-workers were reduced by semi-starvation to a general
state of servile obedience, at times small groups of them,
driven to desperation, mutinied. Having learned of the warning
Malacou had given the murdered Capo, it had occurred to
Loehritz that the occultist might be made use of to give him
warning of such outbreaks.

Malacou had replied that, though he might be able to give
warning should a large-scale mutiny be contemplated, it would
be next to impossible, owing to the vast number of prisoners in
the camp, to predict attacks on individual Capos, which in most
cases arose spontaneously as a result of some special piece of
brutality. He had then offered to read the Commandant's hand.

Loehritz had consented and had been very impressed by
Malacou's insight into his past; but the occultist had cunningly
said that he could tell little about the Oberführer's future unless
he drew his horoscope, and for that he would need sidereal
tables. Like most primitive types, the Commandant believed in
every sort of superstition and ways of attempting to foretell the
future; so he had agreed to send for several works on astrology,
a list of which Malacou had given him.

A week later Loehritz sent for Malacou again and gave him
the books. Malacou then said that he would need time off to
prepare the horoscope and that as he was not good at figures

he wanted Gregory as his assistant, to check his calculations. This led to their being allowed to remain in the hut during the afternoons; so they had achieved their first objective of getting an easier life for themselves. But Malacou did not give much time to drawing the horoscope, and they employed themselves on a new suggestion made by Gregory.

His idea was that, during their dual act when Malacou pretended to go into a trance, it would be a great advantage if he could supplement the thoughts he conveyed by, instead of muttering gibberish, giving straight tips in Turkish. Malacou agreed that this would be a big help; so during the week they were supposed to be working on the horoscope they spent most of the time in Gregory memorizing certain Turkish phrases.

Early in November Malacou reported the horoscope to be ready and spent an afternoon explaining it to the Commandant. Now that winter was about to set in it appeared certain that the war would go on into the spring and this was confirmed by further astral calculations that Malacou had been able to make after receiving the astrological textbooks. He told Loehritz this and that he would not be Commandant at Sachsenhausen when the war ended but would soon be given another post. This was in accordance with the horoscope but he did not add that Loehritz would be sacked from Sachsenhausen and hanged for his brutalities in the following August. Instead, as Himmler was the Commandant's Chief, he predicted that the Reichsführer would succeed Hitler and that after a period of difficulty, which should not last more than three months, Loehritz would be given an excellent job under Himmler supervising the return of displaced persons to their own countries.

Loehritz, who had been dreading the end of the war, was naturally delighted. Then, in order to secure a continuance of an easy time for himself and Gregory, Malacou suggested that the Commandant should get for him the birth dates of his senior subordinates and, by means of drawing their horoscopes, he would check up on their reliability. As the S.S. leaders habitually spied on one another Loehritz thought this an excellent idea; so the afternoons in the hut continued and Gregory was able to make good progress in learning Turkish.

But mid-November brought them a nasty setback. Malacou's prediction that Loehritz would be removed came about. Rumour had it that Himmler had learned that he was diverting a part of the funds received from the brick fields to his own pocket and had reduced him to the rank of Sturmbahn-führer. In any case he went, regretted by none, except Malacou and Gregory, because with his departure the easier time they had secured for themselves abruptly ceased.

The new Commandant's name was Kaindl and he held the lower rank of Standartenführer. They saw him when he made an inspection of the camp. He was a very different type from Loehritz—a fat, jovial-looking man with shrewd eyes and a not unkindly face. But Gregory and Malacou regarded him gloomily, with the thought that if they were to regain their afternoons off they had all their work to do again.

During the month that followed they had good reason for their depression. Winter was upon them; for much of the time the sky was leaden and often it rained for hours at a stretch, while when the sky held only drifting clouds a bitter wind blew from the north-east; but, rain or shine, they were herded out to work as usual.

Gregory had never given up racking his brains for a possible way of escaping from the camp and he thought out a dozen wild schemes, but had to abandon them all as suicidal. The least desperately dangerous ones all required the help of a companion; but he dared trust no-one except Malacou, and the occultist flatly refused to join him or become involved. Having deliberately had a sentence passed on himself as a criminal in order to escape the *Ersatzgruppen*, the last thing he meant to do was to prejudice his chances of remaining where he was till the war was over. But he stoutly maintained that another opportunity would arise to better their situation.

Throughout this period the prisoners woke every day in darkness. By the light of half a dozen oil lamps they wolfed their Linden tea and thin porridge, then were marched out to the building site. Their only protection from the cold was torn and bloodstained Army greatcoats, taken from casualties, with which they had been issued; their faces became a greyish blue and their hands and feet throbbed madly from chilblains.

When frost and snow made bricklaying no longer possible they were put on to carting heavy tree trunks and sawing them into logs; but whatever the labour the days seemed interminable.

When darkness fell they were marched back to the hut and huddled round two small woodburning stoves, which was all the heating provided. Then, at seven o'clock, the oil lamps were put out and, suffering the pangs of hunger, coughing and spitting from colds and sometimes moaning from the pains of frost-bite, they somehow got through another long, miserable night. Every week one or more of them was taken to the hospital to die, and those who survived had become gaunt from privation and hardship.

Yet they were infinitely better off than the political prisoners; for these had no lamps to give them a little light during a few of the long hours of darkness and no stoves to give them any heat at all. Even in summer, owing to starvation and brutality, few of them survived life in the camp for more than six months, and now a thousand or more of them were dying every week. And Sachsenhausen was only one of the Nazi murder camps. Auschwitz was much larger. There were also Buchenwald, Dachau, Belsen and some twenty others in which the Devil-inspired Hitler had decreed a terrible death for so many men, women and children that, had their corpses been stacked in a pile, they would have made a mound higher than St. Paul's Cathedral.

The grim life Gregory led had made him leaner than ever, but his wiry frame was extraordinarily tough and he took all the care of himself he could; so, although he suffered severely from the cold, he managed to keep in good health and he endeavoured to buoy up his spirits with Malacou's prediction that his chances of living out the war were good.

It was on December 17th that there occurred the new break for them that Malacou had so confidently predicted. To their surprise, at half past seven that evening their Blockführer roused them from their bunks and said that the Commandant had sent for them. As they slept in all their clothes they were already dressed, so at once left the hut and were marched to the Headquarters building. Since discipline up to any punishment short of death could be inflicted on the prisoners by the

S.S. Lieutenants in charge of each section, it seemed obvious
that Malacou had been summoned in connection with his occult
activities; but Gregory had never been sent for by the previous
Commandant, so why he had been included in the order he
could not imagine.

Standartenführer Kaindl was still in his office. Having run
his sharp grey eyes over them he said, 'When Oberführer
Loehritz handed over to me, he happened to mention that
among the convicts in E Section there were a couple of mystics.'

Fixing his glance on Malacou he went on. 'I gather that you,
No. 875, told him about his past with surprising accuracy. I
also understand that with the aid of No. 1076 you give sort of
séances, during which you predict the course the war will take.
Personally, I do not believe in such nonsense, and am convinced
that it is done by some form of trickery. But on Christmas
night I am giving a party and it occurred to me that it would be
amusing to have you over as a cabaret turn. You have ten days
to polish up your way of putting your stuff over, and I shall
expect a good show or it will be the worse for you.'

It was Gregory who replied at once. 'Herr Standartenführer,
we shall be honoured to entertain your guests; but permit me
to remark that the predictions made by my friend No. 875 are
not nonsense. For example, he foretold the defeat of the
British airborne landings at Arnhem several days before it
occurred; and if you can spare a few minutes now I am
confident that we can convince you of our bona fides.'

The chubby-faced Commandant suddenly smiled. 'All right.
Go ahead then.'

Malacou sat down in a chair, Gregory made passes at him,
he closed his eyes, his head fell forward on his chest and, after
a short period of silence he began to mutter. As they had
come unprepared for this session Gregory could only hope for
the best and concentrate with all his might on reading
Malacou's thoughts. To his surprise and consternation, for he
could not believe it to be the least likely, the occultist conveyed
to him particulars of a great German victory in the coming
week. Yet while he was still hesitating whether to risk
announcing it, Malacou confirmed the thoughts he had sent
out by a few phrases in Turkish.

Seeing nothing else for it, Gregory turned to the Commandant and said, 'Great news, *Herr Standartenführer*. The Wehrmacht is about to launch a major offensive. It will break through the Allied front in Belgium and inflict great losses on the Americans.'

The Commandant grinned. 'That seems highly improbable; but I hope you are right. Anyway you have committed yourselves. If you are wrong I'll have you put on special fatigues for a month; but if you are right you shall enjoy as good a dinner on Christmas Day as I have myself.'

Swiftly, Gregory seized on the possibility of reward. He said that they would be able to give a far more interesting demonstration on Christmas night if they were given the names and birth dates of several of the guests, and that time to make a study of their astrological significance was essential. He added that Malacou and he were half starved and half frozen, so could not possibly give of their best unless they had better food and a warm place in which to work.

At that the Commandant laughed and said that they were a typical pair of confidence men with wits trained to seize on every chance of getting something for nothing. But apparently it amused him to humour them. He said that he would provide them with certain information and that he would have them put in a heated prison cell where, for the next eight days, they could work things out. Decent food would be sent in to them, but if on Christmas night they failed to produce the goods woe betide them.

The interview resulted in their spending the following week in what was, for them, unbelievable luxury. They were taken to be deloused then given a cell in the headquarters used for S.S. officers who, having committed some misdemeanour, had been placed under arrest. There were iron beds with mattresses to sleep on, a table at which to work and meals were brought to them which, although plain, were of the sort that during the past months they had spent hours dreaming about.

On the third day the Commandant paid them a visit. He regarded them with curiosity and a new respect as he said, 'You were right. General von Rundstedt launched an offensive

in the Ardennes the day before I sent for you; but you could
not have known that by any normal means. His Panzers are
through to Dinant now and the Americans are running like
hares or surrendering by the thousand. It is a great victory. Ask
for anything you want, wine included. And I'll send you some
decent clothes to come to my party on Christmas night.'

The party proved to be the strangest that Gregory had ever
attended. Himmler had long since ruled that no junior S.S.
officer should marry. The obsession which governed his every
thought was the elimination of the Jewish race and the
preservation of a pure Teutonic stock. Only Germans with a
proved descent of three generations on both sides had
qualified for admission into the original S.S., and Himmler
never tired of proclaiming to them their duty, in which he was
heartily supported by Hitler. It was that every S.S. man should
beget children by as many girls as possible who were of the
Aryan type. To facilitate this racial project the girls were
encouraged to bear bastards willingly by appeals to their
patriotism, the provision of luxurious maternity homes, State
support for their children, lavish payments and the promise
that they would be held in honour above all other German
women.

In consequence, in the concentration camps there were no
married quarters for the S.S. guards. Instead, there was a
brothel for the officers and another for the other ranks. So all
the women at the Commandant's Christmas party were the
inmates of the officers' brothel.

Not more than a quarter of them were German girls; the rest
were French, Poles, Hungarians, Czechs, Dutch, Belgians; and
all of them had been picked, on account of their good looks, for
this form of slavery from the many thousands of women who,
for one reason or another, had been interned by the Nazis.
Many of them had been only too glad to exchange hard labour
and starvation for it; and all of them knew that unless they
showed eagerness to please their many masters they would
promptly be returned to the miserable existence of which they
had at first had a sample. In consequence there were no holds
barred at the party.

Soon after it started Gregory and Malacou did their act,

which proved a great success, as they foretold peace in the spring, that the Russians would be restrained by the Anglo-Americans from occupying any but a small part of Germany, and clement treatment of the German people by their late enemies. Afterwards they told individual fortunes for a while by palmistry, but not for long. There was an abundance of good food, and champagne from stocks looted out of France during the German occupation.

Despite Malacou's optimistic prophecies, all the S.S. officers knew that Germany stood on the brink of catastrophe and that this might be the last Christmas they would enjoy. So it was a case of 'eat, drink and be merry and tomorrow be damned'. Everyone got drunk, no-one had any more time to have their fortunes told. By ten o'clock the men were pulling the women's clothes off while the latter giggled or egged them on with ribald jests and shouts of laughter. By eleven nearly everyone present was half naked and leching unashamedly on the sofas and armchairs in the big mess room. Girls danced nude on the tables, drunks of both sexes writhed in heaps on the floor and blond giants who did not care for girls were making love together. It was an orgy that might even have for a while amused the bored Emperor Tiberius. At about four o'clock in the morning Gregory and Malacou staggered back to their comfortable cell, unescorted.

The following evening the Commandant, looking distinctly part-worn and bleary-eyed, came to see them. They congratulated him on his party and he agreed that it had been a great success. It transpired that he was in a talkative mood, for he sat down on the edge of one of the beds and asked them about their lives and why they had been given prison sentences. Malacou said that he was a doctor and in for embezzling funds; Gregory maintained his role as the Lübeck lawyer Protze.

Their visitor then began to talk about himself. He said that he did not like his job. His conscience was troubled by the thousands of slaves working in his charge who were dying and, although he could do nothing about it, he felt certain that when the Allies had defeated Germany he would be called on to account for the deaths of his prisoners.

They agreed with him and, since he had treated them so

handsomely, against their own interests they strongly advised
him to get a transfer to some less vulnerable position before
the war ended. Malacou offered to read his hand; but he
refused, saying that he preferred to rely on his own judgement
about how to protect his future.

Before leaving them he said, 'Well, you two seem to be
good fellows, so at least I can chalk up one small decent act
by letting you stay on here instead of sending you back to one
of those lice-ridden huts.'

They thanked him effusively, then he shook hands with them
and took himself off. Somewhat to their surprise he did not pay
them another visit and for another three weeks they enjoyed
the amenities he had granted them. Then, in the second week
of January, to their acute distress the guard who looked after
them informed them one morning that Standartenführer Kaindl
had been posted elsewhere and had left the camp the previous
evening. They were then marched back to their old hut with no
benefit remaining from the easy time they had had except the
respectable clothes with which they had been provided for the
Christmas party.

This calamitous setback submerged Gregory in a new wave
of depression: for, in spite of the temporary improvement in
their situation that Malacou's activities as an occultist had
twice brought them, he did not see how, even should they
succeed in intriguing yet another Commandant, they could
hope for any permanent relief from semi-starvation and hard
labour. But Malacou begged him to be patient, assuring him
that they were due for an even better break quite soon. And
a fortnight later he proved right.

On the 31st January they were again sent for, but this
time they were not taken to the Commandant. Instead,
having been ordered to collect their belongings, they were
marched to the camp railway station and, accompanied by a
guard, told to get into a train. It took them to Berlin and there
they transferred to another train. As it chugged along, Gregory
asked Malacou if he had any idea where they were being taken.
The occultist shook his grizzled head and replied:

'I know only that one of the great men of the Nazi Party has
heard about my powers and that we are being taken to him. We

are about to enter on the situation of which I told you soon
after we met at Sachsenhausen. We shall be in great danger. I
feel confident that I shall survive it. I think you will, too, but
that depends on your doing the right thing at the right time; and
with the help of the stars I will do my utmost to guide you.'

Half an hour later they detrained at what was evidently a
private siding. They got out and waited there for some ten
minutes. Then a large car drove up. Out of it stepped
Standartenführer Kaindl. He smiled at them and said:

'You see, I hadn't forgotten you.' Then dismissing their
escort he added, 'Jump in and I'll take you up to the house.'

The car set off at high speed. After less than a mile it ran
through impressive gates guarded by a sentry. Gregory had a
vague idea that a long time ago he had passed through those
gates, or a very similar pair. He had already noticed that
Kaindl was wearing a different uniform and he realized now
that it was that of a Colonel of the Luftwaffe. At that moment
Kaindl said:

'I managed to get out from under Himmler. In the First
World War I was a fighter pilot in the Air Force and my old
Chief agreed to take me back. I arranged your release from
Sachsenhausen because I'm sure that the Reichsmarschall will
be most interested to hear some of your prophecies.'

Gregory's heart missed a beat, then seemed to sink to his
boots. Suddenly he had realized that the car was speeding up
the long drive to Karinhall. There he would soon be brought
face to face with Goering, one of the very few people in
Germany who knew him to be a British agent.

22

In the Lion's Den

THE drive up to Karinhall, Goering's huge country house, was a mile long; so as the Mercedes sped through the beautiful park Gregory had several minutes in which to contemplate the ghastly trick that fate had played him. This was the second time that he had been trapped by circumstances into going to Karinhall. His first visit had been in the autumn of 1939, nearly five and a half years ago. He had then been posing as Colonel Baron von Lutz, but had taken a desperate gamble by disclosing his real identity to the Reichsmarschall because only by doing so could he discover if Erika was in the hands of the Gestapo as he feared, and if so secure her release; for he knew that Goering had in the past been a great friend of Erika's, so would almost certainly use his power to save her.

Greatly intrigued by the fact that the loveliest woman in pre-war Berlin was in love with Gregory, Goering had asked him to dine and tell him about himself. During their long *tête-à-tête* it had emerged that they had certain interests in common. Russia was then allied to Germany, so a potential enemy of Britain, and was threatening to invade Finland. But as a long-term policy it was to Germany's interest to weaken Russia; so Goering had wanted the Finns to fight. Gregory had persuaded the Reichsmarschall that if given enough information about the then weakness of the Soviet Army, and with winter coming on to aid them, the Finns would resist the Russians' demands. Goering had agreed and supplied the information from the German Intelligence files. So instead of being shot as a confessed British spy Gregory had gone to Finland as Goering's secret envoy.

But now he could think of no such plan to save himself by

offering to perform some valuable service for the Reichs-marschall. And Goering was not the man to spare an enemy of his country out of sentiment, because he happened to be the lover of a woman who, in pre-war days, had been a most welcome guest at Karinhall.

Grimly, Gregory faced the fact that his only chance of surviving the coming interview was that, after five and a half years, the Reichsmarschall would fail to recognize the gaunt prisoner in ill-fitting civilian clothes, whom he had seen only once before posing as a Prussian aristocrat and dressed in the impeccable uniform of a German Colonel. Against that there was the disconcerting memory that while Goering had sent to Berlin for Intelligence summaries by the three Services and dictated from them an enormously long report for the Finns, Gregory had sat up with him the whole night, then breakfasted with him; and people are not apt to forget a face that has been within a few yards of them for the best part of twelve hours.

The car drew up at the front door of the great mansion and they got out. The sentries presented arms to Kaindl and the Mercedes drove off to park with a score of other cars that were lined up in a wide sweep at one side of the house; for when Goering was in residence he used his home as a headquarters and there were many officers coming and going.

When Gregory had last been to Karinhall the great pillared entrance hall had held a number of good statues and pictures; as they passed through it now, in spite of his anxiety about himself, he looked round with amazement. The old *objets d'art* had been replaced with masterpieces every one of which was worth a fortune. Goering, he knew, loved beautiful things and these priceless treasures were obviously some of the many that he had had carried off from museums and private collections in France, Belgium, Holland and other countries that the German armies had overrun. As an art thief it looked as if he had exceeded even the cupidity of Napoleon.

Kaindl led the way upstairs to the second floor and along to a good-sized room in a side wing of the house. Even here there were furniture and pictures that any rich man would have been happy to possess. The room had two beds, a large table, a

writing desk and a good selection of books; and leading off it
was a well-equipped bathroom.

With a smile, the plump-faced Colonel said, 'No doubt you
will find this a pleasant change after the accommodation to
which you have been used. Your meals will be brought to you
and you are not to leave this room until the Reichsmarschall
sends for you. Naturally, he is always very fully occupied; so
that may not be for some days. In the meantime I feel sure that
you would not be so foolish as to attempt to escape; but as a
formality I must ask you both to give me your paroles.'

Malacou did so at once, Gregory hesitated for a moment.
To refuse would mean being locked up. Even if he could break
out the chances of being able to evade the guards in both the
house and park were slender. Above all, he had neither papers
nor money. Without either and with a full description of
himself being circulated to the police of the whole district his
capture would be as good as certain; and when he was caught
he would certainly be shot. Swiftly he decided that it would
be better to bank on Goering failing to recognize him; so he,
too, gave his parole.

As soon as Kaindl had left them, Malacou, his black eyes
bright with triumph, gave a low laugh and said, 'There; you
see how right I was. I told you that with your experience in
handling these Nazi swine and my powers as an occultist,
between us we'd land on our feet.'

Rounding on him, Gregory snapped, 'Damn you! I've
always known that you derive your powers from the Devil. I
was crazy to have anything more to do with you. It's always
said that Satan only makes use of his votaries then lets them
down. I'm more likely to land up against a brick wall, unless
Goering takes it into his head to have me hanged.'

'What makes you think that? I warned you that we should
be in considerable danger, but——'

Impatiently Gregory cut him short and told him the situation. When he had done, he added, 'And if he recognizes me
he'll never believe that you didn't know that I am a British
agent; so you'll be for the high jump too.'

'No.' Malacou shook his head. 'Unless Hitler dies unexpectedly I shall be safe. At a certain point some months ahead our

horoscopes interlock. Both he and I enter a period of crisis but it is written in the stars that I shall outlive him. As for yourself, you say that when you were at Herr Goering's mercy before you saved yourself by thinking of a way in which you could be of use to him. You must use that agile brain of yours and devise some similar plan to produce should your fears be justified and he does remember you.'

'The situation is utterly different,' replied Gregory angrily. 'When I was last here it was early in the war. Only a few nations were involved. As the others had not then lined up there was still scope to apply power politics to the smaller countries. Now they are all in it up to their necks and there's no way in which I could suggest aiding Germany, even if in this case I were prepared to work against the interests of Britain. Some freak of fortune may enable you to save yourself, but unless Goering's memory fails him, I tell you my number is up.'

After a few moments' thought Malacou said, 'From what I remember of your horoscope your situation is now much as it was when you were trying to find out what was going on at Peenemünde. You have again entered a period of danger, but there is a fair chance that you will come through it. If you will agree to let me help you I could assure your doing so.'

'How?' Gregory asked, giving him a suspicious look.

'At night we can be sure of remaining undisturbed here. I could perform a ceremony. The Lord of this World does not abandon his followers, as you seem to think. If you are prepared to acknowledge him as your Master, he——'

Taking a pace forward, Gregory seized Malacou by the neck of his jacket, shook him violently and roared, 'You filthy Satanist. Get to hell where you belong. I'd sooner die first. For two pins I'd kill you here and now.'

His thick-lipped mouth agape with terror, Malacou staggered back and collapsed into an armchair. Perspiration had started out on his dark forehead. With a long thin hand he wiped it away. Then, when he had recovered a little, he whined:

'I was only trying to help you. Remember we are at one in our hatred of the Nazis, and we need one another. I look on you as my friend. Think back on how I hid you all those weeks at Sassen, and by my skill as a hypnotist saved you much pain.

Were it not for me and the power I derive from my Master you would not be alive today.'

'You helped me then because you had read in the stars that I would save your life later,' Gregory snarled. 'And had I not been fool enough to indulge with you in that damned thought transference I'd not be in this accursed country now, but safe in England.'

'You are unfair. From having established rapport with you I enabled you to do your country a great service by getting the mechanism of the giant rocket out of Poland. I risked my life to achieve that and have since paid dearly for it. I have told you, too, that together we shall soon strike another great blow against the Nazis. Surely it is that which counts above all else.'

Gregory stared down into Malacou's big dark hook-nosed face with its sensual mouth and clever, slightly slanting eyes. Apart from Stefan Kuporovitch, whom he trusted completely, he had never worked with anyone, greatly preferring to play the lone wolf; and he resented it intensely that in this last phase of the war fate should have thrust such a partner as Malacou on him. The man was unprincipled, evil, and to save his own skin would undoubtedly prove treacherous. Yet there was much in what he said. They were allies against the Nazis and in this thing together. Giving a shrug, Gregory said in a calmer tone:

'You are right. Abusing you won't get me anywhere and there's no sense in our quarrelling. As far as I can see our only hope of saving our skins—or mine, if you prefer it—is to impress Goering with our ability to predict coming events to the same degree as we did Loehritz and Kaindl. If we can be useful to him in that way, even if he does recognize me he may anyhow keep me on ice for the time being.'

With obvious relief, Malacou sat up and said, 'That's better. Now tell me everything you know about him, to help me get a sense of his personality.'

Thrusting his head forward Gregory began to pace up and down the room with panther-like strides, while speaking in crisp sentences. 'To look at he is a big, fat, jovial brute whom one would think to be interested only in wine, women and song. He has earned himself the reputation of being greedy for wealth, is ambitious, vain and utterly ruthless towards his

enemies. He is, of course; there can be no doubt about that.
But appearances are deceptive. In that great head of his he has
a first-class brain or, anyhow, he had, although it's said that in
recent years he has ruined it with drink and drugs. Whether or
not he has we shall find out when we meet him.

'One thing is certain. He has bags of courage. In the First
World War he was a fighter pilot. His exploits were second only
to those of von Richthofen. He commanded what was known
as a "circus" and with it shot down scores of Allied aircraft.
When the war ended he refused to surrender its aircraft to the
Allies. Instead he and his officers burnt them and swore to stand
together when the time came for Germany to revenge her defeat.

'I think that by then he had married. The girl was rich and
beautiful and, if I remember, a Swede. Anyhow, her name was
Karin. She was the love of his life. That's why, although he
married again after her death, he called this place Karinhall.
For a while they lived in Sweden. It was then that he first took
to drugs, and for a time he had to go into a home on that
account. But it did not impair his brain.

'In due course they returned to Germany. Hitler was then
no more than a soap-box orator. The two biggest planks in his
platform were the danger from Communism and the injustice
of the Versailles Treaty. Both of them appealed strongly to
Goering. He was one of the very few well-born Germans who
gave his allegiance to Hitler in those early days. And Hitler
owes an immense amount to him. He was in a position to
persuade many wealthy industrialists to support with funds
Hitler's anti-Communist movement. He became the first chief
of the Nazi strong-arm squads that formed Hitler's bodyguard.
Goering is no wishy-washy idealist who just did not like the
idea of the Communists getting control of Germany—as they
might well have done in those days. He went out with a gun in
his hand to break up the Communist Party.

'While Hitler did the talking Goering used every ruthless
means in the book to destroy Communism in Germany,
including kidnapping the leaders and having them shot. It was
that which enabled Hitler to be elected legally as Chancellor of
Germany in 1933. Hitler acknowledged the fact by promoting
him from an ex-Captain to Field Marshal overnight. But

Goering's usefulness did not end there. As I have told you, he has brains as well as guts. Hitler put him in charge of re-creating the German Air Force and for years he worked like a demon at the job.

'He became the head of a vast industrial concern, the *Hermann Goering Werk*, of which you must have heard. By it he not only built the Luftwaffe but became the king-pin in rearming Germany. He is the sort of man who, even if he had been born a poor boy in the Balkans, would have made his millions. He had an extraordinary grasp of essentials and was a glutton for work.

'Today we know the Luftwaffe's initial successes have tailed off into failure. Fat Hermann, as the Germans used affectionately to call him, has lost a great part of his popularity. But he is still too mighty a prop to Hitler's throne for Hitler to dispense with. The other Nazi leaders hate him, because he has never subscribed to the socialist side of National Socialism and he was much too much of a realist to approve the elimination of the Jews, who were so valuable to German industry. He did his utmost to protect Selma's friend, Hugo Falkenstein, the Jewish millionaire, and he is still the leader of the right-wing Nazis who loathe Goebbels because they know that, given half a chance, he'd turn Germany into a 'Workers' State'.

'He is at daggers drawn with Ribbentrop, too, because he never believed that the British people were effete, and he saw the danger of Germany entering on another world war against the British Empire. He did his utmost to stop Hitler going to war; but as he failed in that, being the complete cynic that he is, he's made the best of things and turned this place into a vast Aladdin's cave of looted treasure for his own enjoyment.

'Well, there is Hermann Goering for you. I'm told that at private parties he often appears in fancy dress and that his favourite costume is that of a Roman Emperor. Anyhow, he is the nearest thing to Nero in our age and it's my guess that now the Nazi Empire is cracking right, left and centre he is cheerfully fiddling. But that, and in his ostentation and debauchery, is where the resemblance ends. Because he has what Nero never had: brains and guts.'

'Can you give me his birth date?' Malacou asked.

'No, I'm afraid I can't. But we could get it from some book of reference that is bound to be in the house.'

'We must, so that I can draw his horoscope.'

There, for the time being, they left matters. By luck, Malacou found an old *Wer ist's?* among the books in the room that gave him the date he required, and he set to work on it with the sidereal tables he had brought with him from Sachsenhausen. Having spent twelve hours on Goering's horoscope, Malacou took from the *Wer ist's?* the birth dates of several other leading Nazis and for the following days, with Gregory's help, worked on them.

His previous endeavours to forecast the end of the war had got him little further than any fairly well-informed person could judge from the continued advance of the Allied Armies. This was because although nations, like persons, have associations with the heavenly bodies, the former are much more nebulous as no birth date can be affixed to them. But his calculations concerning the fates of the Nazi leaders enabled him to form a much clearer picture.

It emerged that a great gap would be torn in their ranks early in the coming May. Both Himmler and Goebbels would take their own lives and a number of others would die in one way or another. There followed a hiatus of seventeen months until October '46. Ribbentrop, Keitel, Jodl, Rosenberg, Frank and Kaltenbrunner would then all be hanged and Goering commit suicide. But Borgmann, Doenitz and Speer appeared to have a good chance of escaping similar fates.

That of Hitler remained uncertain. He would be in extreme danger of death during the first crisis, but it might be only that one of the doubles he was believed to use was reported dead; so that it would be thought he had committed suicide, while he went into hiding and continued in secret to direct the war.

Further to this, from the more nebulous data it looked as if by April the Russians would be in Berlin, the Americans on the Elbe and the British in possession of the greater part of Western Germany. It also appeared that at that time General Alexander would inflict a final defeat on the German armies in Italy, that both Himmler and Ribbentrop would try to negotiate a peace and that Goering, as Hitler's already appointed successor, would, temporarily at all events, assume the leadership.

In spite of what looked like the collapse of Germany in May, Malacou was convinced that fighting would continue on a large scale at least until August; but this might be in the Far East and he predicted that, in that month, something like an earthquake would occur in Japan, and that this would have serious repercussions throughout the whole world.

From these predictions they deduced that the arrival of the Russians in Berlin would precipitate a major crisis; perhaps a revolution in the Party, in which Himmler and Goebbels would get the worst of it. But that this would bring about an end to the war did not follow. Goering and the other leaders living on until October '46 appeared to indicate that under them the many S.S. Divisions and hard core of the Nazis, possibly still controlled by Hitler, would continue to resist long after Berlin had fallen. Considering the enormous superiority of the Allied forces this seemed improbable, yet that possibility could not be ruled out in view of Malacou's opinion that the great hanging would take place somewhere in South Germany, and it was obvious that if a last stand were to be made it would be in the natural redoubt formed by the Bavarian Alps.

Meanwhile although Gregory tried hard to keep his mind on these deliberations, he lived in constant fear of the summons that might end his life. He ate the good food that was brought up to them scarcely noticing what it was, and for four nights hardly slept from apprehension of the fate that the near future might hold for him. The long hours of waiting frayed even his strong nerves and he reached a point when he began to pray that Goering would send for them; so that he might know the best or worst.

The summons came on their fifth night at Karinhall, January 25th. At seven o'clock that evening Kaindl came in and said, 'I returned only this afternoon with the Reichsmarschall from one of his tours of inspection. Tonight he is giving a small dinner party and he has ordered me to produce you to entertain his guests afterwards. As he always dines late it will probably be about ten o'clock before I come for you; but you had better be ready well before that. If you do well he will probably keep you here. If not you will be sent back to Sachsenhausen and I shall be on the mat for having misled him. So for both our sakes do your utmost to make yourselves entertaining.'

Malacou assured him that he need have no fears and humbly thanked him for the chance he was giving them. When he had gone they did their best to smarten themselves up, then settled final details about such of Malacou's forecasts as they would give out and those it would be politic to withhold. At eight o'clock their dinner was brought in, but after a few mouthfuls Gregory found it next to impossible to swallow the food and pushed his plate aside. Throwing himself on his bed he lay there and, by thinking of his beloved Erika, somehow got through the final period of waiting.

Soon after ten Kaindl came for them. They accompanied him down to the ground floor and into a spacious dining room. It was so large that a horseshoe table occupied less than half of it, and Gregory saw that Goering's idea of a small dinner party consisted of at least twenty people. Most of the men were in uniforms bedecked with Knight Stars, Iron Crosses and other decorations, but three of them were in dinner jackets and the women were all in décolleté evening dresses.

The Reichsmarschall sat enthroned at the outer centre of the horseshoe. As Gregory had thought might prove the case, he was clad in a white and gold toga and had a laurel wreath on his head. He had become enormously fat, his eyes were pouched, his cheeks loose and puffy and on his sausage-like fingers there gleamed rings worth several thousand pounds. No actor in a play would have given a better representation of one of the most dissolute Roman Emperors.

Kaindl led his two charges into the centre of the horseshoe and presented them as Herr Protze and Herr Malacou. Goering ran his eyes over them and spoke:

'Colonel Kaindl tells me that you predicted our victory in the Ardennes and other matters correctly. Let us hear now what else you can tell us of the course the war will take.'

Gregory drew a deep breath. He was standing within ten feet of Goering and had escaped immediate recognition, but at any moment some expression on his features or in his voice might give him away. With a bow, he replied:

'Excellency, it is necessary that my colleague be seated. He will then fall into a trance and I shall interpret the communications that he receives from the entities of the outer sphere.'

A chair was brought, Malacou sat down, closed his eyes and, after taking several long breaths, began to mutter. As Gregory felt sure that everyone there must realize that Germany could not now possibly win the war, and that if he held out false hopes no-one would believe him, he said:

'Alas, through my colleague, the entities speak of no further German victories; but the soldiers of our great Führer will fight desperately in defence of the Reich. May will be the month of decision. Overtures for peace will be made. At that time there will be dissension in the *Partei*. Many prominent members of it will then die, but Your Excellency will not be among them. By March the Anglo-American armies will be across the Rhine and the Russians across the Oder. In May Berlin will become a doomed city; but it seems that resistance will continue in the south with the object of obtaining better terms from the Allies than they will be willing to give in May.'

Goering shrugged his massive shoulders. 'You tell us little that from the way things are going we might not guess for ourselves.'

Now that Gregory was, as it were, right up in the firing line, he had got back his nerve and was on the top of his form. With a smile, he replied, 'That the views of the Herr Reichsmarschall should coincide with fore-knowledge obtained from beyond confirms the soundness of his judgement. But to obtain more than an outline of general events is not possible. I can only add that war will continue to inflict the world at least until next August, and that in that month a disaster will occur in Japan that will affect the whole world.'

'What kind of disaster?'

'It will be in the nature of an earthquake or a violent eruption, but there are indications that it will be brought about by man.'

Suddenly Goering's eyes lit up. '*Lieber Gott!* Could it be that the Allies are really so far advanced in developing an atom bomb?'

Gregory shrugged. 'That is more than I can say; but many thousands of Japanese will die in the disaster. And now, if it please Your Excellency, my colleague can be the vehicle for much more precise predictions about individuals than about generalities. Would you like to be the first to have your future told?'

Goering shook his head. 'No. I am content to wait and see what fate sends me.' Then he gestured to a woman on his right and added, 'Make a start with this lady here.' Turning to the woman, Gregory bowed and asked her for the loan of something she always carried. She gave him her gold cigarette case and he handed it to Malacou. He then fetched a chair, sat down opposite the woman and asked her to lay her hands on the table, palms up. Smilingly she did so. For a few moments he studied her hands in silence, meanwhile he conveyed to Malacou what he read in them. Malacou, who was seated behind him, was at the same time psychometrizing the cigarette case and communicating his thoughts. By working simultaneously on the same subject in this way they checked their findings, and when Malacou began to mutter Gregory pretended to interpret.

He told the woman that as a child she had had a serious accident that had affected her spine, that she had married twice and that her present husband was an airman, that she had two children, a boy and a girl, both of whom had been sent out of Germany, he thought to Sweden. Then he predicted that she would survive the war, have two more children and go to live in some southern country, he thought Spain.

With astonishment, she declared him to be perfectly right about her past and Goering clapped his mighty beringed hands.

The second subject was a younger woman. Having told her accurately about her past, Gregory said, 'You, too, will survive the war, *gnädige Frau*. But not without injury. I regret to say that in an air-raid you will lose your right arm. You will also become a widow, but you will marry again, an elderly man who will provide you with every comfort.'

The third was a good-looking but rather sullen-faced woman. About her, spontaneously, Malacou sent Gregory a thought. As all that mattered was to impress Goering he decided to use it. When he had told her past, he said, 'Within six months you will become the mistress of a Russian officer.'

Her eyes blazing with anger the woman sprang to her feet and slapped his face. But Goering roared with laughter and the rest of the guests followed his lead.

When the clamour had subsided Gregory started on his next subject. She was what the French term a 'belle laide'. Her hair was a true gold and Gregory thought that he had rarely looked into a pair of more magnificent eyes; but her mouth was a thick gash across her face, and enormous. As he looked at her he suddenly wondered if she could be Sabine's friend, Paula von Proffin of the letter-box mouth. When his reading of her hand and the thoughts Malacou sent him tallied with what Sabine had told him of Paula he felt certain of it. Malacou also conveyed to him that she would be raped to death by Russian soldiers. Looking at her with pity he decided to give her no idea of that. Instead, after telling her that she had had a hard early life as a model, then married a banker who had left her penniless, he added, 'Your life will not be a long one, so make the most of it. At all events you are now married to an immensely rich man who can afford to indulge you in every luxury.'

Again Goering roared with laughter. Then, leaning forward towards a middle-aged man in a dinner jacket who was seated near him, he bellowed, 'Listen to that, Hans. And you pleading poverty before dinner. You'll not be able to deny little Paula anything after this.'

From that Gregory surmised that her new husband must be one of the chiefs of the Hermann Goering Werk, and that was why they were among Goering's guests.

Paula gave Gregory a ravishing smile and he turned to the next woman along the table. Among other thoughts, Malacou informed him that she had a venereal disease. So in her case he ended by saying, 'For the present I would advise you to lead the life of a nun; otherwise you will give anyone you go to bed with a present that he will not thank you for.'

She, too, jumped up in a fury, but Gregory sprang back in time to evade the slap she aimed at him. Again the cruel laughter rang out and, bursting into tears, the woman ran from the room.

'Well done,' wheezed Goering. 'Well done. I shall find you invaluable.'

So it went on through the women, then the men took their turn. Most of them were to survive, but three were to die, and Gregory told them frankly that they would give their lives for the Führer; but he refused to give them particulars or dates. One among them was a Naval Captain and Malacou told Gregory, both by telepathy and by confirming it in the muttered Turkish that at times he used to ensure that Gregory got his thoughts exactly, that the Captain was a traitor in the camp and using his position to spy on Goering.

Gregory made no mention of that, but when he had told all their fortunes he addressed the Reichsmarschall. 'Excellency, these psychic investigations into your guests have revealed one piece of information that I have not disclosed. It is for your ear alone and important to your safety. If you would give me a few minutes in private . . .'

Goering's eyes held his for a moment, then the elephantine Chief of the Luftwaffe nodded, heaved himself up from his great ivory and gold throne and said, 'Come with me.'

Picking up the skirts of his toga, he led the way out to an ante-room. On the walls there was a fabulous collection of paintings by the Dutch Masters. A great curved table desk occupied the centre of the room. With a grunt Goering lowered himself into a chair behind it, signed to Gregory to take another, and said:

'Well, go ahead.'

'That Naval Captain,' Gregory replied. 'I don't know his name. But my colleague is certain that he has been planted here to spy on you.'

A broad grin spread over the Reichsmarschall's fat face. 'I know it. He is my Naval Attaché, but in the pay of Himmler. I keep him on a string. Better the Devil you know than the Devil you don't. As long as he is here Himmler won't send anyone else to spy on me. I feed him with what I want that crazy fool to know.'

Gregory smiled. 'Then my warning is redundant, *Herr Reichsmarschall*. But Herr Malacou and I are deeply grateful for the way in which you have rescued us from prison and are anxious to be of service to you in any way we can.'

For a moment Goering studied Gregory's face intently, then

he said, 'Tell me, Herr Protze, how much of this clever act of yours is trickery? There are no means by which your predictions about the future can be checked, but all my guests are well-known people; so you and this Oriental fellow for whom you appear to act as manager might have obtained particulars about their pasts from ordinary sources.'

'No,' Gregory replied firmly. 'I assure Your Excellency that Herr Malacou is a genuine mystic. After all, both of us have been confined at Sachsenhausen for the past four months; so what possible opportunity could we have had to ferret out facts about the lives of your guests?'

Goering nodded. 'Yes. You certainly seem to have a point there. The Führer and Himmler swear by this sort of thing; but I never have. I'm still convinced that the occult has nothing to do with it. My belief is that you have only the ability to read people's thoughts about themselves, and make up the rest. Still, that's neither here nor there. The two of you provided us with an excellent entertainment, and in these days we haven't much to laugh about. You may go now. Tell Colonel Kaindl to give you a glass of wine and to protect you from those angry women, and that I'll rejoin my guests presently. I've a few notes I wish to make.'

As he spoke, Goering took a sheet of paper from a drawer and picked up a pen.

Having thanked him, Gregory came to his feet, gave the Nazi salute, turned about and walked towards the door. He was breathing freely now and his heart was high. He had come through the ordeal undiscovered and the party had been a huge success. The cold, the hunger, the lice, the stink and the nightly fatigue from which he had suffered for so many weeks at Sachsenhausen were finished with. He was safe now and he had only occasionally to amuse the Reichsmarschall at the expense of his guests to continue enjoying the good food and comfort of Karinhall.

He had just reached the door when Goering's voice came clearly from behind him. 'By the by. When you last saw her, how was my old friend Erika?'

23

The Other Side of the Curtain

'. . . MY OLD friend Erika?' For a moment Gregory strove to persuade himself that his mind had played him some trick and that he had only imagined hearing Goering speak those words; yet he knew it had not. When they had first come face to face that evening or, if not then, a little later, some feature, mannerism or tone of voice *had* struck a chord in the Reichsmarschall's memory. And that chord had resulted in no vague feeling that they had met on some previous occasion. His mention of Erika showed that he had definitely identified Gregory as the British agent whom he had been within an ace of having had shot in 1939.

Gregory was so near the door that his instinct was to dash through it. A second's thought told him that any attempt to escape would be foredoomed to failure. Already Goering might have taken a pistol from his desk and have him covered. At best he could hope only for some desperate minutes blundering down the long corridors before he was cornered by the guards. Since, at last, he had come to the end of his tether it was better to accept defeat gracefully.

Slowly he turned on his heel and faced the monstrous figure clad in the Roman toga. Goering raised a hand with fingers the size of sausages, heavy with rings, and beckoned:

'Come here, Englishman. I recognized you by the scar above your eyebrow, but I forget your name. What is it?'

'Sallust,' Gregory replied quietly, walking back to the desk and standing at attention in front of it.

'I remember now. Before I could recall only that years ago you risked your life by coming here to ask my help because you believed Erika to have fallen into the clutches of the Gestapo.'

'That is so, Excellency. Then you entertained me to dinner. Afterwards we spent the night making a plan to induce the Finns to refuse Russia's demands and go to war.'

'*Jawohl, jawohl.* What a lifetime away that seems. But it all comes back to me. Although our countries were at war it was in our common interest to induce the Finns to fight; and I spared your life because you had the wit to suggest a way in which that might be done.'

Gregory managed to raise a smile. 'Although our countries are still at war it is possible that we may still have interests in common. I served you well in Finland, perhaps . . .'

'No, no!' Goering gave a harsh laugh. 'Times have changed. Neither you nor anyone else can pull us out of the mess we are in. The game is up; and however able you may be, this time I can find no use for you.'

Already, during the past five days, Gregory had racked his brains in vain for some means of intriguing Goering into sparing him should his true identity be discovered. Now, he had made his bid and, as he had expected, having no concrete proposal to offer, it had been rejected. He began to wonder if the Reichsmarschall would have him taken out and shot at once, or give an order for him to be executed in the morning.

Goering again raised his hand. Gregory thought that he was about to press the bell on his desk to summon the guard, but the gems on it flashed as he waved it towards a chair and said, 'Those people in the next room bore me. Sit down again and tell me about yourself. How long have you been in Germany? What have you been up to, and what did you hope to gain by masquerading as a fortune-teller?'

It was seven months since Gregory had left England and even any information that could have been extracted from him under torture was long out of date; so he had no hesitation in relating how he had been flown into Poland to collect the mechanism of a V.2 and had become stranded there.

'What damnable luck,' Goering commented. 'And on account of that stupid firework, too. I always maintained that to manufacture a weapon that was as expensive as an aircraft, yet could deliver only one medium-sized bomb, was the height of idiocy; but the Führer wouldn't listen. Instead he let that loud-mouthed little crook Goebbels build it up as a war-winner, with the result that the people no longer believe our broadcasts. When I think of the millions in money and man hours that went into that damp squib it makes me hopping mad. With the same cash and effort I could have added ten thousand 'planes to the Luftwaffe and made the Normandy beaches present a very different picture. But go on. What happened to you then?'

Having no doubt that within eight hours at most he would be dead, Gregory took some pleasure in describing how he had killed the two S.S. men in Malacou's cottage and disposed of their bodies, then made his way to Berlin dressed in an S.S. uniform. But, having told how he had got rid of it, he temporarily abandoned the truth in order to protect Sabine; simply saying that he had hidden for some days in an empty boathouse on the Wannsee, and during the nights broken into a number of garages until he found one with a car that had a driving licence in the locker and for which there was a good supply of petrol. To that he had only to add that the licence had happened to be that of Prince Hugo von Wittlsebach zu Amberg-Sulzheim to return to a true account of all that had since befallen him.

Goering listened to all this with interest and, at times, amusement; but when Gregory spoke of the success that Malacou had had while at Sachsenhausen in predicting the future, the Reichsmarschall frowned and said, 'Surely that was no more than intelligent guesswork. For a long time past I could have foretold the way things would go for Germany and been right in all but minor matters.'

'No doubt,' Gregory agreed. 'But you had all the information available to go on, whereas Malacou, cooped up as he was in a concentration camp, had nothing other than rumours and news that was often weeks old. Even you could not have foreseen that the British airborne landings at Arnhem would prove a failure.'

'Oh yes I could. Montgomery's successes have been due mainly to his extreme caution and being backed by overwhelming air power; but for once he stuck his neck out. It was clear to us that he had allowed the airborne forces to be put down too far ahead for them to be supported by his armour, since it had to advance along a road that our artillery was able to enfilade from both sides.'

'Perhaps. But remember, you had the battle maps showing the dispositions of the opposing forces to judge from; whereas Malacou had nothing. And the Ardennes offensive. How could he possibly have known in adance about that by any ordinary means?'

'No; well, possibly you are right. Do you really believe what he said about May being the critical month for Germany, with us Nazi leaders at one another's throats and some of us trying to negotiate a peace?'

'I certainly do.'

Goering gave a heavy sigh. 'I would to God we could get peace tomorrow. We are finished. There is no way out. Nothing to be done. The nation is dead already but, still animated by the will of the Führer, refuses to lie down. And to think that we had the game in our hands; the whole world for the taking, in 1941.'

'You still had Britain against you, and the people were solid behind Churchill. We should never have given in.'

'In the end you would have been forced to,' Goering replied with a bitter laugh. 'That is, if I'd had my way. You and I know that the real danger to the civilization of the Western World is Communism—or, to give it another name, Soviet Russia. But Russia could wait. She would not have dared attack us, so we ought first to have devoted our entire energies to putting an end to the Government systems in other countries that tolerated Communist Parties within them. We had already made ourselves the masters of Austria, Czechoslovakia, half Poland, Denmark, Norway, Holland, Belgium, France, Yugoslovia and Greece. Italy, Spain, Rumania, Portugal and Finland already had Governments that had made Communism illegal. Sweden and Switzerland could have given us no trouble. In Europe only Britain remained as the refuge of our real enemies, who continue to take advantage there of your out-worn custom of affording asylum to anarchists, saboteurs and revolutionaries. If Germany had not dissipated two thirds of her strength by invading Russia, we could have brought such weight to bear on Britain that she would have found herself compelled to accept our terms and become our ally in a war to destroy the Soviets.'

'I doubt it, Excellency. And what of the United States?'

'The Yanks, eh?' Goering gave a great bellow of laughter. 'Surely you are too intelligent to share the belief common among Englishmen that the top Americans are really the friends of Britain? Under a screen of good will their State Department never ceases to work for the disruption of your Empire. They care only for making money, and in the markets of the world Britain is still their most formidable rival. For all their vaunted democracy, did they rush to help Britain and France in 1939? Certainly not. They sat back smugly watching their greatest trade competitors exhaust themselves.'

'That is by no means fair. By bringing in Lease-Lend, President Roosevelt gave Britain invaluable assistance.'

'But not until Britain had pawned her shirt; so could no longer find the money to pay for further armaments. Lease-Lend, my friend, was a shrewd move to enable Britain to continue the fight and so further exhaust herself. And even then the Americans got their pound of flesh for it—fifty obsolete destroyers in exchange for a lease of British possessions in the West Indies. Believe me, had it not been for the Japanese attack on Pearl Harbour the United States would have remained neutral to the end. It was Pearl Harbour which gave Churchill his opportunity to force her hand; and that clever old devil seized upon it. Within the hour he declared Britain to be America's ally in her war against the Japs. After that how could the Americans refuse to reciprocate by declaring war on Germany? But if Churchill trusts Roosevelt he's more of a fool than I take him for. When it comes to making the peace those American money-grubbers who behind your backs always refer to you as 'the bloody British' will do you down and bring about the dissolution of your Empire.'

While listening to the views of such a shrewd and well-informed man as the Reichsmarschall, Gregory's fears for himself were momentarily forgotten and he said, 'You are convinced, then, that had Germany played her cards rightly in 1941 she would now be the master of the whole of Europe?'

'I've not a doubt of it; and of Africa as well. That is, had
my advice been followed. Again and again I urged the Führer
to let Russia wait and, with or without Franco's consent, go
into Spain. We could have closed the Mediterranean at the
Straits of Gibraltar and cut off the British Army in Egypt;
leaving it to rot, as did the Army of Napoleon there after
Nelson had cut its lifeline by the Battle of the Nile.'

'After Italy came in, it was in any case virtually cut off
for a long period; but we succeeded in supplying and rein-
forcing it by the long route round the Cape.'

Goering laughed. 'Do you think that having got as far as
Gibraltar we should have stopped there? In '41 the French saw
no hope for themselves except by collaborating with us. They
believed Britain to be finished, so would have given us a free
hand in North Africa, and in Equatorial Africa too. From
there it is a short step to the Belgian Congo. Then we would have
launched a *Blitzkreig* against South Africa. The handful of
aircraft there would have been helpless against the Luftwaffe.
A few nights' bombing of Johannesburg and Cape Town would
have forced the South Africans to give in. Look now at the
strategic picture that would have resulted. With our U-boats
and aircraft operating from bases in Northern Spain, Portugal,
Gibraltar, Morocco, the Canaries, West Africa, St. Helena
and South Africa, we could have made it impossible for you
to send convoys round the Cape. With her army in Egypt
stranded and all supplies to Britain from Africa, Asia and
Australasia cut off, how could Britain possibly have refused
to accept the reasonable terms we would then have offered
her?'

There could be no doubt that Goering's great strategic
conception had been the right one for Germany and, while
Gregory still believed that if Britain had been *in extremis* the
United States would have come to her aid, he said with a wry
smile, 'I can only thank God that Your Excellency's advice
was not taken. No part of Africa could have offered any
prolonged resistance against the might and organizing ability
of Germany, and you could have had the whole continent for
only half the effort that was put into the attempt to conquer
Russia.'

'You're right!' Goering sighed. 'Yet even that false move need not have proved so utterly disastrous if the Generals had been listened to. We could still have fought the Russians to a standstill on a line along the Vistula and the Carpathians down to the mouth of the Danube, and so kept them out of Western Europe, had it not been for the Führer's obsessions about holding every foot of ground, and the Jews.'

'The Jews?' Gregory echoed in surprise. 'What had they to do with it?'

The Reichsmarschall shrugged and adjusted the laurel wreath on his head, which had slipped a little. 'I suppose you could not be expected to realize it, but it is the Jewish question that has bedevilled our entire strategy for the past year. At least you must be aware that Himmler's one aim in life is the complete elimination of the Jewish race, and that the Führer wholeheartedly supports him in his endeavours to achieve it.'

'I know that in Poland they were murdered by the million and that, since then, hundreds of thousands more of them have been collected from all over Europe to be driven into gas chambers.'

'Yes, poor devils. They are not my favourite people, but many of them were intelligent and useful citizens and there was nothing to be gained by their wholesale slaughter. On the contrary, it has robbed Speer and the Todt Works Organization of a great reservoir of slave labour. Far worse, Himmler's policy of "the ultimate solution", as it is called, has led to a great part of the Army being diverted from the job it should be doing.'

'Surely you cannot mean that the S.S. have found the job of rounding up the Jews too much for them, and have had to call on the Army for help?'

'Not precisely; but that's what it amounts to. Even after the loss of von Paulus's Army outside Stalingrad, and our Northern Army that became bottled up in Courland because the Führer refused to allow it to withdraw, we still had ample troops to fight a defensive war successfully. But when Rumania showed signs of collapse the Führer insisted that the front there must be held long enough to get the Jews out to Germany, so that they could be executed. The result was that another

sixteen of our Divisions were encircled and destroyed. The
line of the Carpathians was lost and a great gap torn in our
south-eastern front. To fill it an Army was moved from Warsaw
and its withdrawal so weakened our all-important Russian
front that it caved in.

'And this madness about putting the killing of Jews before
all other considerations continues. We had nothing to gain by
going into Hungary. Up till last spring the Hungarians observed
a favourable neutrality towards us and acceded to all our
requests for supplies and volunteer Divisions to help fight the
Russians. But there were seven hundred thousand Jews there
and the Hungarians refused to have them murdered; so
Himmler got permission to send in his Waffen S.S. troops to do
the job, instead of their being employed on a battle front.
Rounding up and eliminating such hordes of Jews takes time;
so half of them are still alive. The thought that they might be
saved by the arrival of the Russians in Budapest sent the
Führer berserk. Rather than let them escape he has transferred
yet another German Army from our vital Central front to
Hungary with orders to hang on there whatever the odds
against it, until Himmler's man, Eichmann, has administered
"the ultimate solution" to the remainder of the Jews.'

That Hitler's demand that every yard of conquered ground
should be held had led to immense losses of German troops
by encirclement was now common knowledge; but that his
disastrous strategy had been dominated largely by his obsession to eliminate the Jews was a revelation to Gregory.
After a moment he said:

'Had anyone other than yourself told me this, *Herr Reichsmarschall*, I would not have credited it. But, of course, you
know the facts. And how extraordinary it is that indirectly
the Führer's persecution of the Jews should have played so
large a part in Germany's defeat. One cannot help seeing in that
the hand of fate.'

'Perhaps.' Goering shrugged his great shoulders. 'Anyhow,
that's the way things are. This last attempt to hold Hungary
is bound to fail. Instead we should have withdrawn our south-
eastern Armies to the Bavarian Alps. And the price to be paid
for having weakened our northern front will be to have the

Russians in Berlin. I've had a grand life while it lasted so I'll have no complaints when my time comes; but you and I both know that the game is up. We are finished; all of us.'

As the modern Nero ceased speaking he pressed the bell on his desk. Gregory's muscles tensed. He felt certain that during the past ten minutes the Reichsmarschall had been only relieving his feelings by criticizing the Führer to him in a way that he still dared not do even to his personal friends, and that this was the summons for the guard to take the man to whom he had been blowing off steam away to face a firing squad. But when a footman appeared in the doorway, Goering said only, 'Bring champagne.'

Gregory tried not to show his relief. Although he knew that the postponement of his execution could be only temporary, the idea of buoying himself up with a few glasses of good wine before he had to meet his end was most acceptable. To keep the conversation going, he remarked:

'Could the Generals do nothing to persuade the Führer that many of his decisions would lead only to defeat?'

Goering's big belly shook as he sat back from his desk and roared with laughter. 'The Generals! *Gott im Himmel*, no! From the beginning the Führer has paid little heed to what they had to say. And since the July *Putsch* he would sooner take advice from his woman vegetarian cook. He is convinced that every one of them is a traitor. He doesn't trust even that time-serving toady Keitel. It is Martin Bormann who rules the roost today.

'Bormann is a cunning devil if ever there was one. He poses as the humble secretary whose only thought is to take work off his master's shoulders; but he has a finger in every pie. Not even I can get in to see the Führer now without Bormann being present and poisoning the Führer's mind against me afterwards. What is more, as Party manager he controls the Gauleiters and under him they are now absolute rulers in their territories. Even an Army Commander's authority is restricted to within five miles behind the front on which his troops are fighting. At times the Gauleiters even divert and commandeer for their own use trains of supplies intended for the troops. But the protests of the Generals go unheeded.'

'How fantastic,' Gregory murmured.

At that moment the footman brought in a magnum of Krug in an ice-bucket, and glasses. When he had poured the wine, both Goering and Gregory took a long drink. Then the Reichsmarschall went on. 'But that's not the worst the Generals have had to put up with. They are now being overlaid by Himmler's vast private army.'

'The term "vast" may apply to the Waffen S.S. but I should not have thought that in quality it could compare with the regular army.'

'You are out of date, my friend. Contrary to the belief of her enemies, during four and a half years of conflict Germany had not become geared for total war. Right up to last summer there were still hundreds of thousands of young, able-bodied men who continued to enjoy a protected status as Civil Servants, actors, authors, artists, agriculturists, bank clerks, railwaymen, and in a score of other occupations. Then came the Normandy landings and Goebbels persuaded the Fuhrer to order a *levée en masse*. Within a few weeks a million men were winkled out and called up to form what became known as the Replacement Army. But the Generals were not given control of it, because after the bomb plot the Führer openly proclaimed them to be his enemies. He gave the command to *der treue Heinrich*, as he affectionately calls Himmler; and, at the same time, permission to increase his Waffen S.S. without limit by any means he could devise.'

Goering took another long drink of champagne and added, 'Himmler's ambition for power is boundless. Naturally, he drafted the pick of the recruits into his Waffen S.S., and left only the duds for the Army. While he was at it Goebbels scraped the bottom of the barrel; so it may surprise you to hear that the Wehrmacht now has units composed entirely of men who are deaf, others of men suffering from stomach ulcers who have to have a special diet, and others again of epileptics and old dug-outs of over sixty.'

'Surely such troops are a liability rather than an asset?' Gregory remarked.

'Of course they are. They were roped in only on Himmler's insistence. His object was to swell the numbers of the men that could be allocated to the Army, so that when the Generals protested to the Führer he could be persuaded that they had had their fair share of recruits. Meanwhile, that little swine Goebbels had induced the Führer to order me to release half a million men from the ground staffs of my Luftwaffe stations.'

At the memory the Reichsmarschall's fat face turned almost purple. Quickly, Gregory refilled his glass and handed it to him. He took a gulp of wine then spluttered, 'Those . . . those are the fine fellows who are now being sent to die in Hungary, so that more Jews can be exterminated before the curtain comes down. Nine-tenths of them, and the greater part of all that was left of our German youth, have been enrolled in the Waffen S.S. Not content with that, Himmler for once scrapped his race-purity obsession in order to get another half million men under his command. He made honorary Aryans of Bulgarians, Albanians, Slovenes, Hungarians and even Russians. His S.S. Leaders combed the prisoner-of-war camps for anyone and everyone who preferred to put on a Nazi uniform rather than starve to death. To that he added French, Belgian, Dutch, Norwegian and Latvian collaborators by the thousand; so now his private Army numbers scores of Divisions and is nearly as big as the Wehrmacht. That's why the Führer could not refuse him the command of an Army Group.'

'What!' Gregory exclaimed. 'Himmler an Army Group Commander! But he can know nothing about soldiering.'

'Not a thing. But the greater part of the Wehrmacht's armoured divisions had been lost in Russia and in Normandy. The best we had left were the new ones created for the Waffen S.S. by Sepp Dietrich; and he is a good soldier even if he did start his career as the Führer's chauffeur. They had to be used as the spearhead of the Ardennes offensive, and as they were Himmler's troops he claimed the right to command the whole sector. Von Rundstedt would not stand for that and the Führer had to give way to him; so Himmler was bought off by being given command of the neighbouring Army Group, covering the sector between the Ardennes and the Swiss frontier.'

Once more Gregory was so intrigued that he had temporarily forgotten that he was talking to a man who, as soon as he tired of giving vent to his bitterness and rancour, would have him shot; and he asked, 'What sort of showing did Himmler make as a General?'

Goering shrugged. 'He proved not only helplessly incompetent himself, but has continued to be a menace to the success of all the other Army Commanders. You see, Commanders of S.S. divisions that are allotted to Army Groups come under Wehrmacht Generals only for operations, not for discipline; so they owe allegiance only to their own chiefs, the Obergruppenführers and, of course, to Himmler as their Supreme Commander. In consequence, being given an Army Group did not deprive Himmler of the power to interfere on all the other fronts on which Waffen S.S. divisions were employed.

'Sepp Dietrich did a splendid job with his armour in breaking through the Ardennes front. Had he been properly supported he might have reached Antwerp and delayed the Allied advance for several months. But the offensive failed for two reasons. The divisions from the Replacement Army given to von Rundstedt to follow up the attack were of such poor quality that they were not up to the task; and when he asked Himmler to release some of his S.S. Divisions from the neighbouring front to support the armour, Himmler refused. Instead he despatched his reserve divisions to Hungary, in another effort to prevent the Russians from capturing Budapest before all the Jews there could be killed off. There you have our tragedy: the units of two separate armies mixed up on every front, with the Generals of both hating the others, bitterly jealous and refusing to co-operate.'

Gregory shook his head. 'I had no idea of this. It must render all planning hopeless, and in such chaotic conditions I marvel that Germany is still able to maintain any front at all.'

'Planning!' Goering gave a cynical laugh. 'There is none. Each General is fighting only a local battle to stave off defeat. None of them knows what is happening to his neighbours, because they are forbidden to communicate in case they get together and decide to lay down their arms. The Führer sitting in his bunker in Berlin not only decrees the major moves but also directs everything, even down to the movement of battalions, with only the vaguest idea of what is really happening in the battle areas. Quite frequently he orders new units of the

Replacement Army to proceed to places that have been over-run by the enemy a week or more before.'

'That makes it all the more amazing that there has not been a general collapse.'

'Two factors account for that: the Wehrmacht Generals now ignore all the Führer's more idiotic orders, and the dogged determination of our soldiers to protect their homeland. We Germans and you British are the finest fighting men in the world, both in victory and defeat. But the Führer's distrust of the Generals and his fanatical belief that he can direct the war better than any of them has brought us to this shocking pass.'

'Could you not have persuaded him to see sense,' Gregory asked. 'After all, you are Nazi No. 2 and his appointed successor. Surely you must have great influence with him.'

Goering sighed. 'In the old days I had; but now he is barely civil to me. And that goes for the German people, too. They used to call me "fat Hermann", and they loved me. Now they blame me for the failure of the Luftwaffe and curse my name when the bombs come crashing down. That is my personal tragedy and my heart bleeds for my gallant airmen. Today they are humiliated and stigmatized as cowards. But it is no fault of theirs or mine that the Allies have driven the Luftwaffe from the skies.

'Dominance in the air is largely a gamble on which nation has the latest machine in operation when a war breaks out. It was no thanks to your Government, but because Lady Houston gave her millions to the development of fighter air-craft, that you had your Hurricanes and Spitfires operational in 1939. Had the war broken out a year later, we would have had a better type of Messerchmitt and you would have lost the Battle of Britain. But even then it was not too late. I could still have beaten the Allies in the air, or at least have prevented the bombing of our German cities later in the war, had I been allowed to manufacture our new types in sufficient numbers. Instead the fools hamstrung the Luftwaffe by divert-ing irreplaceable technicians and vast quantities of precious materials to the making of the V.1's and V.2's.'

After emptying his glass again, the Reichsmarschall said

bitterly, 'Well, now you know how things really are with us. That's why you find me amusing myself by dressing up like this and fiddling while Rome is burning, instead of ordering such squadrons of the Luftwaffe as are still serviceable into battle. They have to continue to make sorties, of course; but since I realized that our situation had become hopeless I've been trying to conserve the lives of as many of my boys as I can. The awful thing is that unless the Führer ordains otherwise this desperate last-ditch resistance may go on for months yet. I would to God that we could end it tomorrow, but I'm thoroughly discredited and there is nothing I can do.'

'About that I don't agree,' said Gregory firmly. 'You still possess immense powers, and your Luftwaffe troops would obey your orders. Since the Führer will not listen to reason and is clearly mad, you could surround his headquarters with your men, arrest him and, if need be, shoot him; then take over and ask for an armistice.'

Suddenly the elephantine figure behind the desk lurched forward. With eyes blazing, Goering brought his huge fist crashing down on the desk and bellowed, '*Lieber Gott!* For suggesting that I've a mind to have you shot.'

Gregory's mouth fell open. Before he could stop himself, he exclaimed, 'But . . . but, aren't you going to have me shot anyway?'

With the same suddenness as had marked his outburst, the Reichsmarschall sat back, relaxed and shook his head. 'No. Why should I? You're a brave man, Sallust, and I like brave men. What is it to me now that you happen to be a British spy? God knows, I've enough blood on my conscience already. Men and women are dying by the thousand while we sit here. Why should I add yet another corpse to this senseless carnage?'

So certain had Gregory been that he was living through his last hours that it took a long moment for him to adjust his mind to this utterly unexpected reprieve. His face went whiter from relief than it would have done had the guards arrived to lead him off to execution. Then he swallowed hard and stammered:

'For . . . for giving me my life, *Herr Reichsmarschall* . . .

well, I can't find words to thank you adequately. All I can say is that had our positions been reversed I would have acted in the same way towards you.'

Goering nodded. 'Yes, I believe you would. But never again suggest that I play the traitor. All of us know that the Führer is mad and has brought about Germany's ruin. But, all the same, he had the touch of genius. There is not an iota of truth in those stories that he was no more than a brilliant orator that the rest of us made use of as a figurehead. When he came to power Germany had eight million unemployed. It was his brains and courage that saved her from Communism, brought her back to prosperity and gave her again a place in the first rank among the nations. Had he refrained from resorting to war and from persecuting the Jews, he would have gone down in history as a great ruler. We others were no more than his servants and we obtained wealth and power in his shadow. Others may betray him, but I never will.'

'I appreciate your point of view,' Gregory said seriously, 'and your sentiments do you honour. All the more so since you have given me to understand that for some time past the Führer has treated you with little consideration.'

'That is hardly surprising in view of the failure of the Luftwaffe. He constantly rails at it and throws its failure in my teeth. What does surprise me is that he has not deposed me as his successor in the event of his death. Himmler, Goebbels, Ribbentrop and Bormann never cease from endeavouring to bring that about; but he won't listen to them. It may be that because I did more than anyone to gain support for him in the days of his struggle he still feels a certain loyalty towards me. But I'm inclined to think the real reason why he is reluctant to disgrace me publicly is that, if he ever did decide to throw in his hand, he believes that the Anglo-Americans would be more willing to negotiate terms with me than with any other of the Nazi leaders.'

'In that I'm sure you're right. Himmler and Goebbels are loathed, Ribbentrop despised and the name of Bormann is hardly known. Whereas there was a time when, owing to your exploits as an air ace in the First World War, many people in England looked on you as rather a glamorous figure; and even today none of the odium about lying propaganda, concentration camps or the persecution of the Jews attaches to you.'

Taking the magnum from the ice-bucket, the Reichsmarschall again refilled their glasses; then he said, 'Talking of England, you have not yet told me about Erika. Is she still in love with you?'

'It is seven months since I have seen her in the flesh,' Gregory replied. 'But I've not the least reason to doubt that her devotion to me still equals mine to her. Years ago we made up our minds to marry as soon as she could get free of von Osterberg, but that was impossible as long as the war lasted and he remained alive. I . . . well, I heard a rumour that he was involved in the July plot and that when the Gestapo came to arrest him he committed suicide. Do you happen to know if that is true?'

Gregory had spoken casually but his heart was hammering as he waited for Goering's answer. After a moment it came. 'I do remember hearing something of the kind, but I've an idea that he survived. It has been no easy matter to keep track of what happened to all the people who disappeared after the plot. Between August and the end of the year over three thousand men and women were executed for treason, and thousands more were carted off to concentration camps. The Führer's fury knew no bounds and he ordered that no mercy should be shown to any blood relative of those involved. He even signed the death warrant of his favourite General, Rommel, merely on suspicion that he had been implicated.'

'What a terrible thing to do.'

'Yes. Rommel was at his home, recuperating from wounds received when the car he was in was bombed in Normandy. The Führer sent his adjutant, Chief of Army Personnel, General Burgdorf, to him with a phial of poison and an ultimatum. He was given the choice of taking the poison or having his whole family put through the mill; so, of course, he took the poison.'

'God help us! And after the brilliant show he put up in the Western Desert. Such treatment of a national hero is almost unbelievable.'

'Oh, they gave him a hero's funeral, with laudatory orations and all the rest of it,' Goering replied with a cynical chuckle. 'But reverting to von Osterberg. If he was in hospital with a self-inflicted wound he would have escaped the initial massacre, and as he was one of the king-pin scientists in the Secret Weapon racket, it's quite probable that when he came out Himmler decided that he was worth more alive than dead. I've certainly an idea that someone told me he had seen him recently. Tell me more about Erika, though. What is she doing?'

'She's running a hospital for R.A.F. wounded. At least, she is responsible for the non-medical staff, rations, entertainments and general administration.'

'She would do that well, for she had brains as well as looks. *Gott im Himmel*, what a woman! In Munich, in the old days, the help she gave me was invaluable. And what beauty! Her only rival in all Germany was Marlene Dietrich and they might easily have been sisters. What a lucky fellow you are to have gained her love. But that is another reason for my giving you my protection. It would be ungrateful of me to deprive her of you. I did my utmost for her to save Hugo Falkenstein. I could have, had he not been so proud and courageous; but he stood up to the Führer in defence of his people and so signed his own death warrant. Erika never forgave us his death and went over to the enemy. That was a bad day for all her friends and those of us who loved her. I suppose that in order to do this hospital job she has had to take British nationality?'

Gregory shook his head. 'No. She declares that only cowards rat on their own country in the middle of a war. By rights she should be in a concentration camp as an enemy alien. But the big country house which has been turned into a hospital, where she works, is owned by a friend of ours, Sir Pellinore Gwaine-Cust. He has great influence with the Government and has gone surety for her. She has agreed that if she can become my wife she will regard Britain as her country; but until then, having been born a German she will remain a German.'

'Ah, how like her!' Goering smiled. 'Clever, brave, beautiful and a true patriot. Well, I only wish that I could send you back to her. But that is out of the question. Still, there is room and to spare in this lovely home that I have made. You can remain here as my guest; anyway, until those accursed Russians over-run and pillage it of my treasures. For you the war is over. You have only to kill time as best you can until the final collapse. That applies too, of course, to the man you brought with you. The two of you can amuse yourselves consulting the stars and drawing horoscopes.'

Gregory smiled back. '*Herr Reichsmarschall*, I am more grateful than I can say for your clemency and kindness. If I succeed in getting back to Erika and tell her of this she, too, will always bless your name. I only wish, though, instead of idling here for the next few months I could be of some use. I mean, play even a small part in bringing about the cessation of hostilities.'

For a long moment Goering remained silent. Then his eyes lit up and he leaned forward. '*Teufel nochmal!* I believe you might if we played our cards cleverly. The Führer will listen to no-one these days except the astrologers and fake magicians with whom he surrounds himself. Their predictions are the one thing which can still influence his decisions. *Gott im Himmel!* This is an idea! Stupendous! *Kolossal!* I'll make him a present of you and your Turkish mountebank.'

24

The Devil's Court

GREGORY jerked back his head as though he had been hit between the eyes and held up a hand in protest. 'God forbid! I'd rather you had me shot here and now than send me to the Führer's headquarters.'

The Reichsmarschall's eyebrows arched into his broad forehead. 'What an extraordinary thing to say. As a secret agent you must be used to acting a part and I thought you to be a brave man. Why are you so terrified of coming face to face with the Führer?'

'I'm not,' Gregory replied sharply. 'But, as his headquarters is now in Berlin, if I stay there for any length of time all the odds are that I'll run into Gruppenführer Grauber. It was I who bashed out one of his eyes. With the other he would recognize me in a second. He has threatened that if ever he gets me he'll keep me alive in agony for a month before what's left of me gives up the ghost. That's why I'd prefer a bullet now.'

'One does not have to be a coward to dread such an end,' Goering admitted. 'And from what I've heard of Grauber he enjoys doing that sort of thing. But you needn't worry. Grauber is now on the Russian front.'

'What in the world is he doing there? Is he no longer the head of the Gestapo Foreign Department, UA-1?'

'No. I assume he saw a good chance of getting a step up when his Chief became an Army Commander. He did, too. He got himself promoted to Obergruppenführer, and Himmler took him with him as his Chief of Staff when he moved to Russia.'

'But he can't know the first thing about running an Army Group.'

'Of course not, but he is just the man to carry out Himmler's ideas of fighting a war. He has decreed that the commanding officer in any town or village who fails to hold it is to be shot. And behind the lines he has mobile squads of S.D. troops whose job it is to shoot out of hand any officer or man they come upon who is walking away from the front.'

'What an insane way to treat one's troops. But I thought you said that Himmler's Army Group was in the West.'

'So it was until about a week ago. As you know, in the latter part of January the Americans launched their counter offensive in the Ardennes. To relieve the pressure on our troops, von Rundstedt proposed an attack against Strasbourg. The Americans were weak there and the city might quite well have been retaken, but Himmler made a hopeless mess of things; so the Führer kicked him upstairs and gave him command of a more vital sector, our front on the Vistula. General Hausser was ordered to take over in Alsace, but Himmler did not bother to wait for him and tell him what was going on. He cleared out bag and baggage with his staff, leaving only a dirty laundry basket full of unsorted reports for Hausser to make what he could of.'

'This becomes more and more fantastic.'

'Oh, it's the truth all right. Can you wonder that I've long since washed my hands of the whole business? Anyhow, Himmler is now on the Russian front and Grauber with him. All through December the Russians had been quietly preparing one of their great offensives. They launched it on January 12th. Within ten days they reached the Baltic coast east of Danzig and cut off another twenty-five of our divisions that the Führer had forbidden to retreat. Guderian, the Panzer expert, who is now Chief of Staff, wanted General Weichs to command the last troops of the Replacement Army that were being sent to fill the gap that had been torn in our front; but in such a crisis the Führer decided that Himmler was the only man he could trust, so *der treue Heinrich* got the job.'

'You feel confident then that I shan't run into Grauber if, as you suggest, you send me to the Führer's headquarters in Berlin?'

'I'm sure you won't. I have a highly competent Intelligence

service of my own that keeps tabs on all my dear colleagues. If any fish as big as Grauber is moved to another job I am informed of it at once. I would warn you if you are likely to be in any danger and you could come back here.'

'But do you really think there is the least chance of my being able to influence the Führer?'

Goering shrugged. 'It is impossible to say. But it is an indisputable fact that the only things he takes any notice of these days are Bormann's poisonous whispers and the predictions of his astrologers. I've no great hopes that you could persuade him to ask for an armistice; but you never know. Since the bomb plot his health has been steadily deteriorating. He still rules the roost because everybody is terrified of him. But mentally he's gone to pieces. He eats practically nothing and is kept going only on drugs. He lives in constant fear of assassination and is harassed by the belief that everyone except a handful of his toadies is scheming to betray him. The strain upon his mind must be appalling and at times he must long to free himself from it. That's why I feel there is just a chance that a determined man like yourself, who can make use of this occult hocus-pocus, might succeed in tipping him over the edge and getting him to put an end to it all.'

'How about the astrologers?' Gregory asked. 'It's certain they'll do everything they can to prevent a newcomer breaking through their ring and getting at him.'

'Yes. That is a problem. The jealousy and hate of the people who make up the Führer's court have to be seen to be believed. And my stock with him is so low that he may not take my word for it that you are a wizard of the first order; so refuse to see you.'

'Perhaps then it would be better if I were not presented as an occultist, but was sent to him in some other capacity; then, out of the blue as it were, make some startling prediction that comes off a few days later. That is, if Malacou can provide me with one.'

'That is certainly an idea. You are a shrewd fellow, Sallust.' Goering picked up the magnum, saw that it was empty, dropped it back into the ice-bucket and said, 'I don't think I'll order another. We've talked enough for tonight, and to good purpose. The more I think about this plan the more I feel that there is a lot to it. We'll go to bed now; but we must both put our wits to work on how to make you Adolf's new blue-eyed boy. We'll talk again tomorrow.'

When Gregory got to the room he shared with Malacou he found him asleep, so did not disturb him. Next morning he told him how Goering had, after all, recognized him but spared him, and of the Reichsmarschall's idea of sending them to Hitler's headquarters.

Malacou's dark eyes gleamed with excitement. 'I knew something of this kind would happen. The stars foretold it and the stars never lie.'

'Aren't you a little scared at the thought of having to face him and, perhaps, influencing him into committing some act that may come back on us like a boomerang?' Gregory asked. 'I don't mind confessing that I am.'

'Yes; I have not concealed from you that our lives will be in danger. Towards the end of April things look very black for both of us; but I have good hopes that we will survive. This present project causes me no special fears for myself, because I am convinced that I shall outlive Hitler. After that, my horoscope is obscure. To me there comes danger from an impulse of my own. There is a possibility that I may lose my life in an attempt to save someone else. As I am not of the stuff of which heroes are made, I cannot see myself making such an attempt; so perhaps my death may be the result of an accident. But sometimes one survives such periods of danger with only an injury; as was the case with you at Peenemünde.'

They spent most of the day discussing Goering's idea and how best to prepare for it; then, shortly before midnight, Kaindl came to fetch Gregory. On their way the Colonel congratulated him on the excellent show he and Malacou had put up the previous evening and said he felt sure that they need not fear to be sent back to Sachsenhausen. At that, Gregory smiled to himself and again expressed his gratitude to Kaindl for having rescued them from their harsh captivity.

Two minutes later they entered the Reichsmarschall's study at the top of the house. It was as large as a small church and at the far end Goering was sitting at a desk the like of which

Gregory had never before seen. It was of mahogany, inlaid with bronze swastikas and twenty-five feet long. On it stood two great gold candelabra and a huge inkstand of solid onyx. Behind it sprawled the formidable figure, tonight dressed in the silks of a Doge of Venice and with the Phrygian cap crowning his broad forehead. With a smile at Gregory, he said:

'Sit down, both of you; and you, Kaindl, listen carefully to what I have to say.'

When they were seated, he went on, 'As one of my fellow pilots in our fighting days I know that I can trust you, and I am about to confide to you a secret that might land us both in a packet of trouble should it ever get out. We all know that the war is lost, although it is treason to say so. During the past six months scores of people in bars and tram cars have been picked up by the Gestapo and shot for saying no more than that. But we must face facts, and I've thought of a way by which there is just a chance that we may hasten the end of this senseless slaughter.

'Herr Protze here, and his friend the Turk, claim to have occult powers; so I intend to send them to the Führer, as there is just a possibility that they may be able to influence him into asking for an armistice. But for two criminals on parole to gain the Führer's confidence would be far from easy; so I mean to practise a deception upon him. Herr Protze will become a member of my personal staff with the rank of Major. The Turk will accompany him as his batman.

'Now, the only danger to my plan is from people who saw the two of them perform for us last night. Have you any idea how many of them know that Herr Protze and the Turk are on parole from Sachsenhausen?'

Kaindl raised his eyebrows in surprise. 'None of them, *Herr Reichsmarschall*. I naturally supposed you would not wish it to be known that they were convicts; so I have told no-one from where they came.'

'That is excellent. Then you have only to put it about among the household that Herr Protze is one of my staff officers who has been for a long time abroad. You can explain the fact that he was confined to his room with his man for the past week by saying that they had to be for many hours together to carry

out their occult operations, and that they will continue to
share a room while here for the same reason. Meanwhile, I'll
see that it gets to the ears of all who dined with us last night
that Herr Protze is in fact a Major of the Luftwaffe. You, too,
can help in that.'

'*Jawohl, Herr Reichsmarschall.*'

'The next thing is uniforms. Get a tailor out here from Berlin
first thing tomorrow morning and tell him that he must supply
everything necessary within forty-eight hours. Finally there is
the matter of instruction. You have not been with me very long,
but long enough to have met most of the people at the Führer's
H.Q. It is important that Herr Protze should be as fully informed about them as possible. He will be attached as an
extra adjutant to General Koller. I will, of course, see Koller
about that myself. But he will not be in our secret; and I shall
not introduce his new adjutant to him until Major Protze
has his uniform and you have given him some idea of the duties
he will be expected to perform. Is that all clearly understood?'

'*Jawohl, Herr Reichsmarschall.* You may rely on me to do
my utmost to assist *Major* Protze in any way I can.'

Goering nodded. 'Thank you, Kaindl. I felt sure I could.
You may leave us now.'

The Colonel stood up, clicked his heels, bowed sharply from
the waist and marched off down the long room.

When the door had closed behind him Gregory smiled and
said, 'My congratulations, Excellency, on the speed with
which you have thought of a good way to put me in contact
with the Führer in a respectable guise.'

After drawing heavily on a long cigar and exhaling the
smoke, Goering replied, 'It was the best plan I could think of,
but I'm not altogether happy about it. We shall be gambling
on your ability to act and talk like a staff officer.'

'Oh, you needn't worry about that,' Gregory laughed. 'But,
unwittingly, you have demoted me. At home I have the rank
of Wing Commander which, as you know, is the equivalent
of Lieutenant-Colonel.'

'Indeed!' Goering gave him a sharp glance. 'How does that
come about?'

'It was simply a matter of convenience; so that I could be

usefully employed during the long spells I have spent in England between my missions.'

'Where did you work?'

'Air Ministry Intelligence,' lied Gregory smoothly. 'There were lots of other fellows in it who, like myself, had no flying experience: lawyers, schoolmasters, journalists and so on.'

'I see. Yes, that's the case with us, too; and why I can send you in without General Koller—who, by the by, is my Chief Liaison Officer at Führer H.Q.—or any of my other staff officers being surprised to learn that you have never seen active service with the Luftwaffe.'

'I thought as much; but there remains one nasty snag. What am I supposed to have been doing all the five years the war has been on? It is going to be thought very strange that I won't have a single acquaintance in common with any of your other people. And I dare not lie by stating that I was in this or that department as it might easily emerge that I was not.'

For a moment Goering remained deep in thought, then he asked, 'Do you know anything about pictures or *objets d'art*?'

'As much as the average educated man, but not enough to discuss such matters with an expert.'

'But you have travelled, I take it, and at one time or another visited most of the famous galleries?'

'Oh yes. Florence, Madrid, Vienna, Munich, Brussels and the rest. I've been to nearly all of them more than once.'

'Good. That's quite enough. Ever since 1940 I've had eight or ten men going round Europe for me, picking up these sort of things.' The Reichsmarschall waved a hand vaguely round, indicating the Gobelin tapestries on the walls and the Buhl cabinets filled with priceless Meissen. 'You can have been one of them and spent most of the time in some of the remoter places, say Bulgaria and the Crimea. I've a splendid collection of jewelled ikons. You could have found a lot of those for me. But don't be too specific; give the idea that you were also on the lookout for Byzantine armour, silk Persian rugs and golden trinkets found in the tombs of ancient Greece. I've masses of all these things and you can spend a day or two examining and memorizing some of them before you go to Berlin. If you had been one of my collectors and I'd a personal regard for you, now we've been pushed out of all those countries from which I used to extract these little presents there would be nothing at all unnatural about my taking you on as an extra adjutant.'

Gregory nodded. 'That will provide an excellent cover, *Herr Reichsmarschall*. It's quite certain that no-one at Führer H.Q. is going to ask me to give an expert's opinion on such things at a time like this. But it is going to be more than a few days before Malacou and I will be ready to go into action.'

'Why?'

'Because, having Kaindl, and later General Koller, brief me on the men we'll meet there is not enough. If we are to stand any chance at all of putting this over, we'll need the birth dates of as many as possible of them and all the particulars that can be raked up about their pasts. Malacou will draw their horoscopes while I digest all the down-to-earth stuff; but that will take time.'

'How long?'

'A fortnight at least. Let's say till the end of the month.'

'Very well. My Intelligence Bureau has dossiers on all these people. I'll have them sent to you. And from now on, of course, you are free of the house. The Turk had better continue to have his meals in your room; but as soon as you have your uniform you can have yours in the mess, then you'll get to know my officers. When I'm dining at home I'll ask you to my parties, as the greater number of important people you meet and talk with the better. Now; is there anything else?'

'No, Excellency.' Gregory stood up. 'You seem to have thought of everything. First thing tomorrow, or today rather, I'll get down to work.'

In the morning Kaindl produced a tailor, who measured Gregory for his uniforms; then he spent the best part of the rest of the day going round the house. By blackmail, bribery and outright theft Goering's agents had filled it with treasures the value of which it was impossible to estimate, but they would certainly have fetched many millions of pounds. Museums and palaces all over Europe, and some even in Germany, had on one pretext or another been looted of old masters, statuary, gold altar pieces, gem-encrusted crucifixes, jade carvings, precious porcelain, jewelled snuff-boxes and thousands of rare books that were housed in a great, domed library, making it the most magnificent art collection in the world ever assembled by any private individual. In five or six hours Gregory had time to examine only a tithe of it, but he promised himself many more hours of similar enjoyment before leaving Karinhall to again risk his life.

That evening the dossiers arrived and the following morning, with Kaindl's help, he started to study them, while Malacou took notes of birth days and important dates in the lives of those people who, since January 16th when Hitler had made his H.Q. in the bunkers under the Reich Chancellery, had been his most frequent companions.

Martin Bormann, it emerged, was now forty-five. He had been an assistant to Rudolf Hess and first came into prominence as the head of the Party Chancery; but he had won a high position in Hitler's favour by becoming his successful financial adviser. Subservient, self-effacing, but extraordinarily watchful and competent, he had gradually made himself indispensable and assumed the role of confidential secretary. As Hitler took special pride in his abilities as an architect, Bormann had won further favour by supervising for him the building of his mountain palace, the *Berghof*, at Obersalzberg. Then, after Hess's flight to Scotland, Bormann had succeeded in slipping into his old chief's shoes as Controller of the *Partei*, a post which, while not making him as conspicuous as the other Nazi leaders, gave him immense hidden power. He was loathed by the others, who realized his insatiable ambition, but he had now achieved a position in which they could not harm him and had to discuss their business with him before he would even arrange for them an interview with his master.

Dr. Josef Goebbels was the only one of the Nazi satraps who had even a working agreement with Bormann, and that only because both were intelligent and respected one another's capabilities to the extent of feeling it wiser not to quarrel openly. The little club-footed doctor was now forty-eight. He had been a star pupil at a Jesuit seminary, and had acquired an extraordinary ability to argue a case convincingly however dubious the facts on which it was based. Even after the tide of Germany's defeat had clearly set in he had continued to persuade the greater part of the people that victory was still assured by the simple device of putting out in his broadcasts the same flagrant lies repeated again and again with conviction and vigour. Politically, he led the extreme Left of the Nazi Party. Privately, he led an unusual dual existence; for on the one hand he was a devoted family man with several children, while on the other it was well known that as Films came under his Ministry, no good-looking woman could get a leading part in a film unless she first agreed to sleep with him. He was unquestionably devoted to Hitler and was one of the few people still completely trusted by him.

Grand Admiral Karl Doenitz was another of those few and, now being close on seventy, was by some years the oldest of Hitler's courtiers. He had reached the top of his Service through a combination of being both a highly competent officer and a convinced Nazi. Wisely, he had refrained from mixing himself up in the political intrigues of the others and, as a hard, cold man, he had carried out without argument Hitler's wish that the war at sea should be waged with complete ruthlessness. The Army, Hitler had always distrusted and now hated; the Luftwaffe had failed so lamentably that he had come to despise its officers; the Navy alone, in his opinion, had never let him down; so Doenitz had become his favourite of all his Service Chiefs.

Field Marshal Wilhelm Keitel, aged sixty-three, had, from 1938 when Hitler had taken over as War Minister, deputized for him as Chief of the Armed Forces and was still his principal military adviser. Tall, distinguished-looking, correct, he was the lick-spittle to outlick all lick-spittles, and lacked even the courage to say a word in defence of his brother Generals when their troops were forced to abandon their positions on being attacked by overwhelming odds. In his dossier Gregory was amused to read that when, at last, Montgomery had broken out from the Normandy beachhead and von Rundstedt had reported what had happened, Keitel had wailed over the telephone, 'Oh, what shall we do? What shall we do?' to which von Rundstedt had replied tersely, 'Sue for peace, you bloody fools. Sue for peace. It is the only thing you can do.' And for that, within the hour, on Keitel's reporting it to Hitler, Germany's greatest General had been sacked as G.O.C. West; although Hitler had seen no alternative to asking him to come back a few months later to launch the Ardennes offensive.

Under Keitel, Colonel-General Alfred Jodl, recovered from the wounds he had received when the bomb went off at Rastenburg, was again filling the role of expert on land strategy, and doubling up with him was the Panzer General, Guderian, whom Hitler had chosen as his latest Chief of Staff of the Wehrmacht, not because of his undoubted ability but because he was hated and distrusted by all the other Generals.

On a lower strata, but wielding more influence because he was hand in glove with Bormann and Goebbels, was General Burgdorf—another toady. He was both Hitler's personal Wehrmacht adjutant and Chief of its Personnel Bureau.

The principal representatives of the Luftwaffe were Generals Karl Koller and Eckard Christian; the former an elderly, much harassed, long-suffering man; the latter a youngish, ambitious Nazi who had married one of Hitler's two women secretaries. But, as Hitler blamed the failure of the Luftwaffe on Goering, he regarded its officers with less rancour than those of the Army, and for his personal Luftwaffe adjutant, Colonel Nicolaus von Below, he had a high regard.

Heinrich Himmler, who was the same age as Bormann, forty-five, still held a very high place in the Nazi hierarchy and appeared to be the most likely bet as Hitler's successor should he ever be persuaded to rescind his decree of 29th July, 1941, by which Goering had been appointed as Heir Apparent. Yet Himmler's potentialities seemed more apparent than real; for he now rarely saw Hitler and there was good reason to believe that Bormann had deliberately flattered him into asking for the command of an Army Group in order to get him out of the way.

Why Himmler was allowed to continue as the Supreme Head of scores of divisions of fighting troops, large bodies of pro-Nazi partisans all over Europe and countless thousands of civil and secret police, Gregory could not imagine; for he was clearly as mad as his master, hopelessly incompetent and suffering from a series of nervous breakdowns to boot.

Although theoretically commanding an Army Group against
the Russians on the most vital sector, he was now spending most
of his time in a clinic at Hohenlychen, where he was completely
dominated by three people—his doctor, Karl Gebhardt, his
masseur Kersten and his astrologer Wulf, whom, from time to
time, he lent to Hitler. But he remained Reichsführer and
Hitler still often referred to him affectionately as '*Reichheine*'.

It was evident that Himmler's empire was being run for him
by his principal lieutenants: Kaltenbrunner who, after the
assassination of Heydrich, had become the head of the
R.S.H.A.; Ohlendorf, the head of the S.D.; Grauber, Eichmann, Heinrich Mueller, the head of the Political Police; von
dem Bach-Zelewski, the Partisan Warfare Chief, and others
less senior of their kind; all depraved blood-lusting sadists who
for years past had been torturing and murdering people by the
tens of thousands and continued to do so as the only means of
postponing defeat and being called to account for their
appalling crimes.

Himmler's liaison officer at Führer Headquarters was
Obergruppenführer Hermann Fegelein. He was a detestable
little man who had started life as a horse coper and jockey,
then been an early member of the Waffen S.S. In spite of
being almost illiterate he had risen to command an S.S. cavalry
division. With it he had achieved a spectacular success on
the Russian front and it was this, coupled with his abilities
as an unscrupulous intriguer, that had led to his further
promotion.

Joachim Ribbentrop, vain, pompous and self-opinionated,
now aged fifty-two, was both hated and despised by the other
members of Hitler's court. They blamed him equally with
Goering for the disasters that had befallen Germany, but with
more justification. Goering's aircraft replacement programme
had, as Gregory knew, been hopelessly sabotaged during the
past two years, whereas Ribbentrop had suffered no such handi-
cap at the Foreign Office. From the beginning Hitler had given
him a free hand, and by his puffed-up insolence he had made
innumerable enemies for Germany among the statesmen of
both her allies and the neutrals. Yet nothing could persuade
Hitler to change his belief in Ribbentrop, who was a very

frequent visitor at Führer H.Q. and was always warmly welcomed by him.

Albert Speer, aged forty, was a satrap of a very different kind. In his early thirties he had become Hitler's favourite architect. With unlimited millions to spend and the backing of such an enthusiastic builder as his master a brilliant career had opened for him. His outstanding ability and genius for organization had led, in 1942, to Hitler making him Minister of Armaments and War Production. Delighting in his work and totally immersed in it, he played no part in politics and was the one member of the court who, apparently, had no enemies.

After these Princes of the Nazi State there came the less prominent courtiers, although some of them were said to possess more influence over the Führer than his Ministers. For instance his physician, Professor Theodore Morell and his surgeon, Dr. Ludwig Stumpfegger.

Morell was probably the worst criminal ever to have held a medical degree. Having begun his career as a specialist in venereal disease among the demi-monde of Berlin, he was sent for to treat the court photographer, Hoffmann, but soon acquired Hitler as his patient and for the past nine years had been in constant attendance on him. He was a repulsive servile old man who knew little and cared less about the practice of medicine, but had sufficient brains to use it with complete unscrupulousness as a means of gratifying his insatiable avarice. Within a few years he had a number of big laboratories going in which were manufactured vast quantities of quack remedies, some of which were actually condemned as harmful by the medical profession. But that did not deter him, and Hitler, whose faith in him knew no bounds, both granted him monopolies for certain of his products and made the use of his 'Russia' lice-powder compulsory throughout the armed forces.

Stumpfegger was a more recent acquisition. He was a giant of a man with very little brain but an unlimited capacity for hero-worship, and Hitler was his idol. Always prone to adulation, the Führer had taken to him at once and now often chose him for his companion on the walks he took every afternoon round the Chancellery garden.

Others who had frequent access to Hitler were Heinz Lorenz, who brought the news bulletins from Goebbels' Ministry, Artur Axmann the Nazi Youth Leader, the secretaries Frau Jung and Frau Christian and his vegetarian cook Fräulein Manzialy, with whom he often took his meals. In addition to these, there were a score or so of junior staff officers, guard commanders, detectives and servants, all with long service and of undoubted loyalty, who had their quarters in the basement of the Chancellery.

As well as files on all these people, the contents of which Gregory was striving to memorize, there was one that he studied with special interest. Hitler had always presented himself to the German people as so entirely devoted to their welfare that his every thought was given to it, to the exclusion of all private pleasures, including sex. That this was not the fact Gregory was aware, as he had seen British Foreign Office Intelligence reports recording occasions in pre-war days when Hitler had been known to retire from very private parties with young women—generally blonde acrobats, for whom he apparently had a particular penchant. There was also the unedifying case of Frau Goebbels whom, it was reported, he had forced to perform certain services for him that had so disgusted her that she had fled to Switzerland, and had been induced to return by Gestapo agents only when threatened with the death of her children.

But what Gregory had not known was that Hitler had had a regular mistress for twelve years. This woman had first come to his notice as the assistant of his photographer, Hoffmann. Her name was Eva Braun, but it was forbidden to refer to her except by her initials, and mentions of her as E.B. were made by members of Hitler's entourage only in whispers. That the secret of their intimacy should have been kept for so long, Gregory decided, must have been mainly due to her personality and Hitler's.

Other dictators, with such an inexhaustible choice of female companions to amuse them in their leisure hours and with whom to disport themselves in bed, had always taken for their mistresses women who were universally acclaimed either for their beauty, intelligence, wit, charm, breeding or chic; but Eva

Braun did not possess a single one of these qualities. Had she done so she would, no doubt, like the great courtesans, have insisted on recognition and demanded houses, a retinue of servants, splendid jewels and to be the best-dressed woman in her country. As it was, she was no more than a moderately good-looking blonde with a passable figure, lacking both intelligence and wit, and completely unambitious. Hitler had made her independent by making over to her one half of the royalties on his photographs but, although she had been for many years, in all but name, the dictator's wife, she still lived like an ordinary German *Hausfrau*, content to preside over the teacups, to make small talk with his men friends and to sleep with him when required. But that had suited Hitler, for he had never succeeded in sloughing off the mind and habits of a common man, and Eva was a common woman.

These, then, made up the devil-inspired maniac's court of which Gregory was shortly to become a member. Apart from a harem and eunuchs it had, he realized, all the elements of that of an Eastern potentate of the eighteenth century: the unpredictable, tyrannical, sadistic Sultan who handed out rewards, or orders to have people executed, entirely according to his mood of the moment; the grovelling flatterers who throve upon his vanity; the high priests of the Nazi religion, ever urging him to greater blood sacrifices by the murder of countless Jews; boastful paladins who at heart were men of straw; petty thieves who had swollen in that hothouse of opportunity into crooks defrauding the Government of millions; medicine-men who kept their Lord alive on drugs only for their own profit, and even soothsayers by whom he allowed himself to be guided. The more Gregory read the more he marvelled that such a cesspool of hatred, intrigue and corruption could have continued for so long as the fountain-head of power in Germany.

During those February days, while Malacou worked tirelessly on horoscopes, Gregory got to know the members of Goering's entourage. General Koller he found to be a pleasant, elderly man but one whose nerves had been frayed almost to breaking point since, as the Reichsmarschall's chief liaison officer with Hitler, he had daily to listen to furious diatribes

by the Führer about the failures of the Luftwaffe. Koller's
deputy, General Christian, Gregory liked less, and he seemed
stupid enough to believe that in spite of everything Germany
might yet emerge victorious. But with Nicolaus von Below
Gregory got on extremely well, although he met the Colonel
only twice at the dinner parties Goering continued to give,
dressed in ever more fantastic costumes, as an Indian Rajah,
Inca Emperor or in some other array of silks and satins that
enabled him to display his fabulous jewels.

At length the period of preparation on which Gregory had
insisted ended, and on the morning of Thursday, March 1st,
General Koller took him and Malacou into Berlin. The Air
Ministry had been partially wrecked but the damage from bombs
had not harmed its basement and, down there, an Administration Officer showed them to cheerless quarters that had
been prepared for them. Kaindl had seen to it that they were
equipped with everything that an officer and his servant would
normally require and, leaving Malacou to unpack their things,
Gregory accompanied Koller up the Wilhelmstrasse to the
Reich Chancellery.

The vast building was one of Speer's major achievements
and in former days its huge Egyptian-style hall, staircases and
galleries must have been most impressive. But in the past year
bombs had destroyed its upper storeys and brought masses of
plaster down from the ceiling of the lofty hall. No serious attempt had been made to clear up the mess and, instead of the
seething mass of busy people whose clamour used to fill it, it
was now a mausoleum of shadows, the silence of which was
broken only by the crunching of the rubble under the feet of a
few men in uniform hurrying to and fro from the staircase
that led to the several underground bunkers.

At the head of the stairs there was a cloakroom, not for
garments but for weapons. Since the bomb plot positively
no-one had been allowed to enter Führer H.Q. while armed.
Even Goebbels and the other Ministers had to submit to being
searched before they were allowed into the quarters of their
master and, as Gregory found, the search was a really thorough
one.

On going down into the depths he expected to find some

similarity to the fortress basement In Whitehall, in which
Churchill's staff officers planned the High Direction of the war.
But it was totally different. The underground accommodation
of the British War Cabinet and Joint Planning Staff consisted
of the best part of a hundred rooms with every facility which
would have enabled its inmates to withstand in reasonable
comfort a siege of several weeks; whereas the bunker from
which Hitler now directed his war had fewer than thirty rooms,
many of which were no more than cubby holes, and the only
spaces large enough to hold conferences, or in which a number
of people could feed, were the passages. There were other
bunkers in which junior staff and servants had their quarters,
but these were some way off, and the whole system presented
a picture of muddle, acute discomfort and inefficiency.

The difference, as Gregory was quick to realize, lay in the
fact that the British had foreseen that their war leaders would
have to go to earth and had planned accordingly; whereas the
German High Command had never visualized the possibility
that the bombs of the Allies would force them to seek shelter
underground.

Gregory was already fully informed about Hitler's routine.
The Führer rose at midday, held a conference with his principal
executives, which sometimes lasted several hours, went up to
walk for a while with one of his cronies round the Chancellery
garden, returned to the bunker for a meal of vegetables or
tea and cream buns over which he treated those present to
endless monologues about the war situation, then he gave
interviews to Generals from the front and others, ate again,
and went back to bed at between four-thirty and five o'clock
in the morning.

In order never to be absent when his master uttered, Bormann
kept the same hours. Thus, by keeping himself informed of
every last detail of what was going on, he was able either to
prevent visitors from having access to Hitler, or criticize what
they had said after they had gone; and he had become the
channel through which the majority of Hitler's orders were
issued.

Having arrived down in the bunker shortly before noon,
Koller was able almost at once to present Gregory to Bormann.

Hitler's 'Grey Eminence' regarded him with a cold, unsmiling stare then shot at him a few questions about himself. Gregory replied that until recently he had been employed by the Reichsmarschall in buying antiques in the Balkans. Bormann's lips curled in a sneer and he muttered, 'What a way to spend the war! Your fat slob of a master should be choked with the loot such people as you have stolen for him.'

For a moment, Gregory felt that he ought to show resentment at the insult to his Chief, but Koller gave him a quick nudge; so he remained silent. And he was soon to learn that in the bunker such abuse of Goering was quite usual.

With a wave of his hand Bormann dismissed him. Koller then went in to the midday conference while Gregory found von Below, who gave him a friendly welcome and showed him round the headquarters, although not, of course, the rooms occupied by the Führer.

For a time they discussed the war. In the bunker there was no spacious map room, such as that in the War Cabinet basement where Gregory had worked in comfort with half a dozen colleagues—only a small chamber adjacent to the Führer's apartments, barely large enough for three people to move round in. But von Below produced a map of the Western Front on which were marked roughly the positions of the opposing Armies.

On February 8th General Eisenhower had launched his great spring offensive, its main weight being directed towards the lower Rhine. In the extreme north the British and Canadians had succeeded in clearing the Reichwald Forest, but further south the American thrust towards Düsseldorf had been checked by the fanatical bravery of General Schlemm's First Parachute Army. Moreover conditions could not have been more unfavourable to the Allies, as it had rained incessantly; tanks and carriers had become hopelessly bogged down, slowing up the general advance along the whole front. But now the ground was drying out and, placing his finger on a spot west of the Rhine in the Wesel–Homburg sector, von Below said:

'The enemy are massing here for another major assault. Air reconnaissance is almost entirely denied to us these days, but hundreds of officers and men who were overrun by the Allies' advance, then succeeded in hiding and straggling back by night, all report enormous concentrations of guns and armour in that area. I fear there is little doubt that the British will be over the Rhine before the end of the month.'

'They may,' Gregory replied, 'but the Americans will be across before the British. The first crossing won't be made up there either, but further down, south of Cologne.'

That was the conclusion that Malacou had come to as the result of his astrological calculations and mystical communings with occult powers while at Karinhall. The opportunity to use it had arisen sooner than Gregory had expected, but he felt it too good to miss.

Von Below looked at him in astonishment. 'But, my dear fellow, you are talking nonsense. Just look at the map. General Patton's army, in the centre there, is still many miles from the Rhine, and unlike the Allied dispositions further north his troops are widely dispersed. What you suggest is wildly improbable.'

'It is not,' Gregory insisted. 'The Americans will be over the Rhine south of Cologne within a week. If it were not unsporting to bet on certainties, I'd bet you a hundred marks that will be so.'

'*Gott im Himmel!* To talk of it as a certainty you must be crazy. I'll willingly take you for a thousand. On what do you base this extraordinary assertion?'

'On the foreknowledge of my servant. He is a Turk, whom I acquired while travelling for the Reichsmarschall in the Balkans, and he is a genuine mystic. He predicted correctly the defeat of the British airborne landings at Arnhem, the Ardennes offensive and its failure, and many other things. So I have complete confidence in him.'

'How very extraordinary. That is better than any of the Führer's magicians can do. Sometimes they pull a rabbit out of the hat. When the Führer decided to rescue Mussolini our Intelligence people hadn't an idea where he was imprisoned. But an occultist who calls himself the Master of the Sidereal Pendulum located him for us. On checking up we found that he was right, then Otto Skorzeny flew in and got the Duce out.

Most of the time, though, I think they are just guessing, and only last week the Führer sent his two latest wizards packing because they had misled him with false predictions.'

Gregory smiled. 'Most of these fellows are charlatans; but Malacou is not. Perhaps he is granted these powers because he refuses to make money out of them. Anyway, if you would like your fortune told you have only to let me know.'

At that moment von Below was called away; so Gregory continued to familiarize himself with his new surroundings, then returned to the Air Ministry for a late lunch.

During the next few days he made the acquaintance of all his new colleagues in the bunker and settled down to his duties there. They were by no means onerous and consisted mainly in making précis of staff papers for Generals Koller and Christian, relaying orders by telephone and, at times, going in a car to the Tempelhof or Gatow airports to meet senior officers who had been summoned to Berlin by the Führer.

On March 6th he met and brought to the bunker General Siegfried Westphal. This comparatively young and exceptionally brilliant officer had, in turn, been Chief of Staff to Rommel in North Africa and to Kesselring in Italy and was now Chief of Staff to von Rundstedt. He had been sent by his chief to endeavour to persuade Hitler to permit a withdrawal which would considerably shorten the front in the West and so enable it to be held more strongly. After his departure Gregory learned from Koller, von Below and others the course the interview had taken. With great courage Westphal had spoken his mind frankly to Hitler and for five hours stood up to endless tirades of abuse. When he at last emerged from the interview he was sweating profusely but he had managed to wring a partial agreement from Hitler.

He had asked that parts of the West Wall should be given up, on the grounds that it had been so shoddily built that many of the emplacements were death-traps rather than strong points, and that, fearing to be buried in them, the troops preferred to risk their lives in the open. As the West Wall was Hitler's own creation this had sent him into a furious rage; but he had been forced to admit that his own estimate, that a division averaging five thousand men could hold a front of fifteen kilometres, was no longer practical in view of the Allies' great numerical superiority; and had consented to withdrawals in certain places. But General Jodl expressed the opinion that Westphal's success was only temporary, and that the Führer would soon revert to his demand that every foot of ground should be held.

The following afternoon Gregory was sent by Koller out to Karinhall with a confidential document for Goering, which gave him an opportunity to report that he had established himself satisfactorily at Führer H.Q. and had made his first move, although he was now far from happy about its probable outcome. But on his return, when he entered the outer bunker he noticed that its inmates were looking very glum. Suddenly, von Below caught sight of him and cried:

'*Teufel nochmal*, Protze! You were right!'

To Gregory the exclamation could mean only one thing: the Americans were across the Rhine. For the past two days he had been becoming more and more anxious, as Malacou had been unable to give a more exact prediction than that the crossing would take place in the first week in March. Had he for once proved wrong, Gregory would not only have been made to look a credulous fool but also have lost the sort of brilliant opening to his campaign that might not again arise. But this was the 7th; so, much relieved, he was able to smile and ask:

'When did it happen, and where?'

'This afternoon,' replied the Colonel. 'One of General Patton's flying columns reached the Rhine at Remagen. God alone knows why, but our Sappers there failed to blow the bridge in time. Still, the Americans can't possibly have crossed in any strength. They couldn't have had more than a reconnaissance force so far in advance of their main body; so all the odds are that the few who have got across will be driven back into the river.'

But hour after hour next day, as the reports came in, the atmosphere in the bunker grew more tense. 'Two-gun' Patton was proving himself another Murat by his dash and determination. Not only had the Germans failed to retake or destroy the bridge; the Americans were pouring across it and, supported by a thousand aircraft, establishing themselves on its far side.

On the 9th a German counter-attack in force was launched but by evening it was known that it had failed. At eleven o'clock that night Gregory was in his cubicle in the Air Ministry basement and just about to turn in. An orderly from the telephone exchange came to his room and told him that General Koller required his presence at once over in the Chancellery bunker. Hastily he put on his tunic again and hurried off up the street. He found Koller in the main passage that was used as a general sitting room. The General said only 'Come with me,' and led the way through the partition door into the end of the passage that was used for conferences.

There, alone at the long narrow table, Bormann was sitting. Fixing his cold steely eyes on Gregory, he asked, '*Herr Major*, is it true that you predicted the crossing of the Rhine at Remagen by the Americans a week before it occurred?'

'*Jawohl, Herr Parteiführer*,' Gregory replied promptly.

Bormann stood up and said, 'The Führer requires an explanation of how you obtained this intelligence.' As he spoke he pushed open a door on his right and signed to Gregory to go through it. A moment later Gregory found himself face to face with Adolf Hitler.

25

In the Cobra's Lair

GREGORY had had only a few seconds' warning of what to expect, but he rose to the occasion. Halting a yard short of a small table on the far side of which sat a hunched figure, he thrust his right arm out high in the Nazi salute and cried, 'Heil Hitler!' Then he stood rigidly to attention.

Hitler acknowledged the salute by raising a shaking hand a few inches from the table, then he held it out. Gregory would have been less astonished had he realized that, from long habit, Hitler shook hands with everyone. Taking the trembling hand gently in his he bowed over it, then resumed his rigid attitude looking straight in front of him.

But the one good look he had had at the Führer's face had told a tale that had he heard it from others he would have regarded as gross exaggeration. Goering had said that Hitler had aged considerably and was kept going only by the drugs with which Morell injected him thrice daily. Yet, after all, he was only fifty-six and this man looked as if he were well on in his seventies. His hair was thin and, in places, nearly white, his face was grey and furrowed by lines; his eyes were dull and pouched in deep sockets; his body, which had been stalwart, appeared shrunken.

One thing that remained still unimpaired was his voice. Just as it always had, it rasped but held unchallengeable authority. He said, 'Sit down, Herr Major. What I have heard about you interests me greatly. I understand that you have dealings with occult forces.'

Bormann pushed a chair towards Gregory. With a bow, he sat down on it. Taking another Bormann also sat down, crossed his legs, clasped his hands and began to twiddle his thumbs while keeping his gaze on Gregory's face with an unwinking stare.

'*Mein Führer*,' Gregory replied. 'I cannot claim direct communication. But my servant, a Turk whom I brought from the Balkans, unquestionably has the power to call upon entities of the Outer Circle for foreknowledge and guidance.'

'The Outer Circle,' Hitler repeated. 'He is, then, far advanced and must have crossed the Abyss. Continue.'

'He interested me in these matters some two years ago. Since then we have worked together. He puts himself into a trance and so becomes a focus for intelligences beyond. When in that state he has no knowledge of what he is saying and speaks only in Turkish. I have learned Turkish, so I am able to understand the information he is obtaining from the Seventh Plane and take note of his predictions.'

'How often are they right?'

'Invariably, *mein Führer*. For the past year he has foretold to me accurately every major development of the war.'

'*So!* Then I must make use of him. In recent months I have suffered several disappointments in such matters. Predictions made to me have not been fulfilled, so I have dismissed their authors. The Reichsführer's man, Herr Wulf, has been the most reliable occultist I have consulted, but his master can spare him only occasionally. This man of yours sounds promising and I badly need guidance.'

After a moment Hitler went on, 'No-one, *Herr Major*, except my dear friend Martin here, realizes the burden that I carry. It is due to me alone that our country has not yet been defeated. I am betrayed on every side. This catastrophe at Remagen! Just think of it! German soldiers neglecting their duty! Leaving the bridge inadequately guarded! The swine! By my orders they will be shot. Every one of them! Every one of them! And their officers shall pay with the lives of their wives and children too! I . . . I . . . I . . .'

He was off. Neither Gregory nor Bormann dared attempt to interrupt him. For over an hour he never ceased talking. Although he became hoarse the words continued to flow in rhythmic periods. They made a kind of harsh song that dulled the senses and led his hearers to nod automatically in agreement. Gregory had often heard tell of Hitler's hypnotic powers; now he had first-hand experience of them. He had to make a conscious effort to prevent himself from accepting it as a fact that the grey, broken man opposite him was a Messiah who had sacrificed every pleasure in life and been brought to his present wretched state solely by his desire to better the lot of the German people.

He had not wanted war. It had been forced upon him as the only means of saving the country from starvation, anarchy and Communism. He had no wish to be harsh, but he was the father of his millions of children. To spare the rod was to spoil the child. For their own salvation they must be made to fight on until victory was achieved. And by his guidance victory would be achieved. About that there could be no shadow of doubt. But he was betrayed, betrayed, betrayed. Last July the General Staff of the Army had tried to murder him. Him! The true representative of the German people. He had had five hundred of those traitors executed. But those pigs who remained still wished to sell Germany out to her enemies. And so on and so on, and so on.

At last, coughing and choking, he subsided. After a full moment of silence, Gregory nerved himself to take the plunge and said, '*Mein Führer*. The hearts of all true Germans bleed for you in the struggle you have waged for us. And it cannot be denied that the Generals are not showing the defiant spirit that they should in this hour of crisis. That the Americans should have crossed the Rhine virtually unopposed is a terrible thing. How can one account for it except by coming to the conclusion that either the Commander-in-Chief West is no longer capable of fulfilling his duties, or no longer cares what happens? General von Rundstedt is a great soldier, but he is now an old man and one cannot help thinking that the strain of having waged war for so long must have worn him out.'

'Von Rundstedt!' Hitler was off again. 'A great soldier, yes. But you are right. Age has impaired his will to victory and his judgement. He sent General Westphal to me only last week to say that the fortifications in the Siegfried Line are rotten and we cannot hold it. Lies! Lies! Lies! Who should know better about the West Wall than myself? I had it built.

I approved all the plans. When it was finished I inspected it. There is no finer system of fortifications in the world. Of course it can be held. It needs only courage and that our soldiers have. They are the finest in the world and loyal to me. All they require is Leadership! Leadership!'

Suddenly he turned to Bormann and croaked, 'The Herr Major has talked sense. Send a signal to *Ob West*. Every foot of the West Wall is to be held. Von Rundstedt is relieved of his command. Kesselring is to take over. Kesselring is not one of these lily-livered Army swine, but a Luftwaffe General. He will defend the West Wall for me.'

The impassive Bormann simply nodded and said, 'It shall be done, *mein Führer*. I will send the signals right away.'

Hitler staggered to his feet, leaned upon the table and, exhausted by his tirades, muttered to Gregory, 'You must produce this servant of yours. Bormann will arrange it. We will hold a séance. It may be that you and your man have been sent to give us guidance. To achieve victory we must leave nothing untried. There are powers which can aid us. We cannot afford to ignore them.'

Seeing that the interview was over, Gregory had risen at the same moment. Having again given the Nazi salute, he marched smartly from the room. A moment later Bormann joined him in the passage, and said with a pale smile:

'You are a rash man, *Herr Major*, to have offered the Führer advice so freely. Another time it would be wise to confer with me about any opinions you may have before airing them. But in this instance you have done well. For a long time past von Rundstedt has been obstructive and he makes no secret of the fact that he is in favour of asking the enemy for terms. On Kesselring's showing in Italy he will fight a better defensive battle.'

As Gregory walked back to the Air Ministry he could hardly believe that he had not dreamed his interview with Hitler. The thought that without any hocus-pocus or aid from Malacou he had succeeded in having Germany's most competent General sacked, and that Hitler should not even have consulted Keitel, Jodl or Burgdorf before taking such a momentous decision, left him utterly dumbfounded. No clearer proof could be needed that the proper place now for the tyrant was a lunatic asylum.

During the next few days further calamities befell the Third Reich. Himmler had again left his headquarters at Prenzlau and was now directing his Army Group from his bed in Dr. Gebhardt's clinic at Hohenlychen. This direction consisted of Orders of the Day such as: 'Forward through the mud! Forward through the snow! Forward by day! Forward by night! Forward for the liberation of German soil!'—orders that the relatives of soldiers who were taken prisoner un-wounded were to be shot—and an order to his subordinate who had been left to defend besieged Danzig which led to scores of people, including boy ack-ack gunners, being strung up to the poplar trees that lined the principal streets with placards on their chests that read, 'I am hanging here because I left my post.' But such frightfulness did not prevent the ill-armed half-trained troops that now made up the bulk of his Army from being constantly driven back by the Russians, or their capture of Danzig.

Although the Russian advance on the northern front now directly threatened Berlin, disaster in the south-east was felt in the bunker to be an even more shattering blow. Rather than spare Budapest from the horrors of a siege and bombardment, Hitler had sent Sepp Dietrich there with the flower of the Waffen S.S., and they had stubbornly defended the Budaberg until all its beautiful old palaces had been shelled into rubble. Then, on the 13th, the news came through that he had with-drawn the remnants of his Army and was retreating on Vienna.

Two days earlier Hitler had sent detailed orders for a new counter attack. It had taken place on a day of torrential rain and had resulted in a wholesale slaughter of Dietrich's best troops. When Hitler heard of this and that his most trusted General had ordered a general retreat, his rage knew no bounds. He raved for hours on end and that night issued a decree that as a punishment his own pet regiment, the *Leibstandarte Adolf Hitler*, should be deprived of the distinguishing arm-bands that were their special pride, thus inflicting the ultimate disgrace upon men utterly devoted to him.

A few days later it was learned that Dietrich had flatly

refused to promulgate the order; then a parcel arrived at the bunker addressed to the Führer. It contained a chamber-pot in which were all Dietrich's decorations.

It was owing to Hitler's addled mind being so taken up with these disasters that Gregory put down the fact that he and Malacou were not sent for during the week following his interview with the Führer. By then, for over a fortnight, he had spent several hours each day in the outer bunker and although he was not subject to claustrophobia he found conditions there extremely trying. It was always crowded with people coming and going, some in fear of being the victims of the Führer's terrible angers, others bewailing his insane orders that it was their duty to transmit to the Army, Navy and Luftwaffe; all harassed by fears for their families during the air-raids or their own ever more uncertain futures. In consequence, by the 17th of the month he felt that he positively must escape for a while and get a little relaxation.

During the past nine months he had often wondered what was happening to Sabine and since his return to Berlin he had several times contemplated taking a few hours off to find out if she was still in the city. So on that Saturday he asked Koller's permission to absent himself for the afternoon, then set off for the Villa Seeaussicht.

He had not passed through East Berlin since the previous July. It had been depressing enough then, but now it was a revelation of the state to which a great city could be reduced by modern warfare. Although the upper storeys of many of the big buildings in central Berlin had been rendered untenable, their steel, concrete and stone façades, which still stood, saved them from appearing to have been greatly damaged; whereas the older blocks and brick houses, of which by far the greater part of the city consisted, told the full story.

The great highway through Charlottenburg was now a broad defile between two endless mounds of jagged rubble. Hardly a building had its roof intact; not an unbroken window was to be seen. Many of the side streets were now impassable; on either hand lay acre upon acre of burnt and blackened ruins. People with gaunt faces and sunken eyes moved among them, wearily clambering over charred beams and emerging from holes at the roadside that led to deep, crowded shelters or cellars wherein they dwelt like half-starved rats in filth and squalor.

In the suburbs along the Havel the picture was, by comparison, much less terrible, although they had also suffered severely. Here and there houses had been burnt out or partially wrecked. In many gardens there lay uprooted trees, the glass in porches and conservatories had been shattered, gates swung askew on broken hinges and every few hundred yards gaps had been torn in walls and fences. And when, at last, Gregory came in sight of the villa he was greatly worried to see that its upper storey had been blown to pieces.

Since Sabine had hidden him when he was on the run he had no fear that on his turning up again in the uniform of a Luftwaffe Major she might betray him, or that Trudi would do so—if they were still alive and there. But Goering had said he believed von Osterberg to have survived. It was therefore possible that he too was living in the house, and for Gregory to run into him would be disastrous; so he approached the villa with caution.

As he came nearer he saw with relief that although all the windows, bar one downstairs, were broken and had been boarded over, through that one he could make out a pot of hyacinths, which implied that the house was still occupied. Having made certain that no-one was about, he slipped through the side entrance, took the path behind the garage and rang the back door bell. A moment later it was opened by Trudi.

On recognizing him her mouth fell open with surprise, but he smiled at her and said, 'I'm not a ghost, Trudi, and I'm delighted to see you safe and well. I only hope your mistress is, too. Is she about?'

Trudi returned his smile. 'Not at the moment, *mein Herr*. She is at the doctor's. But she should soon be back and, I am sure, will be most happy to see you. Please to come inside.'

'How about the *Herr Graf*?' Gregory asked. 'Is he still living here; or anyone else?'

She shook her head. '*Nein, mein Herr*. For a long time past we have been living here alone.'

'That's good. But what's this about the *gnädige Baronin* having gone to the doctor? I trust it's not for anything serious.'

'*Nein, mein Herr.* Just a slight indisposition from which she has been suffering for the past few weeks.'

Reassured, Gregory entered the house and followed Trudi through to the sitting room. Several large sections of plaster had come down from the ceiling and there were damp stains on the walls, but otherwise it was clean and tidy. Trudi told him then about the house being hit. It had happened in September, but fortunately the bomb had not been a large one; so only the top storey had been wrecked and no-one injured. Gregory was still talking to her when, ten minutes later, he heard the slam of the front door, and as he got up from the sofa Sabine came into the room.

She did not appear ill and was as lovely as ever, but he noted a look of strain on her face. The instant she saw him it disappeared and with a cry of joy she ran to embrace him. After their first greetings were over she stroked his smart uniform and asked how he had come by it.

'That's a long story,' he smiled, 'and I'll tell you it later. The essential points are that after six months in a prison camp I succeeded in getting to Goering, and he has given me a job sticking pins in maps at the Air Ministry.'

'Darling Gregory,' she laughed. 'For audacity you are unbeatable.'

He shrugged. 'Oh, once I succeeded in getting an interview with him it wasn't difficult. He is an old friend of mine.'

'What! Do you mean that he actually knows you to be an Englishman?'

Gregory nodded. 'Yes; but he also knows that I was always pro-Fascist. I told him that I had been put in prison in my own country and that having escaped I felt so bitter about the way I'd been treated that I decided to offer my services to Germany; and that having managed to reach Germany I had had the ill luck to be arrested and again put into prison.'

This mendacious account of himself corresponded sufficiently closely with that he had given Sabine in July for her to accept it without comment; but she asked, 'How is your wound?'

He had been ready for that and, as he was no longer in a situation where expediency demanded that he should give the impression that he longed to make love to her, he replied with a laugh, 'Healed perfectly; but don't let that give you any naughty ideas. I've come only as an old friend, to find out if you were still here and had escaped injury in the air-raids.'

She made a rueful face. 'That's not very complimentary, but perhaps it's just as well. For the past few weeks I haven't been at all fit; so for the moment I'm rather off being made love to.' Before he could ask her what was wrong with her she added quickly, 'I see that silly Trudi didn't provide you with a drink while you were waiting for me. I'll go down to the cellar and fetch a bottle of wine.'

When, a few minutes later, she returned with the bottle of champagne, he saw that she had brought only one glass and he asked in surprise, 'Aren't you going to join me?'

As she filled the glass for him, she shook her head. 'No; for the time being I'm not allowed alcohol.'

'Really!' He raised his eyebrows. Then a possible connection between her surprising abandonment of her favourite pastime and her no longer drinking suddenly struck him and he added, 'Surely you don't mean . . .?'

Tears came into her lovely eyes and she nodded. 'Yes. I wouldn't tell anyone else, but I can tell you. I've been an awful fool. I hate and despise myself. Of course, from fear they'll never live through another night practically every woman in Berlin has become promiscuous, and I suppose at least half of them are in the same state as I'm in. But that's no consolation. I feel so horribly unclean—like a leper. When I realized what had happened I had half a mind to kill myself.'

They were sitting side by side on the sofa. Flopping over towards him, she buried her face in his chest and burst into a fit of uncontrollable sobbing.

Stroking her hair, he tried to soothe her and gradually, as her sobs eased, she told him how she had come by her misfortune.

'It was just a month ago. I went in the afternoon for *Kaffeetrinken* with a friend. She was not in her apartment, but her son was. He told me that his mother had been suddenly called

away because her sister had been injured in an air-raid, and
that she would not be back that night; but he insisted on
making coffee for me. He was only a boy; a child almost,
barely fifteen. But he was in uniform. He had been called up
to join a Hitler Youth Battalion that in two days' time was
being sent to fight the Russians. I've never cared much for
young men; particularly inexperienced ones. You know that.
And when he started to make love to me I hadn't the least
intention of having anything to do with him. But he pleaded
with me desperately. All the usual things about my being the
loveliest person he'd ever seen and the rest of it. That wouldn't
have moved me, but what did was his saying that in a week
or two he would almost certainly be dead; that it would be
terrible to die never having had the experience, and if I'd let
him he'd have something wonderful to think of when he lay
gasping out his life. What could I do, darling? What could
any woman with any decent feelings do but let him have
her?'

After another bout of sobbing, Sabine went on. 'Having
reluctantly decided to let him, I felt it would be mean not to
give him as good a time as I could; so I let him undress me,
then he stripped and we got into his mother's bed. I'd expected
it to be all over quickly, but he recovered in no time and
begged for more. After that, I confess, I rather enjoyed it, so
we stayed there for more than two hours. By that time it was
dark and an early air-raid started; so I was afraid to leave the
building and, as the apartment was on the ground floor of a
big block, we were fairly safe there. If only I had gone home I
should have taken the usual precautions. But I stayed on and
slept with him all night. Then . . . then ten days later I found
that the little swine had lied to me. I hadn't been his first
experience at all. He'd had some little bitch, or perhaps several,
and must have been riddled with it.'

'You poor darling,' Gregory murmured. 'It's a horrid business, but nothing to be really worried about. The same thing
is happening to thousands of men and women all over Europe
every day now that this accursed war has separated so many
people from their wives, husbands and sweethearts. And don't
regret having given yourself so generously to that wretched

boy. If you are receiving proper treatment you'll be as right as rain again in a few weeks.'

Sabine sat up, took a little embroidered handkerchief from her bag and mopped her eyes with it. 'Yes. That's what my doctor says. But in the meantime it's simply ghastly. As I mustn't drink anything I have to refuse all invitations to lunch or parties, in case people suspect what is wrong with me; and God knows if I'll ever be able to look at a man in future without being scared that the same thing will happen again.'

'Talking of men,' Gregory said, 'I heard a rumour that von Osterberg is still alive. Is it true?'

'Yes. Kurt had the luck to make a mess of things. When he shot himself the bullet only fractured his skull. He was in hospital for three months; then, as there was no real evidence that he had been involved in the plot, Speer got him a clearance so that he could go back to his job making explosives for the Secret Weapons.'

'Have you seen him lately?'

'No. It seems, though, the old boy had developed a really serious passion for me. As soon as he was out of hospital he came here several times and implored me to let him come back and live here. But the purge after the conspiracy was so thorough that there was not the least likelihood of its starting up again, so Ribb said there was no point in my keeping tabs on Kurt any longer. That let me out, and I politely but firmly refused to play. He had gone back to his quarters in the underground laboratory near Potsdam and, as far as I know, he's still there.'

Gregory told her about his car smash and how he had been sent to Sachsenhausen as Prince Hugo. Then he said how sorry he was that he had wrecked her car and assured her that he would pay her for it as soon as that became possible.

She shrugged. 'You don't have to. I got the money for it out of the insurance people. Thank God you said at your trial that you had stolen it. When first I heard what had happened I was terribly scared; but I might have known, darling, that you would have the wit to think up some story that would prevent anyone from finding out that I had been hiding you here.'

'That was the very least I could do. But we had planned that the car should be returned to you, so that you could use it to get away if you decided to leave Berlin.'

'You needn't worry on that score either. Now that nobody can get any petrol cars can be bought for a song. With only a small part of the insurance money I was able to buy another, and I've still a good supply of petrol.'

'In that case, what on earth induces you to remain here? If I'd been you I'd have got out of this ghastly city weeks ago.'

Sabine sighed and shook her head. 'I've often thought of leaving, but I hated the idea of not having my own home and I had no other except in Budapest. With the Russians in Hungary to go there was out of the question, and now my lovely little palace in Buda will have been destroyed with all the others.'

'I know; to give orders that the Budaberg should be held and have it reduced to rubble was another of Hitler's crimes. But, my dear, you really must leave. Within a month, perhaps less, the Russians will be in Berlin. If you are still here, God alone knows what will happen to you. It's too frightful to contemplate.'

Again she shook her head. 'I can't leave yet. The best specialist in Berlin is looking after me and I wouldn't be able to find another half as good. My every thought is set on getting well again; so I am determined to remain until I have completed my treatment.'

In vain Gregory begged her to alter her mind. Then, finding her adamant, he changed the subject and told her of some of his experiences while at Sachsenhausen. Later they had supper together. Her larder was nowhere near as lavishly stocked as it had been in July but black-marketeers were still bringing her palatable items from the country, so they had an enjoyable meal.

Afterwards Gregory said that he must get back to the Air Ministry and, since she was so depressed and lonely, he promised to come out again to see her as often as he could; but he told her he doubted if he would be able to get away from his duties more than once a week.

It took him over two hours to make his way through the

blackout to central Berlin and when he did reach the Air Ministry, a little after eleven o'clock, he found Koller waiting for him in his cubicle. In a great state of agitation the elderly General told him that the Führer had asked for him and his servant over an hour ago. Having collected Malacou, they hurried up the street to the Chancellery.

Down in the bunker Gregory was for the second time taken through the partition in the passage beyond which only the very senior members of the Führer's entourage were permitted to go. There, as before, Bormann was sitting at the narrow conference table. He told Koller that his presence was not required, then said to Gregory:

'The Führer has ordered that you and your man should hold a séance for him. But I wish to warn you again that you are not to air your own opinions, as you did in the case of von Rundstedt.'

'*Herr Parteiführer*,' Gregory replied, 'I shall translate only what my man may say when he is under the control of occult forces. But I will keep my eye on you, and should he begin to make any prediction that is displeasing to you just close your eyes for a second, then I will refrain from translating further, or alter the sense of what he has said.'

Bormann gave a pale smile and replied, 'I am glad that we understand one another, *Herr Major*. Go out now and wait in the sitting passage until I call you.'

It was two hours before the summons came and during that time Gregory was as near panic as he had ever been. He tried to take comfort from the fact that, although pale, Malacou seemed calm and unafraid. But there was no way of disguising his markedly Jewish features and in them lay a terrible danger. It was possible that the very sight of them might drive the mad Führer into one of his fits of ungovernable rage, in which he would not listen to assurances or explanations. Should he decide on the instant that a Jew had been brought to him, before either Gregory or Malacou could open their mouths he might order them to be taken up to the Chancellery garden and shot.

Gregory wondered if that possibility could have occurred to his companion and thought probably not; for during their

time in Berlin Malacou had played his role as a soldier servant
admirably, happy in the obscurity that he considered his best
protection, confident that by doing so he would, in due course,
be able to strike a great blow in revenge for the persecution
of his race, and armoured against fear for himself by his
conviction that he would outlive Hitler.

At last the almost unbearable strain ended. Bormann opened
the door in the partition and beckoned, then led them through
the little ante-room to the Führer's study. With a silent prayer
of thanksgiving Gregory realized that this must have been one
of Hitler's good days for, although his face was shrunken and
blotchy, he looked calmer and more normal than the first
time Gregory had seen him.

The moment Gregory had pronounced his 'Heil Hitler!' he
went straight on, 'Mein Führer, permit me to present my
servant Ibrim Malacou. His home is in Istanbul but so convinced was he that you had been sent to regenerate the world
that he left it voluntarily to fight for the great cause.'

Having got out his statement, Gregory waited for a moment
that seemed an eternity. Hitler was just finishing a cup of tea
and a cream bun. Still chewing the last mouthful he smiled,
shook hands with them both and said to Malacou, 'Germany
has always been the friend of Turkey and it is good to meet
Turks who are our friends. You are very welcome, Herr
Malacou.' Then he told them to sit down and to proceed.

Like all the rooms in the bunker, except those that had been
made by dividing its broad central passage, Hitler's study was
not more than twelve feet square, so they were decidedly
cramped. Malacou moved a chair so that he could sit in it
with his back to the door, Bormann sat near but sideways on
to him, and Gregory remained standing at the side of the
Führer's desk so that he faced them both. He then made his
usual passes at Malacou.

They were by now so used to their act that they slid into it
easily and, in anticipation of this critical moment, they had
gone with great care into the question of what Hitler was to be
told. As Malacou's duties while at the Air Ministry had been
very light, he had continued to spend the greater part of his
time checking and improving the results of the astrological

calculations he had made at Karinhall, and they had qualified these by the information about personalities and events that Gregory had obtained from day to day.

For a few minutes after Malacou had closed his eyes he remained silent, then he began to mutter and gradually his mutterings became intelligible to anyone who could understand Turkish. His voice took on a high shrill note and Gregory started to interpret his utterances, which were mostly brief and at times were punctuated by spells of silence.

As previously arranged, some of the things he said had no bearing at all on the situation but appeared to be communings with the spirits about friends of his who were dead and soon to be born again in a new incarnation; but Hitler showed no impatience because these were skilfully interspersed with predictions about the course of the war.

During the three-quarters of an hour that the séance lasted Malacou's forecasts of general interest were: That between five and seven days hence General Montgomery's army would cross the Rhine in force and there would follow several weeks of desperate fighting in the West. German losses would be extremely heavy and some ground would have to be given up to the British and the Americans; but on the Northern front there would be an improvement in the situation. Within a few days the Russian onslaught would be checked and for at least three weeks they would make no further advance of importance. The coming day would be a very trying one for the Führer. He would receive two communications. One would be the request of one of his most trusted Army Commanders to be relieved of his command; the other a letter from one of the pillars of the Nazi regime stating that he had lost faith in victory; but the Führer was advised not to take the letter too seriously, because the writer had a great affection for him and would remain loyal to him to the end. It also appeared that within a week the Führer would decide to make an important change in the High Command of the Army by dismissing one of his Generals. Lastly, in mid-April there would come to him from an unexpected source great consolation for the trials with which he was being afflicted and support in his struggle, but whence this would spring it was not yet possible to divine.

Deliberately, in order to win Hitler's confidence, Gregory had made the general tone of this first occult communication as optimistic as possible, by suppressing several of Malacou's bleaker predictions. At the mention of the two communications he was to receive the following day Hitler had temporarily gone off the deep end and raved about the betrayals of which he was constantly the victim; but after ten minutes he had subsided, and at the end of the session he was obviously pleased by what he had been told. Turning to Gregory, he said:

'Herr Malacou several times mentioned dead people he has known who are shortly to be born again. Do you also believe in reincarnation?'

'Most firmly, *mein Führer*,' Gregory replied promptly; which was the truth, for he had frequently discussed it with Erika and had become fully convinced. Moreover, it was with a definite intention that he had told Malacou to mention the subject several times in his ramblings. Keeping his eye on Bormann in case he indicated disapproval Gregory added, 'To anyone who accepts the survival of the ego after death, which I regard as beyond doubt, reincarnation is the only logical belief, and the wise men of all nations have taken it as a guide for their actions.'

Hitler nodded. 'Several people have told me that they hold that opinion, *Herr Major*, and the subject is a most interesting one. Sometime we must talk of it together.' With a friendly wave of thanks he then dismissed them.

When they reached the conference room Bormann signed to Malacou to go through to the far side of the partition, then turned to Gregory. 'This Army Commander who is asking to be relieved. I saw your hesitation when you spoke of it. You held back something. You know who he is. Tell me.'

There had been other occasions on which Malacou, when uttering on a subject, had suddenly been inspired to add particulars of which he had not previously been aware. That had happened in this case, and it had given Gregory a very nasty moment.

'You are right, *Herr Parteiführer*,' he replied. 'It is Herr Himmler; but I thought it more tactful not to name him.'

Bormann glowered. 'It's as well for you that you did not. Are you sure of this?'

Gregory shrugged. 'How can I be? I can only say that I have confidence in the Turk's predictions.'

'I see. Well, this must be stopped. At the moment, if Himmler were free to come frequently to Berlin he would exert a bad influence on the Führer.'

As Goering had told Gregory that Bormann was scheming to replace him as Hitler's successor and that Bormann, regarding Himmler as his most serious rival, had got him out of the way by securing for him the command of an Army Group, Gregory knew what was really in Bormann's mind. But he simply bowed and said, '*Herr Parteiführer*, you may rely on me to accept your guidance at all times.'

The following afternoon the storm broke. Guderian, the Chief of the General Staff, arrived with a letter from Himmler in which he asked to be relieved of his command on the grounds of ill health. A conference was called and those on the far side of the partition heard a battle royal take place, with shouts and screams, between the Führer and his General.

Later, Gregory learned that Guderian had defied Hitler and told him that Himmler had proved such a disaster as an Army Group Commander that he had forced him to offer his resignation, then insisted that it be accepted. Keitel and Jodl had, as usual, played for safety by saying the Führer was the best judge, while Bormann had insinuated that this was another plot to weaken the Führer's control of the armed forces. After hours of wrangling Hitler, near collapse, had got up from the table and, mumbling that he would 'think it over', staggered off to his room.

On the following day Gregory heard about the other letter. It had been from Albert Speer. In it he had stated his conviction that Germany's situation was now hopeless, so an armistice should be asked for in order to save Germany's cities from further bombing and conserve as much industrial plant as possible to aid in Germany's recovery. The letter invoked another outburst of self-pity in the Führer and vituperation against the young Minister who had made his dreams of magnificent buildings and splendid autobahns come true. But he took no action.

Malacou had told Gregory that it was his belief that Speer was now actively plotting to put an end to Hitler and as that, above all things, was what they desired they had at the séance done their best to protect him. One thing was certain. He was the only decent and honest man in the whole of Hitler's court.

On March 22nd Hitler suddenly made up his mind about Himmler and, despite Bormann's endeavours to prevent him, accepted his resignation.

Gregory immediately took alarm; for that could lead to Himmler visiting the bunker and it was possible that he might bring Grauber with him. He endeavoured to calm his fears by the thought that at least for some days that was unlikely. But, with Koller's consent, he used the private line from the Air Ministry to Karinhall to telephone Goering and also, with apparent casualness, took the first opportunity that offered to discuss the results of Himmler's resignation with his representative at Führer H.Q., the horrid little ex-jockey, Obergruppenführer Fegelein.

From both sources he received reassurances. Himmler had had a breakdown and was unlikely to leave the clinic at Hohenlychen for some time, while Grauber was remaining on the Russian front to keep an eye on General Heinrici, who had been appointed as Himmler's successor in command of the Army Group.

Yet Hitler, with his now chronically illogical assessments, having decided on Guderian's advice that Himmler must be replaced, suddenly made up his mind to get rid of the unpopular but extremely able Panzer expert too; so overnight Guderian was replaced as Chief of Staff by Colonel-General Krebs.

On the 24th General Montgomery launched his great offensive on the lower Rhine and the Luftwaffe's attempts to prevent the crossing proved hopelessly ineffective. When the news came through Hitler sent for the unfortunate Koller, and so lashed him with his tongue for an hour without stopping that when the poor old man emerged from the Führer's sanctum he was white, shaking and in tears.

By then the Remagen bridgehead was thirty miles deep, and further north the British and Americans were streaming

over the new crossings in their tens of thousands. In a frantic
effort to stave off complete defeat another spate of murderous
decrees was rushed out. That issued by Keitel read:

In the name of the Führer.

*Any officer who aids a subordinate to leave the combat zone
unlawfully, by carelessly issuing him a pass or other leave papers
citing a simulated reason, is to be considered a saboteur and
will suffer death. Any subordinate who deceitfully obtains leave
papers or who travels with false leave papers will, as a matter of
principle, suffer death.*

And General Blaskowitz, the Commander of Army Group
H, in Holland, supplemented it by issuing a decree of his own,
announcing that any soldier found away from his unit who
declared himself to be a straggler looking for it should be
summarily tried and shot.

The Replacement Army was scraped to the bottom of the
barrel and new units of teenagers or sexagenarians, for whom it
had not yet been possible even to find uniforms, were sent up
to the front. Their pleas that if captured while still in civilian
clothes they would shot as *franc-tireurs* were ignored, and they
were being driven into battle by S.D. men threatening to mow
them down with machine guns from behind.

From von Below Gregory learned that Hitler had sent for
Speer and in a demonaic spate of words that had gone on for
hours poured out his reaction to the Minister of Armament's
letter. The Führer had said, 'If the war is to be lost, the nation
will also perish. This fate is inevitable. There is no need to
consider the basis of even the most primitive existence any
longer. On the contrary, it is better to destroy even that, and to
destroy it ourselves. The nation has proved itself weak, and
those who remain after the battle are of little value; for the
good have fallen.' In vain Speer pleaded that, for humanity's
sake, those who survived should at least be left the material
means by which they could sustain life. Hitler would not
listen and ordered Speer to go away on permanent leave. Speer
had refused, saying that it was his duty to remain at his post.

When he had gone Hitler, trembling and purple in the face,

issued further orders through Bormann. As the Allies advanced, everything in their path was to be destroyed: factories, railway junctions, power stations, houses; everything was to be blown up or burnt down. Nothing was to be left. Since the German people had betrayed him they were not entitled even to the means to continue to exist after Germany's defeat.

Next day, March 30th, as so often happened the storm was succeeded by calm. After the daily conference Hitler sent for Gregory and told him that he wished him to accompany him on his late afternoon walk round the Chancellery garden. Together they ascended the stairs at the far end of the bunker and emerged into the spring sunlight. Immediately they began their promenade Hitler said, 'Tell me your reasons for believing in reincarnation.'

'*Mein Führer*, they are quite simple,' Gregory replied, and proceeded to produce the arguments he had thought out as most likely to appeal to his megalomaniac companion.

'No sensible person can believe in the Christian God or, for that matter, any personal God. The very conception of a universal resurrection followed by a judgement, awarding all of us either perpetual bliss or consigning us to eternal torment, on our conduct during one short span of life, is absurd. One has only to think of those who are born half-witted or as the children of criminal parents. What chance in life have they? To condemn such unfortunates because they had led evil lives would be a travesty of justice. And what of young people who die when still in their teens? Are they to be held fully responsible for their actions? Were you or I brought before such a tribunal we should feel only contempt for a God who had given life to men on such arbitrary terms; so the teaching that He exists must be false.'

'I agree. I agree,' Hitler said huskily.

'Yet,' Gregory went on, 'that the spirit which animates man continues to exist after death none of us who knows anything about the occult can doubt. If, therefore, there is no personal God to whom our spirits are accountable, it follows that we are our own masters and responsible only to ourselves for our acts down here. But nothing stands still. The declaration of Gautama Buddha, when he said that everything of which we are aware is in a state of either growth or decay, cannot be challenged. It applies not only to vegetable and animal life, but also to mountains, the earth itself and every heavenly body in the universe. Since it is a universal law our personalities must also be subject to it. This could not be more clearly demonstrated, *mein Führer*, than by giving only a moment's consideration to your own personality. One thinks of your wisdom as a law giver, your great abilities as a strategist, your extraordinary flair for creating beautiful buildings, your immense knowledge of every aspect of life of the people over whom you rule. All these abilities could not conceivably have been accumulated in the short space of fifty-odd years.'

'I see that. Yes, you are right.'

'Between your mind and that of an Australian aborigine there lies an immense gulf; and the explanation of that is simple. Such a man can have lived only a few lives whereas, in different bodies, as men or women, rich or poor, healthy or crippled, you have had many hundreds; and in each you have progressed, learning some lesson which is stored up in your subconscious. It is rarely given to people to be able to recall their former lives, but the lessons they have learned remain. How can one doubt that it is owing to this vast experience that in your present incarnation you have emerged as the genius that everyone acknowledges you to be?'

At that moment Bormann came hurrying across the garden, a piece of paper in his hand. Having given his '*Heil Hitler!*' he said, "*Mein Führer*, only my duty and my devotion to you give me the courage to make this report. But it would be wrong to conceal even the worst news from you. This signal has just come in from Field Marshal Model. His entire army has been cut off in the Ruhr, and he asks permission to fight his way out.'

The blotches on Hitler's face stood out more clearly as it drained of blood. Suddenly he screamed, 'Abandon the Ruhr! Never! Never! Dolts! Fools! Traitors! These Generals should be burnt over a slow fire for their cowardice and crimes. Model is to hold the Ruhr to the last man. If they are driven in, as the circle narrows they are to destroy everything. Everything. What good will Krupps be to us if we lose the war?

The plants must be blown up—not one brick or girder left upon another.'

Ignoring Gregory, he trudged off with Bormann, still shouting at the top of his voice and wildly waving his good arm.

Speer was again summoned, but remained in the outer bunker for some time before Hitler would see him. He told the officers there that nothing would induce him to carry out the Führer's orders for the destruction of everything in Germany which could help those of the German people who survived to carry on their lives somehow and, eventually, enjoy prosperity again. On the contrary, he was using his own immense powers as the Controller of German Industry and Labour to ensure that everything possible should be saved from the wreck. He had ordered that no more explosives were to be made and that as the Allies advanced every piece of undamaged plant was to be handed over to them intact. To check the fanatical S.S. in attempts to enforce the orgy of destruction the Führer had decreed, he was now issuing hand grenades and sub-machine guns to the staffs of all factories and installations, so that they could prevent the sabotaging of the plants on which their future would depend.

When Speer faced his master and disclosed what he was doing, yells and curses rang through the bunker; yet when Speer emerged from the ordeal, he left the bunker still a free man. Gregory felt that this miracle could be attributed only to divine intervention.

Of the satraps who visited the bunker in these days, the most frequent were Goebbels and Ribbentrop. The little doctor, with his twisted foot and twisted mind, although normally concerned only with inventing endless clever lies and distortions of fact to boost the morale of the German people, could at times show an unscrupulous brutality rivalling that of the worst of the other Nazis. On one occasion, infuriated by the mass air-raid on Dresden, he demanded that the Führer should repudiate the Geneva Convention, order the massacre of forty thousand Allied airmen prisoners as a reprisal, and bring into use two poison gases that had terrible effects on their victims.

Hitler, so his doctors said, was subject to a pathological blood lust. It is in any case certain that he always became happy and excited after ordering an execution; so the idea of this wholesale slaughter made a strong appeal to him. But Koller hastily sent for Goering who, with the aid of Doenitz and several Generals, all of whom feared mass reprisals on the prisoners of war in their own Services, succeeded in dissuading Hitler from carrying out this heinous crime.

Ribbentrop gave Gregory an extremely nasty moment; for one day they came face to face in the outer passage. It was two and a half years since Gregory had been a guest at a small supper party given for the Reichsaussenminister at a night-club in Budapest, but from the stare he gave Gregory it was obvious that he was trying to remember where he had previously met him. Fortunately, Major Johannmeier, General Burgdorf's assistant, distracted Ribbentrop's attention by coming up just then and saying that his Chief would like a word with him while he was waiting to see the Führer. After that Gregory always kept a wary eye out for Sabine's ex-lover and, whenever he came to the bunker, stayed well out of his way.

For some time past, Gregory had been very worried by the thought of Sabine; for, knowing her unhappy state, he had had every intention of keeping his promise to go out and spend a few hours with her at least once a week. But once he had succeeded in interesting Hitler in Malacou's predictions and the subject of reincarnation he had felt that in no circumstances must he again leave his post for any length of time, in case he or both of them were sent for. Much as he owed Sabine, the war, and the millions involved in it, had to be put first.

To excuse his neglect of her he had several times tried to telephone, but the exchanges and lines in Berlin were constantly being destroyed by the nightly air-raids so he had failed to get through; and he felt it too risky to write, because a great part of the mail was being opened by Gestapo men at the post offices in a witch hunt for grumblers and pacifists, and he did not want it to be known that he was acquainted with her.

During the first days of April the Anglo-American advance

continued unchecked, but the Russian front remained quiet
and, although any piece of bad news never failed to bring on
one of Hitler's screaming fits, there were no special excitements in the bunker. Then, on the night of the 5th, he again
sent for Gregory and Malacou.

The procedure was as before and the gist of Malacou's
ramblings as translated by Gregory were as follows. The
Russians were building up for another major offensive which
would be launched in the middle of the month. The Ruhr
must be written off, because Field Marshal Model was surrounded by traitors and they would force him to surrender.
There were traitors too among the senior members of the
Government; at least two of them were secretly in touch with
the enemy and endeavouring to bring about a peace; but they
would not succeed. In spite of the present successes of the
Anglo-American Armies they would never reach Berlin, and
they were shortly to receive a blow of the greatest magnitude,
which could alter the whole political outlook.

Hitler had been crouching over his desk, looking extremely
ill. At this point his head suddenly fell forward and, although
he made an effort, he was unable again to raise it.

Springing up from his chair, Bormann ran to him and shouted
to Gregory to go and get Dr. Morell. Malacou, arousing from
his state of semi-trance, opened his eyes and Bormann told him
to 'get out'.

Morell occupied two rooms in the further bunker and rarely
left them, so Gregory had no difficulty in finding him and telling
him what had happened; then they hurried back to Hitler's
study. There the slovenly, cringing old doctor gave his Führer
a shot in an arm that was already black with the marks of
injections. Within a few moments he recovered, fixed his dull
eyes on Gregory and said:

'Your Turk is a wonderful medium. I am psychic myself,
you know; so I can readily recognize the true gift in others.
In my case it takes the form of remarkable intuition, and his
prediction that the Anglo-Americans will never reach Berlin
accords with my own firm belief. I am tired now, so we'll
not call him back. But I'll send for you both again soon . . .
quite soon.'

Waiting for him upstairs in the vast Egyptian-style hall on the ground floor of the Chancellery, Gregory found Malacou. With his dark eyes gleaming the Jew asked in Turkish, 'Is the swine dead?'

Gregory shook his head. 'No. His resistance is extraordinary. That unsavoury old brute who looks after him is the worst kind of crook, but he gave him a shot that brought him round almost immediately.'

Malacou muttered a few Hebrew curses. Then, as they left the building, he took something from his pocket. An air-raid was in progress and at that moment a bunch of incendiary bombs exploded in the street some forty yards away. By their light Gregory saw that Malacou was holding in his hand a long piece of cord with a noose at one end. His curiosity aroused, he asked:

'What is that?'

'A garotte.' Malacou smiled. 'I carry it as a talisman for our protection, and a focus by which I can draw down power. If I did not take something of the kind with me to these séances, at a vital moment Hitler's own evil radiations might destroy my contact with the Outer Circle.'

'What is there so special about that piece of cord to give it such a potent occult significance?' Gregory enquired.

Malacou gave a harsh laugh. 'Astrology alone could not enable me to make such accurate predictions. Now and then I must make an offering to . . . well, the source of my power. In normal circumstances one would use a sacrificial knife and that would become the talisman. But as things are I would not be allowed to take a knife down into the bunker; so instead I carry the garotte. And it is highly charged, because I have recently used it several times to take life.'

Halting in his tracks Gregory grasped the Satanist by the arm, swung him round and exclaimed in horror, 'D'you mean that when you sometimes go out on your own at night it is to murder people in the blackout?'

Shaking off his grasp, Malacou retorted, 'If I had we would be far better protected. But, unfortunately, I have not the courage. For my victims I make do with animals.'

'What! Cats and dogs?'

'Yes. I lure them with a little food, throw my coat over them and carry them to the nearest bombed-out church, then offer them up by strangling them with the garotte.'

'Good God, how revolting,' Gregory exclaimed.

'Your scruples are foolish,' Malacou retorted sharply, 'and this is no concern of yours. Be content to make use of my contacts with the Timeless Ones to bring to ruin our common enemy.'

By then they had reached the Air Ministry. As Gregory started to turn into it the Satanist wished him an abrupt good-night and walked on.

For a few moments Gregory remained there and was almost sick at the thought of the bestial act that the colleague whom fate had forced upon him was about to commit. He was in half a mind to follow and stop Malacou; but the thing that mattered above all else was to put an end to Hitler and, if these ghoulish rites performed during the hours of darkness might contribute to that, he realized that his duty to humanity lay in ignoring them. Sick at heart, he went down to the basement of the Air Ministry.

Next day Hitler again sent for Gregory to walk with him in the Chancellery garden, and again questioned him about reincarnation.

Had Gregory been talking to anyone else, he would have said that with every life in which a person's good deeds exceeded their bad ones they progressed; and, although at times they might be sent back to hardship and poverty in order to learn humility or some other special lesson, as a general principle they were born into a higher status where they would have greater responsibilities. And that, on the other hand, should they abuse their powers to inflict grief and suffering on others, in their next several incarnations they were sent back to face situations in which they would be the victims of similar tyrannies themselves.

But he was no unorthodox, though true, priest making a forlorn last-minute bid to save Hitler's soul; so he couched his replies in accordance with his secret objective. Using unctuous flattery he told the megalomaniac who was limping along beside him that, with every life a personality lived, it acquired more knowledge and consequently power: that the Führer had been perhaps in ancient Egypt a minor official, in Rome a Centurion, in the Middle Ages the Abbot of a rich monastery, in Venice a wealthy Senator, in the eighteenth century the ruler of a small Principality, until by his accumulated abilities it had been decreed that he should become the Leader of one of the greatest nations in the world.

Seeing himself in all these roles Hitler readily agreed, then asked, 'But what now? How, in my next incarnation, can I go yet higher? It seems to me that in this one I have already achieved the limit.'

'By no means, *mein Führer*,' Gregory replied. 'Our earth is only one of ten thousand worlds. Science has shown us that the stars are as innumerable as the sands of the sea. With the exception of the handful of Planets in our own solar system, every star is a sun and most of them have their own system of Planets revolving round them. Science has told us, too, that all the heavenly bodies are composed of more or less the same materials and that all of them, like everything else in the universe, are subject to growth and decay. They begin life as molten bodies and through the aeons gradually cool until they become extinct. Yet in their long lives there is, compared to ours, a single moment of time when they have cooled sufficiently for their crust to harden and produce first vegetable then animal life. In view of the incalculable number of heavenly bodies in the universe there must, at this moment, be at least several hundred of them that are passing through the same stage of development as this world of ours. Their inhabitants may not resemble us physically, but it would be unreasonable to suppose that they do not possess intelligence, in some cases almost certainly superior to ours.'

'I see; I see,' Hitler muttered. 'Then you think that when personalities here can progress no further, their next incarnation takes place on another world?'

'Exactly, *mein Führer*. And I feel no doubt at all that when the time comes for you to leave your present body you will be born again in a world where you will be given opportunities to become an even greater ruler than you have been in this.'

'You interest me greatly,' Hitler declared excitedly. 'But I

have walked enough for today. I am tired now. I must go down
and rest.' On that this second private conversation ended.

Considering it unlikely that the Führer would send for him
three days running, on the 7th Gregory decided to risk a visit
to Sabine. When he arrived at the villa she was delighted to
see him but soon began to reproach him bitterly for his neglect
of her.

To excuse himself he told her that there had been several
casualties among the staff in the Air Ministry Map Room and
replacements for them could no longer be spared; so those
remaining had to do longer hours and now, like sailors, had
been put on four-hour watches. As, in the present chaotic
condition of transport, it took four hours to come out to the
villa and return, that had put a visit to her out of the question
until that day, when he had persuaded two colleagues each to
take half of his watch for him. He added that he had hoped
by this time to find that she had left Berlin.

She shook her head. 'I'm better, much better, but not completely cured yet and I won't go until I am.'

'How soon does your doctor think that will be?' he asked.

'Another week or so. Perhaps a fortnight.'

'But my dear girl,' he protested, 'the Russians will be here
in a fortnight. They have just launched another of their great
offensives. Within three weeks they will have captured Berlin.
I'm certain of it. You positively must go before there is any
danger of the city being surrounded and all escape routes cut.'

'Yes, that's what Kurt says.'

Gregory raised his eyebrows. 'So he's turned up again?'

'He has been to see me several times. As I told you he is
genuinely in love with me; so he too is anxious for my safety.
Naturally, I've continued to refuse to let him come back and
live here, but I let him spend Sundays with me.'

'I thought you found him a bore, so were glad to be rid of
him.'

She gave a bitter little laugh. 'It is I who am bored these
days. For the past five weeks I've seen hardly a soul and it has
been getting me down terribly. Anyhow, it was only as a lover
that I found Kurt unsatisfactory; he is always interesting to
talk to.'

Later they had a meal together, and before leaving Gregory again endeavoured to persuade her to leave for the south; but he could not move her from her decision to remain until she was completely cured.

When he was only half-way back to central Berlin a major air-raid began. The thunder of the ack-ack guns was deafening, the sky a great, twinkling carpet of bursting shells, bombs rained down, mostly on the northern part of the city and soon, from the many fires they started, the streets were almost as bright as by day.

During the next few days the situation began to look desperate. Colonel-General von Vietinghoff, who had taken over from Kesselring in Italy, reported that General Alexander had launched a full-scale offensive and that without big reinforcements it would not be possible to continue to hold the Gothic Line. General Model's encircled army in the Ruhr was losing thousands of men in killed and prisoners every day. In Czechoslovakia and Austria two more great armies, consisting of the survivors of the scores of divisions sent to South Russia, the Balkans and Hungary, were cut off. In Holland the Army Group under von Blaskowitz had its communications with Germany threatened by the Canadians. The British armour was driving towards Hamburg and that of the Americans towards Leipzig and the Elbe. In the north the Russians had taken Stettin, outflanked the German line and were overrunning Mecklenburg; while in the centre they were launching attack after attack against the Oder, which was the last line of defence for Berlin. It was now clear to everyone in the bunker that only a miracle could save Germany from being completely overrun by her enemies.

On the night of the 10th Hitler again sent for Gregory and Malacou. When he had given them his usual limp handshake and told them to sit down, he said:

'Gentlemen, things look very black for us. But after the conference today my good friend Dr. Goebbels tried to lighten my depression by reading to me a passage from Carlyle's *Life of Frederick the Great*. You, *Herr Major*, will no doubt know it. In 1796 that great soldier-king was at war with Elizabeth of Russia. His armies had been defeated and the Russians were at the very gates of Berlin. It was thought that nothing could save the city. But on February 12th the old Empress died. Her son, Peter, had always hated her and immediately he succeeded he reversed all her policies. The young Emperor was a great admirer of King Frederick; so he at once ordered his armies to halt and offered Frederick an armistice. Thus at the eleventh hour, by what is known as the "Miracle of Brandenburg", Berlin was saved. Now last time——'

A violent fit of coughing caused him to break off. When he had recovered from it he went on, 'Last time you were here Herr Malacou predicted that the Anglo-American armies would never reach Berlin; yet from the progress they are making I cannot help fearing that they will unless something utterly unexpected happens to stop them. He also predicted that our enemies would shortly be subjected to a great blow that could alter their whole political outlook. It seems that only something of that kind could halt their advance. Can you reassure me that such a miracle is really likely to take place?'

Gregory and Malacou entered on their usual act. For some moments the occultist rambled, then he produced the following predictions which Gregory translated as: In less than a week the Führer would receive the support and encouragement that it had been earlier foretold would come to him unexpectedly in mid April. This support was associated with the Moon and must, therefore, come from a woman. Although the Russian front was holding it presented a greater menace to Berlin than did the breakthrough by the Allies in the West. The Anglo-American armies would be halted while still some distance from the capital, but the Russians would be in the outskirts of Berlin before the month was out. The event which could alter the whole political outlook of the Allies was the death of President Roosevelt, and it would occur on the 12th.

At that Hitler jumped to his feet, exclaiming, 'We are saved! I knew it. My intuition is never at fault. There is to be another Miracle of Brandenburg! The President's death will alter everything. The Americans and British will become our allies against the accursed Communists.'

Then he swung round on Bormann. 'But there remains one danger. We must not be caught in Berlin before the Western

Allies can come to our assistance. We will adopt the plan that we have so often discussed. The Bavarian Alps are a natural fortress. Among them the employment of armour is almost impossible. There is certain to be some delay in agreeing terms with the Americans, so for a while we may have to continue to fight on two fronts. Unless Berlin is seriously threatened, I shall remain here; but preparations must be made for a move to Berchtesgaden. Give all the necessary orders.'

'*Jawohl, mein Führer.*' Bormann shot out his arm in the Nazi salute; the others did likewise, then they all left the room.

Next morning the exodus began. As the Führer intended to remain in Berlin for as long as it could be held, Obersalzberg was too far distant for the headquarters to be established there as yet; but it was decided to form one at Krampnitz from which Keitel and Jodl could come into Berlin daily; so a number of the junior staff officers were sent to make the necessary preparations, while all but a handful of the servants were packed off to Berchtesgaden.

Among those who left was Himmler's liaison officer, Obergruppenführer Fegelein. That evening the ex-jockey got very drunk and took no pains to hide his joy at having received permission from his Chief to join him at Hohenlychen. At intervals between pouring brandy down his throat he mercilessly twitted the others on their ill-luck in having to remain in the hell of Berlin and the madhouse that the bunker had become.

For all the senior officers the following day proved one of the worst they had ever experienced. News came in that the American spearheads had reached the Elbe the previous evening and that the Russians had secured bridgeheads over the Oder. The German front there had broken and the Bolsheviks were crossing the river in many thousands.

At the midday conference Hitler demanded that heads should roll, and that the troops be called upon to die fighting where they stood. From beyond the partition there came an unceasing flow of curses, denunciations, reproaches and abuse. Hours later the Generals who had been present trooped out, white-faced and weary. Old Koller had had such a lashing because of the failure of the Luftwaffe to prevent the Russians gaining a foothold on the west bank of the Oder that he was again in tears.

All through the afternoon and evening Gregory hovered about the outer regions of the bunker waiting for the news to come in from the United States; but midnight came, the 12th April was over and there had been no announcement of the President's death. About two o'clock, by then extremely worried, he went back to the Air Ministry, but only to spend an anxious, restless night.

In the morning he went to the Ministry of Propaganda to see Goebbels' assistant, Heinz Lorenz, and ask if there was any news of special interest; but, apart from reports of fresh disasters on the Oder front, there was nothing. Returning to the Air Ministry he tackled Malacou, who could tell him only that Roosevelt's horoscope had shown him to be in great danger at this period, and that he would actually leave his present body on the 12th had been conveyed by the familiar spirits who, in all other matters, had proved correct.

There now seemed little doubt that on this occasion they had misinformed Malacou, and as Gregory walked over to the Chancellery he dreaded the reception he expected to receive. It was not so much that Hitler would pour out his vials of wrath upon him that he feared, but that all his careful planning would be brought to naught by the failure of this one prophecy to mature, and that having won the Fuhrer's confidence by great art and skill he would now find himself completely discredited.

Down in the passage sitting room Bormann was talking to Keitel and Burgdorf before they went in to the midday conference. On seeing Gregory he said with a sneer, 'How is the President's health this morning, *Herr Major*? It seems that you and your Turk have been made fine fools of by the spirits. I'm not surprised, though. You have lasted longer than most of the occult gentry we've had here and done better even than the Reichsführer's man, Wulf; but you all come a cropper in the end.'

'That is not certain yet, *Herr Parteiführer*,' Gregory replied stoutly. 'It is quite possible that the Americans are holding up the news for reasons of their own.'

'They had better be,' snapped Bormann, 'or the Führer will have your head off for having misled him.'

When they had gone in to the conference Gregory went through to the mess passage, to get himself a badly needed drink. He remained there for some time, talking with some of the other adjutants. He then returned to the sitting passage. Just inside the doorway two men were standing. One was von Below. The other, a shortish man with very broad shoulders and rolls of fat showing above the collar of his black S.S. uniform, had his back to Gregory.

With a smile, von Below said, 'Oh, Protze, I don't think you've met our new colleague. The Reichsführer has sent him to replace Fegelein. This is . . .' The rest of the introduction Gregory did not even hear. The other man had turned towards him and he found himself staring into the solitary eye of Obergruppenführer Grauber.

26

Out of the Blue

FOR a moment neither man moved. On Grauber's face there was a look of incredulity; on Gregory's, before he could check it, one of consternation. It was just such a chance meeting with his old enemy that he had feared when Goering had first had the idea of sending him and Malacou to Führer H.Q.

Since then he had become so immersed in the tremendous drama being played out in the bunker as the Nazi-controlled legions were being beaten to their knees, and in his growing influence over Hitler, that he had not given Grauber a thought.

Now he cursed himself for having failed to realize that in the chaos that was swiftly destroying all organization in the Reich such private Intelligence services as Goering's would have broken down, and that men like Grauber would not remain to die fighting with a defeated Army but scurry back to the seats of Nazi power where, for the time being at least, their lives would be safe.

Had Gregory not been caught off his guard and been able to greet Grauber with bland politeness he might, just possibly, have made the gorilla-like Obergruppenführer doubt the evidence of his eye. But Gregory's jaw had dropped and his eyes had shown acute alarm. In that instant, despite the extreme improbability of a British agent's having penetrated the Führer's headquarters, Grauber identified him beyond all question. With a cat-like agility amazing in a man of his bulk, he jumped backwards and his hand slapped on to his pistol holster.

But it was empty. He had momentarily forgotten that before entering the bunker he had had to leave his weapon in the outer guard room. Knowing that Grauber's recognition of him spelt death, had Gregory been armed he too would have whipped out a gun, in the hope of shooting Grauber first then shooting his way out of the bunker. Being used to having to check in his pistol before coming downstairs, his reaction was entirely different but equally swift.

Raising his eyebrows in surprise at Grauber's backward spring, he glanced at von Below and said, 'I'm sorry, Colonel, but I did not catch the Obergruppenführer's name.'

Grauber's high-pitched voice came in a screech of mingled hate and triumph. 'He knows it well enough! And I know his! He is the ace British Secret Agent, Gregory Sallust.'

Von Below looked quickly from one to the other, then smiled and said, 'My dear *Herr Obergruppenführer*. What you suggest is absurd. I . . .'

'It is not absurd. It is a fact,' snapped Grauber.

Gregory managed to raise a smile and shook his head. 'I had no idea that I resembled this apparently famous character so closely. But my name is Protze, and I am a member of the Reichsmarschall's staff.'

'Then you have tricked him,' Grauber snarled. 'As you have many other people by your perfect German. I know you for who you are and now, at last, I've got you.'

'Really,' protested von Below. 'I'm sure you are mistaken. Major Protze has been with us since the beginning of March. He could not possibly be a British agent. All of us here——'

'You fool!' Grauber piped in his feminine falsetto. 'I tell you I know him! I've known him for years. Ever since the beginning of the war. We've been up against one another half a dozen times and each time he's slipped through my fingers. But not now. Not now!'

At that Gregory resorted to a show of anger and stormed back, 'You are talking nonsense! The strain we are all under these days has addled your wits. I've never met you before in my life. I'm as much a German as you are. The Reichsmarschall will vouch for me.'

'I'll take my oath he can't. At least for only during the latter stages of the war. He cannot have known you as an officer of the Luftwaffe in '39 or '40 or even in '42.'

The rank Grauber held made him the equivalent of a full

General but, like most regular officers, von Below disliked
and despised Himmler's people; so he stood up for Gregory
as an officer of his own service and said sharply, '*Herr Obergruppenführer*, this accusation you bring against Major Protze
rests solely on your word. He has shown himself to be a loyal
servant of the Führer, who has developed a high regard for
him. Should you persist in this and be proved wrong you will
have cause to——'

Grauber's pasty moonlike face had gone white with rage
and he cut in, 'How dare you threaten me in the execution of
my duty! I insist that this man be arrested and taken to the
Albrecht Strasse. Round there we've plenty of ways to make
him admit his true identity.'

Von Below drew himself up. 'Your suggestion is outrageous.
Under torture anyone will admit anything. To have an officer
tortured simply because he resembles a British agent that you
used to know is unthinkable. No-one can stop you from
practising your barbarities on Jews and foreigners. But this
is Führer Headquarters and the loyalty of every man in it is
beyond question.'

For a moment Gregory took heart at von Below's stout
defence of him. But Grauber shrilled, 'That does not apply to
this one. I order you to fetch the guard. Whether you like it or
not, I intend to remove him.'

'They will not obey you. They take their orders only from
Herr Parteiführer Bormann.'

'Then I demand to see him.'

Von Below gestured towards the partition. 'He is in there at
the Führer conference, so cannot be disturbed. And it may
go on for hours.'

'*Gott im Himmel!*' Grauber suddenly exploded, driven to
madness at the thought of the least delay in wreaking vengeance
on his hated enemy. 'Then I'll arrest him myself. There are
plenty of S.S. men upstairs who'll obey my orders and take
him to the Albrecht Strasse.' As he spoke he shot out one of his
enormously long arms and grabbed Gregory.

Once out of the bunker, Gregory knew that he would be
finished. Even if von Below later secured from Bormann an
order for his release, long before he could be got out of

Grauber's clutches the Gestapo would have reduced him to a gibbering, bleeding wreck. Jerking himself away, he hit out but missed. Grauber came at him in a bull-like rush. A chair went over with a crash. They fell to the floor together struggling wildly and yelling curses at one another.

Gregory had Grauber by the throat, but was underneath him and held down by his great weight. The Gestapo Chief had both his thumbs under Gregory's eyes, endeavouring to gouge them out. The pain was excruciating. Gregory screamed, but managed to wrench his head aside. Then he fixed his teeth in Grauber's right hand. The deep bite brought forth a yell of agony.

The door in the partition opened. Bormann appeared and shouted angrily, 'What the hell is going on here?'

Spreading out his arms in a helpless gesture, von Below cried above the din, 'The *Obergruppenführer* declares Major Protze to be a British spy.'

'Stop it!' bellowed Bormann. 'Stop it, you two!' And, taking a pace forward, he kicked at the writhing bodies on the floor. His heavy boot caught Grauber on the thigh. Gregory unclenched his teeth. They rolled apart and, panting heavily, came unsteadily to their feet.

Hitler had emerged behind Bormann and was surveying the scene with dull eyes, as Bormann rapped out at Grauber, 'Explain yourself, *Herr Obergruppenführer*. On what do you base these accusations?'

'I know the man,' Grauber piped. 'I've known him for years. His name is Sallust and he is the most dangerous agent in the British Secret Service.'

'When did you see him last?' Bormann asked.

'In the summer of 1942, *Herr Parteiführer*,' Grauber replied promptly.

'But damn it, that is getting on for three years ago. However good your memory may be for faces that is a bit long for you to be so sure you recognize a man. Can you produce anyone else who could identify him as this British agent?'

Grauber hesitated, sucked at his bleeding hand, then admitted sullenly, 'No, *Herr Parteiführer*. No. But I am certain of what I say. He was then passing himself off as a French collaborator. I ran into him in a night-club in Budapest.'

His hopes rising again, Gregory burst out, 'That's a lie. This whole business is an absurd mistake. I've never been in Budapest in my life.'

'And that is a real lie,' said another voice, that came from the far doorway. In it Ribbentrop had just appeared, having arrived to attend the conference. Addressing Hitler with a smile, he went on:

'The *Obergruppenführer* is right, *mein Führer*. When I first saw this man here a few weeks ago I knew I'd seen him somewhere before, but could not place him. It was in Budapest in the summer of 1942. He is an exceptionally able British agent and his name is Sallust.'

It was the *coup de grâce*. Up to that moment Gregory had still hoped that with von Below's help and by calling on Koller to protect him he might manage to get the issue postponed for long enough to escape and disappear among the ruins of Berlin or, if he were placed under arrest pending investigation, at least get them to insist on his being confined in the bunker and allow him to telephone Goering. What attitude the Reichsmarschall might have taken up there could be no telling. He would certainly not have been willing to admit that he had knowingly foisted an English spy on to his Führer and with everything going to pieces he might cynically have declined to intervene. On the other hand, out of loathing for Himmler, he might have used his still great powers in some way to thwart Grauber.

But Ribbentrop's appearance on the scene had now rendered such speculations futile. It had been Gregory's ill luck that, apart from Goering, the only other Nazi in all Germany who could identify him had arrived at that moment. The Obergruppenführer's solitary eye gleamed with triumph. He passed his tongue swiftly over the thin lips of his mean little mouth and cried in his feminine falsetto:

'I thank you, *Herr Reichsaussenminister*. Your arrival is most opportune. Now I'm proved right I'll have my people take this fellow to pieces and we'll learn what filthy game he has been playing here.'

Gregory paled; but he possessed that fine trait in the British character—he was at his best in defeat. Whatever he said now could not save him, but he might yet win himself a quick death instead of one after prolonged, excruciating torment. Facing Hitler he burst into a torrent of words, shouting down Bormann's efforts to check him.

'*Mein Führer!* You are a just man. I ask you to see justice done. It is true that I am an Englishman. But I am not a British agent. Many years ago I realized that any democratic government dominated by Jews must lead to corruption and the exploitation of its people. I became a Fascist but disguised my beliefs in order to enter the British Secret Service and work against the decadent Government. In the early years of the war I twice managed to get sent to Germany with the intention of offering my services to the Nazi Reich; but on both occasions I came up against the *Obergruppenführer*. He had already known me in London as a member of the Secret Service so would not believe the honesty of my intentions. On both occasions I was forced to go to earth and return to England. Otherwise he would have had the Gestapo torture me to death.'

'You lie!' screamed Grauber. 'This is a tissue of lies. He never offered to come over to us. In Budapest he was plotting to persuade those accursed Hungarians to go over to the Allies.'

'On the contrary,' shouted Gregory. 'I was persuading some of their leaders to give more active support to Germany. And from the Baroness Tuzolto I was receiving invaluable assistance. Everyone knows that she is a wholehearted Nazi.' Suddenly he swung round on Ribbentrop and cried:

'You can vouch for her, *Herr Reichsaussenminister*. Is it likely she would have given me her aid if I had been working for the British? But the *Obergruppenführer*'s vindictiveness wrecked everything. I had to get out to save my skin and to save hers from this ham-fisted lieutenant of Herr Himmler's I had to take her with me. And it was you who enabled us to escape. Isn't that true?'

Ribbentrop had helped them to get away in order to spite Himmler, and he was quick enough to see that, since Gregory had been Sabine's lover, if she were brought into the matter she might side with him. As he could not afford to be accused of aiding a British agent to escape, he decided to hedge and replied:

'I knew only that he was an Englishman and that Sabine Tuzolto vouched for him. I've known her for years and she is above suspicion. When Grauber got after them it occurred to me that by helping this man to escape I might make use of him; so I sent the Baroness with him to London hoping that through her high connections there she would obtain valuable information for us.'

'And she did,' added Gregory. 'With my help she obtained for you the Allies' plans for their entry into the Mediterranean —Operation "Torch".'

Suddenly Hitler spoke. His memory for facts, figures and events was prodigious and, despite the shocking deterioration in his health, his memory had not suffered. In his hoarse, rasping voice, he said:

'I recall the affair. A few days before the North Africa landings, through the help of the Moldavian Military Attaché, the Baroness got back to Germany. She brought the plans with her. But they proved to be false. False!'

'*Mein Führer*,' Gregory cried, 'that was no fault of mine. I had them from a man I knew in the Offices of the War Cabinet. But the swine had sold me the Deception Plan. That, though, is only half the story. M.I.5 had got wise to the Baroness's activities. She was arrested; sent to the Tower of London. She was to have been court-martialled and would have been shot as a reprisal for the Gestapo's having executed British women landed in France by parachute. And what then? Did I leave her there to her fate? No! At the peril of my own life I rescued her from the Tower, and with Colonel Kasdar's help succeeded in getting her away. Is that not proof enough that I believed the plan she took with her to be the genuine one and did my best to serve Germany?'

Ribbentrop nodded. 'That is true, *mein Führer*. She could never have escaped had it not been for this man's skill and daring.'

'And I paid for it,' Gregory went on quickly. 'I was caught within a few minutes of having got her into the motor boat that Kasdar had brought alongside the Tower water front. I was court-martialled and received a long prison sentence. I was let out only because the British knew that I know Berlin better than most of their agents and they wanted an eye-witness account of the bomb damage. They offered me my freedom if I would get it for them and dropped me outside the city by parachute. I went to the Reichsmarschall and laid my cards on the table. He had the sense to see that my intentions were honourable and that I could be of use.'

For a moment Gregory paused for breath, then he went on. 'And, *mein Führer*, I can claim that I have. You have honoured me with your confidence; and during the past few weeks with the aid of my Turkish servant I have obtained for you from occult sources much valuable information.'

Up till that moment Gregory had played his poor hand as though inspired. While succeeding in neutralizing Ribbentrop, he had recalled his extraordinary feat of enabling Sabine to escape from Britain, and it could not be proved that he had not been imprisoned for doing so. He had cashed in on the assumption that the shrewd Goering believed him to be a fanatical pro-Nazi, and derided Grauber as a blundering fool for having earlier refused to believe in his honesty and driven him out of Germany. But in mentioning the occult he had made his one fatal error.

Hitler's face suddenly went livid. His semi-paralysed arm began to shake and he raised the other accusingly. Foam flecked his lips and his rage was such that he could hardly get his words out.

'You . . . you . . . you filth!' he cried. 'You came here under false pretences. Goering must have been insane . . . insane to have believed in you. I put my trust in you and . . . and like all others you have betrayed me. You have used your occult affinities to make predictions. And they came true. But why? Why? Why? So that in the big thing . . . the thing that mattered, I should believe you. You buoyed me up with false hopes. You promised me a miracle. It was a lie! A lie! A deliberate lie because you hoped that when your prophecy failed to mature I should be driven to despair.'

Turning to Grauber he yelled, 'Take him away, *Herr Obergruppenführer*. Take him away. Do what you like with him.'

His outburst was followed by a moment's complete silence. Grauber's thin mouth broke into the sort of catlike smile that came to it when he watched his victims being reduced for his amusement to whimpering idiots, as he had the skin flayed piece by piece from their backs.

Bormann shrugged and said to von Below, '*Herr Oberst*, call the guard.'

Gregory's mouth was parched and he felt the blood going to his head.

During the past few weeks he had frequently contemplated attempting to kill Hitler. Owing to the thoroughness of the search to which they had to submit no one could ever have smuggled a weapon down into the bunker; so to assassinate him would have been extremely difficult and, whether the perpetrator succeeded or failed, it would have resulted for him in a most ghastly death.

But now that a ghastly death at Grauber's hands was inevitable Gregory nerved himself for the attempt. He was standing within two yards of Hitler. One spring and he could be upon him. As none of the others had weapons they could not shoot him through the head. Between them they would haul him off; and in much less time than it would have taken to kill a normal, healthy man. But Hitler was already a physical wreck. A grip on his throat with the left hand, and an all-out blow over his heart with the right, could well be enough to finish him. White as a sheet and with the perspiration standing out on his forehead, Gregory gathered himself for the spring.

He was actually on his toes when a shout came from the outer door of the passage. All heads turned in that direction. Heinz Lorenz burst in among them. Shooting out his right arm, he cried wildly:

'*Heil Hitler! Heil Hitler!* Tremendous news, *mein Führer*. It's just come over the air at the Ministry. I ran all the way here. The President is dead! Roosevelt died last night. It is official, announced by the Americans. *Sieg Heil! Sieg Heil! Sieg Heil!*'

Again there was a moment's pregnant silence. Hitler let out a long whistling breath. Then he whispered, 'A miracle! The Miracle of Brandenburg has been repeated. The Reich is saved. I knew it! I've always known it. The decrees of fate are unalterable and it is decreed that I should triumph over my enemies.'

His voice had risen to a shout. At the sounds of the excitement Keitel, Jodl, Koller, the new Chief of Staff General Krebs and the Admiral Voss, who represented Doenitz, had all come out of the conference room, while several others, including Johannmeier and Hogel, Chief of the Führer's personal S.S. guard, had emerged from the far end of the lounge passage. Now they all raised their arms with shouts of *Heil Hitler! Sieg Heil! Sieg Heil!*

When the tumult had died down Hitler said to Gregory, '*Herr Major*, you have justified yourself. I have been under a great strain—a great strain. For a moment, just for a moment, I lost faith. That a man should not be born a German is not his fault. At this moment there are thousands of Frenchmen, Dutchmen, Czechs, Danes, yes and even Russians, fighting beside us for our ideals. That you should share them is enough. You will remain here and may count upon my friendship.'

Still sweating, but now from relief at his miraculous escape, Gregory shook the limp hand extended to him. As Hitler withdrew it he scowled at Grauber and said, 'You understand, *Herr Obergruppenführer*. You have been mistaken in this man. Your campaign of malice against him is to cease. Should any harm come to him through you, you will answer for it to me with your head.'

Then, smiling round, his lips trembling and slobbering a little, he cried, 'And now we must celebrate. Champagne! Champagne for everyone.'

If ever anyone had needed a glass of good wine it was Gregory at that moment; but never in his wildest dreams had he imagined that he would clink glasses with Grauber, yet ten minutes later that was what Hitler made them do.

The following day Hitler again took Gregory up to walk with him while he gave his dog Blondi a run in the garden. For a while they talked of reincarnation and Gregory was asked what he thought would become of the ego that had been President Roosevelt. He replied:

'According to the ancient wisdom, *mein Führer*, he is thoroughly enjoying himself, not only because he has now cast off all his responsibilities, but because he is meeting again a number of people many of whom were not in incarnation during his most recent life but were dear to him in others. It is

said that between each life we are granted a period of carefree
happiness, like a holiday between terms at school; then, when
we are fully recovered from the strain to which we have been
put here, we are born again and given new tasks to perform.
Having achieved such a high position in his last life it is certain
that Roosevelt's accumulated experience will qualify him for
leadership again in his next. But the probability is that it will
be on a Planet of some distant star.'

Hitler only grunted, as his mind was too occupied with new
plans to pursue the subject. He said that since the opening of the
last Russian offensive, which looked like spelling the doom of
Berlin, he had been seriously considering remaining there and
making the great gesture of sacrificing himself on the altar of
the ideals for which he had striven so hard. But Roosevelt's
death had fired him with a new faith in his star. It could be only
a matter of weeks now before the Americans offered terms,
during which there would be no difficulty in holding the
Bavarian redoubt. Even if the Russians did take Berlin the
Western Allies could not be so crazy as to allow those Communist swine to advance further into Europe. For him, of
course, politically it would be the end. Churchill would never
agree that he should continue to lead Germany against Russia.
That was a tragedy, because the Allies would deprive themselves of his abilities as a strategist, which everyone acknowledged equalled those of Napoleon. But he would make the
final sacrifice for the sake of the German people. When terms
had been agreed he would retire from public life. He had long
wished to do so. He would spend his declining years in his
old home town of Linz. There he would live with Eva Braun,
the one friend he could utterly trust: the only creature other
than his dog Blondi who, whatever happened, would remain
unshakeably loyal to him. He was, too, already planning to
build an Opera House there and a big gallery to hold his
fine collection of pictures.

Uttering hardly a word, Gregory listened for over an hour to
these extraordinary pipe dreams; then they returned to the bunker.

On the following day, the 15th, to everyone's astonishment
Eva Braun appeared. It was said that at times she could be
temperamental if denied the only thing she asked—to be

constantly in Hitler's company. But never before had she been known to disobey an order from him. When it had first been thought that the Russian armies might possibly reach Berlin he had packed her off to Munich. Now news that Berlin was really threatened had brought her back determined to share her Adolf's fate should he decide to remain in the capital.

At first he ordered her to return to the south, but she flatly refused. He then gave way and welcomed her with open arms, declaring that the more he was called on to face calamities and treachery the more his thoughts had turned to her.

Gregory was presented to her, and his stock went up still higher from Malacou's prediction that in mid-April the Führer would unexpectedly receive from a female source great comfort and support in his trials.

Eva was given a bed-sitting room and tiny dressing room adjacent to Hitler's bathroom, which she shared with him. The vegetarian cook, Fräulein Manzialy, with whom he always took his meals in Eva's absence, was banished to the kitchen and Eva again presided over the teacups and cream buns at the interminable evening sessions.

With the object of endeavouring to show herself superior to the roughnecks who made up such a large percentage of the Führer's entourage, she had given some time to studying art, but Gregory soon saw that her culture was no more than superficial and that basically she was a typical, healthy, fresh-complexioned German woman with bourgeois tastes, and that her real happiness lay in an outdoor life of winter sports and mountain climbing.

For the next two days Hitler seemed a new man. He was cheerful, friendly to everyone and laughing off the news of fresh disasters that continued to come in from the battle fronts. But by the third day it had again got him down.

There was no indication whatever that Roosevelt's successor, Mr. Harry Truman, intended to make any change in the attitude of the United States to Germany; and at the midday conference on the 18th it emerged that the situation was rapidly becoming desperate.

The British were reported to have reached the outskirts of Hamburg and Bremen. General Alexander had captured

Bologna and his troops had broken through into the valley of the Po. The French had arrived on the Upper Danube. The Russians were in Vienna and were now threatening both Dresden and Berlin. The Americans had crossed the Elbe and it now looked as if any day they would meet the Russian spearheads, thus cutting Germany in two.

To the acute discomfort of Hitler's so-called advisers, sitting silently round the conference table, he again went berserk. Foaming at the mouth he declared that Stalin had been right in 1937 to kill off nine-tenths of his General Staff. He had been lucky to find out before the war that they were conspiring against him. It was now clear that the Army was deliberately betraying Germany. The weak-kneed cowards wanted peace at any price. And not only the officers. The men, too, were now thinking only of saving their own skins. They should be shot. All of them! All of them!

Hours later, hoarse, exhausted, staggering, the demon-possessed Führer was led back to his room by the ubiquitous Bormann and handed over, first to the ministrations of the slimy Dr. Morell, then to those of Eva. After resting for two hours on his bed, restored to some degree of calmness, he sent for Gregory to walk with him in the garden.

Up there, in a still strained voice, he repeated the gist of the reports that had been submitted to him at the conference; then he went on callously, 'The Russians will capture Berlin. That seems certain now. But what of it? That is the fault of these traitor Generals who ignore my commands. Not mine. If the Berliners have to suffer it is the Army that will be to blame. I now have a more important thing to think of—my own future. The really bad news is that General Patton has begun a drive with his armour towards the Bavarian Alps. Of course, it is difficult country. But he is a determined man. This new drive of his threatens the Obersalzberg—Berchtesgaden itself. Can I trust the troops who are defending it? Shall I be safe there? Shall I be safe?'

At last there had come the moment for which through six weeks of strain and danger Gregory had striven. With Malacou's help, however questionable its source, he had won Hitler's complete confidence. He had never had the faintest hope of persuading him to ask for an armistice; but he had planned a campaign that, if he could achieve his object, might result in shortening the war by several months. Now was the time to risk everything by speaking out. He said firmly:

'*Nein, mein Führer*. You must not seek refuge in the Obersalzberg. Any attempt to prolong the war there would be futile. There is no sign of an American change of heart and, at most, you could hold out there only for a few weeks. You spoke to me a few days ago of remaining here until the end; of going down fighting in your capital as an example for all time of courage and devotion to the German people. That is the course you should adopt; and in future time, which is endless, I am convinced that you will never regret it.'

For a moment Hitler was silent, then he asked, 'Have you any idea what the future holds for me?'

'Yes,' Gregory declared, without a moment's hesitation, 'I have consulted Malacou. You will be reborn on Mars.'

'Mars! But the Planet is almost burnt out. There is no life on it except, possibly, vegetation.'

'*Mein Führer*, on that you compel me to contradict you. Owing to its smaller size Mars has aged more rapidly than Earth. But it has passed through exactly the same stages of development. And what would man do here when the seas gradually began to dry up and shrink? Even with science as far advanced as it is at present he could devise ways to prolong life on the Planet. Alternately, each spring and autumn, a great part of the ice-caps melt. That last reservoir of water would be conserved and used to bring fertility to plains in the old temperate zones in which there are great areas of crops. And that the Martians have done by constructing their fifty-mile-wide canals. But they are now in peril of extinction.'

'Why so, if they have solved their problem?'

'This solution was the best they could achieve; but it could not save them indefinitely. Evaporation decreases their water supply a little every year, and the time has come when the amount of ice that melts is no longer sufficient to fill the more remote canals. They must now seek some other solution to their difficulties, or they will perish. But it is written in the stars that they will find it and continue to survive.'

'How will they do that?'

'Their scientists are far in advance of ours. They have already solved the problem of overcoming gravity and sending manned space-ships up into the stratosphere. Since Mars is becoming uninhabitable they intend to invade and conquer another Planet where crops, fruit and animal life are still abundant. Earth is their objective. They will need thirty or forty years to improve their spacecraft and build a fleet large enough to send sufficient forces to overcome resistance here. But when they do come they will have weapons of a type we have not even conceived; so, just as happened with Cortés in Mexico, a few hundred of them will be sufficient to overcome a whole nation. All they will need then is an outstanding leader.'

'A leader!' Hitler echoed. 'A leader! Do you really think...?'

'You, *mein Führer*,' Gregory lied with every ounce of conviction of which he was capable. 'That is your future. Malacou is certain of it, and so am I.'

'To conquer the world! The whole world! And with a really determined people behind me, instead of these cowardly Germans. What a prospect! It would make death welcome.'

Gregory stole a glance at the maniac beside him, then hammered home his grandiose deception. 'It would, indeed, *mein Führer*. With that in view, to struggle on against overwhelming odds and risk becoming a prisoner of the Allies would be madness. How infinitely better to make a spectacular end of things here in Berlin, with the ruins of your capital about you. My most fervent prayer is that I may be permitted later to join you on Mars and become one of your lieutenants in this new and greater glory.'

'You shall! You shall,' muttered Hitler, now utterly bemused by this prospect that had been held out to him of becoming Emperor of the World. 'You have given me more than new hope: a vision, the sooner to attain which I could die happily.'

It was on the following evening that Goering sent for Gregory. The Reichsmarschall had spoken personally to Koller on the telephone and said that the matter was urgent; so, reluctant as Gregory was to leave the bunker now he had, temporarily at least, manœuvred Hitler into a position where he might soon be dead, he set off in an Air Ministry car for Karinhall.

For a time he thought he would never get there. Now that the Allies had overrun a great part of Germany they had the use of airfields within such easy reach of Berlin that they bombed it not only every night but all night and in the daytime as well. Five out of every six streets had been rendered impassable by bomb craters, or great heaps of rubble that had fallen from wrecked buildings. The obstructions were so numerous and new ones of such frequent occurrence that all attempts to put out diversion signs had had to be abandoned; so the progress of the car was like that of a person in a maze, who comes up against a succession of dead ends and has again and again to turn back and try another way.

Meanwhile a thousand ack-ack guns were blazing away, the explosion of heavy bombs shook the ground, scores of searchlights raked the sky and the flames from dozens of burning buildings, reflected from the clouds, gave the night sky the hue of hell. Even when they at last got clear of the city the car could proceed only at a moderate pace, as the area was now the rear of a battle front. The headlights frequently glinted on water-filled potholes, in places fallen trees partially blocked the road, and from time to time they were held up by convoys of lorries or columns of weary, marching troops. The hideous journey took over five hours; but they made it and, soon after midnight, Gregory arrived at Karinhall.

When he gave his name, an adjutant took him straight up to Goering's vast study. The Reichsmarschall was not in fancy dress but wearing a uniform of pure white silk, the tunic of which was smothered with stars and decorations, for he had collected not only every German order but also those of every country Germany had overrun.

With a curt nod he said to Gregory, 'Sit down. I imagine you had the hell of a time getting here; but I'm glad you've come and I think you'll find the effort worth it. Have you ever heard of Allen Dulles?'

'Yes,' Gregory replied. 'He is the head of the Office of Strategic Services; or, to call it by another name, the American Secret Service.'

'That is so. Well, for some time past he has been operating from Switzerland. Of course, we knew that, as we have plenty of our people there too. He runs all the escape routes for their prisoners of war who can break camp, and a vast espionage system. But recently he's been after bigger game than that. Quite a number of prominent Germans have been into Switzerland and had discussions with him on ways in which the war might be brought to an end.'

'I'm glad to hear it,' Gregory commented.

'Yes. The sooner it's over now the better. No man with an ounce of sanity could contest that. Incidentally, I've been too occupied to give you a thought lately, but are you making any progress with the Führer?'

Gregory did not wish to disclose his hand; so he replied, 'Yes and no. I felt from the beginning that there was very little hope of getting him actually to order a surrender. But I've succeeded in becoming his chief witch doctor. He now treats me as a friend, has long private talks with me and pays heed to what I say; so there is just a chance that I may succeed in persuading him to throw in his hand and let someone else take over.'

'Good luck to you, then. Unless he alters the succession his mantle will fall on me, and I'll open negotiations with the Allies within the hour. But reverting to Dulles. He has sent an emissary to me, and the suggestion is that I should arrest the Führer, or ignore him, and broadcast an order for our forces to lay down their arms.'

'Thank God for that!' Gregory exclaimed.

Goering frowned. 'You go too fast. When we spoke of this before I told you that I would never betray the Führer, and I still stand by that.'

Gregory knew that it would be futile to start an argument, so he simply shrugged and asked, 'Why, then, did you send for me?'

The Reichsmarschall heaved himself to his feet. 'Because I thought it would interest you to have a talk with Mr. Dulles' emissary. Come with me.'

Side by side they left the lofty room, walked down a flight of stairs and along several corridors. Then Goering halted at a door, turned the handle and threw it open. In the room, near the fire in an armchair, sat a woman dressed as a hospital nurse.

Gregory's heart missed a beat. He could hardly believe his eyes. It was Erika.

27

The Great Decision

ERIKA dropped the book she had been toying with, jumped to her feet and, with a radiant smile, cried, 'Gregory! My darling! I thought you'd never get here.' Next moment she was in his arms.

Goering remained grinning in the doorway. When they had exchanged breathless kisses and, still holding hands, come apart, he said mischievously, 'I told Erika I had sent for you and she suggested that you might prefer to spend the night here instead of returning to Berlin. So I had this suite made ready for you. There is, of course, a separate bed in the dressing room. I hope you will find everything you want. *Schlafen Sie wohl.*'

As the door closed behind him, Gregory exclaimed with mingled delight and anxiety, 'My sweet, to see you again after all these months is marvellous—wonderful. But I'm horrified at the thought of the danger you are running. You ought never to have come into Germany.'

'I had to,' she replied quietly. 'There are some duties that one cannot neglect. I know you no longer think of me as a German. But I am one. And my poor country is now *in extremis*. Whatever horrors the Nazis have perpetrated, that does not alter the fact that there are many millions of decent German men and women who did not want the war and have been forced into doing what they have done by the Nazi tyranny.'

'I know it. But that's no fault or concern of yours.'

'It does concern me, darling. They are my people. Thousands of them are now dying every day or suffering from ghastly wounds. And the children. Poor mites, just think what the bombs are doing to them. Nothing should be left unattempted that might bring an end to this horror. Nothing!'

'You really thought you could?'

'I thought there was just a chance I might, because in Germany before the war I was looked on as a very special person. I negotiated many of Hugo Falkenstein's big armament deals, so I'm a competent negotiator. As you know, Hermann was one of my closest friends. I know that he used the most ruthless methods to make his way to power and that now half the time he is sodden with drink and drugs; but he's not like the other Nazis. He is one of the finest and bravest air aces Germany ever had. And he's never allowed himself to become muddle-headed by the Nazi propaganda. Despite everything, he still has enormous will power and is the one man who might save Germany from complete annihilation. Knowing that he would listen to me, it was my responsibility to come here and talk to him.'

Gregory gave an unhappy smile. 'Darling, I honour you more than I can say for your decision to risk your life in such a cause. But how in the world did you succeed in getting here?'

She shrugged. 'It wasn't very difficult. After the Allies had crossed the Rhine I went to London and talked to dear Pellinore. At first he was most reluctant to help me; but he agreed that with Germany obviously on the brink of defeat no possibility of bringing hostilities to an end must be neglected. He secured for me a letter to Allen Dulles and arranged to have me flown out to Switzerland. Dulles was a little difficult to begin with, but when I had convinced him that I was something more than just an old girl friend of Hermann's he agreed to play. For me to make the journey they fitted up the interior of an ambulance like a caravan so that I could sleep in it at night, and they filled it up with fuel and every sort of store. Then they wangled me across the frontier into Germany under the aegis of the Red Cross. Fortunately there was no question of having to go through Russian-held territory and both the Americans and the Germans respect a nurse's uniform. There were plenty of wolf whistles, but they all waved me on my way and the journey took me only four days.'

'For having made it you ought to be given the George Cross,' Gregory told her.

Erika kissed him again and laughed. 'Oh, don't put it all down to my urge to save the German people from further horrors. I had quite an important axe of my own to grind.'

'The hope of finding me?'

'Of course. When that aircraft returned from Poland without you I nearly died from distress. For the first few weeks I could hardly eat or sleep from worrying about what might happen to you. But I was convinced that you were still alive and free. Then I felt sure that you had been caught and were in a prison camp. All through the autumn, whenever I thought of you I got the impression that you were utterly miserable, but towards Christmas my impressions changed. It seemed that you were no longer hungry or wretched. After that I didn't know what to think.

'Naturally, I realized that if I was right about your being in a camp you would not be there under your own name, so it would be very difficult, if not impossible, to trace you. But I meant to do my utmost and I prayed desperately hard that in some way I'd get a lead. Without Hermann's help I wouldn't even have had a chance, and on arriving here today the first thing I did was to ask it. Imagine my amazement when my prayer was answered on the instant. He just laughed and said that he would get you out here for me by tonight, and I knew he wouldn't lie to me about a thing like that. I almost fainted from sheer joy.'

'My poor darling.' Gregory put an arm round her and drew her to him. 'During those long months you must have been through a beastly time. You were right about my being a prisoner. I was until January, and I'm not surprised that your impressions about my state these past few months have been much more vague. To be honest, that is because I haven't thought of you so frequently. But don't imagine for one moment that's because I love you less. It's because I've been up to the eyes in the biggest job I've ever undertaken. Like yours it concerns trying to put an end to the war, but I'll tell you about it later. I gather you haven't had any luck with Goering?'

She shook her head. 'No. Hermann dug in his toes and there is no moving him. It's absolutely tragic, because the Allies would never negotiate with Hitler, Himmler, Goebbels or Ribbentrop; but I think they would with him. What makes his refusal all the more disappointing is that he is the only one of the big four who remains entirely loyal to Hitler. The rest of the gang are ratting now in an attempt to save their skins.'

'Really?' Gregory sat down in the armchair and pulled her on to his lap. 'That's most interesting. Tell me more.'

'Dulles told me. He decided to because he felt that I might stand a better chance of persuading Hermann to act if I could give chapter and verse about how the other top Nazis are behaving.'

'But you just said that the Allies wouldn't negotiate with them.'

'They won't. But that doesn't stop these murderers and crooks from putting out peace feelers of their own. And, of course, the Allies are quite willing to negotiate the separate surrender of any of the German Armies. As far back as February Karl Wolff, the Military Governor of northern Italy, got in touch with Allen Dulles, then in March he went to Zürich himself and saw Dulles in person. General Alexander was informed and sent two American Generals to meet the Germans in Berne. It was agreed that Kesselring should put up only a token resistance in the Valley of the Po in exchange for which the negotiators were to be immune from criminal prosecution after the war. Unfortunately Stalin was told of it and wanted to send Russian officers to participate in the arrangements. The Western Allies refused; so there was a blood row and the negotiations were called off. But they are on again now with General von Vietinghoff, who succeeded Kesselring, and it's probable that the German Army in Italy will surrender within the week.'

'That's splendid news. How about the other German Armies?'

'Just before I left Zürich news had come in that a large part of General Model's Army that is encircled in the Ruhr had laid down its arms. Apparently a Corps Commander named Bayerlein had the courage to ignore Hitler's order and save the lives of his men. He summoned to his headquarters two of his junior Generals who were die-hard Nazis, put them under arrest, then arranged to surrender to the American General opposite.'

'Good for him. All this is news to me. But how about the crooks and murderers?'

'Ribbentrop has been in secret negotiation with both the Swiss Government and the Vatican. Through them he put forward a plan for Germany to surrender to the Western Allies then turn her armies against Russia. But, like the ass he is, he made the empty threat that if the Allies refused his terms he would hand Germany over to the Russians. Of course, the Allies refused even to reply to him. It is Himmler, though, who has come nearest to selling out.'

'You amaze me! I wouldn't have thought the Allies would have touched him with a barge-pole.'

'They wouldn't; but according to report he seems quite oblivious of the fact that he is regarded as a criminal unequalled in history, and rather fancies himself as a successor to Hitler. Himmler is really a very simple-minded man. For a long time past he has been under the influence of two bright boys who are idiots enough to believe that the Allies would accept a German Government with him at its head and themselves as his key Ministers. One of them is an S.S. General named Walter Schellenberg. Under Grauber he was Deputy Chief of Gestapo Foreign Intelligence. The other is the Finance Minister, Schwerin von Krosigk. Both fancy themselves as diplomats. For months past they have been trying to persuade Himmler to rat on Hitler and work his passage with the Allies. In mid-February, while he was still supposed to be commanding an Army Group on the Russian front, he actually had an interview that was arranged for him by Schellenberg with Sweden's Count Bernadotte. And he has had others since. At one of them he said that he had talked to Goebbels and that the prize liar was considering coming in with him to stage a *Putsch*. But his trouble is that he has always been a coward. He is terrified that Kaltenbrunner, who has really run the Gestapo for a long time past, will find him out and denounce him before the Swedes can get a reply to any concrete offer he may make to the Allies.'

'They wouldn't send one.'

'No; that's certain. Poor Count Bernadotte is going to all his trouble for nothing. But, as I said a little while ago, no

possible chance to stop this awful slaughter should remain
untried.'

'With things going as they are it can't last many months
longer.'

'Months!' exclaimed Erika with a shocked expression.

'It could be months if Hitler leaves Berlin and fights a
guerilla war from the Bavarian redoubt; and that's what it
looks as if he means to do. One thing that inclines me to think
he will is a prediction by Malacou, that most of the top Nazis
won't be hanged for their crimes until October '46.'

'Malacou!'

'Yes. He turned up in the same prison camp as myself.
We got out of it together and he is with me now in Berlin,
acting as my servant.' Gregory told Erika then of how he had
used the Satanist's occult powers to win Hitler's confidence,
and of the plan he had evolved in the hope of inducing him
to put a swift, spectacular end to his villainous career.

'Oh, my darling!' Erika cried. 'If only you can. Hermann says
it's certain that the Russians will be in Berlin within a fortnight.
If Hitler does stay and is killed or kills himself that will be the
end. By preventing him from going to the Nazi stronghold in
Bavaria you will have shortened the war by months. You will
have saved countless lives and prevented untold misery.'

Gregory nodded. 'That's what I'm striving for. But it's going
to be an uphill fight. So many of the people closest to him know
that an end to him means death for them. So it's certain they
will urge him to go to the Obersalzberg and fight on, just on
the chance that some unexpected event might alter the Allies'
attitude and enable them to escape being hanged.'

For a moment they were silent, then Erika said, 'Apart
from this great new plan on which you are working now, you've
told me nothing about yourself.'

'Neither have you,' he laughed.

'Oh, I've nothing to tell. Until last month I carried on with
my job at Gwaine Meads. Dear old Pellinore is in greater heart
than ever these days. Stefan and Madeleine are well and your
godson is a poppet. But you? All those months in a concentration camp! And Malacou turning up! And your managing
to get on the right side of Hermann. Tell me everything. First,

how you succeeded in standing up to such terrible privations. And your leg; how is it? Does it still give you much pain?'

'No. I hardly notice it now, except that it aches when I put too great a strain on it.' Suddenly Gregory began to laugh.

'What is there that's funny about that?' she asked.

He kissed her. 'My sweet, it has just come back to me that I used it, or rather the fact that I'd been severely wounded, to excuse myself from having to go to bed with a very lovely girl.'

'Who was she?' Erika asked quickly.

'Sabine Tuzolto.'

'What! That woman again?'

'Yes. When I succeeded in reaching Berlin from Poland I had neither papers nor money and in all the vast city she was the only person who, if she were there, might befriend me. So I sought her out and found her living in a villa on the Wannsee.' Gregory then related how Sabine had hidden him for more than a week, so saved him from being arrested as a vagrant and ending up in the hands of the Gestapo.

When he had done Erika smiled and said, 'She's younger than I am and terribly good-looking; so you get full marks plus for having resisted her allurements. But in the circumstances, if you had succumbed I wouldn't have blamed you; or, for that matter, her, for trying to seduce you, since she apparently finds you as attractive as I do. Anyway, I bear her no malice. In fact I owe her a great debt. She risked her own life to save you and it is I who am the gainer.'

'I'm glad you feel like that,' Gregory said slowly. 'As you know, she saved me in Budapest too; so although I got her out of the Tower she is still one up on me, and at the moment I'm pretty worried about her.' He then went on to tell Erika about Sabine's misfortune and her reluctance to leave for the south.

'Poor girl, how terrible for her,' Erika commented. 'But, of course, with everyone in Berlin expecting the next bomb to blow them to pieces all normal standards of conduct must have gone with the wind. And it was really very generous of her to let that beastly boy have his fun before he went off to the front, almost certainly to die or become a prisoner of the Russians. I only hope she has taken your advice and by now left Berlin.

'I must try to find out. The trouble is, though, that now Hitler is actually nibbling at the bait I've offered him I dare not leave the bunker for long enough to go out to her villa. I wouldn't have left this evening had I not been given an imperative order from Goering to come out to Karinhall.'

'But you're glad you did?'

'How can you ask!'

They embraced again, then Erika said, 'It's many hours since you left the bunker so you must be hungry. Let's eat while you tell me about the rest of your adventures.'

Gregory had already noticed that a side table against one wall of the sitting room had been converted into a cold buffet. On it were arranged the sort of things that in the final stage of the war very few kitchens in all Europe, except Goering's, could provide. There were foie-gras and a cold lobster, part of a Westphalian ham, wings of chicken suprême decorated with truffles, a pineapple with a bottle of Kirsch standing beside it, and a magnum of champagne in an ice-bucket.

While they tucked into this magnificent feast Gregory told Erika about his escape from Poland, his months of misery at Sachsenhausen and how, with Malacou's help, he had got away from the camp only to find himself expecting to be shot on the orders of Goering.

When they had done it was getting on for three in the morning. Gregory then helped Erika to undress. He did not sleep in the dressing room.

At seven o'clock they were awakened from a deep sleep by a footman. He brought them breakfast on a tray and as he set it down he said, 'His Excellency the Reichsmarschall is already up. He requests that as soon as you have breakfasted and dressed you will join him.'

Sitting up side by side, they ate the newly baked bread spread with real butter and gratefully drank down two large cups of genuine Turkish coffee apiece. For ten minutes they allowed themselves to forget everything for the fun of splashing together in the bath. Then they hurriedly got into their clothes, rang for the footman and accompanied him up to Goering's huge workroom.

The Reichsmarschall was dressed in a pale blue uniform with

all the gold trappings appropriate to the Chief of the Luftwaffe in addition to the galaxy of bejewelled orders that scintillated on his broad chest. Beside him on his desk lay his foot-long Marshal's baton of solid ivory encrusted with emblems in gold.

As they approached he stood up, kissed Erika's hand and said, 'I regret having had to disturb your connubial bliss at such an early hour, but shortly we shall be leaving here. The time has come when I must evacuate Karinhall.'

When he had ceased speaking they became fully conscious for the first time of a dull rumble in the distance.

'That booming . . .' Gregory began, 'can it already be . . .?'

Goering nodded. 'Yes. It is the Russian guns. They will be here tomorrow; perhaps even today.'

Erika made a sweeping gesture round the great chamber. 'But all these lovely things. Are you not going to make any attempt to save them?'

The Reichsmarschall smiled ruefully. 'No, my dear. It would take weeks to pack and send them all away. And what would be the sense of my taking a couple of vanloads with me? I am no petty thief to hold on to a few antiques in order to barter them for bread and butter. This phase of my life is over. While it has lasted it has been magnificent. In modern times no man has lived more like a Roman Emperor. Now the curtain is coming down. What happens to me as I pass from the world's stage is of no importance. My only regret is that the German people should be called on to pay such a terrible price for their great endeavour.'

Gregory turned instantly to Erika. 'Where is your ambulance? We must go to it at once. Since your mission here has failed you must not lose a moment in setting off back to Switzerland.'

'Will you come with me?' she asked.

'No, my dear, I can't. And you know why.'

'Of course. Your duty lies here. I had no right to ask you.'

Goering put in quickly, 'Erika cannot return along the route by which she came. The Russians will be in Leipzig by now. In fact, God alone knows how far their spearheads may have penetrated. Even if she made a long detour she might still

fall into the hands of a Russian patrol. To those barbarians
a woman is simply a woman and a nurse's uniform would be
no protection. It would be insane for her to take such a risk.'

Erika smiled. 'Without Gregory I had no intention of
trying to return to Switzerland. If you are both going to Berlin
I'll go with you. If we have to die there, as a German woman I'll
be proud to share the fate of thousands of Berliners.'

Goering took her hand and kissed it again. '*Gräfin*, you
are a true von Epp. Let the rest of the world think what it
likes of us, but we *Hochwohlgeborene* at least know how to set
an example by facing death with courage.'

'But in Berlin,' Gregory said quickly, 'where can Erika go?
I can't take her to the bunker, or to the Air Ministry.'

'We shall not stay in Berlin,' replied the Reichsmarschall.
'Ten days ago, when first it looked as though the Russians
and Americans might meet in the neighbourhood of Leipzig
and cut Germany in half, it was decided to establish two new
headquarters. Doenitz is to become Supreme Commander of
our forces in the north and Kesselring is to assume that role
in the south until the Führer arrives there. Koller telephoned
me last night that the Führer is working on new plans by which
he hopes to save Berlin; so he may not leave immediately.
But his orders are that all key personnel should set out tonight
for the Bavarian redoubt. For Erika to remain and sacrifice
her life to no good purpose is absurd; so I insist that she comes
with me. From Munich she will have no difficulty in crossing
into Switzerland. Now let us go and wish the Führer a happy
birthday.'

'Of course,' Gregory murmured. 'I had forgotten that it is
the 20th of April.'

Down in the great open space in front of the mansion a
fleet of vehicles had been assembled: motor-cycles, armoured
cars, staff cars, small fast trucks, the Reichsmarschall's huge
cream and gold Mercedes and Erika's Red Cross van. Gregory
mounted on to its box beside her. Goering waved his gold and
ivory baton aloft and the cavalcade set off.

For once, although there were aircraft fighting in the sky
overhead, when they reached the outskirts of Berlin no air-
raid was in progress, but on entering the suburbs they met with

the same difficulties and delays as had Gregory the previous evening; so it was one o'clock before they arrived at the Air Ministry. Goering, accompanied by his entourage, went into the building, but he sent Gregory's old patron, Kaindl, to tell him that Erika was to drive her van down into the underground garage and that she was to wait there for further orders.

After nearly an hour had passed they felt hungry and Erika suggested that they should make a meal off some of her stores. The interior of the van had been fitted up with a comfortable bunk, a washbasin, sink and oil cooking stove. On the stove she heated up some soup and a tin of sausages. While they ate they speculated on what would happen that evening in the bunker.

Koller's report that Hitler was planning a new offensive that would save Berlin they took as a good sign; for if he stayed there another week it seemed almost certain that by then the city would be encircled. But it was self-evident that many of the top Nazis must realize that with Hitler's death their own would soon follow; so to prolong their lives they would make every effort to persuade him to accompany them to Bavaria.

Gregory's joy at having Erika with him again was sadly marred by his concern for her safety on her long drive south. He also felt that by rights he should have gone straight to the bunker, in order to take any chance that offered of using such influence as he had with Hitler to dissuade him from leaving Berlin. But he knew that once Erika had gone he might never see her again, so could not bring himself to forgo these last hours with her.

Meanwhile tremendous activity and bustle was going on all round them. Trucks were being loaded up with files, maps and every sort of impedimenta, and every few minutes one of them, or a car packed with Luftwaffe officers, drove off, as the evacuation of the Air Ministry proceeded.

At about four o'clock Malacou appeared and punctiliously saluted Gregory. He said he had heard that he was down in the underground garage and, as everyone was leaving, wished to know Gregory's intentions.

Gregory told him that unless Hitler went they must both remain, then waved a hand towards Erika and said, 'You will

remember the Frau Gräfin von Osterberg, although you knew
her as Frau Bjornsen.'

Malacou made her a low bow, then his thick lips broke into
a smile as he said in a low voice, 'I had foreknowledge that the
Frau Gräfin would arrive in Berlin at about this time; but I
said nothing of it to the *Herr Major* from fear that it should
distract his mind from the great work on which he is engaged.
I am, of course, aware that the Frau Gräfin has no love for
me; but all of us are at a crisis in our lives, and it is my earnest
hope that she will not allow personal enmity to hamper the
common cause we all serve.'

Erika did not return his smile, but she replied gently, 'Herr
Malacou, I could never approve the ways in which you have
obtained occult powers; yet had it not been for them the *Herr
Major* might well have died of privation at Sachsenhausen,
or at best still be a prisoner there. That owing to you he is still
alive and free more than outweighs the ill-will I bore you, and
short of your seeking to persuade him to become a disciple
of the Devil, I promise that I will not seek to influence him
against you.'

Kaindl arrived at that moment to say that the Reichsmarschall wished to see Erika. Leaving Malacou with the van
Gregory accompanied her and the Colonel up to Goering's
office. Members of his staff were still frantically sorting papers
there either to be burnt or sent to the new headquarters in
the south. He said abruptly:

'I am shortly going over to the Führer's bunker. You,
Major Protze, had better come with me. You, *Frau Gräfin*,
will return to your van and be ready to move off with my
personal convoy when it leaves. That will be soon after dark;
probably about eight o'clock.'

Erika shook her head. '*Nein, Herr Reichsmarschall*, I shall not
be leaving with you. The situation between Major Protze and
myself is known to you. I intend to remain in Berlin with him.'

Both Gregory and Goering broke into expostulations and
begged her to save herself while she had the chance; but she
remained adamant. The question then arose of where she could
stay until the fate of the city was decided. After a moment's
thought, Goering said:

'Not far from here I have *une petite maison* where in happier days I used to receive pretty ladies. An elderly couple have always kept it up for me and not long ago I passed a night there. If it is still standing Erika can have the use of it. If not we'll have to find some other place for her.'

For another half-hour they stood about while the Reichsmarschall signed more papers and gave his final orders. At length he told them to go down, collect the van and join him in the street. Ten minutes later, with Malacou in the back of the van, they were following Goering's Mercedes.

It pulled up at a modest two-storey house standing in its own small garden. The note of the musical horn of the Mercedes brought to the door the elderly couple who looked after the house. Goering presented them to Erika as Herr and Frau Hofbeck, then told them that they were to regard her as his honoured guest and that her van was to be housed in the garage. Having given Gregory only a minute to take leave of her, he hurried him back down the short path to the enormous cream and gold car.

With the tuneful horn at full blast and motor-cycle outriders to clear the way, it took them less than five minutes to reach the Chancellery. Its colossal hall was a scene of greater activity than Gregory had ever witnessed there. Apparently every Nazi in Berlin who could claim any status had come to hand in a card of birthday greetings to the Führer, and when they got down to the bunkers they found all the top Nazis had assembled in them.

The Führer was just about to go up to the garden to inspect a delegation of picked boys from the Hitler Youth that Artur Axmann had paraded for him. With him to hear the loyal speeches of these young heroes he took Goering, Himmler and Goebbels. While he was up there Gregory got hold of Koller and asked him the form. The General shook his head.

'Whether he goes or stays is still anybody's guess. So far he has refused to make up his mind. But after the reception there is to be a conference at which it's hoped that he will announce his decision.'

On returning from the garden the Führer received Doenitz, Keitel and Jodl each for a few minutes privately, then everyone

else was lined up and in turn he received their congratulations
and shook hands with them all. The ceremony over, accompanied by the Princes of the Nazi State, he retired to the
conference passage. For once the conference did not last
several hours, and soon after it broke up the waiting adjutants
learned from their masters what had taken place. Goering,
Himmler, Goebbels, Ribbentrop, Bormann, Doenitz and
Keitel had been unanimous in their appeals to Hitler to leave
for Bavaria, but he had declared that he meant to stay where
he was, anyway for the time being.

Gregory overheard Bormann assure his secretary that within
two days Hitler and the rest of them would go south; but
Goebbels was of the opposite opinion. In a corner of the mess
passage he had been having a furious argument with Speer, and
Johannmeier told Gregory that it had been about the hundred
bridges in Berlin. Convinced that the Führer meant to make a
spectacular end of himself, the fanatical little doctor had proposed that when the Russians reached the suburbs all the
remaining troops should be withdrawn into central Berlin
and a final redoubt be formed there by blowing all the bridges.

Speer had protested violently and again went in to see Hitler.
The idea of this *Götterdämmerung*, by which under Russian
bombardment a million Germans packed like sardines in a
square mile would be dying at the same time as himself, had
naturally appealed to the megalomaniac. But Speer's powers of
persuasion were so extraordinary that he succeeded in preventing measures for this holocaust from being taken, and
orders were given that the last fight for the city should take
place on the far side of the bridges.

While Speer was with Hitler, Goebbels and Himmler were
talking together and, as it was the first time that Gregory had
seen the latter, he eased his way through the crush to get a
closer look at him. Bespectacled, paunchy and pasty-faced,
he appeared even more insignificant than in his photographs.
With his head thrust forward he was speaking in a low, earnest
voice and evidently endeavouring to persuade Goebbels to do
something.

Looking in the other direction but straining his ears, Gregory
caught the words, '. . . weeks ago and you agreed with me then.

Together we could save something. I am now in a situation to arrange everything. You are a fool to have changed your mind. But there is still time.'

Goebbels' reply was inaudible but he violently shook his narrow head and, as Erika had told Gregory of Himmler's negotiations with Count Bernadotte, he had heard enough to guess what they had been talking about. It confirmed what she had said about Goebbels having contemplated playing the traitor in concert with Himmler. But he had evidently decided against doing so. The reason, Gregory had little doubt, was because he had the sense to realize that even if he could hand over his Führer bound and gagged to the Allies they would still show him no mercy.

Only the fanatics—Bormann, Burgdorf, Grauber, Christian, Stumpfegger and a few others—showed even a moderate cheerfulness at this extraordinary birthday party. Ribbentrop, his face gaunt with worry and with great bags under his eyes, loathed and despised by all, stood alone, a picture of misery. Goering, now equally hated for the failure of his Luftwaffe, a human mountain of a man blazing with jewels and decorations, showed complete indifference, occasionally addressing a remark to the unhappy Koller or von Below, who were standing near him, and for the rest of the time pouring champagne down his throat as though he had hollow legs.

After a while he came over to Gregory and said, 'I've had enough of this; so I'm off. You'll stay, of course, to do what you can. Koller will be coming in each day from the new OKW headquarters and you can get in touch with me through him if you wish. I don't need to urge you to take all the care you can of our mutual friend. I only hope that in a few days' time I'll see you both in Munich.'

Soon afterwards the party broke up. Himmler, Ribbentrop, Doenitz, all took their leave of the Führer and joined the great exodus from the capital that was taking place that night. Every Ministry was being evacuated either to the north or the south and long lines of lorries were crawling out of the ruined city by every exit still available.

Gregory made his way to Goering's little house. The electricity there had been cut off for some days and there was no

hot water; but by candle light he and Erika had a scratch meal
surrounded by priceless pieces of Louis XV furniture. As the
house was an old one the risk of a bomb burying them in the
cellar was as great as that of their being killed in one of the
upstairs rooms; so they went to bed in Goering's exotic 'love
nest', which might have come out of the pages of Crébillon
Fils.

Next day there was another hours'-long conference in the
bunker. After it Hitler sent for Gregory to walk with him. He
was positively bubbling with excitement and had suddenly
become confident that he could save Berlin. 'My instinct is
always right,' he declared. 'I was against leaving East Prussia,
but Keitel persuaded me to, and East Prussia was lost to us.
But in Berlin I shall remain and as long as I am here the city
will not fall.'

After a moment he went on, 'I have worked out a new plan.
At dawn tomorrow General Steiner will launch a great counter-
offensive with his army, which covers the south of the city. I
have sent him details about the part that every one of his
battalions is to play. He is not one of those Army pigs but an
Obergruppenführer of the S.S., so he will not betray me.
Besides, I have taken precautions. It is to be an all-out attack
and I have given orders that any commanding officer who holds
back his men will forfeit his life within five hours. I have spoken
to Koller, too, about his miserable Luftwaffe. I told him, "You
will guarantee with your own head that every aircraft that
can leave the ground goes into action." '

For half an hour Gregory's role remained that of an audience
to these absurd blusterings and callous threats, but at last they
petered out in breathless gasps. It was not till Hitler turned to
re-enter the building and go downstairs that he managed to get
in a few words. He said:

'*Mein Führer*. Under your personal direction one can hardly
doubt that this new offensive will prove successful. Should it
fail that will be through no fault of yours, but owing to a decision by those controllers of the Universe who decree the
body into which each of us is to be born on reincarnation,
and a limit to the length of each life that no power on earth
can enable us to exceed. Failure, I am convinced, would be

a clear indication that those powers are averse to a delay of even a few months before you begin to prepare yourself to become the leader and saviour of the great people who inhabit Mars.'

When Gregory spoke of a possible failure he was betting on a certainty. Keitel, Krebs, Jodl, Burgdorf, everyone in the bunker, knew that two-thirds of the formations that Hitler had ordered into battle had already ceased to exist; yet such was his mesmeric power and their terror of him that none of them had dared say so.

Next morning, the 22nd, a stream of contradictory reports followed one another into the bunker's telephone exchange. Some said the attack had started well, others that the Luftwaffe had not even left the ground. By three o'clock there was still no definite news; but gradually, while Hitler held his conference with Keitel, Bormann, Krebs, Jodl, Voss, Koller, and Burgdorf, the truth emerged. Steiner had not attempted to take the offensive. He was hard put to it even to hang on where he was. Still worse, owing to Hitler having ordered the transfer of troops on the northern front to support Steiner in the south, the front from which they had withdrawn had been so weakened that the Russians had broken through and their armoured spearheads had actually penetrated the northern suburbs of Berlin.

At that the storm broke. Gregory, von Below, Grauber, Hoegl and the others who were in attendance on the far side of the partition heard through it the spate of curses and denunciations that came pouring from the Führer's mouth. He shrieked, screamed and bellowed to a degree that could not have been exceeded had he suddenly become a victim of the worst tortures the Gestapo could inflict. He yelled that he had been deserted by everyone; treachery was universal. The Army he had always known to be packed with cowards. Every man in the Luftwaffe should be shot. Now even the S.S. had failed him. On every side he was surrounded by treason, corruption and lies. This was the end. He could bear no more. The Third Reich had failed, so there was nothing left for him to do but die.

That he should at last make such an admission left everyone

gasping. But apparently he meant it, for when he had calmed down a little he went on to declare that he had now definitely decided not to leave for the south. Anyone else who liked might go, but he would meet his end in Berlin.

All his adherents protested vigorously, but he could not be moved. The liaison officers telephoned the astonishing news to their chiefs. Himmler, Doenitz and Ribbentrop came on the line in quick succession and pleaded with him to alter his mind; but he would not listen to them. He sent for Goebbels and directed that a broadcast should be made announcing his intention of holding Berlin to the last and dying there. Goebbels protested volubly, but was ordered to obey.

Meanwhile in the dining passage and outer bunker consternation reigned. The Generals and Obergruppenführers had been shocked out of their wits. Their Führer had declared that he would hold no more conferences, give no more orders, take no further part in anything. For years he had dominated their minds, made every appointment, personally directed the movements of every Army formation. Without his rasping orders ringing in their ears they were utterly at a loss. They had not an idea what to do.

It was Jodl who, with his ingrained sense of discipline and responsibility, at length had the courage to say, 'We cannot allow him to act like this. He is still Supreme Commander of the Armed Forces and has a duty to perform. He must either tell us what to do or delegate his authority to someone else.'

Jodl and Keitel then went in to see Hitler. They begged him for orders, but in vain. He declared that the whole Reich was falling to pieces so there was no need for further orders. When they protested, he said, 'I have no orders to give. You had better apply to the Reichsmarschall. It is no longer a question of fighting because there is nothing left to fight with. If it is a question of negotiating Goering can do that better than I.'

So in the early hours of April 23rd ended the momentous session brought about by the news of the failure of Steiner's attack.

When Gregory reached Goering's little house Erika was asleep, but the situation that had now arisen was so exceptional that he woke her to tell her about it. With shining eyes she drew him to her, kissed him and said, 'Oh darling! How wonderful that it should be you who have destroyed the power of that mighty, evil man.'

He shook his head. 'The idea of becoming Lord of Mars and conquering the Earth certainly appealed to him. But he was in half a mind to make a spectacular end of himself here in Berlin anyway. We can't say more than that perhaps I supplied the feather that weighed down the balance.'

'Anyway, thank God it's over. First thing in the morning we'll leave for the south.'

Again Gregory shook his head. 'I only wish we could. But I can't. There is still a chance that he may change his mind. I've got to stay and remain on hand, so that I can do my utmost to counteract the pressure that is still bound to be brought to bear on him to go to Berchtesgaden. But you——'

'No, darling! No! I'll not leave without you. And now that Hitler has surrendered his powers to Hermann there's no longer the same danger in remaining here. It's certain that he will order a surrender on the Western front immediately. Given a free run, British tanks should be in Berlin within twenty-four hours.'

'That's true, and the Russians will find it tough going actually to penetrate the city. General Wenck's army should be able to hold them off for some days at least.'

Several hours later, back in the bunker, Gregory had reason to be glad that he had decided to stay, as another battle raged round the Führer. Ribbentrop telephoned again to say that he was about to pull off a marvellous diplomatic coup that would save the whole situation, if only the Führer would go south and give him a week to complete his negotiations. Bormann also did his utmost to persuade his master to leave Berlin. But Speer, who was also there, refused to support him and argued forcefully that with the German capital in ruins it would be more dignified for the Führer to die there rather than seek to prolong his life for a few months at what had been his holiday home. Hitler then summoned Goebbels who, with fanatical zeal, endorsed his Führer's decision to have a 'Viking's funeral' and even sought to persuade him that if he stayed in Berlin the city might yet be saved.

Meanwhile the Propaganda Ministry was going up in flames; so it was agreed that Goebbels, his wife and their five children should become permanent inmates of the bunker. During Hitler's brainstorm on the previous night he had declared that he needed no more drugs to see him through; upon which the revolting Dr. Morell had gladly joined the exodus; so the Goebbels family were given his two rooms.

Throughout all the rumpus Hitler, as was often the case on the day following one of his exceptional rages, remained calm, and in the afternoon held a tea party presided over by Eva Braun. Gregory was among those present and with relief listened as he reiterated his intention of dying in Berlin. He said that his state of health would not permit him to go out into the streets and die fighting, and he was determined that his body should not fall into the hands of the enemy; so he and Eva Braun had decided to shoot themselves and afterwards their bodies were to be burnt.

But evening brought a new crisis. A telegram arrived from Goering. It later transpired that Jodl had repeated to Koller that morning at the OKW headquarters what Hitler had said when asked for orders the previous night. Koller had decided that it was his duty to fly at once to Munich and inform his Chief that he was now the arbiter of Germany's fate. Goering had at once summoned a Council which included Mueller, the Gestapo chief, Frank, the leader of the S.S. at Berchtesgaden and Lammers, the head of the Reich Chancery. Goering had declared himself ready to fly to General Eisenhower but insisted that he must have direct confirmation of his authority to arrange a surrender; and, as a result of their deliberations, a telegram was sent, copies of which were despatched to Keitel, Ribbentrop and von Below. It read:

My Führer,

In view of your decision to remain at your post in the fortress of Berlin, do you agree that I take over, at once, the total leadership of the Reich, with full freedom of action at home and abroad, as your deputy, in accordance with your decree of 29th June 1941? If no reply is received by ten o'clock tonight, I shall take it for granted that you have lost your freedom of action, and shall

*consider the conditions of your decree as fulfilled and shall act
for the best interests of our country and our people. You know
what I feel for you in this gravest hour of my life. Words fail
me to express myself. May God protect you and speed you quickly
here in spite of all. Your loyal*

Hermann Goering

Von Below showed Gregory the copy he had received and
they agreed that the message could not have been more proper
to the occasion or shown greater devotion. But for years past
the mole-like Bormann had lost no opportunity to discredit
all the Nazi leaders powerful enough to put a check on the
influence he was acquiring over the Führer; and now he saw
his chance to dispose finally of Goering. He could not question
the fact that the Reichsmarschall had been legally appointed
by the Führer as his successor; but one sentence in the telegram
enabled him to pour his poison into Hitler's ear. It was, *If no
reply is received by ten o'clock tonight.* That, he pointed out
indignantly, was an ultimatum. Goering was holding a pistol
to his Führer's head. To give him a time limit was the greatest
effrontery. If a reply was sent, owing to the chaotic state of
communications, Goering could later say that it had arrived
after the deadline. For all his fair-seeming words Goering had
clearly decided to usurp the Führer's power and arrange a
surrender. He was a traitor.

Hitler's mind was so obsessed by the thought of treachery
that he immediately accepted Bormann's vicious interpretation
of the telegram. He began to rave that it was Goering's mis-
handling of the Luftwaffe that had lost him the war; that
Goering was corrupt, a drug-addict, a drunkard, a liar.
Working himself up into a fury he came out into the passage
and, striding up and down, shouted to everyone that Goering
had betrayed him.

Bormann demanded the Reichsmarschall's death; Grauber
loudly supported him. But Speer was again in the bunker, and
when Hitler had exhausted his first outburst of rage he intervened. Von Below and Gregory followed his lead and the
three of them urged Hitler to remember the immense services
Goering had rendered to the Nazi movement in its early years.

Their efforts saved Goering from the worst. Hitler at length
agreed that telegrams should be sent to the two senior S.S.
officers at Berchtesgaden stating that Goering was deprived
of his right of succession, his rank and all his decorations; that
he was to be arrested for high treason and that all his staff
were also to be placed under arrest. The telegram ended: *You
will answer for this with your lives.*

So ended another late-night session in the bunker that for
the past month had become a madhouse.

After a few hours' sleep Gregory discussed the situation with
Erika. Bormann having stabbed Goering in the back had
shattered their hopes of a quick finish. There would now be no
immediate surrender in the West, no British troops streaming
into Berlin that evening, and the city was already partially
surrounded by the Russians. But at least it seemed certain that
Hitler really meant to commit suicide. The strain of the past
six weeks had told terribly on Gregory and he was so desperately anxious to get Erika out of Berlin that at length he agreed
that should Hitler show no signs of changing his mind that
day they would leave in her van the following morning.

Despite his weariness and preoccupations Gregory had
several times thought of Sabine and wondered if she had left
for the south. Now he felt that before leaving himself he must
find out. When he mentioned this to Erika she said at once:

'If Sabine is still at her villa why shouldn't we take her with
us? There is plenty of room in my van, and after the way she
and her servant hid you in July the least we can do is to save
them from the Russians.'

In consequence Gregory wrote a brief letter to Sabine,
telling her that he could not be certain but hoped to leave
Berlin the following morning and if he did he would take her
with him; then he gave it to Malacou with careful directions
how to find the Villa Seeaussicht and sent him off with it.

Down in the bunker that day things were much quieter, but
towards evening there arose a development which was most
disquieting for Gregory. A telegram came in from Field
Marshal Schöerner. His headquarters were in Prague; the
Army Group which he commanded numbered many Divisions
and was still in good shape. He reported that he was capable

of holding out for months in the mountains of Bohemia, and begged Hitler to join him there.

Although Berlin was now being shelled as well as bombed Gatow airport was still operative, so Hitler could have set off in an aircraft for Prague with a fair chance of arriving there safely. In spite of Bormann's pleading he refused to go; but the telegram had the unfortunate effect of re-arousing his interest in battles. Sending for maps, the latest situation reports and General Weidling, the Commandant of the Berlin area, he again assumed the role he had said, two nights earlier, that he meant to abandon for good, and began to issue orders right and left for the employment of both existent and non-existent units. In addition he had a telegram sent off to Colonel-General Ritter von Greim of the Luftwaffe to join him in Berlin immediately.

That night Gregory went back with a heavy heart to Erika. He told her what had happened and said that now that Hitler had changed his mind about no longer taking any part in directing the war he might also change it about remaining in Berlin; so it was imperative that he should stay on and do everything possible to keep him to his decision to die among the ruins of his capital.

Malacou had safely accomplished his journey to and from the Villa Seeaussicht. He had found Sabine still there and brought from her for Gregory a hastily scrawled letter, that read:

My dear,
In these frightful times it was good of you to think of me. You know the reason why I've stayed on here for so long, but thank God I'm completely cured now and you have no need to worry about me. Kurt has been to see me several times and has persuaded me to go with him to his family place, Schloss Niederfels, not far from the Bodensee. As he has not had the money to keep the old castle up, life there will be pretty grim; but at least I'll be safe from the Russians. His own departure has been delayed for a few days while he has been hiding his scientific paraphernalia, so that it should not fall into the hands of the enemy. He expects to be able to report to Speer by midday that he has

finished the job, and as soon as he gets back from the Ministry
he'll join me here, so Trudi and I are packing like mad to be ready
to leave with him. Blessings on you, darling. I pray that we may
meet again in happier times. Sabine.

That was one worry off Gregory's mind, although it did
little to ease it because he was so terribly concerned for Erika.
But she cut short his pleas that she should leave without him
by saying, 'It's not very complimentary of you, darling, to
suggest that I haven't got as much guts as a woman like
Eva Braun.'

Next day, the 25th, 'Corporal' Hitler was up to the ears in a
wildly impractical new plan by which, not Berlin, but he,
personally, was to be saved. Artur Axmann's battalions of
Hitler Youth were to hold the bridges to the west of the city,
over the Havel, while the Twelfth Army under General Wenck,
which was fighting on the Elbe, was to disengage itself, fight
its way round towards Potsdam, cross the bridges, rescue the
Führer, then turn south and fight its way out of the city again.

Keitel, true to form to the last, declared it to be a Napoleonic
conception and set off to take Wenck his orders personally.
Jodl returned to the new OKW headquarters which had been
moved further out to Fürstenburg, while Krebs remained in
the bunker as, theoretically, the Führer's military adviser.

When Gregory arrived there on the morning of the 26th
he found his friend von Below sitting gloomily at the table in
the dining passage with a bottle of brandy and a half-empty
glass in front of him. There was no lack of good liquor in the
bunker and everyone who frequented it habitually drank
heavily, in an attempt to keep up his spirits. Jokingly Gregory
remarked, 'The morning's news must be worse than worse for
you to start tippling so early in the day.'

Von Below looked at him with lacklustre eyes and said
heavily, 'No, I've just come from a hospital where I watched
my nephew die. He was a boy of only fifteen and such a fine,
happy lad; but, of course, he'd been called up and a Russian
bullet got him.'

Gregory stammered such words of sympathy as he could
find; then von Below went on, 'There's no damned justice in

it. That's what one resents. In the next bed there was a middle-aged man I used to know. He was mixed up in the July *Putsch*, but had the luck to escape being executed. When they came to arrest him he tried to commit suicide, but only wounded himself. Two days ago a lump of ack-ack came down on his head, but not on the part of it that was vulnerable from his previous wound. So he's still alive, and unless the hospital is bombed he'll be out of it inside a week. Yet my young nephew is dead.'

Even as Gregory asked the man's name, his sixth sense told him what the reply would be. It was, 'Graf Kurt von Osterberg.'

So unless Sabine had set off on her own she was still at the villa. And the advance elements of the Russian Armies had now surrounded Berlin. From all quarters reports were coming in of Russian tanks and armoured cars ravaging the outer suburbs. But for the time being Gregory could do nothing about her, for it was imperative that he should remain in the bunker.

All through the afternoon the Führer continued to issue new orders, to battalions and even companies. Then in the evening Ritter von Greim arrived. He was carried down to the bunker wounded and in considerable pain. While the giant Dr. Stumpfegger, who had remained there out of loyalty to Hitler, attended to the General's wound, Hannah Reitsch, who had accompanied him, gave a graphic account of the hair-raising journey they had made at the Führer's command.

Fräulein Reitsch was a famous test pilot and no-one could deny her courage; but in all other respects she was an odious woman with a neurotic mentality that led her to regard people either with vitriolic hatred or passionate devotion and dramatize herself to them accordingly. She was, of course, a fanatical Nazi and regarded Hitler as her god.

Early that morning they had landed at Rechlin. From there von Greim intended to go on by helicopter to Gatow. Only one had been available and that was damaged, but its sergeant pilot had made the trip before so von Greim ordered him to take it up. The aircraft was intended for only two, but Hannah, determined to be in at the death, had squeezed herself into its tail.

Forty Luftwaffe fighter 'planes were ordered into the air to act as escort and most of them were shot down, but the heli-copter reached Gatow with only a few bullet holes in it. There von Greim found a training aircraft. Boarding it, he took the controls himself. By a miracle he escaped being shot down by the Russian 'planes overhead, but as he hedgehopped over the ruins of outer Berlin, where desperate street fighting was in progress, a shell-burst had wrecked the belly of the aircraft and a splinter from it had torn open his right foot. Hannah had then leant over his shoulders, zig-zagged the 'plane wildly and performed the extraordinary feat of landing it safely on the broad East-West Axis near the Brandenburg Gate.

And this desperate venture, involving the death of a score or more of German pilots, had been undertaken solely that Hitler, instead of sending von Greim a telegram, might tell him personally about Goering's treachery and that he was to succeed him as a Field Marshal in supreme command of the Luftwaffe.

On the morning of the 27th Russian shells were falling in all parts of the city and their troops had completely encircled it, so it seemed that the end could not now be long postponed. But the suburbs and built-up area to be occupied consisted of more than a hundred square miles. To the south the Russians were still thin on the ground and many people were managing to escape by dodging their flying columns.

Worried that Sabine might not know that von Osterberg had been wounded and still be waiting for him to pick her up, Gregory decided to send Malacou out to the villa again. By him he sent a note, telling her about the Count and urging her not to lose another moment in getting away before the Russian ring became too thick for there to be any chance left of getting through it. Still armoured in his belief that his time had not yet come to die, Malacou accepted the mission placidly and set off to dodge his way through the ruined and burning city. Gregory then went over to the bunker.

That day, for some unaccountable reason, Hitler was in high spirits, and such was still his extraordinary dominance over those about him that everyone else was too. Old Koller, Gregory learned, had been released from arrest at Berchtes-gaden and, horrified at what had resulted from his repeating to Goering the Führer's remark to Jodl, had attempted to fly to Berlin in order to exonerate his Chief. But he could get no further than the OKW headquarters. From there he telephoned von Greim who, lying in bed on account of his wounded foot, simply said that Goering was a good riddance anyway; and that he was not to worry. 'Don't despair!' hc cried. 'Everything will be well. The presence of the Führer and his confidence have completely inspired me and victory is assured.' In the evening Bormann got drunk and danced a two-step with Burgdorf.

Utterly sickened by the sight of this mass insanity, Gregory left the bunker soon after midnight. Outside in the street the crashing of shells, the explosion of bombs and the roar from burning buildings was deafening. He had covered not much more than a hundred yards when he was hit a terrific blow on the back of his head. Stars and circles wheeled before his eyes then, his mind engulfed in blackness, he crashed forward on to the pavement.

He was brought to by cold water being sloshed into his face. His bleary eyes took in the fact that he was in a low-ceilinged room and that opposite him, with an empty glass in his hand, stood a big man dressed in a grey lounge suit. As he made to move it suddenly came home to him that he was trussed like a chicken to the chair in which he was sitting. His bemused brain sought an explanation and found one.

For weeks past, owing to terror of death and acute privation, Berlin had become completely lawless. The Police could not possibly control the thousands of deserters and desperate foreign workers who hid by day in the vast acreage of ruins. By night they came out in gangs, broke into the food shops and held people up in the streets for their ration cards and money. Unheard by him owing to the deafening din, one of these thugs had come up behind and coshed him.

But why had the man not just taken his wallet and left him lying on the pavement? Why had he been brought here and tied up?

His sight cleared a little and he had the answer. The man in the grey lounge suit was Herr Obergruppenführer Grauber.

28

In the Hands of a Fiend

SLOWLY the water dripped from Gregory's eyebrows, nose, lips and chin. His sight was still blurred and the back of his head was throbbing violently. Instinctively he looked from side to side for any possibility of help or escape. As he made the movement his brain seemed to roll inside his skull, causing him exquisite agony.

The room was about fifteen feet square and it had no window. That suggested that it was in a basement; but it was obviously not one of the cells or torture chambers below the Gestapo headquarters in the Albrecht Strasse, because it was comfortably furnished. The only evidence of pain-infliction in it was a collection of whips hanging from a rack above a backless leather couch on which there was an open suitcase crammed full of clothes. But those slim, springy, silver-mounted strips of birch, hide and whalebone were not, Gregory knew, for flicking the skin from the backs of prisoners. Grauber was not only a homosexual but also a sadist. In the old days he had always travelled with a specially selected S.S. bodyguard of blond young giants who painted their faces and addressed one another with endearments. Those whips had been used on them and, probably, by them on Grauber himself.

Suddenly Grauber spoke. 'Our last round, Mr. Sallust. And I win it hands down. You are a slippery customer, if ever there was one. But your extraordinary feat of getting yourself into the Führer's bunker gave you a swollen head. At last you have made the fatal mistake of underrating your opponent.'

It was true. Had Gregory been less preoccupied with his endeavours to keep Hitler in Berlin and his anxieties about Erika and Sabine, he would have given more serious thought to Grauber and the possibility that his old enemy would devise some subtle way of bringing him to grief. But the terror Hitler inspired among his followers was so universal that, once under his protection, Gregory had thought the risk of Grauber taking any action against him to be negligible.

He had been further lulled into a false sense of security during the past five days by Grauber's attitude. Their respective duties had entailed being at the same time for long spells in the passage outside the conference room and taking meals together in the mess passage. Naturally, neither of them had been more than barely civil to the other, but Grauber had treated Gregory with a certain deference, which Gregory had put down to his having become one of the Führer's intimates, and that had strengthened his conviction that his old enemy fully accepted the situation.

Too late, he realized that, outside the bunker, Grauber still possessed almost limitless powers and could on any night have him kidnapped by Gestapo men while making his way home through the blackout.

Pain made it difficult for him to work his jaw, but now that his wits were coming back to him he managed to croak out, 'Yes, you've got me . . . but you'd better watch your step. You seem to have forgotten that . . . the Führer is my friend. He . . . he warned you not to lay a finger on me at the peril of your life. At any time he may ask for me . . . to talk about the future. If I'm not to be found he'll guess that you are at . . . at the bottom of my disappearance. . . . Then you'll be for the high jump.'

'That maniac!' Grauber suddenly spat. 'Do you think I any longer give a damn for him? He has brought Germany to ruin, and himself. He is now through. Finished!'

'Not yet. You and the others still quail every time he opens his mouth . . . And he has a memory like an . . . encyclopædia. He won't have forgotten that we are enemies. Just wait until you get back to the bunker. The moment he sees you he . . . he'll hand you over to his private police. He'll have them take you to pieces on . . . on the assumption that you'll be able to tell him what has become of me.'

Grauber gave a high-pitched laugh. 'You poor fool. What

do you think I am doing out of uniform and in these clothes?
I'm not going back to the bunker. I'm leaving Berlin tonight.
Tomorrow it may be too late.'

That contemptuous statement hit Gregory as though it were
the last nail being hammered into his coffin. The moment he
had grasped the situation he was in he had realized that his
chances of getting out of that room a free man were about as
good as those of a man surviving who puts the barrel of a
loaded pistol to the roof of his mouth and pulls the trigger.
But there had been just the slender hope that he might use
Hitler's knowledge of his feud with Grauber to frighten him.

Now that, too, was gone. But he felt sure that his end would
be no more horrible if he twisted Grauber's tail a little; and,
his words coming more easily, he said, 'I see. Another rat
leaving the sinking ship. You're off to join the king rat, eh?
But don't flatter yourself that Himmler will succeed in making
a deal with the Allies. He'll not be able to save your skin, or
his own. Count Bernadotte's intentions are of the best, but——'

Leaning forward, Grauber snapped, 'What do you know of
that?'

'Enough to be certain that if we were way back in 1940 and
Britain had really been at her last gasp Churchill would still
not have negotiated with a swine like Himmler. As things are,
it's already been announced that he and his kind are to be
tried as war criminals. That goes for you and it won't be long
before you are dangling from a beam by a rope round the neck.'

'Others may, but not I.' Grauber shook his massive head.
'Again you underrate me. About Himmler you are right. He is
a brilliant organizer but in all other respects a fool, and he has
always gone about with his head in the clouds. Now he has
become almost as mad as Hitler. His acceptance of Schellenberg's belief that the Allies would treat with him through
Count Bernadotte is the proof of it. I've no intention of mixing
myself up with such a pack of dreamers.'

'Whether you do or don't the Allies will get you,' Gregory
said tersely. 'You are too big a fish for them to allow you to
slip into obscurity. They will comb Germany for you; and
you've plenty of enemies here. Sooner or later the Allies' agents
will catch up with you or someone will give you away.'

Grauber's pasty face took on a cunning look. 'You are wrong. I shall be neither caught nor betrayed, because I shall not be here. There are many good Nazis in our Navy and I made my preparations weeks ago. A U-boat is waiting to take me to South America, where I have a large ranch and sufficient money invested for me to live as a rich man for the rest of my life.'

To that Gregory could find no reply. Von Below had said that there was no justice in the world and if, instead of paying the penalty for his crimes, this arch-fiend was to enjoy an old age of comfort and plenty it seemed that von Below had been right.

'And now about yourself,' Grauber went on. 'I have always promised myself that if I caught you I would cause you to die very gradually and very painfully, with the best medical attention between whiles; and I should have considered myself unlucky if your heart had given out in less than a month. But present circumstances render that impossible, as I must leave here in about an hour. In consequence I have decided to let you live.'

Gregory swallowed hard. That Grauber should show mercy and, of all people, to him, was beyond belief. He stammered, 'You . . . you're playing with me.'

'No. I assure you that I am not. Within an hour you shall leave here a free man.'

It is said that hope springs eternal in the human breast. Despite his every instinct Gregory could not prevent a sudden lifting of the heart. 'I . . . you really mean . . . to . . . to let me go?'

'Yes.' Grauber's small mouth twisted into a smile. 'But there is a little matter we must attend to first. You will recall that in November '39, you bashed out my left eye with a pistol butt. You therefore owe me an eye and I propose to claim that debt. Since it has been so long outstanding it is only fair that I should receive interest, and the destruction of your other eye seems appropriate for that.'

Gregory felt a cold shiver run through him as Grauber went smoothly on. 'That evens up our score. But I must also protect myself; for you have made it clear that you will run to our crazy Führer and complain about me. I greatly doubt if he could now have me caught once I have left Berlin; but you and I have survived all these years of war only because it has become second nature to us to take precautions. In the present case I must prevent you from talking. I've seen a tongue torn out by the roots, but doubt my ability to perform such an act; and anyway it would be a very messy business. I shall therefore break a small phial of vitriol on your tongue. After that you will tell no tales for many months to come—if ever again.'

In vain Gregory strove to prevent himself from listening. His hands were tied down so he could not stop his ears, and the gloating effeminate voice continued to penetrate his brain. 'Lastly, I have always had a passion for thoroughness and I should not feel happy if we parted without my having made a proper job of you. I shall therefore pierce both your ear-drums with a knitting needle.'

For a moment Grauber was silent, then he added, 'So, you see, although I must deny myself the pleasure of actually watching you scream for mercy daily for some weeks, I shall be able to think of you during my voyage to South America undergoing a mental stress greater than that caused solely by physical inflictions. As I promised, in less than an hour you will be a free man. I shall remove your uniform tunic and put you out into the street; but you will be blind, deaf and dumb. Then I shall pray for you.' Suddenly he gave a high, cackling laugh. 'I shall pray that you are not killed by a bomb or a Russian shell.'

At that Gregory's control snapped. Hurling curses and abuse at Grauber he violently wrenched with wrists and ankles at the cords that bound him to the chair. But it was of Jacobean design with a high strong back made of heavy ebony. The most he could do was to rock it and the Obergruppenführer ignored him. With his mincing gait he walked over to a cabinet, took from it a box of cigars, selected one and, sitting down in front of his prisoner, held it up.

'One of my best Havanas,' he said, his solitary eye gleaming with sadistic delight. 'To bash out your eyes with the butt of a pistol would be much too crude. Instead I intend to burn them out with the lighted end of this excellent cigar. But not yet.

Oh no, not yet. When it has singed your eyeballs it would have an unpleasant flavour; so first I shall smoke three-quarters of it. You see, we still have plenty of time; time for you to think about what I mean to do to you, time in which you can watch the cigar gradually burning down until there is just enough of it left for me to deprive you of your sight for ever.'

It was the last refinement of cruelty. Gregory was compelled to sit there, sweating with terror. As no-one in the bunker knew where he was he had no possible hope of rescue. The underground room was heavy with a pregnant silence. Down there even the bombardment could be heard only as a faint rumble, and exploding bombs did no more than cause the floor occasionally to give a slight quiver. Obviously Grauber had sent away the men who had kidnapped Gregory, so there was no-one to whom he could appeal for help, even had they been willing to listen. The knots in the thin cord that held him to the chair had been tied by experts and, strain as he might, he could not even ease them.

To attempt to bargain with Grauber was as futile as to ask him for mercy. Had he been going to join Himmler, Gregory could and would have used all his powers to drive home the fact that within a short while now Germany must collapse, and that soon after their victory the Allies would bring to trial and hang all the Chiefs of the Gestapo. Then, counting on Sir Pellinore's great influence, of which Grauber was aware, he would have offered to guarantee his life if allowed to go unharmed. But Grauber was going to South America, where a fine estate and ample money awaited him. So he had nothing to fear, and Gregory nothing to offer.

Maddeningly, a clock on a bookcase ticked away the minutes. Grauber continued placidly to smoke his cigar. The blue haze of the smoke and admirable aroma began to fill the room. Three times he carefully tapped an inch of ash from the cigar end into an ashtray on a nearby table. Each time he did so he looked critically at the cigar, then at Gregory. After removing the ash for the third time he said, 'We are getting on. About another five minutes, I think.'

It was at that moment that a bell rang. The sound acted like an electric shock on Gregory. His heart missed a beat and his muscles tensed. Grauber gave a swift, surprised look towards the door. But he did not move.

The bell shrilled again. Still Grauber did not move. With a frown he looked at Gregory and said softly, 'Don't delude yourself with false hopes, my friend. It is only some neighbour making a chance call. If I don't answer it he will go away.'

For some twenty minutes Gregory had been almost out of his mind from visualizing the awful torments that Grauber intended to inflict on him. Suddenly his wits came back and he opened his mouth to shout. In one catlike spring Grauber was upon him and had seized his nose between a finger and thumb. Dropping the butt of his cigar, he pulled a silk handkerchief from his pocket with his other hand and thrust it into Gregory's open mouth, effectively gagging him.

Again the bell rang, this time insistently. Evidently whoever it was had his finger firmly pressed on the button.

Picking up the cigar butt Grauber stood in front of Gregory, mouthing curses below his breath.

The bell stopped ringing but after a moment there came the muffled sound of heavy blows on the outer door.

For nearly two minutes Grauber remained irresolute. But the blows did not cease and it became evident that someone was endeavouring to break in the door.

With a blasphemous oath Grauber stepped over to the sitting-room door and pulled it open. From where Gregory was sitting, trussed and helpless, he could see that it gave on to a narrow hall. The noise of the blows now came louder to him; then the sound of splintering wood. There followed a confusion of raised voices. Grauber had evidently unbolted the door and was shouting, 'What in thunder do you mean by this?' Someone else cried, 'The light showing under the door told us you must be here.'

His nerves as taut as violin strings, Gregory wondered who these people who had forced their way in could be. As he made desperate efforts with his tongue to force the handkerchief out of his mouth, he prayed frantically that they would save him. A heated argument was going on outside in the passage. He was petrified with fear that it would be settled and that before he could shout for help Grauber would have got rid of his unwelcome callers.

Stretching his mouth to tearing point, Gregory did his utmost to vomit. The effort ejected a part of the handkerchief but the silk of the remainder clung to his gums. He was now able to gurgle, but not loud enough to be heard outside the room. Thwarted in his attempts to shout, he flung all his weight sideways. The heavy chair tipped, hovered, then went over with a crash. His head hit the floor. It had still been aching intolerably from his having been coshed. This second blow sent such a violent pain searing through it that he passed out. But only for a few moments.

He caught the tramp of feet. When his mind cleared the room was full of S.S. men. At the sight of their black uniforms he groaned. These were Grauber's people. The noise of the chair going over must have brought them in from the passage, but his hopes of rescue had been vain.

Two of them heaved the chair upright. Then Gregory saw Grauber and an S.S. officer facing one another in the open doorway. The latter had his back turned, but Gregory heard him ask sharply, 'What has been going on here?'

'A private matter,' piped Grauber angrily. 'A private matter. I have been interrogating an English spy.'

The officer turned and looked at Gregory. Instantly they recognized one another. He was S.S. Standartenführer Hoegl, the Chief of Hitler's personal bodyguard, and he exclaimed:

'*Donnerwetter!* It is Major Protze! He is no spy!'

'He is!' insisted Grauber. 'He is a pig of an Englishman.'

'You can tell that to the Führer,' retorted Hoegl. Then he added to his men, 'Release the Herr Major.'

Half fainting from strain, shock and relief, Gregory was untied and stumbled to his feet. Meanwhile a furious altercation was taking place between Grauber and the Standartenführer.

'How dare you address me in this way!' shrilled Grauber. 'I demand that you treat me with the respect due to an Obergruppenführer.'

'Not while you are in those clothes,' sneered Hoegl.

'What I wear is my business. I am about to change back into uniform.'

'Oh no you're not. You are coming with me as you are.'

'I'll not take orders from you.'

'Yes you will. The Führer asked for you this evening. You weren't to be found in any of the bunkers. He sent me to fetch you. Naturally, we expected to find you at the Albrecht Strasse. You weren't there but they said you might be at this underground apartment of yours. And here you are. What game you were about to play in civilian clothes and with that suitcase already packed that I see over there it is not for me to judge, but——'

'My Chief, the Reichsführer, has sent for me to join him.'

'Then he'll have to wait until you've seen the Führer and explained to him why you left the bunker without his permission. He will want to know, too, what you have been up to with Major Protze. Come along now.'

Two minutes later they had emerged from a deep basement and were all packed into a big S.S. car that had been waiting outside the ruined block. By the flashes of the ack-ack guns Gregory saw that they were driving along the north side of the Tiergarten, but his head was still splitting and he was so exhausted that he was hardly conscious during the journey.

When they arrived at the Chancellery he asked if the car might take him on to Goering's house. As it was not he for whom the Führer had sent and he was obviously near collapse, Hoegl agreed. With an S.S. man on either side of him Grauber, white and shaking, was hustled into the building to face the wrath of the Führer. The car drove off and within ten minutes Gregory, between gulps of brandy, was giving Erika an account of his ghastly experience.

But his trials that night were not yet over. At half past four in the morning there was a terrific detonation. Both he and Erika were blown out of bed. Picking themselves up they put on their coats and went through the wrecked doorway to find out the extent of the damage. A Russian shell had blown in a part of the back of the house. The kitchen quarters were wrecked and the Hofbecks, who slept in a room adjacent to them, had both been killed. Malacou, although sleeping in the room above them, the outer wall of which had collapsed, had, miraculously, come to no harm.

When they had helped him move his bedding downstairs to the small dining room he told Gregory that the previous day he had found Sabine still at Seeaussicht and handed him a letter from her. It read:

My dear,

Poor old Kurt having been wounded explains why he never came for me. These past two days I've been in half a mind to set off with Trudi on our own, but everyone says there are now thousands of Russians to the south of here, so I haven't had the courage to risk it. I must have been out of my mind not to have gone weeks ago, when you tried to persuade me to. But I'm sure you can't mean to stay in Berlin to be captured, and you have always been so full of resource. When you leave, I implore you to come here first and take me with you.

Always your devoted Sabine.

Having shown the note to Erika, Gregory said, 'I don't wonder that having left it so late she's scared to run the gauntlet on her own. But the Russians can't be very thick on the ground to the south of the city yet. And this can't go on much longer. If I find that Hitler is still set on doing himself in we'll leave this coming night and pick up Sabine on our way out.'

After another few hours' sleep, weary, haggard and with his head still aching, shortly before midday Gregory went to the bunker. There he learned that on the previous evening Goebbels had raised the question of the *Prominente*. Not the German *Prominente*, with whom Gregory had for a time been a prisoner. Of them Goerdeler, Popitz, Nebe and others had been executed several weeks earlier. The remainder had been transferred to Flossenbürg and, on orders given by Hitler on April 9th, Canaris, Bonhoeffer, Oster, Dohnanyi and the majority of the others had been butchered. Goebbels, thirsting for blood, had referred to the other group of *Prominente*, which consisted of the most distinguished British and American prisoners of war. The latter had been removed from Colditz and were now being held as hostages in Bavaria. At his mention of them Hitler had gone purple in the face and, his whole body trembling, yelled:

'Shoot them all! Shoot them all!'

It was to transmit orders for this massacre that Grauber had been sent for and, on learning that he had disappeared, the Führer, now ever ready to suspect treachery, had sent Hoegl to try to find him. When he had been brought in there had been another scene, but his wits had saved his life. He had said that his Führer's need of reliable troops was much greater than the Reichsführer's and that Himmler's personal body-guard, consisting of a whole battalion of crack S.S. men, was at Hohenlychen doing nothing. His idea had been to go and fetch it and he was in civilian clothes because that would give him a better chance of getting through the Russian lines.

Hoegl had begun to report having found Gregory tied to a chair in Grauber's apartment. But by then Hitler had appeared so near collapse that Eva Braun had insisted that he should go to bed. Supported by her he had staggered off, but shouted over his shoulder that Grauber was to be deprived of his rank and placed under arrest until his questionable conduct could be gone into further. So the ex-Obergruppenführer was now a prisoner locked in a cell in one of the outer bunkers.

The news that came in continued to be as black as ever. The Allies were advancing rapidly on all fronts, Russian shells were now falling in the Chancellery garden and their troops were said to have captured Potsdam. Yet Hitler continued to cling to the idea that General Wenck's Army would rescue him.

Then in the evening he received his most terrible blow. Heinz Lorenz arrived from the ruins of the Propaganda Ministry. With him he brought a transcript of a broadcast that had just been put out by the B.B.C. It was a full report of Himmler's negotiations with Count Bernadotte.

When given the news by the eager Bormann, Hitler broke into agonizing wails. '*Der treue Heinrich*', of all people, had betrayed him. It was unthinkable, yet incontestable. Soon his distress gave place to fury. As he mouthed curses, his face became almost unrecognizable. He saw everything now. Steiner was one of Himmler's men. It was on Himmler's orders that the General had refrained from launching the attack that could have saved Berlin. It had been a deliberate plot to ruin him. Suddenly he remembered Grauber and gave orders that

Heinrich Mueller, the Chief of the Political Police, should interrogate him.

Hoegl told Gregory afterwards that when they went into Grauber's cell his sagging face had broken out in a sweat of terror, and that in twenty hours he had lost at least two stones of his surplus fat. They had carried out the usual drill of beating the calves of his legs with steel rods until he could no longer stand, pulling out his fingernails and so on, and had extracted a confession from him. He had admitted that for weeks past he had known of Himmler's negotiations with Count Bernadotte and in a desperate attempt to escape further torment he had even invented a story that in exchange for a guarantee that his own life should be spared Himmler had offered to hand Hitler's corpse over to the Allies.

On receiving Mueller's report Hitler flared, 'So the fat swine was aware of all this yet did not tell us. Take him up to the garden and shoot him!'

Gregory was by then so drained of emotion that he could not even take pleasure in the thought that his incredibly brutal and malicious enemy was to die; so although he had intended to witness the execution he was not particularly sorry when, as he was watching Grauber, now a gibbering wreck, being dragged by the guards up the concrete stairs, he was sent for by the Führer.

After referring briefly to Gregory's having been kidnapped the previous night, Hitler said, 'I am now taking the necessary steps to prepare for my end. No leader has ever been served as badly as myself or suffered so many betrayals. Yet I still have a few friends who have demonstrated their loyalty by expressing a wish to take their lives at the same time as I take mine. You, *Herr Major*, came into my life too late for me to bestow on you such honours and rewards as I would have liked to do; but you have been a great support to me in these past terrible weeks, and it has occurred to me that I may be able to show my gratitude to you later. I refer, of course, to your being reincarnated with me on Mars. To ensure there is no time lag and your being reborn there about the same time as myself, it has occurred to me that you may wish to join those who are about to leave this earth with me.'

Completely taken aback by this horrifying invitation, Gregory did his utmost to prevent his features from showing his true feelings. Hastily stammering out that it had been a great privilege to have been of service to his Führer, he rallied his tired wits to take a quick decision. It was that he dared not refuse to play the game out, and could only pray that he would escape this new threat to his life by Hitler giving an example to the rest and taking his own life first. In a steadier voice he added:

'*Mein Führer*, I seek no reward. But it would be an honour to die in your company.'

'Good! Good!' said Hitler cheerfully. 'I expected no less of you.' Then he took from his pocket a poison capsule and pressed it into Gregory's hand.

By then it was a little after midnight and von Greim and Hannah Reitsch were about to leave the bunker. In anticipation of their departure everyone had been writing farewell letters to their relatives for Hannah to take with her; and now Hitler went into von Greim's room to give him his last instructions. Both the newly created Field Marshal and Hannah expressed the opinion that it was no longer possible to escape from Berlin by air and begged to be allowed to remain and die with their Führer. But he insisted on their going.

When they had left he was suddenly seized by a fit of renewed confidence. He announced that his intuition told him that von Greim would get through and carry out his orders. These had been to arrest the treacherous Himmler and use the whole of the Luftwaffe to support Wenck's Army. Von Greim, he said, was a very different man from that decadent traitor Goering. He would put new life into the Luftwaffe and it would now cover itself with glory. The bridges over the Havel were still being held. Under cover of the Luftwaffe Wenck would reach Berlin and save them all.

To Gregory's despair there was no more talk of suicide. Instead the Führer declared his intention of conferring the status she had long desired on his faithful friend of many years. He meant to marry Eva Braun. A minor official named Walter Wagner, whom nobody knew but who was competent to perform a civil marriage, was produced by Goebbels. The ceremony took place in the narrow map room with Goebbels and Bormann as witnesses. So, at long last, Eva Braun became Frau Hitler.

Afterwards they came out into the conference passage and shook hands with everybody, then retired to their private rooms for the wedding breakfast to which Hitler invited the two witnesses, Frau Goebbels and his two women secretaries.

Gregory got away as soon as he could to find that Erika, having slept for a good part of the day, was sitting up waiting for him, and that she and Malacou were all ready to start, as had been agreed the previous morning.

As gently as he could, he broke it to her that he still could not leave. Having told her about Grauber's end, the marriage and the poison capsule, he stilled her new fears for him by saying that he meant to empty the capsule of its deadly contents and refill it with water then, if he were forced to swallow it, throw a fit and sham dead. As she sighed with relief, he went on:

'The last thing I heard before leaving the bunker was that von Greim got away safely after all. He is a fanatic and he'll sacrifice every 'plane in the Luftwaffe in an attempt to save Hitler. If with von Greim's help Wenck succeeds in reaching Berlin the odds are that Hitler will be tempted to abandon his alternative plan of committing suicide. I've simply got to stay and persuade him that it is not in his own best interests to cling on to life for another few months. Maybe as many as a million lives depend on that.'

Erika sighed. 'Of course you are right, darling. You are playing for such tremendous stakes that we mustn't even think of our own lives. All the same if I stay here for another twenty-four hours I may be dead next time you get back. The Russian shells have been coming over all day at the rate of one a minute. Half the roof of the house has gone and three fell in the garden. But don't think I'm suggesting leaving you. I'll never do that.'

After a moment's thought Gregory said, 'Look, central Berlin is now the Russians' main target. The city is vast and they can't possibly have enough guns to bombard the suburbs with anything like the same intensity. Why shouldn't you and

Malacou take your van out to Sabine's villa? He knows how to find it and you would be much safer there.'

'That's certainly an idea,' Erika agreed. Then she added with a smile, 'But don't you think your girl friend might spit in my eye?'

'Of course not; since for your part you've already said you are willing to bury the hatchet. She will be only too pleased to see you, because it will be a guarantee to her that when we do make our attempt to get through the Russian lines we will take her with us.'

When full daylight came they roused themselves from their few hours of troubled sleep. Erika dressed herself in her nurse's uniform and Malacou, as calm as ever, loaded into the Red Cross van all the oddments they thought might prove useful. Gregory promised to join them as soon as he possibly could and, after a heartrending parting from Erika, waved them away on their perilous journey.

Over in the bunker he found nearly everyone still asleep. The wedding party had gone on till dawn. After Gregory had left, Krebs, Burgdorf, von Below and the vegetarian cook had all been called in to join those already with the newly-weds. They had drunk lashings of champagne while talking of the glories of the Nazi rallies at Nuremberg in the old days and of how Hitler had been Goebbels' best man.

It emerged that, at intervals between declaiming to his friends, Hitler had dictated his personal will and a testament addressed to the German people. But this did not prevent him from holding his usual midday conference.

Reports were made at it that the Russians had advanced in Charlottenburg and in Grunewald and had taken the Anhalter Station. Gregory, hovering with other adjutants in the outer side of the partition, learned, too, that the Russians had established themselves in force in Potsdam. At that piece of news his stomach contracted and he was almost sick from apprehension; for Sabine's villa was less than half the distance from Potsdam than it was from central Berlin. Erika was on her way there and there was no possible means by which he could recall her.

When he managed to concentrate again, from the hushed and

stilted conversation of his companions he took in the fact that the Führer, in his will, had appointed Admiral Doenitz as his successor and that three copies of the will had been sent off that morning by Lorenz, Johannmeier and Bormann's adjutant, Zander. Also that Hitler's imitator in immolating a nation for his own glorification, Mussolini, had been caught by partisans and shot the previous day. A mob in Milan had later kicked his body and that of his mistress, Clara Petacci, to pulp, then hung them up by the ankles.

Soon afterwards three other officers were called in to the conference: von Loringhoven, Weiss and Boldt. No news had been received from General Wenck and, at Burgdorf's suggestion, these three were to be despatched in an attempt to get through the enemy lines and urge Wenck to hurry, otherwise the Chancellery might be captured before he reached it.

That afternoon von Below had the courage to go in to the Führer and ask permission to leave. Hitler was then in one of his calm spells and readily agreed; but added that he must wait until after the evening conference to take, if he could, a despatch to Keitel at the OKW headquarters, which had now been moved to Ploen in Schleswig-Holstein.

The long, terrible hours dragged by while the Russian shells crumped into the upper storeys of the Chancellery. At ten o'clock the evening conference began. General Weidling reported that the Hitler Youth still held the bridges over the Havel, but that the Russians had penetrated as far as the Wilhelmstrasse and almost reached the Air Ministry. Later Krebs came out, handed von Below a despatch and, in case he had to destroy it, told him its contents. They were to the effect that the situation in Berlin was now desperate, they could no longer hope that General Wenck would come to their rescue, and the Russians would capture the Chancellery within twenty-four hours. But the Führer expected the troops on all fronts to fight to the last man.

To the envy of most of the others who, had they dared, would willingly have risked death in the streets rather than remain with their mad Führer in the bunker, von Below said good-bye to his friends and set off into the flame-torn darkness.

The score of men and women left in the bunker had received orders that they were not to go to bed; so they stood about, drinking heavily. At last, at half past two in the morning, Hitler emerged and took a ceremonial farewell of them all. He shook hands with everybody, but his eyes were glazed with a film of moisture, his walk was unsteady, he seemed dazed and could do no more than mumble inaudible replies to those who spoke to him.

When he had retired they continued to stand about, expecting to hear the shot that would release them from their thraldom. But no shot came. Instead, the Führer's valet emerged with an order. In the upper basement there was a canteen for the use of the guards and orderlies. With the desperation of despair they were holding a dance and the strains of the music were penetrating to the bunker. Hitler had sent out to say that the music must be toned down because it prevented him from getting to sleep.

Some of his staff lurched drunkenly up the stairs to join the dancers. Gregory, with the awful feeling that this nightmare would never end, went to von Below's now vacant bunk, flung himself fully dressed upon it and fell into a troubled doze.

Next day, the 30th April, the old iron routine was followed, just as though Hitler were still directing armies fighting on fronts many hundreds of miles from the capital. But for once he listened in silence to the reports of the Generals, who were now conducting the defence of central Berlin. Overnight the enemy had captured the whole of the Tiergarten and reached the Potsdamer Platz. The underground railway tunnel in the Friedrichstrasse was in their hands and they were fighting their way through the Voss Strasse tunnel towards the Chancellery.

At two o'clock Hitler had lunch with his two women secretaries and his cook, while Eva remained in her room. Over the meal he conversed quite normally, but before it he had made his final preparations. The guards had been told that they were not to enter the bunker again and his chauffeur, Erik Kempka, had carried two hundred litres of petrol up to the Chancellery garden in preparation for the funeral pyre.

After lunch Hitler came out into the passage with Eva and they again shook hands with all those who had remained to the last. They then returned to their suite. At two-thirty a single shot was heard. For a few minutes those outside stood as though petrified, then they went in. Hitler had shot himself through the roof of the mouth. Eva was also dead, but she had taken poison.

The Devil's emissary who, for so many years, possessed by the spirit of Evil, had done his work in the world so well had, at last, gone to join his Infernal Master. It was as though an almost tangible black cloud, that had stifled clear thought, honest aspirations and all humane instincts, had suddenly been lifted from the bunker. The place had been reeking with treachery, fear, cruelty, blood-lust, and suddenly the atmosphere they breathed had become clean again.

They looked at one another in astonishment, seeing faces they hardly recognized because the features had become relaxed and the eyes no longer held the wary glint of animals intent only on self-preservation.

Smoking had never been permitted in the vicinity of the Führer, but one of them lit a cigarette. The others quickly produced their cases and followed suit. Calmly, not even bothering to bow their heads, they watched the guards carry the bodies of Hitler and Eva up to the garden to be burned.

Goebbels heavily declared that there was now nothing left to live for; so he meant to honour his promise to Hitler that he would kill his wife and children and himself. Krebs and Burgdorf agreed that it was better to put bullets through their brains than risk falling into the hands of the Russians. But the others were throwing away the poison capsules that Hitler had given them. Bormann had already begun to draft a telegram to Doenitz as a first move in an attempt to establish a similar relationship with the new Führer to that he had had with the old. The rest were eagerly discussing the chances of escaping through the Russian lines that night under cover of darkness.

Gregory, knowing that the Russians had captured Potsdam on the previous day, was almost off his head with fear that by this time they might have reached Sabine's villa. Reports were coming in from all the suburbs overrun by the Russians that their brutal Mongolian troops were shooting every man and raping every woman that they captured. If they had advanced up the

east shore of the Havel, what might now be happening to
Erika, Sabine and Trudi did not bear thinking about.

As long as some eleventh-hour twist in Hitler's disordered
mind might have led him to attempt to leave Berlin and,
perhaps, owing to the dark power that had so often protected
him, succeed in reaching Bavaria where he would have
bludgeoned the German Armies into fighting on, Gregory had
felt it his inescapable duty to remain. But now that malignant
beast in human form was dead nothing would have induced
Gregory to postpone until darkness his bid to save Erika.

Without a word of farewell to anyone, he ran up the stairs
and snatched from a pigeonhole in the arms depository the
first pistol he could lay his hand on. Deciding to leave by the
way the officers sent off on the previous day had taken, he ran
on through the empty echoing corridors to the back of the
building, where the garages faced on to the Hermann Goering
Strasse.

A pall of smoke hung low over the city and the air stank
from the fumes of high explosives. There were great holes in
the road from one of which a burst water main was fountaining.
Broken paving stones and shell splinters littered the sidewalks.
In three directions flames from burning buildings lit up the
sulphurous clouds with an orange glow. The noise from
bursting shells was deafening but through it came the clatter
of machine guns: a clear indication that the Russians had that
morning fought their way to within a few hundred yards of the
Chancellery. From close at hand there came the dull rumble of
falling masonry. It seemed impossible that anyone could
remain alive for more than a few minutes in the flaming heart
of the stricken city. But great love begets great courage.
Without hesitation Gregory plunged into the inferno.

29

Death Intervenes

TURNING left, Gregory set off at a run. A shell exploded fifty feet above him and he narrowly escaped the shower of bricks that it brought down. A minute later another crumped some way off in the middle of the road and he was half blinded by the dust it threw up. He had covered no more than three hundred yards when ahead of him the murk was stabbed by the flashes of rifle and machine-gun fire. Then he saw that a high barricade sealed off the end of the street. Beyond it lay the Potsdamer Platz and there fierce fighting was in progress.

Finding his way blocked he entered a ruined building on his right and began a laborious climb over piles of rubble and fallen beams. On the far side he came out into another street. Keeping under cover he looked swiftly from side to side.

A hundred yards to the north of him there was another barricade, but this time he was on the Russian-held side of it. Taking his life in his hands he sprinted across the road towards the ruins opposite. A Russian coming up the street saw him, raised his Sten gun and fired a burst. By a miracle the bullets whistled past him and he was able to dive into a stone porch that was still standing. Fearing that the Russian would pursue him, he clambered up a sloping girder to the first floor of the wrecked building. There he waited for a few moments with his pistol at the ready; but the Russians had so many people to shoot at that the one who had fired on him did not bother to give chase.

Another long perilous climb, with bricks and plaster slithering under his feet, brought him to the Potsdamer Strasse. In it a line of Russian tanks was moving north-eastward. Hiding behind a jagged piece of wall he waited until they had passed, then made his dash across the road. This time he was not spotted. Again, his hands and knees now bruised and bleeding, he crawled, slithered and staggered over the mountains of wreckage until he reached a block of which a part was still intact. By an iron fire escape he made his way to a first-floor window that had been shattered. It gave on to a landing with a stone staircase. Descending it he climbed over a fallen door and found himself in the pillared hall of a large bank. Next moment he heard a movement. Before he had time to draw back a Russian soldier emerged from behind the nearest pillar and was facing him less than six feet away.

For a second they stared at one another in mutual surprise. But Gregory's luck was in. The Russian, intent on loot, had left his Sten gun lying on the bank counter. Before he could turn and grab it Gregory had put two bullets through his head. Things might have gone very differently but, as they had turned out, Gregory looked on the encounter as a special gift from heaven. He now had the thing that above all he had hoped to secure but feared it almost impossible to obtain and change into without being seen—a Russian uniform.

Swiftly, he undressed the dead man and himself. The soldier, a flat-faced yellow-skinned Mongolian, was short but broad, so his tunic was very loose on Gregory and his cloth pantaloons too short, but their ends just tucked into his calf-length leather boots and those, to Gregory's relief, were, if anything, a little large. As a precaution against any Russian officer he might meet calling on him to take part in the battle, he tore a long strip from his victim's shirt, wet it with the dead man's blood and tied it round his own head. Also, much to his regret, he had to abandon his steel helmet and, instead, put on the pointed cloth cap worn by Mongolian troops. But he found the Sten gun was fully loaded so would serve him better than the few bullets left in the pistol, which he tucked into its holster.

By making a half-circle through the ruins he had bypassed the Potsdamer Platz and emerged opposite the Potsdamer Station. At the sight of its gaping roof it occurred to him that it might prove quicker and safer if he followed the straight course of the railway rather than worked his way south-west through miles of half-blocked streets.

Inside the station he found great activity going on. Although it was roofless, and in places great girders had fallen across the tracks, the Russians were using the platforms for dumps of ammunition and stores. Gregory saw too that, although trains could not enter the station, the Russian engineers must have got some of the lines working as, in the distance, several engines were puffing.

Now that he had got out of the Chancellery area he no longer had to fear being blown up by a shell or shot by a Russian, but there was still the danger that an officer might speak to him and discover that he was wearing a stolen uniform. Since he had tied the bloodstained strip of shirt round his jaw as well as his head he was in hopes that if accosted it would provide an adequate excuse for not answering; but there was an unpleasant possibility that some well-meaning 'comrade' might take him by the arm and insist on leading him to the nearest first-aid post.

Keeping a wary look-out, he walked out of the far end of the station and along the tracks to a great open siding where two trains were being unloaded by fatigue parties. A third, he saw, was empty and in the process of shunting, so it looked as if it was about to move out to fetch up another cargo of supplies. Now that he was in full sight of the unloading parties he slowed his pace, let his head hang forward and staggered a little, as though in great pain. Then, as the shunting train came to a halt, he lurched forward in a stumbling run, grasped the ledge of an empty cattle truck that had its doors open and pulled himself up into it.

For some minutes the train remained stationary while he lay in the semi-darkness, fearing that at any moment a transport officer would come along, find him there and, perhaps, accuse him of attempting to get away from the battle without permission.

At length the train jerked into motion. Travelling at not more than twenty miles an hour it covered some three miles, then for about a quarter of an hour it continued on between the vast areas of ruined buildings, frequently stopping and starting until, Gregory judged, it must be a good five miles from central Berlin. His belief that it had passed Lichterfelde was confirmed as it moved on into comparatively open country. So next time it jolted to a halt he jumped from it to the ground.

To his alarm, as he crossed the neighbouring track to the edge of an embankment he heard someone shouting at him. Turning his head he saw that in the rear truck of the train a heavy machine gun had been mounted and that its crew were making violent signals to him to return. Ignoring them, he slithered down the embankment and climbed a fence into a garden.

He had no sooner got over it than the machine gun started to chatter and individual rifle shots rang out. Believing that he was being shot at he flung himself flat among some low bushes, but no bullets came anywhere near him. After a few minutes he peered out. Machine guns both at the front and rear of the train were being fired by the Russians, but not in his direction. As he watched one of them fell wounded, hit by a bullet fired from somewhere along the side of the track. Gregory then realized why the Russians, believing him to be one of themselves, had yelled at him to come back. The train was passing through an area still held by the Germans.

The knowledge filled him with dismay. By taking the Russian soldier's uniform and getting on the train he had covered in three-quarters of an hour a distance that, dodging about on foot, would have taken him at least three hours. But he had come out of Berlin by the main line, not the one further west which served the Grunewald and the suburbs along the Havel; so to reach the villa he had still some four miles to go across country, and since it was held by Germans he was now liable to be shot on sight at any moment.

For a few minutes he contemplated hiding until darkness came down, but he knew that if he did thoughts of what might be happening to Erika would drive him insane. Taking off his pointed cloth cap, so that from the distance his Russian uniform would be less readily identifiable, he stuffed it inside his tunic. As he did so he saw that the pistol was no longer in its holster. The flap must have been wrenched open and the weapon have fallen out as he climbed the fence; but, as he had the Sten gun, the loss of the pistol gave him no concern.

Getting to his feet he warily approached the house at the other end of the garden.

It had been bombed, but appeared to be only slightly damaged. Tiptoeing round it, he looked in through several shattered windows; then, as the house was apparently deserted, he climbed through one of them. The floor of the room he entered was covered with fallen plaster and broken ornaments. In the hall he saw there had been a fire that had burnt part of the staircase. As he went up it the boards creaked ominously, but took his weight. In one of the bedrooms he found, as he had hoped, a wardrobe containing several suits of clothes. Laying the Sten gun close at hand on the unmade bed, he got out of his uniform.

He was still in his underclothes when he heard the stairs creak. Grabbing up the gun he took cover behind the bed. Next moment a big bull-necked crop-headed German, who had evidently been down in the cellar, came into the room. He was in his shirtsleeves and holding a Mauser pistol. As he raised it threateningly and called to Gregory to come out, Gregory ducked. On the floor beside him there was a pair of heavy shoes. Taking one of them in his left hand, while still covered by the bed, he threw it in the direction of the door. The German jerked himself sideways to avoid it. At that instant Gregory bobbed up and fired a burst from his Sten gun.

As he traversed the Sten gun its bullets thudded into the German's chest and both his arms. He coughed, blood spurted from his mouth and he fell dead, doubled up on the floor.

Gregory would have preferred only to wound him, but he had not dared risk being shot himself or chance the man's shouting for help and perhaps raising a hue and cry. At all costs he had to get to Erika. Quickly he got a suit out of the wardrobe and put it on. It was much too big for him but that could not be helped, and the turn-ups of the trousers served to conceal the greater part of the Russian's regulation boots. On the top of the wardrobe there was a light weekend case. Getting it down he crammed the Russian uniform into it on the chance that it might again prove useful. It then occurred to him that a civilian carrying a Sten gun might have it taken from him by some soldier who had run out of ammunition; so he threw it on the bed, retrieved the German's Mauser and thrust it into his jacket pocket.

Two minutes later he was out in the street, looking cautiously to right and left. No-one was about and he soon realized the reason. As the Germans still held this area, the Russians were shelling it; so all the inhabitants had taken refuge in air-raid shelters or their cellars. Taking his direction from a watery sun, he hurried through several streets that were similar to that in Dahlem where Ribbentrop had lived, but with smaller houses.

Half of them had been gutted by fire and many of the trees in their gardens were black and leafless from having been set alight by incendiary bombs. Two German armoured cars rattled past but their crews took no notice of him. Every few minutes a shell whined over or burst a few hundred yards away. No-one can judge where a bomb will fall, but anyone who has had experience of being shelled can guess roughly where a missile is likely to land; so whenever one seemed likely to fall near him, Gregory was able to take cover behind a low wall, or throw himself flat. Here and there he glimpsed German troops posted in ruined buildings that they had made into strong-points, and twice on looking down roads leading south he saw that manned barricades composed of wrecked cars, tree trunks and paving stones had been erected.

He had passed several corpses both of soldiers and civilians and scarcely given them a look, but when he had covered about two miles he caught sight of a young woman running down a side road. Her stockings were down round her ankles, a part of her torn skirt was trailing behind her, her upper garments had been ripped away leaving her breasts bare, and her hair was in wild disorder. It was obvious that she had been assaulted and, apparently, driven crazy.

Since Gregory had left the railway he had seen only troops in German uniforms; so it might be that some of them, knowing that within a day or two they must be dead or prisoners, had seized the girl and raped her. On the other hand it was possible that she had fallen into the hands of the Russians and had only just escaped from them. From Potsdam the Russians might by now have come up the Havel and landed on the west side of the long lake towards which he was heading. The thought of their bursting into the villa and what would follow caused him more agony of mind than had even the fear two nights earlier that Grauber would burn out his eyes.

Weary in mind and body, but imbued with an overwhelming urge to reach the villa at the earliest possible moment, he pressed on; at times running a few hundred yards, at others pausing to crouch down when a shell came over. As he progressed he continued to see German troops here and there and, to his heartfelt relief, when he reached the shore of the Havel there was no sign of the Russians.

He had left the bunker a little before three o'clock. Having come by train for over half the distance he had made the journey in only a little more than three hours. It was ten past six when he crossed the causeway to the small island on which the villa stood. At his first glimpse of it through the still-standing trees his heart gave a lurch. Another bomb had hit it squarely, reducing it to a pile of rubble.

When had the bomb fallen? Less than three days ago Malacou had been at the villa and had brought back a letter from Sabine; so it must have been since then. Erika had driven out there the previous morning and, if she had arrived there safely, must have been in it for the past thirty hours. If she had been there when the bomb came down it was a hundred to one that her mangled body lay buried somewhere among the pile of bricks and masonry.

Gregory began to run again, and as he ran he prayed, 'Oh God, don't let it be! Don't let it be!'

It took him five agonizing minutes to reach the remains of the villa. Even the partition walls that had formed the rooms were unrecognizable. The upper storeys had buried the lower rooms in a great pile of debris from which, here and there, pieces of smashed furniture protruded.

In a forlorn hope he turned and ran to the garage, on the outside chance that they had escaped the bomb and taken refuge there. That too had been partially destroyed by the blast, but he forced his way through the shattered doors. It was empty. There was no sign that anyone had temporarily occupied it and neither Erika's van nor Sabine's car was there.

Tears started to his eyes and ran down his lean haggard

cheeks. Dazed by this last terrible blow after having survived
so many perils to reach the villa, he staggered round into the
garden behind it. For some moments he stood staring dull-eyed
at the pile of ruins, then he turned and looked towards the lake.
On the roof of the boathouse there was a splash of colour.

Could it be? Yes, by God it was! A small Red Cross flag had
been spread out and weighted down on the boathouse roof. A
surge of new strength suddenly animated his limbs. He pelted
across the lawn and burst in through the door. On a bench
inside Erika and Malacou, propped up by cushions from the
boat, were dozing.

For the next few minutes Gregory and Erika were incoherent.
Both had almost given up hope of ever seeing the other again.
With tears of joy streaming down their faces they clung
together.

In jerky sentences between kisses they gave one another the
gist of what had happened to them during the past day and a
half. Gregory gasped out that Hitler was dead; that he had
actually seen his body being carried up to be burned. That meant
that the war was as good as over.

Erika then told him of her drive out of Berlin with Malacou.
It had been a ghastly journey. Two-thirds of the streets they
had tried had been blocked by craters or rubble. A low-flying
Russian 'plane had then machine-gunned them from the air,
riddling the roof of the van with bullet holes. Finally, driving
down the road along the shore of the Havel a Russian shell had
exploded within twenty yards of them. Blast from it had turned
the van over and they had been lucky to escape only with bad
bruises. But the van had then caught fire, so had to be
abandoned. They had walked the last two miles, only to find
the villa in ruins and, it was to be assumed, Sabine and Trudi
buried somewhere under them.

Malacou added his quota and gave full vent to his delight
that Hitler was really dead. With sudden gravity he added, 'I
was right in my prediction that I would outlive him. Now I
have nothing left to live for. I have a small fortune in Sweden
and could make more money if I wished; but my beloved
Khurrem is dead, so I can foresee no future happiness for
myself. As you are both aware I have made obeisance to Him

whom you term the Evil One, but that has enabled me to avenge my race; so I do not regret it. He is the Lord of this World and to this World I shall return, perhaps again as His henchman with a further opportunity to penetrate the great mysteries. Or it may be that as a child of ignorance I shall be set upon another path to atone for such ill as I have inflicted on my fellow beings in this and my past lives. Whatever may be my present fate and unforeseeable future, I am now content at any time to pass on.'

Erika said quickly, 'God's mercy is infinite, and you used such weapons as you had to fight for your people. Hitler's death will save the lives of many thousands of them in the Bavarian and Austrian camps whom he would have had murdered if he had lived on for another few months.'

'That's true,' Gregory nodded, 'and it encourages me to hope that I'll be forgiven for having countenanced the methods that we used.'

There was a moment's embarrassed silence, then Erika said to Gregory, 'Darling, have you brought any food in that little case you were carrying? All of ours was destroyed when my van was burnt. The only thing I managed to save was the flag from its bonnet. We've had nothing to eat for twenty-four hours so we're absolutely starving.'

Instinctively, Gregory had clung on for the past two hours to the weekend case he had stolen and he had thrown it down only to embrace Erika. He shook his head. 'No, it contains only a Russian uniform. But there's plenty of food in the villa if only we can get at it. Sabine kept a big store of tinned stuff in the cellar.'

The three of them quickly crossed the lawn and climbed up into the rubble. Having known the house so well Gregory had no difficulty in locating the place beneath which lay the stairs down to the cellar. As twilight fell they set about heaving aside loose bricks and lumps of masonry. Fortunately no beam too heavy to move had fallen across the cellar entrance. After three-quarters of an hour's hard work they succeeded in uncovering it and, with a small torch that Erika had in her handbag, Gregory led the way down.

The cellar was undamaged, although the floor was an inch

or more deep in wine, for the concussion of the bomb had broken the greater part of the bottles. As he descended the steps Gregory feared that he would find Sabine and Trudi, dead from the shock of the explosion that had taken place immediately above, but to his relief they were not there. There were two beds, a table, chairs, an oil stove and cooking utensils, so it was evident that Sabine and Trudi had slept and spent a good part of their time down there during the worst of the bombardment. There were two candles on the table and oil in the stove. Malacou lit them and Erika selected from Sabine's stores some tins of soup, sausages and fruit to make a meal. Gregory removed the broken glass from a bin of hock until he came upon two unbroken bottles.

While they ate they discussed the situation and their prospects of getting away. Gregory said he thought it certain that the Chancellery would fall that night; but the last news to come in had been that Axmann's fanatical Hitler Youth were still holding the bridges over the Havel, and there were still many large pockets of resistance such as that in which the villa was situated.

He added that he had learned from General Krebs that German units were now surrendering right, left and centre and that Berlin would have fallen several days previously had it not been for the foreign contingents incorporated in the S.S. These were composed of men from almost every nation in Europe: tens of thousands of collaborationists, many of whom from quite early in the war had volunteered to fight for Germany. For them there could be no future if they returned to their own countries, only death as traitors; so most of them would fight on to the bitter end.

There could be no doubt that Berlin was completely surrounded and, in spite of the scores of miles that such a belt of encirclement must cover, Gregory felt that by now the Russians must be thick enough on the ground everywhere to prevent any vehicle getting through. Even if they had still had Erika's van all the odds were that in spite of its Red Cross the Russians would have commandeered it for their own use and, suspecting them to be spies or escapers, have made them prisoners. As things were it seemed that their best hope was for them to set off when full darkness had come, keeping away from the roads as far as possible and, by using the cover of woods and buildings, endeavour to dodge the Russian patrols.

While eating their meal they had kept their feet up rather uncomfortably to prevent the soles of their shoes from becoming soaked through by the flood of wine in the cellar and, when they had finished, as they did not mean to make a start for another hour or two, Erika decided to lie down on one of the beds. Before doing so she went over to tidy her hair at a small dressing table that had been brought down and stood at the far end of the cellar. Wedged in the corner of the mirror there was an envelope that in the dim light none of them had previously noticed. Across it was scrawled the one word, 'Gregory'.

It could have been left there only by Sabine. Eagerly he tore it open and read out the note inside:

'My dear, I've waited for you all day, but as you haven't come I greatly fear that you must have been killed. Now night has come I feel it's my last chance to get away. So Trudi and I are setting off in the car on our own. God knows if we'll get through. I can only pray that we will and that you are still alive and will somehow get here and read this. If you do, but have no car in which to run the gauntlet of these bloody Russians, take the motor launch. I had plenty of petrol, so filled its tank before I left. Thank you and bless you for everything. May God preserve us both. Sabine.

'Then she's alive!' exclaimed Gregory happily. 'They must have left before the bomb fell. And the launch! I'd regarded it as useless without petrol. But she's filled it up for us, bless her!'

Swiftly, they began to remake their plans. Gregory's knowledge of Russian was hopelessly inadequate to stand up to an interrogation if they were halted on a road. But while in Moscow and Leningrad in '41, he had picked up enough to answer a challenge, and he could change into the Russian uniform. By going down the Havel they would have to pass Potsdam, but if a searchlight were turned on to the launch his uniform would be seen and he could shout a few sentences which should prevent their being fired on from the shore.

Deciding that it would be wise to take some provisions with them, Gregory took the uniform out of the weekend case and stuffed that full of tins, then he and Malacou went out and down to the launch. As it had not been used for many months they had to spend some time working on the engine and getting it running. Satisfied that it was in good shape they returned to the cellar, where Erika was still lying on one of the beds. As they did not intend to start until midnight, while Gregory changed into the Russian uniform Malacou replaced with two fresh candles the stumps that had nearly burnt down and found another bottle of wine.

The two men had been sitting drinking at the table, with their feet up on a spare chair, for about a quarter of an hour, when they suddenly heard the noise of slithering rubble up above. Gregory quickly pulled out his pistol. When picking it up from the floor of the bedroom where he had shot the German he had been so obsessed by his urge to get to Erika that he had not thought of examining it. Now, as he really grasped it for the first time, it struck him that it was surprisingly light. At that the disturbing possibility flashed into his mind that the German had been bluffing with a weapon that was not loaded.

By then they could hear footsteps at the top of the stairs and a voice called anxiously, 'Sabine! Sabine! Are you there?'

As they stared upwards they saw the lower part of a man in German uniform and the barrel of a Sten gun. A powerful torch flashed out. Its beam chanced to fall directly on Erika's face as she lay on the bed. Next moment there came an exclamation of astonishment:

'Erika, by all that's holy! What the devil are you doing here?'

Instantly Gregory realized who the man was. It could only be Kurt von Osterberg, now out of hospital and come there in the hope of getting Sabine away. Knowing the Count's hatred for Erika and himself his whole body tensed with awful apprehension. To have survived such dangers throughout this terrible day and now, at its end, to be faced by yet another well-armed enemy seemed an unbelievably cruel trick of fate.

Gripped by an anxiety that made his temples throb, he prayed frantically for the ability to handle this menacing situation.

Sitting up with a jerk, Erika cried, 'You, Kurt!' Then, after a moment, she added, 'Sabine's gone and I . . .'

The brilliant beam of the torch far outshone the light from the two candles on the table and von Osterberg, his gaze fixed on Erika, who was immediately below him, had not yet realized that there was anyone else in the cellar. As he ran down a few more steps they saw that his head was heavily bandaged, but he showed no sign of weakness.

Suddenly he shouted at Erika, 'You bitch! You filthy traitress; going off with an English spy while your country is at war. At least I can settle accounts with you before the Russians get me!'

As he raised his Sten gun Gregory sprang to his feet and squeezed the trigger of his pistol. It gave only a loud click. His fears of a few moments before were only too well founded. It had no bullets in it.

At the sound of his movement von Osterberg swung round. He was holding the torch alongside his weapon, so its beam swept across Malacou then focussed on Gregory. Giving a gasp, the Count cried:

'*Mein Gott!* A Russian!' Then, while keeping the gun trained on Gregory, he sneered for Erika's benefit. 'So, my lady wife, you have again changed your allegiance. First a Jew, then an Englishman, now a Russian. It's clear that you'd stoop to any iniquity to save your lovely skin. You slut! You lecherous harlot! When I've put him and the fellow with him out of the way I'll see to it that you don't live to take another lover.'

Raising his gun a little, he aimed it at Gregory's chest.

'Stop!' shouted Erika. 'For God's sake, stop! He's not a Russian. He is . . .' Her terrified voice trailed away.

Under the broad bandage the Count's eyes suddenly lit up. '*Himmel nochmal!*' he whispered. 'It is! It's the Englishman. Now indeed God has been kind to me.'

Gregory knew that although he could expect no mercy from von Osterberg, the man was not a Grauber. One death might quench his urge to kill so, if he could concentrate the Count's hatred on himself, that would, perhaps, save Erika. Bursting into speech, he cried:

'Yes, it's me all right. I am the man who gave you that scar across your face with my knuckles for having allowed the Gestapo to make use of you to trap your wife. And if I were near enough to use my fist I'd lay your other cheek open to match it.' As he spoke he stepped round the table and threw his empty pistol at the Count's head.

Von Osterberg jerked his head aside. The pistol went harmlessly over his shoulder, struck the wall behind him and clattered down the stairs. Seeing that Gregory was about to rush him he raised the barrel of his gun and shouted, 'Move a foot closer and I'll riddle you.'

At the same moment Erika screamed, 'Gregory! No! Stay where you are! I implore you. If he must kill someone let it be me.'

'What a pair of turtle doves,' jeered the Count. 'The gallant Englishman about to offer himself for slaughter in the hope that I haven't enough bullets for you both, and his nymphomaniac whore wailing to be allowed to sacrifice herself for him. But don't worry. I couldn't bring myself to part you. Like Romeo and Juliet you are going to share a common tomb.'

For a moment he was silent, then he snapped at Gregory, 'Tell me. How is it that you come to be here?'

'We came to pick up Sabine Tuzolto, in the hope of taking her through the Russian lines with us.'

'I had no idea you even knew her.'

Gregory laughed. 'I've known her for years; and this villa. She was hiding me here from the Gestapo at the time of the attempt on Hitler's life. I was up on the roof when they came to arrest you and you tried to commit suicide, but lacked the guts to put the gun in your mouth and make a proper job of it.'

'Where is Sabine now?'

'God knows; I don't. But she left a note for me containing a suggestion about how we might get away.'

'Yes, Kurt,' Erika put in eagerly. 'Before she went she filled the tank of the motor launch with petrol. We meant to start in about half an hour and go in it down the Havel. Please, please forget the past. Anyway until we are all safe again. Put these terrible thoughts of revenge out of your mind and, instead, come with us.'

'Thank you, my dear, for the information,' replied the Count drily. 'That is an excellent plan and I shall adopt it. But as I dislike the company of spies and loose women I shall go alone.'

'Then you'll get yourself killed,' said Gregory quickly. 'The Russians are in Potsdam and they are certain to have searchlights trained on the river. They will shoot you and the launch to pieces.'

'Oh no they won't. Not when I've stripped that uniform you're wearing from your dead body and they see me in it.'

'They will; unless you can speak Russian and answer in it when they challenge you.' Gregory was standing some eight feet away from the Count, so too far off to rush him. He knew that he would be mown down before he could even clutch the Sten gun; and there could be no question about the extreme peril with which he and Erika were faced. Their only hope of saving themselves lay in talking von Osterberg out of his declared intention to murder them both, so he hurried on:

'Erika is right. Surely you have seen enough of violence and death in Berlin these past few months? Try to remember that we were once all decent civilized people, and now that this ghastly war is as good as over we should cease from acting like savages. You are not a Gestapo thug but a German nobleman. It's your duty to your caste to behave like one. Only a few years ago you would have been horrified at the idea of shooting two people in cold blood. I know enough Russian to get us through, and it's your life as well as ours. For Christ's sake be sensible and let's all go together.'

The Count gave a frosty smile. 'You would make a good barrister; but, in this case, not quite good enough. If they challenge me I'll shout some gibberish and as I will be wearing a Russian uniform they'll take me for a Kalmuck or a Tartar, and let me pass. Then somehow I'll find Sabine Tuzolto. No; when I've had the pleasure of shooting you two beauties I'll set out on my own.'

As he ceased speaking Erika began to plead again, but he cut her short and snarled at her, 'Silence, you bitch! Get up off that bed and stand with your face to the wall.'

Pale as death she shook her head. Suddenly he swivelled his gun and fired three shots into the end of the bed within a few inches of her feet. As the detonations reverberated through the cellar, with a little cry she jerked up her legs, half fell off the bed and did as he had ordered.

His eyes starting from their sockets, Gregory sprang forward. But Malacou grabbed him by the arm and pulled him back. Von Osterberg swiftly turned his gun in their direction. As they struggled together, Gregory shouted:

'Wait! Listen! You can't do this! You must have loved Erika once and she is still your wife.'

Von Osterberg nodded and said bitterly, 'Yes, she is my wife and I once thought her the most beautiful thing I had ever seen. But ours was a marriage of convenience. She accepted me only to please her dying father and resuscitate the family name after she had been prostituting herself to the millionaire Hugo Falkenstein. She made a bargain with me that I was never to enjoy her but she was to be free discreetly to sleep with anyone she liked. In exchange I was to have the prestige of being the husband of the most beautiful woman in Germany and she would supply me with all the money I needed for my scientific experiments. But she did not keep her bargain. She ran away to England with you, and as an enemy of her country the Nazis confiscated the great fortune that Falkenstein had left her, leaving me nearly penniless. For that, and for having dragged my name in the mud by betraying her country, I've nursed a growing hatred for her for years. She is a heartless, treacherous bitch and deserves to die.'

He passed his tongue over his dry lips, then went on with a sneer. 'No doubt you would have liked me to die so that you could marry her. But it is going to be the other way about. By killing her I'll gain my freedom. Then when I find Sabine Tuzolto I'll be free to marry her. She was my mistress; the most wonderful mistress I've ever had, and although that did not last we are still good friends. After all, I am von Osterberg, and my family is older than the Hohenzollerns. A little Hungarian Baroness, however beautiful, is not likely to reject such a match.'

'You poor fool.' Gregory gave a harsh laugh. 'The only

reason Sabine ever became your mistress was because Ribbentrop set her to spy on you. When I was hiding here she spoke of you with contempt as a poor old once-a-weeker. She wouldn't have you as a gift.'

'You lie!' yelled von Osterberg, his face going crimson with mortification and fury. 'Not one word of that is true.' In his surge of rage he ran down the last few steps of the stairs and levelled his gun. From the glare in his eyes it was evident that he was about to press the trigger.

Gregory stiffened, realizing that for him the end had come. But at that moment Malacou hurled himself forward. The Sten gun belched flame and the cellar echoed to its thunder. As the bullets buried themselves in Malacou's body he gave a gasp but by a last effort of will he seized the barrel of the gun before slumping to the ground at the Count's feet.

It was Gregory's opportunity. He seized upon it. With a cry of triumph he hurled himself at the Count. His arms were outstretched, his fingers spread wide. In another moment they would have closed on the neck of the older, weaker man in a strangler's grasp and borne him down. But the wine had made the stone floor of the cellar horribly slippery. Gregory's feet slid from under him and he fell backward with a loud splash, measuring his length beside the table. By the time he had regained his feet von Osterberg had wrenched the gun barrel from Malacou's dying grasp, kicked him in the face and had the gun pointing again at Gregory.

Malacou moaned, shuddered and lay still. He had said only a few hours before that he had nothing left to live for and was ready to die, and he had given his life to save a man whom, however different their standards of conduct, he had regarded as his friend. But his sacrifice had been in vain. Erika still stood with drooping shoulders facing the wall and Gregory, now dripping with the spilt wine, was still covered by von Osterberg's murderous weapon.

Wiping the muck from his face with a shaky hand, Gregory said hoarsely, 'There! You've killed a man; and one who never did you any harm. You'll have to answer for that in the hereafter. Isn't that enough to have on your conscience?'

'No,' replied the Count quietly. 'The fool got himself killed only because he threw himself in the way. Although I suppose I would have had to eliminate him later. Otherwise, as he was a friend of yours he might have played me some trick. Now we've talked enough. Turn round and face the wall.'

At that moment they all caught the sound of light footsteps on the upper stairs. For a second Gregory hoped that the sound would distract von Osterberg so that he could spring upon him. But the Count did not turn his head. Keeping Gregory covered he snarled, 'Stay where you are.'

Looking up over his head, Gregory saw Sabine come into view. Her hair was disordered and she was dirty and bedraggled. As she took in the scene below her in the cellar her face showed her amazement, and she gasped:

'Kurt! Gregory! Whatever is going on down there?'

Still not looking round, the Count, recognizing her voice, cried, 'Sabine! You're safe! Thank God! Where have you been?'

At the sound of Sabine's voice Erika had turned round. Her face and Gregory's both showed their unutterable relief. Sabine's arrival at the last minute of the eleventh hour spelt their reprieve. Both were convinced that the Count would not commit a double murder under the eyes of the woman he had said he loved. In breathless silence they listened as Sabine stammered:

'Trudi and I . . . we tried to get away. We left in the car the day before yesterday . . . But when I had driven about three miles we saw some Russians. We . . . we turned off the road and hid in a wood. This morning we made another attempt to get through but were held up by a group of men in German uniforms. They weren't Germans but French or, perhaps, Belgians. Anyway, these swine were set on having my car. They hauled Trudi and me out and . . . I suppose we were lucky that they were so desperately anxious to get away in it. They threw poor Trudi and me into a ditch, piled into the car and drove off. About an hour after we had pulled ourselves together we saw another lot of Russians, so we ran into a garden and hid ourselves in a bombed-out house there until this evening. As soon as it was dark we decided that the best thing to do was to make our way back here.'

'Where is Trudi now?' asked von Osterberg abruptly.

'She's gone down to the boathouse. I sent her on ahead and told her that if the launch were still there she was to wait for me until I found out if I could possibly get down into the cellar and collect some supplies. The launch is our last chance of escaping from the Russians. But what are you doing pointing that gun at Gregory? And that dead man on the floor. I just don't understand.'

Still keeping Gregory covered, the Count moved round from the bottom of the stairs so that his back was against a wall and he could now see Sabine. With a grim laugh he replied:

'Don't you, my dear. It's plain enough. Between them this man and woman made my life a misery until you came into it. I mean to kill them; then we'll set off in the launch.'

Sabine's big, dark eyes went round with horror. 'You can't!' she burst out. 'Kurt, you can't! Gregory is an old friend of mine. When I was a prisoner in London he saved my life.'

'He is an English spy. He stole my wife and she has brought dishonour on my name. By the grace of God I found them both here. You keep out of this. When I've shot them we'll get away.'

'Kurt! For God's sake, listen!' Sabine cried. 'Of course he is an Englishman, but don't you realize that if only we can get past the Russians he will be able to save us both? If we can reach the British they may make us prisoners but they won't kill us. He'll see to it that we're treated decently. He is the friend of one of the most powerful men in England. As soon as he can he'll arrange for us to be released. Won't you, Gregory?'

'Indeed I will,' replied Gregory promptly. 'The *Herr Graf* has everything to gain by doing as you say. I've only to let Sir Pellinore know that it was due to you and him that Erika and I got away and he'll see to everything, including an ample supply of money for you both to live on till things settle down again. I give you my word on that.'

Giving a quick glance at Sabine, von Osterberg shook his head. 'No! To this man and my traitor wife I'll be beholden for nothing. They are going to die here. We'll take our chance about what happens afterwards.'

'You are mad!' Sabine shouted at him. 'Mad!' Then opening her bag she fumbled in it. After a moment her hand emerged clutching a tiny automatic. She pointed it at von Osterberg's head and gasped, 'To escape with them is the only thing to do. If you can't see that so much the worse for you. Drop that gun or I'll shoot!'

Again the hopes of Gregory and Erika rose with a bound. The Count had his back to the wall and was facing Gregory. Erika was on his left staring at him with distended eyes. Sabine was to his right, still on the stairs and a little above him. Without exposing himself to attack by Gregory he could not turn and cover her, so she had command of the situation.

Yet he would not be baulked of his vengeance. Apparently convinced that Sabine would not carry out her threat he again aimed his weapon at Gregory's heart while shouting to her, 'Don't act the fool, girl.'

At that moment, she fired her pistol. But the bullet missed and thudded into the table. Erika threw herself forward and grasped her husband round the legs. He staggered but did not fall. Sabine fired again, but the lurch he had given saved him. The bullet sang past his ear.

Gregory was still fully exposed to the muzzle of the Sten gun. For a fraction of a second his life hung in the balance. As the gun spat flame he leapt aside. At the same instant Erika thrust up her hand and knocked the barrel of the gun in the opposite direction. This time Gregory did not slip and, as he moved, he grasped by the neck the hock bottle from which he and Malacou had been drinking.

His spring brought him to within four feet of von Osterberg. Before the Count could traverse the gun to fire another burst Gregory brought the bottle crashing down on his head. It shattered into flying fragments on the place where the bone had been fractured when he had attempted to commit suicide. Without a sound he dropped the Sten gun and fell dead.

For a moment there was utter silence while the three survivors stared at one another. Then Erika got to her feet and Sabine came down the last few stairs. Utterly overcome by strain and emotion, although the two women had met only briefly once before and then as rivals they fell sobbing into one another's arms.

Gregory hoisted Malacou's body on to one of the beds. Erika and Sabine between them got von Osterberg's on to the other. Gregory and Erika knelt down on the wine-washed floor and said a prayer for Malacou's soul. Sabine said one for that of the Count. Then they went up the stairs and out into the night.

When passing Potsdam, as they had expected, they were challenged, but standing up in the launch Gregory shouted in Russian the phrase that Stalin had so often used in his broadcasts, 'Death to the Hitlerite bandits,' and they were allowed to pass. They landed next morning about eight miles below Potsdam, near Schwielow, at the far end of the Havel lake. Two evenings later they met British tanks, manned by men some of whom had fought their way gloriously three thousand miles from Cairo to Sicily, half-way up Italy, then from Normandy via Brussels into the heart of Germany.

There followed another anxious day before Gregory could get a telegram sent to Sir Pellinore. After that everything went swiftly and smoothly. Gregory, Erika, Sabine and Trudi were flown back to England in an R.A.F. aircraft. In London that night they saw the lights at last go up, signifying that the war with Germany was over.

On June 6th, the first anniversary of D-Day, Erika again became a bride. From his mansion in Carlton House Terrace, where everything that money could then buy had been provided for the wedding reception, Sir Pellinore escorted her to church and gave her away to become the beloved wife of her beloved Gregory.

A Selected List of Fiction Available from Mandarin

While every effort is made to keep prices low, it is sometimes necessary to increase prices at short notice. Mandarin Paperbacks reserves the right to show new retail prices on covers which may differ from those previously advertised in the text or elsewhere.

The prices shown below were correct at the time of going to press.

☐	7493 0003 5	**Mirage**	James Follett	£3.99
☐	7493 0134 1	**To Kill a Mockingbird**	Harper Lee	£2.99
☐	7493 0076 0	**The Crystal Contract**	Julian Rathbone	£3.99
☐	7493 0145 7	**Talking Oscars**	Simon Williams	£3.50
☐	7493 0118 X	**The Wire**	Nik Gowing	£3.99
☐	7493 0121 X	**Under Cover of Daylight**	James Hall	£3.50
☐	7493 0020 5	**Pratt of the Argus**	David Nobbs	£3.99
☐	7493 0097 3	**Second from Last in the Sack Race**	David Nobbs	£3.50

All these books are available at your bookshop or newsagent, or can be ordered direct from the publisher. Just tick the titles you want and fill in the form below.

Mandarin Paperbacks, Cash Sales Department, PO Box 11, Falmouth, Cornwall TR10 9EN.

Please send cheque or postal order, no currency, for purchase price quoted and allow the following for postage and packing:

UK   80p for the first book, 20p for each additional book ordered to a maximum charge of £2.00.

BFPO   80p for the first book, 20p for each additional book.

Overseas   £1.50 for the first book, £1.00 for the second and 30p for each additional book including Eire   thereafter.

NAME (Block letters) ....

ADDRESS ....

....

....